P9-DBZ-086

DEATH OF
A LAKE

PAPERBACK
EXCHANGE
v. fiesolana 31r.
tel. 2478154
Florence Italy

L. 5000

PAPERBACK
EXCHANGE
v. fiesolana 31r.
tel. 2478154
Florence Italy

Arthur Upfield

DEATH OF A LAKE

**HINKLER BOOK
DISTRIBUTORS** PTY
LTD

To Mr James L. Hole

Editorial Note

*Part of the appeal of Arthur Upfield's stories lies in their authentic
portrayal of many aspects of outback Australian life in the 1930s and
through into the 1950s. The dialogue, especially, is a faithful
evocation of how people spoke. Hence, these books reflect and depict
the attitudes and ways of speech, particularly with regard to Aborigines
and to women, which were then commonplace. In reprinting these books
the publisher does not endorse the attitudes or opinions they express.*

An Angus & Robertson Publication

Angus&Robertson, an imprint of
HarperCollins*Publishers*
25 Ryde Road, Pymble, Sydney, NSW 2073, Australia
31 View Road, Glenfield, Auckland 10, New Zealand

This edition published in 1994 for
Hinkler Book Distributors Pty Ltd
32-34 Graham Road
Highett, Victoria 3190, Australia

Copyright © Bonaparte Holdings Pty Ltd 1954

This book is copyright.
Apart from any fair dealing for the purposes of private study,
research, criticism or review, as permitted under the Copyright
Act, no part may be reproduced by any process without written
permission. Inquiries should be addressed to the publishers.

ISBN 0 207 18618 9

Cover illustration by Russell Jeffery
Printed in Australia by McPherson's Printing Group

1 : 94

1

Lake Otway

LAKE OTWAY WAS dying. Where it had existed to dance before the sun and be courted by the ravishing moon there would be nothing but drab flats of iron-hard clay. And then the dead might rise to shout accusations echoed by the encircling sand dunes.

The out-station crowned a low bluff on the southern shore, and from it a single telephone line spanned fifty miles of virgin country to base on the great homestead where lived the Boss of Porchester Station, which comprised eight hundred thousand acres and was populated by sixty thousand sheep in the care of some twenty wage plugs, including Overseer Richard Martyr.

There wasn't much of Richard Martyr. He was short, dapper, wiry, every movement a hint of leashed strength. His face and arms were the colour of old cedarwood, making startlingly conspicuous his light-grey eyes. Always the dandy, this morning he wore well-washed jodhpurs, a white silk shirt and kangaroo-hide riding-boots with silver spurs. Why not? He was Number Two on Porchester Station, and this out-station at Lake Otway was his headquarters.

Martyr stood on the wide veranda overlooking the Lake, the Lake born three years before on the bed of a dustbowl, the Lake which had lived and danced and sung for three years and now was about to die. The real heat of summer was just round the corner, and the sun would inevitably murder Lake Otway.

Short fingers beating a tattoo on the veranda railing, Martyr gazed moodily over the great expanse of water shimmering like a cloth of diamonds. It was a full three miles across to the distant shore-line of box timber and, beyond it, the salmon-tinted dunes footing the far-flung uplands. To the left of the bluff, the shore-line curved within a mile; to the right it limned miniature headlands and tiny bays for four miles before

curving at the outlet creek, where could be seen the motionless fans of a windmill and the iron roof of a hut named
Johnson's Well. When Lake Otway was dead, that windmill
would be pumping water for stock, and perhaps a man or two
would be living at the hut six hundred rolling miles from the
sea.

The cook's triangle called all hands to breakfast. Martyr
again puckered his eyes to read the figures on the marker post
set up far off shore. He had seen the figure 19 resting on the
water; now he could see the figure 3. Only three feet of water
left in Lake Otway. No! Less! Only two feet and ten inches.
Were there a prolonged heat-wave in February, then Lake Otway wouldn't live another five weeks.

The men were leaving their quarters to eat in the annexe
off the kitchen. The rouseabout was bringing the working
horses to the yard. The hens were busy before the shade
claimed them during the hot hours. The chained dogs were
excited by the running horses. The crows were cawing over
at the killing pens, and a flock of galah parrots gave soft greet-
ings when passing overhead. A city man could never
understand how men can be captivated by such a place . . .
six hundred miles from a city.

Martyr turned and entered the dining-room, large, lofty,
well lighted, and sat at the white-clothed table to eat alone.
He could hear the men in the annexe, and Mrs Fowler, the
cook, as she served them breakfast. Then he looked up at Mrs
Fowler's daughter.

'Morning, Mr Martyr! What will it be after the cereal?
Grilled cutlets or lamb's fry and bacon?'

She was softly-bodied and strong and twenty. Her hair was
the colour of Australian gold, and her eyes were sometimes
blue and sometimes green. Her mouth was small and delic-
iously curved when she was pleased. But her voice was hard
and often shrill.

'Cutlets, please, Joan. No cereal. Plenty of coffee.' Noting the
set of her mouth, he asked: 'A war on, this morning?'

'Ma's in one of her moods.'

Tossing the fine-spun hair from her broad forehead, she
departed as though trained to walk by a ballet master, and he
remembered she had walked like that one morning when the
Lake was being born, and she was just seventeen, and the Boss

6

had come close to dismissing her and her mother because she could be dangerous ... among men without women.

'What upset your mother?' he asked when she was placing the covered dish before him.

'Oh, one thing and another.'

'You haven't been nagging, have you?'

She moved round the table and stood regarding him with eyes he was sure were green. She lifted her full breasts and lightly placed her hands against her hips, and he knew that to be a wanton a woman needed no training.

'A girl never nags, Mr Martyr, until she's married.'

'I believe you, Joan. Go away, and don't annoy your mother.'

'Well, she started it.'

'Started what?'

'Oh, nothing,' she said, and walked from the room rippling her bottom like a Kanaka woman.

Martyr proceeded with his breakfast, which had to be completed at a quarter after seven. Mother and daughter were constantly warring about nothing which came to the surface for men to see. As cook and housemaid they formed a team the like of which Lake Otway had never known. The food was excellently prepared and the house managed expertly. The main cause of contention between these women, Martyr shrewdly guessed, was their closeness in age, for the mother was still young, still vitally attractive, retaining that something of wantonness she had bequeathed to the girl. The husband? No one knew anything of the husband.

Martyr recalled Lake Otway on his accepting the appointment. The Lake was dry then, and the domestic staff comprised a man cook and the black wife of one of the hands. The house was merely a place to sleep in; these two quarrelling women gave it life.

When he was entering the office the telephone rang twice. The call would be for George Barby, who cooked for stockmen at Sandy Well, midway between the main homestead and the out-station. Martyr seated himself at the desk and filled a pipe, and had applied a match when the telephone rang thrice ... the Lake call. He counted ten before taking up the instrument.

'Morning, Dick!' spoke a deep, tuneful voice.

7

'Morning, Mr Wallace.'

'How's the Lake this morning?'

'Two feet ten. Gone down an inch since yesterday afternoon.'

'H'm! No sign of rain, and Inigo Jones says we needn't expect any till March 18th. Feed still going off?'

'Within a couple of miles of the Lake, yes. Rabbits in millions. More 'roos, too, this last week than I've ever seen. Moving in from the dry areas. White Dam is down to four feet.'

'Better shift those hoggets, then,' advised the Boss. 'In fact, Dick, we'd better think of shifting a lot of sheep from your end to the Sandy Well paddocks. When the Lake goes, it'll go quick. The last foot of water could dry out in a day. It did last time, I remember. We lost two thousand ewes in the Channel that time. What d'you intend doing today?'

'I'll send Carney out to ride White Dam paddock. And MacLennon to Johnson's Well to make a report on the mill and pump and tank.'

'Better get Lester to go along with Mac, and remind 'em to lower a light down the well before they go down. The air will be foul after all this time.'

'All right, Mr Wallace. What about the horses? Any sight of a breaker?'

'Yes, I was coming to that,' replied the Boss. 'Feller here now, wanting breaking work. Good references. I'll send him out tomorrow on the truck. Let me know tonight what you want out there.'

'The breaker, is he to have a free hand?'

'As he'll be working on contract, yes. Feed with the men, of course. The name's Bony.'

'Bony what?'

'Just Bony. Talks like a uni' professor. Queenslander, I think. When you've drafted off the youngsters for him, better send all the spares in here. We'll put 'em in the Bend. Well, I'll ring again tonight.'

The line went dead, and Martyr replaced the instrument and reached for his wide-brimmed felt. On leaving the office at the side of the house he faced across a two-acre space to the men's quarters. Backed by a line of pepper trees to his right stood the store, the machinery and motor sheds, the harness room, the stable for the night horse, and beyond this line of buildings were the stock and drafting yards, the well and windmill, and the pumping house. The hands were waiting at the motor shed for orders.

There were seven men ... five white and two black. The aborigines were flashily dressed, the white men content with cotton shirts and skin-tight trousers which had been boiled and boiled until all the original colour had gone with the suds.

The overseer called a name, and one of the aborigines came to him and was told to ride a paddock fence fifteen miles in length. The other aborigine he sent to see that sheep had not huddled into a paddock corner. A Swede, who had been unable to conquer his accent despite forty years in Australia, he sent to oil and grease a windmill, and a short, grey-eyed, tough little man named Witlow he despatched to see if cattle were watering regularly at a creek water-hole. Carney, young, alert, blond, smiling, was sent to White Dam to note the depth of water again. There was left MacLennon, dour, black-moustached, dark-eyed and with a prognathous jaw. A good man with machinery.

'Want you to look-see over Johnson's Well, Mac. You'll have to take the portable pump to lower the water in the shaft. Get the well pump out and inspect. Have a go at the mill, too. Make a note of everything that needs replacement. The truck will be coming out tomorrow.'

'Just as well. The ruddy Lake won't last much longer by the look of her, Mr Martyr.'

'And send a light down the well before you go down.'

'Oh, she'll be all right.'

'That's what the feller said up on Belar,' Martyr coldly reminded MacLennon. 'That well is still all right, Mac, but the feller who went down without testing five years ago has been dead five years. You'd better take Lester to give a hand. Use the ton truck. I'll tell Lester to draw your lunches.'

Lester was coming from breakfast and Martyr met him. He was middle-aged, shrivelled like a mummy by the embalming sun and wind. He affected a straggling moustache to hide his long nose. His pale-blue eyes were always red-rimmed and watery, and he was cursed by a sniffle which deputized as a chuckle. A good stockman, a reliable worker, for the time being Bob Lester was acting homestead rouseabout, doing all

9

the chores from bringing in the working hacks early to milking cows and slaughtering ration sheep at evening.

'Morning, Bob!'

'Mornin', Mr Martyr!' The watery eyes peered from under bushy grey brows.

'Not up your street, Bob, but would you go with Mac to Johnson's?' Without waiting for assent, Martyr concluded: 'Draw your lunches, and give Mac a hand with the portable pump. By the way, the breaker will be coming out tomorrow.'

Lester sniffed.

'Tomorrow, eh! Do we know him?'

'I don't. Goes by the name of Bony. A caste, from what the Boss implied. Ever hear of him?'

'No ... not by that name. Them sort's terrible good with horses when they're good, and terrible bad when they're crook.' Lester claimed the truism. 'You giving him an offsider?'

'Haven't decided,' replied the overseer, abruptly distant, and Lester sniffled and departed to ask Mrs Fowler to provide lunches.

Martyr strolled to the shed housing the power plant and started the dynamo. From there he crossed to the stock-yards, where the men were saddling horses. The night horse used by Lester to bring in the workers was waiting, and Martyr mounted the horse to take the unwanted hacks back to their paddock, a chore normally falling to the rouseabout. On his return, he assisted MacLennon and Lester to load the portable pump and saw they had the right tools for the work at Johnson's Well, and after they had driven away he went into the house and stood for the second time this morning on the front veranda overlooking Lake Otway.

Although Richard Martyr was acknowledged to be a stock expert and a top-grade wool man, it had been said that he didn't seem to fit into this background of distance and space bared to the blazing sky, but, in fact, he fitted perhaps a little too well. Moody, Mrs Fowler said of him; deep, was the daughter's verdict. A psychiatrist would have been assisted had he known of Martyr's secret vice of writing poetry, and could he have read some of it, the psychiatrist might have warned the patient to resist indulgence in morbid imaginings.

Even the coming dissolution of Lake Otway was beginning

to weigh upon his mind, and his mind was seeking rhyming words to tell of it. Actually, of course, he was too much alone: the captain of a ship, the solitary officer of a company of soldiers, the single executive whose authority must be maintained by aloofness.

Because he had watched the birth of Lake Otway, he knew precisely what the death of Lake Otway would mean. He had watched the flood waters spread over this great depression comprising ten thousand acres, a depression which had known no water for eighteen years. Properly it was a rebirth, because Lake Otway had previously been born and had died periodically for centuries.

Where the 'whirlies' had danced all day, where the mirage had lain like burning water, the colours of the changing sky lived upon dancing waves, and the waves sang to the shores and called the birds from far-away places ... even the gulls from the ocean. Giant fleets of pelicans came to nest and multiply. The cormorants arrived with the waders, and when the duck-shooting season began in the settled parts of Australia the ducks came in their thousands to this sanctuary.

All that was only three years ago. Nineteen feet of water covered the depression three miles wide and five miles long. Then, as a man begins to die the moment he is born, so did Lake Otway suffer attrition from the sun and the wind. The first year evaporation reduced the depth to fourteen feet, and the second year these enemies reduced it to eight feet.

It was the second year that Ray Gillen came over the back tracks from Ivanhoe way on his motor-bike and asked for a job. He was a wizard on that bike on all kinds of tracks and where no tracks were, and he was a superb horseman, too. Even now the sound of his laughter spanned the ridges of time since that moonlit night he had gone swimming and had not returned.

He ought to have come ashore. It was strange that the eagles and the crows never led the waiting men to the body, for there were exceptionally few snags in Lake Otway, and no outlet down the Tallyawalker Creek that year.

If only a man could strip that girl's mind and forget her body. She used to catch her breath when Ray Gillen laughed, and when he teased her, her eyes were blue ... like ... like blue lakes.

The Golden Bitch!

2

Bony comes to Porchester

IT WAS NOT an event to be forgotten by those closely associated with it. The details were recorded by the police and
studied by Detective-Inspector Bonaparte many months later.

Ray Gillen arrived at Lake Otway on September 3rd, and
the next morning was taken on the books by Richard Martyr.
As is the rule, no questions were asked of Gillen concerning
previous employment or personal history, the only interest
in him by his employer being his degree of efficiency in the
work he was expected to do. And as a stockman he was certainly efficient.

Nine weeks later, on the night of November 7th, Gillen
was drowned in Lake Otway, and late the following day the
senior police officer at Menindee arrived with Mr Wallace,
the owner. To Sergeant Mansell Martyr passed all Gillen's
effects, he having in the presence of witnesses listed the contents of Gillen's suitcase and the items of his swag.

At that time the men's quarters were occupied by Lester,
MacLennon, Carney and George Barby. The quarters consisted
of a bungalow having three bedrooms either side of the living-
room. Lester occupied one room and MacLennon another.
Carney occupied the same room with Gillen, and Barby had a
room to himself.

November came in very hot and the men often descended the
steps cut into the face of the bluff and bathed in the lake,
which at this date was twelve feet five inches deep. Neither
Lester nor MacLennon could swim. Barby could, but never
ventured far from the shore. Of about the same age ...
twenty-five ... both Gillen and Carney were strong swimmers,
especially the former, who boasted that, with a little training,
he would swim across the lake and back.

On the night of November 7th the moon was almost at full.
The day had been very hot, and the night warm and still. The
men played poker, using matches, until a quarter to eleven,
when they went to bed. Carney stated that shortly after he and

Gillen got to bed, Gillen announced his intention of going for a swim. Carney, on the verge of sleeping, declined Gillen's invitation to accompany him. He stated that it wasn't until he awoke the following morning that he discovered Gillen hadn't returned.

The last Carney saw of Gillen was when he put out the light on leaving the room. Gillen then was wearing only his pyjama trousers. A quick check of Gillen's clothes proved that he could not have returned from the lake, slept, awakened early and dressed and gone out. It was after breakfast, when Martyr appeared to give his orders for the day, that Gillen was reported missing.

For Sergeant Mansell a routine job. He examined Gillen's clothes, his swag of blankets, and the contents of his suitcase, the suitcase being of good quality. There was no clue to Gillen's people. He examined the man's motor-bike, a powerful machine in good condition, noted its registration and engine numbers, and went back to his office.

Wallace and his overseer organized the hands. Aborigines were brought from the River, and meanwhile Lester and Carney and MacLennon scoured the country about the Lake in the extremely unlikely event that Gillen had wandered away and become lost.

On the third day, and subsequently, all hands patrolled the shores to await the coming in of the body. The wind direction and the currents set up by the wind were carefully calculated. But the body did not come ashore, and it was ultimately assumed that it had been trapped by a wire fence crossing the lake which was, of course, submerged when the depression filled with water.

Among Gillen's effects was neither a driver's licence nor a registration certificate for the machine he rode. It was learned that the registered owner of the motor-cycle was a timber worker in Southern Queensland. He was traced to Toowoomba, where he was living at a good hotel and spending freely. He said he sold the bike to a man named Gillen, and described Gillen. He said that his present state of affluence was due to having a half-share with Gillen in a lottery ticket which won £25,000.

Asked how the money was divided, the timber worker told of an agreement to draw the full amount in cash from the bank into which the cheque for the prize had been paid. In an hotel room they had portioned out each share in Treasury notes. They wanted to look at a lot of money, and Gillen had left the next morning on his bike, saying he intended to tour Australia.

And the extraordinary facet of this tale of luck and division of so large a sum in notes of low denomination was that it was true. Gillen had left Toowoomba with something like £12,500 in his possession.

When his effects were examined first by Martyr in the presence of Lester and MacLennon, there was no money.

All the banks in the Commonwealth were asked if an account in Gillen's name had been opened. Result negative. Gillen's journey south into New South Wales and still farther south was traced. Here and there people remembered him. Debonair, handsome, a man seeking adventure. Plenty of money? Well, no, he didn't give that impression. What had the timber worker said of Gillen? 'Money! Ray never cared a hoot for money. Twelve thousand odd in his kip wouldn't worry him.'

Questions: Had he arrived at Lake Otway to accept a job when he possessed twelve thousand pounds? Again according to the timber worker, it was likely. Significantly, the timber worker added: 'Ray would take a job anywhere where there was a "good sort" around.'

There was a 'good sort' at Lake Otway. That £12,000 could not be traced. Gillen was known to be an excellent swimmer. The statements of four men tallied in that they all played poker with Gillen and always with matches. Fifteen months after Gillen was thought to be drowned, Inspector Bonaparte happened to peruse the case file.

There were several angles which, although unusual, were by no means psychologically improbable. Firstly, the personality of the man Gillen. He had been born and educated in Tasmania. On leaving school he worked on an uncle's farm, but the farm, apparently, was too cramped, and the boy crossed to the mainland, where he passed from job to job until, as a stockman in Northern Queensland, he had volunteered for service in Korea, where he had completed his term of service. Returning to Queensland, he joined two men in a timber contract.

14

After leaving the Tasmanian farm, there had never been lack of money in Gillen's life. The sudden acquisition of a large sum of money did not cause Gillen to rush to the fleshpots, as it had done to his partner in the lottery ticket. That lucky ticket provided Gillen with additional means to freedom, and many a man wants just that.

Therefore, that Ray Gillen had stuffed about £12,000 into his kip and set off on a motor cycle to see Australia was in keeping with the psychology of many young men in Bony's experience. Again, in accordance with the known personality of the missing man, Bony was confident that Gillen had asked for a job at Lake Otway after and not before he had met the 'good sort'. It had been the girl and not the job which decided Gillen to seek work at Lake Otway.

There arose the inevitable doubt when a strong swimmer takes a swim shortly before midnight and is drowned, and has among his possessions a large sum of easily spendable cash. A telegram to the senior officer of police at Menindee produced a result which could be looked at from several points. The Sergeant replied that none of the people employed at Lake Otway left after Gillen was drowned. Then no one of those employed with Gillen could have stolen his money, for surely had one done so he wouldn't stay on, but leave to enjoy the spending of it. But the fact that not one person *had* left was also decidedly odd, for all of them save the overseer could be typed as members of the great floating population who seldom stay in one place for more than a year.

And so, fifteen months after Gillen was assumed drowned, Inspector Bonaparte climbed into the cabin of a three-ton truck in the guise of a horse-breaker, Sergeant Mansell and Mr Wallace, the owner-manager of Porchester Station, being the only persons aware of his identity.

The horse-breaker was smoothly dressed in brown twill shirt and trousers, well worn elastic-sided riding boots, and an old broad-brimmed felt. And on the load was his neatly rolled swag of blankets and normal equipment. The truck driver wore a patched pair of greasy grey trousers, a blue denim shirt, whiskers seven days old and no boots. He was twice Bony's weight and one inch shorter. The Boss had referred to him as Red Draffin.

Once clear of the homestead paddocks and the obstructing

gates, Bony rolled a cigarette and settled for the long run. The sun this day of late January was hot and the air was clear. Bony was home, and the simple people like Red Draffin are at home here, too. Red trailed a shower of sparks from his pipe by knocking it against the outside of the door, and said:

'So you're from Queensland, eh? From old Uradangie. Long time back when I was up there. Usta be five pubs in my time. They still doing business?'

'Four are. The Unicorn was burned down.'

'That so! Hell! Remember the Unicorn. She was kept by ole Ted Rogers. Ruddy doer he was. So was his ole woman. They took turns in minding the bar ... week and week about. Neither could last longer than a week at a time. End of the week's spell in the bar, and both of 'em was a cot case. I did hear that Ted Rogers died in the horrors.'

'So did Mrs Rogers. She was in the horrors when the pub went up.'

'Was that so!' Red Draffin spat with vigour and almost automatically drove the loaded vehicle along the track twisting about low sand dunes, across salt and blue-bush flats, over water-gutters, and across dry creeks. 'Well, Ma Rogers could always drink as good as Ted, and he was extra. I seen him open a bottle of rum and drain the lot without winkin'. Hell! Men was men in them days. What brought you down south?'

'Change of country,' Bony replied. 'I get around.'

'I usta,' admitted Red Draffin. 'Never stayed on one fly-speck more'n a month.'

'You have settled down?'

'Yair. You blows out in the end, y'know. You find that the sandhill beyond the next one's just the same, and that Orstralia is just a pancake dotted with pubs wot are all alike. Course, times have changed a lot. The coming generation is too sap-gutted with fruit juices and milk in their tea, and nowadays if a man has a go of the horrors he ain't liked. Once on a time if a man didn't have the horrors he wasn't reckoned a man's shadder.'

'Had a bender lately?' Bony politely inquired.

'No, not for a long time now. I'm gettin' on, and after a bender I suffers something terrible from indigestion. Got to take a bit of care of meself.'

'How old are you?'

16

'Don't rightly know. Last census time, the Boss estimated me at sixty years. What d'you reckon about carb soda?'

'For the horrors?'

'No, me indigestion.'

'I've been told that carb soda is good for anything.'

''Bout right, too. Read in the paper that a bloke in Russia lived to be a hundred and forty 'cos he washed every day in carb soda. Might take that on meself. Carb soda's cheap enough.'

Bony thought the suggestion an excellent idea, but asked: 'How long have you been working on Porchester?'

'Me? Nine years and a bit. I've kinda settled on Porchester. Wallace is a good boss, and, as I said a mile or two back, the pubs in Menindee is just the same as they usta be up at Uradangie. Whisky's got more water in it and they charges six times more, that's all.'

'You'd know this run, then?'

Red Draffin spat at the passing wind, flexed his shoulders.

'I know every water-hole, every sandhill, every blade of grass on Porchester. Every ruddy sheep knows me be name, and this year there's over sixty thousand of 'em. Never took much to horses, though. You like horses . . . musta.'

'Yes, I like horses. What's the overseer like at Lake Otway?'

'Mister Martyr? Good enough,' replied Draffin. 'Knows his work. Done no one a bad turn that I ever heard about. Keeps his place and expects us to keep ours. You married?'

'Yes.'

'Me, too. Lasted eleven days and a bit. Found out me wife was married to a butcher in Cobar. She cleared out with a shearer, and me and the butcher's been good cobbers ever since. Women! You go careful with the women at Lake Otway.'

'There are women?'

'Two. Mother does the cookin' and the daughter does the housemaiding.' Draffin chuckled. 'Ruddy termites, both of 'em.'

'How so?'

'They eats into a man's dough from the inside out. And there's blokes wot likes it. Wouldn't leave the place. Reckons they got a good chance with the daughter or the mother. They sends away to Sydney or Adelaide for presents for 'em. You'll be a wake-up in no time.'

They passed a deserted hut built of pine logs, used only at the shearing season. An hour later they sighted a windmill and two huts partially surrounded by a high canegrass wall.

'Sandy Well,' Draffin said. 'Get a bit of lunch here.'

'Half-way house?'

'That's right. Twenty-six mile to the homestead and twenty-six on to the Lake. Feller called George Barby cooks here when he ain't fur-trapping. Good bloke, George Barby, though he is a pommy.'

Three dogs came racing to meet the truck and escort it to the door in the canegrass wall. From the view of the surrounding sandhills Bony deduced that the wall was essential when the storms raged.

Through the door there emerged a slightly-built man, dark of hair and pale of skin. He was wearing white duck trousers and a white cotton vest. After him came an enormously fat pet sheep, and after the sheep came two outsized black and white cats. Finally there appeared a tame galah, red of breast and grey of back. The parrot waddled forward absurdly, flapped its wings and raised its rose-tinted comb while shrieking its welcome.

The pet sheep chased Red Draffin round the truck, and George Barby said to Bony:

'Come on in and have a cuppa tea.'

3

The Thinker

FOR A MAN of sixty, Red Draffin could move. So, too, could the pet sheep. The bootless, whiskered man appeared from behind the truck and raced for the door in the wall, the large wether hard astern and bouncing the sand with legs like props. Shouting with laughter, the truck driver kept the hard, butting head at bay with one hand and with the other he thrust a plug of black tobacco between his teeth, bit off a chunk and presented it to the sheep. The sheep almost spoke his thanks and retired placidly chewing.

Throughout this exhibition, the pale-faced cook never smiled; in fact, Bony fancied he detected disapproval of Red Draffin's undignified behaviour. He led the way through the door in the wall. After him went Bony, and after Bony came Red Draffin. Following on came the two enormous cats, and after the cats waddled the galah. The dogs only remained without. The sheep arrived later.

Inside the wall of canegrass were two huts, and the cook led the procession to that which served as the kitchen-dining-room.

'Boss said you were coming out,' he remarked, waving to the table set for three. 'Did you bring me stores and mail and things?'

'Get 'em off the load later, George,' replied Draffin. 'Meet Bony. He's goin' out to the Lake breakin'.'

George and Bony nodded the introduction, and Draffin went on:

'Bony's come down from Uradangie. You never been up there, George?'

Barby asked to be told why he should have been up at Uradangie and Bony looked about the hut. It was surprisingly clean and tidy. The cooking was done with camp ovens and billies on the large open hearth. There were crevices between the pine log walls and several holes in the corrugated iron roof. But the place was cool this hot day, and what it was like when the wind blew the sand off the summits of the surrounding dunes he could imagine.

Barby served roast mutton, potatoes and tomato sauce. The bread was well baked and the tea was hot. He sat on the form at the table opposite his visitors, and the conversation at first excluded Bony. Slightly under fifty, he had been so long in Australia that his Lancashire accent had almost vanished. His face was long, his chin pointed. His eyes were dark and, in the soft light, brilliant. And like the great majority of bush dwellers he was intelligent and well read.

To Bony's amusement the galah suddenly appeared above table-level. Using beak and claws, the bird climbed the cook's cotton vest to gain his shoulder, and once there distended its rosy comb and emitted a screech of defiance at the guests. Barby went on talking as might a mother pass off the misbehaviour of her child, but the effort was ruined when the bird said softly and confidentially in his ear:

'Bloody ole fool.'

'Lake's getting low, they say,' Barby remarked, offering no sign of annoyance, or of being conscious of the 'brat'. The bird proceeded to preen his feathers, and Draffin said:

'Down to three feet. Bit under, accordin' to the Boss this morning. She'll go out like a light when she does throw a seven.'

Barby politely wiped his mouth with a pot rag, and the bird lovingly scraped its beak against his ear.

'Ought to be good money in rabbits,' he said. 'And now that Royalty's taken to fox furs the skins ought to be high come May and June.'

'Yair. But rabbit skins are low now, though. Only three quid a hundred.'

'Quantity would make the dough,' Barby pointed out. 'There's quantity enough round that Lake, and when she dies there'll be more rabbits than could be handled by a thousand trappers. I'm thinking of giving it a go. What d'you reckon?'

'Could think about it,' answered Draffin. 'You said anything to the Boss?'

'This morning. Boss said he'd try for another cook. You size up the possible take out at the Lake, and we'll decide when you come back.' To Bony he said: 'You going to work contract?'

'Yes. On a dozen horses to start with.'

The galah screeched, and the noise would have upset a stoic. Barby puffed into its near eye and the bird screeched again, and at once, insulted, proceeded to descend from the shoulder as it had climbed. It fell off the stool to the ground and nipped a cat that spat and fled. Quite unconcerned, Barby said:

'Nice place, Lake Otway. Good tucker. Good quarters. You ought to do well. Tell the women you're married and got fifteen kids, and you're hard put to it to buy fag tobacco.'

'I tipped him off,' said Red Draffin.

'I am married, and I have three children,' Bony told them. 'I can easily add another twelve. Termites, Red said they are.'

Barby regarded Bony with prolonged scrutiny.

'As I told you, Lake Otway's a nice place. Best policy is to know nothing, and see everything, and give nothing away.

Some of the fellers out there been there too long. You know how it is.'

'I have known a similar set-up,' agreed Bony. 'I'm all for the move on.'

'And we'd better get going, too,' said Draffin, rising.

All went out to the truck ... dogs, cats, sheep and galah. Draffin climbed the load to take off stores and a bag of mail and papers. The sheep nudged at Bony's hip, persisted, and the cook said:

'He wants a pinch of tobacco.'

Bony produced the 'pinch' and the sheep daintily accepted it and chewed with evident delight. The galah waddled to his feet and ducked its head and turned over on its back. For the first time Barby smiled. He clicked his tongue and the sheep went to him. He picked up the cats and placed them on the sheep, and the bird he put with the cats, and as the truck rolled away, Bony waved and was always to remember that picture.

When a mile had passed under the wheels, Red said:

'If the Boss wants to shift flocks from the back end of the run where it's pretty dry already this summer, I can't see him agreeing to George taking on the rabbits. Cooks ain't that easy to get. If the Boss says no, George might stand by it, but I don't think so. For a long time now George has had his mind on trapping when the Lake dried out. Funny bloke.'

'How so?' pressed Bony, turning his sea-blue eyes to the driver.

'Well, he don't spend and he don't drink and he don't go for skirts. They sez never to trust that kind of bloke, but George is all right even though he's got a mania for saving money. Now me, I reckon money's only good for booze. But what does George do? He saves his dough till he's got enough to buy a good ute and a trapping outfit. When fur prices is good he slings in the cookin' and goes trapping, and when the trappin' is finished he goes back to cookin'. No between spell, no guzzle on the honk. Not even a trip down to the city. Why? Search me! Tain't like he was savin' to buy a pub, or a race-horse or something. He ain't got no wife to drain him, neither. Leastways he never owned to one.'

The wind came after the truck and the cabin was hot and fouled with burned gas and oil. Only at Sandy Well had they seen animals on this trip, and the naïve would have complained that the land was a desert. Invisible animals hugged the shadows of trees and bush, and deep underground the warrens were packed with rabbits.

They were travelling over a treeless plain extending for twelve miles when Draffin broke a long silence.

'Crook, the Lake dryin' up like she is,' he said as though speaking of one close to him. 'Lot of fish in her, too. Cod up to nine pound and brim up to seven.'

'The floods filled it, of course,' encouraged Bony.

'Yair. Record flood what began up your way. The River got miles wide, and the overflow brought water into the Lake. Nineteen feet of water she took, and with it she took enough fish spawn to feed Orstralia for a year.'

'And now the water has drained from the Lake?'

'No. Evaporation took six or seven feet a year. Then there's the birds. Ruddy thousands of birds from pelicans down to moorhens. And this summer there's been millions of rabbits drinking at her. Cripes! No lake could stand for that.'

'Do any fishing yourself?'

'Now and then.'

'Boat, of course.'

'There was a boat, but she broke up on the beach one windy day. You hear about the bloke what was drowned? In the Adelaide papers?'

'No, I didn't read about it. Working for the Station?'

'Yair. Bloke by the name of Ray Gillen. Goes to bed a hot night and then says he'll go for a swim. Good swimmer, too. Usta go a hell of a way out and muck about before he came in. Boasted he'd swim across the Lake and back. Could swim, all right, but he got himself drowned. About eleven at night, it was. Full moon. Left the quarters with only his 'jama trousers on. Never came back.'

Yet another gate stopped them, and after Bony had opened and closed it, and they were moving towards scrub-covered dunes which appeared an impassable barrier, he said:

'The body was recovered?'

'No, it wasn't,' replied Draffin. 'There was no body come ashore, no 'jamas, no nothink. Ray Gillen just went for a swim and the next morning they wondered wot in hell had happened to him. Got blacks out from the River. Scouted around for a week. They tracked him down to the water but couldn't track him out again. They nutted out the wind and drift of the tide and such like, and argued Gillen had to come ashore along the west end of the Lake. But he didn't. He stopped right down on the bottom somewheres. Funny about that. I always thought there was . . .'

'What?' Bony softly urged, and it seemed that the noise of the engine prevented the question from reaching the driver. Louder, he added: 'What did you think?'

'Well, just between us. Tain't no good stirring up muddy water, but I've always thought there was something funny about that drowning. You see, Ray Gillen wasn't the sort of bloke to get himself drowned. He was the sort of bloke wot did everything goodo. Fine horseman. Make you giddy lookin' at him ride his motor-bike. Swim like a champion. Goes through Korea without battin' an eyelid.'

'And nothing has been heard or found since?'

'Right, Bony. Not a trace. Trick of a bloke, too. Always laughin' and teasin'. Good-lookin' and a proper skirt chaser. The young bitch out there was eyeing him off and puttin' the hooks into him, but I reckon he was too fly for her. Anyhow, bad feelin' worked up with the other blokes, and one evening there was fireworks, Ray and MacLennon getting into holts. I wasn't there, but Bob Lester told me they hoed into it for half an hour before Mac called it a day.'

'But Gillen must have been drowned,' Bony argued. 'Wearing only his pyjama trousers, he couldn't have cleared away to another part of the State.'

'That's so,' Draffin agreed.

'Well, then, he must have been drowned,' persisted Bony, prodding the simple driver to defend himself.

'Could of been, and then he could of not. George Barby told me he reckons Gillen went after a woman that night.'

'Wearing only pyjama trousers?'

'It was a hot night, and it ain't necessary to be all dressed up.'

'Well, he went visiting, then disappeared. That it?'

'Yair.'

Red Draffin braked the truck on a hard claypan and silently cut chips from a black plug. Without speaking he rubbed the chips to shreds and loaded his odorous pipe and, still without speaking, lit the pipe and again settled to his driving. When

23

they had covered a further three miles he voiced his thoughts.

'Don't know what you think about things, Bony, but I reckon booze is a safer bet than women. You can trust booze. You know just what it can do to you. But women! All they think about is what they can get out of a bloke. Look! Only the blacks get their women in a corner and keeps 'em there. Do they let women play around with 'em? No fear. They gives their women a beltin' every Sunday morning regular, and there's never no arguing or any funny business during the ruddy week.'

'There's an old English custom. Are you sure the blacks choose Sunday mornings for the belting?' Bony asked, and Red Draffin, noting the smile and the twinkling blue eyes, roared with laughter.

'Could be they makes it Sat'day night sometimes so's not to miss out,' he conceded, a broad grin widening the spaced flame of hair on his face.

'What makes you think Gillen mightn't have been drowned?'

'Well, you being a stranger, sort of, I can talk to you, and you can keep it under your bib. As I said, it's no use stirring up mud. When you get a bird's eye view of Ma Fowler and the daughter you might feel like me about Ray Gillen. Y'see, it was like this. Ray had a good suitcase, and one day I'm having a pitch with him in his room when he was changing his unders. He pulls the case from below his bed, and he unlocks it with a key what he kept on a cord with a locket, what he always had slung round his neck. The case was full of clothes. He took a clean vest and pair of pants off the top of the stuff in the case, and he had to kneel on the lid to get it locked again.

'That was a week before he went missing. I wasn't at the Lake when he drowned, if he did, but George Barby was, and the next day, or the day after, the overseer got Bob Lester and George to be with him when he opened the case and made a list of what was inside. And accordin' to George Barby, the case was only three parts full of clothes and things. I never said nothink to no one except George about that, but I've thought a lot of what happened to make the tide go down like it did.'

'And did the overseer discover anything in the case, or find anything about Gillen's parents or relatives?' Bony asked, to

24

keep the subject before Red Draffin.

'Not a thing. Ray's motor-bike's still in the machinery shed 'cos nobuddy's claimed it, and the police took the suit-case and things. I'll tell you what I think. I think Ray got wise to them women, or someone got wise to him, and that sort of started someone off. I tell you straight, I don't believe he got himself drowned, and I wouldn't be surprised if they come across his skeleton when the Lake dries up and find there's bones broken what the water couldn't of broke. So don't go muckin' about these women. Keep to the booze and you'll be all right, like me.'

'I will,' Bony promised, and there was no further oppor-tunity to discuss the disappearance of Ray Gillen.

So swiftly as to provide a shock, the ground fell away before the truck, to reveal the track winding down a long red slope, the buildings clustered at the bottom, and the great expanse of sun-drenched water beyond, shaped like a kidney and pro-mising all things delightful after the long and arid journey.

'Beaut, ain't she!' remarked the ungainly, uncouth driver, and added with genuine regret: 'Just too crook her going to die.'

4

'I am what I am'

THE TRUCK STOPPED outside the store and Bony's world was filled with sounds common to every outback home-stead. Chained dogs barked and whined. The power engine chugged in rivalry with the clanging of the lazy windmill. Cockatoos shrieked and magpies chortled. People appeared and gathered about the truck.

Bony opened his door and stepped out. To him no one spoke. He saw Red Draffin pass the mailbag to a dapper man and knew instantly he was the Boss of the out-station. The other men were types to be seen anywhere beyond the rail-ways. He was conscious first of a big-boned woman with flashing dark eyes and raven hair, and a moment later was gazing into eyes as blue as his own. In them was reserved approval. His eyes registered points ... deep gold hair, oval face, wide full-lipped mouth ... and again his eyes met the eyes of the girl, and they were green and smiling and approving.

'Now you two wash and come in for your dinner,' the elder woman told Red Draffin. 'I've kept it hot for you, so don't delay by gossiping.'

Draffin grinned at her, and took Bony to the men's quarters where they shared a room. In the shower house at the rear of the building they washed and then Bony needs must return to the bedroom to comb and brush his hair.

'Never mind making yourself look like a fillum star,' Red said.

Bony was sure that neither comb nor brush had been applied to the red hair for many years, but his own lifelong habits could not be interrupted by Red's impatience. He was conducted across the open space and into the men's dining annexe off the kitchen. Mrs Fowler appeared carrying loaded plates.

'Well, how's things, Ma?' Draffin cheerfully asked as he slid his enormous buttocks along the table-flanking form.

The woman's dark eyes flashed and her mouth became grim.

'You should have been smothered at birth.'

'Now, now, no offence meant,' placated the driver. 'All widders are natural mothers to me. You're a widder, aren't you? Hope so, anyhow.'

'Eat your dinner. And don't waste your time. I told you last time you were out that you haven't a chance.'

'So you did. Never mind. Next time I'm out here you won't. Or it might be the time after.'

Mrs Fowler sat on the end of the form nearest the door to the kitchen and regarded Bony with slow appraisement. He was supposed to be a horse-breaker and to be casual in manner and careless in speech, but he was too wise to adopt in the beginning idiosyncrasies which with the passage of time would be difficult to maintain. As, ultimately, he would be judged by his acts, he decided to be himself.

From glancing at the man of cubic proportions and slovenly habits he studied the woman. That she was the mother of

26

Green Eyes was very hard to credit, for there was no hint of the matron about her figure. She smiled at Bony with her lips and not her eyes.

'D'you think Red would have a chance, Mr . . . er . . . ?'

'Call me Bony,' he replied, beaming upon her, and noted the fleeting shock he gave. 'I cannot believe that Mr Draffin has the merest ghost of a chance.'

'Chance of what?' asked Joan Fowler, who appeared at the kitchen door and came to sit opposite her mother. She sat slightly sideways, that she could the better see Bony who was sitting on the same form.

Bony hesitated to explain, and was glad when Red took the lead.

'The chance of marrying your mother, Joan. What do you reckon?'

The smoky blue-green eyes were insolent and the girl smiled. 'Not a hope, you would never be able to fix her.'

The mother rose hastily, saying:

'That's enough of that.' Then she looked at Bony, her dark eyes casual, but incapable of masking her mind. 'You'll like being here, Bony,' she said. 'How long are you staying?'

Although returning her gaze, he was conscious of the girl's eyes.

'It depends,' he replied. 'A month perhaps.'

'Where have you come from?' asked the girl.

'Down from Uradangie,' Red gave the answer. 'Up at Uradangie women never arst questions.'

'You hurry with your dinner, Red, and get out,' Joan told him.

'I'm not leaving without Bony,' Red stated. 'I like him too much to leave him alone with you two.'

'Bony can look after himself,' snapped Mrs Fowler.

'Not with you, he can't. He ain't old enough yet to hold his own with either of you.'

Mrs Fowler gathered the plates on a tray and departed to bring in the sweet course. Red winked at Bony, and tore a crust of bread with teeth able to smash walnuts. The girl watched him, a sneer on her face, and determined to 'sit' him out. Her mother reappeared to ask:

'Do they bake better bread up at Uradangie, Bony?'

'Madam,' Bony gravely began, 'neither at Uradangie nor

elsewhere in Australia do they bake better bread than yours. And, please, permit me to compliment you on your cooking.'

The woman's smile of appreciation was almost tender, and then Draffin intruded.

'Talks like Ray Gillen, don't he?'

The smile was wiped from the woman's face.

'He does not, Red Draffin,' she said, venomously.

'Something like,' purred the daughter. 'We are going to like him, too.'

Bony almost bowed sitting down, and Draffin had to toss in the final spanner.

'Well, well, it won't be long now 'fore the Lake dries out and we can collect poor old Ray and find out if he did die from no air. Wouldn't be surprised if . . .'

'Stop that kind of talk, Red,' commanded the elder woman.

'All right! All right! Don't go crook at everything I say,' complained Red and lurched to his feet. 'Come on, Bony. Let's go 'fore there's blood spattered all over the walls.'

'Do you play cards, Bony?' asked the girl. 'Come over one evening. You'll be welcome.'

'Thank you. Yes, I like a game of poker now and then.'

'I like poker, too,' the girl said, sleepy green eyes challenging alert blue eyes. But Bony smiled at both women and followed Red Draffin out into the sunset.

Red introduced him to the other men, and they were not greatly interested, superficially, in the stranger. The two blacks had withdrawn to their own camp, an old hut farther along the lake shore, and the whites were excusably engrossed in their mail and papers, which were irregularly delivered. He felt their reserve and decided it was too soon to worry about the precise classification of their attitude. The only man with whom he had conversation was called Earle Witlow, middle-aged, rotund, grey and cheerful, and the subject of mutual interest was horses. Another, elderly but alert and addressed as Swede, invited all and sundry to play cards and received no co-operation. He didn't meet Martyr until the following morning when orders were issued for the day, and by then he had summed up this small community.

The two aborigines, of course, were a section to themselves. Earle Witlow and the Swede appeared to be joined in some

28

kind of alliance, and the remainder were peculiarly individualistic. These individualists were Lester, MacLennon and Carney. They were the 'old hands', who, with George Barby, had been working here when Ray Gillen was drowned.

MacLennon and Carney were sent out for the youngsters and half an hour later their whips could be heard like exploding rifles, and soon a spear of dust speeding down the slope to the homestead became a river of horses, and ultimately the head of the spear was rammed into the open gateway of a yard. They emitted a cloud of red dust for a minute or two before the restless animals quietened.

Men sat on the top rail of the yard and watched the horses – the overseer and Bony, Lester and MacLennon and Carney. No one commented, and Bony quickly felt he was being appraised rather than the youngsters.

Fifteen taut-eyed young horses who had never known bridle and saddle, or the caress of a rope, stared at the men on the rail, and the men rolled cigarettes or filled a pipe and waited. They would have to be satisfied that he, Bony, could break in horses, for they must be made to accept him as such, and so enable him to fit into their own background.

Without being a horseman one could watch the change from the exhilaration of the open gallop, to the uneasy fear of the trap which held them, to the acceptance of the trap and men immobile on the top rail. And then when Bony slid to the ground within the yard, fifteen pairs of eyes pricked and fifteen pairs of nostrils whistled wind.

Martyr and his three stockmen moved not a fraction. Their faces were blank, but their eyes were quick and hooded, as though eager to detect errors. And although he hadn't handled horses for years, Inspector Bonaparte fancied he could disappoint them.

Standing in the centre of the yard, he clicked his tongue, and the horses could not choose a corner where they might be safe. He sauntered after them as they rushed from corner to corner, deliberately taking time to judge their points and sum up their characters. For a little while he leaned against the yard rails and slowly rolled a cigarette, like a man unable to make up his mind which horse to back for a race. He put on a good act, but at the same time shrewdly chose the animals most amenable to begin with.

Then with slow deliberation of all movement, which is the greatest weapon in the breaker's armoury, he opened a gate to an inner yard. A bay filly made a hesitant step forward, hoping that through that gate lay freedom. A black sister nudged her, and as one the fifteen sprang for it. Twelve got through before the gate barred three.

With the patience of a row of Jobs, the rail-sitters watched for thirty minutes Bony merely sauntering after those three horses, round and round the yard walls. They could hear his tongue clicking, and the seemingly careless slapping of hand against a thigh, and they watched as the three animals slowly tired and became bored with this seemingly endless round-about.

When Bony finally stood in the yard centre, the three horses also stilled to watch him, ears thrust forward, nostrils quivering. He moved quietly towards them, talking softly, and they stiffened and shivered and whistled through pink-lined nostrils. Then they would break and rush to another corner. The watchers lost count of the number of 'tries' before one horse stood, forefeet braced, nostrils flaring, muscles trembling, and waited for man's next movement.

Bony walked to this horse, his eyes upon the eyes of the horse, his voice low, crooning, himself creating the impression of irresistible power. The horse became as of hewn marble. The gap between it and the man narrowed till but two feet separated them. The horse couldn't back, for the yard wall was hard behind it; it could lunge forward, but it didn't dare. Instead, it brought its soft muzzle towards the man, and its body seemed to lean forward over the braced forelegs.

'He's hypnotizing the bastard,' hissed Lester to the overseer, and Martyr ignored the comment.

Bony's right hand rose slowly to touch the animal's jaw. The horse shivered violently. The human hand slid from the jaw to the rippling shoulder muscles, and the watchers witnessed fear die away and muscles gradually calm. They saw Bony patting the shoulder, slip a hand under the horse's throat, pass up the arched neck to the ears. Then Bony slowly turned his back to the horse, remained in that position for half a minute before walking away.

The second horse proved more difficult, but the third was like the first, and finally Bony climbed the rails to sit beside the overseer, and roll a cigarette. No one spoke. Having applied a match to the smoke, Bony said:

'You have a handy paddock for the mokes?'

'Yes. What do you think of them?'

'Passable. I'd like the lot taken out to the paddock and yarded again this afternoon.'

'Why?' asked Martyr. 'You've got 'em for the day, haven't you?'

'I want them to become used to yarding without rebellion. I want them to become so accustomed to these yards that they will never give trouble when being driven to any yard. And I want to handle them so that they will stand while I climb over them, under them, all round them. They have to be quiet before I ride them, because I'm no buck-jumper rider. I don't break a horse, I train him.'

'All right, if that's the way you want it.'

'Thanks. You might ask your riders to leave their whips behind. There's too much noise, too much excitement. Later, I'll get them used to a whip cracking against their ears.'

Martyr ordered Carney and MacLennon to return the youngsters to the paddock and to bring them to the yards again after lunch. Lester seemed inclined to remain, and was told to get on with his chores. Alone, Martyr said:

'Haven't seen you in this district before.'

'First time I've been down this way. The Diamantina's my country.'

'Oh. Then why come?'

Bony chuckled.

'Woman trouble,' he said, and from Martyr's nod knew he had been accepted.

5

Below Surface

AT THE CLOSE of his first week as horse-breaker, Bony knew he had successfully 'edged' himself into this small community, and further, he was confident that there were strange under-currents in this community, opposed to him and to two other men . . . Kurt Helstrom and Earle Witlow.

Helstrom, always addressed as Swede, was grey and tall and long-jawed. He had a strong sense of humour which he himself appreciated most and it made no impression upon his ebullient nature when others appreciated it not at all. He preferred the company of Earle Witlow to anyone else's and it appeared that Witlow liked the Swede. Witlow, much younger, looked much older, for he was a sun-dried raisin of a man who spoke but rarely to anyone other than Helstrom.

The others, that is Lester, Carney and MacLennon, for the two aboriginal stockmen were quite apart, while not openly hostile to each other were bound by an invisible cord which would have been accepted by anyone less intuitive than Bony as the clannishness of old employees.

Witlow had been employed at Porchester Station for four years, but at Lake Otway for only the last seven months, and the Swede had been put on the pay-roll eight months back. Neither had been at Lake Otway when Ray Gillen came, or when Gillen was drowned. Lester had been working on Porchester for fifteen years and he had gone to the city every year for a spell, but not after Gillen had come to Lake Otway. MacLennon's service had begun three years ago, and Carney had ridden paddocks about Sandy Well for two years before being transferred to the out-station shortly after Lake Otway had been born.

Lester and MacLennon and Carney had been working here when Gillen vanished that moonlit night. That was fifteen months back, and not one of them had left the place for a spell since then. One man of several working under such conditions of isolation might decide not to take a spell, his ambition to knock up a good cheque, but it was rare enough to be an oddity for three men to work more than a year without a holiday.

The same tag applied to the Fowler women. They had come to Lake Otway shortly after its birth and had remained ever since without once leaving the out-station. Like the men, they bought their clothes per mail-order, but, being women, it was a trifle odd how they had so long resisted the shops.

There was another matter to spur speculation. The two women, the three men and Barby, the cook, were much more concerned by the coming death of Lake Otway than seemed normal, certainly more so than Witlow and the Swede, and when Bony coloured the known facts concerning Gillen with impressions gained during this first week breaking horses he felt that the death of Lake Otway could coincide with the climax of a drama which began when Raymond Gillen came.

He had had no further opportunity to probe Red Draffin, as Draffin had returned to the main homestead the day after he brought Bony and the load to the Lake. Draffin had certainly voiced suspicions, but it had been to a casual worker who would not long remain, concerning especially the suitcase and contents belonging to the vanished Gillen. In view of the fact that it was officially believed that Gillen possessed twelve thousand odd pounds in notes of low denominations. Draffin's remarks about the 'tide' having ebbed in that suitcase appeared significant.

As Bony had foreseen, this was not an investigation wherein he could bamboozle suspects with questions and hope to bring out the solution with the slickness of city detectives backed by willing informers. Actually he had but one problem: to establish Gillen's fate, which, because of the non-location of twelve thousand pounds, cast grave doubt that the man's fate had been accidental drowning.

Seven people were here when Gillen vanished, and those seven people were still at Lake Otway, including George Barby, who was only twenty-six miles distant and who wanted to return for the trapping.

Twelve thousand pounds is quite a sum. No bank held it in safe keeping, it being reasonable to assume that as Gillen came into possession of the money lawfully there would have been no cause for him to have banked the money in an assumed name. It was also reasonable to assume that Gillen would have done something about it had it been stolen from him. Thus, until proved otherwise, it must be assumed that Gillen arrived at Lake Otway with twelve thousand pounds 'in the kip'.

Twelve thousand pounds in notes of low denomination make up quite a parcel. A bank manager had demonstrated the size of the parcel to Bony before he left Brisbane, and that parcel could be the difference between the high and the low 'tide' noted by Red Draffin.

T—D.O.A.L.—B   33

Further, if one of the men had stolen the money from the suitcase when it was thought Gillen had drowned in the Lake, would that man have continued working at Lake Otway? Assuming so, then the reason for sticking to his job must indeed be extremely powerful.

Yes, questions here and now would be out of order. A prodding perhaps, a good deal of listening and working out sums, plus the aid of the old ally, Time, would provide a break soon or late. His role was to be unobtrusive, subtly diplomatic, acceptable to all seven suspects.

Seven suspects! The overseer, Martyr, was run-of-the-mill. Public school education . . . apprentice jackaroo . . . sub-overseer . . . undermanager. Next step up, manager. But that final step a very long step, indeed. Martyr knew how to handle men and, according to Mr Wallace, he was proficient in handling sheep and cattle. He was introspective, imaginative and ambitious.

There was Bob Lester, uninhibited, nervy, earth-bound, with a wonderful memory for sporting details. MacLennon was restrained yet virile, slightly morose, determined, and could be dangerous. Carney was young, fearless, imaginative, well read, and not as well educated as he claimed to be. Barby was something of a mystery, conforming to no type. Well read, quietly observant, careful with his money and ambitious to make more.

The women had to be considered, for either could have raided Gillen's suitcase. The mother was still young and attractive, man-hungry and avid for conquest. Not the type to stay put for so long. The daughter was alluring and knew it. Bring her in contact with a good-looking and daring young man and a bush fire could start in the centre of Lake Otway. Or would the flame be kindled by twelve thousand pounds?

It was after five in the afternoon that Bony actually came in contact with the hands, for they and Martyr had been engaged in moving several of the huge flocks of sheep from the back of the run to those paddocks around Sandy Well. Even Lester, the rouseabout, was called on to assist, so that during the day Bony was the only man about the place. He suffered but one hardship: to keep track of the lies he told, for the way of the liar is, indeed, hard.

As is the custom, one of the women would tap the triangle

with a bar to call him to morning smoko-tea and again in the afternoon. Lunch, which he took with them, was more formal. He was amused to find both mother and daughter piqued because he failed to progress according to their assessment of him.

At morning and afternoon 'smoko' they talked intelligently of everything excepting Ray Gillen, to whom he never referred, but as the days slipped by their interest in the falling level of Lake Otway sharpened. At the close of that first week of Bony's employment, the Lake fell by four inches.

The men's interest in the Lake was just as marked. Often they returned to the yards with only a few minutes in hand to wash before the dinner gong was struck, but always they scanned Lake Otway to note the imperceptible changes taking place. At this time of day, Bony was usually sitting in a broken arm-chair on the veranda of the quarters overlooking the Lake.

Then came that late afternoon when the first sign of volcanic emotion surged above surface. Bony sensed that the beginning occurred before the men returned from work, before they came trudging across from the horse yards where they had freed their mounts to roll on the sand and take their fill at the trough.

'I'm going in for breaking,' remarked Harry Carney when passing to his room. He was cheerful of voice, but anger lurked in his eyes.

'Yair, better'n stock-ridin', anyhow,' agreed Lester, and sniffled. 'You just hypnotizes a youngster for an hour or two each morning, and then lays off all afternoon in a comfortable chair well in the shade, with a book or addin' up the dough you've earned. Wonderful job.'

MacLennon, stocky and powerful, said nothing. He stood at the end of the veranda looking down at the Lake, now as placid as a road puddle. Overseer Martyr appeared on the house veranda, also obviously interested in the Lake.

'Been hot today,' Bony remarked. 'Mrs Fowler said at lunch it was a hundred and two in the pepper-tree shade.'

'Four hundred and two in the sun,' rumbled MacLennon. 'I hate these windless days. Makes the flies real vicious.'

He passed off to the shower, and the Swede came and laughed at Bony and asked how it felt to be a 'cap'list feller'

– asked with the usual roar of laughter. Witlow merely grinned and went in for his towel.

Presently Carney reappeared, cleaned and his fair hair slicked with water. He stood by Bony's chair and rolled a smoke.

'No mail out, I suppose?' he asked, gazing down at the Lake. Bony shook his head, and Carney added: ' 'Bout time someone brought it. Hell! The Lake looks like someone's poured gold into it.'

The gong thrummed through the heated evening air, and Bony took his old and tattered Charles Garvice to his room. On coming out, he found Lester looking at Lake Otway, as Carney and MacLennon had done, and he called:

'It will be still there after dinner.'

'Yair, that's so, Bony.' Lester joined him and they walked after the other two men. 'Going down fast, though. Another four weeks will see her out.'

'A pity.'

'Yair. She was beaut up to last Christmas, and when she was full there was no need to go down to the seaside for a cool-off beer. Given a good wind the waves would come curling in a white surf, and at night you could hear it miles away. It never seemed hot in the paddocks, when you could come home to it.'

'Have you seen this place when there's no water?'

'Too right. Just a flat all over, covered with bush rubbish. Blasted heat trap, too. Water comes into her every seventeen to twenty years, and then stays only for three years at most.'

They ate without sustained conversation, what there was of it being carried on by Witlow and the Swede. They were, of course, tired from the heat and the burning sun and the pestiferous flies, but they seemed taciturn when a normal gang could have tossed chaff at each other. Only towards the end of the meal did one address Bony, and he was Lester, who inquired of his progress with a brown gelding. Bony was making his progress report when Joan Fowler came to the door leading to the kitchen and waved to Bony, saying:

'Cards?'

Bony rose and bowed.

'At eight?' he said, smilingly.

The girl laughed and disappeared. Bony sat down conscious

of the hostility in MacLennon and Harry Carney. Witlow, the bow-legged, whimsical Witlow, dryly chuckled, and his apparent friend, the Swede, jibed:

'You tink Bony been pawing the ground whiles we's been working all day?'

'Could of been,' conceded Witlow. 'You can never trust these horse-breakers, Kurt.'

'What you reckon?' asked the Swede, grinning at Bony. 'Better for us to sit in on cards, too – just to make sure he keep all right?'

'Yair, better,' Lester put in. 'Bony isn't old enough to play cards with grown wimmen. He'd be fleeced for a monte.'

'Perhaps I shall need a little support,' Bony laughingly agreed.

MacLennon crashed his eating utensils down on his plate, got up and left. In the silence, Lester sniffled, and Carney drawled:

'You can cut out the fleecing idea, Bob. Sounds bad.'

His round face was flushed and his eyes were void of the usual good humour. The Swede leered wickedly, opened his mouth to say something and shut it in pain when Witlow kicked his ankle under the table.

That was that, and it fell out that Bony and Witlow were the last to leave the annexe. When crossing back to the quarters, the little man murmured:

'Keep your hair on, Bony. That Bitch likes to make trouble. You might be able to use yourself, but Mac's an ex-ring champ.'

'Thanks for the tip. I'll tread lightly,' Bony said, and added: 'There wouldn't be anything in treading on other people's toes here.'

'Wise feller. They're a funny mob. Best to let 'em cook in their own camp fire.'

Bony chuckled, and they paused to look out over the Lake and at the sea-gulls that came winging in to land with the hens who were waiting to be fed.

'Long way from the sea for the gulls,' Bony observed.

' Six hundred miles from the nearest salt water at Port Augusta. It could be they've never seen the sea.'

'Yes, that's likely. Get the Swede to come in for cards. Safety in numbers, you know.'

Bony pondered about Witlow, and decided he would ask this stockman a few questions.

6

Fish and Fowl

AT THE CLOSE of the first week Bony had his first horse far enough in training to be ridden outside the yard and sensible enough to be trusted to permit its rider to concentrate on matters having nothing to do with a sparkling young filly.

Thus he gained freedom to examine Lake Otway, allegedly the scene of the death of Raymond Gillen. One morning he rode round the Lake, saw where the flood water had flowed into it at the northern end and where it had spilled over a sandbar into a creek at the southern end. He noted with interest the large area opposite the out-station taken over by pelicans for their hatchery and nursery, and where the swans had selected sites for their nests. Rabbits were everywhere in plague proportions, for the surrounding dunes and the slopes of the uplands outside the dunes were honeycombed with burrows. Often a 'swarm' of rabbits would dash ahead of him, and when he shouted they would burrow and he could see the sterns of animals at every hole, unable to get in for the crush. Everywhere, too, claiming every major shadow were kangaroos, and away up the slopes back of the dunes were black dots of countless emus.

A paradise for fur trappers. A mighty harvest ready for the reaping, and soon to be calcined by the sun.

Barby arrived one morning driving his utility loaded with camp gear and trapping equipment, his three dogs, two cats and the tame galah. The Boss had found another cook to relieve him, but had been unable to spare Red Draffin, and Barby had gone along the track to Johnson's Well and farther round the Lake to begin operations.

The afternoon of that day found Bony interested in Ray Gillen's motor-cycle. He had gone to the large machinery shed which housed the station trucks, machine parts and materials, in order to repair a girth buckle. The motor-cycle was completely covered by a tarpaulin, and the dust on the tarpaulin supported statements that the machine hadn't been used or moved after Gillen vanished.

Bony lifted the hem of the covering. It was obviously a powerful machine, and had been maintained in good order. Bony felt the tyres, and they were firm. About the cap of the petrol tank was a wide ring of dust darker than the rest, and Bony smelled petrol. He removed the cap, and found the tank was full to capacity. The tank had been filled some time during the past two weeks, and Bony was confident it must have been done during the week before he arrived at Lake Otway.

He was sure that whoever had filled the tank and perhaps pumped air into the tyres had, like himself, not wholly removed the tarpaulin. When he dropped the hem of the covering, the dust remained heavy on the level surface. All evidence indicated that the machine had not been moved since its owner vanished fifteen months ago, and yet someone had prepared it for a journey.

Came the evening when he decided to take Witlow partially into his confidence, and it happened that the wiry little stockman himself provided the opportunity. Dinner was over and the Swede had started a game of banker in the sitting-room of the quarters, and Bony joined Witlow, who was darning a pair of socks on the veranda. Witlow lost interest in the socks and stood to wipe perspiration from his face.

'What about taking a swim in the Lake?'

'In two feet of water?' objected Bony.

'Two feet six inches,' corrected Witlow. 'Do a bit of wading. Splash about a bit. Cooler, anyway. Rux up the birds, too. Something to do.'

'Yes, all right,' Bony assented. 'As you say, it will be something to do.'

Witlow changed into a pair of shorts and Bony put on a pair of drill trousers needing to be washed, and in bare feet they descended the bluff steps to the 'shore' of the Lake and stepped into the water.

It was distinctly warm, and the bottom was hard beneath an inch of sludge. They had to proceed fifty-odd yards before the water reached their knees, and another fifty yards before it rose to their hips. The water was loaded with algae, faintly green in colour, and it was impossible to see far below the surface.

Witlow gave his humorous chuckle and splashed Bony, and Detective-Inspector Bonaparte shed thirty years. Gasping, yelling like small boys, they showered each other, and the nearer birds indignantly skidded away.

They continued wading towards the centre of the Lake, the depth not increasing. Before them the water was almost constantly disturbed by fish, the surface being ribbed, being sliced by dorsal fins, often for a moment broken by the broad back of a large codfish.

Like flotsam pushed aside by the bow of a ship, the ducks and moorhens swam to either side of the two men, and closed in again behind them. The great fleets of pelicans appeared to be motionless and yet kept their distance, and so with the swans and the cormorants. Some fifty-odd gulls accompanied the men as though expecting to be fed with crusts.

The water came no higher, and its temperature remained cloyingly warm. The air above it was hot to the skin, and the westering sun was the blinding centre of a vast flame. When Bony looked back and estimated they had waded a mile from shore, the distant homestead was aureoled in conformity with the crimson face of the bluff.

'A fortnight of this weather will finish the Lake for another twenty years,' predicted Witlow, and knelt on the bottom so that his head looked like the head on Salome's platter. 'A hundred and four again today in the pepper-tree shade. It'll go twenty degrees higher before this summer busts.'

Bony knelt and managed to sit back on his heels, when the water tickled his chin. He could not forbear smiling at Witlow, who said:

'We shoulda brought a couple of chairs out here. Funny, ain't it, being so far from land. Crook if the tide came in quick like it does up Broome way. Hey, stop your tickling, Jock. Oh, you will, will you? All right, brother.'

He appeared to lunge forward, his face going under. He came up, crouching, and lifted from Lake Otway a codfish weighing in the vicinity of twelve pounds, the fingers of one hand up under the gills. Then he lowered the fish into the water, played with it for a moment, and let it go.

'D'you know what, Bony, that feller just came and leaned against me. I put me hand on him, and he still leaned. Just like a lovin' cat.'

'There's one leaning against me right now,' Bony said. 'I'll try to grab him.'

He failed, and then, being abruptly serious, he said:

'Don't much like the idea of groping after fish. Might catch hold of Gillen's skeleton.'

'Yair, could do,' Witlow agreed, also sobered by the thought. 'He must be around somewhere, all the meat eaten off him by the yabbies.'

'Were you here when it happened?'

'No.'

'Good swimmer, too, wasn't he?' Bony nonchalantly asked.

'So they say,' answered Witlow. 'Still, fresh water ain't like the sea, and although it was a clear night the wind had been blowing all day and the currents out here musta been still running. Some say that after a windy day the currents run round and round like a whirlpool, and having swum out about this far Gillen woulda been in the centre and couldn' swim out again to the land. Anyway, he must be around somewhere. Crook if you or me happened to kick him up.'

Bony stood, feeling a chill down his back which had nothing to do with the prevailing temperature. He recalled a man much older than Witlow who had kicked up a corpse in a lake surrounding a place known as Venom House, and it was not an experience he wished to share. Witlow chuckled.

'Ain't likely,' he said. 'No more likely than winning Tatts. Big lake this, and a body's mighty small. Look at those birds.' A vast fleet of pelicans had drawn closer. 'An idea! Let's shift 'em. Both of us yell and splash at the same time.'

The effect of their efforts was explosive. The entire surface of the great Lake was thrashed with spurts of spray as the fleets of pelicans, the swans and wild geese, the countless ducks and the cormorants all skidded over the water to take to the air, the alarm passing from bird to bird with the speed of light.

'Look at 'em! Look at 'em!' shouted Witlow.

A chain of swans swung by, low above them, and the swans were bright red. The gulls fluttered as though nervous of being rammed; they were crimson and reminded Bony of Dampier

Bay and Broome where the widows were murdered. Crimson fire flashed from the plumage of whirring ducks, and the white markings of the pelicans grandly wheeling in great wedges looked to the men like splashes of blood.

'What d'you know about that?' yelled Witlow. 'The bleedin' Battle of Britain. What d'you . . .'

Abruptly he sat down, floundered, came up again spitting water.

'Strike me pink if a flamin' fish didn't charge through me legs,' he complained.

The birds gained height. The pelicans and the swans and the geese became armadas of heavy bombers, pounced upon, attacked by the meteor-swift ducks. The cormorants weaved as though completely bewildered, and the moorhens dived to the surface and huddled together as though in conference. And higher than the mighty bombers and the streaking fighters, the eagles spun their invisible webs beneath the scarlet sky.

Sudden and powerful pressure was applied to Bony's left leg, and he could feel the slimy body of the fish cannoning off him. It seemed, too, that all the fish had gone berserk, for his legs registered continued collisions, and the limpid surface of the lake was like a huge pot on the boil.

'That's worth wading out here for,' he said, and Witlow nodded agreement.

The sun went down behind distant trees whose ghostly shadows raced to them, passed them by, yet held them with threat of inevitable night. The water slowly became placid, and the fish quietened. The smaller ducks came tumbling down the airways to shoot long arrows of lilac spray as the water braked them. But the big birds remained aloft.

The two men began the journey to the shore, without haste, a little awed, for both were close to this spirit of Australia so impervious to Time and such finite matters as the birth and death of a lake. The distant bluff and the buildings upon its summit now were purpling, the shadows between the buildings like jet. The gulls flew on ahead, their colour now of gentian blue.

'What do you reckon about the blokes around here, Bony?' asked Witlow a trifle too casually.

'They aren't very pally,' Bony replied, easily.

'Can't nail 'em down. Must be the women what's upset 'em.'

'One would think most of them were old enough not to be upset by women.'

They plodded onward for a space in silence before Witlow said:

'You could be right, but the conditions ain't usual. I hitched to a drovin' outfit one time bringing cattle out of the Territory. Two men run the outfit, both of 'em older than either of us. Hard doers, too. Fight and booze artists. Been cobbers for twenty years. They thought only about cattle and grog and racehorses. And then an abo joined up, and he brought his gin with him. Young gal she was, and ugly as hell. Inside a week them two old bastards were in holts, and if I hadn't given the abo the wink to get going and take his gin with him, them two blokes would have murdered each other and the cattle would have scattered all over Australia. Day after the gin departed, they was back to usual. Beats me.'

'They say a man is apt to slip when he's seventy, or is it sixty?' Bony said, laughingly. 'There's certainly something eating the lads here at Lake Otway.'

'Sure thing, Bony. Remember the night you got asked to play cards with the women, and me and the Swede went with you to see there was no cheating. And then what? Ten minutes after we started playing, in comes Bob Lester, all friendly and interested, sniffle and all. After him comes Mac ... you know, just dropped in to borrow the flat-iron or the fry-pan or something. Next comes Harry Carney, joking about being scared of being in the quarters all by himself. Me and the Swede was talkin' about 'em yestiddy. We never got close to them three, and somehow they stick together and yet snarl at the drop of a hat. Remember that brooch Ma Fowler was wearing that night?'

'Yes. An opal set in gold. Good stone, too.'

'Lester give her that,' Witlow went on. 'A hundred and twenty quid he paid for it.'

'What!' ejaculated Bony.

'A hundred and twenty. He told me. The emerald ring she's wearing she got from MacLennon, and Lester give Joan the wristlet watch she had on that night. He paid forty-five guineas for it. Then the ear-rings and the thing she had in her hair

Carney give her. Cost him twenty pounds for that lot.'

'How the devil do you know who gave what and what was paid?' asked Bony.

'That's the screwy part of the set-up,' replied Witlow. 'You see, those mutts simply got to tell someone about it. Lester tells me about the brooch, and skites that when he's saved a few more hundred quid Ma Fowler will be taking a trip with him to Sydney, and he gives Joan the watch to back him up with Ma. Mac tells me about the ring he gave to Ma, but he don't know that Ma promised Lester the Sydney trip; he tells me Ma promised to go on a bender with him to Adelaide soon as he's got plenty of money to pay for the trip. Then Carney tells me about the present he gives to Joan, and says he's keeping sweet with the mother till he pays up for Joan on the lay-by. See? All just between 'em and me or the Swede, if you know what I mean. J'u know what?'

Bony asked.

'There's going to be crackers and volcanoes before long. You can see it hotting up. Them two women are schemers all right. Proper trollops. Take a mug's advice and go easy, Bony. Better spit at 'em than smile. Me and the Swede could see what they was up to, that night we played cards. Smiling all over you. Cooing at you, and giving me a glad eye now and then, just to work up those mutts to send in to the office for a big cheque for more jewellery or something. And I ain't so sure that Martyr ain't a mutt, too.'

'Martyr!'

'Yair. Joan has a sort of bracelet all made with opals. Could be worth anything.'

'But why d'you think Martyr gave it to her?'

' 'Cos none of the others told me or the Swede about that, and that bracelet is something to boast about, believe me.'

'Did they ever put it on you for a present?' Bony asked.

'No. But Joan put the hard word on the Swede for the loan of fifty quid, and Kurt told her he had to support six kids in Norway, pay alimony to a wife in Sydney and keep a woman up in Cairns. Them big birds is coming down. Let's watch.'

The pelicans came down in wide curves and spirals. The swans dropped in steeper descent. A pelican fleet turned to line ahead, followed the leader like black-and-white links of an everlasting chain. The leader skimmed water less than thirty feet from the two heads, and every succeeding bird touched water at the same spot, followed the same braking line, moved to the right or left of the leader to form a vast crescent, each ship with its yellow 'bowsprit' dipped in salute to the Lake. The ducks continued to dive and skate in foam to a cheeky halt at the men, then swam lazily about them as they proceeded to wade to the shore.

'Be interested in a little bet?' drawled Witlow.

'You name the odds,' suggested Bony.

'All right! Betcher there'll be a murder within five miles of this out-station before Easter. Four to one in favour.'

'Sporting enough,' agreed Bony. 'In for a pound.'

7

It Pays to be Dumb

HAVING GAINED FREEDOM of movement without arousing speculation, Bony rode one of the youngsters along the sandy track leading to Johnson's Well. From the Well the track flowed over uplands of belar, pine and mulga, for thirty miles to the eastern border of Porchester Station, on and on to pass by the homesteads of two settlers and so to the railway at the town of Ivanhoe. It was by this track that Gillen had come to the out-station of Lake Otway.

It could be conceded that there are better places for meditation than the back of a young horse on a very hot afternoon, but the heat gave the horse something to think about and, being entirely devoid of humidity, was not unpleasant for the rider.

So far Bony could make nothing square in this mystery of Ray Gillen and his vanished treasury.

All that had emerged for the intuitive Bony was that those men and women who were at the out-station when Gillen announced his intention of going for a swim now waited with anxiety for Lake Otway to die. What did they expect, or dread, or hope from the death of the Lake? Did they foresee that, when the sun had sucked up all the water, the skeleton of Ray Gillen would prove he had not died from accidental drowning and thus start a murder investigation? Were that so, then five men and two women were associated in the murder, and this would seem exceedingly unlikely. Did they hope that, when Lake Otway dried out, the missing money would be exposed, and was it for this reason that every man and both women had continued in their employment here?

They were united by two bonds: their anxiety concerning the coming death of the Lake, and their front to everyone not present when Gillen went swimming for the last time. In all else, each of them was opposed to all the others.

Having reached this stage of his investigation, he was not dissatisfied with his progress, and again decided all he need do was to wait, when the people concerned would inevitably reveal exactly what did happen to Ray Gillen and his twelve thousand pounds.

At Johnson's Well he dismounted and neck-roped the horse to a shady cabbage tree. The well was situated on the bank of a creek some two hundred yards from the sandbar which prevented water running from the Lake when the level there was nineteen feet.

The hut was built with pine logs and had an iron roof. There was no glass in the one window, and the door required new hinges. Near the hut was the well, spanned by the windmill, and flanked by large iron tanks from which water could be discharged into lines of troughing for the stock. There was an engine shed and a supply of oil to work the auxiliary pump when the wind failed. Beyond the well were the horse yards, and an apparently abandoned reservoir tank stood in isolation between these yards and the engine shed.

A familiar scene for Bony: composed of sand and drowsing box trees, grey creek banks and flats, summer heat and flies, and, in winter, icy winds sweeping over the low dunes to keep the air heavy with gritty particles. A mere living place for men willing to put up with utter absence of comfort in order to earn a cheque.

Evidence of the work done by MacLennon and Lester was plain. The mill had been greased and the reservoir tanks were full, but the ball-cocks had been chocked with wood to prevent water running into the troughs. The oil engine had been serviced and run. There was, too, evidence that George Barby had been here with his utility.

The interior of the hut hadn't been touched. The floor was of packed rubble from termite nests. The long table was flanked by the usual forms. There was a bench under the glassless window, and white ash still lay heaped on the open hearth. When Bony entered he disturbed a dozen rabbits, and they crowded into a corner and wished they had wings.

He had boiled water in his quart-pot and brewed tea, and was sipping the scalding liquid when he heard the rising hum of a motor engine, and was not at all surprized when Barby's brown utility heaved over the hard sandbar and came along the creek bank, empty water tins rattling, and three dogs barking at the tethered horse.

Barby stopped at the tanks, waved to Bony and proceeded to fill his tins. The dogs came across to make friends and then lie in the hut shadow with Bony. One of the rabbits charged out through the doorway, and the dogs simply were not interested. They accepted rabbits with the boredom with which they tolerated their stick-fast fleas.

Barby eventually came over to squat and load a pipe.

'What are you doing here?' he asked. 'Layin' off?'

'Toughening a youngster,' replied Bony. 'Where are you camped?'

'Couple of miles round the Lake. There's millions of rabbits coming to water, and I'm gonna fence a strip of coast and trap 'em.'

The cook was no longer a cook. He wore a grubby grey flannel vest, old and patched tweed trousers and rubber-soled sand-shoes which once could have been white. The sun already had sizzled his face and bare arms, had puckered his hazel eyes and stiffened his brown hair.

'If I had a farthing for every rabbit around this Lake,' he said with slow emphasis, 'I'd claim to own half Australia. Heard over the air once that there's five million rabbits in Australia. Well, all but ten of 'em is drinkin' at Lake Otway.'

'All but ten million?'

'All but ten. Eight, nine, ten. Those ten is down at Canberra laughing at the scientists. You think that mysotis any good to bump off all the rabbits in Australia?'

'Myxomatosis!' corrected Bony. 'No. It's partially effective,

I think, on small farms and along rivers where the mosquitoes are busy.'

'The rabbit'll beat the scientists, don't you reckon?' Barby persisted.

'The rabbits will beat any germ, any man, any thing,' Bony said with conviction. 'What the people in the cities and towns cannot grasp is the immensity of this land mass called Australia, and another thing they cannot grasp is that the Australian rabbit has been fighting droughts, sun, eagles and foxes, poison baits and George Barbys for a hundred years, and is still winning.'

'Too right they have,' Barby agreed, earnestly. 'Nothing's going to stop 'em. Why, the young does when they're six weeks old begin to litter fives and sevens every six weeks after. They're the greatest breeding machines that ever was. Let 'em multiply, I says.'

'They do eat feed and drink water needful for stock,' Bony mildly countered.

'So what?' Barby asked. 'They ain't doin' no real harm to Australia. The rabbit is the poor man's food and always has been. If the scientists do knock them out, which they won't, and if the squatters do rear twice as many sheep, will the price of mutton be any lower? Will the cost of blankets and clothes be any cheaper? Or the price of tobacco and booze come down any? No hope. But the squatters and the farmers will be able to buy more motorcars and machinery to rust away in the paddocks, 'cos they're too damn lazy to put 'em under cover, and they'll pay a bit more in taxes to let the blasted politicians have more world tours and get higher pensions when the people heaves 'em out into the cold, cold snow. And that's all the scientists are being paid to bump off the rabbits for.'

'Don't worry,' soothed Bony. 'Brer Rabbit will last for ever. How are you to clean them up here?'

'Drop-netted fences. Stop 'em getting to the water. Or stop 'em makin' back from water. Water they must have. And feed they must have. Wish Red could turn up. Me and him can skin five thousand a day. He's a champ. And five thousand a day for five years wouldn't be missed round Lake Otway. How are you gettin' on with the gals at the out-station?'

The unexpected question momentarily rocked Bony.

'Pleasantly enough,' he replied disarmingly.

'Bit stuck up with you?'

The indirect reference to his birth was not missed. As it was not intended to hurt, Bony took firm hold of the cue and played the stroke.

'Perhaps they think I'm dumb. A caste earning good money. Be nice to him, and he'll be persuaded to send down to the city for expensive presents.'

'That's about it, Bony. They never tried it on me, but there's them they have. Chisellers, they are. Been here too long. But blokes like me and you can see through them. You hear about the feller who was drowned in this Lake?'

'Yes. Red mentioned him at dinner one day.'

'Name of Gillen, Ray Gillen. Went swimming in the Lake one night and stayed put. So they say. Me and Red has other thinks about that. I was trapping at the time, but living at the men's quarters. Things were getting sort of tense, if you know what I mean.'

'Oh! How, tense?'

Barby had let his pipe get cold, and he picked up an ember from Bony's fire, balanced it on the bowl and drew noisily.

'It's a sort of history,' he said. 'Beginning from when them women came out from Broken Hill. Everything was smooth as pie then and they certainly made a difference. The young 'un could ride; Martyr used to take her out to look at the Lake and things.

'Then, accordin' to Red, there was a sort of bust-up. Red added a sum and probably got the wrong answers, but Martyr suddenly stopped taking the girl out riding. Seems that the mother complained she was left to do all the work, but it could be she was jealous at the daughter getting off with Martyr.

'Anyhow, after that it got sort of quiet, right up to the time Gillen came. He came from Ivanhoe way, and he had to push his bike the last half-mile to this place 'cos it broke down. He had tucker with him, so he camped a day or two right here and tried to fix the bike. When he couldn't, he walked to the out-station with the part that wanted fixing, and it happened all the blokes were out. So he stayed there till Martyr came home, and Martyr repaired the part and gave him a job the next morning.

49

'From then on things hotted up at the out-station. Both the women fell for Gillen, and he was supposed to be after the girl. Then there was a fight between him and MacLennon, and although Mac's done some ring work, Gillen beat him. He'd take the girl out on his bike. Then he'd take the mother for a ride, and they didn't know which of 'em he was after. He almost came to bashing Carney who camped with him and, being of about the same age, they sort of stuck together. Lester said something cross-eyed, and Gillen floored Lester, and apologized next morning. The women got into holts over nothing, so they said, but under it was Gillen. Then one night we all goes to bed, and he decides to go swimming, and that was the last anyone seen of him.'

'Any trouble that day?' Bony asked.

'No. Been no trouble for a week. The night he went for a swim we was all playing poker in the quarters.'

'Money?'

'No. Matches.'

'Gillen had a suitcase,' Barby went on. 'It was a flash case, too. He kept the key on a cord with a gold locket round his neck. And one day Red was sittin' on Carney's bed yarning to Gillen, and Gillen wanted a change of undies, and takes off the cord to open the case. And after he took 'em out he had to kneel on the lid to lock the case, it was that full.

'The day after Gillen was missed, Martyr got me and Lester to look see while he goes through the case to find out who Gillen's relations are. I didn't know then what Red saw about Gillen kneeling on the lid, not when Martyr opened the case. The case wasn't full at all. It was less than three parts full. It's only after Red and me talked it over that we wonder what happened to the inside of that case from the time Red seen Gillen open it to the time I seen Martyr open it. It wasn't as though Gillen's few things on the bed table made up for it. They didn't.'

Opportunity favoured Bony.

'You say Gillen always kept the case locked. And the key on a cord round his neck. How did Martyr open it?'

'How? Why, he just pushed the catches aside. Cripes, Bony! You're all there. I never thought of that angle. That case wasn't locked when Martyr opened it.'

'Martyr didn't have the key and the locket on the cord?'

'Not that I remember. No, he couldn't of had. Gillen had the cord round his neck. He never took it off, that I do know as well as Red.'

'And you think someone took something from that case?' Bony prompted.

Barby nodded, slowly, significantly.

'Yair, Bony. Money was took from that case.'

'Money!'

'A lot of money. I'll tell you why I'm sure it was money. Seven or eight days before Gillen got drowned, I was along the shore one night looking at me traps. There was a moon, good enough for me to work without a light, and I'm coming back from the end of me trapline . . . I was workin' a hundred spring traps . . . when I heard voices, and I just had time to slip behind a tree.

'I seen it was Harry Carney with young Joan Fowler. They wasn't walkin' arm-in-arm. Just walkin' polite. Joan says, calm as you like: "I'm not marrying on a few hundred pounds, Harry." And Harry says: "Well, the four hundred odd I've got saved up would give us a good start." She says: "That's what you think. It wouldn't go far these days. When I marry you you'll have to be rich. And you know what to do."

'Harry says: "Now look, Joan, I couldn't do that, even though the money musta been stolen, and he wouldn't dare to make a song and dance about it being stolen from him." Well, that's what I hear 'em say before they got too far away. I waited by that tree and presently they comes back, still arguing about a lot of money someone's stolen and what could be stolen in turn. Joan says: "Aren't I worth it, Harry? Think of the wonderful times we'd have. You know I love you." Harry still says he couldn't do it, whatever she wanted him to do about stealing stolen money. And she was still kidding him on when they got out of my hearing.'

'And you think Carney knew there was a lot of money in Gillen's suitcase?' Bony pressed, nonchalance well acted.

'Yes. I didn't know what to think at the time, but I thunk it out since.'

'But Joan didn't marry Carney, so Carney couldn't have taken money from Gillen's case.'

'That's so, Bony. But Carney knew the money was in the

case, and he told Joan about it. I'll bet he looked inside the case that morning he woke up and found Gillen hadn't come back. He could have taken the money then and planted it somewhere. Or someone could have beaten him to it. If it was the money missin' what sunk the tide in Gillen's case, then someone's got it and whosoever is still at the out-station, 'cos not a man left the place since Gillen was drowned.'

Bony looked dumb, frowning perplexedly at the cook-trapper.

'I don't get it,' he admitted. 'If anyone took a lot of cash from Gillen's case, then why didn't he go on a bender? If Carney took it why didn't he run off with Joan?'

'That beats me, too, Bony. But I'm as sure as we're sittin' here that Carney and Joan knew about a lot of money in Gillen's case, so much money that it must have been stolen. P'raps, when Carney wouldn't lift it, Joan got someone else to do it, and that someone double-crossed her. There's double-crossing all round, if you ask me. They're all like hungry dogs watchin' each other to find out where the bone's buried. And nicely planted that bone is, I'll bet.'

'You may be right,' conceded Bony, feigning admiration of Barby's perspicacity.

'I'm right enough,' Barby averred. 'And you and me could do a deal. You keep your eyes and ears open. Tip me off about what goes on over there. We might find that planted dough, and then we go fifty-fifty. We can easily face out in my ute, and nothing could be said by nobuddy.'

8

Effervescence

ANOTHER WEEK WAS devoured by the year, and nothing happened save that the two aborigines were sent with sheep to Sandy Well and Lester returned to his chores as rouse-about. Now the thermometer registered above the century every day, and the Lake began to look grey and tired.

One still morning an audience waited within the deep

shade cast by the pepper tree, an audience comprising nine
dogs chained to roughly-made kennels and a young woman
dressed in white. Her hair held the sheen of bronze, and her
eyes . . . well, dogs, of course, are colour-blind.

Bony came riding a grey horse, and the girl laughed because
the horse trotted. Only once had she seen a horse trotting
with a rider up, and that at a Ceremonial Parade in Adelaide.
When a hundred yards past the audience, Bony turned and
rode back at a canter, and now the girl could but admire the
action of the horse and the seat of the rider. They passed for
the third time, at a gallop, the red dust springing away from
the grey-tipped arrow.

Horse and rider returned again to pose for the audience,
the horse standing like a statue. The pose was broken abruptly
when Bony fell off the horse and lay on the ground with a
foot trapped within a stirrup-iron. The girl became genuinely
concerned. The horse remained a statue. Bony twisted his leg
in an effort to free the foot, and the girl cried:

'Can I help? Shall I grab his bridle?'

Bony tugged at a thong, and the stirrup-leather parted from
the saddle. He stood, smiling at the astonished girl. He
returned the stirrup-leather to the saddle, dropped the reins,
walked a little way from the horse and pretended to shade his
eyes to admire a view. The horse flicked a fly away with an
ear-waggle. Bony went back to him, leaned against a shoulder.
Nothing happened. He shifted position and leaned hard
against the animal's rump, the toe of one foot resting neg-
ligently on the instep of the other. He lit a cigarette, blew
smoke elegantly skyward, and asked:

'D'you think he'll do?'

Joan Fowler's eyes shone, and Bony was immensely pleased
with himself, for he was experiencing one of the lesser
triumphs so vitally necessary to the maintenance of the
pride which sustained him in the eternal war of the two races
fighting for his soul. The feeling of triumph passed, leaving
him refreshed.

'He's not one of the youngsters, is he?' Joan doubted.

'He was a youngster three weeks ago. Too soft yet for real
work. Like to ride him sometime?'

'I really would.'

'You shall. But no prolonged gallops.' He smiled and she

53

forgot he was twice her age. 'D'you think I've earned my morning smoko?'

'Of course. It must be time.'

'Then we will return this gentleman.'

He removed the saddle, slipped the bridle, and the horse found a sandy patch and went down for a roll.

With the girl beside him, he ignored the horse and walked to the yards, in through the gateway. The horse got up, undecided what to do until he heard Bony's whistle, whereupon he trotted into the yard and bunted Bony's back.

'I expect he wants his piece of cake.' Bony produced a handful of crumbly cake from a pocket and, leaving the horse in the yard, they proceeded to the annexe for smoko.

'And Mother's been thinking you men got down on her cake extra well these last two weeks,' Joan remarked.

'You have no idea how your mother's cake has been appreciated,' he said gravely, although his eyes twinkled.

'I do now.'

'Keep the secret of training horses ... until I've trained my last horse at Lake Otway.'

Mrs Fowler was sitting at the men's table, her dark eyes smouldering, her lips smiling. Joan poured tea for Bony and herself, saying:

'The Boss ought to be here soon. He left at seven, so Mr Martyr told me.'

'You're not dressed up like that because the Boss is coming,' her mother stated vehemently. 'What's the idea?'

The veneer of sophistication returned to the girl. Her eyes were masked by insolence, and deliberately she baited:

'Don't be jealous, Mother.'

Faintly perturbed by the expressions on their faces, Bony suavely intervened.

'No quarrelling, now. It's much too hot. A hundred and nine in the shade.'

'You keep out of it,' snapped the elder woman. 'And while I'm on the subject, let me tell you this. You're only a temporary hand here, and I won't have you and Joan slinking away and scheming.'

'Mother! That's enough.'

'That's what you think. I'm not blind nor soft.'

'You are both, my dear parent,' sneered the girl.

'And you're nothing but a brainless clot. You've proved that time and again. You're so full of yourself you think no one can see round corners.' The woman swung back to Bony. 'And you're a bigger fool than you look if you believe anything she tells you.'

The girl attempted to speak, was shouted down. Bony calmly sipped his tea, hoping to learn more about women.

'She's only using you up,' Mrs Fowler continued, her voice raised and dark eyes blazing. The storm of anger suddenly increased so that her voice shook and syllables slipped. 'She's got you in and she'll bilk you, like she's bilked others. Young and luscious, eh? The itch of any man. But I'm warning you she's more poisonous than a bottle of strychnine. Don't you . . .'

'Why don't you go and jump in the bloody lake?' asked the 'young and luscious'. 'You've had your day and can't take it, that's what's wrong with you. Shut up!'

'You . . .' Mrs Fowler fought for control enough to scream the words. 'You fool, you couldn't even seduce a sailor.'

'Enough, my lady mother. Let's have a cup of tea in peace.'

'And I'm not soft,' went on the older woman. 'Neither is MacLennon. He'll stop your slimy tricks. And if you think we don't know about your little schemes you're mistaken. You won't get away with any more. You won't . . .'

Joan snatched up the milk jug and dashed its contents against her mother's face. She held the jug behind her shoulder to throw that, and Bony hastily removed it from her hand before she could resist. The mother gasped and wiped her eyes with the hem of her apron, and the girl turned on Bony.

'Get out and leave me to calm her down.'

There is a time for masculine discretion, and this was it. Bony filled his cup, took another slice of cake, and retreated. The door slammed shut behind him, and he sat on a case and continued his smoko. He had been there less than a minute when Lester appeared, and the watery eyes lit with momentary interest and the sniffle was almost an explosion.

'You chucked out?' he inquired.

'Requested to leave,' corrected Bony.

'Are they at it again?'

'They are at it again, Bob. Pause awhile to give them time

to cool. Otherwise you may have the tea-pot thrown at you.'

Lester sniffled and squatted on his spurred heels with admirable dexterity.

'Seems they got things on their minds.'

'What things?'

'Oh, this and that. Could be each of 'em thinks the other's got something they haven't.' He stood up, 'Well, I'm goin' to chance my luck. I'm dry.'

'Then take my cup in. You might need ammunition.'

Bony chuckled and brought another sniffle, and he left a little hurriedly as Lester made for the door. Glancing back he saw Lester on the step, his hand turning the door-knob, and a look of cunning concentration on his face.

Other than himself and Lester, no other man was in for lunch. The cold meal was set out for them. Neither woman appeared. Throughout, Lester was thoughtful and spoke but little. Witlow came in from his day's job just before the afternoon smoko, and when they were strolling to the annexe, the Swede joined them. The tea and cake were on the table, but the women were still absent.

Lester was still moody, and Witlow was about to chaff him when the irrepressible Swede cut in with:

'How hot today, Bony? 'Undred and eighty?'

'A hundred and nine.'

'Looks like March won't see no water in the Lake,' observed Witlow.

'Pelicans leave soon, I bet,' Helstrom laughed at an undisclosed joke. 'P'raps tonight. I bet level pound no pelicans here tomorrer.'

'Keep it,' said Witlow.

'You not sports, eh?' He stood up and tapped his chest. 'Me, I real Australia. All yous New Australians. Not sports. You too soon in Australia for to be sports.'

'You were, I suppose, born at Snake Gully,' smiled Bony.

'Me! Na! I been in country forty-one year. I real Australia. How long you been in Australia?'

'Forty-one minutes.'

Helstrom roared with laughter.

'Ya! I tink now why you spik like Bob Menzies. What place you born, eh? London?'

'Yorkshire.'

'Yorkshire!' The Swede indulged in ponderous thinking. Then he grinned and shouted: 'Ya! You got any brass?'

The Swede certainly was one big bright boy, and only Lester failed to appreciate him.

'What's wrong with Sniffler?' Witlow asked when they were on the veranda, and the rouseabout had saddled a horse and gone for the cows.

'Maybe he's worried because the women had a fight at morning smoko,' Bony surmised. 'They ordered me out, and I told him to give them time, but he would go in and probably had his ears blistered.'

'Ah,' murmured Witlow, smiling satisfaction. 'Working out, eh! Well, you're going to have it all on your own. Me and Kurt's shiftin' camp in the morning.'

'Oh! Where?'

'Takin' ewes into the River. Fifty miles is too far to be handy when it happens.'

'When what happens?' Bony asked quickly.

'You took me up on the murder bet.'

'So I did,' Bony drawled. 'I shall be collecting four pounds from you.'

'I'll bet a pound you won't.'

'Now we're becoming involved. Straighten out.'

'All right. I lay you four to one there'll be a murder hereabouts before shearing starts. And I lay you a level pound I win that bet. Sort of a bet behind a bet.'

'It's as well for me that you are leaving. When were you told?'

'This morning at orders.'

'Sorry about the move?'

'No. Much better on all counts at the River.'

'You will have your cobber with you.'

'Yair. Me and Swede get along. You're gonna be lonely.'

Bony agreed and crossed to the yards, and had been there only a few minutes when a new and large American car brought the large Mr Wallace, owner of Porchester Station. Wallace must have noticed the dust being kicked up by the horse Bony was handling, for he walked stiffly from the car and hauled himself up to sit on the top rail. There Bony joined him.

'How's things?' asked Wallace.

'Could wish for a spell of cooler weather,' replied Bony. 'The grey there has turned out well. You want him, Martyr said.'

'Yes. Always liked that gelding. My second daughter's coming home next week. Good enough for her?'

'Should be. Leave him with me for another week.'

'All right.' The large man eyed Bony sideways. 'How's the other business coming along?'

'My interest is being sustained,' replied Bony, and Wallace was astonished to see no smile accompanying the statement. 'How long will the Lake last?'

'A week at most if the heat continues. Important?'

'It seems to be,' admitted Bony. 'Don't ask me why. You could perhaps work out a small problem. I understand that Kurt Helstrom and Witlow are leaving here tomorrow for the River. You knew of that?'

'I knew that forty-four hundred ewes would begin the move to the river country in the morning.'

'Not that the Swede and Witlow would be taking them?'

'No. I leave the hands at this end of the run to Martyr. Martyr is a good man. The best overseer I've had. Always believed in loading responsibility on those who can take it. What's the problem?'

'I am presented with what is probably a coincidence, and if coincidence or not, I must determine,' Bony said. 'It's a subject I must ask earnestly that you treat confidentially. When Witlow and the Swede leave Lake Otway tomorrow, there will remain the seven people who were here when Gillen vanished.'

Wallace produced a pipe and filled it, taking his time, and lighting up before he spoke again.

'Coincidence.'

'But ... When did MacLennon and Carney and Lester last go down south on a spell?'

'I must think that one out. The book-keeper will know.'

'Inform me later. I know that these men haven't taken a holiday since before Gillen vanished fifteen months ago. That applies also to Mrs Fowler and her daughter. What about Martyr? Doesn't he take annual leave?'

'Yes, of course ... What the hell is on your mind? He was due for leave after Christmas, and the Christmas before last

58

he didn't take it; said he couldn't afford to as his mother had to undergo an expensive course of treatment for something or other and he was her sole support.'

'Very well. We can leave Barby out as he has a reputation for saving money. You have six people, all here when Gillen vanished. Not one has left even for a holiday. Normally everyone would insist on taking a break from this isolated place. Martyr, you say, selected the Swede and Witlow to move the ewes. Could you invent a reasonable excuse for suggesting to Martyr that Witlow be retained and one of the others sent?'

'Yes. What's the point?'

'I want to know if Martyr purposely selected those two men, or if he offered the move to one or two of the older hands and they refused it. Living conditions at your homestead by the River would be superior to those ruling here, don't you think?'

'Yes, of course. Regular mail. Close to Menindee. Fair amount of traffic passing through. I see what's on your mind. Any man here ought naturally to want to change to the river homestead.'

'That is so. When anyone doesn't react naturally, I am elated,' Bony said, beaming at Wallace.

9

A New Experience

BONY RELAXED ON the edge of the bluff. It was almost totally dark, and he had watched the night extinguish the furnace colours on and above Lake Otway. The Swede would have lost his bet had anyone taken his odds on the pelicans leaving, for last seen by Bony they were gathered in close-packed mobs like crowds about road accidents. Now it was night and the only sounds to reach Bony were the conversations of water-birds and the radio in the house behind him, for the men were at dinner in the annexe.

All the people who were at Lake Otway when Gillen

vanished were here this night, save Barby in his camp across the Lake. The only addition to this community was himself, a supposedly itinerant horse-breaker. Before Wallace had left to return to the big homestead he had made clear the selection of Witlow and Helstrom to take the ewes to the River, having ascertained from Martyr that the overseer had offered the change to MacLennon and Carney as they had been working much longer at the out-station. Both these men preferred to remain, the former because he did not like change and the latter because the pubs at Menindee couldn't be far enough away.

This cleared up a minor point concerning Martyr, a point which would have had to be considered had the overseer not given those two old hands the opportunity of change, but it stressed the significance of the fact that those two men had remained constantly at Lake Otway, and were determined to stay on.

Wallace had agreed to probe Red Draffin and the point to be raised was the suitcase key, the key to the true fate of Ray Gillen. Draffin had said Gillen always kept his case locked and the key on a cord round his neck. This was supported by Barby. When Martyr, with Barby and Lester, examined the contents of the case the day after Gillen was missing, it was not locked and the key wasn't seen by Barby. Draffin said the case was so full that its owner had to kneel on the lid to close it; Barby said the case was but little more than half full when they had listed the contents.

That neither Draffin nor Barby had informed the police or even Wallace of their suspicion that something of value had been removed from the case was quite in character, for neither had closely associated with Gillen and, like the average bushman, they would not want to be drawn into a police inquiry. In none of the police reports was there mention by Gillen's room-mate, Carney, of the key worn by the missing man ... or mention of it by anyone else.

Bony was considering the implications behind the progress of his own investigation when there was a light step behind him and he turned to see a dark figure approaching.

'I was hoping you were still here, Bony,' Joan Fowler softly said. 'I want to talk to you. You won't mind?'

'No. I won't be lonely now.'

Together they sat on the edge of the low bluff where steps had been cut. The girl said :

'We must talk quietly, 'cos voices carry, and I've sneaked out. I saw you here before it got dark. You know, I've been thinking a lot about you. D'you think I was very terrible to sling that milk at Mother?'

'Red Draffin, I think, would have suggested even sterner measures. It would seem that your mother can be very difficult.'

'She won't believe I've grown up and all that. You don't really like me, do you?'

'Not to like you would be plain silly,' was his cautious response.

'I don't mean just that way. I mean, well, you know how I mean, don't you?'

'How do you mean?'

'Now you are being difficult. Just imagine. When I go to meet a man, he wants to kiss me to show how much he likes me.'

'Ah! But you see, Joan, I am married, and you are Temptation.'

She restrained her laughter . . . and moved close to him.

'Being married's got nothing to do with it, Bony,' she whispered. 'You men! You aren't all the same, no matter what Mother says. Some want to smother me; others, you for instance, have to be told. Kiss me, please.'

The danger of being seduced had never been previously encountered by Inspector Bonaparte, but one kiss would be both pleasant and ungallant to refuse.

'That was nice,' Joan sighed, resting her head against his shoulder. 'Do it again. You like me now, don't you?'

'Yes. You are very desirable, but I . . . I am unseducible.'

'I haven't really tried yet.'

'What else can I do for you?' hastily Bony asked.

'Would you do anything for me, Bony?'

'Bar throwing milk at your mother.'

'Are you still my friend?'

'I have, I hope, proved that.'

'I must go back.' She swung her body round to confront him, and he could see the starlight in her eyes. 'Mother will wake up to me if I don't. Will you do something for me . . . please?'

'Tell me.'

'What would you think about a man who promised to marry you and, because he came into money, wanted to get out of it?'

'If you are the lady, the man needs the attention of a psychiatrist.'

'A what?'

'Mental doctor.'

'Oh! Yes, he does ... Now you've made me admit I'm the girl. Well, so I am. Mind you, I wouldn't marry him now, but I'm not letting him get away with it.' Joan moved closer. 'Pity you are pure, Bony, but I'm glad you'll help me. I've no one I could trust to see that I get a fair deal.'

'I shall make sure that you get a fair deal,' he told her.

The girl fell silent, and Bony waited.

'A long time ago,' she resumed, 'Harry Carney made love to me. You know how it goes in a place like this. No amusements, nothing much to do, nowhere to go. He promised to marry me, and I believed him. Then he went cold and called it off, and I made him tell me why. He said it would be silly to marry on a station hand's wages, and that's all he'd have until his uncle died and left him a pile. When I said we could wait, he said his uncle might live for another thirty years even with a sick heart.'

Joan fell silent again, possibly expecting Bony to jump in with indignant sympathy. Instead, he asked:

'How long ago was that?'

'Just a year. And lately I've been wondering about Harry. He's moody and restless, and I think his uncle died. I think Harry's come into his money, and I'm worried he'll sneak off and leave me cold. That's why I want you to help me.'

'How?'

'Just by watching him. You know, without him knowing. Just tell me when he starts packing up ready to go.'

'But he couldn't go without you seeing him put his things into the Boss's car or Barby's utility.'

'He could get away all right, Bony. There's Ray Gillen's motor-bike still over in the shed. Harry's good with a motorbike. We took it out one afternoon when Mr Martyr and the other men were away at the lamb-marking. We went for miles on it.'

'The lamb-marking? Last May?'

'Yes.'

'Only that time?'

'Yes.'

'But everyone would hear him start the machine. You would, too.'

'It would be too late then. Harry would be on it and off.'

Bony did not trouble to point out that before Carney, on the stolen machine, could arrive at Menindee to the south, Ivanhoe to the east, or Wilcannia to the north, the telephone could cripple the plan. Nor did he state the fact that Carney was intelligent enough to devise a far more subtle plan. Nevertheless, the motor-cycle in the shed had been prepared for the road.

'He'd persuade George Barby to give him a lift from here, Joan.'

'No, he wouldn't,' she argued. 'I know, because he's already got the bike filled with petrol. I watched him. It was the day before you came here, and he was supposed to be out riding. I happened to see him sneak into the shed, and ran over and looked through a crack in the wall. He was filling the petrol tank. I saw him unscrew things and clean them. Then he pumped the tyres and put the sheet back, and tossed sand on it to make it look dusty like it was.'

'H'm! Could be serious,' conceded Bony.

'I know what I'm talking about.'

'You have given that impression. You want me to watch him?'

'Please, Bony.' Her hands pressed his shoulders. 'Will you . . . for me?'

'Very well. Now off you go, and you don't have "to be kind to me".'

Flippantly, she tilted his chin, jumped to her feet and ran, and he waited a minute before strolling to the men's quarters. Someone cut the dynamo motor, and the result relieved the mind and freed the ears to register other noises. Within the house a radio gave music. From the Lake the birds called. In the men's sitting-room Carney was writing a letter and Lester was reading a paper through spectacles perched on the end of his long nose.

Instead of entering, Bony sat on the broken chair and rolled a cigarette. He wondered what lay behind Joan Fowler's inducement to persuade him to watch Carney, discarding the absurd story of the rich uncle, and having to accept the fact of the motor-cycle being prepared for a getaway by Carney.

A figure loomed into the light from the living-room, and when the man mounted the veranda Bony saw MacLennon. MacLennon obviously noticed the glow of Bony's cigarette, for he paced the veranda and sat with his back against a rail post.

'Took a chance and cut off that damn engine five minutes ahead of time,' he said. 'Gets on my nerves nights like this. I hate it when the wind don't blow.'

'Could be no wind for weeks at this time of year,' Bony pointed out. 'Getting near the end of the sheep lift?'

'Yes. Passed the last flock to go to the fellers at Sandy Well. Martyr's given us a day off tomorrow. Crook on the sheep, too, movin' them in this weather. Not so good, either, on the horses, I suppose.'

'That's so.' Bony tossed the cigarette butt over the rail and began to roll another. 'The Swede and Witlow are lucky to be going to the River.'

'They can have it,' MacLennon said, a trifle sharply. 'Too much spit and polish there. Martyr's easy compared with the Boss. You see the end of your contract in sight yet?'

'About three weeks.'

'You'll see the Lake dry out.'

'Looks like it,' agreed Bony. 'Pelicans seem to be preparing to go for good. Water down under two feet by the marker this evening.'

'It'll go quick at the end.' MacLennon struck a match and held it against his pipe, and the illumination revealed his square face and powerful shoulders. The black moustache, always trimmed and snipped short, partially balanced the broken nose. He spoke with the slow deliberation of the punch-drunk, and often put a punch into his speech to emphasize a point important only to himself. 'Find Ray Gillen when she dries out, I expect.'

'The feller who was drowned some time ago?' queried Bony.

'Yes. Went swimming one night. Musta got cramp. Ruddy fool.'

'How so?'

64

'Been a hot day. Hot night, too. First heat of the summer, it was. He always tore into the water at the run. Worst thing out for getting cramp. Owed me forty quid, too.'

'Bad luck,' sympathized Bony.

'Yes. I won it at cards. Not all at once; over a coupler weeks. He said he would pay up some time. Offered to give me a gold locket as security. Me, I'm a fool. I told him I'd wait for the cash. Ought to have took the locket. He always had it on a cord round his neck. Musta wore it when he went swimming.'

'Then it will be with his skeleton. Close by it, anyway, if the cord hasn't rotted by this time.'

'That's what I've been working out,' MacLennon said, keeping his voice low. 'I was thinkin' you might do me a favour if you happen to find Gillen.'

'How?'

'There's no knowing where the skeleton will be now. Could be anywhere on the Lake floor. Good place to exercise young horses . . . on the Lake when she's dried out. If you happened to find the skeleton, would you nab the locket for me? It's mine actually.'

'Yes, all right.'

'Good for you. And keep it dark from the others. Suspicious lot of . . .'

Above the noise of the radio reverberated an explosion, the house walls making the sound deep and hollow.

'Gun!' exclaimed MacLennon and heaved up from the veranda. Bony vaulted the railing and ran to the house, raced up the wide steps to its front veranda. There were lights seemingly in all the front rooms. The door behind the fly-netted door was closed.

Bony was conscious of the others behind him.

'Gun, wasn't it?' queried Carney.

'Sounded much like it,' Bony said and pulled open the fly-door. He was about to knock on the inner door when somewhere within the house a woman screamed hysterically. Then came Joan Fowler's voice raised to shouting pitch.

'Stop it, you damn fool!'

There was a bumping sound and the noise of pounding feet. Bony knocked heavily on the door, and behind him MacLennon rumbled :

'Get in! Get in! Sounds like a rumpus.'

Bony thrust the door inwards to bang against the wall of a short passage. At the end of the passage stood Martyr in his pyjamas. In his right hand he held a 12-bore shotgun.

Somewhere along a cross-passage Mrs Fowler was hysterically crying, and they distinctly heard the face-slap momentarily stopping the hysteria. A door slammed, cutting the whimper threatening renewal of the screaming.

'What happened?' asked Bony, and was relieved of tension when the overseer leaned the weapon into a wall corner and advanced to them.

'An accident,' he said, evenly. 'Nothing for anyone else to worry about, when Joan can pacify Mrs Fowler. I was cleaning my gun when it went off. Didn't know it was loaded, and I could have sworn it wasn't.'

'Funny time to be cleaning a gun,' growled MacLennon. 'Do any damage?'

'No, I don't think so. The charge went into the floor. Everything is all right.'

The air was heavy with burned powder. From a distant room Mrs Fowler could be heard sobbing.

'It's quite all right, Mac. You can get back to the quarter,' Martyr told them.

He was unusually pale, but his voice was steady. He stood with his hand on the door preparatory to closing it. Lester sniffled and that touch of normalcy killed unreality. And unreality was buried when Martyr said:

'Good night!' and closed the door.

10

An Unsolvable Mystery

DUE TO HIS lifelong habit of waking at dawn Bony witnessed the first throe of the coming death of Lake Otway.

On waking he proceeded, as usual, to roll a cigarette and while doing so recalled how the pelicans had congregated in great crowds on the previous evening. He had slept on the top of his bedclothes, and it was now as hot as when he had fallen alseep.

On bare feet, he passed out to the veranda and sauntered to its end overlooking the Lake.

The birds still congregated. He counted eleven masses of them in a rough line along the lake's centre, each mass looking like an island on which now and then someone waved a white flag. The flag was the white of under-wings when a bird raised itself and flapped its wings as a cat will stretch to limber up.

The sky slowly acknowledged the threat of the sun. The surface of the Lake caught and held the same threat, and when the edge of the sun lifted above the trees behind Johnson's Well, the first bird took off.

The unit detached itself from a mass, flapped its great wings, paddled strongly and began to lift. When air-borne, the bird took the long upward slant as though bored with flying. Another bird followed, a third, and so on to form a chain being drawn up to the burnished sky by a magnetic sun. The same routine was followed by the other congregations of pelicans, until there were eleven long black chains over Lake Otway, each link rhythmically waving its white flag.

When a thousand feet above the water, the leader of each chain rested upon outspread pinions, and those following gained position each side of the leader and also rested. Thus a fleet was formed, which proceeded to gain further height, every 'ship' of each 'fleet' alternately winging and resting in perfect unison.

The chains having been wound up and the fleets formed, the sky was ribbed and curved with black-and-white ships, each with its golden prow. Like ten thousand Argosies, they sailed before the sun, fleet above fleet, in circles great and small as though the commanders waited for sailing orders.

Presently the fleets grandly departed, one following the other, the units of every fleet in line abreast, sailing away to the north till the sky absorbed them. Fifteen, twenty years hence that same sky would produce similar fleets of Argosies to sail down the air-ways and harbour on Lake Otway reborn.

'They must have felt the bottom with their paddlers,' Carney said, and Bony turned to the young man whose face defied sunburn and whose large brown eyes seemed always to be laughing.

'What's the tally?'

'Be a wild guess. Ten thousand, perhaps,' Bony essayed.

'Could be more. The swans took off some time in the night, looks like.'

'One foot ten inches of water left, by the marker. Bottom of the Lake flat all over?'

'Like a billiard table excepting at Johnson's Well end,' replied Carney. 'There the creek extends into the Lake for about a hundred yards. They call it the Channel. Water will stay there for some time because the Channel is twenty feet deep, and the sandbar keeps it from running out. The banks being steep and slippery, it's a trap for stock, which is why the flocks watering at the Lake had to be shifted.'

'You will be sorry to see the Lake die,' Bony said, and Carney nodded and his eyes, Bony fancied, became wistful.

'When she's full, Lake Otway makes this place worth while,' Carney said. 'I'd like to own this country and have Lake Otway full all the time. How would it be with a light yacht to sail on windy days and an aquaplane to pep things up?'

'You forgot the fishing-boat,' Bony added, to make the picture complete.

There was a boat here, brought out soon after the Lake filled. We used her for fishing and bathing from. Then we got an east wind, a real beaut, and it raised short up-and-down waves that pounded the boat to splinters. We ought to have had sense enough to pull it well up the shore-line. Now there's barely enough water to float a loan.'

Carney was propounding a 'brilliant idea' to keep Lake Otway permanently filled when Lester appeared to give his first sniffle for the day. On being told that the pelicans had departed, he said no respectable bird could be expected to 'lollop around on a plate of soup,' and Bony noted that Carney's moment of loquacity ended.

Who had cooked the breakfast this morning was not evident. The dishes were placed on the table for the men to help themselves. Nothing was said of the gun incident, and afterwards the men loafed about the quarters and Bony went for his horses, including the grey. At the morning smoko gong everyone crossed to the annexe, and again neither woman appeared.

'Wonder how George's getting on with the rabbits?'

Carney said, obviously to lighten the general mood. He was supported by Lester.

'Ought to be doing pretty well. I never seen so many rabbits around this Lake before, and nowhere else for that matter. You can go anywhere and holler and choke the burrows with 'em. It's goin' to be the fun of Cork when the water dries out and leaves only the Channel. There'll be so many rabbits drinking at the Channel, old George and his dogs and cats and galah will all be buried under the rush.'

The sniffle was almost a snort, and Bony said:

'As I am going to spend the night with him, I'd better warn him.'

'You oughta give up breaking and go in with George,' suggested MacLennon. 'Make more money in one night at the rabbits than any of us would make in a month. Wouldn't mind giving it a go meself.'

'Not me,' supplemented Lester.

MacLennon scowled into his tea-cup.

'We'll all go in with George,' he said. 'Harry'll want to, I bet. And Martyr won't be left out. The women could come along, too, and cook for the gang.'

'Suits me,' drawled Carney. 'But no guns.'

'No guns,' agreed MacLennon. 'Guns go off on their own account late at night. George wouldn't like that. Make him nervous.'

Lester cackled, and raised a laugh.

'A grain or two of strychnine if you like, but no guns.'

'Seems to be a joker in the wood heap,' Bony mildly surmised, and MacLennon glowered.

'Yes. Bloody funny. We'll cut the talk and stick to rabbits. If we're all going, we'd better get Red Draffin out to lend a hand. Told me he could skin five hundred an hour when he got his hand in.'

'Bit over the fence, that one,' objected Carney, and Lester argued.

'You want to see Red in action. If he can't do five hundred, I'll back him to do four ninety-nine. Tried myself out once and got up to ninety-nine.'

Bony left them discussing famous tallies and went back to his work, and an hour later was surprised to see Joan sitting on the top rail of the yard watching him. Today she wore

69

navy-blue slacks and a blue blouse, and blue wasn't her colour. When he joined her to roll a cigarette, he asked:

'How is your mother? Recovering from the fright she received?'

'She's all right now. Sleeping it off. Shock, you know. The sound inside the house was terrific.'

'It must have been. Who did fire the gun?'

He looked at her, watching her mouth frame the words:

'Who fired the gun? Why, it went off when Mr Martyr was cleaning it. The idiot! Messing about with a gun at that time of night.'

'Where was he cleaning the weapon?'

'It sounded in his room. Said it went into the floor. When are you going to let me ride the grey?'

'Tomorrow afternoon. Suit you?'

'Yes. I'll be able to manage him?'

'I shall be riding with you.'

He swung his legs over the rail to sit facing across the open space and the light-drenched Lake beyond.

'All the pelicans left this morning,' he said. 'The swans went during the night.'

Joan swung herself round to face the Lake. The house was then slightly to their left. Bony said:

'I have been wondering what caused the hole in the house roof above your bedroom.'

Receiving no support at this turn of the conversation, he looked directly at her. Her face was expressionless, and her eyes were green, like bottle glass.

'You don't believe Mr Martyr when he says the gun went off while he was cleaning it?'

'The hole in the roof wasn't there yesterday. Martyr could have been cleaning the gun in your room, and the gun could have been pointed at the ceiling when it was discharged. The iron roof is quite low to the ceiling, and the Number One shot did not expand to make a cullender of the roof, as you can see.'

'You were outside looking through the window?'

'I wouldn't dare.'

'Then how did you know where my room is?'

'Because the slacks you are now wearing, and which are so nicely pressed, were lying over the window sill. What did happen last night?'

70

'I told you. You wouldn't know, anyway.'

Joan climbed down to the ground, where she turned and looked at him, head up, an insolent smile curling her mouth. He smiled at her, and her mind was held by his eyes, deep blue and unwinking, and they grew in size and threatened to read her secrets. Then he released her.

'You'll ride the grey tomorrow?'

'Of course. And we're still friends?'

'If you will permit.'

'Then say nothing about the hole in the roof.'

'As your friend, why should I?'

She laughed, turned to make for the house, said over her shoulder:

'Thanks. You're improving. See you sometime.'

Bony found Martyr working in the office after lunch, which was served by Mrs. Fowler, now her usual self. Tentatively, he told the overseer his intention of spending the night with George Barby; the alert pale-blue eyes in the weathered face were speculative until their owner nodded agreement.

'How are you travelling . . . per horse?' Martyr asked, and when told Bony would walk, he offered the use of the station utility. With assumed shyness, Bony declined the offer, saying he would prefer the walkabout, and Martyr nodded understanding of the urge which often cannot be resisted by aborigines.

Thus, in the late afternoon, Bony went down to the Lake and followed the short line round to Johnson's Well. The clear burning heat dried his throat, and the glare of the water seared his eyes, so that he turned a tap in one of the reservoir tanks and drank the comparatively cool water. Thereafter, he sat in the shadow cast by the tank and fell to making another of the everlasting cigarettes.

Relaxed, he went over again the reactions of those whom he had told of this trip to Barby's camp for the night, and arrived at the same conclusion – that no one of the men appeared abnormally interested, or betrayed even a hint of pleasure at being relieved of his presence. The short conversation with MacLennon the previous evening during which emerged the ex-fighter's interest in the gold locket worn by Gillen occupied him for five minutes.

Then he wandered about this Johnson's Well, hauling himself up to look down into the water filling the reservoir tanks. Wire netting was stretched across the tank-tops to prevent birds drowning and fouling the water. He removed the boards covering the well, and would have gone down the ladder fixed to the shaft had he been certain about the air below. The discarded tank attracted him. It was smaller than those in service, and he guessed its capacity to be three thousand gallons. Its circular wall appeared to be in fair condition, but then it is always the floor of an iron tank which first rusts out.

Without difficulty, he hauled himself up to look inside, and received one of the great surprises of his life.

It was filled almost to the brim with the carcasses of cormorants. They had been there so long that the sun had mummified them, and there was no evil smell other than the faint musty odour. How many? There must have been several thousand birds that had piled into this tank to die.

11

The Trapper's Camp

BONY FOLLOWED THE creek bank to the dune blocking it at the shore of Lake Otway, and on his walking over the ramparts of blown sand the Lake in all its mystic colour stretched before him.

The continuance of the creek beyond the sandbar and out into the bed of the Lake was plain enough, the Channel being forty yards wide and said to be one hundred yards in length.

The buildings of the out-station were blobs of red-and-white atop the red bluff, and much nearer, on the opposite shore, was the white patch of Barby's tent set up in the meagre shade cast by an ancient gum. Everywhere in the shallows extending from both sides of the Channel, ducks were busy, but the herons and other waders fished with such marked indifference as to cause Bony to wonder why they wetted their feet. Flocks of moorhens ran about the dry flats, and galahs sped under the arches of the metallic sky as though to prove to earth-bound men that nothing created by nature has straight lines.

On the wide strip of dry land between Barby's camp and the dwindling water of the Lake, Barby had erected a flimsy fence of wire netting in the form of a very broad V, the point of the V thrust into the wall of a high netted trap about ten by ten feet. Now the netting was lifted off the ground and hooked to the top of the posts, mere sticks hammered into the earth. The rabbits would soon begin their evening journey, from burrows and every inch of shade on the sand dunes and the uplands beyond, to drink at the Lake, and after dark they would be out on the flats in countless numbers. And then Barby would lower the netting, making sure of a wide selvedge on the ground, and in their efforts to return to their burrows and feeding grounds, the rabbits would drive to the point of the V, pass through a hole at the point and so into the great trap.

Barby was cooking at his fire. Close by the tent was the utility, the tailboard being Barby's table, and a wooden case his chair. Under the vehicle were his three dogs, who on sighting Bony ran excitedly to meet him. The black-and-white cats came from somewhere to add their welcome, and the galah, who had perched on the tent ridge-pole, became so flurried it forgot to fly and slid down the canvas to 'flop' on the ground and emit screams of injured dignity.

'Day, there!' Barby shouted long before Bony drew near. 'Seen you coming, so I've boiled the billy. How's things?'

There being nothing to shout unnecessarily, Bony deferred an acknowledgement of welcome until he stood watching the trapper laying a bread dough in a bed of hot white ash.

'Thought I would put in a night with you,' he said. 'How is the fur coming?'

'Staying the night! Good on you. Fur's coming in like a ruddy flood. Two thousand pelts last night. Could have got five thousand if Red had been with me. You sighted him at all?'

'No.'

'Give us a bit of a hand in the morning?' Barby asked, anxiously. 'Tea's in the billy. Sugar and pannikins on the table.'

'I could lend a hand for a couple of hours,' Bony said.

73

He filled a pannikin, added a morsel of sugar. The dogs sub-sided. The cats daintily rubbed against his legs. The galah waddled over the ground on its clumsy pigeon-toed feet, tumbled on its back and looked up at him with hard bright eyes.

Barby covered his bread dough with the ash, plus an addi-tion of tiny red coals, careful to spread the heat. Because his face had been darkened by the sun his eyes were inconspicu-ous, but they were no less quick, no less alert.

'Goin' to be even hotter tomorrow, by the look of that sun,' he remarked. 'Hope it keeps up. Hotter she is the thirstier the rabbits.'

'Did you see the birds go?'

Barby nodded.

'You don't see a sight like that down in the stinking cities,' he said with emphasis. 'Or that.'

Bony followed the direction of his out-flung hand and wit-nessed a rabbit unhesitantly come running from the dunes, its normal timidity vanquished by the onslaught of thirst. It followed a straight line to the truck, stopped in its shadow for a moment, moved on and over the foreleg of one of the dogs. The dog lifted its upper lip in a sneer of disdain and con-tinued panting. It did snap at a fly. The rabbit ran on to the flat, seeking the water it must drink or perish.

'Why in hell I own dogs I don't know. Fat lot of use, ain't they? Well, I'll knock up a stew for dinner.'

'What can I do?' asked Bony.

'Do! Nothing, just yabber. How's things on the other shore?'

'Everyone is a little moody.'

'Watchin' each other, eh?'

'And the Lake.'

The galah determinedly tried to detach tabs from Bony's riding boots . . . until a flock of galahs whirled overhead, when it twisted its head to look up at them. Barby shouted to Bony to 'grab him', but Bony was too late. The bird took wing and sped upward to join his kind.

'Now we'll see something, I hope,' Barby predicted. 'But one day he won't be coming home.'

Barby's bird joined the flock, which proceeded to put on a turn of aerobatics for the benefit of the stranger. The stranger

could not be distinguished, for its performance was as flaw-
less. They flew about the camp tree, shrieking at each other
and the watchers, and presently there emerged from the general cacophony a sepulchral voice:

'Ole fool! Ole fool!'

The same line was repeated several times, when the entire
flock converged upon one member. The movement revealed
the Ishmael, who, uttering a wild shriek, headed for the camp
and arrived fast, to land on the cabin of the truck, skate off to
fly in a semicircle to Barby's feet, skid to the ground and then
swear with extraordinary fluency.

'That'll be enough out of you for one day, my lad,' Barby
said, severely. 'Where you got that Australian language, I
don't know. You never got it off me.'

Taking up the bird, he locked it in the netted cage and,
continuing to glare like the parent of an unruly child at a
party, proceeded with the preparation of the stew, saying
not a word until a vast shadow moved over the camp.
The caged bird muttered threats, but not at the passing eagle.

'Plenty of them about,' Barby told Bony. 'Ordinary times
they keep to their own beats. Now they're here in thousands.'
The eagle, golden of neck and wedge-shaped tail, swung out
over the flats, and the trapper carried forward the argument
whether eagles do greater good by killing rabbits than the
reputed destruction of young lambs.

The sun went down when the stew-pot was simmering, and
Barby lifted from the ashes the feather-light loaf of baking-
powder bread. The rabbits were leaving the uplands, crossing
the dunes like drops of dark-brown ink, passing the camp on
either side, taking no fright of the dogs and the cats, and un-
noticed by them. An uncountable host was beginning to con-
verge on Lake Otway.

Barby fed his dogs on kangaroo meat and filled their
drinking dish. The cats received smaller pieces of meat, and he
put a handful of sunflower seeds on a plate with damper crusts
and passed it to the galah. The galah promptly emptied his
dinner on the floor of the cage and threw the plate away.

Night appeared ... stepping from the Lake. Night draped its
garments over the surrounding flats, pulled down the red
dunes, reached for the slopes of the uplands. The pestiferous
flies went home, and the men ate at peace with themselves and

with this land which never has been and never will be the servant of man.

Barby went to work on one of the wings of the fence-V, and Bony attended to the other, lowering the netting, making sure the selvedge lay flat. The hole at the apex of the V inside the great trap was examined by Barby. The stars were hazy, and the silence was hot.

Afterwards they squatted on their heels either side the camp fire, where Barby drew at his pipe and Bony smoked cigarettes and betrayed his maternal ancestry by constantly pushing together burning ends of wood.

'I looked into that discarded tank at Johnson's,' he said. 'D'you happen to know what is in it?'

'I do. Shags. Millions of 'em.'

'How do you think they died there?' prompted Bony.

'Don't know. No one does. It happened after the flood came down, when the Lake was pretty full, so there was miles of water for them birds to swim in.'

'How soon after the floods arrived?' pressed Bony as Barby appeared to be thinking on something quite different.

'How soon? It must be about three months after the Lake filled up that I was at Johnson's, and the shags were in that tank then and ponging high.'

'Although the tank was discarded, it could have held rainwater?'

'That tank wasn't discarded,' Barby said. 'She was took there from the River to make an extra reservoir tank, but before the stand could be built the flood was coming, and nothing was done about it.

'Martyr and me and Ray Gillen was deciding about them shags one night. Just after the flood entered Lake Otway it rained more'n five inches in one hit. That was the first rain for fifteen months, and the last decent rain we've had. It must have put five inches into that tank.

'The shags, of course, are flying round. You know how they get wet and sit on fence posts and up in dead trees, droopin' their wings to dry off. There's water then in a bit of lake down the creek, too, and those birds was flying from one to the other. One of 'em sits on the tank to dry off, and he could've seen a tadpole in the rainwater and went down for it. Then there isn't flying-room for him to get up, and while

76

he's flopping round, a cobber sees him and went in, too. Then the others followed on to get trapped in the same way.'

'It could have been like that,' Bony conceded, doubtfully.

'Never heard of a better argument to explain it.'

One of the cats jumped to Barby's shoulder, settled there and purred like an engine. Foxes barked near and distant. The faint sound of rabbits passing by could be heard when the men were silent. Presently Bony asked:

'D'you think Martyr is careless with guns?'

'Didn't ought to be,' replied Barby. 'Been handling guns since he was three and a bit. Why?'

'It appears he was cleaning a shot-gun late last night and it was accidentally discharged.'

'What time last night?'

'About twenty minutes after ten.' Bony related the details. 'There's an inaccuracy in Martyr's story. He said that the shot went downwards in the floor, but there's a hole in the roof which wasn't there in the afternoon. The situation of the hole in the roof is peculiar. When the gun was discharged it must have been pointing upwards at the ceiling in Joan Fowler's room.'

'Perhaps the gun was pointing at someone, and someone else knocked the barrel up just in time.'

'If it was like that, George, then the two women and Martyr are hanging well together. There was no one else in the house.'

'And Ma yelled and screamed, and had to be slapped down.'

'We could hear the slaps.' Bony repeated the talk in the men's dining-room at the morning smoko, adding: 'It appeared to me that Lester, for preference, thought one of the women might be in the kitchen and wanted her to know that the tale of the accidental gun discharge wasn't believed.'

'Could be that way,' agreed Barby. 'Lester's more cunning than the other two added up. Born and reared in this part of the country. Like me, the other two wasn't. Where d'you reckon Harry Carney could have planted the money he took from Gillen's case?'

The tacked-on question astonished Bony, but gave him an instrument to use in the near future.

'Under that load of cormorants,' he replied, chuckling.

'By heck, you may be right at that, Bony. Fancy burrowing

77

down among all them birds to plant a wad of money. Imagine the pong while he was doing it. Well, we'd better think of some shut-eye, for we're due to rise at sparrow-chirp. I can lend you a wool-pack to lie on.'

Bony slept on the wool-pack until an hour before dawn, when Barby beat him to the bell by announcing breakfast consisting of kangaroo steak, damper bread and coffee.

Soon after the meal, the Lake began drawing Night down from the upland ridges, and Bony sat with Barby on a low dune providing a clear view of the latter's trapping plan. A little wind came from the north, and even after all the sunless hours it was hot.

The rabbits that had been drinking when the netted arms of the V were lowered had, of course, found their way back to the shore dunes blocked by the fence, and taking the course of least opposition had arrived at the point of the V. Inside the trap all the ground was covered with them, and at each corner living rodents sought freedom by standing on a heap of suffocated rabbits.

Outside the trap the animals were vainly seeking passage to the dunes and, like drops of water trickling from a tap, so they found the hole at the V point and trickled into the trap. Farther out on the flats rabbits ran as though from an enemy, to be slewed by the fence arms and so to run towards the point.

'You'll see something in a minute,' forecast Barby.

Bony saw the eagles, winging low along the verge of the water. One angled and skimmed the ground, then shot upward: another came on and delayed its swoop until opposite the camp. The rabbit leaped but failed to evade the talons. It screamed when a thousand feet high. Now all along the shore the eagles worked, their wings spanning six to seven feet and as rigid as the wings of a plane until they needed power for the lift. To and fro flew the eagles, and all the rabbits out in the open raced for the dunes and cover, and all the rabbits inside the tips of Barby's V raced dunewards, to arrive at the trap.

No eagle missed. Some snatched the victim without touching the ground with a claw; others paddled like the pelicans for a yard or two. Some dropped their catch from a height and swooped to retake the victim before its muscular death-twitching ceased.

'They do that every morning for me,' Barby said 'Good workers, eh?'

'Saves you a lot of rushing about,' agreed Bony.

'They don't last, though. One rabbit to each eagle and the supply of eagles soon runs short. We'd better get out there and stop them rabbits breakin' back.'

The dogs went with them as they circled eventually to walk inwards between the extremities of the fence. The men shouted and hoo-hoo-ed as though droving sheep, but the dogs were blasé and useless.

The rabbits crowded into the V point. Many hundreds did manage to break back, and when Barby cursed a bored dog, the animal deigned to grab one and break its neck.

Bony assisted Barby with the skinning, raising his hourly tally to eighty-three. At the end of the third hour, thanks to Barby, they completed this chore with the night's catch of close on two thousand rabbits. Barby was most appreciative when Bony left him slipping the skins over U-shaped wires to be stuck upright in the sand to dry.

12

A Night Out

WITHIN BONY'S PHILOSOPHY of crime investigation was the conviction that if the criminal became static immediately following the unlawful act he had every chance of escaping retribution, and when this, rarely, happened in an investigation he was conducting, he countered by prodding the suspect to activity.

On his way back to the out-station, he decided on a little prodding, and the opportunity came at the afternoon smoko when again he met the two women, Lester, MacLennon and Carney, the men having returned early.

'Have a good time?' asked Carney, and MacLennon raised his dark brows and seemed to await the answer with unusual interest.

'Yes. Quite a change from horses,' Bony replied. 'Helped

George to trap and skin just under two thousand. He netted the same number the night before.'

'My! What a big pie,' exclaimed Mrs Fowler, again vivaciously dark and off-setting her daughter's vivid colouring.

'You wouldn't believe how thick they are a bit away from here,' Lester put in. He sniffled before adding: 'This side of Johnson's Well they're thicker than sheep being druve to the yards. And foxes!'

Bony, munching cake, was conscious of Joan's eyes, but resisted looking at the girl in order to outwit the watchful Carney. MacLennon grumbled :

'And after what they said the myxotossis would do, too.'

'If the floods and droughts can't wipe out the rabbits, the mosquitoes and germs haven't a chance,' Lester said. 'Look, four years ago there wasn't a rabbit anywhere within a hundred and fifty miles of this place, and I hadn't seen a rabbit for eighteen months. Then one day I saw a rabbit on a sandy ridge, and a month afterwards rabbits were burrowin' and breedin' like mad. Them city fellers can't even imagine how big Australia is. They think the rest of Australia is another suburb or something.'

'And they won't believe rabbits drink water, either,' declared Mrs Fowler. 'When I said they did, I was called a liar.'

'Caw!' Lester sniffled twice. 'Rabbits'll drink water and they'll climb trees and gnaw off the suckers and then go down to eat the leaves. When there an't no grass, they'll scratch up the roots. And wild ducks will lay their eggs a mile from water, and lay 'em up in trees, too. Won't they, Bony?'

'Yes. And cormorants will fill a three-thousand-gallon water tank up to the brim.'

'Ah! You had a look in there?' asked Joan, and Bony now met her eyes and, while nodding assent, decided they were blue.

'George was telling me how it must have happened,' he said. 'But what I don't understand is why the topmost birds died there when they could have waddled to the side, stepped up to the rim and flown away.'

'But ...' Carney began and trailed, and impulsively Lester asked :

'How far down from the rim d'you reckon them birds is?'

'Three inches. Not more than six.'

The almost colourless eyes dwindled, then flashed examination of the others.

'Them birds was down eighteen inches when I seen 'em
last.'

'When was that?'

'When? Year ago, could be. You tell George about that?'

'That the level of the birds was almost up to the rim?
No.'

'I wonder what raised them,' murmured Joan, gazing
steadily at Bony.

'Some chemical change which has gone on since Lester
looked in the tank. The action of heat and the air and what
not might have caused each carcass to expand a fraction.'

'Sounds likely,' supported MacLennon. 'I still can't believe
the yarn how they got there.'

'Give us a better one, Mac,' urged Mrs Fowler.

He shook his head, grinned and lurched to his feet. 'I'm no
good at inventing lies,' he said, and went out. There was silence for a space, broken by the girl.

'You sure, Bony, about the level of the birds?'

'Reasonably so, but I could be mistaken,' replied Bony. 'I
merely pulled myself up to look over the rim just to see what
was inside. A few inches down from the rim was the impression I received.'

'I expect the crows got at the carcasses and stirred them
up,' Carney volunteered. 'Say, Bony, did you ever see the sun
suck a dam dry?'

'Only once,' recalled Bony, aware of the effort to change
the subject. 'It was one of those days when the sky is full of
dusty-looking clouds that never pass under the sun to throw a
shadow. I happened to be heading for a dam containing
seven feet of water in a twelve-thousand yard excavation.
It was 112 degrees in the shade, like today, and no wind.
When I first saw it the water was being sucked up in a fine
mist you could see through. The mist thickened to a light-
brown rod, and then the rod densed and became dark brown,
almost black, and suddenly it looked like a water spout upside down. At the top it formed a white cloud, and in two
minutes the bottom of the rod was drawn up like those pelican chains we saw. When I reached the dam there wasn't
enough moisture, let alone water, to bog a fly.'

'It doesn't often happen, then?' asked Mrs Fowler, keenly interested.

'So rarely that people who haven't seen it won't believe.'

'I believe it. I believe anything can happen in this country,' Mrs Fowler claimed, and Lester sniffled and told a story about fish coming up three thousand feet from an artesian bore. After that the 'party' dispersed, Bony satisfied with the initial effect of his prodding.

When darkness spread over the Lake he was sitting on his favourite dune well to the right of the bluff, and when the night was claiming the dunes, he caught sight of the figure stealing between the dunes and taking advantage of the low but sparse scrub trees. He thought it could be Lester.

It was dark when he moved. The light was on in the sitting-room, but the bedrooms were vacant. He drifted across to the house. There was a light in the annexe, but no one was there. On the side veranda the two women were listening to a radio play. He did not see Martyr.

In his room at the quarters, he stripped and put on sand-shoes. Because the light in the sitting-room could reveal him leaving, he slid over the sill of the bedroom window at the back, and drifted down to the Lake to follow the flats to Johnson's Well.

On arrival at Porchester Station, he was all Inspector in an efficient police department, but quickly assuming the role of horse-breaker, he travelled far from that lofty appointment towards the normal occupation and status of the half-caste. When he started out for Johnson's Well this early night on a mission of stealthy observation, he travelled beyond the half-caste to become all aborigine ... save in the ability to assess the psychology and bushcraft of the white man.

The men at the out-station were expert in this bush of the Continent's interior where open space separated the flat plane of earth and sky. They knew their stars, and were familiar with the importance of sky-lines . . . the shape of things against the sky ... so that movement in the normal dark of night was barely less curtailed than by day. Set against the aborigine standard the bushmanship of these station men was poor, but none the less to be respected.

Bony followed the flats all the way till barred by the sheen of water he knew to be the Channel. This he swam and continued towards Barby's camp before turning 'inland' and so reaching Johnson's Well.

Any tracks his sand-shoes might leave would be attributed to the trapper, and presently against a sky-line appeared the shapes of remembered trees, and then the short straight lines abhorred by Nature ... the shape of the hut.

Here he waited to prospect with his ears. He could detect the scurry of rabbits, now and then the warning signal made by a rabbit thumping a hind foot on the ground, and a methodical thudding as of wood on iron. This last came from the direction of the discarded tank, and he guessed correctly it was made by a fork or shovel being used in emptying the tank of dead birds.

He had to bring the tank to a sky-line, and because the man at work was almost certainly being watched, the watcher or watchers had to be located.

He moved in a wide arc to cut the drift of the faint air-current bearing the musty odour of the dead cormorants, and then moved up-wind, progressing on hands and toes to reduce the danger of crossing an enemy's sky-line. Eventually he could see the level rim of the tank regularly broken when the worker tossed out carcasses.

In the air-line of the bird-odour lesser scents could not be registered. He moved to the right, and so was aware of the smell of a white man. The white man was lying against the steep bank of the creek, his head protruding above the bank, so that he had a clear night-view of the tank. He located the second white man positioned near the engine shed, and he also had a clear view.

Three men ... one inside and two outside the tank ... Lester, Carney, MacLennon. He doubted it was Lester among the carcasses because Lester hadn't been carrying a fork or shovel when last seen among the dune scrub at dusk.

He returned over his course to cut again the odour of the dead birds, and then warily proceeded up-wind to draw as close to the worker as possible in order to identify him on a skyline when he clambered out. And he had been in the selected position less than three minutes when he heard a suspicious sound ... down-wind.

Bony brought his face close to the ground to obtain a sky-line to see what made this sound, the air current passing from him making his nose useless. The place was alive with rabbits. He saw the skulking shape of a fox moving swiftly and with enviable silence, and was sure the fox hadn't betrayed itself. Then he saw a shape without identifiable form, and knew it must be within a dozen feet of himself. It was advancing with extreme caution, slowly, silently, until its breathing identified it for Bony as a man. A fourth man.

Like an iguana Bony slid to one side, keeping that low-to-earth figure in view. It passed close by, continued towards the tank till it vanished in the complete darkness against it.

The fourth man? George Barby, or Richard Martyr?

The phrase 'It's gonna be good!' stirred in the well of his mind. He ordered memory to haul it to the surface while he lay inert, vision strained to register any movement against his sky-line. The implement being used to empty the tank was a garden fork. He could see the load of carcasses lifted above the tank rim, see the fork shaken, hear the handle bumped against the iron to free it. The man laboured diligently, yet it was some time before Bony heard the tines scrape over the iron floor as though searching for something.

'It's gonna be good!' Ah! An aborigine had said that nine years previously when he and Bony were about to witness, from the top of a tree, a brawl between two sections of a tribe.

A dark bulge grew atop the tank. Before it became recognizable a greater mass rose between it and Bony . . . that fourth man . . . When the fourth man moved slightly to the side as he advanced, the shape on the tank rim was like an enormous spider walking its web. On dropping to the ground he vanished and the sound of his landing came clearly.

Other sounds reached Bony, soft and sinister noises culminating in a sound like a snake being slammed against a tree branch by a kookaburra. A man shouted the one word 'You . . .' and then this same voice shouted 'By . . .' Again the snake was slammed against the branch, and the man said softly this time 'No!' as though saying it dreamily to himself.

There was a low scuffling in the black void against the tank. The man lying against the creek bed withdrew, rolling rubble down to the dry bed. Over by the hut, someone ploughed with devastating noise through the heap of tins and refuse. Then a shapeless thing loomed over Bony, and he slid to one side to avoid tripping the fourth man, who departed

to the point from which he had first appeared. Thereafter
there was nothing but the soft movements of the rabbits and
the incessant conversation by the birds on the distant lake.

Bony retreated, covering a hundred yards without creating
sound enough to upset the rabbits playing all about him. Now
on his feet, he strode to the drafting yards, circled wide the
horse yards and the hut and so arrived at the Lake on Barby's
side of the Channel. He sprinted to the Channel, swam it with
least noise possible, and began the four-mile journey to the
out-station at a lope.

He had to be in bed before the men returned to the quarters,
and first must ascertain who was about. That Mac and Carney
had followed Lester, Bony was sure, but it could be that
neither was aware of the other having trailed Lester. It could
be that Lester had been trailing either Carney or MacLennon.
Who the fourth man was, was a further item to accompany
Bony as he ran silently over the flats.

The morning would reveal who had been bashed when he
left the tank, either by his appearance or by his absence. Were
his own absence from the quarters discovered, the guise of
disinterested horse-breaker would be shot to pieces.

13

Lester is Confidential

THE HOUSE WAS without light, but the bulb still blazed in
the sitting-room at the quarters. The dogs were quiet, yet
the darkness might well conceal a watcher. Bony circled wide
to reach his room via its back window, and found a watcher.
She was within the deeper darkness of the machinery shed,
and from her the exceedingly gentle wind conveyed to Bony
her perfume. Joan Fowler's presence made him gamble with
time. He spent five minutes seeking out other watchers, found
none, and slid over the sill of his bedroom window.

Soundlessly he removed the sand-shoes and donned his
pyjamas. That was easy. It was not easy to lay himself on
his bed without making it complain, but he achieved it as
the result of previous practice.

Silence was an empty stage upon which not even the calls of the water-birds intruded. Silence was an enemy defeated by inherited instincts and aboriginal training, but it triumphed over the white man. Bony heard the faint noise made by Carney, who entered the room next to his by the same ingress, the window.

Long, long minutes passed into limbo. Then the bed beyond the room occupied by Carney squeaked when MacLennon put his weight upon it.

As Lester occupied the bedroom on the far side of the sitting-room, Bony could not blame himself for failing to hear Lester's return.

More long minutes passed, when Carney moved and uttered a soft expletive. Bony heard him leave his room, then light steps on the veranda. He saw his dark figure looming in the oblong of the door-frame.

'Hey, Bony!' Carney called. 'You awake?'

'Wash that? What's marrer?' asked Bony.

'Got any aspirin? I've a rotten headache.'

'Aspirin! May be some in my case. Put the light on.'

Carney the bird digger? Carney making sure the horse-breaker hadn't been up to tricks?

Swinging his legs off the bed, Bony withdrew his case from under the bed and groped under its lid. He blinked at Carney. Carney was in night attire. His fair hair was ruffled. He looked undamaged.

'Don't know what I ate to bring it on,' he said. 'Thanks. I'll get some water. What time is it?'

'No idea,' Bony replied. 'Time for a smoke, anyway. Have you been out on a jag?'

'Been playing cards with the women. Only coffee to drink.'

The brown eyes were round and wary, and Bony purposefully fumbled with the cigarette paper and tobacco. They missed nothing, taking in the condition of Bony's bedding, his clothes, his boots. The canvas shoes they failed to see, for they were inside the case.

'Last man in left the light on, Bony. What time did you go to bed?'

'About half-past ten, I think. There was no one about, so I left it on.'

'Well, switch the ruddy light off and shut up,' shouted MacLennon.

'All right! All right!' Carney called, and winked at Bony.

He passed to the door, paused with his hand on the switch. Bony nodded and he switched off the light. Bony heard him pouring water from the bag suspended from the veranda roof. Then the sitting-room light was flicked off and Carney dropped on his bed as though intentionally making it complain.

The next morning he met Carney coming from the shower-house and inquired about the head.

'Good! Those tablets fixed it in five minutes,' replied Carney. 'Goin' to be a stinker of a day by the feel of the sun.'

'Seems likely.'

Bony showered and towelled. He heard MacLennon on the veranda when he was combing his straight black hair, and MacLennon was advising Lester to 'rise and shine', else he'd be late for breakfast. MacLennon needed to shave, but otherwise was tidy and clean, and he nodded to Bony when turning from Lester's room, saying:

'Bob must have gone off early after the horses.'

Carney carelessly agreed and joined Bony at the end of the veranda. They looked upon Lake Otway, an unruffled sheet of molten metal seemingly making afraid the gulls hesitant at the verge, and a cormorant perched on the marker. The level was thirteen inches. Carney said nothing. The breakfast call was given.

As usual, Mrs Fowler served the breakfast. Other than the 'good mornings' and the question and answer concerning Lester, conversation was at zero. Joan didn't appear. Carney was first to leave the table, and when Bony passed outside the annexe he found Carney gazing narrowly towards the horse yards.

Coming round the outside of the yards was Lester. He was on foot and carrying a bridle.

'Seems like Bob got tossed,' Carney remarked. 'Looks for trouble, Bob does. Won't put a saddle on the night horse, and that mare can't be trusted.'

Together they walked to the end of the buildings backed by the pepper trees and waited for Lester, who was dragging a foot. MacLennon joined them, and it was he who asked Lester, without evincing much concern, what had happened, Lester's jaw was dark with contusion. His head was awry. The right eye was bloodshot but not bruised. He sniffled and tried to jeer at himself.

'Heaved off,' he said. 'Treacherous bloody mare. Caught me bending as I was rounding up the mokes. The neck strap broke and she got free and cleared off on me.'

'Feelin' a bit sick, by the look of you,' MacLennon snapped, his lip lifted in a sneer of derision. 'Looks like you been fighting or something.'

Lester's eyes hardened and became small, like wet beach pebbles. He would have snarled a counter had not the quiet voice of the overseer slipped it aside.

'Go and lie down on your bunk, Bob,' Martyr ordered. 'I'll come later and practise on you. Mac, ride out to Sawyer's Dam after you bring in the workers. Bony won't mind you using his hack. Take a deck at the weaners. And get back as soon as you can. It's going to hot up properly, and there's no necessity for any of us to fry. By the way, you fellows, your light was on too late again last night.'

'Yair,' admitted Carney, who occasionally slurred his speech. 'Last up forgot.'

Martyr's pale-grey eyes hardened as Lester's had done, and he clipped :

'If it happens again, I remove all the bulbs. Some of the batteries are sick. The dynamo is sick. I'm sick of talking about it.'

They dispersed, Bony to saunter to the yards to await the return of MacLennon with the horses. He rolled a cigarette and watched the overseer walking to the office. Martyr suffered a slight limp. He came from the office carrying a medical kit and crossed to Lester's room. Ten minutes later he returned to the office, and five minutes after that Mrs Fowler crossed to the quarters carrying a breakfast tray.

At the morning smoko, Mrs Fowler had Bony to herself. She was wearing a coral-pink overall, which suited her, and she was evidently pleased with the situation.

'It's going to be unbearably hot today,' she said while filling the cups with strong tea. 'I do hate this heat.'

'Thermometer under the pepper trees says it's 108 degrees. It must be 208 degrees in your kitchen,' Bony guessed, and wasn't far off the mark.

'Must be ... with bread baking. Your work must be exhausting.'

'Unfair to the horses. I'm knocking off at lunch for the day. Took a filly along to Johnson's Well to work off some steam. The Lake seems about finished, doesn't it?'

'Looks just yellow mud to me.'

'Who won last night?' Bony asked, and the woman's dark brows rose questioningly.

'But we didn't play last night. Joan was out somewhere till late. With you?'

'I've been here three weeks,' Bony said with assumed severity. 'Candidly, do I appear to you as a skirt chaser?'

'No – no, you don't, Bony.' Then she smiled. 'You could try yourself out some time. Keeps a man young ... and a woman, too. Everyone's a bit slow here, you know. I'll bet you've had plenty of women chasing you before now. You can't make me believe you're not scientific.'

'Ah!' Bony breathed, and smiled his beaming smile. 'Once upon a time when I was young and bold I rode away with a squatter's daughter. The squatter and his men pursued us, soon caught up because my horse was carrying a double load. I'll take a cup of tea and a portion of cake over to Lester, if you don't mind.'

He stood and filled a pannikin.

'What happened when the men caught up with you?' demanded Mrs Fowler, and Bony wondered if she was being naïve.

'I dumped the lady upon a saltbush and rode on and on.' he said. 'And I never went back to that station. In fact, there are so many stations to which I cannot return that I have to think hard before asking for work at one.'

Smiling deep down into Mrs Fowler's warming eyes, he placed a piece of cake on his own plate and, with a cup of tea, wended his way to Lester, who was sitting on the broken arm-chair on the verandah. An expertly placed bandage was about the stockman's neck and much adhesive tape fixed lint to his jaw.

'How is the neck?' Bony asked.

'Not so bad. Bit stiff. Sort of ricked it when I hit the ground.'

'It mightn't have happened if you hadn't forgotten to wear your spurs.'

'You could be right,' Lester agreed. 'Tain't often I forget 'em. Musta been dopey. I woke up at dawn and couldn't get back to sleep, so I decided to go for the workers 'fore breakfast.'

'The first time you forgot them, too. The spurs, I mean.'

Lester glanced direct, then swerved away from the bright blue eyes. Quietly and with slow emphasis, he asked:

'You talkin' double?'

'For your sake, Bob.'

'How come?'

'If MacLennon tracked you when he went after the working horses, he mightn't find the place where the stable horse threw you this morning. Of course, if you thought to mess up the ground somewhere, and faked the horse's tracks where she was supposed to have bucked you off, it would substantiate your story.'

'Are you tellin' me I wasn't dumped this morning?' Lester asked.

'Yes. There is something going on here I don't understand. I'm here only to do a spot of breaking, and it's nothing to do with me, but I couldn't help seeing that neither Carney nor MacLennon believed you were dumped. After all, you've never done me a bad turn, and I'm only giving you a warning.'

There was another long silence, which Bony terminated.

'You see, Bob, it was like this. MacLennon could have noticed you forgot your spurs. You always wear spurs. You put them on when you dress in the morning as sure as you put on your trousers. There is something else, too. Someone has forked all the shags out of the tank at Johnson's Well. Was done last night. When you limped back this morning and told us your story, I could smell on you those dried birds. The smell wasn't strong, but you were to windward of MacLennon and Carney as well as me. It's no business of mine why you went to Johnson's Well and emptied that tank.'

The inevitable sniffle. A chuckle without humour.

'What else did you see at Johnson's?'

'Nothing.'

'Tracks you musta seen.'

'No. The rabbits wiped out your tracks.'

The possessive pronoun was not missed.

'You seen no other tracks?'

'As I said . . . the rabbits . . .'

'Yair, I heard.'

Lester pondered and Bony patiently waited. The veranda roof creaked under the torture of the sun. Beyond its shade the earth was polished by the sun, light red on the summit, dark red in the gullies of the miniature dunes kicked up by human feet all the way to the house on the far side of the open space. The shadows cast by the distant house, the out-buildings backed by the pepper trees, were black. White patches in one such shadow were the gasping hens.

'You know, Bony,' Lester drawled, 'there's something up between Ma Fowler and Mac and between Harry and Joan what's different to just playing ring-a-ring-a-roses. Right now those two women will be watching us, wondering what we're saying, wondering what we know and what we don't know. If I talk, you keep it to yourself?'

'Don't talk if you'd rather not,' urged Bony. 'As I've told you I'll be gone with my cheque in a couple of weeks. I mentioned those birds at Johnson's merely as a warning because I saw how suspicious Carney and Mac were this morning.'

'I know, and I'm not liking you less for it, Bony. It's because you're only casual, and because you got eyes, that I reckon you could do me another good turn. If y'would.'

'Of course.'

'Well, I got to start with them two women,' Lester proceeded and at once proved he could think straight. 'They came here, and mighty soon got everything changed over at the house and with the cooking and such. We could see they was on the make, but they was good sports and played around. You know how it is for a few blokes in a place like this.

'After Ray Gillen come here, things were stirred up a bit. Mac had been chasin' Ma Fowler and Harry had been after Joan when she was passed up by Martyr, who, I suppose, reckoned he'd have to be careful, or take the sack from Wallace. Ray was a good bloke in all ways. Them women played up to him, but he was too cunnin' to be properly caught. He'd take one and then the other out of an evening on his motor-bike. He'd tease 'em and make 'em wild, and kiss 'em when they wasn't expectin' him to, and all that. He was always crackin' jokes and bettin' he'd do anything better'n the next . . . and always winning, too.

'One day me and Ray was sent to patch up the yards at

Johnson's Well and we went there on his bike. We took our lunches as it was a long job. And that day Ray told me he was suspicious that someone had opened his suitcase and gone through his things.

'He swore he always kept his case locked, and that the locks weren't just ordinary and easy to pick. Always had the key with a gold locket on a string tied round his neck. I seen it there. Everyone did. Even when he went swimming he had that key and locket round his neck.

'We nutted out who could have got to his case when Ray was out in the paddocks. There was Carney who slept in the same room as him, and there was them two women always home when every man Jack of us would be out working. Any of us others could have tackled Ray's case, but would take a hell of a risk of being seen, going in or coming out of his room, by one of the women.

'I arst Ray what was in the case he was so particular about, and he said there was two hundred quid he had saved up. When I told him he ought to take it to the homestead to be locked in the book-keeper's safe, he said he could look after his own dough.

'Two nights after we pitched that day, he was drowned. Then Martyr got me and George Barby to be with him when he went through Ray's case to find out about his people or such. The case wasn't locked, that stonkered me, but I was more stonkered when there wasn't any money in it.

'I've never said anythin' about Ray tellin' me he had two hundred in his case, and ever since I been wonderin' if he planted the dough some place, or if it was stolen by someone who dun him in for it.'

14

A Business Proposition

'TWO HUNDRED QUID makes a tidy packet,' Lester said, sniffling. 'I thought about who might have took it, and if no one did, then where would Ray plant it? He had time to plant it, see! I got to workin' it out. It couldn't have been Mac, 'cos he'd have rushed off to the nearest pub. Harry, yes. Carney is shrewd, and he don't drink. Then there's George Barby. George is always careful of his money. He likes a drop, but not enough to blow two hundred on a bender.

'Then something happened what hit me to leg. It was about three weeks after Ray went off. I was repairing the fences round the horse paddock when a wire snapped back and gashed me arm. It bled a lot, and I came home for something to stop it. All hands were away, so I went over to the kitchen to get Ma Fowler to fix me arm properly. And when I walked into the annexe, them women was arguing in the kitchen, spittin' at each other like a coupla cats.

'Joan was saying that she didn't have any of the money, and that if Carney had found it he was keepin' it to himself. She goes on to say that it's more'n likely Mac dug it up somewhere, else where did he get the money to buy Ma that emerald ring. Ma threatened to smash Joan's face in if she bilked her for her share, and Joan laughs and says: if ever she did lay her hands on that twelve thousand five hundred quid her Ma would never know.

'They goes at it, and I'm quiet and listening in the annexe, and after a bit Joan says something about Ray's gold locket. Ma tells her to forget about the locket, saying it'll be many a year before anyone finds Ray Gillen. Joan says it'll be about a year before the Lake dries out, and first on the body gets the locket, and whoever gets the locket gets that twelve thousand five hundred of the best.

'With that Joan goes out of the kitchen and I cleared back to the pepper trees and went in again as though for the first time, and Ma Fowler doctored me arm. And sweet as sugar, she was.'

Lester's watery eyes encountered Bony's steady regard, and Bony nodded.

'It sorta come plain to me why them women and Carney and Mac always seem to be watching each other,' Lester said. 'I knew them four was up to something, and when I heard the women quarrelling I knew what about. I could never make out how the locket came into it, unless it was a sort of clue telling where Ray had planted his money.

'But the thing that stuck in me mind was the amount of

dough the women mentioned. I wrote it in words on a bit of paper. Then I wrote it in figures with the pound sign in front, and I knew I had seen them figures in a paper some time. I got a good memory for horses and performances and sporting dates, and I stewed over them figures for weeks before they hit me between the eyes.

'I could tell you where I seen them figures and when I seen 'em. I couldn't contact any names by them figures, but I remember suddenly the yarn told about 'em. There was two blokes up in Queensland what won £25,000 in a lottery, and they divi'd the cash between 'em in a pub bedroom. I musta read about it in a sportin' paper, 'cos I don't read no other kind except the sport pages.' Lester closed his eyes. 'I can see them figures now, Bony. £25,000 and some words I can't remember, and then £12,500, as plain as I can see you.'

'Are you telling me, Bob, that you believe Gillen had £12,500 in his case?' Bony prompted.

'I am, Bony. I am tellin' you just that. Look! Ray comes here from nowhere. Has a suitcase what he always keeps locked and the key around his neck. He gets worried when someone has a go at his case. He tells me he's got two hundred in it. Two hundred quid is a nice wad, but not so big that anyone here would of done him in for it. Even take it out of his case. But £12,500 is something, Bony.'

'I agree, but . . .'

'What?'

'A man would be a fool to get around with all that money in a suitcase.'

'Ray Gillen was a fool,' countered Lester.

'All right, then. But would he take a job here when he had all that money?'

'Yair. And I know why. He told me. His bike had broke down beyond Johnson's, and he walked here the next morning to get repairs. We was all out except the women. He was asked in for morning smoko. He seen Joan. So he asked Martyr for a job. He said so.'

'But £12,500!' Bony persisted, and Lester sniffled.

'Caw! Be your age. I carried a swag once with over four hundred quid and cheques for another two hundred in me hip pocket. Stormy Sam had a cigar-box in his swag when they come on his body up near Wilcannia. Full of opals and gold

94

sovereigns and English bank-notes. And Sam died just naturally. I reckon Ray Gillen got suspicious and planted his money
until he was fed up with Joan and ready to clear out.'

'What about the locket? How does that enter the picture?'

'I don't get the locket, Bony, and that's dinkum. But that
locket is important to the women. They think it will lead
'em to the dough, which is why they're so interested in the
Lake dryin' out, which is why Mac and Carney is so interested
in the Lake, too. I reckon he planted his money and put 'em
off somehow with a yarn about the locket. But they didn't
get the money 'cos they're all still here ... waitin' for Lake
Otway to die to find Ray's body. You help me find that money,
and we go fifty-fifty.'

'You thought Gillen might have buried his money among
the dead birds in the tank?'

'Yair,' replied Lester. 'Good place, too.'

'And you haven't an idea who waited for you to get out of
that tank?'

'Too dark to see. Can't understand why he waited for me.
I never seen him till after he punched me on the jaw. He
picked me up like I was a bag and caught me on the side of
me neck. He musta been there when I was forking out
them birds, and he musta known I didn't chuck anything
out before I got out meself. Pity the bloody fork didn't drop
on him.'

'Perhaps he thought you had found the money and had it
inside your shirt.'

'Could have.'

'Did he look when he had you down?'

'Don't know. I passed out. Musta been lyin' there a coupla
hours before I come to. It was just breakin' day when I got
back here and nutted out how I could explain me condition.
I'd like to know which of 'em bashed me. I'd get him if I
waited ten years.'

'Concentrate on the money,' urged Bony.

'Ain't I concentratin' on it?'

'How often did Gillen go riding on his bike?'

'How. ... Oh, pretty often of an evening. Usta take one or
other of the women on the back.'

'Which direction, which track did he take?'

'Mostly to Johnson's Well.'

'What other track?'

'Don't recall he ever went another way. Sometimes he'd ride right round the Lake, keeping on the edge of the flats.' Lester sniffled, and Bony wished he wouldn't. 'I reckon I know what you're headed for, Bony. I thought he might have planted his dough at Johnson's Well 'cos he came here from Ivanhoe and he would prob'bly go back that way, pick up his money when passing the Well. There ain't a holler log, or a holler tree, I haven't delved into. I been down the Well, thinking he might have dropped a tin with the money in it and a wire hitched to the tin, or he might have planted it behind a board holding the shaft. I been up every tree round the Lake looking for a likely hole.'

'Then what about the Lake? The deepest part is at the Channel, isn't it?'

'Yes, but ...'

'If I wanted to plant money ... notes ... I'd stuff them into treacle tins which have press-on lids,' Bony said. 'The treacle tins I'd put into a twelve-pound cyanide tin which also has a press-on lid. The notes would be safe enough under water for twelve months.'

'Cripes, Bony, you got a head on you. Gillen knew about the Channel, of course. Diving for the tin of dough wouldn't stonker him. Funny if after he got drowned he was sorta steered about the Lake to drop into the Channel and be lying on top of his dough, guardin' it sort of.'

'Think it likely?'

'Could be. When Gillen was drowned, there was more'n twelve feet of water. Like a sea it was when the wind blew hard. You could hear the surf a mile away. The tide would go out along that side off where the wind blew and rise high on the opposite side. That set up currents. You could see the birds ridin' 'em. And Gillen never come ashore.'

'What d'you think prevented the body coming ashore?'

'Well, if he drowned, and he needn't, Ray was probably well out near the middle. But where he went down don't really matter, as I'll prove. Anyhow, he drowns in twelve feet of water. After three days up he comes. We're all waitin' for him to come ashore. He's like a small raft ... the middle of him 'cos his legs and his head is just under. If he was murdered and his body heaved into the Lake, it would float back upward : if he drowned, then he would float stummick up. His stummick would be the raft, get me?'

'Yes,' replied Bony.

'Then what happens? I'll tell you. The raft gives landing ground to the crows, and the crows goes for the belly. They always go for the belly of anything dead. The crows tear at the belly and lets out all the gas what made the body rise. With the gas out, the body sinks again.

'The body don't rest hard on the bottom, Bony. In the water he ain't got much weight, if any, so it just touches the mud. Then the currents moves it slowly round and about until it tangles with the old fence crossing the Lake or among the branches of one of the two red gums what fell long before the flood. Or it could have moved all over the place till it fell over the edge and down to the bottom of the Channel. You any good at swimming?'

'Not good enough to dive among a dead man's bones,' answered Bony with conviction.

'Me, neether,' Lester said. 'Still, twelve thousand of the best is worth a bit of horrer.'

'The water has receded from the two ancient trees,' Bony said.

'Yair, I know. The tops of the posts of the old fence showed up more'n a month ago. With me feet I prodded that fence from shore to shore feeling for Ray. He ain't tangled with the fence. Nor the trees. So he's in the Channel. Even if he wasn't drowned but bumped off and thrown in dead, he'd be in the Channel . . . ten or eleven feet down.'

Bony stood, saying:

'I'd better get back to my horses and turn them out. Too hot for work. I haven't been round the Lake for a week. When did you circle it last time?'

'More'n a week ago.'

'And the others? D'you know?'

'They give up going round her when the water went down and left the trees high and dry. I beat Carney to the fence-proddin' by a coupla nights.' Lester sniffled. 'I been watchin' all of 'em. They ain't missed much, especially Joan. Do we go fifty-fifty?'

Bony half sat on the veranda rail and rolled another cigarette. His back was towards the house, and he 'felt' green eyes and dark eyes boring into him. His answer to Lester's question was given with a nod.

'Good on you,' approved Lester. 'We work together. You get around the Lake as much as you can on your youngsters, just to make sure Ray ain't lying out in the sun. I'll keep my eyes on the others. They're thinkin' of the locket, and how they expect that to lead 'em to the dough beats me. Still, we got to keep ahead of 'em even with the locket. Then one night when the water's gone from both sides of the Channel, we'll do a bit of draggin'.'

Again Bony nodded.

'Then when we find the money we divi up, and I'm telling you we got to go careful when we do. No lashin' it out in the pubs. No buying flash cars and clothes or women. We spends it quiet like, slow, and steady, so nobody will wonder where we got a hell of a lot of cash and ask questions. Some I know would write to the income-tax bastards, and they would ask why, see?'

'Yes, I see,' admitted Bony. He moved from the rail and took a few steps from Lester. Then he turned about and asked:

'Where did you learn about bodies in water, and how they come up and what happens to them, Bob?'

Once again the sniffle mixed up with the chuckle.

'Sort of come to me through the family,' replied Lester. 'Me grandfather got the licence of a shanty on the river up near Bourke. Long time back, 'fore I was born. Then me old man took over the pub when the grandfather fell into the river one night and got drowned. Times were wild. Lots of cheque-men sort of fell into the river and was drowned. Me grandfather, an' me old man, often come on a dead body. Quite a cemetery growed around the pub, and they could tell what bodies was drowned and what wasn't.'

'Did you inherit the pub?' smilingly asked Bony.

'Not a chance. The old man drank hisself outer the pub in less'n eight years and went bullock-drivin'. Had a fight one day with another bullocky. With their whips, old style. The other bloke accidentally got his whip round the old man's throat and before he could get it clear the old man was a body, too. Terrible hard doer, the old man.'

That was the only occasion when Bony forgave Lester his sniffle.

15

Passing of Lake Otway

WHEN THE GROUND at foot was still hotter than the rays of the setting sun, they went down to the Lake ... everyone, including the women. When the overseer and the two women had emerged from the house, the men had automatically joined them, as though magnetized by inevitability. No one spoke as they crossed the iron-hard flats to the softer marge which had been covered with water only that morning.

The pale-yellow solidified light that had been Lake Otway this last day of its existence was now a tarnished wafer of old gold, heavy, metallic, flat. Far outward from the 'shore' blemishes constantly appeared, dabs of darker-brown which moved to draw silver lines quickly erased. The divers couldn't dive any more, and they sat upon the metallic wafer like little china ducks, and here and there in grand but terrible isolation the ibis and the heron and the crane stood motionless as though dead.

Far out beyond them the ducks were congregated as the pelicans had gathered, and they waited for the leaders to take off along the sky-ways to far-away waters. Two cormorants perched atop the marker post, their wings drooping to dry as though in mockery of the Lake. The only note of joy in life was struck by the gulls who rode upon the golden wafer, high and clean and beautiful.

Bodies rested on the marge, bodies rested along the edge of the water, the countless bodies of fish. Beyond the dead fish the doomed sought frantically to evade the inevitable. Their broad backs were the dark dabs on the wafer of gold, their bodies drawing the silver lines upon it. The marker post no longer registered.

After the sun had gone the colour of Lake Otway swiftly changed, taking from the western sky its coating of crimson, and Mrs Fowler cried:

'Isn't it awful? It's like a plate of tomato soup.'

And MacLennon said :

'By this time tomorrow we'll be able to walk across without getting our boots muddy.'

Yet again the night came upwards from the ground. It turned the water to molten lead. It crept like a mist over the flats, about the feet of the watchers, dimming the greyish legs of the cranes. It drew everything down and down as though Earth and everything upon it was a hell being banished from the glory of the sky.

The sky was salmon-pink to the west, merging with emerald-green, passing to the blue of Bony's eyes down by the eastern horizon. They could not see the beginning of the bird migration, but through the rising night there came to the watchers the whirring of wings, faint and yet momentous. Then beneath the celestial canopy appeared the ducks in formations, moving fast and sure. The wading birds flapflapped their way upwards, and the cormorants weaved about them. Presently only the gulls remained. The gulls hovered about the watchers like the ghosts of the departed.

'I'm going to the house,' Mrs Fowler decided, hysteria in her voice. 'I've had enough.'

She moved away through the rising night towards the bluff. The face of the bluff and the walls of the buildings were dovegrey, but the windows were oblongs of blood. Lester spoke, and the woman spun about as though struck.

'Tomorrer we'll be able to look around for Ray Gillen.'

'Why bring that up?' drawled Carney.

'Why not? We all been waitin' to find him, ain't we? Ray's somewhere about . . . what's left of him.'

'Don't count me in,' flashed Carney. 'I'm not interested in finding Ray Gillen. Never was. I had nothing to do with him . . . not like some people.'

'Well, you can all ride out tomorrow,' Martyr said, quietly. 'Gillen ought to be found and be decently buried. And then we ought to suffer less from bickering.'

Mrs Fowler hurried away, and the gulls fluttered after her, flew on beyond her and vanished against the dark face of the bluff. Bony felt a hand rest lightly on his forearm, and brought his gaze down to Joan's face.

'I didn't think the Lake would die like that,' she said, slowly 'It's left it all naked and stiff like a . . . like a real body.'

'You have seen a real body?'

'I read books, stupid.'

They proceeded to the bluff steps. He asked :

'What did Lester mean when he said everyone has been waiting for the Lake to dry out in order to find Gillen's body?'

'It's been in our minds for a long time,' replied the girl. 'You see, Ray Gillen was a . . . he was hard to forget. If Lester or Mac had been drowned, we'd have forgotten all about them by now. Did you hear what Carney said?'

'That he isn't interested in finding Gillen's body, yes.'

'When he goes riding tomorrow you keep close by. He's interested all right. Ray used to wear a gold locket round his neck. Probably still there. Ray promised me that locket, and if Carney gets it he won't give it up. You get it and give it to me. Will you?'

'If he promised it to you,' Bony said, with assumed doubt.

'He did, I tell you. Now no more. But remember, that locket belongs to me.'

Having arrived at the steps hewn into the bluff face, she ran up them and was nowhere in view when Bony reached the top. Lights sprang up in the house and someone switched on the light in the men's quarters.

Bony found Carney already in the sitting-room settling down to read a magazine. Lester slumped into the arm-chair on the veranda, and Bony joined him to sit on the boards and roll a cigarette.

'Stinker of a night, ain't it?' Lester complained, and Bony agreed. 'Sort of night that dynamo engine gets on me nerves. Bang, bang, bang, right into me head.'

'I think I'll carry my bunk outside for the night,' Bony decided. 'Too hot in the room.'

'Good idea. You might give me a hand with mine. Set 'em up back of the building where they'll be in the shade first thing in the morning. Blasted heat-waves. Can't stand 'em like I usta. Hear how Carney bit just now when I said about huntin' for Gillen?'

'Methinks he doth protest too much.'

'Caw! You musta got that off Martyr. He knows a lot of them sayings. Puts 'em into his poetry, too.'

'He writes poetry?'

'Pretty good at it. You understand it?'

'Genuine poetry, yes.'

'Can't stand a bar of it.'

MacLennon appeared from the darkness.

'Took a screw at the thermometer,' he said. 'A hundred and three. In the shade! In the night! A hundred and three! Be a bitch of a day tomorrow.'

'We're sleeping outside,' Bony told him. 'Give me a hand with the beds?'

At break of day the flies woke every man, and Carney said he had had the bush and would quit.

'Better not,' advised MacLennon. 'Mightn't be safe.'

They glared at each other, and Carney, becoming angry, drawled:

'If I want to quit, I quit, Mac. What you might be thinking don't trouble me.'

'No? Well, go ahead and see what happens. No one quits on his own.'

'Yair, that's right,' interposed Lester. 'No one quits till we agrees on the divi.' The interjection appeared to calm the others. They both stared at Lester, and Carney said:

'It's up to you, Bob. Spill it.'

'Oh, no, it isn't. It's up to you or Mac.'

'Aw, what's the use,' snarled MacLennon. 'Shut up talkin' like kids. You goin' to work the horses in this heat, Bony?'

'This morning, anyway,' replied Bony. 'Mustn't let up on two I'm taking through the hoops. I'll put in a couple of hours before breakfast.'

They lapsed into sullen silence. Bony dressed and walked to the stables for the fed horse, and knew they watched him. The risen sun already burned his flesh when he rode out for the youngsters, and when the breakfast gong was struck no living thing voluntarily ventured from the shade.

'If only the wind would rise,' Carney said as, with Bony, he paused to look out over the Lake as they crossed to the annexe.

'If only to shoo the flies from pestering our eyes.' Bony heartily agreed. 'As you did this morning, I feel like quitting. Too hot to work. Might put in a week with George and the rabbits. That's not water down there. The water has vanished.'

'Yes. Bloody shame.'

The gleaming shield still covered Lake Otway, but now areas of mottled grey dulled the shield, and Bony fancied that, even as he watched, these areas were expanding. Following breakfast, he looked again at the Lake. Those grey areas were spreading fast as the last of the surface moisture was sucked up by the murderous sun.

At morning smoko, the temperature in the pepper tree shade was 117 degrees, and on Lake Otway there wasn't sufficient moisture to service a postage stamp.

Nevertheless, the depression wasn't yet hard enough to bear a horse, and Martyr had sent MacLennon out on a job, and he himself had taken Carney on the utility to work some miles away. Lester, who had been told to take life easy, was hugging the shade of the quarters veranda and reading a sporting paper when Bony rode off to visit George Barby.

He found the trapper had shifted camp to Johnson's Well, and that he had begun the erection of his fence around the Channel. Barby was cooking at a fire outside the hut when Bony arrived and neck-roped his horse to a shady tree.

'How's things?' shouted Barby. 'Come in out of the sun and have a cuppa tea.'

The dogs barked with no enthusiasm. The galah, perched on a biscuit tin, kept its beak wide open and panted, its wings drooping and reminding Bony of the cormorants. The cats watched Bony, their mouths wide and pink, and their flanks working like bellows. And Barby, lean and tough, was naked save for the towel tethered about his middle with string.

'Pretty flamin' hot, ain't it?' he said, pouring the 'cuppa' into a tin pannikin for his guest. 'Sugar on the truck. Bit of brownie in the box.'

'A hundred and seventeen when I left,' Bony told him.

'Don't talk about it. I give up labour. Even the blasted cats can't take it. Look at 'em. Got to nurse 'em. Watch!'

Taking the canvas water-bag from the hook suspended from the hut veranda, he stroked one of the cats and without difficulty persuaded it to lie flat on its back. Slowly he tipped the bag and poured the comparatively cool water on the animal's tummy, and the cat squirmed with pleasure and began to purr. In like fashion, he treated the other cat and, to Bony's amusement, the galah flopped off the biscuit tin and came staggering to them, wings trailing, beak wide with distress.

'If you think I'm goin' to keep on doing this all day, you're mistaken,' Barby protested.

The galah tumbled over its head to lie on its back like the cats. Barby scooped a rough hole in the sand and poured water into it. He held a finger low and the bird clasped it and suffered itself to be lifted and lowered into the hole, back downward. Then Barby sloshed water over it, and the bird sat up like an angry old man and swore. Then it lay down again and would have purred if able.

'Ruddy characters,' Barby claimed. 'Poor bastards, they can't stand this heat.' Genuine pity stirred his voice, and he tried to hide it by saying: 'There's seven or eight crows in that tree where you tied your horse. If it gets much hotter they're goin' to perform. You know who chucked all them birds out of that tank?'

'Should I?' countered Bony. 'When was it done?'

'Night before last. Anyone missing from the quarters night before last?'

'MacLennon, Lester, Carney.'

'What about Martyr?'

'I don't know about him,' Bony smiled. 'I mentioned to the men that the birds in the tank were to within a few inches of the top. It puzzled them, and Lester said they were not that high when he looked in some time ago.'

'Wonder what they expected to find,' chortled Barby. 'Money? Hell! Gillen? Perhaps. You got no idea who it was?'

'Lester. He was bashed on leaving the tank.'

Bony told of Lester's ruse to allay suspicion by saying he had been tossed, and Barby grinned.

'I knew it was Lester,' he said, triumphantly. 'I was over here at sun-up yesterday morning, getting drinkin' water, and right against the tank I found his old beret. He never went anywhere after dark without it. So Bob Lester can't know where Ray Gillen's money is planted. Wonder why they bashed him.'

'You don't know who bashed him?'

Barby's dark eyes were abruptly hard.

'No. Think I should?'

'As I see it, George, Carney and Mac followed Lester. They waited for him to empty the tank. When he jumped out, one of them bashed him ... hard enough to knock him out for several hours. Doesn't it appear to you that Carney and

MacLennon both were after the money and thought it possible that Lester found it among the dead birds?'

'Looks like it, don't it?'

'Therefore, Carney and MacLennon also cannot know where Gillen's money is.'

'H'm!' grunted the trapper. 'Bit of a mix-up, eh?'

16

Smoke on the Bluff

ANYTHING MORE BEEN said about the gun going off?' Barby asked, when they were eating lunch.

'Not a word,' Bony replied. 'You make a good curry, George.'

A bag nailed to the window-frame of the hut would have darkened its interior against the flies, but the heat within was unbearable. They defeated the flies by making a smoke fire in the shade cast by the hut and squatting on their heels either side this small fire to envelop their heads and the meal within smoke.

'Only tucker worth eating this weather,' Barby said. 'I been thinking about that gun, and where it went off, and what was workin' up. Something or other will bust before long. You got any idea where that money could of been hid?'

'Afraid not. It wasn't buried among those dead shags.'

Had Bony been able to forget he was a horse-breaker, Barby quite unconsciously would have repeatedly reminded him, for deep inside the English Barby was ever the superiority towards the 'native'. It was Barby's opinion that his own intelligence and powers of reasoning were far higher than that of the heathen, and this attitude amused and gratified Bony because it cloaked his work as a criminal investigator.

'I see you are going to trap the Channel,' he said, casually.

'Yair. I done a bit to the fence along one side and the trap, and I'll finish this evening and start. What about coming in with me?'

'I'd like to. Seems to me you could do with twenty assistants.'

'I could do with fifty.' Barby tossed his tin plate to the ground and groped for the pannikin of tea. 'You and me together can't deal with the mob of rabbits round here. We couldn't trap 'em and skin 'em fast enough to beat the sun. Then there's millions right round the Lake what'll be headed this way tonight for water. All we can do is skin what we can.'

'The 'roos are going to be a nuisance to your fence,' Bony reminded him. 'Any guns with your gear?'

'Couple of Winchesters and a twelve-bore shot-gun. We'll have to sit up most of the night to keep 'em off the fence. Got plenty of ammo, fortunately. Blast! It's hot, ain't it. Don't remember being so hot for years.'

Bony washed the utensils and Barby crossed to the trough and let water gush into it from the reservoir tank. The dogs loped over to him and plunged into the trough. He brought a bucket of water back to the hut shade, scooped a hole, splashed water into it, and the two cats lay in the water and rolled in the wet sand after the water had soaked away. The galah demanded attention and was given a wet hole all to itself.

Bony sat with Barby, their backs to the hut wall and with gum-tips whisked the flies from the their faces. Barby explored the possibilities of generating power from the sun's heat, and climaxed the subject by asserting that the capitalists would never allow it.

'D'you think the scientists will ever make rain when they want to?' he asked.

'Quite likely,' replied Bony.

'If they do, they'll ruin Australia,' predicted the trapper. 'What keeps the rabbits down, and the foxes, and the blowflies, and the kangas? What d'you reckon?'

'The droughts.'

'Course. If it wasn't for the ruddy droughts no white man could live in the country, and the remainin' blacks would migrate to Blighty. Myxotitis! Rot! Just as well spray the rabbits with hair oil.'

'It seems you wouldn't like the rabbits to be wiped out,' dryly observed Bony.

'Because why? There's hundreds of blokes making a good

living outa rabbits and the fur, and while rabbits run there's no excuse for any man to be out of work in Australia. I know trappers what take live rabbits into country where there ain't any, just to let 'em breed up. Why not? Done it meself, but don't you ever tell the Boss.'

Bony laughed.

'The Boss would be annoyed?'

'He'd drop dead,' Barby agreed and chuckled. The mood passed, and the note of indignation crept back into his voice.

'Fancy wiping out all the rabbits what give rich women albino fox furs and coats, and Kohinoor mink and Alaskan capes and things. Fancy killing all the rabbits what could give cheap meat to the working people who got to pay four bob for a pound of measly mutton chops. And just to let farmers buy more cars and crash-bang boxes for the kids. And dirty politicians putting more and more racket money down south in wads we couldn't lift off the ground.'

Bony thought it was hot enough without becoming worked up over a mixture of economics and politics, but the wads neither Barby nor he could lift off the ground spurred imagination, and imagination did help to make the heat bearable. Lucky politicians.

'Yair,' continued Barby. 'Something wrong somewhere. Old age pensioners freezing all winter in their one rooms down in the stinkin' cities, and the politicians rushing round the world on holiday trips we pay for. They calls it the March of Science. What's science done for us, anyhow? Me and you's still stuck here in this flaming joint, and millions of workers still got to toil day and night for a crust. Australia! Look, Australia would be the finest country in the world if it wasn't for the morons running it.'

'Agreed, George, agreed,' murmured Bony. 'Do you happen to see what I see?'

Bony pointed to the low dune barring the Lake from the creek. Beyond the dune a stark pillar of smoke appeared like a fire-blackened tree supporting a snow-white cloud. Together they stood, and without speaking walked to the dune, oblivious of the sun on exposed arms and the heat striking up from the ground through their boots.

The base of the smoke column was shot with crimson.

'Don't remember seeing any fire alarm, I suppose?' queried

Barby, his voice thin. 'Better hop into the ute and light our fags at the last ember.'

They shifted unnecessary dunnage from the utility. The dogs were chained. The galah was thrust into its cage. The horse was left in the shadow of the cabbage tree. Without undue speed, Barby drove the oven-hot vehicle over the sandy track to the homestead.

'Who was there when you left?' he asked.

'Lester and the two women.'

'Would've made no difference if there'd been a hundred men about the place,' Barby said. 'All pretty old buildings. Bit of a spark ... pouf ... few ashes ... all in two minutes ... day like this.'

They passed through low scrub and over ragged ridges and the world was utterly still and strangely stereoscopic, the only movement being the twisting column ahead. They saw that the quarters were safe, and the tops of the pepper trees were thrashing in the updraught created by the red remains of the large house. The machinery shed and the store and other buildings were warped but not ignited.

Lester they found bending over someone sitting in the armchair on the veranda of the quarters. He didn't notice the arrival of the utility, or of the travellers until they stepped up to the veranda and Barby said:

'You been tryin' to singe the flies, Bob?'

Lester straightened, and they saw the occupant of the chair was Joan. Lester's face was drawn by obvious shock, and he forgot to sniffle.

'Yair,' he said. 'Ma got caught.'

The girl stared at the smouldering ruin, her hands pressed between her knees. As though whimpering she said:

'I couldn't get her out. I tried ... I couldn't.'

'I was sitting here having a cat-nap,' Lester put in. 'I hear a roar and I thinks it's a willi passing by, till Joan run over and woke me up. Then the ruddy house was going up swoosh, and there wasn't a chance to get near it. Burned faster than dead buckbush in hell.'

'It would in a shade temperature of 117 degrees,' agreed Bony, and Lester snorted without sniffling.

'Hundred and seventeen!' he echoed. 'A hundred and twenty-one when I came back from lunch.'

'No one else home?' asked Bony, who had unconsciously taken command of the situation.

Lester shook his head. Joan repeated her whispered statement, then she sat upright and looked dazedly at Bony.

'I was reading in my room, and Mum was lying down in her room. All of a sudden I was surrounded by smoke and flames. I ran to Mum's room, but she had fainted or something, and I dragged her off the bed, but I had to leave her. The house was crashing . . . I couldn't stop with her.'

Smoke stains and ash streaked her face and arms. As she continued to stare at the ruins, Bony turned her chair from the picture of desolation. Her hands remained clasped between her knees as though to control their trembling, and he left her to procure aspirin and water.

'Take these,' he said, his voice hard in an effort to defeat possible hysteria. 'Bob, boil a billy and brew some tea. Make it strong.' The girl swallowed the tablets obediently. Gently Bony patted her shoulder. 'Cry if you can, Joan. It'll help.'

He left Barby with her. Lester was making a fire behind the building. He crossed to the machinery shed, noted how close it and the store had come to destruction. The smoke column was now a thin spiral, and high in the sky the smoke had solidified to a huge white cloud. Wherever the overseer was, he must see that cloud.

Of the house nothing remained bar the roof iron now lying upon the grey ash. Even the three chimneys had collapsed. He was able to draw close enough to see the remains of the iron bedsteads and their wire mattresses, the cooking range and several iron pots and boilers, the piping carrying the power lines, the steel safe where the office had been.

Joan Fowler was fortunate to have escaped, for certainly she would have been given no more than a few seconds to get out of the inferno.

It occurred to him that the heat of the ruin was barely higher than the heat of the sun. There was no doubt concerning the abnormal heat of the early afternoon, and he could imagine the temperature within the house before the fire started. Even the bedrooms would be like fired ovens, and to lie on a bed, fully dressed, would be an ordeal. Joan had said she was reading in her room when smoke and flame surrounded her, and that her mother was lying in her bedroom.

That worried him as he sauntered about the huge oblong of grey ruin which had been a house.

On the far side of the site the few citrus trees were beyond salvation, and the garden was destroyed. At the bottom of the garden stood the fowl-house, intact, and within the netted yard were the bodies of several hens. Their white shapes drew Bony. He wondered if they had been killed by the heat of the sun or the heat of the fire. His own throat was already stiff with thirst.

Farther on beyond the garden fence grew an ancient red gum. It stood on the slope of the bluff and when Bony went on to the fence he was out of sight of those on the veranda of the men's quarters. There was a gate in the fence, and he wasn't mistaken by that which had drawn him to it. On the red ground was a gold ring set with sapphires. It lay in the half-moon depression made by the heel of a woman's shoe, and because, as always, he had noted and memorized the tracks of everyone living here, he knew that the impression had been made by Joan when returning through the garden to the house, from one of the two house lavatories.

These structures were farther down the slope and fifty yards apart. The imprints on the path leading to each revealed which of these was used solely by the women.

He retrieved the sapphire ring, and remembered having seen this ring worn by Mrs Fowler. He recalled that Joan was now wearing her lounge clothes, a jewelled bow in her hair. Also that she was wearing the wristlet watch given her by Lester, and an opal bracelet thought by Witlow to have been subscribed by Martyr.

He followed the path to the lavatory visited by the women.

Behind the door, suspended from a hook, was an old and shabby handbag, and as he examined the contents his eyes were hard and his mouth grim. There was a lipstick in a studded holder; a gold-etched compact and cigarette-case; a few bobby pins; a bank-book in Joan Fowler's name showing a credit of £426 6s.; and a roll of treasury notes bound with darning wool. And a gold brooch set with opals, an emerald ring, and a wristlet watch.

The jewellery belonged to the late Mrs Fowler.

17

After the Fire

B ONY RETURNED THE items to the handbag and the bag to
its nail behind the door. He crossed to the other toilet,
found nothing, and detoured to arrive at the pepper trees
behind the outbuildings. The dogs welcomed him, unconscious of their good fortune, unaware of the effect of the fire
upon the upper portion of the trees. He spoke to them, patted
several, and passed round to the front to regard with studied
interest the warped walls and doors of the machinery shed
and other buildings. Like a man shocked by the catastrophe,
he wandered to the edge of the hot ruin, remained for a while,
and finally joined Lester and Barby, with Joan Fowler, on the
quarters veranda.

They barely noticed him, each seemingly engrossed by a
private problem. Lester had brewed tea, and Bony helped himself and squatted on his heels to roll and smoke a cigarette.
Presently Barby said:

'No hope of phoning to the homestead, I suppose?'

'Don't think,' replied Lester. 'There was a coupla spare
instruments, but they were inside the office when I last seen
'em.'

'Where did Martyr go?'

'Went out to Winter's Mill with Carney. Took the ute.'

'Take 'em an hour and a half to get home ... after they
seen the smoke,' Barby estimated. 'Just as well make ourselves comfortable.'

'Can't we get Mum out of that?' complained Joan, and
wasn't answered till she repeated her remark.

'She ain't feelin' nothing,' Lester pointed out. 'Hell, it's hot,
all right. Couldn't be worse droving a mob of rams on the
plains. What d'you reckon, George? Reckon Martyr'll take the
lot of us to the River homestead?'

'Don't think. Take Joan in, of course.'

'Go to the River!' the girl exclaimed. 'I'm not leaving here.'

The suggestion banished the lethargy of shock, and her

eyes blazed at Barby as though he dictated her future. He stroked his moustache with the mouth of his pipe and regarded her, calmly frigid.

'There's no argument. I'm not the Boss.'

'But why should I leave here?' persisted the girl. 'I'll be all right. I can cook here when you bring things from Sandy Well to cook with. Besides, I'm not leaving Mum . . . like that.'

Barby got up from the packing-case, and strolled into the sunlight and over to the smouldering ash. The girl watched him under partially lowered lids, her mouth twitching and her hands never still. Now and then the light was caught by the jewelled hair-clip and opal bracelet. Abruptly, she stood, and, as abruptly, Lester stood, too.

'Better not go over, Joan,' he advised. 'Better stay here. Nothink to see over there, anyhow. Ash'll cover up everything.'

'I . . .' Joan resumed her chair, and Bony knew she was as surprised as he was by the revelation of Lester's mental strength under crisis. Lester refilled the pannikins, and presently Barby came back. He nodded acceptance of the tea, stirred it with the splinter of wood serving as a spoon and sat upon his heels with the ease of the native-born. And the girl waited a long time before she burst out with:

'Well, did you see anything of Mum?'

'Pipe down, Joan,' snarled Barby. 'Nothing to see. Think about something pleasant, can't you?'

'No, I can't, and don't talk to me like that, George.'

'Got to, Joan, or you'll start a tantrum, and then I'll have to slap you out of it. It's too hot to argue.'

'Well, I'm not going to leave here, no matter what Martyr says.'

She looked at each of them as though hoping they would argue with her. Lester sniffled and snorted noisily. Barby seemed interested in the last spiral of smoke rising straight and slowly from the twisted iron sprawled upon the ground like the backs of sleeping beasts. Bony pretended to doze. It seemed hours before they heard the returning utility.

Martyr stopped his truck at the machinery shed, and he and Carney remained in it as they stared at the débris. Those on the veranda waited and watched, until the overseer and

Carney left the vehicle and walked to the edge of the ashes. They stayed there for several minutes before Martyr came to the quarters. His light-grey eyes were steel discs in his weathered face.

'How did it happen?' he asked.

'Don't know,' replied Lester. 'I was having a shuteye after lunch. I heard what I thought was a passing willi-willi, and took no notice until Joan shook me awake and I seen her going up . . . the house, I mean.'

'Mrs Fowler?'

'She got caught.'

The light-grey eyes turned to the girl, concentrated on her for a second, seemed to leap away from her to Barby, and returned to Joan. 'Tell me about it,' he said, and the girl faltered:

'I ran to her room. I tried to drag her out. She was in a faint or something, or unconscious from the smoke. I got her off her bed, but I couldn't get her out of her room. The place was full of flames all round. She was too heavy, and I couldn't breathe. I . . . We must get her out of that.'

Martyr sat on the case. Carney leaned against one of the veranda posts, his face blank but his brown eyes nervous. The girl lay back in the arm-chair, her eyes closed, restless fingers rotating the opal links of her bracelet. The men waited for the overseer, who apparently needed time to plan action. And Bony felt rather than witnessed growing elation in him.

'It's a rotten mess,' Martyr said in his terse manner. 'How much spare tucker have you, George?'

'Enough for a couple of days, but flour only for tomorrow,' replied Barby, anticipating the questioner's mind.

'Where are you camped?'

'Johnson's.'

'Take the men back with you. You fellows roll your swags and camp with George.' A faint smile flickered about Martyr's mouth. 'Give George a hand with the rabbits tonight . . . to earn your tucker. Harry, fill the ute tank and look to the oil. Joan, you'll come with me to Sandy Well, and then on to the River.'

'But why?' Joan sprang to her feet. 'I'm all right here. I can cook here instead of Mum.'

'What in? What clothes? What'll you cook?'

The girl's eyes grew big and almost baleful. There was nothing of resignation in her, or supplication. Carney stilled against his veranda post to watch her with admiration, her head flung back, breasts lifted high and her green eyes flashing. Bony thought of Boadicea.

'What in?' she shrilled. 'A pair of Mac's spare pants and one of your silk shirts.'

'My silk shirts are fired to ash.'

'Then Lester can lend me one. What's it matter? You bring back some cooking things from Sandy Well. And flour and rations. I'll manage to cook on the open hearth of the sitting-room. I'm not leaving, I tell you.'

'All right,' Martyr said slowly and with emphasis. 'But you are not staying here. You can go with the fellows to Johnson's Well, and you can damn well do the cooking there. There's no window to the hut and the door won't shut, but no one will mind that. I'm sure. Come on, Harry. Help me fuel the ute and I'll get going to Sandy Well and the telephone. I'll leave you to see that Joan goes to Johnson's. And no fighting over her before I get back with the Boss and the police.'

Save for Carney, who crossed to the utility, they presented a tableau. The girl defiant, her mouth curved upwards; the overseer silently taunting her to stick to her guns; Lester and Barby waiting with cynical tensity for her final choice.

'That'll do me,' she said, and Martyr turned and walked after Carney.

Ten minutes, and the utility was served, and the overseer returned to the quarters, to address the men.

'No one is to interfere with the remains of the house, you understand. As soon as practicable. Sergeant Mansell will be out from Menindee, and he'll be in charge. That's the drill.'

'Righto, Mr Martyr,' Lester said and sniffled before adding: 'We'll get along.'

The overseer cogitated, regarding each of them in turn, coming in the end to Joan Fowler and staying with her a fraction longer than necessary.

'Wait for Mac, George, before you push off,' he said, and turned away.

He backed into the utility, slammed the door, started the

engine. They watched the dust rising behind the wheels as it sped up the long rise, and no one spoke till after the machine disappeared over the distant crest dancing in the heat. Carney sat on the veranda step and rolled a cigarette. Lester appeared to expect to see the utility reappear and come speeding down the rise. Bony drank more tea.

It was not a situation the girl could stand. She jumped to her feet, and Carney swung round to look at her.

'Well, if you all won't talk, I've something to do,' she said, almost shouting, and made to pass Carney.

'You heard what Martyr said,' Carney quietly reminded her. 'No interfering with the fire ashes.'

'Damn you, Harry! And the fire ashes, too. Let me pass. You can come with me if you like . . . right to the door.'

Carney was young enough to blush his embarrassment, but he managed a chuckle and airily replied that such a walk would be fine. The others watched them skirt the house site, to pass beyond the back of the bluff and towards the lower garden gate. When Carney's head only was in sight, he stopped and the girl went on. Lester sniggered, and Barby pointed out MacLennon, who was arriving at the yards.

MacLennon didn't dismount. He rode on to the quarters, astonishment depicted clearly on his unshaven, broad face.

'Someone play bonfires?' he asked.

'Yair,' replied Lester.

'Thought the wild blacks had attacked the joint,' MacLennon remarked, with ill-disguised casualness. Slipping off the sweat-drenched horse, he tethered the reins to the veranda rail, and almost fell upon the tea billy. 'What a bloody day! Anyone under the iron?'

'Ma Fowler.'

'You don't say, Bob! You shove her back in after the fireworks started?'

'S'far as I know, she never got out to be shoved back in,' Lester drawled. 'I was having a shut-eye when Joan woke me up with the news.'

'Where's she?'

'Over in the Little Bungalow. Harry took her halfway.' MacLennon put down the empty billy-can, wiped his mouth with a forearm, regarded Lester with sombre eyes, and Lester added hastily: 'Martyr said none of us was to go delving for Ma. Harry's seeing to it that Joan don't do no delving, see?'

'D'you think you're gonna stop me doing a bit of delving?' enquired MacLennon.

'Caw, blimey!' exploded Barby. 'Pipe down, you blokes. What's rasping you all the time? A woman gets burned up in a fire, and it's a police job. You got brains, I suppose. Martyr's gone for help, and tucker, and other things ... including the Boss and the police. And you're all coming over to camp at my place.'

Bony slipped into his room, selected a few things and rolled his blankets into a swag. He dropped the swag outside the bedroom window, climbed after them, carried it to Barby's utility. He was 'meandering' about the machine shed when Carney and Joan returned to the quarters, and when the men were rolling swags for the move, he slipped away down the shoulder of the bluff and so to the 'Little Bungalow'.

The handbag behind the door was empty.

He emerged from behind the line of partially burned pepper trees when Lester and Carney brought their dunnage from the quarters to the utility and MacLennon was freeing his horse, and he was confident that none of them had been observing him.

Carney loosed the dogs, and they raced the horse to the trough. Bony was first aboard the truck, standing immediately behind its cabin on that side where Joan would enter. He was thus able to look down at her when she drew near and when she was about to step into the cabin. She was wearing a blouse of cream pleated silk, now soiled by smoke and ash. The plunging neckline, as he had anticipated, revealed a glimpse, nestling deep down, of the blue bank-book he had seen in the old handbag.

It was ten to five. The water-saturated dogs loped behind the vehicle which Barby drove unhurriedly. Nothing else stirred in all the land, the invisible host of rabbits crouching in shade and burrow, the invisible birds clinging to the shadows falling upon branches and even upon the ground. Nothing else moved but the eyes of watchful kangaroos, and the sky was void save for the watching, waiting eagles.

It was a relief to gain the comparative dimness of the trees about Johnson's Well, where they were welcomed by Barby's dogs and his now vociferous galah. Bony jumped to the ground immediately the truck stopped. With a flourish, he opened the door for Joan Fowler.

'Welcome to the bandits' lair, my lady!' he cried, and bowed.

Her clouded eyes widened, brightened. She smiled, wanly. As she stepped from the utility, he moved swiftly to offer a helping hand. The act was spoiled, for he tripped, lurched slightly, almost fell against her. Their hands missed contact, and his palm was pressed against her breast.

'Forgive my clumsiness,' he pleaded gravely. 'I hope I did not hurt you.'

The suspicion leaping in her eyes was beaten back. He was so confused, so contrite, so damn silly like all men. She smiled again, graciously.

He wondered if the jewellery he had felt inside her blouse had hurt her.

18

The Riddle of the Safe

THE TENSION CONTROLLING these men had broken during the short journey from the homestead, and for the first time they appeared to Bony as normal individuals. Lester sniffled and chortled and swore at the dogs, who were threatening Barby's dogs; MacLennon even laughed when Carney suggested bathing in the troughs, and George Barby waved to the hut and invited Joan Fowler to take possession.

Joan presented a character facet which might have astonished anyone other than these bushmen ... and they were gratified. She looked into the hut and walked round it. She studied the position of Barby's camp fire, and the contents of his tucker box she surveyed with marked contempt. She looked at the salt-encrusted meat-bag hanging from the branch of a nearby tree, and finally inspected the men, who had paused as though for orders.

'You think again if you're thinking all this is going to beat me,' she said. 'You thought I'd weaken when Martyr slung me into this. Thought you'd get rid of me, didn't you? What a hope! All you can offer me is a couple of clean blankets and a clean suit of pyjamas. And if you have a clean pair of trousers, Harry, I'll borrow them. A skirt and scanties won't do here.'

No one argued. Bony assisted Carney to carry the bedstead, brought from the quarters, to set up at the far side of the hut. Barby carried the mattress, and Carney supplied two blankets which happened to be comparatively new. Lester tore the dirty covering off a feather pillow and expertly covered it with one of Barby's snowy cooking aprons. They even placed a wool-pack on the ground beside the bed to serve as a mat. With unspoken mutual consent, they left it to Harry Carney to conduct the girl to 'her room'.

It was after five o'clock, and seemed to be even hotter than at noon. When removing the horse's neck-rope from the tree, Bony glanced upwards into its shadowy arches and saw the mynah birds and several crows, every beak wide agape, every wing drooping as though to permit a cooling draught of air to reach their breasts. He said nothing of his intention to ride the horse back to the homestead and release it in its own paddock.

It was too hot to ask the animal even to canter.

Human reactions to the destruction of the homestead he reviewed with calm detachment, and found himself now rather in the role of spectator than of director, for he had been content to watch human reactions and unfolding events and evade interference.

Excepting for that one incident of prodding the suspects by focusing interest in the tank filled with dead birds.

There could be no better example of stirring lethargic suspects than the destruction by fire of the homestead, for this event exerted strong influence on minds as well as the circumstances governing the lives of these people. And Bony experienced neither regret nor jealousy that he had not been the agent.

As the horse carried him at a fast walk, itself anxious for freedom and a drink, Bony surveyed the results of the fire upon all those vitally concerned. To begin with, the overseer.

Hitherto, Richard Martyr had appeared to be reticent, aloof, moody, given to introspection and far too much exercise of imagination. Then, being confronted by the ruin of the homestead, instead of dismay, even rage, because of carelessness, he had betrayed elation.

The effect of the fire hadn't been manifested in the others until they reached Johnson's Well, when they welcomed the change of living conditions. That was out of focus, because stockmen do not welcome a change from homestead food and homestead comfort to a rough camp where they would have to sleep on the ground and battle with the flies for stew on a tin plate, or kangaroo steak on a slab of baking-powder bread.

The reason for their satisfaction, Bony thought, was that they were still free to watch each other and hunt for the remains of Gillen.

The determination displayed by the girl not to leave these men was one of several interesting pointers in the progress of the human drama being played against the drama of the death of Lake Otway. Her possession now not only of her own bank-book and jewellery, but also of her mother's jewellery, proved that she had placed them in the old handbag behind the door of the toilet which no male would enter.

That collection had been made and secured before the house caught fire, and had been retrieved by Joan Fowler after the house had burned to the ground.

'You know, Starface,' he said to the horse, 'despite this devastating heat, I'm quite enjoying myself. A nice little cheque for training you and your friends added to my salary, plus the antics of half a dozen men under the influence of green eyes, plus the phenomenon of a dying lake to encourage my interest in natural history, combine to make me look upon criminal investigation as a lost cause.

'I ask myself, why wrestle with a problem which others will ultimately solve for me? All I need do to earn my salary is to wait upon events, because the Spirit of Drama impels the actors to play their cues. A comfortable attitude to duty, don't you think, Starface?'

They emerged from the dune scrub and took the last slope to the homestead bluff. The upper portion of the pepper trees marred the now familiar view, but only this scar was evident, for the fire ruin lay beyond the men's quarters. The windmill was still, had been for days. The unmistakable silence of the abandoned received Bony, and made the horse restive. It was at this moment that Bony saw the dust mist.

It lay like a brown fog atop the ridge where passed the track to Sandy Well and the River, and it had certainly been produced by the passing of a motor vehicle. Martyr's utility had raised dust at that place one hour earlier this afternoon, and the dust now hovering above the ridge could not possibly have lingered for so long a period.

Bony unsaddled and slipped the bridle, knowing the horse would find feed after drinking at the mill trough, and having stowed the gear in the harness room, he strode to the veranda of the quarters and there recalled the exact movements of Richard Martyr from the moment he arrived in the utility until he left in it for Sandy Well and the telephone . . . one hour earlier.

He then proceeded to check and prove that Martyr had returned to the homestead after everyone had departed in Barby's utility, and that he had left for the second time shortly following Bony's departure from Johnson's Well. Thus the reason for Martyr's return was quickly established.

The office safe had been moved, probably stood upright, and then replaced as formerly. It was situated four yards in from the edge of the bed of grey ash, and it was plain to Bony that the overseer had attempted to obliterate his tracks on the ash bed by blowing ash into them, using his broad-brimmed hat to create the draught.

Heat caused by the fire would now be negligible, but the safe was exposed to the sun and not to be handled with bare hands. Bony had to procure an empty sack to protect his hands and having memorized its position, he stood it up, when he found that the key was in the lock and, like the safe, bore plainly the effect of fire. Bony turned the key, and the door was easily swung open. The condition of the contents was a compliment to the safe maker. There was a stock book, a ledger, a time book, and taxation stamp sheets. In a small compartment were treasury notes, a little silver and taxation stamps. In the second compartment was the out-station work diary.

Bony relocked the safe, leaving the key in the lock. There

was no doubt that the key had been in the lock when the house burned, indicating that the safe hadn't contained anything of great value, and, therefore, what had brought Martyr back to open it and take pains to obliterate his tracks over the ash bed?

Having turned the safe to its original position, Bony scattered ash over its topmost side and, as Martyr had done, whisked ash over his tracks when retreating to the clear ground. The following ten minutes he spent studying the ruins and decided against delving among them. He did circle the ruins twice, hunting for traces having the slightest significance; finding none save those left by the overseer.

Martyr's examination of that safe nagged him, and he wished he knew if the overseer had returned to it to correct an omission of duty, such as to report the condition of the contents to his employer, or if he had purposely delayed the examination until all hands were cleared to Johnson's Well.

A cawing crow recalled the passing of time, the approach of evening. The sun was westering, and its decreasing heat was now permitting the birds to venture from the shadows to slake their day-long thirst. He must not remain here longer if he was to prevent suspicion, and while crossing to the quarters to obtain a packet of tobacco from his room his mind tore at the covering of this mystery.

What had brought Martyr back to his office safe? What had occurred to make the hands so cheerful, especially Lester? And why had Joan Fowler so strenuously rebelled against leaving Lake Otway, now dead? And why the defiant front following her arrival at Johnson's Well?

He sat on his stripped bed to open the packet of tobacco and roll a cigarette. He stood on the veranda smoking and hesitant to hurry back to Barby's camp. He gazed long at the rising land-swell and at its summit where he had seen the faint dust fog raised by the overseer's second departure. Nothing moved on that shadow-etched track.

Lester! Lester had been comforting the girl when Barby and himself had come. The girl had been sitting in the arm-chair, dabbing at her stained face.

That tableau could have been an act.

Lester! Bony entered Lester's room. He moved the mattress, finding between it and the wire under-mattress a ready-made suit layered between newspapers and kept there for pressing. Under the bed was a small tin trunk, its lock broken, its interior holding a jumble of old clothes, new town shoes, a horse bridle and books devoted to racing statistics. Also under the bed were old boots and, hard against the wall, a paper-wrapped parcel. He removed the string, opened one end and felt with sensitive fingers the notes compressed to wads.

The parcel was about the size of that made up for him by the bank manager at Brisbane. There was neither name nor mark on the outside of the wrapping paper. The wrapping might yield fingerprints. He put the parcel in a saddlebag on Gillen's motor-bike.

Passing down the bluff steps to gain the flats, he followed the old shore line, his mind tearing at several facets presented by these two developments ... the fire and the fortune in notes under Lester's bed. First the fire. The fact that Joan Fowler had collected her own valuables, and also her mother's jewellery, and concealed them in a safe place to preserve them from destruction strongly indicated that she knew the homestead would be destroyed, and also that her mother would perish in the fire, or her mother's body would be consumed by the fire.

Following the fire, she had collected the valuables from the hiding place. That clearly indicated forethought, planning. Had Joan been in possession of the parcel of notes, would she not have hidden it in that safest of safe places ... the women's toilet? Subsequently, however, she could not have thrust the parcel down inside her blouse, and it seemed feasible to assume that she had taken Lester in as an accomplice-in-part. She could have told Lester that she had escaped the fire with the parcel of money, not mentioning to Lester her mother's jewellery.

Secondly, Gillen's money. When in possession of twelve thousand pounds or more, would Joan Fowler have bothered about her mother's jewellery worth not more than two hundred pounds? Wearing her own jewellery after lunch, and when the fire began, she could explain, and be believed, by saying she had dressed for the afternoon, and had put on all her trinkets, really as something to distract her mind from the heat. Would she be silly enough, when possessed of twelve thousand pounds, to risk her mother's jewellery being associated with her escape from the burning house?

There was a fact not to be denied.

The parcel of notes under Lester's bed was free of the dust which lay upon the trunk and the other odds and ends, proving that the parcel had not been under the bed for more than a day or two at most.

Despite the annoying flies that seemed anxious to drown in his eyes and burrow into his ears, a slow smile stole over Bony's sharply-moulded features, and aloud he said:

'It seems, Detective-Inspector Bonaparte, that you will now have to work.'

19

The Channel Trap

BARBY ADOPTED THE plan of trapping rabbits at water holes and dams, and the construction of his fences and traps was much more intricate than the wide-wing fences he had built on the Lake flats.

The entire Channel was enclosed with wire netting and here and there the wire was brought to a point facing the water, an opening at the point being made to permit rabbits to squeeze through. Thirst-crazed rabbits thus able to reach the water and take their fill could not retreat by the way they had come, and when searching for the way of escape would find it in an outward-pointing V inside one of the two large netted yards.

Bony arrived in good time to contribute his labour ... physical ... to the work of building the Channel trap. The men worked with good will. What energized them? What drove them despite the heat? Barby's offer of a fair division of the 'catch' had its influence, but this was over-shadowed by the sporting instinct. Even Lester, with thousands of pounds under his bed, worked like a slave.

The job done, Barby went off to see how Joan was getting on with the cooking, saying he would bring her and

Plan of Barby's netted fence and traps enclosing the Channel

refreshments, 'to be in at the finish'. The others sat on the low mound spanning the mouth of the creek, and rolled smokes and tried to evade the glare of the sun striking at them across the great depression.

'I still reckon George oughta been satisfied to fence only one side of that water and have only the one trap,' MacLennon argued. 'If all the 'roos I've seen this last two weeks arrive here tonight, the ruddy fence will be flattened.'

'Have a try and keep 'em off,' Carney said in his easy manner. 'We've plenty of guns and ammo.'

'Yair,' agreed Lester. 'By midnight them traps should be two big blocks of fur.' He sniffled . . . as Bony knew he would. 'Give George a job skinning 'em. Last him a week at least. When we goin' to look for Ray Gillen?'

Easy attitudes visibly stiffened. Following a loaded silence, MacLennon asked:

'You in a hurry?'

'Yair,' replied Lester. 'Like everyone else.'

The sun touched the far horizon over which the flood water had raced to create Lake Otway. The galahs and the white cockatoos came seeking the water and found it, whirling down to settle on the flats either side the Channel.

Birds that had been watering every evening for three years at Lake Otway now came to the Channel. They alighted on the flats either side the thin ribbon of water, made suspicious at first by the fence and traps, massing in great patches of colours. The galahs crowded together their grey backs and the dots of pink combs, and the Major Mitchell cockatoos splashed white and raised their combs to produce pink dots on white.

They topped every inch of the fence and the trap-yards and tumbled to the verge of the water and lowered and lifted their heads like mechanical toys. Every minute additional flocks arrived. The crows came to whirl among those aloft and deliberately generate deeper suspicion in the vociferous parrots, and make still more shy the hundreds of emus who stalked the flats wide out.

'Better have a go for Gillen in the morning,' suggested MacLennon, his voice raised to defeat the cacophony of the birds. 'When d'you reckon Martyr ought to be back?'

'Some time tonight, if the Boss doesn't want him to go on

to the River,' replied Carney. 'Better hunt for Gillen in the morning, because after the Boss and the rest get out we won't stand a chance. It seems to be a matter of pulling together . . . or else.'

'Should have looked for him today,' Lester said.

'You seem mighty anxious, Bob,' sneered the ex-fighter.

'Yair,' agreed Lester with ill-feigned nonchalance. 'Seems we all got a stake in Gillen. Even me and George and Bony.'

'Meaning?' demanded MacLennon.

'You don't need tellin', Mac. Gillen had a lot of dough. He had a locket. The locket leads to the dough, don't it?'

'What the hell are you talking about?' asked Carney.

Lester actually giggled before he sniffled.

'Not much gets past me,' he claimed, triumph pictured on his unshaven face. 'Caw! Look at them birds.'

MacLennon wriggled sideways like a crab to bring himself closer and able to talk with less demand on his vocal chords. His broad features were distorted by anger.

'That locket belongs to me,' he shouted. 'I won it off Gillen, see? What's mine is mine. So you keep out of it, Bob. I'm meanin' that.'

'Quite a few birds around, eh?' remarked Carney to Bony, obviously with the intention of easing the strain. Of these three men, his was the firmest character and he was now beginning to assert it.

The appearance of Barby and Joan Fowler could have been the cause of MacLennon's withdrawal from argument. The trapper carried a bucket of hot coffee and the girl had brought a loaded dish of sweet scones. Wearing a pair of light drill trousers and a man's shirt, her almost blatant femininity was a travesty despite her powdered face and scarlet lips.

The first rabbit appeared to their right, running over the sandbar, running fast and direct, never pausing to look for possible enemies, flogged by the craving for water after the hours of terrible heat. The fence stopped it, flung it back, and it crouched obviously not understanding what had barred its progress.

The animal was recognizable only by its colour and shape, all its natural attributes of caution, of swift alertness, of gentle and graceful movement having vanished during the hours of its torture by the sun. It pawed the netting, frantically, standing on its hind legs, and not having the sense to climb the netting like a cat. It tested the wire with its teeth before running along the fence, to reach at last an inward pointing V, and so finding the hole to pass through. It thrust indignant birds aside to lap the water.

Carney touched Bony's arm and pointed over the depression.

'Fence won't stand up long after dark,' he worried.

Beyond the birds the kangaroos were gathering. The nearest were squatting, erect, ears attuned to catch the sounds about the trap, nostrils twitching to register suspicious scents. Beyond them others came loping over the dry lake bed, and already the dust rose from their passage.

The birds maintained their uproar, filling the air about the men. Birds were drowned in the Channel. Birds were staggering about on the marge inside the fence, their feathers wet, shieking anger and defiance, being buffeted by others and by rabbits.

There were now a dozen rabbits drinking. There were a hundred outside. They came like speeding drops of brown water over the dunes, over the flats, never halting, minus caution, motivated only by the urge to drink. They joined those at the fence, trickled through the holes to the water where they parted the birds to drink. The men watched the first water-laden rabbit enter a trap-yard.

An eagle appeared floating through the bird cloud. It tipped a wing and side-slipped to snatch a running rabbit. The rabbit hung by its rump from the iron beak, and they could see its pink mouth widen in a scream when, to stop its struggles, and to clear the lesser birds, the eagle drove its talons into its vitals. Through the birds on the flats, like a ship moving at sea, a dingo loped, betraying exhaustion, its red tongue lolling, its flanks tucked to its backbone. The dog took no notice of the rabbits or they of it. It butted the fence as though it were blind, sat and stared. The lolling tongue was drawn up under the snarling upper lip, and with the resolution of despair the animal drove at the netting, rose on hind legs to paw its way up and over. It plunged into the water and drank as it swam.

'I better fetch the guns,' Barby shouted.

'Bring mine, George!' requested MacLennon. 'And that red

box of cartridges on top of me swag. We gotta keep them 'roos off, or they'll flatten the fence.'

Lester went with George, and Bony glanced at the girl sitting with her hands clasped across her drawn-up knees. Her eyes were hooded. The evening light tended to soften her features, to give her hair a more brilliant tint. Carney moved to sit close to her, but she did not speak in answer to what he said, did not permit the intrusion to disturb her evident absorption in the terrible struggle for survival.

Bony went down to the fence where the rabbits were beginning to mass in a wide ribbon. They were pouring through the V points. They were jammed against the wire. They were gnawing at it, and none took notice of Bony's boots as he edged through them. A V point was choked by a rabbit that had died in the act of passing through, and he cleared the hole. He straightened the netting where the dingo had pawed it, and he witnessed the dog clamber over the opposite fence and lope slowly away.

The dusk was creeping over the depression, but the birds would not leave. They whirled about him like coloured snow-flakes, and continued to cover the flats, and when he walked wide of the fence they reminded him of that evening Witlow and he had waded in Lake Otway and the ducks had parted before them and closed in after them.

On coming to the far end of the Channel he paused awhile to marvel at the number of kangaroos and to note that of all the animals they only still retained their normal attributes, and he was wondering if this was due to higher intelligence when his attention was caught by what could be the body of a large fish now beneath the coverlet of massed galahs. Had not the light been tricky, he might not have noticed this hump where one ought not to be.

Recalling Lester's theory of what had happened to Gillen's body, he walked on through the birds, who at this moment chose to rise with a roar of wings and screams of defiance and depart for roosts. Even when fifty yards off the hump he could not now see it, but eventually coming to it his curiosity was richly rewarded.

The skeleton was shrouded with tiny weeds which covered the floor of once Lake Otway, the weed now dead and brittle as it lay over the depression . . . a perfect camouflage.

128

He turned and slowly walked back to the Channel.

The 'roos crept after him. The rabbits came running between them, running after Bony, passing him, to run onward to the magnet of water. Without trouble, he caught one. It screamed and struggled. He put it down, and it ran on as though it had not been hindered.

Well, there was the unfortunate Gillen, and there were the men and the woman on the distant sandbar who had waited long for Lake Otway to die that they might find his remains. According to Lester, what the others wanted was the locket about the skeleton's neck, the locket giving the clue to Gillen's money. But Gillen's money was under Lester's bed. And Mrs Fowler was dead under the ruins of the homestead.

Again skirting the Channel, the last of the birds continued their struggle for water. Scores were drowned, others were drowning. The bodies of rabbits floated on the black surface. There were more living rabbits inside the fence than could find space at the water's edge, and now and then one of the drinkers was bitten and it leaped forward to plunge into the water and swim. They swam like dogs. All headed away from the land as though strongly determined to reach the other side, but in every case when they had proceeded a yard or two they panicked and swam in an ever-narrowing circle until they lowered their heads below the surface as though compelled to suicide.

The traps were deep with animals. At each corner they were standing on hind legs, biting the wire to get out, and, like little chickens who crowd into a corner and smother, so did the rabbits.

The party on the sandbar was breaking up, and Barby came hurrying to Bony, offering a Winchester rifle and a box of cartridges. The excitement in the trapper's eyes, the tremor in his voice, did not escape Bony or estrange his sympathy, for Barby was like a man who has stumbled on an outcrop of gold-loaded quartz.

'Goin' to be big, Bony,' he cried. 'I never knew it could be like this, did you?'

'No, George not like this,' Bony admitted. 'I'll go back to the tip of the Channel. Be sure to make the others understand where everyone is positioned, for when the moon goes down it will be very dark, and accidents can easily happen.'

'Yair. Right! I'll tell them. No firing at the fence, or along it, either. Thanks for giving a hand.'

Bony made his way back to the extremity of the Channel ... made his way because he had literally to kick the rabbits from his path. The dusk was eating the salmon-pink dunes and the eagles were compelled at last to seek roosts on the topmost limbs of dead gums ... that is, if they roosted at all, which Bony, like many bushmen, doubted.

He waved his gun and shouted, and the Channel behind him was now itself a living thing. It actually appeared to breathe, to pulsate, to moan and heave. Rabbits brushed against his legs. Rabbits sped over his feet. Rabbits surged over the now invisible ground like ocean waves on shingle.

Although he hated it, he had to do his share of defending the fence. He shot a kangaroo that rose up within two yards of him, and thereafter shot many others, taking small comfort in that the slaughter would provide Barby with hides for his market.

All about the Channel the foxes were gathering and barking as though in sadistic approval of this flameless hell.

20

The Skinners' Reward

IT WAS ALMOST dark before the birds ultimately gave up and retired. The guns barked spasmodically, and the crescent moon gave sufficient illumination to see creeping 'roos when but a few yards from the defenders. Had not thirst subdued caution the defenders might have won the battle : but what is to be done with a kangaroo who, taller than a man and twice his weight, bumps him aside like a woman determined to reach a bargain counter?

Barby came along the fence, chanting a lurid parody to give warning of his approach. Bony struck a match and, before the light expired, the trapper found him and sat with him on the ground.

'Keep 'em off for an hour if we can,' he said. 'How you going?'

'So far so good,' replied Bony. 'There will be quite a few 'roos around before midnight. Look at this gentleman.'

Bony struck another match and they found themselves confronted by an unusually large animal resting on its short forepaws and staring at them from what appeared to be the base of the small mountain of its hindquarters.

'Caw!' muttered Barby, and fired. 'Funny the noise of the guns and yelling and screaming don't have any effect, ain't it? Y'know, if I told me relations in England about this they'd call me a bloody liar to me face. Even if I had a camera and flash-bulbs they wouldn't believe the pictures. If only we had a movie camera. The chaps are going to look for Gillen at daybreak.'

'Oh! No skinning, then?'

'Me and the rabbits can go to hell. Even the cook's goin' to hunt for Gillen soon's it's light.'

'Joan?'

'Yair. Carney was trying to get the others to search by a plan, but it looks like they'll keep together for fear one finds and the others miss out.'

To all points, far and near, the foxes barked. The moon hung low across the depression, and now and then it was temporarily eclipsed by a moving animal.

'Let them hunt, George. I'll give a hand with the skinning.'

'Thanks, Bony, old feller. They won't find him. Gillen's down on the bottom of the Channel, and by morning there'll be a ton or two of dead rabbits on top of him. We'll keep our eyes on 'em, all the same. I'll make me way back to see to the V holes. Must keep 'em clear. I'll shout and bawl when we knocks off and lifts the netting to let the mob in for a drink. They'll be back tomorrow night.'

Barby left, and shortly afterwards a fox came close. Bony heard its panting, and then felt its breath strike against his face. He thrust the rifle forward and the muzzle encountered the fox, who snapped at the steel. Hastily Bony stood. Better to have an ankle bitten than his face or an arm.

It was only a few minutes after nine when he heard Barby

shouting and the men answering and he proceeded to roll the netting up from the ground and sling it from the top of the stakes. Every step he took he trod on rabbits. They surged about his feet like strips of blanket energized with power. Then the netting ahead of him jerked under his hand and he knew, although he could not see, that a kangaroo was entangled in it.

Lights appeared in the direction of the sandbar, and someone carried a lamp along the fence to him. It was Carney, and Carney took his rifle to allow him to use both hands.

'Martyr should be here. Write a poem about it,' commented Carney. 'The place is going to look sort of peculiar in the morning.'

'Probably just one big heap of rotting fur,' Bony predicted.

The light revealed a scene of such prodigious struggle for survival that both men were awed. A huge kangaroo squatted at the water and drank, flanked by a seething mass of rabbits, Gulliver crowded by the Lilliputians. A fox stood drinking with the rabbits under its belly, with a rabbit crouched between its forepaws and lapping the water. Another 'roo appeared, moving like a spider, flinging rabbits out of its path, its muzzle stretched forward as though the head was impatient of the lethargic body. It ranged alongside the fox, which continued imbibing. A half-bred dingo appeared in the radius of the lamplight, and it seemed to run on rabbits to reach the water it lapped and lapped as though determined never to stop.

Then men moved along the fence lifting the netting, before them a carpet of frantic animals trying to reach water, and after them a violent mêlée. Bony saw a 'roo turn from the water and accidentally swipe a fox with its tail. The fox was knocked into the water, and it continued to drink even as it swam.

'Aw, let the netting stop,' Carney urged when another kangaroo was entangled with the roll they had left suspended on the stakes. 'There'll be no fence in the morning, and the netting will never be fit for anything again.'

'I think you're right,' Bony agreed, but they went on with the task till they were met by Lester on the same work.

'Cripes! You oughta see what's in the traps,' he chortled. 'Four million rabbits in each of 'em.'

'Have you counted them?' Bony inquired, and wished he hadn't, for the question brought the sniffle.

'No. I give up when I got to ten thousand.'

They came to a trap-yard. The interior was a block of animals, only those on top of the mass being alive.

Barby came, saying dolefully:

'What a ruddy mess! Stonker the crows! You blokes will have to lend a hand in the morning. Money! Money! Money! Come on! Let's eat.'

On the sandbar, Bony paused to listen. Mercifully hidden by the night, the titanic struggle for life-saving water created sound which could be likened by the imaginative to the snoring of a prehistoric beast, and that sound dwindled as Bony passed on beyond the sandbar, dwindled till he could no longer hear it, and was glad. But memory retained a picture of the green and the red lights which had ringed them as they lifted the netting ... the lamp-light reflected by the eyes of tortured animals.

Later, when they had washed and eaten and drunk enormous quantities of sugarless coffee, Barby brought up the subject of skinning his 'catch'.

'We'll get on with that later,' insisted MacLennon, and Lester sniffled and said:

'Yair. After we've found Gillen and the locket.'

'You remember what happened to you when you'd dug out them Paddy's ducks,' snarled MacLennon. 'That locket's mine. And no bloody arguing.'

'Oh no it's not,' Joan exclaimed, and, being near MacLennon, turned to smile contemptuously at him.

Bony spoke coolly:

'Where do you expect to find the remains of Gillen?' Everyone turned to him, everyone save Barby.

'On the Lake somewhere or other,' replied MacLennon. 'You keep out, anyhow. Nothin' to do with you.'

'Perhaps not,' conceded Bony. 'On the other hand perhaps you would like to be saved much walkabout in the heat tomorrow.'

They crowded him. He looked at them in turn, their faces clearly revealed by the leaping firelight.

'Well, what's to it?' demanded Carney.

'Merely that you should walk in circles and never find the

remains of Ray Gillen. I will lead you, all of you, to the remains in the morning. After.'

'After! What d'you mean, after?' Lester asked.

'After we have skinned the rabbits in George's two traps.'

'Strike me flamin' blue!' exploded MacLennon. 'What a hope.'

'Good on you, Bony,' chortled Barby, and Bony said:

'Fair's fair. You help to skin the rabbits, and I take you to Gillen's body. You don't skin the rabbits, and you promenade in the gentle heat of western New South Wales. It's all yours, dear brethren.'

The girl confronted Bony, mouth uplifted, eyes blue-green like opals.

'Truly, you know where he is?' she asked, admiringly.

'I know where the body is, as I told you. When the rabbits are skinned, I'll take all of you to the place. Quite simple.'

The smile settled about her mouth, and on her turning to the men her voice contained an underlying note of steel. 'You heard what Bony said, Harry, Mac and Bob. That's final. You'll skin the damn rabbits. We'll all go with Bony in the morning . . . and don't try to be clever.'

'Suits me,' agreed Carney.

'Me, too,' added Lester, and Bony silently complimented him.

Thereafter a truce settled on them and the subject of Gillen and his locket was not mentioned. For a while they squatted or sat inside the circle of firelight, and all agreed when Carney said that Martyr must have gone on to the main homestead after telephoning from Sandy Creek.

'No one will get here till about eleven tomorrow,' Lester estimated. 'That'll give us time to skin them blasted rabbits for George and then Bony will do what he promised.'

Half an hour later, Carney announced his intention of having some 'shut-eye', and the girl rose, saying she needed sleep if no one else did. And yet they waited for Bony.

Bony brought his swag and unrolled it in the firelight. He undressed only by removing his boots. Lester brought his swag and laid it on the ground nearby, and MacLennon and Carney did likewise. They were not going to lose Bony to any artful dodger, and he was highly amused when the girl staggered from behind the hut, carrying the bedding so carefully arranged for her.

To see them composed for sleeping within a few feet of the camp fire, it would be difficult to believe that the temperature of the night was above the century.

When the sky proclaimed the coming of the day, Barby had the coffee bubbling and was frying flapjacks and grilling kangaroo steaks, and before it was possible to read a newspaper away from the firelight, they trudged over the sandbar armed with skinning knives and bags to take the rabbit skins.

The Channel wasn't to be seen. It was marked by the sturdy corner posts of the two trap-yards, and a few of the fence stakes. The rolled netting appeared here and there above the dun-coloured mass which covered the ground and stiffened the surface of the water invisible beneath the bodies of the drowned. Back from this dreadful immobility, the living were dazed like zombies. Kangaroos were gouging among the dead with their paws, thrusting their muzzles among the dead to make space to get at the water. Hundreds were sitting up at varying distances, with rabbits moving among them, and among the rabbits the foxes were walking with grotesque daintiness.

The men skinned diligently, and Bony noted their reaction to this work. The girl mystified him, for she watched the skinners and now and then regarded the background of their work with undoubted enjoyment. MacLennon was sullen; Carney was, as usual, cheerful; Lester worked fast and automatically, because his mind wasn't on the job.

Some of the kangaroos returned ... those who hadn't reached the water. The rabbits were gathering into heaps about the dead 'roos, and these were doomed as they had not taken in water and instincts were shattered. Now and then a flock of birds came to whirl above the Channel and depart at high speed as though aware they must find water before the sun again became a killer. The crows attacked the living rodents gathered in growing heaps, for when a rabbit died others crowded on it, too stupefied to run for cover from the risen sun.

'Righto, blokes, no more,' Barby called. 'The sun's rotting 'em already. We musta got through four thousand.'

The fur was gathered into bags to keep till dried on the wire bows. Thousands of carcasses were left in the one trap-yard: the other wasn't touched and now the sun was destroying hundreds of pounds worth of fur. MacLennon said:

'It's up to you, Bony. We got to go far?'

'No. You understand, I hope, that if you interfere with the remains the police will be annoyed?'

'My troubles!' snorted MacLennon.

'And that the locket, if still with the body, is the property of the State?'

'Just too bad,' sneered Lester. 'Caw! You talk like a judge.'

They proceeded, the four men and the girl keeping close to Bony.

'I don't understand your avid interest in a locket you claim was worn by Gillen when he was drowned,' he said. 'I'm not going to be drawn into any trouble with you or the police. If, as I said, you interfere with the remains, the police will want to know why. They would say that until the authorities prove Gillen was drowned, it could be that one of you murdered him. They will certainly want that locket. Why is it so important to all of you? What d'you want the locket for?'

'Just to see what's inside it,' replied Lester.

'You ain't got no right . . .' MacLennon began, when Carney stopped him.

'Now look, Mac, let's recognize facts, and let's behave decently. It wouldn't get us anywhere if we all rushed it like a pack of dingoes. We'll let Bony find the locket, and we'll let him open it for us all to see.'

'Fair enough,' agreed Lester, but MacLennon started again to argue, and this time Joan stopped him with a verbal lashing which stunned Bony and caused Lester to sniffle thrice.

They did not see the weed-shrouded remains of Raymond Gillen until Bony stopped and indicated the skeleton. Silently he waited, and one by one they looked up and into his wide and ice-blue eyes.

Carney was grave and self-possessed. Lester licked his upper lip, and the watery blue eyes were avaricious. The girl's mouth was compressed to a straight thin line of scarlet. Barby was white about the nostrils, and MacLennon's face was twitching at the corners of his mouth and under his cheek-bones.

'Go on, Bony, get it,' cried Joan.

'All right! Now stand away, all of you.' They drew back,

and he ordered them to retire still farther. They obeyed. He sank to his knees, continuing to watch them. He delved with his hand under the skeleton. The cord had vanished. A little groping, and he found the key. The locket was half-buried in the sludge. He stood, showing the locket to the watchers, and they surged forward to surround him. Carney exclaimed:

'Good on you, Bony! Open it for us.'

21

The Locket

UNHURRIEDLY, BONY rubbed the locket against his trousers to clean it of weed and dried mud. The four men watched his hand manipulating the locket; the girl watched his eyes, enigmatically. He was smiling. A lesser man might have so reacted to this situation creating self-importance, but to Bony it was merely the prelude.

MacLennon twisted his great hands about each other; intent like an eagle ready to pounce. Carney stood with hands against his hips, balanced on his toes, an easy smile about his mouth and faint amusement in his eyes. Lester forbore to sniffle. His mouth was slightly open, and for once his eyes were strong and steady. George Barby's teeth were worrying his upper lip. There was a vertical frown between his brows, and perplexity was clearly defined. For a long second Bony's eyes clashed with the girl's green eyes, suddenly wide and probing.

The locket was heart-shaped, of modern design and was studded with a solitary square-cut sapphire. When Bony displayed it on the palm of his hand, the others crowded about him.

He was unable to open it with a thumb-nail, and Barby presented a clasp-knife. Deliberately, he prised the locket apart on its hinges, to reveal on the one side the picture of a woman and on the other that of a man.

Suspended breathing hissed from MacLennon, and Lester sniffled and deserved a cuff.

'Get the pictures out, Bony,' urged Carney. 'Could be writing on the back.'

With slight difficulty, Bony managed to lift out the picture of the woman. There was writing on the back of the print ... the word 'Mum'. On the reverse of the picture of the man was the word 'Pop'.

'There doesn't seem to be anything else,' drawled Bony.

'Lemme look,' rasped MacLennon, and Carney said, warningly:

'Go easy, Mac. Look again, Bony. Look for small letters scratched outside or inside the locket. There's something we want to see.'

'There is nothing,' Bony said after a swift examination of the locket. 'What did you expect to see?'

MacLennon cursed and grabbed, but Bony's fingers imprisoned the locket. He stepped back to avoid MacLennon's punch and then Joan was confronting the ex-pugilist and shouting:

'You animal, Mac! Behave yourself.'

'It's my locket, Joan. It's mine.'

'Shut up,' cried the girl furiously. 'It's mine more than yours.' She swung about to confront Barby. 'You look at it, George. Bony can't see anything. I can't see anything, and Mac can't, either. But you look at it to satisfy him.'

'Damned if I know what all the botheration is about,' Barby said, flatly. 'There's nothing inside the locket bar the two pictures, and there's nothing on the back of them except "Mum" and "Pop". Why the fuss?'

'Gillen had a lot of money, that's why,' bawled MacLennon, surging past Joan.

Joan opened her mouth, caught back the words. Carney grinned, and this abused word is the correct one to describe his expression. Lester licked his drooping moustache like a dingo watching a fox being killed by eagles. Still perplexed, the trapper said:

'Gillen had money, so what? Did one of you murder him for it?'

They became still, and passivity was smashed by MacLennon.

'He could of been, George,' he shouted. 'I wouldn't know. He had a lot of money in his case, wads and wads of it. Must have stolen it from a bank or something. He woke up to some-one after it, and planted it and put the clue to the place in the locket. We been waiting for the tide to go down to get at that locket . . . all of us.'

'Not me,' chirped Lester. 'I knew nothing about no locket.'

'Lot of rot, seems to me,' drawled Carney, rocking on his heels. 'Better quit and pass it up.'

'No damn fear,' roared the heavy man. 'Someone's got Gillen's dough. And I'm having me share, or else.'

'Me, too,' interjected Lester. 'Find anything, George?'

'Nothing,' replied Barby, and slipped the pictures into place and closed the locket.

'But there is. There must be. Gillen said there was,' persisted the enraged MacLennon.

'All right, Mac. You look.'

MacLennon snatched the locket and opened it easily with his thumb-nail. He dug the pictures out with his dirty nail, peered at them with screwed-up eyes, and at the locket inside and out. And with varying reactions the others waited, united only in contempt for this Doubting Thomas. Bony stood a little to the rear of the group, his fingers working at a cigar-ette but his eyes missing nothing. He hoped for more from MacLennon, and was given more. The big man threw locket and pictures to the ground and with hands knotted into clubs glared at them.

'One of you got here first. You got here 'fore we did, Bony.' The limelight played on Bony, and Bony nodded.

'Yes, just before dark last night. You asked me to get the locket for you if I should find the remains. Joan did, too. But the locket belongs to the State, who will hold it for the right-ful owner at law. The State is going to ask us a lot of questions, such as how did the locket come to be forced open and the pictures tossed on the ground. And what is this yarn about a lot of money in a dead man's suitcase. In fact, the State is going to be most tiresome.'

'I told you to shut up, you fool,' snarled the girl at Mac-Lennon. 'Harry tried to shut you up, too. Now spit out the rest of it and be a bigger fool.'

'All right, I will,' roared MacLennon. 'Harry showed us a letter writ by Gillen, saying he'd spotted his case being inter-fered with, and that he'd planted his money and put the clue to the place inside his locket. So if the one who mucked about with his case really wanted his dough he'd know where to find the clue but they'd have to get the locket off him first. Twelve thousand quid and some was what Gillen had, according to you, Joan. You told us Gillen had showed you that dough to make himself sweet with you. And Harry found the letter in the case instead of the money . . . accordin' to him.'

'Could of been some double-crossing,' followed Lester's sniffle.

'Yair, of course,' shouted MacLennon. 'One of you got in first. One of you got that money. And by hell I'm gettin' my share of it. I'll . . . smash your rotten . . .'

'You'll drop in a fit, that's what you'll be doing,' sneered the girl.

She received a slap to the face which sent her backwards. Carney sprang at MacLennon and got in a right royal haymaker which splayed the ex-pugilist. Then they went to it, and Carney quickly proved he was no gentleman in a real Australian brawl . . . boots and all.

The girl scrambled to her feet. Lester danced and sniffled and shouted:

'Four to one, Carney! Sock it in, Harry. Four to one Mother's boy. Let 'em alone, Joan! Get off it! Cripes! Odds is short now. Two to one, Carney. Caw! Let 'em alone!'

Joan was hanging to the big man's shirt and kicking at his ankles. Carney got in a walloper, and Lester began the count. Calmly, without the trace of a smile, George Barby remarked to Bony:

'When thieves fall out, honest men like you and me steps in.'

Bony was reminded of a picture of hounds pulling down a stag. He retrieved the locket and the miniatures, replaced the pictures, and pocketed the locket. Then he smiled at Barby:

'It must be time for smoko, George.'

'Yair. Very dry argument this morning, Bony.'

Carney was kneeling and waving his hands as though in obeisance to King Sol. Joan was behind MacLennon and doing her utmost to scalp him. MacLennon was yelling, and Lester was urging Joan to 'pull his ears off'. Then Carney left the ground in a flying tackle and the combatants became a heap. Bony turned away, and Barby walked at his side and said:

'Did you hear Ray Gillen laughing and laughing?'

'Yes, I heard it,' Bony replied, gravely. 'I thought it was ghostly merriment.'

They came to the Channel, invisible beneath the covering of drowned animals. The crows were now the flakes of a black snowstorm, and dotted on the flats the eagles were gorging. Here and there, farther away, daintily walked the emus, their tail feathers billowing like the skirts of a ballerina. The kangaroos had gone, but a few of the galah host still lingered about the dunes.

'Funny about that letter MacLennon said Carney found in Gillen's suitcase,' Barby drawled. 'What d'you make of it?'

'I wish that MacLennon had been a little more elucidative, George. It does seem that Carney found such a letter in Gillen's case, and we may assume that Carney found that letter after Gillen went swimming, that he was anxious about the money, having been told by Joan how much there was, Joan having been told by Gillen. Which supports what you overheard that night when Joan and Carney discussed money. We now know why no one left Lake Otway after Gillen was drowned. Why everyone was so interested in Lake Otway's inevitable demise. Did you ever see Gillen writing letters?'

'Can't say I ever did,' replied Barby, taking up one of the bags containing rabbit pelts. 'Never said anything about his mother or father, or about any pals.'

Bony heaved a bag to his back, and together they went on. Near the sandbar, Bony turned to see the three battlers and the referee walking slowly after them. They were widely spaced, and obviously not engaged in friendly conversation.

'It is going to be abnormally hot today,' he told Barby. 'I wonder what has happened to Martyr. Someone ought to have arrived by now. Must be after nine o'clock.'

'Ought to come any time. I'm goin' to get on with stretchin' these skins. Won't have a chance after the mob gets here. Betcher the Sergeant'll be out askin' questions. What do we say about the locket?'

'Haven't decided. I think the police will be far too interested in the fire and the fate of Mrs Fowler to bother about Gillen's remains just now. Have you enough bows for all these pelts?'

'Not near enough.'

'Then I'll cut some more after smoko.'

They dumped the heavy loads in tree shadow. The dogs welcomed them dispiritedly. The cats yawned and went to sleep again. The pet galah screeched, and Barby opened its cage door and it fell over itself, such was its haste to gain freedom. A rabbit had found a bread-crust at the edge of ash marking the fire site . . . and continued to eat.

Bony took empty water-buckets to the reservoir tank, and saw rabbits crouching under the long trough. The trough was empty and he removed the chock from under the ball valve and permitted water to gush into it. Immediately, crows appeared to caw raucously, and galahs came to perch on the trough edges. Barby's dogs jumped into the water and lapped as it ran under their tummies. The rabbits beneath the trough waited for the water to drip from the iron seams.

The warriors entered camp, Carney carrying the third bag of skins. They were sullenly silent, and the men stripped to the waist and carried towels to the trough to bathe their bruises and abrasions. On his way with filled buckets, Bony encountered Joan, whose left cheek was still inflamed by the smack from MacLennon. She actually smiled at him, but it didn't raise his blood pressure.

In sullen silence a meal was eaten, and afterwards Bony took a file to a heap of old fencing wire and cut lengths to be bent to U shape. Lester assisted Barby to stretch the pelts over the bows and thrust them upright by pushing the points into the soft ground. The skins were board-hard and dry in less than twenty minutes, and eventually were removed and packed into a wool sack.

When it was ten o'clock, the heat was almost combustible. Lester estimated the temperature to be about 112 degrees; Carney 115 degrees. The cats demanded watered tummies, and the galah sought similar attention from the solicitous Barby. Immediately the tea-billy was empty, another was placed on the fire, smokeless and almost invisible in the glare of the sun.

The men and the girl clung to the shadow cast by the hut. Whenever they drank, perspiration oozed from face and body within minutes. Joan had a basin of water and she saturated somebody's shirt and draped it about her head. Carney wished they had a pack of cards.

It was just before eleven, and Lester was voicing doubt

that Martyr could have reached the telephone at Sandy Well, when the crow fell from the cabbage tree where Bony had tethered his horse. It uttered a long-drawn c-a-a-h as it nose-dived to the ground without a flutter

'Last time I seen anything like that,' Lester said, 'the local shade temperature was 123 degrees.'

'That's what it is here and now,' Carney stated with conviction.

'Assuming that Martyr's utility broke down between Lake Otway and Sandy Well, what would he do?' Bony asked, and Carney answered him.

'He'd try and fix the trouble. He had a full gallon water-bag for himself, and a tinful for the radiator. And a mile off the track midway there's a well called The Shaft. If he couldn't get the lump of junk to go, he'd wait till night and walk on to Sandy Well.'

'And if he didn't get to Sandy Well by nine last night, more'n likely there'd be no one in the River office to answer his ringing,' supplemented Barby. 'That would mean he'd camp there and wait for the Boss to ring at half-past seven this morning.'

'What do you think Wallace would do on being told about the fire?' persisted Bony, actually to break up a moody silence.

'He'd tell Martyr he'd be out as soon as he could. He'd know we was all right, and Martyr was all right,' replied Barby. 'Mr Wallace would ring the police at Menindee, and the Sergeant would have to get a doctor, and as far as I know the nearest doctor would be at Broken Hill, seventy miles off. Or he might come out without a doctor. I reckon Wallace would come out without waiting for the Sergeant.'

'What good would a doctor do? Tell us that,' sharply urged Joan.

'A doctor has to certify how your mother died,' Bony said, adding: 'And also how Gillen died.'

22

Something to do

AFTER DAYS AND nights when the air had remained still, the wind came. It was neither strong nor gusty: a gentle wind in pressure, but hated for its heat. It came from over the depression, came over the sandbar and down along the creek bed to destroy even the imaginary coolness of the shadows. It lacked even the virtue of strength sufficient to worry the flies.

They could escape the flies by entering the hut, but the interior of the hut wasn't to be borne longer than a few seconds. Two could have gone down the well and stood on the platform supporting the pump seventy feet underground. There the temperature was about sixty degrees, but the cramped position would be too much and the climb down and up the ladder fastened to the wall of the shaft not lightly to be undertaken by the allegedly weakest of the party, Joan Fowler.

Barby plunged an old cooking apron into a water-bucket, and with this about his head and shoulders he took the bucket to refill. There were no birds attempting to drink the water in the trough; there wasn't a bird on the wing. The water in the trough was hot.

While filling his bucket from the tank, Barby heard the crows in the tree from which one had fallen dead, and threw an old jam tin among the branches. Several crows flew from the close-set foliage, loudly complaining, and before they had proceeded a dozen yards from the shelter they turned and almost fell back into it.

'Hot water on tap,' Barby said on his return to the hut shade. 'See them crows? They'll put on a turn soon, believe you me.'

Bony alone appeared interested.

Barby set down the bucket and the galah fell into the hole made for it before water could be poured into the hole. The cats didn't move, and he poured water on them. They refrained from licking the water from their fur. One of the dogs looked as though about to die, and he procured a pair of hair clippers and proceeded to shear it, for something to do.

'Hell of a long time since she was as hot as this,' Lester said. 'Must be over 120 degrees in this shade, anyhow. The old man usta tell of a heat-wave they had when he run the pub. It was so hot all you had to do to light a match was to hold it in the sun for a sec.'

Carney extracted a wax vesta from a box and tossed it from the shadow. He lay watching it for some time before saying:

'Not as hot as your old man's pub, Bob. I say, George, what about taking a run to the homestead in the ute? Something to do to pass the time.'

'Too hot to shift the ute,' Barby objected. 'Besides, we'd go less than a mile when her petrol would be all gas and she'd stop dead. I'm staying right here. Look! Your match is burnt.'

'You'd be right . . . about the petrol turning to gas,' Carney agreed. 'That's it! That's why no one has come from the River. Car's stuck up on the track somewhere. Hell, they'll be hot if they are.'

He tossed another match to fall on the shadeless ground and waited for it to ignite. A second crow fell from the tree, but he didn't remove his gaze from the match.

Something to do was becoming a powerful need, even for Bony. Merely to sit and wait was, psychologically, to add another ten degrees to the temperature. He draped his shirt over his head and shoulders and went for a bucket of water. That was something to do and he felt better even though the short journey back with the filled bucket made him feel slightly giddy.

The gentle wind direct from an imagined furnace continued. It softly rustled the leaves of the cabbage tree. It sent the sap from all the tree branches down the trunks to the roots, and branches weakened by termites or dry rot began to crash to the ground. Bony saw one branch fall, and heard others fall from distant trees along the creek. To Carney he said:

'Supposing that Martyr's utility held him up and he was

unable to reach Sandy Well, what would have happened at the River homestead?'

'Well, the Boss would have tried to raise the out-station last night at seven as usual,' Carney replied, having waited for the sun to fire his second match. 'Not being able to raise anyone he might get the cook at Sandy Well to have a go. Then he'd decide that the telephone at the out-station must be out of order, and he'd know Martyr had a spare one and would ring through sometime. This morning when the Boss rang through at half-past seven, and got nothing, he'd reckon the line was down between here and Sandy Well.'

'And knowing nothing about the fire, and there being nothing important to discuss, the Boss would patiently wait?'

'Yair. Wait on the cool homestead veranda, while one of his daughters supplied him with iced gin slings.'

'Has the cook, or anyone at Sandy Well, a motor vehicle?'

'No. If Martyr don't contact him by this evening, the Boss might get one of the riders at the Well to follow the line out from here. And if no one turns up here by nine tonight, I reckon something serious has happened to Martyr.'

'I am beginning to think that,' admitted Bony. He glanced at MacLennon, who was lying on his back and hadn't spoken for more than an hour. The girl was sitting against the hut wall, her eyes closed, a spray of gum leaves serving her as a fly-whisk. Barby spoke:

'What we all want this warm day is a good feed of trebly-hot curry. I'm goin' to make one that'll turn your eyes back to front.'

Lester voted the curried tinned meat 'a corker'. Barby certainly put everything he had into it, but no persuasion would induce MacLennon to get up and eat.

'Let the hunk starve,' advised Joan, and when Lester was about to jibe, Barby restrained him.

Bony saw the white cockatoo drop dead from a near box tree, and he anticipated that, despite Barby's attention, the pet galah would not live the day through. The hot wind died away, but its departure gave no relief. What did bring relief, although of short duration, was the shouted declaration by MacLennon that he was 'going home'.

'To hell with the lot of you,' he told them when on his feet. 'I'm going home now.'

'Oh well, have a nice time,' drawled Carney.

The big man strode into the sunlight, and Bony called after him that he had forgotten his hat. MacLennon mightn't have heard, for he walked on, his over-long hair matted with sweat and dust.

'Come back for your hat, Mac,' shouted Barby, but the big man did not turn, did not halt, and they watched him pass over the sandbar and knew he intended following the flats.

'Ruddy idiot,' snorted Barby, and poured water over his cats.

Bony drenched a shirt with water and draped it about his head. He picked up MacLennon's hat and took down a water-bag from a wire hook.

'Let the fool go if he likes, Bony,' Joan urged.

'Yair,' supported Lester. 'He won't go far. Thirst'll hunt him back here.'

'It will be something to do,' Bony told them, and set off after MacLennon.

The sunlight burned his arms and 'bounced' off the red earth to hurt his eyes, but these discomforts were little to what he met when he passed over the sandbar to the depression.

The rank water in the Channel, its banks, the man-made traps and the wreckage of wire netting were a horrible picture which Bony tried to shun. Beyond the Channel, MacLennon was walking direct over the depression towards the distant out-station, and the mirage heightened his massive figure, making him a giant wading into the ocean.

Bony shouted but the man took no need. To run after him, even to hasten, would be to fall victim to the power from which he hoped to save MacLennon. As bad as the burning heat was the fierce light, which had no colour and contained an element of density, itself threatening to impede movement. His eyes shrank inward to the shade of the garment protecting his head, and for long moments he was compelled to keep the lids tightly lowered.

He did not see MacLennon struck by the sun, did not see him till about to pass him, and then MacLennon was groping on his hands and knees, and was blind and babbling.

'Get up and come back with me,' commanded Bony.

MacLennon did not hear. He was following a small circle,

and Bony was horribly reminded of the drowning rabbits. When Bony poured water from the bag upon the back of his head, neck and shoulders, he betrayed no reaction, and continued his unintelligible babbling.

Bony slapped a naked shoulder and shouted in an effort to make the man stand. Beyond this, common sense halted effort, for physical exertion beyond the minimum would bring collapse. He did think his urging was successful when MacLennon abruptly stood. He made five long strides, bringing the knees high and keeping his arms flung wide as though in balance. Then he crashed, falling on his face and lying still.

Bony knelt beside him and sheltered him with his own shadow. The warning to himself was unmistakable. The ground about the fallen man was magnified with such brilliance that the pin-points of rusty clay on a sliver of débris, the hairs on MacLennon's neck, even the nodules of dust on the man's back, appeared as large protuberances.

Despite the warning, Bony succeeded in turning MacLennon on his back . . . when death was evident.

During a long moment Bony fought for self-control. The bad moment passed, and his maternal ancestors crowded about him, whispering and cajoling. They pleaded with him to remain passive if only for a minute. They told him of their battle with this homicidal sun, brought to him their lore and wisdom. They implored him to drink and pour the remainder of the water on his head.

But the bag was empty.

Presently he felt a little better though vertigo remained a threat. He peered from the protection offered by the shirt to estmate distance to the sandbar. He found that the shore dunes were closer, and he could see a tea-tree bush growing between two dunes. It looked black against the red sand, and black spelled shade.

In the act of standing he remembered the crows, and couldn't leave MacLennon entirely to them, so he stepped from his trousers and made the garment a covering for his head: the shirt he laid over the dead face.

The ground heaved as he walked away from MacLennon. He fought back the impulse to run to the tea-tree shade, and slowly the bush grew in size, and slowly its shade came to meet him and became large enough to accept him.

He remembered he had once seen a thermometer at a homestead registering a point above 122 degrees, but that day the wind was blowing strongly. Today, here and now, there was no wind, not a current of air to be felt by the skin. The windless day is opportunity for the sun.

He was debating the subject of heat apoplexy, and the relation to it of perspiration, or lack of it, when he realized he could not remain in this shade without water. Already thickening saliva was swelling his tongue and gumming his lips.

He espied the nearest shade fifty yards towards the creek, a black ribbon lying over the ground cast by the trunk of a dead belar. Where the shadow joined the foot of the tree crouched a rabbit, and he did not see the rabbit until, struck by his foot, it fled into the sunlight. He watched it run to a steep sand dune, watched it scrambling upward and dislodging a minor avalanche. The animal was near the summit when it gave a convulsive leap, rolled down the slope and lay still.

'That was quicker than MacLennon got it,' he said, and knew he couldn't have been vocal.

Thus from shadow to shadow he accomplished the journey back to the creek trees, and, remembering the guest at Johnson's Well, he put on his trousers and crossed the creek with the empty water-bag on his head for protection.

They noted the absence of his shirt and MacLennon's hat.

'You caught up with the fool,' Lester stated as fact.

Bony nodded and sat with them in the hut shadow, now larger in area. There was a pannikin of warm tea beside Lester, and he 'sloshed' his mouth with the liquid because he couldn't part his lips.

'A bit generous, giving him your shirt,' snorted Barby, and again Bony nodded, now able to draw the liquid in between his lips and about the swollen tongue. Pride was digging into him. It would never do to permit these men and the girl to realize how soft he was, how close he'd come to meeting Sol's bolt. They were watching him closely, and with well-acted casualness he emptied the pannikin and borrowed Lester's tobacco and papers. Having made the cigarette, and having fought down the desire for more tea, he accepted a match from Carney.

'MacLennon didn't go far,' he said, and was inwardly pleased

149

he was able to speak clearly. 'About half a mile on from the Channel.'

'What d'you mean?' asked the girl, impatiently.

'What he said,' Carney told her. 'Without a hat, and no shirt on, course he wouldn't get far.'

'Well, I hope he's dead,' Joan snapped, and, without looking at her, Bony related his adventure.

'And you left your shirt on him,' Barby said.

'I remembered the crows,' Bony told them, and the girl sneered.

'More fool you, Bony,' she jibed, and laughed.

23

Proceed as Usual

HOURS LATER, when the shadows were noticeably longer, Bony suggested that someone should accompany Barby to the out-station and, if no one was there, take the track to Sandy Well to locate Martyr and the main homestead. The suggestion found favour, and everyone wanted to go with Barby.

'All right! We'll all go. Better than sitting on our sterns. What's to be done about MacLennon?'

The question was put to Bony, and the others, waiting for his views, didn't realize how much his ego was boosted. Lester sniffled:

'Could do with a morgue, there's bodies all over the scenery.'

He was told by Carney to shut up, and Bony said:

'Because of the birds and the dingoes, the body should be put inside the hut. We could make a start now. While the body is being brought in, perhaps someone could bake something to go with George's tins of beef. We must take plenty of water in case we break down when trailing Martyr.'

It was arranged that Lester get on with baking scones, the girl would prepare another curry, and Bony would fill petrol tins with water. Carney went off with Barby in the utility. Eventually, the dogs having been fed, the cats attended to and the pet galah imprisoned in his cage, the party left Johnson's Well.

The sun was then a mighty crimson orb low over the depression, and it was setting when they arrived at the out-station. No voice hailed them, and Lester insisted on leaving the vehicle to look at the thermometer under the pepper trees.

'What next?' snarled Barby, but stopped none the less. 'Sun going down, getting a bit cool, and he wants to see if it's true.'

Lester jumped to the ground and slouched to the instrument. They saw him peering at it. He straightened and peered again. Then he shouted:

'A hundred and nineteen and a bit. Caw! Wonder it ain't busted.'

Forgetting to sniffle, he climbed on to the body of the ute.

'You sure?' demanded Carney.

'Take a deck yourself,' snapped Lester. 'A hundred and nineteen now. What must she have been round about two this afternoon? A flamin' record, I bet.'

They left the empty out-station, took the track up the long slope, and passed over the crest where Bony had observed the dust left by Martyr. No one looked back. Those on the tray body stood to look over the cabin top. They could see the track winding ahead for several miles. It was empty.

The normally red land, now covered by areas of dry grass dotted by clumps of belar and mulga, was apricot and silver in the waning evening light. They were grateful for the breeze created by the speed of the utility, and for the conquest of wind over flies.

Now and then Lester, clinging with Bony and Carney to the cabin top, sniffled and snortled.

'A hundred and nineteen at six o'clock!'

It was dark when they topped the following swell, and there Barby braked the vehicle to a stop, for far away blazed the lights of several vehicles coming their way. It being obviously unnecessary to go further, Barby turned the ute, cut his engine and climbed from the cabin.

'Three,' he said. 'Martyr in his ute, the Boss in his chromium chariot, and Red driving the juggernaut.'

'Hardly be Red, George, He wouldn't be able to keep up,' Carney pointed out.

'There's three coming, anyhow.'

'The third is probably being driven by a policeman,' offered Bony, and after that no one spoke.

Presently the lights caught them, and ultimately the first car stopped a few yards away. From the driver's window the overseer called:

'Righto, George! Get going back. I can give room here.'

The girl got in beside Martyr. Carney went with Barby, Lester seemed undecided, but followed Carney. Bony vanished. He reappeared beside Sergeant Mansell, who was driving the third vehicle.

'Been a hot day, Sergeant,' he remarked when climbing into the rear seat.

'Terrible,' replied the heavy man in plain clothes and, being uncertain of the identity Bony wished recognized for the benefit of the man sitting with him, added:

'A hundred and twenty-four at Menindee. One degree lower at Porchester homestead.'

'Must be a record, surely.'

'Easily. Broken Hill radio just said it's been 117 degrees down in Sydney. Dozens of people collapsed. Nearly did myself. Fires raging in Victoria. Doctor here wouldn't leave till four o'clock.'

'Too damned hot to move,' declared the doctor.

'You might introduce us, Sergeant.'

'Sure. Detective-Inspector Bonaparte . . . Doctor Clive.' The acknowledgements were given. 'How do we go,' Inspector?'

'As we were for the moment,' replied Bony. 'I am thankful you were able to come along, Doctor. There are three bodies to be dealt with : death by fire, assumed; death by drowning, assumed; and death by heat, easily established.'

'Quite a job,' murmured the doctor, and would have put a question had not Sergeant Mansell interrupted.

'The drowning case Gillen, by any chance?'

'Yes. I located his remains yesterday resting on dead Lake Otway. Man named MacLennon – you know him, perhaps – was struck by the sun. We were camped in the shadow of a hut, and I believe the heat upset him even before he determined to walk back to the out-station without a hat or a shirt. You can deal with the heat case on the spot, but the other two must be referred to a pathologist.'

'Ah-ha!' exclaimed the sergeant. 'Suspicious circumstances?'

'Yes.'

'As you will remember, Inspector, I was never satisfied about Gillen's disappearance, even before the money interest came out. Is this fire business mixed up with the Gillen affair?'

'It might be,' cautiously replied Bony, recalling that Mansell's first report on Gillen cast no doubts on accidental death. 'Is Draffin coming on behind us?'

'Yes. Loaded with stores and gear and stuff, including a coffin.'

'Did you bring a constable?'

'Too right, Inspector. He's travelling with Mr Wallace.'

'Good. Until the morning carry on as though everything is routine. Let no one suspect you think anything wrong in the case of Mrs Fowler. Tomorrow I will begin my inquiry into the deaths of Mrs Fowler and Raymond Gillen, following which you, Doctor, can with Sergeant Mansell decide your subsequent actions.'

'The fire victim is to be our first charge, Inspector?'

'Yes. On our arrival there will be much confusion till the place is put in order by Wallace and his men. The remains of Mrs Fowler, and the office safe, must not be tampered with until daylight.'

*　　*　　*

Confusion there was, and yet order was eventually established by Wallace. Barby was dispatched to Johnson's Well to transfer his camp and return the men's belongings. In the hearing of all, Doctor Clive said he would like to examine the body of MacLennon as quickly as possible, and that the remains of Mrs Fowler could be retrieved at daylight. That brought sobs from Joan, and Wallace himself took her to sit in the old arm-chair on the veranda.

Martyr went off with the doctor to Johnson's Well; Lester and Carney proceeded to build a camp fire and erect over it a beam from which Barby could suspend his billies and dixies. The fire illumined the front of the quarters and the line of out-buildings, and, when Draffin arrived, it aided the helpers to unload the stores and gear ... and the coffin, so handled that Joan did not see it.

With utensils Draffin brought from the main homestead, Lester brewed coffee, and opened tins of biscuits, meat and cheese. Oil-lamps were lit and Wallace took a large suit case to an empty room, then told Joan his wife had packed it for her. The room was next to that occupied by Lester.

Barby returned with his load, and at once washed and then took charge of the fire and the cooking. All the dogs were loosed, and the two cats cleaned themselves under Barby's feet and his galah in the cage woke to mutter words which disgraced its owner. With tragedy absent, it could have been a festive occasion.

A kind of buffet dinner was set out on a trestle table distant from the fire for comfort and yet advantaged by its light. They stood around to eat, and spoke in subdued tones because of the dead and the presence of Joan Fowler, now arrayed in a lime silk dress once packed in that suitcase.

Nothing about her registered the strain she had undergone for many hours. Firelight burnished the red-gold hair, and the silk dress gleamed as greenly as her eyes.

'What happened to you, Mr Martyr?' asked Carney when the chance offered.

'Had fan-belt trouble a mile this side of The Shaft,' replied the overseer. 'Spent a couple of hours messing about with it. Didn't get to Sandy Well till after eleven last night and then no one was in the office.'

'Don't wait up on the chance of hearing disaster on the phone,' remarked Wallace. 'Heard about it, of course, this morning. Mr Martyr wanted to return here, on a bit of rope for a fan-belt and a prayer. Just as well he didn't, with the heat rocking the mercury all over the States. Could easily have perished. As for us ... we left about five this afternoon, and even then the petrol almost exploded a dozen times before we got to Sandy Well.'

Lester came to sniffle and announce that the thermometer still registered 101 degrees, and when told by the sergeant of the record at Menindee he was as pleased as though he had backed a Melbourne Cup winner. Obviously he was trying to be cheerful ... as the others were ... and it did not appear that Joan ignored their efforts.

'We weren't to blame, Mr Wallace,' she entreated Wallace. 'Mother was always so careful with the stove and the frig. It was so quick, so sudden.'

'Try not to think about it too much, Joan,' advised the big man. 'We'll straighten it all out tomorrow. The place was old and the heat would make it tinder-dry. You did your best, and all of us can imagine how quickly it happened.'

Reaction set in and she burst into tears. Martyr stared hard at Barby's fire. Carney turned his back on her and sipped coffee. It was Lester who gently patted her shoulder. Wallace looked meaningly at the doctor, and Clive nodded. She did, however, insist on helping Barby to clean up.

It was not unusual for the 'government house' party to camp apart from the men, and Red Draffin put up stretchers for Wallace and the doctor, the sergeant and Martyr outside the store which was the closest to the site of the burned homestead. The men gathered in the light given from the cooking fire, and presently Red Draffin joined them.

He was barefoot as usual, his trousers and shirt were greasy and stained, as usual. And, as usual, his face was enlivened by his smile and twinkling eyes. Joan happened to be in her room.

'How did the rabbits go, George?' was his first question, and Barby glowered.

'Still going,' he answered, carefully stepping over a cat. 'Fenced the Channel yesterday. This morning the Channel is yards under dead rabbits and 'roos and birds.'

'I oughta been with you.'

'No good. The 'roos tore the fence down, and the sun did the rest. There'll be millions of rabbits digging under the dead uns to get at the water this very minute.' The glower lifted, the dark eyes cleared. Triumph crept into Barby's voice. 'But we needn't worry about the rabbits. A bit of a heat-wave can't knock them out. There'll be millions get through this summer, and when she rains they'll breed like hell. You ever seen a picture of the mouse licking up the drops of wine leaking from a barrel, and the cat's sitting on the top step of the cellar? The mouse says: "Now where's that bloody cat?" And that's what all the rabbits will be saying, Red: "Now where's that bloody myxotocksis?"'

24

Inspector Bonaparte Works

AFTER BREAKFAST, eaten before sun-up, everyone went into action, determined to accomplish as much as possible before the intense heat once again singed the earth and them. By nine o'clock the heat was severe, but a high-level haze smoked the sky and forecast a change accompanied by wind.

Sergeant Mansell and his constable appeared much interested in the interior of the machinery shed, whilst the others, including the owner and the overseer, relaxed on the veranda of the quarters.

Then the constable crossed to the group on the veranda to address Bony:

'Sergeant would like a few words with you.'

The general conversation petered out as Bony accompanied the policeman to the machinery shed. The doors were wide, the roof was high, the temperature was not yet unbearable. Packing-cases had been placed to form a desk and serve as seats, and the sergeant was taking from his brief-case paper, pens and ink.

'This do, Inspector?' he asked a little stiffly.

'Yes. We'll sit, so. As we deal with each of these people they must be kept here, not allowed to circulate. We'll begin with Carney. All right, Constable. Produce Henry Carney.'

Like those who were to follow him, Carney received a succession of surprises. He was surprised by finding Bony sitting with Mansell behind the 'desk', and was surprised by the invitation to sit on a tea-chest before them. Carney had been told that the sergeant wanted a few words with him, therefore the culminating surprise came when Mansell said:

'This is Inspector Bonaparte, Harry. He wants to ask a few questions.'

'Concerning Raymond Gillen, Mr Carney,' Bony said smoothly. 'We won't waste time by going into what is general knowledge but keep to essentials.'

Carney stared, knew he stared. The easy-going, softly-spoken horse-breaker had undergone a remarkable metamorphosis, for he sat squarely, his eyes were deeply blue, and there was no trace of the previous reticence of the aboriginal part of him. The voice was precise and authoritative.

'Mr Carney. Did you ever have a serious disagreement with Raymond Gillen?'

'No. Never,' answered Carney, barely side-stepping the 'sir'.

'What was your feeling towards Gillen?'

'Friendly enough. We got on all right. Camped in the same room. Most of us liked him. I know I did.'

'Despite the fact that you were both in love with the same girl?'

'That's only partly true. Ray wasn't in love with Joan. He thought he had a chance, that's all.'

'You were in love with her, were you not?'

'Yes. I was, then.'

'You imply you are not in love with her now. Would you tell me what changed your feelings?'

'That had nothing to do with Gillen,' prevaricated Carney. 'Gillen was a good type. Dare anything; try anything. He had a try for Joan, and it didn't upset me because I thought he would never get her. I know what she is. Yes, I loved her and hoped she'd marry me. I knew that Gillen meant to buy her, and I knew that because Gillen told me, and showed me money enough to buy a dozen women. It was in his case ... rolls and rolls of it.'

'Did he tell you where he obtained the money?'

'Spun a yarn about winning it in a lottery.'

'Do you know what happened to the money?'

'No.'

'You will remember that when MacLennon was shown the locket belonging to Gillen, he became enraged and said that Gillen had left a letter in his suitcase which you had found. Was that true?'

'Yes,' replied Carney. 'I'll tell you what happened from the time Ray had been here about a month. We'd become good friends, and he knew I was keen to marry Joan. He asked me, and I told him straight. He asked what I thought of my chances, and I said they were good ... until he came to the Lake. He said "Look, Harry. Don't be a mug. You've got no money and that's all she's after. She's a teasing bitch." '

Carney's mouth was grim, and his brown eyes were empty of the laughter Bony so often had seen.

'I knew what Ray said was right,' he went on. 'And then he said if I gave away the idea of marrying Joan, he'd give me a hundred to get her out of my system. When I laughed at him about the hundred, he opened his case and told me to help myself. He said again he'd won it in a lottery, but I couldn't believe that. But he did offer me a hundred to work off on Joan. I wouldn't take it. But I thought a hell of a lot of Ray Gillen.

'Then one night Joan said she wanted to go for a walk. She told me that Gillen had a case full of notes, and that he must have pinched it, and she wasn't being mixed up with hot money. She said she'd marry me if I stole it from Gillen, because then Gillen couldn't do anything about it, as he stole it in the first place. That woke me up to her properly. I didn't hate her exactly. I still loved her, or what I thought she could be. I still love her that way. I'm sorry if I can't make you understand.'

'I do understand,' Bony said slowly. 'Go on.'

'It turned out that Gillen got to work on her, offering her a thousand quid to clear out with him on his bike. She wouldn't fall for it. So he raised the ante ... just like he would. She said she didn't believe his yarns, and so he took her to his room and opened his case for her to see for herself.

'D'you know what, Bony? Joan planned to get all that money for free. She told her mother about it, and then the mother sooled MacLennon to steal it for her. Mac must have thought it over, and must have tried to open Gillen's case, because Ray found marks on the locks.

'Four days after that, or four nights after, Ray went for his last swim. Or so it turned out. When he wasn't on hand the next morning I looked at his case. It wasn't locked. Instead of the money, there was a letter. And the letter read: "What you want isn't here. It's well planted, and the clue is inside the locket around my neck. Try for the locket if you have guts enough. Ray G."

'I thought one of them had murdered Gillen, for the money. I don't think so now, not after you opened the locket for everyone to see.'

'Did Gillen tell you he was going to plant the money?'

'No. Not a word.'

'What did you do with the letter?'

'I gave it to Joan for a birthday present,' Carney grimaced. 'She didn't even thank me.'

'Did Gillen write letters?'

'No. He told me his parents were dead.'

'Did he seem to be worried ... just before the night he disappeared?'

'No. I've been trying to tell you what Gillen was, a chap who feared nothing, and no one. He never lost his temper.'

'He did fight Mac. Why?'

'Over what he said about Ma Fowler. But he didn't lose his temper about it. Mac did, and got a hell of a thrashing. Gillen laughed all the time he was dealing it out.'

'Let us return to the suitcase. The rooms are small, and each contains two beds. You camped with Gillen in the same room. When on your bed could you see Gillen's case under his?'

'At times. Depended on how far he pushed it under.'

'Quite so. When you could see the case, it was invariably locked?'

'The locks were in place and the catches were up. By looking at the case, I wouldn't know if the key had been turned in the lock.'

'When did you first find the case unlocked?'

'That morning Gillen was missing. I sat up and found Ray wasn't in his bed. I could see his suitcase under the bed. The ordinary catches weren't in place, and the slides were open. In fact the lid wasn't closed properly. That's why I pulled the case out and looked for the money, and found the letter.'

'In an envelope?'

'No. Just folded three times. It was lying on top of the clothes.'

Bony lit a cigarette.

'You have been candid, Mr Carney. Now tell me why you did not hand that letter to Mr Martyr, or to Sergeant Mansell.'

'I thought it might be a forgery, put in the case by whoever had taken the money, and could have murdered Gillen. I decided I'd stand by and wait to see who left here, and then

I'd have the satisfaction of reporting it to the police. But no one left the place.'

From the floor at his feet, and hidden by the cases from Carney, Bony picked up the parcel of money.

He was satisfied by Carney's reactions that Carney did not know its contents, but he asked the question:

'Have you seen this parcel before?'

Carney shook his head, and was directed to relax on the row of cases placed along one wall of the shed.

'Produce Robert Lester.'

The constable disappeared. The sergeant lit his pipe. He was the senior officer of a police-controlled district, and yet refrained from asking questions of the man who could give orders like that.

Lester sniffled before he came on. On seeing Bony, he sniffled again, and for the third time when told to sit on the tea-chest. On being informed that Inspector Bonaparte wished to ask a few questions, his watery eyes dried up. The bright blue eyes were expectant, and he knew there was a trap baited to take him, and wished he were far, far away.

Nonchalantly Bony removed the trap and placed it on the ground at his feet . . . the parcel of money. He reached for pencil and paper and drew a sketch of the front of the men's quarters, the while Lester sharply watched him, the sergeant curious, and the audience of one, Carney. Then the voice so different from the easy drawl of the horse-breaker:

'Now, Mr Lester, tell me: do you sleep soundly at night?'

'Fairish, I think,' replied Lester.

'Do you sleep soundly in the daytime?'

'Caw! Hell of a hope sleepin' in daytime. I can't answer that one, Bony.'

The sergeant coughed disapprovingly at such *lèse-majesté*.

'You remember that afternoon when you were feeling off colour following a nightmare in which you were climbing in and out of a tank? You were awakened by Miss Fowler and told the house was on fire. You were having a nap on the veranda, remember? Were you sound asleep then?'

'Must have been. Never heard the fire; leastways, I thought it was a willi-willi passing by.'

'You had lunch at the usual time . . . half-past twelve. After lunch you returned to the quarters. Who served the lunch?'

160

'Joan.'

'Did you see Mrs Fowler?'

'No.'

'Did you hear Mrs Fowler talking in the kitchen, or moving about in the kitchen?'

Lester proved that he had indulged in retrospection.

'Not a sight or sound of her.'

'After lunch, did you dally at table .talking with Miss Fowler?'

'No. She seemed in a bit of a temper.'

'With whom? You? Her mother?'

'Didn't let on.'

'So that you must have left the kitchen after lunch at about one o'clock?'

'Yair. Musta been.'

'What did you do after leaving the annexe?'

'Went over to the quarters. I had a smoke, and wanted a paper to read, but there wasn't any and so I made meself comfortable and took a nap.'

'Would you say you were asleep before one-thirty?'

'I would,' answered Lester, adding confidently: 'And by the shadders I'd say it was just before two when I was awoke by Joan to see the ruddy house going up.'

'Thank you! Now look at this sketch of the quarters showing the room doors, the steps up to the veranda.' Bony rose and passed round to stand beside Lester. 'Was the old armchair about here?'

'She was. Yes, that's about where she was. Always is, remember?'

'I should do, Mr Lester. Was the back of the chair towards the steps?'

'Yair.'

'Would the door of the sitting-room be, say, ten feet from the chair?'

'About that, I reckon.'

'Then the back of the chair would be sixteen to twenty feet from the door to your room?'

'Yair. That's so.'

'And even if you had been awake, you would not have seen anyone move up the steps, walk across the veranda and enter your room?'

'I might have heard 'em.'

'But you were asleep.'

'Dead to the wide, matter of fact.'

'Right!' snapped Bony. 'See that brown paper parcel?'

'Yair,' assented Lester, staring at the trap brought up from the floor.

'What was it doing under your bed after the fire?'

'Search me.' Lester was plainly puzzled, and Bony was satisfied.

'Thank you, Mr Lester. Please join Mr Carney.'

He slouched away to sit with Carney. He sniffled before automatically biting a chew from a plug. He sniffled when Bony said:

'Produce Richard Martyr.'

25

Telling Tales

MARTYR SAT ON the tea-chest. He looked to Sergeant Mansell. The light-grey eyes, invariably in startling contrast with his complexion, were almost lazy until the sergeant said that Inspector Bonaparte wanted to ask questions. When Bony looked up from his notes, the pale-grey eyes were small, and the firm, determined mouth was small, and there was a paleness about the small nostrils.

'Mr Martyr, what time did you leave the homestead on the morning of the fire?'

'Ten past eight.'

'You did not return until after the fire, accompanied by Carney?'

'No. We saw the smoke plume from Winters Well . . . sixteen miles away.'

'I was here with Barby, Lester and Miss Fowler when you returned with Carney after the fire. You gave instructions to the effect that we were to accompany Barby to Johnson's Well, and remain there until you returned from reporting the fire to Mr Wallace. You left before we did. When you had passed over the first ridge, you stopped the utility, watched the out-station to see us depart for Johnson's Well, and then you returned to the out-station. Why?'

'I did not return from beyond the first ridge.'

'You did. Your tracks betrayed you.'

'All right! I remembered that the Boss would ask me did I look into the safe to see if the books had been destroyed. I ought to have done it before I left. The stock books and records are important, and the Boss would be anxious about them.'

'You opened the safe and found the books . . . in what condition?'

'Fairly good, to my relief.'

'What did you do then?'

'I locked the safe and carried on.'

'Leaving the key in the lock?'

'I . . .' Martyr automatically touched the pockets of his jodhpurs.

'Must have done. Damn!'

'What else is in the safe besides the books?'

'Oh, tax stamps, a few pounds in petty cash.'

'Do you customarily carry the safe key in your pockets when you leave the out-station?'

Those pale-grey eyes stood by their owner.

'No. Usually it's kept on a little nail in the wall behind the desk.'

'And yet a little while ago when the key was mentioned you unconsciously tapped your pockets.'

'Why not? I remembered I took the key from the safe that morning and pocketed it because I was in a hurry.'

'Of course, Mr Martyr. Obviously the contents of the safe were of such great value that you would not habitually carry the key in a pocket when out on the run. The books found not to be seriously damaged, forgetting to relock the safe and remove the key is understandable. To replace the safe and cover it with ash is, however, curious. Well, now, I don't think there is anything else.'

Martyr rose and strode to the open door. Bony called:

'Oh, just a moment, Mr Martyr. Won't keep you long.'

Martyr turned, walked back to the desk. There he stood looking down at the brown-paper parcel Bony was holding.

From the parcel, his eyes flickered to encounter the blue eyes from which he couldn't hide. Actually, Bony was a little surprised when Martyr sat down.

'Where did you find that?' he asked, thinly.

'In Lester's room.'

'Lester's room!' echoed the overseer. Then came the one word, loudly: 'When?'

'After the fire . . . after.'

Martyr placed his elbows on the desk and cupped his chin in his hands. He put a question to the sergeant:

'Have I got to tolerate this inquisition?'

'No, there's no compulsion, Mr Martyr,' replied Mansell. 'Would look bad if you refuse, of course.'

'Yes, I suppose it would.' Martyr removed his gaze from the grey eyes to the bright blue eyes, and the blue eyes detected neither fear nor despair, but resolution.

'I don't like answering questions,' Martyr said sharply. 'I'm used to asking them. Do you know what's in that parcel?'

'Money. Shall I tell the story, or would you care to?'

'I will. I can tell it better than you. Two days before Gillen vanished, he came to the office after dark and requested me to take custody of a parcel which, he said, contained personal effects he treasured. I consented to do so, saying I would place the parcel in the station safe. I told him I would write a receipt for the parcel, and he laughed and said that wasn't necessary. I waxed the knots and at one place got him to press his thumb.

'I didn't think anything more of the parcel until, on the phone, Mr Wallace told me to run through Gillen's effects to establish his connexions, and when I opened the parcel I was astounded to see the large amount of money it contained.

'Not having found anything among Gillen's effects leading to his parents or friends, or where he came from, and feeling sure he could not possibly have gained the money by honest means, I decided to forget about the parcel in the safe. I realized that it mightn't do to resign right away and start off on my own, but that I must be patient and wait on here, perhaps for several years. My mother is almost an invalid, and I am her only support. I was able to send her a few pounds now and then together with a salary cheque.

'Naturally, when the house burned down, I was anxious

164

about the parcel, and you know that when I got here the safe would have been too hot to touch, and I didn't want the men to see me interested too much in it. Which is why I ordered them to go with Barby to his camp. So I returned, as you said, and opened the safe, and took the parcel to Lester's room, intending to retrieve it on my return and before I went to Johnson's Well for the men. It was my intention to steal the money. I believed Gillen had stolen it, or that it was stolen money, so that my action didn't seem to be so bad.'

'H'm!' Bony added a note to his pad. 'Having taken the parcel from the safe, you forgot to take the key. You threw ash on the safe and over your tracks as you withdrew from the ruins. Then you took the parcel to Lester's room and hid it under the mattress on Lester's bed. Why? Why didn't you take the parcel with you? You were in no possible danger of being searched.'

'I couldn't be sure I would not have to take over another ute, or drive Mr Wallace's car. And having lost everything bar what I stood up in in the fire, possession of the parcel might have been noticed.'

'Didn't you think that Lester might return from Johnson's Well, and might have found the parcel under the mattress?'

'No. Anyway, that was a chance I had to accept.'

'Yes, of course.' Bony regarded the overseer for a long moment. 'I think, Mr Martyr, I could tell the story better than that. Just where did you hide the parcel in Lester's room?'

'Where? Under the mattress, as I stated.'

'Think! Think, man!'

Martyr reddened with anger.

'If you didn't find it under the mattress, then someone found it before you. That's where I put it.'

'I rode back from Johnson's Well, and saw the dust raised by your utility after your second departure,' Bony went on. 'After you left for the second time, and before I arrived here, there was certainly no other person in sight. Therefore, no one could have removed the parcel from under the mattress, because it was never under the mattress.'

'All right! Then where was it?'

'You don't know, Mr Martyr?'

'Under the mattress was where I put it.'

'I repeat, Mr Martyr, you don't know where I found the

parcel, because you did not hide the parcel in Lester's room.'

'I tell you I did. And my word is as good as yours.'

Bony bent over and brought to view the station books.

'See the slight damage done these books by the heat in the safe, generated outside the safe. The covers are brittle. Here are the tax stamps, curled by the heat to thin spills. Now regard the parcel of money. The wrapping does not bear any such effects of heat. So, Mr Martyr, the parcel was taken from the safe before the fire ... when you were miles away on a job with Carney.'

Martyr said nothing, looking at Bony, trying to evade the ice-blue eyes, being compelled to face them again and again.

'You returned from just beyond the first ridge,' Bony continued. 'You opened the safe to remove the parcel, which already had been taken, and you began then to guess about the fire, and you knew who took the parcel from the safe before the fire began. And those questions you asked yourself, and hated to answer, because you don't like answering questions, are questions I have asked myself, and have supplied the answers. Nothing you can say will affect the result to the person who removed the parcel of money from the office safe. I suggest that you concentrate on Gillen.'

The only sound within the shed was the occasional creaking of the roof iron tortured by the sun. Martyr bit his lip, and then his finger-nails. Bony rolled a cigarette. Sergeant Mansell stared at the overseer and was glad he wasn't the object of this suavely polite interrogation. Martyr sighed, moved to roll himself a smoke, as though to steady his fingers. His voice was flat.

'I was sitting on the house veranda. The moon was full. It was late, after eleven. I saw Gillen walk down to the water. He was wearing only pyjama trousers and once the moonlight was reflected by the golden locket suspended from his neck.

'He ran into the water, and then he splashed it over himself, as he continued to run, getting deeper and deeper until he lunged forward and began to swim. For some time I could see his dark head on the silvered water and watch the outward-running ripples under the moon. Presently, he swam from my sight, swam on towards the far shore.

'I sat on the veranda, thinking. Then I heard a cry. It was

far out on the Lake. At first I thought it was Gillen playing the fool. Then I heard, low but distinctly, his cries for help, including the word "cramp". I did not get up. I knew Gillen wasn't playing the fool, but I didn't get up from the chair. I sat on and listened to Gillen drowning.

'You must understand why I hated Gillen, and why I let him drown.

'Living conditions here were rough before Mrs Fowler and her daughter were employed. But, life was smooth for all of us. I had my first big job. The men were easy to get along with. There was no clashing and no unpleasantness. The women changed all that. They brought order and cleanliness and decent living, but they also brought hate and pain.

'That was three years ago, and I thought Joan was innocent and sweet as well as beautiful. I asked her to marry me. She said she would like to think about it. I took her riding, gave her little presents. She asked me how I stood financially. I told her I hadn't been able to save because I had to support my mother. I offered her the partnership in my job here, and was confident one day of becoming a full manager. She said she wouldn't marry a man in my position and with my prospects. The man she married must be rich. When I pressed her, she told me I was too dull, and too old, anyway.

'That was before Gillen came. Carney was trying his luck when Gillen asked for a job. I used to watch the play. I was asked by this one and that to obtain a wages cheque from the Boss, and then when making up the mail I'd see a letter addressed to a Sydney or an Adelaide jeweller. I became satisfied to wait, and bet with myself which of the men would finally murder her.

'Gillen came and he fancied Joan, and Joan seemed to fall for him. Gillen must have been fifteen years younger than I am. In modern parlance, he had everything it takes. She played with me, and she played with Carney, but she meant business with Gillen ... until she came to me one evening and was sweet and loving and told me that Gillen had a lot of stolen money in his suitcase. She suggested that I take it, saying it must have been stolen by Gillen, and what was stolen would not be real stealing the second time. And that when Gillen discovered his money was gone he wouldn't dare make a fuss about it, and we could go away and be married and start with plenty of cash. The Golden Bitch! I told her to use someone else.

'The very next night, Gillen came to me with the money in a parcel, and after he had gone back to the quarters, I opened the parcel, made sure that it contained a fortune in bank-notes, and retied and resealed it and put it in the safe.

'I stayed on the veranda a full two hours after I heard Gillen shouting for help from the middle of the Lake, and by then was sure he had drowned. Because all the time he'd been here he had never written a letter, but had signed the employ-ees' work-book, I imitated his handwriting and wrote a note saying he had planted his money and that the clue to the plant was in his locket and daring anyone to take the locket from him. I knew someone had been after the money, because Gillen told me his case had been tampered with.

'At four in the morning the front of the quarters was in deep shadow, and I took the note and crept into Gillen's room and put it into the case. If someone came after the money and took the note, they'd be ready to get in first for the locket when the body came ashore. And if by chance it didn't, they'd have to wait for the Lake to dry up. If no one opened the case, I'd give the note to Joan for the pleasure of seeing her reac-tion. But when I listed the contents of the case, the note was gone, and as Gillen's body didn't turn up, I sat back and watched the play go on.'

'Who knew where the safe key was normally kept?' asked Bony.

'No one other than Mr Wallace and myself.'

'And on the morning of the first you inadvertently left the key in the safe lock?'

'I did. That morning when Mr Wallace rang through he wanted stock figures and I had to refer to the stock book. I forgot to relock the safe. That is the story, Inspector. I have nothing to add to it. I shall continue to sit back and watch the play, because I know now that you know the end of it.'

26

Who Wins?

JOAN APPEARED, escorted by the constable, and behind them came Mr Wallace, who had been requested by Bony not to leave the poor girl alone to brood.

She looked cool and confident in a lilac dress and sling-back sandals. Her hair was gloriously, vividly alive and her make-up was, as usual, lightly applied. She gave Bony a tender smile and then concentrated on Sergeant Mansell, who had sent word that he wished to ask questions. It was when Bony was presented as Inspector Bonaparte that she froze.

'You, a detective-inspector!'

'When I am not breaking-in horses, yes. Now be easy, Miss Fowler. I just want you to tell us about the fire so that this matter of your mother's unfortunate end may be cleared up. Would you tell Sergeant Mansell just what happened?'

'What, again?' Joan tossed her hair, settled herself on the hard tea-chest, and related her experience as previously given to Bony and others.

'Thank you,' murmured Bony. 'Let us be quite clear. Your mother was lying down on her bed. She occupied a room other than yours?'

'Yes. When I ran to her she was lying on her bed and I tried to wake her up and couldn't. So I pulled her off the bed and tried to drag her from the room, but the fire and smoke was too much for me, and I just got out myself. As I told you.'

'When you first noticed the fire, you were lying down on your own bed?'

'Yes.'

'Fully dressed, of course?'

'Oh, yes. I had had a shower and dressed for the afternoon. I was reading a book when I saw smoke pouring into my room and then I heard the crackle of the flames.'

'It was, if memory serves, a very hot afternoon, Miss Fowler. You would have found the shade cast by the garden trees much cooler. During the morning you swept out the office, I understand.'

'No. I didn't. Mother did, I think.'

'Supposing you tell us about the money in the unlocked safe.'

'Money in the safe!' echoed Joan. 'What are you talking about?'

'This money,' replied Bony, and brought up the parcel to place it on the desk. 'Gillen's money. It was in the safe before the house caught fire. It was not in the safe when the house was burning. After the house burned to ash, it was in Lester's room . . . under his bed and pushed as far back as possible. Can you tell us anything concerning this strange angle?'

'I still don't know what you are talking about!' persisted the girl, her eyes indignant, but voice controlled.

'You knew, of course, that Gillen possessed a great deal of money, and that everyone thought he had stolen it?'

'It's the first I've heard of it. And if you believe tales told you by Harry and Mr Martyr about me, you're a fool. They're spiteful liars. They've always been sore because I wouldn't give in to them. This has never been a safe place for a decent girl, but Mother and I had to live, and we could save something from our wages.'

'These tales about you have to be checked, you know,' Bony said soothingly. 'It's my job. Let's return to the fire. Of course, you know there will have to be an inquest, and it's better to have it all straightened out for the coroner. Would you prefer to sign a statement covering your actions from the time you realized the house was on fire?'

'Yes, I would.'

Bony wrote down the details.

'There you are. Please read it carefully before you sign it. Then we'll witness your signature, and make it hard and fast.'

The girl read the document. She picked up the pen provided by Mansell. She looked at Bony, who was rolling a cigarette. She glared at Martyr and Carney, who had drawn close at Bony's beckoning.

'That is what happened,' she said. 'Every word of it. I don't tell lies about people.'

With angry deliberation she wrote her name, and sat

back while Carney and Martyr and Lester witnessed her signature.

'You might confirm the document, Mr Wallace,' suggested Bony, and Wallace signed as a Justice of the Peace. The men were waved away, and Bony continued. 'Now that subject is covered, Miss Fowler, let us make clear the subject of your mother's jewellery.'

Bony thought to make the girl betray shock, and when he saw no evidence of it he could not but wonder at the manifestation of a one-track mind, unable to anticipate a trap. Here was a woman so sure of her power, made so vain by her victories, that even the subject of her mother's jewellery did not, at this moment, disturb her, as she deftly renewed her make-up.

'Well, what about Mum's bits and pieces?' she demanded, slipping the gold compact into the pocket of her skirt. Bony smiled ruefully, saying:

'I find this as irritating as you must do, Miss Fowler. Do you remember Lester giving your mother a gold brooch set with opals?'

'Yes. She showed it to me when Lester gave it to her.'

'Did you see the emerald ring given your mother by Mac-Lennon?'

'Yes.'

'And the pendant?'

'Yes. Why all this?'

'Where did your mother usually keep her jewellery?'

'Oh, I don't know. Never interested that much.'

'Do you think she would keep her jewellery in an old hand-bag behind the door of the ladies' tante?'

'Tante! What's tante?'

'Aunt.' The girl laughed, and Bony said suavely:

'Constable, take Mr Wallace and Mr Lester to the room now occupied by Miss Fowler, and bring here any jewellery you may find.'

The girl jumped to her feet and stormed, her voice harsh, her words raw. The sergeant stood and towered over her. The constable and Lester departed, the mystified Mr Wallace following after them. Bony glanced across at the two men again seated by the wall. Martyr was leaning back and resting his head against a wall support. His eyes were closed, and he was smiling. Carney sat tensely, his eyes wide, as horror strangled an ideal which had striven to live.

'Sit down, Miss, and keep calm,' urged Mansell. 'The Inspector's only getting things straightened out.' She looked up at him searchingly, her hands clenched. Abruptly she turned to Bony. Bony was writing a memo, and she sat again and from the cigarette section of the gold compact she extracted a smoke. The sergeant struck a match for her. She inhaled clumsily, and as she spurted smoke through pursed lips, Bony looked up and the light in his eyes caused her to flinch.

'You don't know where Gillen planted his money, do you?' he asked, softly. 'I do. I know how his money came to be in Lester's room, and who conveyed it thereto. I know why it was hidden under Lester's bed. And I know who took your mother's jewellery to the tante, before the fire, and who removed it from the tante just before we all left for Johnson's Well. Greed is a loathsome vice, Miss Fowler. Beauty is a wonderful gift which should make the recipient deeply humble. When beauty is allied with greed and a lust for power, beauty is as nothing. You, with your possession of beauty, with the addition of a little intelligence, might have created a world of happiness.'

'Clever, aren't you!'

Sadly, Bony looked into her green eyes, mocking, cold, empty. Wallace came into the shed. The constable entered with Lester. The constable put on the desk gold and gems which caught the hot light from without.

'Lester! Is that the brooch you gave to Mrs Fowler?'

'Yair, it is. And that's the ring that Mac gave her. And here's the necklet Harry gave her, too. Isn't it, Harry?'

Carney made no move from his seat against the wall, and Bony said:

'Would you like to make a statement telling how your mother died?'

'I signed it.'

'That one isn't quite accurate.'

'I'm signing no other statement,' the girl said, contemptuously tossing her cigarette butt on to Bony's papers.

'Very well, I'll tell you how she died, and what you did afterwards. The case is so simple and so clear that the best lawyers in the country would fail in your defence. There is only one point which eludes me, and it is not important, and that is whether you or your mother found the office safe with the key in its lock.

'For years there has rested on the top of the safe a brass figurine, and this morning it was found where the passage door of the office originally swung.

'The doctor is sure that your mother was killed by a blow from that figurine. He is confident that the Government pathologist will support his opinion, and further will agree with him that the body was dragged on its back for some distance to the bedroom where the fire partially consumed it. The fact that a dustpan has been found on the place where the office stood indicates that one of you went there to sweep out the office. And there murder took place over the parcelled money taken from the safe.

'You dragged your mother's body from the office, along the passage and so to her room. That was before lunch, and Lester would be expecting to hear the gong struck. You called him to lunch at the right hour, and afterwards you collected all your mother's jewellery, your own bank-book and what loose money there was, as well as your toilet aids, and hid them in the handbag behind the door of the ladies' tante, dropping a ring on the path as you went there or returned.

'You foresaw that after setting fire to the house you would escape with nothing save what you were wearing. You could wear your own jewellery but not that belonging to your mother, and what place more secure against men than that you selected?

'Doubtless you were a trifle upset by the body in the house. What to do with the brown-paper parcel containing some twelve thousand pounds? The jewellery you could eventually hide down inside your blouse and in your skirt pocket. But not the parcel. That was too large. You would have put it in the tante, but you could not be sure what Mr Martyr would decide about your immediate future. So you looked across to the quarters and saw Lester dozing with his back to the steps, and you stole over with the parcel, silently gained the veranda and slipped into Lester's room because it was the first room you came to.

'After the fire, you gained your way with Martyr, or

thought you did, to let you stay at the out-station, but when compelled to accompany the men to Johnson's Well for a space, you retrieved the loot you had put in the handbag and stuffed it down your blouse. The parcel, however, you could do nothing with because one of us at least would see it. So I found the parcel under Lester's bed within two hours after we left in Barby's utility, and Mr Wallace with the constable and Lester found your mother's jewellery in the room given you since yesterday.'

'In the suitcase my wife packed and I brought here for her,' supplemented Mr Wallace.

'Damn clever, eh?' commented Joan, calmly.

'Heavens, no, one hasn't to be clever with you,' replied Bony, pleasantly. 'You know, actually, you are extremely dumb. Just listen to this. This is what you said and what you signed before witnesses: "I found Mother unconscious from the smoke and I dragged her off the bed. I couldn't lift her. The smoke was getting my breath, and the room was full of flames. I dragged Mother by her feet to the doorway, then I had to leave her and rush out because the house was all on fire." That is what you stated, and signed as the truth.'

'Well, so what, cocky?'

'Come, come, Miss Fowler! You cannot really be as dumb as that. If you dragged your mother off the bed and then by the feet to the doorway, her body would have been found by police and doctor with its feet to the doorway. She was found with her head to the doorway, proving that you had dragged her body by the feet to that place from the passage. From the passage, Miss Fowler, not from the bed. That'll be all, Sergeant.'

*   *   *

'Just a little conference before I depart with the Boss,' Bony told Lester and Carney and Martyr, he having drawn them to the edge of the bluff overlooking the dreary depression.

'Much will depend on the Crown Prosecutor,' he went on, 'but I fancy he won't take action against either you, Martyr, or you, Carney. Martyr, don't let this episode in your life spoil it. There was no action you could have taken to rescue Gillen that night, for had there been a boat he couldn't have been reached in time. As for the money . . . well . . . with no

174

one to claim it and a mother desperately ill, I believe I would have ... thought about it.

'As for you, Harry, cling to your dreams and remember that what one woman kills another can resurrect. Tell me, who did trounce Bob when he climbed out of that tank?'

'MacLennon,' sighed Carney, and Lester sniffled twice.

'The fourth man there that night? Was it you, Martyr?'

'Yes. I was keeping watch from the creek bank.'

'Who prepared Gillen's bike for a get-away?'

'I did,' Carney said. 'I was fed up with the place and all. Then I thought how silly I'd be.'

'You would have been, and it would not have been like you. And had you attempted to ride away after I came here, you would have found that the carburettor had been removed. We won't say anything more about Gillen's motor-cycle and, unless the matter crops up, we'll say nothing of the accidental discharge of the shot-gun, Mr Martyr. What did happen that night?'

'The women had been nagging each other for days, and I ought to have anticipated a showdown,' Martyr replied. 'The gun was kept on the wall in the hall, and cartridges are about anywhere. I was in my room, and I heard them arguing. A moment or two later, I heard the gun-breech snapped shut. It was a sound I couldn't mistake, and I raced to Joan's room and was just in time to push up the barrel of the gun as the mother pulled the trigger. I didn't make a song and dance about it, Inspector, as it would have spoiled my star act.'

'Yes, it would have been an anticlimax,' agreed Bony. He gripped Lester's forearm. 'Now, Bob, you cannot gossip without stones crashing through your windows. Remember, you have lived in a glass house. Imagine giving a woman a brooch worth £120 merely on a promise. Imagine what people would say. It made the gamble frightfully expensive, didn't it?'

'Yair, I suppose it did.' Lester forgot to sniffle, but he did chuckle. 'Still, if a bloke never gambles, he can't ever win, can he?'

'That's quite true, Bob,' agreed Bony, smiling. 'Yet when it comes to gambling on a woman, no man can win ... ever. Now I must go. *Au revoir*, and grand luck for you all. Should you be here at the time, let me know when Lake Otway is born again.'

P9-EES-05?

Praise for Michael Slade

"*Swastika* will please Slade's legion of fans and anyone who enjoys a good thriller with a historical bent."
—*Quill & Quire*

"[Slade] goes the extra mile to authenticate his tales."
—*Ottawa Citizen*

"Slade has that rare ability to create tension on the page, to make your mind race ahead as the chapter unfolds before you."
—*North Shore News*

"Slade has developed a hell-bent style that rivals that of the master of cop/crime fiction, James Ellroy … it works like a ticking bomb."
—*The Province*

"Masterfully written and thoroughly researched."
—*The Record* (Kitchener-Waterloo)

"Slade runs a three-ring circus of suspense."
—*Booklist*

"Captivating and wonderfully written."
—*The Leader-Post*

PENGUIN CANADA

SWASTIKA

MICHAEL SLADE is the pen name of JAY and
REBECCA CLARKE.

 Swastika was inspired by the
Second World War archives of
Flight Lieutenant Jack "Johnny"
Clarke, who flew forty-seven
combat missions against the Third
Reich in Europe, and in North
Africa for the Battle of El Alamein.

 As a criminal lawyer, Jay Clarke,
Jack's son, has fought more than
one hundred murder cases. He
specializes in the law of insanity.

 Rebecca Clarke, Jay's daughter,
has a degree in history and English
literature.

Michael Slade is the author of eleven Special X
thrillers.

Visit the Slade website: **www.specialx.net**

Also by Michael Slade

SWASTIKA
MICHAEL SLADE

PENGUIN
CANADA

PENGUIN CANADA

Published by the Penguin Group

Penguin Group (Canada), 90 Eglinton Avenue East, Suite 700, Toronto, Ontario, Canada M4P 2Y3
(a division of Pearson Canada Inc.)

Penguin Group (USA) Inc., 375 Hudson Street, New York, New York 10014, U.S.A.
Penguin Books Ltd, 80 Strand, London WC2R 0RL, England
Penguin Ireland, 25 St Stephen's Green, Dublin 2, Ireland (a division of Penguin Books Ltd)
Penguin Group (Australia), 250 Camberwell Road, Camberwell, Victoria 3124, Australia
(a division of Pearson Australia Group Pty Ltd)
Penguin Books India Pvt Ltd, 11 Community Centre, Panchsheel Park, New Delhi – 110 017, India
Penguin Group (NZ), cnr Airborne and Rosedale Roads, Albany, Auckland 1310, New Zealand
(a division of Pearson New Zealand Ltd)
Penguin Books (South Africa) (Pty) Ltd, 24 Sturdee Avenue, Rosebank, Johannesburg 2196,
South Africa

Penguin Books Ltd, Registered Offices: 80 Strand, London WC2R 0RL, England

First published in a Penguin Canada paperback by Penguin Group (Canada),
a division of Pearson Canada Inc., 2005
Published in this edition, 2006

1 2 3 4 5 6 7 8 9 10 (OPM)

Copyright © Headhunter Holdings Ltd., 2005
Excerpt from *Kamikaze* by Michael Slade copyright © Headhunter Holdings Ltd., 2006

All rights reserved. Without limiting the rights under copyright reserved above, no part of this
publication may be reproduced, stored in or introduced into a retrieval system, or transmitted in any
form or by any means (electronic, mechanical, photocopying, recording or otherwise), without
the prior written permission of both the copyright owner and the above publisher of this book.

*Publisher's note: This book is a work of fiction. Names, characters, places and incidents
either are the product of the author's imagination or are used fictitiously, and any
resemblance to actual persons living or dead, events, or locales is entirely coincidental.*

Manufactured in the U.S.A.

LIBRARY AND ARCHIVES CANADA CATALOGUING IN PUBLICATION

Slade, Michael
Swastika / Michael Slade.

ISBN-13: 978-0-14-305326-2
ISBN-10: 0-14-305326-4

I. Title.

PS8587.L35S93 2006   C813'.54   C2006-903557-1

Except in the United States of America, this book is sold subject to the condition that it shall not, by
way of trade or otherwise, be lent, re-sold, hired out, or otherwise circulated without the publisher's
prior consent in any form of binding or cover other than that in which it is published and without
a similar condition including this condition being imposed on the subsequent purchaser.

Visit the Penguin Group (Canada) website at **www.penguin.ca**

Special and corporate bulk purchase rates available; please see
www.penguin.ca/corporatesales or call 1-800-399-6858, ext. 477 or 474

In memory of
Flight Lieutenant Jack "Johnny" Clarke,
who flew forty-seven combat missions
against the Swastika
in Europe and North Africa

Rem Acu Tangere

Under conditions of peace,
the warlike man attacks himself.

—FRIEDRICH NIETZSCHE

Hitler's Bunker

BERLIN, GERMANY
April 3, 1945

The swastika crouched on the armband of SS-General Ernst Streicher's Nazi uniform like a crooked-legged spider at the center of its web. The uniform was midnight black, broken only by silver braids, Schutzstaffel emblems, and the striking brassard of the Nazi Party on the upper left sleeve. Bordered by a black tress at top and bottom, to signify the SS—Hitler's Black Corps—the armband was as red as the German blood currently saturating the soil of the Fatherland. A circle of Aryan white on the red band backed the black spider.

Stomp, stomp, stomp …

The heels of Streicher's jackboots echoed down the hall.

The uniform was the man in Hitler's Third Reich, and Streicher took great care to ensure that his appearance was impeccable. Black riding breeches, flared at both thighs, were tucked into his knee-high boots. The single-breasted black tunic, with its four silver buttons and flapped pockets, was cinched in a black leather belt with a round swastika buckle. Holstered on his hip was a 7.65 mm Walther PPK. The SS-Obergruppenführer's rank was signified by his collar patches: three oak leaves on black velvet with two pips. The open collar at his throat flaunted the Knight's Cross, the highest German decoration for valor. On the band of his black, peaked, high-front cap glittered the *Totenkopf,*

the silver skull and crossbones that denoted the SS Death's
Head. Hand-tailored by captives in the concentration camps
he ran, this uniform was as pristine as it was feared.
Streicher had had the Polish slave who'd sewed the swastika
armband crookedly on his sleeve publicly hanged in the
yard at Dora-Mittelbau.

Clomp, clomp, clomp …

Lesser footfalls mimicked the stomping boots.

The Nazi general was flanked by his teenage sons. Fritz,
fifteen, and Hans, fourteen, boasted the same Nordic blond
hair and icy blue squints as their father. Seemingly parading
their hardiness in the teeth of bitter April, both boys
proudly wore the summer uniform of the Hitler Youth: a
small-peaked cap with the Hitlerjugend badge on the front,
and the brown shirt, black tie, black shorts, calf-high socks,
and shoes inspired by the Brownshirt thugs of the Nazis'
rise to power. The brassard on each of their left biceps bore
the swastika in a horizontal white stripe. A leather strap
crossed each lad's chest from the right shoulder to the left
hip, where Fritz and Hans Streicher sheathed their Hitler
Youth daggers. Each blade was inscribed in German script
with the motto *"Blut und Ehre"*—"Blood and honor."

Stomp, stomp, stomp …

Clomp, clomp, clomp …

Father and sons strode in lockstep through the bowels of
the New Reich Chancellery toward the *Führerbunker*.

On January 16, Hitler had gone underground in
downtown Berlin, never to see a sunrise or sunset again.
Inexorably, the war he had created was grinding to a close,
while day and night the Allies steadily pulverized the Nazi
capital with saturation-bombing raids. By sunlight,
American Liberators and Flying Fortresses unleashed their
rain of death upon those cowering below. Ninety percent of
the city was flattened, and groggy Berliners struggled to

survive in hovels of crumbling rubble. By moonlight, British Lancasters and Halifaxes droned above, preparing to drop their incendiaries on the heart of Hitler's Third Reich. Firestorms raged with such ferocity that they sucked people off the street and into the hellish flames. Everything—trees, rivers, asphalt, lakes—was ablaze, as the phosphorous maelstrom reduced the city to a molten morass. Meanwhile, unknown to all but those in his inner circle, the führer commanded the defense of the Fatherland from a rathole under the garden of the chancellery, buried twenty feet deeper than Berlin's sewage system.

The bombs began to fall again as the three reached the far end of the tunnel that ran from the cellar of the chancellery to Hitler's bunker. It was nearly midnight when they descended the stairs to the narrow butler's pantry (dubbed "Kannenberg Alley" for its fat chief steward). Having taken to the skies in Britain at dusk, the Royal Air Force was now overhead, using the wide artery of the East–West Axis—built by Hitler for his victory parades—to guide them like an arrow to the Brandenburg Gate. The bunker was buried just to the south, at the corner of Wilhelmstrasse and Voss, with the great green lung of Tiergarten park off to the west. Close by was the most terrifying address in the Third Reich: 8 Prinz Albrechtstrasse, headquarters of the Gestapo, the SS Secret State Police, whose agents arrested, tortured, and killed the enemies of Adolf Hitler.

Boom!

Boom!

Boom! …

The thundering roar of the British bombardment seemed muffled and distant down here. It would take a near hit by a two-ton blockbuster to make the bunker shudder. Hitler's hidey-hole was a cement cave fifty-five feet below ground level. Up where the bombs were exploding, there was little to give it away. The chancellery garden, hidden from public view, was a spacious interior court designed like a Roman atrium. A square blockhouse and a round watchtower encased the bunker's emergency exit, and forty-four steps led down to its door. The tower and the bunker were still under construction, so a big cement mixer blighted the surface décor. A curious trench, designed as a moat, was gouged from the soil around the exit. Berlin itself had been built on soft alluvial sand that cushioned the bombs like a shock absorber. So did the tons of earth on top of the buried bunker's sixteen-foot-thick roof and around its six-foot-wide exterior walls. As the general and his sons presented their papers to the guards, queasy trembling from the blasts overhead made the lamps sway as if they were being rocked by a subterranean wind.

The bulkhead between Kannenberg Alley and Hitler's bunker was secured by SS bodyguards armed with machine pistols and hand grenades. Entry by the emergency exit was strictly *verboten,* and even high-ranking generals summoned by der Chef—"the boss," as Hitler was called in the bunker—had to pass muster and present their identity papers at three checkpoints. For Streicher, it was an ominous taste of the fascist suspicion with which his Black Corps had viewed the German people since Hitler's rise to power in 1933.

The guard, a strapping young Prussian of six-foot-four, gave the general back his papers but didn't withdraw his hand.

"Pistol," he demanded.

Streicher unholstered his PPK and slapped it onto the outstretched palm.

"Daggers," ordered the other bodyguard, a man an inch shorter than the Prussian.

The general snapped a curt nod at his sons.

Fritz and Hans Streicher relinquished their Hitlerjugend daggers.

"Enter," said the Prussian, and the bodyguards stood aside.

Last July 20, German army officers had tried to assassinate Hitler in his bunker at Rastenburg headquarters. Operation Valkyrie had failed through mischance: an officer had kicked the briefcase that held the bomb behind a table support, effectively shielding the führer from the blast. Four men died, but the intended target did not. Hitler's vengeance was merciless. The SS executed five thousand soldiers and civilians, rooting out once and for all anyone suspected of disloyalty. For the ringleaders, der Chef decreed special attention: "I want them strung up like carcasses of meat." His demand was carried out to the letter by the Black Corps. In the death chamber at Plötzensee prison, SS executioners secured a row of hooks to a beam suspended from the ceiling. One by one, the naked plotters were hauled in. A hangman's noose of thin cord was looped around each neck, and the man was hoisted up, then left to strangle by his own weight from one of the meat hooks. Not only was his kicking and thrashing witnessed by the next conspirator to hang, but the slow and agonizing deaths were filmed for Hitler's pleasure.

Traitors, jerking like macabre marionettes.

The SS general crossed the threshold to enter the upper level of the bunker, but he didn't know what to expect inside. As each day brought more depressing news from both fronts, rumors ran rampant through what had once been strongholds of Nazi power. On March 7, the first American troops had crossed the Rhine, exploiting to their advantage the unblown railway bridge at Remagen. Now Patton's Third Army was rampaging deep into the Fatherland, and Montgomery's whole Twenty-first Army Group was overrunning the Reich. To the east, a far greater threat was closing in on Berlin. Bent on revenge for what the Nazi Einsatzgruppen had done to the

Russians during the Barbarossa invasion of 1941, the Red Army was laying waste to everything in its path. German men were forced to watch as Soviet soldiers raped their wives, daughters, and mothers—and were castrated and shot if they struggled. Women who fought back were either bayoneted or nailed to barn doors. The heads of babies were bashed in, and any German soldiers captured alive were doused with gasoline and turned into human torches.

"The Ivans are coming!"

That was the cry of panic heard retreating from the east.

But what of Adolf Hitler, the defender of the Reich? The rumors among the SS elite had the führer locked away in a madhouse run by the inmates. There, he was attended by a few SS guards, some servants and aides, and a morphine-addicted doctor, a notorious quack who was said to be injecting der Chef with drugs that had him shaking as if he had the DTs. The course of the war was being waged according to Hitler's horoscope, which Dr. Göbbels, his propaganda minister, took from the stars. Hitler was linked to his generals at Zossen, twenty miles away, by only a switchboard, a radio, and a radio-telephone. He was directing the OKW, the Armed Forces High Command, with a parody of the efficient, high-tech electronic network that had once spun orders across conquered Europe.

War reduced to war games.

Fantasy had usurped reality down in Hitler's bunker. A fascination with maps had always been the führer's hallmark. The map rooms in his *Führerhauptquartiers*—there had been thirteen FHQ command posts for waging war—were where he had once moved tiny paper flags around a chart table to deploy real Panzer divisions in France or along the Volga and around the Black Sea. Rumor had it that the military briefings still went on, with each day weighed down by more Nazi defeats, a lurid litany that tracked the shrinking of the Reich.

Dresden, Cologne, Bonn … all rubble and ruin.

Mannheim, Frankfurt, Danzig … wiped off the map.

Hitler's chart table had a jigsaw of local maps put together to form a large-scale coordinate grid of the Third Reich. Hard-bitten front-line veterans summoned from surface battlefields to brief the führer on losses arrived with the dust, blood, and grime of reality on their field gray uniforms. In astonishment, they stood and watched as their neurotic, paranoid leader maneuvered army divisions that no longer existed into territory that had been captured by the Allies. He demanded that some fallen city be defended to the end, that some phantom battalion not yield an inch, and that hordes of ghosts launch blitzkriegs that would never take place to turn the tide of this war back to victory. Since Hitler saw Nazi traitors as the root cause of military defeats, the generals who went down to the bunker played self-defense war games, too. As each German city fell, it vanished from the table. "Situation adjustments"—discarding that local map from the jigsaw grid—erased reality from the fantasy that der Chef was spinning at the center of his web.

But the hooks were real.

Meat hooks like those at Plötzensee prison.

Meat hooks cemented into a wall at 8 Prinz Albrechtstrasse, down in the cellar at Gestapo HQ.

Meat hooks, rumor had it, that didn't use nooses, but instead were spiked directly into the necks of traitors.

Traitors, real and imagined.

As SS-General Ernst Streicher entered the bunker and strode with his sons along the dining passage, he wondered yet again, Why has Hitler summoned me?

Had the treason that Streicher had recently hatched somehow been exposed?

Was one of the meat hooks waiting for him?

Underworld

Mosquito Creek came rushing down from the confining Vs
of the North Shore Mountains like a convict on the run.
Since long before human feet first crossed the land bridge to
North America, the creek had been gouging a gully toward
the natural harbor at Inspector Zinc Chandler's back, and its
depth narrowed his view of the peaks that soared from both
banks farther upstream. Pacific storms blowing in over
millennia had filled this canyon with rainforest green.

It wasn't raining this morning.

It was a fine spring day.

Of all the months of the year, May was Chandler's
favorite. What more could a man ask of nature than a stroll
like this? Having parked his car on Fell Avenue, beside
Mosquito Creek Park—his just one of a long line of police
cruisers at the curb—he had descended the steep path to
the Trans-Canada Trail, the western leg of an 11,233-mile
coast-to-coast-to-coast trek. Veering left, the Mountie
followed the rapids like a salmon leaping upstream to spawn.

Zippity-do-da …

It was that kind of plenty-of-sunshine hike.

The fish habitat was protected by a rustic wooden fence,
which was discreetly backed by wire mesh to keep dogs out
of the creek. Water dappled with whitecaps foamed over

algoid rocks. Songbirds warbled in the trees that flanked the winding path: cedars, firs, and alders with moss on the north side of their trunks. Sunbeams streaked through saplings to checker a forest floor carpeted with fresh fern fronds and last year's leaves. A birdhouse up one tree was an anomaly.

So was the cop standing in the pathway.

Having recently returned from five weeks in the South Seas, Zinc Chandler of Special X—the Special External Section of the RCMP—was sporting a tropical tan around his dark sunglasses. The tan clashed with both the pale scar left by a knife wound along his jaw line and the metallic tint of his hair, the color, since birth, that had given him his name. His jacket was slung over one shoulder of his muscular frame, exposing both his Smith & Wesson 9 mm pistol and the bison-head regimental badge clipped at his waist.

"Chandler. Special X," he declared.

The uniformed cop blocking the path let him through. "You'll find Sergeant Winter under the overpass. Hug the creek and you'll see a gap in the fence."

The hum of the city had retreated with his descent into the gully, and from there to here, it hadn't been able to compete with the gurgling gush of the rapids. But now the hum returned, stronger with each step he took along the banked stream, until he caught sight of the overhead span through the curtain of creek-side saplings.

Foom … foom …

The Trans-Canada Highway cut across the face of the North Shore Mountains on its way to a screeching halt a few miles to the west, where the Pacific Ocean lapped into Horseshoe Bay. The original bridge across this creek and the Trans-Canada Trail had been widened not too long ago with a second span. Now for every *foom* of the cars whizzing by, disturbing the peace of nature, there was twice the noise—*foom, foom*—to pollute tranquillity.

Ahead, the path zigged right toward the water, and the rustic fence ceased for several yards. The gap between the creek and the first pickup post where the fenced path zagged inland around the bridge supports was just wide enough for Chandler to sidle through. Ducking into the foliage, he detoured up the path of contamination, the forensic route cleared by the Ident techs.

One minute, the Mountie had the sun on his back.

The next minute, he was in the chill of the underworld.

CONCRETE Ts supported one span of the double overpass. Vertical pillars met the horizontal beam of a highway trestle. The parallel span to the north was held up by a concrete arch. Chandler felt as if he was gazing out through the mouth of a sewer.

The waste of the over-world collected down here. The dual spans were no more than a few feet apart, but that left enough room for the garbage of a throwaway culture to slip through. Packaging from fast-food joints and discarded candy wrappers had wafted down from passing cars like confetti at a wedding, or had been flushed down the open corrugated culverts during rainstorms. Other junk had come in by land: empty cases of beer and rusty shopping carts, spray-paint cans left by graffiti artists, a wayward motorcycle helmet. The artists had festooned the concrete pillars with colorful tags, most of them street names in a bubble-like mural. The black helmet, discarded on the garbage-strewn earth, was also a gilded work of art. Golden jaws with sharp fangs decorated the front, a hand with an upright middle finger the side. And on the back, the words "Go fuck yourself" in what could pass for Old English script.

Poetry in motion, Chandler thought.

The cop coming toward him on the path of contamination seemed as tall as Zinc, just over six feet. Like Zinc, he was athletically built, but he was slimmer than the inspector. Basketball, not football or hockey, would be his game. Sandy-haired and cobalt-eyed, he wore the dull plainclothes of GIS, the General Investigation Section of North Van Detachment. The Mountie carried a plastic evidence pouch in one hand and held the other out to shake as he neared Chandler. Behind him, where the arch of the upstream span met the bank, a saddle of Horsemen worked around a body that had been staked to the earth.

"Sergeant Winter, I presume?"

The cops knew of each other. Several of Winter's case reports had crossed Chandler's desk.

"Nice tan."

"Just back from the South Pacific."

"On account of me? Hope my call didn't interrupt your vacation," Winter kidded.

"Planes don't fly that fast. Thankfully, you pulled me away from a pile of paperwork."

"Here's another sheet to add to the pile," the sergeant said, passing Chandler the see-through pouch.

The inspector held the crumpled note up in front of his eyes. It had been torn off the corner of a larger sheet of paper. Scrawled on the scrap was "Zinc Chandler" and his home address on Kitsilano Point, across the harbor.

"What's that doing in the pocket of a cannibal, Inspector?"

"*Alleged* cannibal," Zinc said dryly.

ACROSS THE CREEK and up the bank on the opposite side of the water, sunlight flashed off the telephoto lens of a top-end digital camera. The glint came from the bushes just to the right of the overhead spans, at the point where the multi-lane highway left the mountain slope to bridge across Mosquito Creek's gully.

"Did you get it?" the reporter asked.

The photographer nodded.

"Both the patch and the stake through the other eye?"

"If you don't believe me," the cameraman said, "see for yourself." He held out the Nikon and pressed the monitor button to display the digital images on the camera's LCD screen. The last three shots, taken down through the forest of concrete pillars, had caught in sufficient detail the head impaled by a stake.

"Good," said Jantzen. "The cops on the path—"

He had to pause while a car passed on the nearby off-ramp, its stereo so loud that it drowned out the noise of the never-ending traffic on the Trans-Canada Highway. Fittingly, the tune that blared was AC/DC's "Highway to Hell."

"The cops on the path to the body are Inspector Zinc Chandler and Sergeant Dane Winter," the crime reporter continued as again he focused his binoculars on the under-world. "Shoot some of them with the stiff—hey, they're moving across to it—then let's stake out the cars on Fell and catch 'em coming up."

"RECOGNIZE HIM?" Winter asked, raising his voice to counter the rumble of traffic overhead.

"Yeah," said Chandler, squatting beside the body at the foot of the arch. "I saw him yesterday at Colony Farm. Just before they sprung him from the mental hospital."

"You went there to see him?"

"No, to question the Ripper. The Ripper's a psycho who wants me dead for locking him up in the nuthouse. He recently tried to orchestrate a hit from inside the psych ward by talking a visitor into stalking me to the South Pacific."

"Obviously he failed."

"But not for want of trying. I spent the next month relaxing, and when I got back, I went out to face the Ripper at Colony Farm. He refused to meet me, but I caught sight of him in the exercise yard with this guy, who I hadn't seen before. The nursing staff called him the Congo Man because of some calypso tune."

"What were they doing?"

"Fooling around with a deck of tarot cards. The Ripper's obsessed with the Tarot. He was doing a reading. The Congo Man left when it was time for his release."

"Anything else?"

"Yeah," said Chandler. "The Ripper glimpsed me as he went back to the ward. Grinning like the maniac he is, he ran a finger across his throat."

"Sounds like the Ripper may have enlisted this Congo Man to finish what the earlier killer failed to do."

The inspector nodded. "That would explain why my home address was in the dead guy's pocket. And I'm pretty sure this handwriting is the Ripper's."

"Not very cautious."

"He doesn't have to be. The Ripper is about as psychotic as a man can be. He's already in the psych ward. There's nothing worse the law can do to him. He wants me dead and won't stop until one of his psycho henchmen succeeds."

"Well, you're safe from *this* guy."

"That's for sure."

"So who killed the Congo Man?" Winter asked.

THERE WAS NO NEED for either cop to fill the other in on the background of the Congo Man. *The Vancouver Times* had been reporting on the case for the past few days. In fact, that morning's edition had run a front-page story under the banner "Alleged Cannibal Freed by Appeal Court." The story was by Cort Jantzen.

VANCOUVER—A Liberian refugee alleged to be the cannibal killer of a six-year-old girl was released from custody yesterday by order of the B.C. Court of Appeal. The court ruled there had been insufficient evidence produced at trial to support his detainment in the Forensic Psychiatric Hospital at Colony Farm....

The trial had been a *cause célèbre* because of the lurid details of the crime. The victim was a white schoolgirl who'd been snatched off the street; the accused was a black refugee from war-torn Africa. The girl's body was found cooking in a canning pot under a bridge where down-and-outs—like the refugee—often slept in the rough. The discovery had conjured up nineteenth-century cartoons depicting pale explorers bubbling in black cannibal pots.

As near as the immigration department could tell, Marcus Cole—the Congo Man—was from Liberia, an African nation founded in 1822 as a haven for freed American slaves. He had arrived in Canada with just the clothes on his back, claiming to be a refugee from the Liberian civil war.

The horrors of that war were familiar to those who watched the news. From 1989 to 1997, seven warlords had used every barbaric tool they could think of—including sorcery, blood-drinking, and cannibalism—to terrify their rivals and seize control of the country. Ragtag armies of teenage killers, stoned on drugs and alcohol, had fought the war with red scarves, dark glasses, and AK-47s. The Poro was a bush school where elders initiated these soldiers into the ancient rites of the secret Leopard Societies. A Leopard Man's *borfimor* was a talisman that powered his virility once it was anointed with human fat that had been boiled down in a pot. The "bush devil" had to be fed, so each initiate also ate human meat from the same pot to assimilate the power of those slain and cooked.

The article went on:

Marcus Cole wasn't a refugee, the prosecutor alleged. He was a cannibal killer fleeing from the outcome of that war. By 1997, Charles Taylor had become the strongman in Liberia. It's said that he tortured, dismembered, and cannibalized enemy captives in the presidential palace at Monrovia....

The trial had been a minefield of evidentiary bombs. Marcus Cole was one of the homeless sleeping under the bridge, but no credible testimony linked him to the cannibal pot. The testimony there was came from a camp of drunken bums, two of whom had past convictions for sexual perversions. Not only had Cole refused to confess to the police, but he'd refused to speak to pretrial psychiatrists as well. The shrinks were left to psych him from the details of the crime, a murder that the Crown could barely pin on him.

So incensed was the trial judge by the nature of the case that she had flouted the law to put the Congo Man away, shipping him off to the psych ward at Colony Farm to get his head shrunk. The appeal court, however, was less cavalier, and yesterday had overturned the original verdict and ordered that the Forensic Psychiatric Hospital turn Marcus Cole loose.

On hearing the appeal court quash the trial verdict, the outraged father of the murdered girl stormed from the law courts building. "If the law won't give us justice," he swore, "I'll hunt that African monster down and kill him myself...."

"YOU LOOK HEALTHY," said the pathologist, Dr. Gillian Macbeth. She, too, seemed the epitome of wellness and youth, thanks to the best rejuvenation money can buy. She wore the same white hood, jumpsuit, and foot coverings as the other forensic techs combing the area around the body.

"He just returned from the South Seas," Winter explained.

"I know," said Macbeth.

The sergeant caught an exchange of looks between the pathologist and the inspector that made him wonder if any hanky-panky was going on. In fact, Gill Macbeth was dating Chandler's boss, Chief Superintendent Robert DeClercq. In addition to being the Special External Section of the Mounties—the cops responsible for investigating crimes with links beyond Canada's borders—the squad did double duty as the Horsemen's psycho-hunting unit. Consequently, at lots of crime scenes in the past, Gill and Zinc had stood together over bodies on the ground.

"Something different," Chandler said.

"I don't get many stakings. Vampires are foreign to this part of the world."

"Missed the heart by a mile."

"Don't touch the stake," cautioned Macbeth. "There's blood up on the handle."

The pathologist had moved back to let the inspector squat near the body. Crouched on the balls of his feet, Chandler felt the earth vibrate as heavy rigs crossed the overhead span. The Congo Man was sprawled face up on the bank, with his crown toward the arch support and his soles toward the creek. With arms as big as other men's legs, a chest the size of King Kong's, and a skull that seemed to reduce a bowling ball to the girth of a pea, he was a giant of muscular power. Tussling with him, Chandler had thought yesterday at Colony Farm, would be like having Tyson going for your ear.

"Cause of death?" he asked Macbeth.

"His skull was caved in with a blunt instrument just before he was spiked through the eye. See how splinters of the zygomatic arch sink into the socket around the stake? Someone approached him with a weapon in hand, clubbed him across the side of the head, shattering his skull, then rammed the stake into his eye after he hit the ground."

"Dead either way?"

"Uh-huh. He was probably in his death throes when he was spiked to the earth."

"What sort of blunt instrument?"

"It could be the stake. The handle's made of wood, but the lower shaft is metal."

"Like the head of a spear?"

"It's about the length of a walking stick. The killer would seem to be hiking as he approached, then suddenly the walking stick would turn into a baseball bat. A whack across the side of the head and down would go the giant. Plunging the tip into his eye socket would spike him to the ground."

"Wicked."

"And effective. Three tools in one."

"The killer's lucky the bat didn't break."

"But unlucky if the blow cracked loose this splinter." Gill pointed to a sliver of wood still attached to the handle. "See the blood on the tip? That could be from the killer. Even wearing gloves, he might've pricked his hand as he drove the stake through the skull. Perhaps he didn't notice at the time."

The Congo Man wore a black patch over his other eye. He looked like a pirate who had seen his last doubloon.

"Check under the patch?"

"The eyeball is missing. Probably lost it in the Liberian civil war," said Gill.

"Anything else?"

"Examine his forehead, Zinc. You'll find a possible motive hidden in the blood."

The Congo Man's face was a mess of gore. Blood had bubbled out of the spiked socket like an erupting volcano. The red lava had begun to clot on his black skin. Moving in for a closer look, the inspector breathed in the sweat of insanity wafting up off the cadaver. Then he discerned the symbol that had been carved into the forehead of the African refugee, above and equidistant to the pirate patch and the vertical stake.

The symbol, covered with blood, was instantly recognizable:

"Motive?" Chandler asked, glancing up at Winter.

"Hate crime? Possibly. Lots of hate around. Sikh stomped to death by skinheads outside his temple. Jewish graveyards desecrated. Refugees waylaid. Cole might have been sleeping rough under these spans when a neo-Nazi gang chanced along."

"Or?"

"Or the swastika might be a red herring. Someone killed him for a personal motive and masked it as a hate crime."

"To avenge the dead girl?"

"Perhaps," said Winter. "Or it could be a hit gone wrong. The Ripper enlisted the Congo Man to kill you. Maybe

Cole teamed up with a partner, and they had a falling-out."

"Who found the body?"

"A jogger with a wayward dog. He's clean."

"That's several leads. It's your case, Sergeant. Where do you plan to start?"

"Feel like a drive?"

"Where to?" asked Chandler.

"Inland to Colony Farm."

CORT JANTZEN, the crime reporter for *The Vancouver Times,* waylaid them as they crested the path to their cars.

"Is it true that the vic is the cannibal killer who got released yesterday because of a foul-up by the courts?"

"I wouldn't put it that way," Winter replied.

"Is the vic Marcus Cole?"

"Yes," responded Chandler.

"Do you suspect that an outraged relative of the cannibalized girl took justice into his own hands?"

"The investigation is ongoing. No comment."

"A vigilante?"

"No comment," echoed Chandler.

"The jogger who found the body says it was nailed to the bank by a stake that had been rammed through the head. Do you have any reason to suspect it's a hate crime?"

"We have inquiries to make," said Winter. "Media Relations will issue a press release."

They left the reporter scribbling empty words in his notebook. For decades, the Mounties had used "key-fact hold-back" evidence as a sneaky trip-up tool. Key facts known only to the primary investigators and those involved in an offense were held back from the media as a means to weed out false confessions and expose those with *inside* knowledge of the crime. In this age of the Internet and people willing to say and do anything for their fifteen minutes of fame, "key-fact hold-back" evidence was even more crucial.

Cort Jantzen had been closing in on the key fact in the Congo Man killing when the cops had ducked away. They didn't want him to catch them on record with a lie.

The key fact was the Nazi swastika that had been carved like a Cyclops eye into the cannibal's forehead.

Blind Alley

PORT COQUITLAM

The traffic out here is a nightmare. Geography creates it. Vancouver sits at the mouth of a river that cuts west to the ocean through a north–south range of mountains. Exacerbating an already tight situation, the Pacific balloons inland, creating a major harbor. For physical setting, there are only six great cities in this world, and Vancouverites populate one of them. Cram a million outdoorsy Lotuslanders onto a few geographically bottlenecked arteries and the bumper-to-bumper gridlock is enough to enrage even the most laid-back tree hugger.

"Man," said Winter, banging his palms against the steering wheel as if that would make the car move faster, "I could live two lives with the time I waste on this highway."

"Try yoga," said Chandler soothingly.

"If this keeps up, I'll try my nine-mil instead."

"Cars with dead drivers. Somehow I doubt that will help."

From the North Shore murder scene, they had U-turned south on Fell Avenue to bridge Mosquito Creek by the lower road, before angling back up to the Trans-Canada Highway. Cutting east across the mountain slopes and fording the harbor on the Ironworkers' Memorial Bridge— the building of which had cost twenty-five lives in four accidents, inspiring the 1962 hit "Steel Men" by Jimmie Dean—had put them onto this snail trail up the Fraser

Valley. Cars inched forward on this highway toward urban sprawl. Finally, just before another bridge stepped across the mighty Fraser River, they branched off onto the old Lougheed Highway, which ran parallel to the freeway. Ahead, in the crook where the meandering Coquitlam River snaked south to empty into the headwaters of the Fraser Delta, stretched the marshy flatlands of Colony Farm.

"Your family name's Winter?" said Chandler. "Are you one of the Air Division Winters?"

"My dad and my granddad. Not me," Dane replied.

"That must have been hard on you. Losing your parents and your grandmother in a single crash."

"I was young. Somehow that cushioned the blow. It was worse for my granddad. He lost his wife, his only child, and his daughter-in-law in the blink of an eye. All he had left was me."

"Still living?"

"No, he died on Wednesday. Tomorrow morning, the undertaker will deliver his ashes to me."

"Sorry to hear."

"In the end, it was a blessing. Pancreatic cancer is an ugly route to go."

"I loathe hospitals."

"So did my granddad. Until just before the end, he wasted away in the house he purchased fifty years ago."

"Sounds expensive."

"It was," replied Dane. "I had to create a mini hospital at home for him. Now I'm in the process of cleaning it out. I feel like I'm working an archeological dig. All those layers of family history. Last night, I came across his pilot's flying log from the war. He flew forty-seven bombing missions over Nazi Europe and North Africa. Ironic, huh? The odds of his surviving the war shrunk to about two out of a hundred. The Nazis couldn't get him, and he came back.

Then Mother Nature got his family on a *civilian* flight."

"Hit the Razorback, right?"

"Yeah. Up the valley. Several miles east of here. Strange, but I've never been up to the Mountain. I was too young for the memorial service at the time of the crash, and then … well, it's like I have a psychological aversion to the place."

"Perhaps one day?"

"Oh, it's gonna happen. Sooner, not later," said Dane. "Depending on the weather and the avalanche warning. Within a day or two, I have a date with the Mountain."

IT USED TO BE that you would turn south toward the Fraser River off the Lougheed Highway onto Colony Farm Road to drive the eeriest mile on the West Coast down to the Riverside Unit for the criminally insane. Back then, the hills surrounding the murky marsh were thick with primal woods, and the right side of the road was overhung by a line of towering elms. Colony Farm dated back to the era when masturbation was thought to be one of the four causes of insanity, and the haunted-house asylum at the end of that postcard-perfect byway seemed fit for the likes of Karloff and Lugosi. In fact, mad scientists did once work for Riverside, lobotomizing patients with razor-sharp scalpels and unscrambling fried brains with jolts of electricity. One look at that Gothic madhouse, with its cross-hatched bars on triple tiers of windows along both wings and black crows perched on the eaves of its flat roof, and you could imagine the screams of those long-ago inmates.

The flip side of that historical coin was Colony Farm today. Gone was the wooded landscape around the marsh flats; now god-awful monster houses blighted the denuded hills. Root rot from neglecting the drainage had toppled most of the elms, so swaths of sunlight played across the roof of the cop car as it closed in on the vacant riverside lot that once had housed the decrepit asylum. The replacement for that archaic booby hatch was the $60-million Forensic Psychiatric Hospital. Just to the right of the demolished institution spread a spacious lot where Winter parked the car.

"It looks like a country club," he said.

"That's the idea."

"Fancy a round of golf?"

The gate was forged from vertical bars that were strengthened with a bull's-eye circle. The lawns beyond were as manicured as putting greens. From the hub of a central hall, where the patients attended school and chapel, a ring of spoke-like paths radiated out to the patient residences. The structures were named Fir, Cottonwood, Dogwood, Birch, and so on. The administration building—Golden Willow— flanked the gate. Opposite it, on the right side, sat the stronghold of Central Control, beyond which was hidden Ashworth House, where the high-risk psychos were caged.

Psychos like the Ripper.

And until yesterday, the Congo Man.

"Back so soon?" the security guard asked Chandler.

"Unfinished business."

The inspector and Winter signed the visitors' log and handed in their guns.

The nurse who came to fetch them was Rudi Lucke. Meticulous, wiry, fine-boned, and in his mid-forties, Rudi had given the Congo Man his nickname. Years ago, at Carnival in the Caribbean, "Congo Man"—the calypso tune by Mighty Sparrow—had caught Rudi's ear. Since the lyrics about never eating white meat seemed to fit the crime that had sent the Liberian refugee to FPH, Congo Man was the ideal sobriquet for Marcus Cole.

Yesterday, Rudi had informed Chandler about the Ripper's refusal to see him, just before pointing out the conspiratorial meeting between those psychos in the yard. Today, from the look in Rudi's eye, Chandler knew the nurse suspected why the Mounties were here.

"The Ripper?" Rudi inquired.

"Yes," said Zinc.

"His body is in his room. Don't know about his mind."

Buzzing the key reader with his fob—the personal electronic pass that registered who opened which door at what time in Central Control—Rudi led the cops through a security door that led to an interview room. The hall, with its cinder-block walls and window slats instead of bars, seemed common enough. But those blocks encased a steel grating that turned the hall into a cage. The "glass" was really Lexan, an unbreakable polycarbonate resin, and rotating rods were hidden within the slats to foil the bite of hacksaw blades. The pen in Rudi's pocket was an alarm. Triggering it would bounce a beam off the peach walls and peach floor with its blue stepping-stone squares to a sensor on the ceiling that would summon the entire staff of Ashworth House within thirty seconds.

You couldn't be too careful with psychos like the Ripper.

The interview room, eight feet by ten, was starkly furnished with a table and two chairs. The sterile box had no art or atmosphere. The door didn't lock.

"He might not see you," Rudi said.

"Bring him anyway," replied the inspector.

FOR RUDI, it was the eyes.

It bothered him that he judged people by a physical characteristic, but the eyes were different, weren't they? The windows of the soul? Eyes weren't like noses, cheekbones, and lips: racial characteristics. Eyes—the eyeballs, at least—were more than that. "If thine eye offend thee, pluck it out ..."

But still he felt guilty.

His guilt, he suspected, went back to something his grandfather used to say about reading the eyes of the Nazis in order to stay alive in the camp. Lucke was a name with centuries of Jewish history in Prague, so when the Aryans occupied Czechoslovakia during the war, "Good Lucke," the old man said bitterly, "won me a trip to Terezin."

Terezin, a concentration camp north of Prague, had been established in a fortress from the eighteenth century. During the trip there, the Gestapo had stopped the truck convoy of political and Jewish prisoners on an old stone bridge across the Vltava River. They selected five men from each transport group and had them line up along the plunge to the water. Next, they looped a double noose around the men's necks, joining the five chosen Jewish prisoners to the five non-Jewish political prisoners, who were then shot in the head. As each dead man tumbled toward the river below, the still-living Jew was yanked off the bridge and into the water like jettisoned cargo weighed down by a human anchor.

"We don't waste bullets on Jews," the SS commandant warned the convoy prisoners.

To this day, Rudi couldn't glance over the side of a bridge without momentarily glimpsing phantom eyes staring up from the depths of the water.

Once at Terezin, however, the SS had no qualms about wasting bullets. Prisoners who tried to escape were stoned to death in the courtyard, and others were locked together a hundred at a time without food and water in a cramped room where the SS could watch them die. But past the quarters where the commandant and the ranking guards resided was a target range. There, Jews were forced to run from one side of the yard to the other so the SS could enjoy shooting practice.

"You can spot a Nazi by his eyes," Rudi's grandfather maintained. "I survived the camp because I learned to read their eyes. Nazis escaped after the war and are hiding around the world. Study their eyes, Rudi, so that you can spot them too."

On Saturdays, it was Rudi's chore to accompany the old man to the library. He would lean on the boy and hobble along the street with his cane. Inside, they would find a book on the Third Reich and sit together at a reading table to study the eyes. Hitler's eyes, flashing as he shrieked fiery oration. Himmler's eyes, as cold as ice behind his wire-rim glasses. Göring's eyes, in that piggy face. Eichmann's eyes, in Israel, on trial in the glass booth. Streicher's eyes, in one of the few photographs of him to survive the war.

One day, they had shared their table with a blond man who was also reading a photographic book on the Second World War. "What they did to us was awful," said Rudi's grandfather, rolling up his sleeve to expose the number tattooed on his forearm, "and pictures cannot capture the torment we endured." Frowning, the stranger set his book down on the table, and Rudi saw the photo that he had been perusing. It was of a Nazi with a weird measuring device, some sort of calipers he was applying to the face of a Jew to prove him "subhuman." Then Rudi noticed the blond man's eyes. He wasn't looking at the tattoo on his grandfather's arm. He was staring intently at the old man's nose.

Rudi felt suddenly guilty.

For staring as unreasonably at the stranger's eyes.

Decades had passed since then, but Rudi's ocular compulsion had not. Some days he was convinced that was why he had sought this job as a psychiatric nurse in Ashworth House. The link went back to the trial of the Manson Family in 1970, when Charles Manson and three female disciples, Susan Atkins, Patricia Krenwinkel, and

Leslie Van Houten, had carved swastikas into their foreheads as they prepared to face the jury judging them on multiple counts of murder. "I have X'd myself from your world," that hypnotic guru had declared. Rudi had stared, transfixed, at newspaper photographs of Manson's maniacal eyes looking out from under the swastika he'd gouged into the flesh above his nose.

The killer had Nazi eyes.

The eyes of those in Ashworth House were haunted by psychosis, and none were more unfathomable than those of the psycho in room A2-13. Before he entered the Ripper's realm in the high-security ward, off a hall that was constantly monitored by watchers in the fortified nursing station at one end, Rudi peeked in through the oblong judas window in the blue door. Though the ward was sealed, the door wasn't locked. The Forensic Psychiatric Hospital wasn't an asylum, and its patients were free to leave their rooms to go to the toilet, the dining room, the TV room, the smoking room, and the quiet room for reading. The Ripper, however, rarely left his realm, except to travel.

To time-travel back to London.

To 1888.

Five inches wide and three feet tall, the judas window was a slit in the door. Positioned near the handle, it gave Rudi an overall view of the room, except for the corner by the hinges. A bed with a brick headboard was bolted to the left-hand wall. The Ripper lay stretched out on it with his feet in the far corner. Scrawled on the wall beside his head were Einstein's theory of relativity and jottings from Hawking's *Brief History of Time*. The notes segued into a jumble of occult symbols that spiraled like a time tunnel from the Ripper's insane mind across the opposite wall, to end in a mishmash of morgue photos and maps on the right-hand wall. The big map was of the East End of London in

1888. Marked on it, and detailed by smaller maps, were the five spots where the notorious Jack the Ripper had struck. Surrounding them were morgue photos of his victims, slashed to ribbons, disemboweled, and relieved of various organs. And ringed around all that, to represent the mouth of the time tunnel, was a deck of occult tarot cards.

Rudi opened the door.

The Ripper didn't move.

He must be off time-traveling through the wormholes bored into his diseased brain, thought the nurse.

"There's news," Rudi announced.

The Ripper didn't stir.

"Marcus Cole," he suggested.

That did the trick.

The Ripper had not been told that the Congo Man was dead. Rudi sensed that something had brewed in the yard yesterday, so if the Ripper had tried to have the Mountie who put him here killed in the South Pacific—as the hospital's rumor mill maintained—then wasn't it likely that the Ripper would try again?

"What news?" the psycho asked.

"Come see," said the nurse.

THE TWO MEN coming down the hall were a study in contrasts. The athletic nurse was about as fit as a featherweight. Rudi sported his street clothes—plain, short-sleeved shirt, jeans, and loafers—with all the panache of a runway model. His bland attire was dictated by a strict dress code: no ties or anything else that might be seized, cinched, or converted into a noose; no logos or T-shirt prints that might set off the unstable.

The Ripper, too, wore unremarkable clothes. His jogging suit was standard issue for Ash 2 patients: a navy blue sweatshirt over matching sweatpants, with a pair of Velcro runners.

But so anorexic and emaciated was the phantom cannibal that he resembled the walking skeletons who were freed from Nazi concentration camps at the close of the war. Rudi's granddad had shown him in *Life* magazine photos snapped by army cameramen as Allied troops were pressing east into the Third Reich. Death-camp images from Nordhausen, Gardelegen, and other hellholes—showing gaunt slaves worked almost to death in secret tunnels that SS-General Ernst Streicher had bored into the Harz Mountains to protect Hitler's *Vergeltungswaffe* from the RAF—were the first to shock the Allied nations. The way the baggy blue jogging suit hung on the patient's skin-and-bones frame reminded Rudi of those starved wretches.

As they paused outside the door to the interview room in which the cops were waiting, Lucke's obsessive-compulsive fixation on abnormal psychology made him stare deep into the black holes that were the windows to the Ripper's soul, and for a moment he glimpsed a symbol that sent a chill down his spine.

Both pupils had blown their irises and dilated into fathomless tunnels to a hellish dimension. So intensely had the Ripper sunk into his internal weirdness that the skin of his fleshless face seemed to have been sucked into his skull, crinkling and creasing into the squint of all squints. If what he grasped in his bony fingers was all he would eat, it was no wonder the psycho's body was cannibalizing itself for carbs. As he gnawed at the imaginary organ meat he'd harvested during his most recent trip back to 1888, he smacked his lips with relish and sucked the non-existent juice out of the phantom flesh that fed his soul.

"What do you *see*?" the Ripper snarled.

Startled, Rudi blinked.

What he saw—in the same way that he saw ghostly eyes gazing up from rivers—was a swastika that had been formed by the squinty furrows between the psychotic's eyes.

"What do you see?" the Ripper shrieked, lunging at Rudi with his long-nailed claws.

What Rudi saw—or thought he saw—was the last thing he would ever see.

THERE ARE SCREAMS, and there are *screams!* And Rudi Lucke's was one of those *screams!*

A scream to wake the dead.

Chandler, being the cop nearer the door, was first to rush into the hall. A second or two behind him, Winter was relegated to the role of backup. Never having seen the Ripper in the flesh—or lack of flesh, more aptly—he might as well have burst in on the filming of a horror movie. A wiry man was being pinned to the floor by what Dane would have described as a ghoul. An animate skeleton of a creature in humanoid form loomed over its thrashing prey, its bony arms outstretched so that it could drive the overgrown nails of its knob-knuckled index fingers deep into the eye sockets.

"What do you see?" the ghoul repeated like a graveyard refrain an instant before Inspector Chandler locked that skull-face into the crook of one muscular arm and wrenched it around like the head of the possessed girl in *The Exorcist.*

Snap!

Crack!

Pop!

The ghoul dropped as limp as a doll.

A foul, metallic smell like rancid goat cheese permeated the hall—the same chemical sweat of insanity that earlier had oozed off the corpse of the Congo Man—and Winter realized that this corridor was now a blind alley in his investigation.

Help arrived as Chandler hauled the ghoul off the nurse. The staff worked frantically to try to save Rudi's life. Had the inspector not done what he did, the nurse wouldn't have had a chance, so Winter knew he would have no difficulty justifying this kill to all the investigators who would have to be called in.

"Problem solved," Chandler said in a voice that Dane could barely hear.

Which problem? the sergeant wondered.

Werewolf

Not every man gets to meet God on this side of the grave. Fifteen-year-old Fritz Streicher would hardly have qualified as a man if this were peacetime, but with Hitler embroiled in an all-out, total-war struggle for the survival of his Reich, both sons of SS-General Ernst Streicher had bypassed their teenage years. German boys were dying like men on the western front, and they stood ready to battle the Russians at the gates of Berlin. Fritz, like all the young Germans who had joined the Jungvolk at age ten, had sworn a lifelong oath on the Blutfahne—the Reich's Blood Banner—a flag soaked in the gore of the Nazi martyrs who'd been killed in the failed Beer Hall Putsch of 1923: "In the presence of this Blood Banner, which represents our führer, I swear to devote all my energy and my strength to the savior of our Fatherland, Adolf Hitler. I am willing and ready to give up my life for him, so help me God!"

God in heaven.

God on earth.

Combined in one man.

"Heil Hitler!"

Fritz Streicher's idol was Kurt Meyer, the buccaneering daredevil who had led the 12th SS-Panzer Hitlerjugend Division—the so-called baby milk division—on D-Day.

"Panzermeyer" was everything that Fritz yearned to be. The youngest divisional commander in the Reich's armed forces, that SS-Standartenführer was a Hitler Youth veteran of hell-raising tank battles in Poland, Greece, and Russia, where his unorthodox combat style had spearheaded him deep inside enemy lines. His followers—their imaginations filled since childhood with tales of valor, triumph, and sacrifice for führer and Fatherland—were all fanatical furies from the Hitlerjugend. The ferocity of their fighting had spawned the myth of the Hitler Youth: how young Nazis blitzkrieged as if possessed by that battle madness the Vikings called *beserkr*.

Fritz's favorite fantasy cast him in the role of Kurt Meyer after D-Day in Normandy. Commanding the Hitlerjugend, Panzerfritz fought the Canadians, led by that bogus British hero Montgomery of El Alamein, at the Battle for Caen. Monty and his Desert Rats—a fitting name, Fritz thought, for rats the British were—would never have forced the Desert Fox to retreat in North Africa had the Yanks not armed the Eighth Army with Sherman tanks, and had Rommel's Afrika Korps not suffered rot in its ranks from swarthy Italian cowards. Fritz, however, gave Monty a cut with German steel at Caen, for that's what the führer demanded from his Hitler Youth: "Be as slim and slender as greyhounds, as tough as leather, and as hard as Krupp steel."

Bwam! Bwam! Bwam! …

In his mind, Fritz summarily executed twenty Canadian prisoners of war at Abbey Ardenne, like they said Panzermeyer had, dispatching each with the Walther PPK holstered on his hip.

A Walther identical to the one his father wore today.

Like Panzermeyer had, Fritz pitched his Hitlerjugend division of seventeen- and eighteen-year-olds into a blazing tank battle with Monty's Canadians. As night fell, the cannon-fire raged on, and infantrymen shot each other at point-blank range or chased the enemy down into cellars to bayonet hand-to-hand. For thirty-three days, Fritz kept the smug victor of El Alamein from taking Caen. Monty was no match for a titan of Krupp steel with the Iron Cross first and second classes glinting on his heart and the Knight's Cross at his throat.

A cross identical to the one his father wore today.

Hitler Youth not old enough for the 12th SS-Panzer, those who had yet to reach seventeen, were destined for the Volkssturm. Boys fourteen and older—though Fritz had seen some as young as eight—joined men over sixty and soldiers just out of hospital to form the People's Militia, a last-ditch home guard to defend the Fatherland. Had they both not been the sons of an SS general, Fritz and Hans Streicher might have attacked the U.S. 9th Armored Division as it crossed the Rhine over the bridge at Remagen. A horde of Volkssturm Hitler Youth had hurled themselves at the rumbling tanks of the Yankee invaders, forcing shocked GIs to fight for their lives against armed children young enough to be their own.

But they *were* the sons of an SS general.

So Fritz and Hans were now Werewolves.

FOR AS LONG as they could remember, the sons of Ernst Streicher had been raised to fight for Adolf Hitler. Fritz's earliest memory was of a Hitler Youth rally staged before a medieval Nuremberg castle that had once been the headquarters of the Teutonic Order of German Knights, a Christian organization of warriors who'd participated in the Crusades of the twelfth century. The SS general had taken his son along at such a young age so the boy would be keen to join the Jungvolk at ten. That would graduate him into the

Hitlerjugend at fourteen, and from there the Schutzstaffel—
the SS—would recruit him into the Black Corps.

Like father, like son.

How the soaring ancient walls of that great castle had
loomed up out of half darkness, lit only by flickering torches.
How the thunderous overture of Wagner's monumental
opera, *Der Ring des Nibelungen*—so loved by the führer—
had captured the boy's heart, overwhelming Fritz with waves
of melody and stirring orchestration, extolling the heights of
heroism and sacrifice to which the assembled Hitler Youth
must aspire. How the beat of drums and the fanfare of
trumpets had heralded the torchlight parade of boys, most
of whom had walked to the rally from Berlin and other far-
off places in a display of physical endurance. Gazing up at
that castle draped with swastika flags and Nazi icons,
young Fritz had known instinctively that Hitler was his
God, for no mere man could be as awesome as this führer.

"Here he comes!" his father shouted, lifting up his son.

Fifty thousand voices cheered in unison as if those
gathered at Nuremberg had been forged into one. From
where Fritz sat, high up on his father's shoulders, he could
see the shiny limousine as it crept into the stadium and the
small standing figure that drove the crowd into fits of
hysterical fervor. Bonfires were ignited and booming
fireworks filled the night sky. As Hitler mounted the
platform, the Reich youth leader read the Lord's Prayer.

"Adolf Hitler," he shouted, "you are our great führer!
Thy name makes the enemy tremble. Thy Third Reich
comes. Thy will alone is law upon this Earth. Let us hear
daily thy voice. Order us by thy leadership, for we will
obey to the end, and even with our lives. We praise thee.
Heil Hitler!"

The responsive roar from the ralliers almost knocked
Fritz from his perch.

"Loyalty is everything!" the youth leader yelled. "And everything is the love of Adolf Hitler!"

The throng went wild.

"The führer commands, and we follow! Everyone says, 'Yes!'"

"Yes!" clamored the mob.

From high above on the castle's towers, trumpets blared to launch the trooping of banners. As fifty thousand voices sang "Holy Germany," flags that had been flown during the Adolf Hitler March were slowly carried in. They had already been sanctified on the tomb of Frederick the Great, and now they brushed across the Blutfahne. The Hitler Youth had a martyr of their own. Twelve-year-old Herbert Norkus, stabbed to death by Communists in 1932, had died for his faith in Adolf Hitler. The flag dipped in Herbert's blood led the parade.

The führer reviewed the banners as a hymn rang out:

Let the flags fly
In the glorious sunrise
That guides us to new victories
Or into flaming death!

"Heil, my youth!" Hitler, a tiny man flanked by gigantic swastikas, greeted the rally with fire in his voice. "These are exciting days!" he declared with a flourish. "We are accustomed to battle, and no attack can defeat us!" he seethed, shaking his fist. "You, my youth, will always stand at my side!" he assured one and all. "You will raise our flags on high!" Hitler bellowed. "Our enemies may attempt to assault us once more, but our flag will always win the day!" he yelled to the heavens. His right arm shot forward, straight as an arrow, angling up to God, hand flat, palm down, in the Nazi salute.

"Sieg heil!" the Hitler Youth screamed in a frenzy, returning their führer's salute with outstretched arms of their own. SS-General Ernst Streicher seized his son by the right wrist and shot his arm out too, father and son fused in parallel fealty.

"Sieg heil!

"Sieg heil!

"Sieg heil!" Fritz shrieked, until his voice went hoarse.

THE JUNGVOLK had expanded on that early experience.

"Aryan purity," Fritz was told by his first leader, a multi-chinned fat man who taught the boys through class examples, "is the new religion of *our* Germany."

For each lesson, he ordered one of the ten-year-olds to strip off his Young Folk uniform and stand naked before the class. Then, with a ruler and calipers, he took physical measurements to ensure that no subhuman features tainted the boy's blood.

"Guido von List," the fat man said the day that Fritz was assessed. "He's the occult philosopher who proved that mystical Aryans were the sole founders of culture and civilization. We—the Nordic and Germanic people—are the most noble of all Aryans, so God's will is that we keep our bloodline clean."

The Nazi fingered Fritz's hair as if it were spun gold.

"Consider this boy, the blondest in our pack. We know that he is Aryan from the purity of his features. Hair so blond that he blinds us out in the sunlight. Eyes so blue that they match the clearest sky. And as we measure his body …"

With intimate touches, the fat man applied his ruler and calipers to Fritz's head, torso, limbs, and genitals.

"… we find appropriate shapes and dimensions."

The teacher turned and pointed to a picture on the class-room wall, a Nazi rendition of the crucifixion of Christ. The

Savior hanging on the cross had Nordic features, the portrait an icon of SS Christianity.

"Know the swarthy Jew for what he is, Young Folk. Jesus died an Aryan martyr to save the world from Jewish influence. That's why dirty Jews killed him. Now the Jews are on the rise again. So God has sent us the führer as our new messiah to rescue Germany. Worship Hitler. Keep our race pure."

To illustrate that point, the teacher had taken his Jungvolk on a field trip to a Nazi institution for Germans afflicted with physical or mental defects. Led by a limping doctor in a crisp white lab coat, Fritz's pack had toured the wards. Hunchbacks, men with club feet, people who swore vociferously for no apparent reason ... the cells were a virtual freak show of *Untermenschen*.

"Subhumans," the doctor said, "disgrace our race. An able-bodied Reich must not be crippled by their burden. The way to protect ourselves from their inferiority is to nip it in the bud. Human dignity demands that they be sterilized."

Gazing out the window at the pure white snow, ten-year-old Fritz had wondered if that was the answer to all subhumans.

To Jews ...

To Gypsies ...

To queers ...

To Slavs ...

There were so many *Untermenschen*!

THE HITLERJUGEND built on what Fritz had learned in the Jungvolk.

Wearing a different uniform—the same one he wore today—Fritz had studied the difference between Jewish and German physics. Science held a special fascination for him because of his father's role as the keeper of Nazi secrets at

Dora-Mittelbau, the concentration camp that Streicher and his sons called home.

"Jewish physics," his new instructor told him, using Hitler's term for *Untermenschen* science, "has no place in the Third Reich. It is a plot by world Jewry to suppress our German physics of quantum mechanics. In the theory of relativity, by the Jew Einstein, we see the workings of an alien mind bent on world domination and the enslavement of the German race.

"That, you must fight," snarled the instructor, glaring at the Hitler Youth through a pair of glasses so thick that his eyes resembled oversized fish in undersized glass bowls.

"Professor Johannes Stark! Honor that name. The Nobel Prize–winning head of the Nazi state organization for scientific research, Stark declared his allegiance to our führer as early as 1924. All Jewish physicists, Stark warned us, are egocentric liars interested solely in personal publicity and commercial gain. All Aryan physicists, Stark implored us, must focus on quantum mechanics aimed at technological breakthroughs that will win this war!"

Panzer had barked in agreement.

"Professor Pascual Jordan! Honor that name. The genius of theoretical physics at the University of Rostock. The founder of quantum mechanics and the *Führerprinzip*. The 'leadership principle,' Jordan has proved, is present in the molecular structure of all matter. The *Führerprinzip*! And who is your führer, boys?"

"Adolf Hitler!" Fritz and his classmates shouted in unison.

"Would you die for our führer?"

"Yes!"

"Would you kill for our führer?"

"Yes!"

"Without remorse, boys?"

"Yes!"

"Does your obedience to the *Führerprinzip* outweigh attachment to anyone or anything else?"

"Yes!"

"Prove it, boys. Draw your daggers!"

One and all, the Hitler Youths unsheathed the steel blades slung at their waists.

"Blut und Ehre!"

"Blood and honor!" they echoed.

"Now do it, boys."

Each boy had been told to bring a favorite pet to study in Aryan science. The class was full of dogs and puppies, cats and kittens, and exotic birds. Panzer, the Alsatian pup that Streicher had given his sons at Christmas, wagged its tail between them. Fritz and Hans shared a dumbfounded look as the first shriek shrilled the room, then ...

"Blut und Ehre ...

"Blut und Ehre ...

"Blut und Ehre!"

Both boys plunged their knives repeatedly to prove their love for Hitler.

Though he would never admit it, Fritz was sometimes wrenched from sleep in a cold sweat by the nightmare howls of all those pets killed for the *Führerprinzip*.

THE SS WOULD REAP what it had sown in Fritz and Hans Streicher. The Hitler Youth was designed to create for the Black Corps dynamic recruits instilled with physical toughness and ideological fervor. The zigzag Sig Runes on their belt buckles mirrored the dual lightning strikes of the SS symbol. Many recruits were earmarked for the Death's Head units of the SS-Totenkopfverbände, from which the Black Corps drew its concentration camp guards. They might guard the subterranean secrets of Dora-Mittelbau, or

the other underground factories run by SS-General Ernst
Streicher. But not *his* sons.

"Fritz, Hans," their father had confided a month ago,
"you are the future of the Third Reich. It used to be that
candidates for the SS had to prove that their Aryan heritage
had been untainted by inferior blood for eleven or twelve
generations, back to the year 1650. *That,* my sons, was
racial purity."

"Like us, father?" Hans asked.

"Yes, but others are suspect. The demand was later
shortened to a span of two generations. That requires clean
blood no further back than 1885. Here we see the result of
that weakening."

The concentration camp for recalcitrant Hitler Youths
had been set up at Moringen, near Göttingen, in Lower
Saxony in 1940. Some of the inmates were boys whom
Fritz and Hans had run with in their Jungvolk packs. The
infractions that could land an outcast in here were varied
and many: drinking, smoking, singing prohibited songs,
improper or sloppy saluting, violating curfew, or creating
disorder in billiard or dance halls. The general had brought
his sons here to drive home a point: no one could be trusted
to be taint-free, even with the ever-present threat of
punishment.

At Moringen, boys collapsed from brutal exercise,
shrank thinner from withheld meals, were thrashed with
hickory sticks, and were confined alone for weeks on end.
One boy—"A recidivist," sneered the general—screamed
hysterically for his mother from behind a cracked door in
the dank cellar.

"Take a look," the general said. "He just wouldn't learn.
The taint is too deep."

Fritz had widened the crack to peer into the chamber. A
frantically struggling youth, stripped from the waist down,

was strapped to a table. His ankles were chained to hooks screwed into the far corners. Between his splayed legs stood a Totenkopf guard with what appeared to be long-handled bolt cutters.

"Mutter!" beseeched the about-to-be eunuch.

That earned him another sneer.

"Only Red Ivans believe in a *Mother*land," scoffed the general.

THE SLAVE who had etched the tattoos over Fritz's and Hans's hearts was a French prisoner of war at Dora-Mittelbau. The SS general had designed different crests for his two sons, and the POW had been forced at gunpoint to engrave them exactly as sketched. Streicher himself had held the pistol to ensure that the only witnesses to the tattooing were him, his sons, and the captured navy artist. As soon as both inkings were done to his satisfaction, the general passed the Walther to Fritz and said, "Seal our secret."

Bwam!

Without hesitating, Fritz blew the Frenchman's brains all over the wall portrait of Adolf Hitler.

NOW, THE COLD MOON shone down on the Nazis' Fatherland while packs of marauding Werewolves prowled and howled in the night.

Down in the *Führerbunker,* fifty-five feet underground, Fritz was itching to go out and kill for Adolf Hitler.

But first, this honor.

Not every man gets to meet God on this side of the grave.

Stealth Killer

VANCOUVER
May 24, Now

In the newspaper business, battles are waged over the Story, a scramble for the Scoop. Scoop-scrambles ignite checkbook journalism. Checkbook journalism infects the newsroom too, since those reporters who land the huge Scoops find their paychecks fattened. Consequently, there are newsroom battles over the Byline.

Byline is the name of the reporter credited on the front page with breaking the Story.

And if the Story is Watergate—or something of similar importance—it takes only one to make your career.

Woodward and Bernstein got the Byline for the Story that broke Watergate.

Joe Schmo didn't.

Who's Joe Schmo?

Exactly.

The Vancouver Times wasn't in the same league as *The New York Times* or *The Washington Post,* but it had its Byline fights too. For the past few weeks, the paper had been running a series of articles on missing down-and-outers who might be unknown victims of foul play. All had been on the streets one day and were gone the next, as was common with transients who pass through this city's skid road and along its prostitute strolls. The impetus for the series had come from Bess McQueen—a brassy, bleach-blonde queen bitch, in Cort Jantzen's opinion. Jantzen and McQueen shared the crime beat at *The Vancouver Times*. For a piece of investigative journalism that widespread and time-intensive, they had tackled divergent angles and shared the Byline—until yesterday.

Disposable People
By Bess McQueen and Cort Jantzen

The "high track" stroll on Seymour Street is run by pimps and organized crime. The "low track" stroll on the Downtown Eastside is for women who will turn a trick for the price of their next fix. The "kiddie stroll" on Commercial Drive has runaway girls as young as twelve working the sex trade. And "boy's town" at the end of Homer Street caters to men who want sex with teenage males.

Are they disposable people? Those prostitutes who have been forced by poverty, sexual abuse, alienation at home, bullying at school, and drug addiction into a dead-end life of victimization on our meanest streets? And if foul play should claim their lives, do we view them as less dead? …

That first story in the series had been followed by other McQueen–Jantzen joint bylines:

Does the Criminal Code Kill Hookers?
By Bess McQueen and Cort Jantzen

On the street, perverts can be as cruel as they want to be.

It used to be that sex-trade workers did business in rooming houses. Back then, hookers walking the stroll knew there was a hotel they could safely use within a short distance. Car dates were frowned upon. It's dangerous for hookers to corner themselves in cars.

But the Criminal Code was changed in 1986 to make it illegal to communicate in public for the purpose of buying or selling sexual services. Climbing into cars to transact business became the best way to beat that law. Soon, most street hookers were being driven away to who knows where for whatever sexual acts were ordered by their captors. Lock the doors of a car and it becomes a prison....

Last week, the joint McQueen–Jantzen byline amalgams had ended with this:

The Less Dead
By Bess McQueen and Cort Jantzen

Vancouver targets prostitutes. It always has. There are now close to 2,000 prostitutes working the strolls of Vancouver, and they may as well have bull's eyes on their backs. To politicians, the police, and the pious, prostitutes are a nuisance. Vice laws are designed to drive them from one location to another, in the vain hope that one day they'll simply disappear—and if one does, mission accomplished. That's one less to worry about.

Out of sight, out of mind. That's how most people view them.

To pimps, pushers, and predators, prostitutes seem like easy prey. All the talk of ridding our city of prostitutes gives those who victimize them a reason to do what they do. Kill a prostitute and does anyone really care? It's not the same as killing a police-woman or a nurse. Good riddance to bad rubbish is the theme we send to predators. We expect the police to focus on crimes against the "more dead," not the culling of the "less dead." Those we physically marginalize by forcing them into darkly lit industrial back streets where serial killers hunt....

The series had been a success. It had raised circulation. The public had reacted with a lively flow of letters, pro and con. That had prompted the managing editor to go to the well again … well, actually two more times, since Bess McQueen and Cort Jantzen had been sent out separately—"A little friendly competition," according to their boss—to try to scoop each other with the best incendiary follow-up to their joint-byline series on Vancouver's "disposable people."
Friendly?
Ha!
That bitch!
Cort Jantzen had filed first with this story:

Sex Trade a Leghold Trap for Kids
By Cort Jantzen

What begins as a game of catch-me-if-you-can for runaway kids ends as a leghold trap for those snared by the sex trade.
They come from troubled families or a background of sexual abuse. "It's easy to vanish down here," says a twelve-year-old girl. "Lots of cheap rooming houses where I can hide during the daytime, then come out at night." What brings her out at night is the need to turn

tricks. Sex is all she has to barter with to pay for her room and her fix. Within a month of leaving home, that girl was a heroin addict.

The Internet has helped to make Vancouver a well-known destination for sex tourists. Pedophiles sneak in to stalk the "kiddie stroll" and "boy's town." Websites provide the locations and a price list for sexual acts....

The following day, Bess McQueen had filed this story:

Is a Killer Stalking "Boy's Town"?
By Bess McQueen

Too many boys have gone missing from one of the city's prostitute strolls. Since the early 1990s, at least thirty young males known to have offered themselves for sex with men who cruise the "boy's town" area of Homer Street have lost all contact with friends and family....

The day before yesterday, Bess McQueen's story had appeared on the front page of *The Vancouver Times,* and before the morning was out, the paper had received a request from Chief Superintendent Robert DeClercq of Special X to brief the reporter of the "boy's town" piece on the status of the Mounties' investigation. Suddenly, that story had taken on dimensions of the Story of the week, and possibly the year, and that—given how pushy the queen bitch was—had resulted in yesterday's Byline battle, which erupted in the office of the managing editor.

"It was *my* story," Bess declared. "So the interview with Special X is *mine* exclusively. And so is the byline on any piece that emerges from that scrum."

"We had a *joint* byline."

"Had, Cort. *Had*. Remember what you said in this very office, Ed? 'A little friendly competition.' Well, that's what happened. And now that I have a scoop, Cort is trying to horn in."

"You don't own boy's town," Jantzen fumed. "It came up in our joint 'Disposable People' piece, and I mention it in my 'Leghold Trap' story."

"Give me a break," scoffed Bess, rolling eyes that were bloodshot from too many gin-and-tonics in the press club watering hole. "The idea for the series was *mine*. You were brought in as backup, nothing more, Cort. Do your own thinking. Don't plagiarize *me*!"

The mention of the P-word had galvanized Editor Ed into frog-leg action. He didn't want any complaints made to the publisher, the press council, or God knows who. He'd rather have a pit bull tearing at his ass than the queen bitch.

"'Friendly competition.' That's what I said, Cort. The byline was split. There's no denying that. Special X asked to brief the reporter who wrote Bess's piece. Ipso facto"— Editor Ed's favorite coffin nail—"Bess gets the interview, and the byline."

"Ed—"

"That's it! The press gods have spoken. Now, go write me a scoop about that African cannibal whom the courts, in their infinite wisdom, just sprang from the funny farm."

DON'T BELIEVE EVERYTHING you read in the papers.

DeClercq didn't.

"If it bleeds, it leads" is the time-honored mantra of newspapers everywhere. Fear-mongering sells papers; comfort articles encourage people to turn on the tube.

The past few weeks' bleeding-heart series on "Disposable People" in *The Vancouver Times* was a case in

point. It fostered the false impression that Special X was
flat-footed when it came to catching those preying on the
down-and-out. Reading between the lines exposed a well-
worn and troubling subtext: Serial killers are free to murder
the weakest members of society because the police suffer
from linkage blindness—the inability, or lack of will, to see
patterns in murders or disappearances, especially when the
victims lack power and prestige. The dispossessed are
refused the attention that should come automatically from
investigators and those who pull the priority strings of
Special X. Having been victimized throughout their miserable lives, they suffer a final victimization at the hands of
apathetic cops.

The problem, of course, was more complex than the
Times' articles suggested. Psycho-hunters were hamstrung
by prostitution laws that had been designed to keep the
most vulnerable on the move. Hookers elude arrest by
criss-crossing the country and working serial strolls in
Vancouver, Calgary, Winnipeg, Toronto, and Montreal, or
down the West Coast into the States. Girls on the kiddie
stroll and the "chickens" of boy's town are trafficked by
pimps in a circuit that links cities in the western provinces
and states. Systems of dispersal are what thwart the police,
for it's hard to detect missing persons when those living on
the edge *want* to get lost, and when the stealth killers who
pick off the unwary sneak around the fringes of large,
vague, general hunting grounds.

But that didn't mean that DeClercq had no detection
card up his sleeve.

So that's why the chief was here.

To set the record straight.

RETURNING TO THE NEWSROOM from interviewing the
parents of the girl killed by the Congo Man, Cort Jantzen

found the briefing by Special X about to get under way. The fact that DeClercq had come to the *Times* was a draw in itself, but when Cort saw who he had brought with him—the famed Kim Rossmo—the tug was irresistible. Poised pen and notebook in hand, with a tape recorder running, Bess McQueen sat front and center in the chair nearest the two psycho-hunters. As DeClercq began to speak, Cort slipped into the boardroom and found a seat among the editorial hounds who'd gathered to hear what the chief had to say.

DeClercq, the head of Special X, was in his fifties, lean and wiry in build, with dark hair graying at the temples and even darker, brooding eyes. This afternoon, he wore the blue serge uniform of commissioned officers, with his rank—one crown above two pips—displayed on the epaulets, the badge of the force as collar dogs on the jacket, and above the breast pocket his long-service medal: a ribbon with a gold clasp and three hard-earned stars known within the RCMP as "the Milky Way."

A Horseman's Horseman, thought Jantzen.

"Stealth predators," the Mountie told the press, "are the hardest of all serial killers to catch. Why? Because the core strategy of such killers is to commit their murders in ways that will fail to attract notice. Bluebeards and black widows are good examples. These are males and females, respectively, who secretly kill off their spouses. Others have occupations that lure potential victims to them. The best recent example is Dr. Harold Shipman. As a family doctor in Britain, he probably murdered in excess of two hundred elderly patients in their homes. And then there are stealth killers—as you point out in your paper—who prey upon fringe members of society. The homeless, runaways, and sex-trade workers. Jeffrey Dahmer fits your profile. He picked up gay males and later ambushed them in his apartment, then used their skulls to build a shrine. The police in Milwaukee, Wisconsin, were unaware that a serial killer was stalking the homosexual community, even though dark rumors about missing men had circulated through that city's gay bars."

DeClercq held up *The Vancouver Times*.

"'Is a Killer Stalking "Boy's Town"?'" he read. "The investigative piece that follows seems to imply that Special X is unable to see patterns in the disappearances of those you call the 'less dead.' While that might have been true not so long ago, it isn't true now. Though you leave that headline unanswered, we're here today to provide that answer for you.

"Is a killer stalking 'boy's town'?" DeClercq repeated.

"Most likely," he replied.

VANCOUVER'S LOSS was America's gain.

In hindsight, it seemed inevitable—given the number of psychos loose down there—that the United States would welcome Kim Rossmo with open arms. The man who took over the stealth-killer briefing from DeClercq had revolutionized the way that state-of-the-art psycho-hunters bring predators to bay. The first cop in Canada to earn a Ph.D., Rossmo, a math whiz, had come up with the concept of geographic profiling from what he observed while walking a beat in Vancouver's skid road. Step one in psycho-hunting is to consolidate the pieces. You must gather a serial killer's murders together to know he is stalking prey. For that, the FBI created the VICAP system, a nationwide databank that searches for links among crimes that might suggest a serial killer is operating. Step two in psycho-hunting is to profile the warped behavior inherent in the signature that lies behind those links in that consolidated series of crimes. For that, the FBI created psychological profiling, which has now been flogged to death in too many TV cop shows. What = why = who.

But what had been missing from that equation was "= where," and by tackling that puzzler with geographic profiling, Rossmo had entered the ranks of the world's supercops.

"The Hound of the Data Points," according to *Popular Science*.

"Mapping Evil," according to *Reader's Digest*.

His theory is simple. Each time a serial killer meets, attacks, kills, or dumps a victim, he leaves a point on a map. Because his hunting ground overlaps his "awareness space"—the areas of the city he moves through quite innocently from day to day—his crime sites are linked to anchor points like his home or his place of work. That which is predictable can be mathematically quantified, since by definition the laws of probability apply. By researching known killers' typical journeys to their crime scenes, Rossmo created a computer program that plots a serial predator's crime sites on a map, then draws a box around his hunting ground and divides it into a grid of thousands of pixels. Next, the computer calculates the probability that each point on the grid is an anchor from which the killer began. Finally, points of equal probability are linked together and color-coded according to a scale, and what results is a geographic profile of the hunting ground that shows the likelihood that any given area is the killer's home or place of work.

What = why = who = where.

Build a better rat trap and the world will beat a path to your door. The first person to grasp the awesome forensic potential of what Rossmo had created was C/Supt. Robert DeClercq. If Special X psycho-hunters knew *where* to look for their prey, they could focus their attention on that neighborhood and apply the psychological profile generated by the crime scenes to the psycho possibilities within its confines. So as Rossmo the beat cop catapulted up the ranks to detective inspector in the Vancouver Police Department, the Mountie had embraced his creation and used it to hone Special X into a razor-sharp squad.

Psychos respect no boundaries.

Neither do supercops.

What Rossmo had to offer was in demand around the world, so he was now a new breed of *international* cop.

THE LAST TIME Cort Jantzen had seen Kim Rossmo in the flesh—assuming that phrase applies to an image on TV—was when he appeared with Chief Moose on CNN during the Beltway Sniper Case. The Americans had called Rossmo in to geographically profile those murders. Back then, the cyber cop was living in Washington, D.C., having accepted an offer he couldn't refuse as director of research with the Police Foundation. At the same time, he was establishing—as he had done earlier for Scotland Yard in Britain—a geoprofiling division for the Bureau of Alcohol, Tobacco, Firearms and Explosives. Now Rossmo was ensconced at the Texas State University in Austin, where he was rumored to be at work on the next generation of psycho-hunting tools.

Shorter and stockier than the Horseman who handed him the reins, Rossmo was a physically fit man somewhere in his forties who had let the cop's mustache grow into a beard. His eyes were those of a night owl, not of a lark, and the reporter had the suspicion that they exposed his mind. The darker the landscape, the more intense the hunt.

"The stealth killer," Rossmo warned, "is a tough nut to crack. No crime reports, no crime linkage. No crime scenes, no behavioral profile. No points on a map, no geographic profile. Our forensic tools become impotent. The stealth killer isn't out for notoriety. His core strategy is to kill in such a way that nobody knows he's on the hunt. The stealth killer sees himself as the Invisible Man."

"So how do you find him?" Bess asked.

"We have to smoke him out."

"You've done that?"

"Yes."

"For the boy's town missing persons?"

Rossmo nodded. "We have a stealth-predator pattern."

"Done how?"

"Spatial-temporal clusters."

As the cyber cop explained his methodology, he turned around his high-end laptop computer so that Bess and the gathered editorial hounds could follow visually.

"Vancouver is divided into different prostitute strolls based on the income level and sexual orientation of potential clients. The locations of the various strolls have shifted over time, but that hasn't prevented us from analyzing and computerizing their historical patterns. We know the number of missing-person reports that each stroll has generated in the past, as well as the 'survival rate' for a missing person—how long before he or she is usually found. From that, we've derived a mathematical formula that tells us what to expect in the future. The statistical graph for boy's town looks like this."

A graph hit the screen.

"The formula is built into ViCLAS, the Violent Crime Linkage Analysis System, the Mounties' equivalent to the FBI's VICAP. As each missing-person report is fed into the system, it is analytically compared to the past. In other words, ViCLAS is a front-end system programmed to routinely scan crime data and missing-person reports to identify unusual levels of activity or abnormal clusters. If, based on historical crime patterns, too many things start happening, in too short a time and too small an area, the alarm goes off. In short, your so-called disposable people are watched over by an early warning system designed to detect stealth predators."

Bang. The cyber cop hit a button that caused the graph onscreen to spike abnormally.

"That's boy's town. See the mark of the stealth predator?"

"Wow," said Bess. "Where'd you get the idea?"

"It's a redesign of models created by epidemiologists to track outbreaks of virulent disease."

THERE IS A NATURAL TENDENCY among hyper-conservative cops to deny that a serial killer might be preying on their patch. This springs not only from a desire to avoid having to commit limited resources to the bottomless pit of a major investigation, but also from the irrational feeling that such an admission is tacit acknowledgment that past policing has failed.

DeClercq saw matters differently. Foolish and negligent would be the cop who dismissed a Rossmo warning, he believed, for what sort of dimwit blinds himself to the laws of mathematical probability? The chief knew of one force that had done just that. The dinosaurs in the path of the comet thought they knew better than some egghead who could use a computer. They said that they had no bodies, so there was no proof. That's tantamount to a fire station's refusing to roll its trucks because reports of smoke aren't proof of fire. They snubbed the cyber cop's warning that it was time to swing into action, and ended up with several more victims on the ground.

Talk about fumbled footballs.

"Your series on disposable people reflects bygone attitudes," DeClercq told the staff of *The Vancouver Times*.

"At least at Special X, we've studied and learned from the successes and failures of past serial-killer manhunts. We don't suffer linkage blindness. We don't ignore the 'less dead.' We know how to organize overwhelming information. We coordinate with other police jurisdictions. And we don't see ourselves as adversaries of the media. History shows that it is usually some member of the public who provides the key to solving any serial killings, and you are our link to the community.

"It's probable that a stealth predator has been stalking boy's town for some time. To take him down, we need your help. First, we ask that you publish an alert in tomorrow's paper, advising the public that we have the area and those prostitutes whom the killer is targeting under blanket surveillance. Second, we're asking that anyone who saw, knows, or suspects something contact Special X. There may be someone out there who knows something without realizing its significance. To stop this killer, we need that person to get in touch. Ted Bundy was caught because he was seen backing out of a middle-class driveway in the dead of the night. Peter Sutcliffe—the Yorkshire Ripper— was overheard dropping a hammer and ice pick onto the concrete in an effort to hide them."

CORT JANTZEN and Bess McQueen crossed paths at the boardroom door as the briefing let out for a coffee break. From the gloating expression on her face, you'd think the queen bitch had just scored an honorary Stetson.

"Eat your heart out, baby," Bess cooed as she sashayed off to the powder room.

Teeth grinding and blood pressure rising to a boil, Jantzen sat down at his desk in the newsroom to write his story on the death of the Congo Man. He spread prints of the photos he'd surreptitiously snapped at the crime scene across the cluttered surface, studying the patch over one of the cannibal's eyes and the stake rammed into the other. He tried to fathom the motive that would induce a killer to leave a signature like that.

It wouldn't come to him. But a story angle did. An angle with the potential to turn his story into the Story and seize the Scoop from the byline bitch.

Pandora's Box

May 25, Now

The blood of the Congo Man stained the tip of the SS dagger in Swastika's right hand. Carving the symbol into the *Untermensch*'s brow had bloodied the Damascus steel of the SS-Dienstdolch's point. Now, as the Fourth Reich Nazi wiped away the subhuman's slime with a chamois cloth, the steel polished up to a mirror finish along the center-ridged blade that had been etched with the SS motto *"Meine Ehre heisst Treue"*—"My honor is loyalty." The ebony grip of the service dagger was inset with the silver eagle-and-swastika emblem of Hitler's Third Reich. The handle was capped by an enamel circle struck with the two lightning bolts of the SS runes.

Sieg heil, thought the killer.

Satisfied that he had cleansed the dagger back to Aryan purity, the Nazi assassin slipped the gleaming blade into the sheath of its scabbard. The scabbard was anodized to a black finish, and a coat of lacquer gave it and the interlaced swastikas across its middle a Black Corps shine. Attached to the scabbard was a double chain made of alternating links of *Totenkopf* skull and crossbones and SS runes. Triangulating up to a clover-leaf clasp, the edged weapon could be slung from the metal loop that hung from the lower-left tunic pocket of an SS officer's black dress uniform.

But not tonight.

The interior of the black walnut case was lined with black satin for a plush display. Gently, Swastika returned the dagger to its resting place, after first wrapping a silver cord with a slide, stem, crown, and ball around the upper part of the grip and cross-guard of the dagger's handle. Known as a portepee, the cord designated the status of the wearer. Here, the dagger would rest until the next "solution."

Lowering the lid, Swastika closed the case.

The original owner's name was engraved on a silver plaque.

"SS-Obergruppenführer Ernst Streicher."

NAMED FOR the University of British Columbia, University Hill—surmounting the cliffs out at the tip of Point Grey— is the area with Vancouver's finest real estate. Above Chancellor Boulevard was the habitat of retired professors who had bought into this pricey area before the cost went sky-high. The realm of *real* money was below Chancellor Boulevard, where the half- and whole-acre spreads on the bluff commanded a panoramic view of the white-capped waters of English Bay and the snow-crowned North Shore peaks. The title to one particular estate was held by a law firm in Switzerland, and had been ever since the years just after the Second World War. Buried underground in the cellar of the $10-million mansion was a reconstruction of the *Führerbunker* from the dying days of the Third Reich.

The map room was an exact replica of the room in which Adolf Hitler had wed Eva Braun, fifty-some feet under Berlin as the Red Army rushed to raise the hammer and sickle over the blasted ruins of the Nazi Reichstag. The map table around the SS dagger box displayed newspaper cuttings from editions of *The Vancouver Times* in which Cort Jantzen had covered the court-ordered release of the cannibal killer.

Armed with a pair of scissors, Swastika seated himself
at the table to mutilate that morning's edition of the *Times,*
which had hit the streets at about one a.m. A pair of articles
on the front page required his attention. "Stealth Killer
Stalks 'Boy's Town'" was the headline of Bess McQueen's
story. That string of disappearances posed the greater threat
of arrest, so Swastika studied the piece for clues that might
lead Special X to the abandoned Skunk Mine where Ernst
Streicher's companion Nazi sword—his SS-Führerdegen—
continued to pigstick young blood.

Nothing.

At least not in print.

With no indication that he was in jeopardy on that front,
Swastika switched focus to the other story. This one—
written by Cort Jantzen, who was following up on his
earlier coverage—had a headline that matched that used for
the boy's town piece, as if the editor had decided to set both
stories up as rivals. "Vigilante Kills Alleged Cannibal" it
reported. The subhead added, "Settling the Score?"

After he absorbed the angle adopted by the reporter, the
Nazi killer nodded in agreement with the heroic myth that
had been boxed in a sidebar next to the main text. "Blinding
the Cyclops" was its title. The myth wasn't Nordic, but it
appealed to Swastika's imagination.

Snip, snip, snip …

Having cut the vigilante piece out of the *Times,* Swastika
arranged it with the earlier stories on the "taken care of"
side of the dagger box. Then he turned back to the paper to
find something suitable for the bare surface on the other
side of the desk.

Snip, snip, snip …

From the business section, he removed a story about a
corporate exec who had viewed his company as a personal
piggy bank, emptying the employee pension plan and

divesting stockholders of their life savings. No one knew where the cash was now, but some of it had surely lined his lawyers' deep pockets, for they had kept the case from coming to trial for several years and would probably hold it off for several more. The money worries he'd caused had driven a distraught investor to suicide. The dead man was the father of three. But there would be no murder charge.

Swastika grinned.

Before leaving the map room, the Fourth Reich assassin snipped a Scrabble tray of letters out of various headlines and arranged thirteen pieces along the edge of the desk.

The word described how he viewed the social outcasts of the *Times'* pieces, for whom his final solution was extermination.

The word was "*Untermenschen.*"

WHEN HE STOOD in the deathly quiet corridor outside the map room, a replica of the *Führerbunker* conference hall where Hitler had said farewell to his diehard disciples, Swastika thought he could still hear the footsteps of all the fugitive Nazis who had slipped into this city in the post-war years to plot the rising phoenix of the Fourth Reich. Hidden in the secret storage passages behind these walls had once been a fortune in Nazi gold. It had been smuggled out of the Third Reich just before it fell, and later was buccaneered up from South America with *Flugkreisel* hardware in the only U-boat ever sanctioned by the Pentagon to sail this coast. Those whose phantom footsteps Swastika heard haunting this hall were the most elusive Nazi war criminals, all unaccounted for in 1945.

But now those disciples were gone.

And so was Hitler's gold.

Except for the gold in Switzerland, which maintained the family trust that kept this far-flung estate in Swastika's hands.

This mansion in Vancouver.

And the ranch in the Cariboo.

The phantom footsteps came to life as Swastika walked along the narrow corridor, reviewing the waxwork figures against the far wall. The rheostat that controlled the ceiling fixtures was dimmed so the lamps would cast evocative shadows. His mother—a woman of many talents—had sculpted the wax much as the display artists do at Madame Tussaud's. Fittingly, the first figure he came to was the führer. But this führer was taller, to match his father's height. It wore the uniform Hitler had worn during those last days in the bunker, perfect in every detail. Its glass eyes were riveting, as if fired up for one of Hitler's Nuremberg speeches.

Swastika snapped his arm up in the Nazi salute.

Sieg heil, Father.

The memory was as sharp as Streicher's dagger: the first time his father had whipped off the belt of his führer's uniform to thrash his son for spying on something he shouldn't have seen. That was back in the hazy days of his early childhood, just after he had somehow discovered— had the door been left ajar?—the secret passage where the Nazi gold had once been cached. He remembered descending the staircase to the bunker. He remembered seeing light coming through the peephole in the false wall. He remembered sneezing from the dust as he placed his eye to the spy hole. He remembered the terror of witnessing his father's rage. He remembered the pain of the beating. But there was a blank in his mind. Whatever he had spied had been wiped from his memory by the fury of the führer's belt.

Only later had he uncovered clues in his mother's closet.

That was shortly after the fall of the Berlin Wall in 1989, when his parents had both vanished in East Germany.

The female waxwork was supposed to be Eva Braun. The facial features, however, were those of Swastika's mother. In fashioning the wax to fit her husband's fantasy world, she had morphed the face of Hitler's submissive wife into her own. The figure wore a replica of the black taffeta dress in which Eva had wed.

The door off the hall at Swastika's back led to an anteroom to the study in which Hitler had blown out his brains. Off the study to the right was Hitler's bedroom. Off the study to the left was a reconstruction of Eva Braun's boudoir that included a closet full of role-playing costumes, all of them, like the wedding dress in the hall, copied by Swastika's mother from varied historical sources.

Half of the closet lay open, flaunting knock-offs of Eva Braun's clothes, from dirndl country attire to haute couture fashions looted from occupied Paris. As a boy, Swastika would watch his mother undress in preparation for one of their cuddly bed-rests, and she would neatly hang her clothes, garment by garment, in the open half.

The other half, the *verboten* half with the big lock, was to him, as a young lad, akin to Pandora's box. Pandora's box, his mother had told him one day when they lay naked together in Hitler's bed, was where the gods had hidden all the evils of the world. If the box were ever opened, all hell would break loose.

That's how he had imagined the locked half of his mother's closet throughout his prepubescent years. Like Pandora's box, full of delicious secrets. So once his parents were gone and the mansion belonged solely to him, Swastika had busted open the lock on his mother's subconscious Freudian kinks.

It was a man's world in the years that followed the Second World War, and GIs returning from overseas had snapped up pulp magazines with lurid covers of hot nympho babes in peril or imperiling. These appealed to their basest male instincts of sex, power, and war. For thirty-five cents, a vet could purchase *Swagger, Rage, For Men Only, Escape to Adventure, American Manhood,* or any of the other rags that Swastika had found on a shelf in his mother's secret closet. The cover of *Climax: Exciting Stories for Men* said it all: a burly, shirtless he-man straddled a flagpole flying a tattered American flag.

The women in the mags were all bursting at the seams. With shirts unbuttoned to bare ample cleavage and skirts torn up their legs, the ones on the pages earmarked by his mother were captives trussed up in Nazi chains. Other pages depicted dominatrices—busty women in unbuttoned shirts with swastika armbands, Nazi helmets on their heads, and skin-tight jodhpurs sheathing their showgirl waists and thighs—tormenting red-blooded American POWs in concentration camps flying swastika flags.

There were also canisters of film.

Ilsa: She-wolf of the SS read their labels.

On the shelf, beside the fantasy pile, Swastika had also discovered an album of Second World War photographs of the two most notorious Nazi women.

Both Ilses.

Irma Ilse Grese. Born 1923. She became a camp guard at the age of nineteen and transferred to Auschwitz in March 1943. There, she rose to the rank of senior SS supervisor and was placed in charge of thirty thousand female prisoners. Her murders, tortures, and sexual excesses were legendary. Irma enjoyed shooting prisoners in cold blood, or beating them to death with a plaited whip, or allowing her half-starved dogs to tear them to pieces. She ordered guards to cut off the breasts of Jewish and gypsy women, and personally selected victims for the gas chambers. She demanded that she be brought their skins, which she stitched into lampshades, book covers, and household items. At Auschwitz, she had a love affair with Dr. Josef Mengele, and later, at Bergen-Belsen, she had one with Kommandant Josef Kramer.

The first photo in the album showed Irma Grese in her SS uniform, complete with jackboots, pistol, and whip.

On her arm was the swastika.

Ilse Koch. "The Bitch of Buchenwald." Married to Karl Koch, the kommandant of that camp. Ilse was especially fond of riding her horse through Buchenwald, whipping any prisoner who attracted her attention, and selecting those with distinctive tattoos for gassing. Like Grese, Koch had a sexual fetish involving human skin. But in addition to making those tattooed hides into lampshades, book covers, and shrunken heads, she had them tanned into human leather and stitched into gloves and a lady's handbag. Those, Ilse wore as proudly as any South Seas cannibal did his harvested human trophies.

The iconic photo of Ilse in that album showed her in her riding attire, with whip and spurs.

Beneath the shelf of that closet full of inspiration, Swastika's mother had hung her Freudian role-playing costumes. She had imitations of the bodice-rippers and SS Black Corps uniforms like Ilsa wore on film and copies of the dominatrix wardrobes favored by Grese and Koch.

What she had done with them, Swastika had no inkling. For try though he might, he couldn't get backstage of that iron curtain in his tortured mind to whatever sadistic burlesque had gone on in the master bedroom.

That's where the peephole was.

Whatever the trauma his father's belt had masked, it still shook him to the core. When he broke open the closet that day to release the evils of Pandora's box, Swastika had inexplicably burst into tears.

His sobs had gone on for an hour.

RED, WHITE, AND BLACK swastika banners flanked the trio of waxworks that captured the ideal Aryan family. The third figure was that of a young lad in a Hitlerjugend uniform. His mother had sewn that for Swastika at an early age, lengthening both it and the wax mannequin as he grew up.

As soon as he was old enough to learn how to kill, Swastika and his dad had gone hunting with a crossbow, a rifle, and a skinning knife up in the Cariboo.

"Fire!" his father had whispered, so fire he had, and the bolt of the crossbow had shot through the trunks of the forest trees to strike a doe in the flank with a sickening thud. "She's down," his father said, handing him the skinning knife. "Now go finish her off with your bare hands," he ordered.

If you'd seen them stalking through the brush toward the wounded deer, you might have thought they were Lord Baden-Powell and one of his Boy Scout cubs. In a way, they were. The Hitler Youth version, with him in the uniform sewn by his mother. His father had taken him roughing it in the woods near their Cariboo ranch—in that part of central British Columbia that seems to speak to the Black Forest yearnings of Germans today—for the same survivalist training that Nazi instructors had drilled into his dad as a youth.

"Kill her," came the order as they stood over the downed deer.

"I can't." Quivering.

"Toughen up!" demanded his dad.

His hands were shaking. He began to cry. He pointed to the forest clearing, where two Bambis stood watching.

"They'll survive. I did. Now wash your hands in blood!"

He hesitated, frozen.

Too long for his dad's temper.

The führer clenched his son by the scruff of his neck and whipped him with his belt until the pain was more than he

could take, giving him no alternative but to plunge down
the blade.

Jabbing a finger into the gaping slit in the deer's neck,
his dad had blooded him with the warm, red war paint,
signing a swastika on his forehead.

"Wear it with pride!" commanded the former Werewolf.

SWIVELING 180 DEGREES in the waxwork corridor, the
Nazi killer clomped across the threshold into the replica of
Hitler's private quarters. Jackboots echoed through the tight
confines of this bunker, for tonight Swastika was all
dressed up in the same Black Corps uniform that had once
been worn by his grandfather, SS-Obergruppenführer Ernst
Streicher.

Untermenschen

At heart, he was a nihilist. He hated everyone. His upbringing on a pig farm behind the Iron Curtain had warped his outlook on this shitty world and all the subhumans in it. Total and absolute destruction of everybody *and* himself had been his impossible dream. But now he actually had the means to bring that about, thanks to the treasure trove of long-lost Nazi secrets that he had recovered from the Knight's Hall at Castle Werewolf in what was now Poland.

As a boy in East Germany, he had often heard the Teutonic myth of Götterdämmerung, the twilight of the gods, which told how the end of the world had begun with the birth of a brood of wolves fathered by the great wolf Fenrir in a forest to the east. One of the pack had chased the sun and caught it in its jaws, extinguishing light and plunging the landscape into endless winter. As snowstorms swirled, war broke out all over the earth, culminating in an epic battle between the Norse gods and evil giants on a battlefield in front of the gates of Valhalla. Its upper jaw touching the heavens and its lower jaw brushing the ground, Fenrir, the demon wolf, spurted fire from its eyes and nostrils and dripped blood from its fangs. The wolf swallowed up Odin, the king of the gods, with a single snap of its jaws, and the rest of the combatants slaughtered each other chaotically. With all their gods dead, men were abandoned, and the human race was swept from the surface of the world by a cataclysm of fire, earthquakes, and tidal waves that subsumed everything into an abyss of nothingness.

Only now did the East German boy, having grown into a man, see the myth of Götterdämmerung as a prophesy. Of late, he had watched with interest as America veered toward the political right, nodding with agreement when the Christian crusade was launched against those "sand niggers," and recognizing the echoes of his ancestral past in the tortures of Abu Ghraib and the concentration camp at Guantanamo Bay. That's why he had sent a sample of the treasure trove from Castle Werewolf to the Pentagon by way of Switzerland, along with an extortion demand for a billion American dollars.

Götterdämmerung!

As a nihilist, he would gladly sacrifice his life to the cause of the end of the world, but not before he had a money-is-no-object blowout of sky-high proportions to compensate for all the suffering and deprivation he had once endured.

Meanwhile, there was the hunt …

HE THOUGHT OF HIMSELF as "the Aryan" when he was on the hunt, prowling the streets of boy's town in this dusty farm truck, just another hick from the sticks looking for male ass. Oh, he was looking for ass, was *obsessed* with ass. But not male ass for perverted sex like all these *Untermenschen* cruising Davie Street.

Davie Street was the club scene for fags in Vancouver. There was a sewer to fit every subhuman debauchery in the five-block stretch from Jervis to Howe. After midnight they came out on the street in force. They should be wearing pink triangles, thought the Nazi killer, and peering through the barbed wire of a death camp, waiting for him to drive a stake through their hearts.

Mein Kampf.

My struggle.

He tensed as he touched the cover of the book that he'd tucked into the map pocket of the farm truck's door.

Someone had to die.

The SS-Führerdegen—Ernst Streicher's sword—offered his only relief.

"Pigsticking," the Aryan called it down in the mine at the Cariboo ranch.

THE HOT NEW CLUB on Davie Street was Cabaret Berlin. Harking back to the sophisticated depravity of the cabaret cellars of the Weimar Republic, this club was so buzzed with collective lust unashamedly flaunted that the sexual energy crackled out onto the street through its swinging door.

Marya Delvard was onstage, singing "The Lavender Song."

Yuri could see her as he paced, paced, paced.

He couldn't get in to the club.

He was only fourteen.

They styled her "The Valkyrian Dominatrix" on the poster outside the door. Like her Austrian namesake from a hundred years ago, the drag queen exuded femme fatale. She was wearing a slinky floor-length gown the same inky hue as her hair, which fell to bare shoulders on either side of her chalk white face. The gown was slit to her waist to expose garters and a fishnet stocking up one thigh as she poised her stiletto heel above the groin of a prostrate man who was naked except for a codpiece with a thong up the crack of his ass. Draped behind the drag queen's neck and flouncing as she sang her sultry song was a boa that extended from her fingertips like dual bullwhips.

Marya Delvard.

Chanteuse of "I am a Vamp!" "I Don't Know Who I Belong To." "It's All a Swindle." "The Washed-up Lover." And her favorite, "Streets of Berlin."

Pace, pace, pace …

"Jib, cryssie, ice, speed," the street kid mumbled as a mantra.

Yuri was going snaky.

He was desperate for crystal meth.

THE LICENSE PLATES on the farm truck were neither legitimate nor stolen. A natural when it came to mechanical things, the Aryan created miracles in a basic workshop. If you had the willpower of Nietzsche's superman, you could teach yourself to do anything from texts in the library, postings on the Internet, and dogged trial-and-error experiments.

Hadn't he proved it in his makeshift lab down in the Cariboo mine?

So creating license plates that weren't genuine and couldn't be traced as stolen was a snap.

For years, the Aryan had stalked the dingy alleys of boy's town. A better urban hunting ground didn't exist. The youths skulking back in the shadows were hiding from everyone. Almost all were misfits, runaways who'd ended up peddling their asses to make ends meet. Not only were they hiding from the law and from nosy social workers, but they were hiding from their families as well. Picking one of them off was like kidnapping a ghost.

Boy's town was Valhalla.

"YOU'RE A DRAG HAG, honey," Marya had teased Yuri that first time she'd taken him back to her place from the street. "I dress in drag. You dress in drab. D-R-A-B. 'Dressed as a boy.' Get it?"

"You're a transvestite."

"Ugh," said Marya, dropping a limp wrist. "Don't say transvestite. That's *sooo* passé. I'm a cross-dresser who lives *en femme*. I'm always in stealth mode."

"What's a drag hag?"

"You're a homovestite," Marya said, laughing. "You dress in the garb of your birth sex, but you hang with me."

Never had Yuri seen a more feminine residence. Portraits of divas decorated the walls. Ute Lemper sang like a dream from the CD player, a bust of Marlene Dietrich sat on a table stacked with 1930s- and 1940s-style hats, and everywhere there seemed to be outrageously flamboyant gowns draped over or within easy reach of several full-length wardrobe mirrors.

"You're welcome to stay for a while, honey. Until you get on your feet. I know what it's like to run away from being misunderstood. There is, however, one rule you must never breach. It took a lot of pain for me to kick drugs. I won't have drugs around, and I won't coddle a druggie. If I catch you high, you're out the door like this."

The snap of her fingers had the crack of a whip.

And so it was, for several weeks, that Yuri had stayed with Marya. On show nights at Cabaret Berlin, over dinner, she would ask, "What drag should I wear in the show?"

For the next few hours, Yuri had watched her prepare. Marya used a gaff to hide her penis, an elastic waist-cincher for that figure-eight contour, foam padding for shapely hips, and a cleavage-creator for boobs. Next up was a runway fashion show in front of the mirrors so that Marya could select her lingerie and frock. Finally, to impersonate whatever diva held her fancy, she put her false face together through makeup wizardry at a dressing table once used by Gypsy Rose Lee.

Marya Delvard.

Queen of the drag ball.

How Yuri longed to return to that womb of security, to again have a mother figure who understood her adopted son, so he could stop peddling his ass in boy's town just to survive on the street. If only he'd played by her golden rule of no drugs, Marya wouldn't have made good on her threat to kick his sorry ass out the door.

Please, Marya!

Help me!

God, I need a fix!

"Jib, cryssie, ice, speed."

Pace, pace, pace ...

If only Yuri could get word to Marya inside this club; beg her to leave the stage and come outside; promise to shake the monkey if only she'd take him back in; tell her how crystal meth had sunk his life to hell on earth; explain that jib was a popular drug with kids at raves, that ecstasy was laced with it and that's why he'd begun, that there was an aphrodisiac kick in it, that it made you feel sexy as hell. Who knew it hooked you worse than crack or junk? He only knew that it was cheaper and a longer high, then— *fuck!*—this jib monkey was in way over his head.

Yuri peeked in the door.

The bouncer scowled at him.

"No way, kid. Move on down the street."

What time was it?

How long till the end of her act?

Sweating, twitching, paranoid, and fearful of seeing things.

He wasn't ready for detox.

Not here on the street.

Just one more fix would see him through ...

Through till Marya got offstage ...

Then he'd go straight ...

No more jib monkey, nosiree …

But first, he had to score cash fast for that fix …

And that's when Yuri saw the farm truck idling at the curb.

THE GOOSESTEP and jackhammer pounding of East German industrial rock, with its blitzkrieg assault of Teutonic drums and guitars and its battering-ram vocals, blared deafeningly in the Aryan's ears. Having grown up behind the Berlin Wall, where this music had been spawned, he could relate to songs like *"Du Hast"* (You hate) and *"Weisses Fleisch"* (White flesh) historically. The music spoke to his cauldron of hate through the headphones clamped over his ears and covering the swastika studs punched through both lobes.

The person who glowered back at the Aryan from the rear-view mirror was an *Über*-blond Eurotrash punk like those you'd find headbanging in a Hamburg underground club. The purest of the pure, yet he had once wallowed in dirt back on the East German farm where he had learned to hate. The Aryan's hair was close-cropped and his eyes were ice blue. The tattoos partially hidden by his black leather skin were Nordic runes, and the barbed wire inked around his neck dangled an Iron Cross scar.

The Aryan personified the master race.

The sandwich board outside the cabaret across the street announced that tonight was a homo event titled "Getting Clocked." It was some sort of dress-up affair for drag queens, transgenderists, cross-dressers, and female impersonators, or whatever they called themselves. They played for prizes, trying to pass themselves off as members of their fantasy gender, instead of "being read" as masqueraders hiding their birth sex.

Who was a he?

Who was a she?

Who fucking cared?

If Hitler had won the war, there'd be no shit like this on the streets of Berlin, be none of these *Untermenschen* alive in Germany, be no need for him to journey here to claim what was rightfully his, be no compulsive attraction to this toilet of a club to stoke his seething wrath before he drove several blocks east along Davie Street to hunt his prey in boy's town.

Wait a minute.

What have we here?

Coming toward the truck?

The Aryan's heartbeat quickened as he watched the druggie cross the street and round the front of his vehicle to the passenger's side. He knew enough about street kids to know that this one would die for a fix. The kid had Slavic cheekbones. What more could he ask?

Punching off the Discman to silence the music, the Aryan turned in the driver's seat to face the opening door. He could hear through the lightweight headphones hiding the swastikas.

"Want me?" the kid asked, poking his head inside.

"A suck and a fuck," the Aryan said. "I'll pay you in cash, meth, or crack."

The kid was so hungry for one of the drugs that he didn't quote his price, just swung into the passenger's seat and said, "I know a dark place nearby."

"Buckle up," the Aryan said. "It's a bumpy ride."

"Bette Davis, right?" The kid's voice was shaky. "'Fasten your seatbelts, it's going to be a bumpy night?'"

As soon as the kid was cinched in against the padded L-frame of the passenger's seat, the driver pulled a lever that compressed a metal plate against the back of the seat frame, jabbing numerous tranquilizer needles out of miniature tubes that had been drilled like Swiss cheese holes through the seat's chassis. Like a first strike of tiny missiles launched from secret underground silos, the needles pierced the padding and spiked into the rump and back muscles of the boy. Impaled by what was tantamount to an iron maiden, he let out a squeal of surprise like the pigs did back home at the ranch, then passed out.

No need to go to boy's town.

Boy's town had come to him.

The Aryan put the truck in gear and pulled away from the curb, turning at the next corner to bypass boy's town and wend his way toward the Trans-Canada Highway. He had a long night's drive ahead of him, up the Fraser River and the Fraser Canyon to the pigsticker waiting in the Cariboo mine.

Angel of Death

Entering Hitler's bunker was like descending into the claustrophobic confines of a cement submarine. It reminded the SS general of the tight squeeze Wolf Pack crews had to endure on torpedo runs under cold Atlantic waves, cut off physically and mentally from surface reality.

Firebombs devastated Berlin up there.

Down here, utensils rattled.

The *Führerbunker* was an underground tomb on two levels. Behind the bulkhead that separated it from Kannenberg Alley, where the guards had confiscated Streicher's pistol and his sons' daggers, were the upper-level servants' quarters. A long oak table laden with food, cognac, wine, and bottled beer ran the length of the central dining passage. The aromas from the hearty German cooking prepared in the kitchen still lingered in the stuffy recycled air. Single file, the general and his sons skirted one side of the table, where several drunks slept off the booze with their flushed faces cradled in their arms, and made for the spiral staircase at the opposite end.

Clang …

Clang …

Clang …

The general's jackboots stomped down the dozen wrought-iron steps.

The lower level continued under the chancellery garden. As this was the innermost sanctum, and Hitler rarely left it, another team of armed sentries guarded the steel door through the last bulkhead. Beyond this point, rumor was, lunatics ran the asylum.

"General, der Chef is waiting for you," a voice chastised Streicher as he and his sons stepped past the point of no return. If there was a meat hook waiting for him in the torture chamber at Gestapo HQ, he would soon know. "I see you've come dressed for the occasion," said Martin Bormann, head of the Nazi Party chancellery and Hitler's private secretary.

"He *is* the führer," Streicher replied.

"Follow me."

With the Reich crumbling around them and fear of traitors lurking everywhere now that the Nazis' *Kriegsglück*—war luck—had all but run out, the SS general and his sons had dressed up to remind the führer of his glory days. After a downtrodden cavalcade of wartorn, bloodstained officers reporting military defeats in field gray battledress, would Hitler not yearn to feast his eyes on the black dress uniform of his SS elite? And—even though it was unseasonable attire for the first week of April—would not the summer uniform of his Hitler Youth, a version of what Nazi Brownshirts had worn during their climb to power, warm his heart?

Hopefully, the garb was meat-hook insurance.

Inside the bunker, it was ghostlike and bleak. So low was the ceiling and narrow the central passage that Streicher felt as if he were being buried alive in a crypt. So poor was the mechanical ventilation that the rough, bare concrete of the rusty brown walls dripped moisture and in places was

splotched with mold. The relentless bombardment of Berlin
had kept the masons from finishing their plasterwork. As
the SS general and his sons followed the odious Bormann
toward the center of the Third Reich's unraveling web, they
passed from a cocoon of sultry warmth to a pocket of
clammy cold. The resulting shivers felt like the bony finger
of death caressing their spines. At this hour of the night, it
was eerily quiet, except for the sound of their echoing
footfalls and the loud hum of a diesel generator in the
powerhouse to the right. On their left, a steel door opened
into the toilets. To the musty odors of fungous boots,
sweaty woolen uniforms, and coal-tar disinfectants was
added a wretched stench. A drainage backup had befouled
the bunker, turning it into a public urinal.

A divider split the central passage into a general sitting
area and a conference hall beyond. Passing the switchboard
room, next to the powerhouse, Bormann entered the conference hall, stopped, swiveled, and ushered the Streichers
toward a threshold just inside the divider and to their left.

Hitler's anteroom.

Martin Bormann brought to mind a stuffed *weisswurst*
sausage. Like the Munich delicacy, his puffy face was
blanched white by the artificial light. Streicher knew
Hitler's take-charge toady by reputation. Universally hated
and feared by the staff of the bunker, this stocky, hard-
drinking bully had maneuvered his own desk into the
anteroom and was always hovering at Hitler's elbow. By
controlling access to der Chef, he could pull strings for
personal gain in these dying days of the Nazi power game.

A sycophant.

A fawner.

An obsequious turd of a yes-man.

The measure of Martin Bormann was the extent of his
lying. Since Hitler didn't drink, the toady hid his own

drinking. Since Hitler didn't smoke, Bormann hid that too. The ultimate hypocrite, he even professed to being a vegetarian. Hitler and Reichsführer-SS Heinrich Himmler— Streicher's boss in the Black Corps, the head of the Gestapo and architect of the final solution—had an aversion to the hunting of animals. "Pure murder," in Himmler's lexicon. The führer's vegetarianism dated back to 1931, when the love of his life, his niece Geli Raubal, committed suicide by shooting herself in the heart. From that point on, Hitler could no longer stomach meat. "It's like eating a corpse!" he would tell dinner guests as they cut into their schnitzels. Bormann, the fawning "vegetarian," was known to hang a salami for midnight snacks from a hook on the back of his cot.

"The führer!" Bormann announced as the SS general and his sons stepped into the anteroom.

The glare that Hitler's henchman shot Streicher was ripe with malevolence. He was a dangerous foe who was jealous of what Streicher controlled down in the SS mines.

At Dora-Mittelbau.

And east in the Sudeten.

Clicking the heels of his jackboots, the general shot his right arm forward in the Hitler salute. Flanking him, Fritz and Hans acknowledged the führer too.

"*Heil* Hitler!"

In the next room, they could see him.

And the Angel of Death.

THE CANDLELIGHT reminded Fritz of the Nuremberg rally and his first Nazi salute. Of the thirty rooms on both levels of the *Führerbunker,* the three that made up Hitler's private quarters were slightly larger than the rest, ten by fifteen feet. The anteroom fronted the study where he now sat in flickering gloom, staring at the wall. Off the study to the right was his bedroom, and to the left was a toilet and shower. In keeping with Hitler's monastic nature, his spartan cells were furbished with but a few sticks of furniture. In Hitler's study, the candlelight burnished the couch on which the führer sat, a coffee table, three chairs, and—the only wall decoration—a portrait of Frederick the Great.

"Come with me, boys."

It was the angel who summoned.

As the son of an SS general who moved in Himmler's inner circle, Fritz had heard rumors and whispers about females offering up their bodies to the führer. Women around Hitler were prone to suicide. Two had thrown themselves from apartment windows. One had jumped in front of Hitler's car. Another had slashed her wrists. And two had shot themselves. It was said that the führer's current mistress—was she this angel?—had tried to kill herself twice. First, she had shot herself in the chest, narrowly missing her heart, because the führer had built a shrine to a woman named Geli Something-or-other. Later, she had swallowed too many pills. All should have known, Fritz thought, that they couldn't have him. Even had the führer not stated publicly, "My bride is Germany!"

"Go with her," the general ordered.

Fritz and Hans stepped forward to join the beckoning angel.

"Hello," she chirped with a buoyant Bavarian accent. "My name is Eva Braun."

The Todesengel! The Angel of Death. Fritz wondered why the SS had dubbed her that. Eva seemed perfectly charming to him. Slim and demurely girlish, she was a strawberry blonde in a stylish black dress. Hitler liked his females *"weich, süss, und dumm"*—soft, sweet, and dumb—so they could fulfill the primary role of women in the Third Reich: giving birth to lots of Aryan children destined to rule the world. Girls were trained to be mothers in the Bund Deutscher Mädel—the German Girls' League—their equivalent to the Hitler Youth. As he and Hans neared her, Fritz fell under the seductive spell of Eva's French perfume, and wondered if this was what the mother he had never known had been like.

The angel set her champagne glass down on the coffee table. With the siren song of silk lingerie looted from the Champs Elysées shops of occupied Paris rustling beneath her skirt, she led the boys past the führer and headed for the dark bedroom beyond like a heavenly Pied Piper.

"My youth," Hitler murmured as Fritz moved within reach. His right hand rising as if to return the Nazi salute, he instead paternally patted the Hitler Youth's cheek.

His touch was like an electric bolt, like the touch of God, like God in that ceiling painting in the Sistine Chapel, where he extends his finger to touch the hand of man. It felt to Fritz as if the führer was passing the torch of the Third Reich's thousand-year future to him.

"*Sieg heil,*" the Hitler Youth replied.

Were those tears in God's fire-sparked eyes?

Eva Braun stood aside at the bedroom door and allowed the boys to precede her into this holiest of holies. Here was where the führer slept and mounted the Todesengel. Only after closing the door did she switch on a weak lamp. The pool of yellow revealed more bare-bones furniture: a single bed, a night table, and a dresser. On the dresser sat a photograph of Hitler's mother, Klara, whose death in 1907 had severely traumatized her teenage son.

"Sit on the bed, boys," Eva suggested.

As Fritz and Hans sat, the bedsprings squeaked.

The squeak became a shriek of sexual ecstasy in the fantasy world of Fritz's Freudian mind. From this position, Eva Braun loomed between the Hitler Youths and the lamp.

Fritz could see the silhouette of her long legs through the fabric of her skirt. The image reminded him of Marlene Dietrich—that sexy traitor—in *The Blue Angel,* one of those *verboten* films the camp guards liked to watch. Before the Nazis had crushed their "anything goes" degeneracy, the *Kabaretts* of Berlin had steamed with unbridled sex. Now, backlit Braun stirred both Fritz's loins and his post-pubescent imagination, conjuring up that Hollywood queen in her early German role—with the top hat, the tight top that clung to her breasts, and the skirt that split at her waist to reveal the frilly knickers of a whore and the dark stockings that sheathed her long, long milky legs.

You bitch in heat, thought Fritz. When *I'm* führer, I'll have an Angel of Death like *her.*

THE SS CALLED her the Todesengel because Braun's mid-March arrival in Berlin meant that the führer planned to make his last stand here, smack dab in the path of the vengeful Russians—who were raping, pillaging, and killing their way in from the horrific graveyard of Stalingrad—rather than moving his Nazi elite to the Berghof complex, high in the Bavarian Alps, where the surrender, if it came to that, would be into the gentler hands of the Western Allies.

Berlin meant suicide to the Black Corps.

The Death's Head for *them.*

By candle glow, the SS general watched the Angel of Death spirit Fritz and Hans away from Hitler's study. No sooner had Eva Braun shut the bedroom door than the führer dismissed his secretary with a flick of his hand. The scowl that Bormann cast at Streicher was as sharp as the daggers he'd confiscated from the Obergruppenführer's sons, but the oaf had no option but to retreat to the anteroom.

As Bormann closed the padded door, he switched on the generated light.

The SS general stifled a gasp. Hitler was now a mockery of his former dynamic self. From 1942 on, this man who had conquered an empire from the North Cape of Norway to the African deserts, from the Pyrenees of Spain to the Caucasus of Russia, had been aging at a rate of five visible years for each calendar one. Since he went underground, the slide had hastened.

Plus, he was addled by drugs.

Hatless, tonight the führer wore the same familiar uniform that he had donned on the first day of the war: the once spotless, simple, pearl gray tunic and long black trousers. On the breast pocket were his golden Nazi Party badge, his First World War black wound badge, and—for bravery in the trenches—his Iron Cross. But soup slop and mustard spots now stained the rumpled jacket, into the baggy shell of which he seemed to have withdrawn like a turtle. His head hunkered into his shoulders. His spine was hunched. As he struggled to his feet, he seemed in danger of losing his balance. Unable to stand erect, his body twitching and trembling, the führer braced his left leg against the coffee table for support. Obviously, Streicher had to go to him, for whatever that quack of a doctor had shot into his patient—at best, mysterious tranquilizers; at worst, morphine—der Chef was a palsied wreck.

He's done, thought the general.

And so am I.

At almost fifty-six, Hitler could have been taken for seventy. His eyes, once ice blue and lustrous, were now as gray and filmy as the skin of a grape. His eyeballs were sunken, the whites bloodshot. Glazed and unfocused, they registered no expression as Streicher approached, and neither did his immobile, vapid face. His brown hair had turned suddenly gray, and drooping black sacs beneath his eyes betrayed lack of sleep. Through the wrinkled mask of a sickly, sallow complexion ran deep folds from his pulpy nose to the corners of his mouth. Up close, the SS general could see the spittle on Hitler's lips and the drool down the front of his tunic, and he could hear him whistling through his teeth.

"My führer," Streicher said. "You sent for me?"

With a cold-fish, flapping gesture that was little more than a jerky reflex, Hitler listlessly took the Obergruppenführer's hand and didn't let go. That was telling indeed, for Streicher—like every survivor in the upper ranks of the Third Reich—knew that the führer recoiled from physical contact.

Something was up.

Like a child leading his parent across to a candy store window, the führer, dragging his left leg, shuffled toward the portrait of Frederick the Great on his study wall. Everyone in the SS had heard about "Old Fritz," the oil painting by Anton Graff that Hitler had purchased in Munich in 1934. As der Chef had moved from HQ to HQ, through six long years of war, it was the perquisite that always flew with him. Chefpilot Hans Baur's irksome chore was to handle Old Fritz with tender care, and nothing inside the führer's plane took precedence over the special bulky packing crate. Even generals were left behind to make room for it in the narrow corridor between the Condor's seats, where the wood-and-steel obstacle scratched the fancy leatherwork of Baur's flying domain. Of flaming Bavarian temperament, Hitler's pilot had complained, but his murmured exasperation always fell on deaf ears. Back and forth across the Reich, Old Fritz had flown, before ending up in the bunker for the last stand.

"Argonaut," muttered Hitler. "That was the code name. Churchill, Roosevelt, Stalin. Used by the Big Three."

"Code name, Führer?"

"For Yalta. The Crimea. On the Black Sea. Where they met to plot how to conquer me."

"Argonaut? From the Greek myth?"

Hitler nodded. "To the Black Sea. That's where they sailed. Jason and the Argonauts. On their hunt to find the land of the mythical Golden Fleece."

"I see."

Actually, Streicher didn't see at all. So addled was the führer after nine years of injected poisonous drugs that he was barely able to speak a coherent thought. From 1942 until April 1944, the Crimean peninsula had been held by the German army. In selecting it as the place for their recent rendezvous, the Allies were trumpeting that the Nazis were in full retreat.

"Frederick the Great. Remember, General?"

The führer let go of Streicher's hand to gesture at the painting in a shaky sweep. The portrait of Old Fritz—was that a wig or his own hairstyle?—showed him with a huge medal on his chest. So jittery was Hitler's other hand that he had to corral it with his good arm and pin it against his Iron Cross.

"The enemy at the gates," der Chef added.

So that was it. The Frederick the Great connection. The reason the führer had sat in the dark, motionless, as if in a trance, his chin buried in his hand, gazing at the portrait by candlelight. He was looking for hope, inspiration, a reason to believe. What the SS general had interrupted was a besieged man at prayer.

The triumph was a familiar tale to every German schoolboy who'd been raised on the drum-and-trumpet history texts of Streicher's generation. In 1762, toward the end of the Seven Years' War, the king of Prussia—Old Fritz himself—was holed up in his ruined palace in Silesia, with his capital of Berlin under siege. His army was greatly outnumbered by a coalition of Russian, Austrian, and Saxon forces, so Frederick the Great was left with two options. He could fight to the death in a losing battle, or he could swallow the poison in a small glass tube.

A tube like the one that Hitler now pulled from his pocket.

"Cyanide," said Hitler, holding up the vial.

Streicher recognized the tube as one of those that Himmler had distributed to those Nazis who might be forced to commit "self-murder" in the days to come. The cylindrical container looked like a lipstick: a translucent plastic ampule encircled with a blue band. It went into a leather pouch that could be worn around the neck. At the moment, the SS general's own poison was in his cheek, ready for him to bite down on if he learned that a Gestapo meat hook was his fate.

"Kriegsglück," mumbled Hitler.

Now, two centuries later, Hitler faced the same catastrophe as Old Fritz. That Yalta coalition of Britain, America, and the Soviet Union was tightening around Berlin, where the führer—like his predecessor—was holed up in a ruined palace. Der Chef faced the same choice between the lesser of two evils. Fight to the death in a losing battle. Or crunch the vial of poison with his teeth.

Unless …

"Dr. Göbbels has seen it!"

"Führer?"

"In the stars!"

"Seen what?" Streicher asked, taken aback.

"Victory!"

"When?"

"Before the end of this month. Herr Doktor had them bring forth my horoscope."

"Who?"

"The astrology department of his Propaganda Ministry. The stars foretold of disaster in the early months of 1945, followed by an overwhelming victory in late April."

"That is good news," said Streicher.

"It is written in the stars."

This physically senile has-been was fueled by shredded nerves and dubious medicaments, but abruptly the general caught a spark of that old fury and willpower that had driven the führer to the apex of Nazi influence. Grabbing Streicher by the arm, Hitler sank his fingers into the engineer's biceps.

"Is it safe?"

"Führer?"

"The secret down in the mine?"

"The Mittelwerk is in crisis. It has about a week. That's when the U.S. First Army will reach Nordhausen."

Hitler dismissed that concern with a flap of his trembling left arm.

"The East!" he snapped.

Streicher sensed instantly that he, too, was in jeopardy. The wrong answer now would cost him his life.

"The *Flugkreisel* works!" the general confirmed.

Another flap of the arm dismissed that breakthrough as well.

Hitler was getting angry. His yellow-gray face flushed. As his lips nervously nibbled each other, a strand of drool dribbled from the corner of his mouth.

"Die Glocke!" he shouted at last. "Is it safe?"

"It is, Führer."

"And does it slow time?"

SS-General Ernst Streicher carefully weighed his answer. "If time doesn't run out on us, you *will* see the glorious future of your thousand-year Reich."

Cyclops

Sgt. Dane Winter awoke the next morning to learn that whoever had carved that Nazi swastika into the forehead of the Congo Man had been turned overnight by *The Vancouver Times* into a hero straight from the pages of Greek myth.

Dane was an early riser. Morning was his time. He liked to get the jump on dawn to start his day, which invariably began with orange juice and the newspaper while he steeled his resolve for his five-mile run along the seawall of False Creek to watch the sun come up. So with juice glass in hand and still in his dressing gown, he fetched the morning paper from the mat of his second-story condo overlooking the narrow inlet that English Bay surveyors had mistaken for a creek back in the 1850s and read this:

Vigilante Kills Alleged Cannibal
Settling the Score?
By Cort Jantzen

In a crime that had striking parallels to the killing of the Cyclops in Homer's *Odyssey*, a vigilante may have settled the score with an alleged cannibal killer who was released from the Forensic Psychiatric Hospital just two days ago by the Court of Appeal.

"Whoever killed him is a hero to me," the father of the six-year-old girl allegedly murdered by Marcus Cole, a Liberian refugee, told *The Times* in an emotion-charged interview. "This vigilante gave us the justice we were denied by the court...."

The story was accompanied by a front-page photograph that had been shot with a telephoto lens from across Mosquito Creek. It showed two Mounties—Winter and Chandler—standing over the huge hulk of the "one-eyed" monster on the bank under the bridge. It caught the patch over one eye and the stake rammed through the other to pin the head to the ground, but thanks to the bloody face and the camera angle, the "hold-back evidence" of the Nazi swastika carved into the African's forehead wasn't visible.

In addition to the photograph, the main story had a sidebar next to it. It read:

Blinding the Cyclops
By Cort Jantzen

Odysseus was the Greek hero who thought up the ruse of the Trojan Horse in Homer's *Iliad*. During his ten-year voyage home in *The Odyssey,* Odysseus—known as Ulysses in Latin—stopped at the island of Sicily for provisions. There, he got trapped in the cave of a Cyclops named Polyphemus, a gigantic, one-eyed cannibal who feasted off Odysseus' crew. To escape, the Trojan War hero hatched another plot. He got the Cyclops drunk on potent wine, and when the man-eater passed out, the Greeks blinded him by ramming a big, heated, pointed stake into the single eye in the center of his forehead....

The other half of the front page was taken up by a rival story on a stealth killer who was loose in boy's town. Between them, those two scoops had pushed the report about Zinc Chandler's killing of the Ripper at Colony Farm to the inside pages. Dane read, then reread, everything on the Congo Man, satisfying himself that there was no leak concerning the swastika. That secret, had it been known, would have changed public perception. As it was, the paper focused on the idea of a vigilante hero "settling a score."

Bottom line: Dane was investigating the murder of a monster that the public was glad to have dead, and the killer he was stalking was seen as a mythic Greek hero.

The Mountie changed into his jogging suit and went for a run.

THE UNDERTAKER KNOCKED on his door at just after eight and handed him a cardboard box containing the cremated remains of his grandfather. He signed for the ashes—all that was left of the man who had raised Dane after the deaths of his parents and his grandmother in that plane crash in the Cascade Mountains—and carried the box into the living room. Opening the package, he took out a plastic bag filled with six pounds of human soot and elemental bone fragments as dismal gray as a bout of chronic depression.

Ashes to ashes, dust to dust, he thought.

So at last, at long, long last, he too was on a collision course with the Mountain.

HIS USUAL DRIVE to work took him due north from the south shore of False Creek, across Burrard Bridge to the downtown core, and through Stanley Park on its bisecting causeway to Lions Gate Bridge. Spanning First Narrows, the constricted seaway that joined English Bay to the west with the harbor sheltered behind the park, the suspension bridge reached across to the peaked North Shore. Dane's detachment policed the southern slopes of the towering mountains as far east as you could see.

Today, however, he was required at HQ.

So he headed south along Cambie Street, the warm rays of the sun shooting in through the driver's window until they were blocked by the green hump of Little Mountain. As he wheeled his way through the post–rush hour traffic, Dane mulled over the status of the stalled Congo Man case. In breaking the neck of the Ripper, Inspector Chandler had also snapped their best lead. Assuming the Ripper had convinced the African to snuff his nemesis in the Mounted Police, who had a motive to impale the Congo Man to the bank of Mosquito Creek? And why gouge a swastika into his forehead?

The Congo Man was dead.

So was the Ripper.

So if the death of the African was the result of a falling-out between the partners of a killing team, that lead was dead too.

The strongest motive for killing the Congo Man belonged to the parents of the six-year-old girl he had allegedly kidnapped, killed, and cannibalized. But both had watertight alibis for the time period in which the crime could have occurred. They were at a convention in San Francisco with at least a thousand corroborators.

Dane had checked yesterday afternoon.

Of course, that's one of the oldest tricks in the book: contract with a hired killer to do your dirty work, then set yourself up with an ironclad alibi. There's always the possibility that your hit man will squeal, of course, so if you're really cold-blooded, you cover your tracks by taking out the contract killer yourself.

The recent death of his granddad had Dane grieving too, so he wanted to make sure he had the evidence he needed before he closed in on the bereaved parents of the cannibalized child. At the moment, he didn't have that evidence.

So what was left?

Perhaps the Congo Man was the random victim of a gang of neo-Nazi thugs. Or perhaps *The Vancouver Times* was right, and a vigilante had taken justice into his own hands. If so, then unless someone phoned in a tip, Dane would have to wait for forensics to indicate the path of investigation.

One thing was certain: the killer was no hero. You could never be a hero if you adopted the Nazi swastika as your calling card of revenge and retribution.

LITTLE MOUNTAIN was crowned by Queen Elizabeth Park. The park—which was named not for Elizabeth II but for the Queen Mother, whom Hitler had dubbed "the most dangerous woman in Europe" for her defiant stand in London during the Blitz—ended at 37th Avenue. Dane turned right off Cambie and found a parking space at the curb.

RCMP headquarters was an L-shaped complex of buildings. Dane entered the administration building on 37th, which made up the short arm of the L. His first stop at HQ was Internal Affairs, where he wrote out a statement backing Inspector Chandler to the hilt. Medical opinion held that Rudi Lucke, the psych nurse at Colony Farm, would have died, and not just been blinded, if the Mountie hadn't stopped the assault at that exact moment.

Exiting the admin building, Dane crossed Heather Street to the operations building, in the crook of the L, then turned right along the side street that ran parallel to Cambie, walking back in the direction he had just driven.

The RCMP forensic laboratory at 5201 Heather was a mushroom-shaped building that had lost its uniqueness when the stem was recently bricked into a square to create more space. The lab was halfway between the ops building and Special X. After being buzzed in, Dane signed in at the counter just inside the automatic door, then the sergeant was ushered into the case receipt unit. A large, open space, the unit was full of benches with computers. Yesterday, Dane had electronically transmitted a C-414 request for analysis, so the tech dealing with him—a petite East Indian woman—pulled that filing up onscreen.

"Known document?" she asked.

Dane passed her a sample of the Ripper's handwriting that he'd seized from his room at Colony Farm. After documenting that exhibit, she attached a barcode label so it could be tracked every step of the way by LIMS, the laboratory information management system. The RCMP lab ensured that *nothing* got lost.

"Questioned document?" she asked.

Dane handed her the crumpled scrap of paper with Zinc Chandler's home address. He knew the procedure from here. Both exhibits—and the third one in his evidence case—would be packaged up and couriered off to the documents section in Edmonton. There, both known and questioned documents would be compared visually and by a low-power microscope for similarities. The exhibits would also be swabbed for DNA traces, and their paper would be checked for telling indentations. Tomorrow, he would receive a report directly from Edmonton.

For Dane, the lab work was backup. He already knew the answer. Having examined both documents himself, he was convinced that all the words had been penned by the Ripper.

"Tool marks?" the lab tech inquired on receiving the exhibit from Dane's evidence case.

"It's a blown-up photo. They were carved into a victim who's still in the morgue."

At the autopsy—performed late yesterday afternoon by the pathologist, Dr. Gill Macbeth—the sergeant had taken detailed photos of the swastika in the skin of the Congo Man's forehead. If a similar signature showed up in another murder, it would be crucial to know the order and direction in which the cuts were carved to determine if the same killer had left both swastikas. The documents section, which tested indentations, also matched tool marks.

Before leaving the lab, Dane checked to see if the blood found on the handle of the stake in the eye of the Congo Man had been analyzed. If it belonged to someone other than the victim, he might have a link to the swastika killer.

No results yet.

DANE'S TREK up the long arm of the L on Heather Street came to a halt at the corner of 33rd. Special X was unlike the clichéd cop shops seen in thousands of movies and TV shows. The Tudor building on the corner had begun life as the barracks for two hundred Mounties and the stables for 140 horses in 1921. It was still referred to as the Heather Stables, even though it now housed the thoroughly modern manhunters of Special X. An expanse of green lawn fronted the beamed façade of what could have been, from the look of it, Shakespeare's country home.

My kingdom for a horse, thought Dane.

Inside the front doors, Dane passed security, then paused in the high-vaulted entrance hall to take it all in. What he wouldn't give to police here. This was the elite posting that every Horseman yearned for. You didn't apply; you were chosen. And there was only one way around the long wait for C/Supt. Robert DeClercq to notice your service record, and that was for Special X to usurp one of your cases.

DeClercq's way of quelling the resentment caused by commandeering files was to second the investigating officer on the case to his unit for the duration of that particular manhunt. Maybe—just *maybe*—you'd be asked to stay on. That crack was almost worth having the North Shore Vigilante settle another score, turning the single-victim Congo Man case into a serial-killer manhunt that would call for Special X.

Almost. But not quite.

A wide staircase angled up to the second floor, where DeClercq's corner office faced 33rd and Heather. Alongside the stairs were hung historical sketches and photographs that traced the mythic heroics of the thin red line from the frontier days, when Superintendent James "Bub" Walsh and a handful of redcoat lancers had dismounted in the camp of Sitting Bull to lay down the law to the fugitive Sioux.

Coming down the stairs was a woman who was almost tall enough to be an Amazon. Black ankle boots under navy pants with a yellow side-stripe. Gun belt cinched around an hourglass waist, the nine in its holster, with a pouch for two more magazines, another pouch for handcuffs, and a radio. Short-sleeved gray shirt, open at the neck, bison-head crest on both shoulders, corporal's chevron on both epaulets. Pretty face with little makeup, emerald green eyes, flaming red hair pulled back in a bun so it wasn't grabbable in a fight.

As she reached the foot of the stairs, Dane dropped his eyes to the name tag pinned to the pocket bulging over her right breast. "J. Hett."

Working with her would be a definite perk if the sergeant ever got the chance to join Special X.

Ooh-la-la.

Turning on her heel, the redhead entered the ground-floor squad room. From what Dane could see though the threshold, the room seemed more like a museum than a bullpen for cops. Mannequins displayed the various changes that had been made to the red serge uniform over time. The walls were decorated with Wild West firearms.

ViCLAS was housed in the cyber cellar of Special X. It shared a clutch of offices at the bottom of the stairs that descended from the entrance of the Tudor building. Joining the online bloodhounds in the basement were the psych- and geo-profilers. Mounted on the wall of the staircase was the huge, horned bison head seen on the regimental crest. The moth-eaten mascot was periodically removed from Special X and used to decorate colorful force functions, like regimental dinners or the formal red serge ball.

Staff Sergeant Rusty Lewis, another redhead who had a freckled face to go with his ruddy hair, was sitting in his office next to the officers' mess. A whiff of curry lingered from a recent ceremony. Dane's knock on the doorjamb caused the cyber cop to break away from the digital dragnet on his monitor screen.

"Saw you in the morning paper, Sergeant," Lewis said. "What can I do to help?"

"I need a database check on hold-back evidence. A signature that I wish kept out of public knowledge."

"How wide do you want the case search?"

"ViCLAS across Canada. HITS in Washington State. And VICAP for the rest of America."

"What's the signature?"

"A Nazi swastika carved into the flesh of the victim."

The three crime-linkage systems all worked the same way. When a murder occurred within the ambit of each dragnet, the investigator filled out a questionnaire that fed pertinent information into a database of previous offenses. Then a powerful search engine compared the current murder to all those in the past to spot links that might reveal a serial killer. What Dane hoped his query would uncover was any killing in North America signed with a swastika.

In the case of hold-back evidence, a special procedure took effect. The "Nazi swastika" was segregated off in an access-controlled link that no one else could see without Dane's authorization. Only Staff Sergeant Lewis could search the ViCLAS files, and he would make personal contact with secure counterparts in Washington State and Quantico, Virginia, to ask them to troll HITS and VICAP on the sly. That would keep the Nazi link "for your eyes only."

In theory, at least.

Big Bad Bill

In the black world of the Pentagon, you can do whatever you want. Lie, cheat, steal, cover up, or kill at random. No one can stop you, because the black world doesn't exist.

In this office like any other office off the long, wide corridors of the five-sided HQ of the U.S. Department of Defense sat a man like any other man in Uncle Sam's military-industrial complex. Just from the look of him, you knew this guy had the right stuff in spades. In the cool, low-lighted atmosphere of this windowless environment, you might mistake him for just another aging career soldier riding a desk into the sunset of his retirement. He still sported the haircut—flat top, short back and sides, salt-and-pepper gray—and boasted the physique of the has-been fighter who continued to heft weights in the gym. You might conclude that his Pentagon power, like his body, had waned.

You'd be wrong.

Exactly what Bill did, no one seemed to know, but everyone knew better than to ask. Bill didn't wear the stiff, blue uniform of the company man, the harness that told the world you came out of West Point and were a force to reckon with. Instead, he wore a white, short-sleeved button-down shirt and a nondescript tie that made him look more like a payroll clerk than a warrior.

But there were clues.

The wings of his desk were as wide as those of an eagle hunting for a kill. *Uncle Sam Wants You* was the title of the framed picture centered on the wall behind it. But this Uncle Sam wasn't the one commonly seen on recruitment posters: the bearded dandy of a Colonel Sanders in a top hat emblazoned with a star, accusatorily pointing the index finger of his right hand at duty-shirking *you*. That "Uncle Sam" was actually Samuel Wilson, the meat packer who supplied the U.S. Army with grub during the War of 1812. The image backing Bill, however, was of an American eagle in a full-throttle dive, its wings crooked for attack, its hooked beak open in a shriek as it goes for your eyes, its forward-thrust talons abnormally elongated, razor-sharp, and spread to sink into the guts of its prey.

Uncle Sam Wants You was a double entendre.

Sam was the bald eagle.

The picture was Bill's "read between the brushstrokes" in-joke.

How Sam wanted you differed according to which side of the beak and talons you were on.

Big Bad Bill was head of the Pentagon's "Weird Shit" Division.

He was in the beak-and-talons business.

An art critic with an eye for hidden subconscious form might have been able to discern the shape of a Stuka dive-bomber in the outline of the eagle. That's because Bill had designed the painting. With its inverted gull-wings and ugly silhouette, the Junkers JU-87 had triggered "Stuka fright" in the soldiers and refugees fleeing across Europe in 1940. In a steep dive of eighty degrees, the sirens in the plane's wheel covers, called Jericho trumpets, would begin to scream, terrorizing those below as the bomber plunged. So precipitous was its dive that the Stuka came with an automatic pull-up system in case the pilot blacked out from the high g-force. The plummeting dive enabled it to attack a target with surgical precision. As soon as the payload had been released, whistles in the bomb fins shrilled, shattering the morale of enemies below, who could track death coming down to greet them. As its *coup de grâce,* the Stuka would circle to strafe survivors with its machine guns.

All through his childhood, a Nazi Stuka had dive-bombed Big Bad Bill's bed. Other plastic models had dangled from the ceiling of his room—a B-24 Liberator, a B-25 Mitchell, a B-17 Flying Fortress, and a P-51 Mustang—but none had captured his imagination quite like the shrieking "Stuke."

That was another clue to Bill's trade.

Nazi weapons.

The music playing softly in his office wasn't Wagner. The music was Bach, another German.

There was something binary about Bach that spoke to the genes in Big Bad Bill. Bach's music, so ordered and contrapuntal, had technology as its soul, so naturally it appealed to the highly organized ciphers that sparked in Bill's brain.

The bookshelf to Bill's right offered another clue.

Commander Ian Fleming had been a British intelligence officer during the Second World War. As such, he'd organized a ragtag commando unit to plunder Nazi technology. Called 30 Assault Unit RN, it ignored the rule book in its roughshod exploits. In the battle for Cherbourg, the unit was assigned the task of capturing German naval headquarters. Their behavior in savoring the spoils of war was described as "merry, courageous, amoral, loyal, lying toughs, hugely disinclined to take no for an answer from foe or *fräulein.*" Later, Fleming's private army was subordinated to the team of British tech-pirates dubbed T-Forces. Five thousand strong, T-Forces advanced with Monty's Twenty-first Army Group and the U.S. Army, looting any Nazi secrets churned up in the onslaught.

Out of that experience, and the roguish exuberance of 30 Assault Unit RN, Fleming created 007, James Bond.

Because the Weird Shit Division was in the same line of work as Fleming's factual and fictional creations, Bill was a fan of the Bond books. Most of his first editions were signed by the author. Not only did he have all the Richard Chopping covers, but he also had the rarest Bond book of all: the recalled first edition of *The Man with the Golden Gun,* with the cover whose embossed golden gun had oxidized.

Bill identified with Bond.

They were both licensed to kill.

THE WEIRD SHIT DIVISION was spawned by the atomic bomb.

On August 2, 1939, about a month before the start of the Second World War, Albert Einstein wrote his famous letter to the president of the United States:

Sir:

Some recent work by E. Fermi and L. Szilard, which has been communicated to me in manuscript, leads me to expect that the element uranium may be turned into a new and important source of energy.... Certain aspects of the situation which has arisen seem to call for watchfulness and, if necessary, quick action on the part of the Administration.... This new phenomena would also lead to the construction of bombs....

Roosevelt appointed a Uranium Committee and gave it $6,000 for experiments. By 1940, the press was full of speculation about nuclear fission. If uranium was bombarded with neutrons, the theory went, that might induce a nuclear reaction, producing more neutrons in a massive chain reaction that might escalate into a huge explosion in the blink of an eye. The result: an atomic bomb.

But by the time the U.S. entered the war in 1941, you couldn't find a mention of fission in the papers. It was as if the subject had never arisen. In Pentagon-speak, the bomb had "gone black."

Ironically, the large-scale U.S. atomic project started on December 6, 1941, the day before Japan attacked Pearl Harbor. August 1942 saw it named the Manhattan Project. Right from the beginning, the secret had leaked like a sieve. Sure, it held until the dropping of the bomb on Japan, but in the meantime, the Soviet Union had acquired the most classified American technology in U.S. history. It exploded its own bomb within a few scant years.

But if the Manhattan Project was a faulty security model, there was successful subterfuge with the Philadelphia Experiment.

How's this for science fiction?

In 1943, scientists experimented with making navy ships invisible to radar by charging them with intense electromagnetic fields. The ship used as a guinea pig was the USS *Eldridge,* a navy destroyer berthed in Philadelphia. Huge electric generators and radio-frequency transmitters were used to wrap the ship with an electromagnetic cloak. The first test that July rendered the *Eldridge* invisible to the naked eye, with only the trough of displaced water under its hull proof that it was still there. Fifteen minutes later, it reappeared, and the crew complained of severe nausea and memory loss. The second test that October caused the *Eldridge* to vanish from its berth in Philadelphia and reappear a moment later some 250 miles away, at a shipyard in Norfolk, Virginia. During the time lapse, the ship and its new crew had been transported into a "parallel dimension." Some of the crew had been atomized and were never seen again.

Those who made it back with the *Eldridge* were either physically disabled or driven mad by the ordeal. Five of them had suffered a worse fate. While being transported through the other dimension, the ship had materially transmuted to accommodate human flesh. The Philadelphia Experiment had fused them right into the metal of the destroyer.

Weird shit, huh?

Some sort of paranormal mystery?

An outlandish myth with a psychotic whiff of paranoia wrapped in conspiracy?

In fact, the Soviets had a word for truth masked by fiction. *Disinformatsiya.*

That marvel of disinformation had been the brainchild of Big Bad Bill's predecessor in this office. Code-named Hardware, he was a legend both in and after his time. What Hardware had realized was that the best way to hide a super-classified secret in plain sight was to mix the truth with so much unbelievable science fiction that anyone divulging it would appear to be nuts. If the Pentagon was going to develop weird shit weapons like the atomic bomb in its non-existent black world, then what America needed was a keeper of its secrets: a Weird Shit Division in Washington that would function as an airlock between that black world and the white world of Uncle Sam's public face.

The British had used disinformation during the war. To protect the nation's radar secrets from the Luftwaffe, RAF intelligence agents had leaked the myth that fighter/bomber command pilots could see in the dark because of all the carrots they ate as kids. Hardware had learned from that that disinformation takes on a life of its own once you seed it in the public's imagination. Even today, it's damn near impossible to avoid parents who pass on that disinformation as worldly wisdom: "Eat your carrots. They're good for your eyes."

Bouncing off that, Hardware had crafted the mandate of the Weird Shit Division: If you spin the weird shit going on in the black world into even weirder shit and serve it to the public as "low-hanging fruit," their collective imagination will spin your subterfuge into the weirdest shit of all.

Ergo, Hardware's lie about the phantom ship.

Disinformation.

The Philadelphia Experiment had indeed taken place. The test was known as "degaussing"—that is, trying to cancel a ship's magnetic field by cloaking it with such intense electricity that nearby light and radar waves would distort. That optical illusion was supposed to render the vessel invisible to both the human eye and electronic sensors. What more could the navy ask for than invisible ships? Unfortunately, the degaussing degaussed the brains of the crew as well, since thoughts are nothing but nerve impulses triggered electrically. The Pentagon didn't want mind-scrambled sailors babbling far and wide about what had happened to them, so the Weird Shit Division had mixed a lot of hooey with the facts to neutralize the truth.

To this day, the Philadelphia Experiment is equated with kooky stuff like wormholes and parallel dimensions.

And Stealth.

BIG BAD BILL had a Stealth cover-up of his own to augment Hardware's disinformation.

The UFO had crashed in the small hours of the sweltering night of July 11, 1986. Those in the immediate area, and for many miles around, had heard a supersonic boom up in the black sky, then felt a thunderous pressure wave flatten the scrub on the ground. A moment later, whatever it was slammed into Saturday Peak, in a desert canyon twelve miles away from Bakersfield, California. The whole horizon lit up like the Fourth of July, with flames flashing heavenward as if they were shooting stars and the thunderclap from that enormous explosion deafening the ears of shocked onlookers.

Within minutes, Bill had scrambled a Pentagon "red team" to lock down the site. Helicopters full of soldiers brandishing assault rifles and wearing night-vision goggles had swooped down on the area, which bordered the Sierra Nevadas and Sequoia National Park. Challenge their authority and you would get shot. Bill's order was simple: Don't let the secret out at any cost.

With dozens of brushfires blazing on the edge of the forest, a cleanup crew from the Weird Shit Division set to work, gathering up every trace of what had crash-landed and then sifting the dirt within a thousand yards of the point of impact, before finally seeding the UFO's crater with obsolete bits of metal that would have alien-hunters and conspiracy theorists scratching their heads for years.

The seeded clues were from a vintage 1960s fighter.

The fighter was a Voodoo.

Disinformation, with black superstition attached.

Hardware would have been proud.

THE MAN who let the secret out was President Ronald Reagan. In November 1988, with the Soviet Union crumbling and the Pentagon itching for daylight tests—and the man himself on his way out of the Oval Office and yearning to be given credit—the commander-in-chief had revealed that a secret squadron of F-117A Stealth fighters had been flying out of a classified Nevada airfield for over five years. Unfortunately, one had crashed near Bakersfield in 1986.

The Stealth was a weird-shaped thing. The product of pure math, physics, and algebraic formulae, it was a bunch of geometric angles somehow fashioned into the silhouette of a jet. It had none of the aerodynamic curves of a regular warplane. Instead, it carried a multitude of flat, ugly panels. Each surface—or facet—was angled in such a manner that it would reflect an incoming radar beam away, and thereby shrink the "radar signature" of the Stealth fighter down to the size of a wasp's.

You can't shoot down what you can't "see."

That the Stealth—unlike the bomb—had been kept secret for half a century, since the days of the Philadelphia Experiment, was testimony to the effectiveness of the Weird Shit Division and its commanders, Hardware and his successor, Big Bad Bill.

How had they kept a secret that big for so long?

You don't fuck with Uncle Sam if you know what's good for you. Those who had tried had mysteriously disappeared and never been seen again.

Of course, of all the dirty little secrets of the black world, none was dirtier than the cover-up by the Weird Shit Division of what had happened in July 1947 at Roswell, New Mexico.

That crazy UFO yarn, complete with clandestine autopsies on big-headed aliens.

There was a clue to the baffling secret behind the Roswell Incident in the clutch of framed photos on the wall above Big Bad Bill's shelf of Bond books. One photo, taken at Fort Bliss, near El Paso, Texas, in 1947, captured the Peenemünde Rocket Team. These 126 Nazi rocketeers were blasting off V-2 missiles for the Pentagon at the White Sands Proving Ground in New Mexico. Heading them was SS-Sturmbannführer Wernher von Braun. In the group photo, he was the man in the front row with his hand in one pocket of his dark slacks. Roswell, New Mexico, was 125 miles east of the White Sands Proving Ground.

The UFO that crash-landed there had been the darkest secret of the black world for well over half a century, and now that secret was in danger of public exposure on two fronts.

A secret to acquire.

And a secret to keep.

The pile of papers stamped with the Nazi swastika had reached the Weird Shit Division by way of a dummy address in Switzerland. A little coercion had revealed that the package really came from a post office in central British Columbia. That had set off alarm bells in Big Bad Bill's mind, for shortly after the Roswell Incident in 1947, the Skunk Mine in the Cariboo Mountains of that same Canadian province had imploded.

Where there's smoke, there's fire.

Was this confirmation?

For here, on the computer screen in Bill's Pentagon office, was a supposedly secret signature check by an FBI cyber cop at VICAP in Quantico, Virginia, on behalf of an RCMP cyber cop named Rusty Lewis at ViCLAS in Vancouver, British Columbia. The officers were searching for any case with a "Nazi swastika" signature. In the aftermath of 9/11, Bill had acquired unfettered access to everything known about everybody. So the Weird Shit Division's search for links to "Nazi swastika" signatures like the one stamped on the pile of wartime documents had quickly revealed the RCMP's own search for matches to hold-back evidence in a B.C. murder case.

What kind of hold-back evidence?

Bill had to know.

According to the Mounties' request to the FBI, authorization for information on the Vancouver case had to be obtained from the investigating officer, Sgt. Dane Winter.

Bill reached for the last truly secure phone in America.

This was a job for Mr. Clean.

Tomorrowland

NORDHAUSEN, GERMANY
April 4, 1945

SS-Sturmbannführer Wernher von Braun had stood on this very spot not long ago and placed one hand on Fritz Streicher's shoulder as the Hitler Youth gazed up at the vast night cosmos. Von Braun had come to Dora-Mittelbau to check on the progress of the concentration-camp slaves he himself had handpicked at Buchenwald. You could never be too paranoid in the Third Reich, as von Braun had learned at two o'clock in the morning on March 22, 1944, the day before his thirty-second birthday. That was the morning when, by the direct order of Reichsführer-SS Heinrich Himmler, three Gestapo agents had knocked on his apartment door and then shuffled him off to prison in Stettin for defying the SS. Even though time was now tight in the production of the V-2 "wonder weapon," the rocketeer had nevertheless found a moment for the son of the slave-driving commandant who oversaw every aspect of the Third Reich's secret armory.

"One day," von Braun had said, choosing his words with care, for he'd been arrested for voicing the fact that his future interest in the V-2 wasn't as a weapon, "our rockets will have blown the Allies away. The same technology that will annihilate our enemies will then launch us into outer space."

The doctor of physics was a handsome, haughty man, the son of a German baron. As a boy, he had entered a school established by Frederick the Great, and soon became obsessed by the book *Die Rakete zu den Planetenräumen (The Rocket into Interplanetary Space)* by Hermann Oberth. As a teen, von Braun had experimented with space-age propulsion by strapping a cluster of solid-fuel rockets to a wagon that he shot down a crowded street. From there, he moved on to tests at a vacant army proving ground, quickly winning a contract to develop weapons for the Nazis. Under a military grant, he earned his Ph.D. in the theoretical and practical problems of liquid-propellant rocket engines. By the age of thirty, von Braun was the head of technical development at Peenemünde. This area—south of Sweden, east of Denmark, north of Berlin—was an isolated, secure, wooded pocket of Germany, on the island of Usedom, where the mouth of the river Peene met the Baltic Sea. A huge complex at Peenemünde was home to two thousand rocketeers and four thousand other personnel. It was there, on October 3, 1942, that von Braun had first launched the best of Hitler's *Vergeltungswaffe*—revenge weapons—the awesome V-2.

The space age had begun.

So here von Braun and Fritz had stood not so long ago, gazing up into the outer reaches of a new frontier while the Nazi rocketeer wowed the enthralled Hitler Youth with this promise of tomorrow.

"Big, reliable, powerful rockets. That's what the Reich needs. And the same rockets that we fire to defend our Fatherland will soon take us up to orbit the earth."

"Battle stations," Fritz said, "shooting death rays. Missile shields raining rockets on the *Untermenschen*. Control space and we will control the world."

"Think bigger," von Braun urged Fritz. "Think of the moon and beyond. Before you are my age, young man, I *will* land a man on the moon."

"You *and* my father," Fritz corrected.

"Yes," von Braun said quickly. He glanced behind him at the tunnels burrowing into Kohnstein Mountain to reassure the SS general's son. "Without your father, I couldn't build such rockets. One day, men will look back on what we created here and realize that this was the birth of everything to come."

OPERATION HYDRA—the opening raid of Operation Crossbow—had brought the Nazi rocketeer to Dora-Mittelbau.

At 1:10 a.m. on August 18, 1943, the *bam-bam* of anti-aircraft guns had jerked Wernher von Braun awake in his Peenemünde home. His head was muddy with confusion, but that disappeared when the first high explosives rocked his residence. The bombers were trying to catch and kill the V-2 engineers as they slept in their beds.

Leaping out of bed, von Braun began to dress. He was interrupted by a blast that shattered his windows and blew the doors off their hinges. Half-dressed in a pajama top and trousers, with a trench coat draped over his shoulders and bedroom slippers on his feet, the rocketeer rushed out into the garden to stare up at the moonlit sky.

Lancasters by the hundreds …

Halifaxes, too …

It looked as if RAF Bomber Command had ordered every plane it had to hit Peenemünde.

Boom … Boom … Boom …

The ground shook beneath him.

Nearly eighteen hundred tons of bombs came tumbling out of the sky as waves of four-engine shadows—close to six hundred in all—passed across the mocking face of a cruel moon. The bomber stream was endless. Those who created the V-2s were targeted first, and then the bombers shifted their merciless sights to the production plant and the development works.

Artificial fog from smoke generators obscured the rocket complex as von Braun made his way through the British bombing raid to the V-2 factory and his brain trust—the experimental station. Searchlights swept under the full moon while shells from Peenemünde's flak batteries exploded in the sky. Target-marking flares descended from the British planes and were followed by deafening bomb blasts amid bursts of blinding light. By the time von Braun arrived at his think tank, at least twenty-five buildings in that development works—including House 4, the headquarters— were ablaze or damaged.

Finally, at 2:07 a.m., the bombers flew away, tailed by Messerschmitt 110s with new *Schräge Musik* guns. For von Braun, however, the battle had just begun. He spent the rest of that long night repeatedly risking his skin to try to salvage the secret documents of his lifelong obsession from the fire that was consuming House 4.

With the light of dawn had come a stark realization.

Von Braun had a mortal enemy in the British air marshal who was planning the Crossbow raids.

Henceforth, he would be up against Sir Arthur "Bomber" Harris.

THE PEENEMÜNDE RAID had set off a whirlwind of fury at the Wolf's Lair, Hitler's remote headquarters in the forests of East Prussia. December 1941 had marked a jolting turnabout in the *Kriegsglück*—war luck—of the Third Reich. Operation Barbarossa, Hitler's overwhelming assault on the "Bolshevik horde" of the Soviet Union, had

resulted in months of Nazi triumphs over the Red Army ...
until the blitzkrieg got mired in the snows of the Russian
winter. That same month had seen America enter the war
after the Japanese attack on Pearl Harbor. Not only did
Germany suddenly have to match the industrial output of
three major powers, but the climactic Battle of Stalingrad
had—in Churchill's words—torn the guts out of Hitler's
army. More than one million Nazi soldiers had been lost on
the eastern front, three hundred thousand of them at
Stalingrad. Only ninety-three thousand had survived to
surrender to the Bolsheviks on January 31, 1943. Faced
with a manpower crisis, the führer had but one hope: the
wonder weapons—the *Wunderwaffe*—of SS-Major Wernher
von Braun and his fellow scientists.

Now this!

"The Bomber hit Peenemünde," Himmler said. He had
traveled to the Wolf's Lair from his own nearby headquarters, High Forest, on the morning of that British attack
twenty months ago.

"Harris!" Hitler fumed, his color rising.

"Yes. Overnight."

"How bad is the damage?"

"Deployment of the V-2 has been set back months."

"Months we don't have."

"Yes," agreed the SS leader. "The Bomber wants our
rockets. The RAF will come again and again. The Bomber
won't stop until every V-2 is useless scrap."

"What do you suggest?"

"Pass control of the rockets to the SS."

For years, Heinrich Himmler had wanted to turn the SS—
established as Hitler's bodyguard service—into a private
fiefdom. Assigned the task of maintaining security throughout
the Reich, he had expanded that into building a huge network
of concentration camps to supply slave labor for factories he

wished to have dependent on his SS—and to exterminate "racial degenerates." From twenty-five thousand inmates on the eve of the war, the population of the camps had climbed to well over half a million by 1943—and that didn't include the millions of *Untermenschen* who'd already been gassed and cremated in Auschwitz, Dachau, and the other death camps. The power of the SS had grown to such perverse proportions that the Black Corps had its own combat force, the thirty-eight fighting divisions of the Waffen-SS, which didn't take orders from the Wehrmacht, the regular German army. Cross Himmler and his Gestapo agents would come knocking on your door. The SS leader was the most sinister warrior of the Reich, and all that he required to make his power base absolute was complete control over all the secret wonder weapons in Nazi development.

Here was his chance.

The henchman who stood before the führer didn't look like a man of violence. He looked more like an intelligent elementary schoolteacher than he did a monster. Today, Himmler wore the less-threatening field gray SS uniform that he'd had tailored to his slender, middle-sized physique. With an air of quizzical probing, his gray-blue eyes peered out through the round, thin-rimmed lenses of his glittering pince-nez. The trimmed mustache beneath his straight nose slashed a dark line across his pale features. The even white teeth that backed his constant, set smile were flanked by a hint of mockery at both corners of his colorless mouth. The most telling feature of his less-than-Aryan face was his conspicuously receding chin, for it revealed a defect in his genes. As Himmler addressed Hitler—another master racist who lacked the coveted features—he clutched his peaked SS cap in his slender, blue-veined, almost girlish hands, so the skull and crossbones of the Death's Head badge winked at the führer.

"Harris doesn't fight like an Englishman. He fights like *us*."

"Fire with fire," Hitler said begrudgingly.

"The Bomber is no Montgomery."

Himmler was alluding to Monty's gentlemanly behavior after the Battle of El Alamein, when he had invited his dust-covered adversary from the trounced Afrika Korps into his tent for dinner so they could analyze the tank war they had just fought.

"Harris plans to bomb us into submission. That man will stomach casualties that make his cohorts blanch. The only way to protect the V-2 is to produce it underground."

"Build a factory?"

"Yes," said Himmler.

"We don't have enough workers."

"I do. In the camps."

Hitler shook his head. "We must use *German* labor. Or we'll have security leaks."

"We already do. The V-2 was betrayed by spies. How else would Harris have known the location of Peenemünde?"

"The risk is too great."

"No," said Himmler. "It's the ideal solution. We can use slaves to burrow the tunnels and to build the V-2s. Having the prisoners underground guarantees secrecy. They can be cut off, with no escape, from the outside world. We can send in criminals as *Kapo* bosses. The plan is watertight."

"But can it be done?" asked Hitler.

"I have just the man to do it."

SS-GENERAL ERNST STREICHER was a rocket himself. His climb through the ranks of the SS had been meteoric over the past two years. And unlike those Aryan rejects Hitler and Himmler, Streicher was as Nordic as an *Über*-Nazi could be. Not only was he the blondest man in the Third

Reich, but his eyes were the iciest of blue. An architect and a civil engineer by training, the forty-two-year-old construction whiz had been a Nazi Party insider since 1931 and a member of the SS since 1933. Utter ruthlessness and endless energy had turned him into a driving force that got things done.

Streicher had made his bones in the agriculture and air ministries by perfecting a way to mass-assemble hangars, barracks, and such. Recognizing that the Aryan poster boy was cut from the same cloth as SS-Obergruppenführer Reinhard Heydrich, Himmler had tasked him with building the ultra-secret extermination camps and gas chambers of Auschwitz-Birkenau, Belzec, and Maidenek.

Streicher's meticulously crafted design for Auschwitz had caught the attention of a delighted Hitler. The führer had instantly grasped that he had the ability to retain control of the minute details of a project without losing sight of its strategic goals. That, Streicher had proved in blood by drawing up plans to increase the capacity of the death camps to fourteen million, and by upping the daily output of their gas chambers and ovens from ten thousand to sixty thousand victims.

That engineer was the ideal tool for this job.

One week after the Peenemünde raid and Himmler's meeting with Hitler at the Wolf's Lair, Streicher had dispatched the first contingent of slaves from Buchenwald to Nordhausen, in the Harz Mountains of central Germany. Their arrival on August 27, 1943, was witnessed by Fritz—then thirteen—and his brother, Hans. Their father planned to toughen up his motherless sons.

"Kretiner!"

Idiot!

"Arschficker!"

Ass-fucker!

"Dreck!"

Shit!

"Krematoriumhund!"

Crematory dog!

The insults and the blows began as soon as the first trucks from Buchenwald disgorged their human cargo outside the yawning mouths of a pair of tunnels that wormed into Kohnstein Mountain. The site selected by the SS for its new "hardened" underground V-2 factory had begun life as a gypsum mine in 1917. In 1936, following Hitler's seizure of power, the mine had been transformed into a highly secret petroleum reserve for the Reich. Two parallel tunnels, "A" and "B,"—each one a mile long and big enough to swallow two railroad trains, with enough space left over for service trucks and towering machinery— were bored into the mountain. A series of cross tunnels— each five hundred feet long—connected the main runs at regular intervals like the rungs of a ladder. With a total subterranean capacity of thirty-five million cubic feet, the S-shaped network had the potential to become the biggest underground factory in the world.

Once it was completed.

"Pay no attention to the human cost," Fritz had heard the general tell the SS guards that day. "The work must get done, and in the shortest possible time."

With their body hair freshly shaved against lice, their emaciated bodies shrouded in the striped prison garb common to all SS camps, and their blistered, bleeding feet shuffling along in wooden clogs, those first 107 slaves were driven like cattle by blows from the guards' *Gummi* cudgels—electric cables wrapped with rubber—into the mountain to get to work. Tunnel B had already exited through the mountain's southern slope. The first job for the slaves was to finish Tunnel A and dismantle the petroleum dump so that machinery salvaged from the RAF bombing raid on Peenemünde could be installed in this new, hardened, top-secret factory.

It was grueling work.

Work Camp Dora quickly became the satellite hell of Buchenwald. A steady stream of slaves—all male and predominantly of Russian, Polish, or French background— were trucked in from the main concentration camp to construct tomorrowland. No Jews among them: Jews were for gassing and burning in other camps. So grinding were these hellholes, which minced up human flesh like sausage meat, that one worker was heard to scream, "Compared with Dora, Auschwitz was easy!" The following day, his body was among the truckload of corpses being shipped back to Buchenwald for incineration in the main camp's ovens. So horrified were those who saw the homecomings of so many crushed and mangled slaves that some committed suicide on learning that they were slated to go to Dora.

"Vernichtung durch Arbeit."

That's what the general had called it.

"Annihilation through work," Streicher had explained to his sons as he led them toward the carnivorous caves to inspect the progress of the first month's labor. On the same day, September 24, 1943, Mittelwerk GmbH (Central Works Ltd.) was incorporated and received an order for the fast delivery of twelve thousand V-2s to knock Britain out of the war.

The entrance to one of the caves was covered with a camouflage net. The huge work yard out front was cluttered with dusty machines, railroad stock, metal ducting, piles of cement bags, rolls of electric cable, stacks of reinforcing bars, and heaps of mining timber. The wind down the valley howled through the man-made canyons, but it was overpowered by the eerie wailing from the hole, a shrill amalgam of slaves' screams, metal grinding on metal and rock, and explosions deep within.

The agony thrilled Fritz.

The inferno inside brought to mind a beehive gone berserk. Fumes of burnt oil and choking dust hung heavy in the air, which was already thick with humidity and the stench of death. Gray beings staggered through the fog with their backs bowed by the weight of crushing loads, or else they struggled to haul long lengths of railroad track at a run, lurching through pools of dim light like ghosts in a grave-yard. The *Kapos* who lashed them viciously had much to lose, for they were real criminals who'd been selected from the Reich's prisons for their perverse sadism, and they would do anything to keep their pain-free—and pain-dispensing—positions in the hierarchy.

"Los! Vorwärtz!" "Quick! Forward!" barked the *Kapos* from behind a hail of *Gummi* blows while SS thugs watched for any reason to shoot.

The guards called it *Premiënschein,* meaning "Good for a prime." An SS man "forced" to kill a slave had earned himself a prime, or a few days' leave.

Some notched their guns to record vacation time.

Passing the glint of mica deposits winking from the rock walls, then hills of gravel and hoppers loaded with rubble and broken bodies, the SS engineer and his sons sank deeper into the mountain. Frantic activity swarmed around them as slaves used shovels, pickaxes, and their bare hands to hollow out and tear away at the would-be factory. The distant blasting added to the chaos, causing slaves atop thirty-foot scaffolds to plummet down onto teams of other workers who were hauling huge skids or pushing heavy handcarts on rickety rail lines. As the skids stopped and the skips toppled, the *Kapos* whipped and clubbed the slaves until each had either fixed his setback or was dead.

The general nodded his approval.

And so did Fritz and Hans.

The first twenty cross-tunnels were functional, but conditions grew more primitive after that. There was no time to construct a barracks outside, so the SS had walled off cross-tunnels 43 to 46 to make some living quarters at the unfinished end of Tunnel A. The shift was changing as Streicher, Fritz, and Hans reached these quarters. Four thousand wretches were caged here underground. At first, the slaves had slept on straw or naked rocks, but then they'd hammered together tiers of bunk beds four levels high. From these, sleepy slaves would be rousted with whips and herded out to the shit barrels.

Toilets were non-existent in this netherworld. Fritz and Hans tried to plug their noses against the retching stench, but their father knocked down their hands.

"A barn should smell like a barn," he said.

The *Arschtonnes* were oil drums that had been cut in half and topped with planks for squatting. They stood in the cross-tunnel exits from the rows of bunks. The general and his sons arrived in time to catch the guards' favorite game. To hurry those squatting on the makeshift toilets at the end of their twelve-hour shift, and to clear the planks for those about to work the other half of the day, the SS guards were pushing some of the slaves into the full barrels. The besmeared workers had nowhere to go but into the already filthy and lice-infested bunks, and nothing to clean themselves with except their own urine.

The guards were laughing.

Here in the center of the mountain, there was little air. The manmade cave was damp, dark, and perpetually cold. The walking skeletons on the work crews were entitled to only one cup of water a day, a cup of coffee, a piece of bread, and a bowl of swill in which swam a few rotten vegetables. Dysentery, typhus, tuberculosis, thirst, and starvation plagued the camp. Whimpers, screams, shouts, and threats of execution echoed throughout the tunnel.

Exhausted slaves stumbled into the now vacant bunks or collapsed onto the ground. Those behind, pressed on by the *Kapos,* trampled across any comrades who fell, and soon thousands of men were desperately crying out for sleep. But the blasting had started up again, and the noise was ratcheting up to a level that shredded nerves and bored into the brain, until there was no escape from dementia even in sleep.

Untermenschen, Fritz thought.

This is what they deserve.

To suffer, slave, and die in the bowels of the earth.

BY NOVEMBER, there were eight thousand slaves underground.

By December, those subterraneans numbered ten thousand.

That didn't include the thousands who'd died and were cremated at Buchenwald.

By the end of the year, Streicher was the toast of the Nazi elite. It had taken him only four months to evacuate the bombed remnants of the V-2 factory at Peenemünde and restart rocket production in this hellhole at Nordhausen. Even Albert Speer, the armaments minister who'd lost control of the wonder weapons program to Reichsführer-SS Heinrich Himmler, had sent the general a note of begrudging respect for an accomplishment "that far exceeds anything ever done in Europe and is unsurpassed even by American standards."

On New Year's Eve, 1943, Streicher—sporting the dress uniform of the Black Corps and flanked by his sons in their Hitler Youth garb—had cracked a bottle of schnapps at the mouth of the tunnels to celebrate the rollout of the first four V-2s.

The rockets were destined for the hands of the aerospace scientist for whom the slaves had toiled.

SS-Sturmbannführer Wernher von Braun.

ROCKETS, ROCKETS, ROCKETS ... they were the driving obsession of Wernher von Braun. To perfect them, he was willing to sell his soul to any devil. The end justified the means.

The brilliant young aristocrat had joined a horseback riding unit of the Berlin SS in 1933 as a sign of political loyalty at a time when Hitler's Nazis were consolidating their power. In 1937, he had joined the Nazi Party, and on May 1, 1940, at Himmler's personal request, he had formally joined the Black Corps with the rank of lieutenant. Promotions in late 1941 and 1942 had elevated him to the rank of captain, or Hauptsturmführer. Von Braun—like Streicher—was shooting up faster than his rockets. It paid to have friends in high places.

On June 28, 1943, Himmler had visited Peenemünde for a tour of the blast-off site, and was tickled pink to be greeted by von Braun in the black uniform of the SS. So pleased was the Gestapo chief to see the scientist flaunting the *Totenkopf* that he promoted von Braun to the rank of major, or Sturmbannführer.

The sky was the limit for most men, but not for the Third Reich's V-2 wunderkind.

On July 7, 1943, von Braun had reached the top. The boomerang blows of the war had shot the V-2, Germany's potential knockout punch, to the head of the Nazi elite's priority list. On that day, the rocketeer was summoned to meet Hitler at the Wolf's Lair.

The audience had opened with a propaganda film. With von Braun narrating as the V-2 blasted off onscreen, the führer—degeneration already showing in his unhealthy,

hunched-over appearance—could hardly contain his
fidgeting excitement. The sleek, single-stage rocket—
filmed at the first successful launch, on October 3, 1942—
stood 14 meters high, von Braun explained, weighed
12.9 tons, sped at a maximum velocity of 5,760 kilometers
an hour, and could strike an enemy target at a distance of
330 kilometers. The logo on its side was from Fritz Lang's
1929 film, *Woman in the Moon*.

As von Braun spoke in a "proud papa" manner, the
rocket lifted off, smoke whooshing down from its tail fins,
then steadily climbed at a rate of 1,340 meters per second
as it arced out over the Baltic Sea through a perfect autumn
sky. It continued straight on its intended trajectory until all
that was visible was a glowing dot at the end of its white
exhaust contrail. High-altitude winds blew the jet stream
into a zigzag of "frozen lightning" after the dot disappeared, its engine having cut out after fifty-eight seconds.
However, the Doppler tone that represented the rocket's
velocity still whined from the projector's loudspeaker. Just
before the five-minute mark, it stopped.

"Boom!" said von Braun.

The führer was clapping his hands.

"How high?" Hitler asked.

"Eighty kilometers."

The V-2 had brushed along the edge of space at a soaring
altitude of fifty miles.

"How far?" Hitler asked.

"One hundred and ninety kilometers."

The V-2 had smashed into the sea 120 miles away. World
records for altitude and speed had been obliterated.

"The spaceship is born," von Braun said, beaming.

A flick of the führer's hand knocked that stupendous
achievement aside.

"How big a warhead will it carry?"

"One ton."

"I want a ten-ton warhead."

The rocketeer blinked.

"I want a production rate of two thousand missiles a month."

The rocketeer swallowed hard.

"And I want a string of concrete bunkers built in Normandy so we can bombard the cities of southwest England and Wales."

"Führer," one of his generals said, "your wants are impossible."

But so intoxicated was the Nazi despot with the power of the V-2 to wreak revenge upon Churchill and Bomber Harris that a weird, fanatical light flared up his eyes.

"Launch! Launch! Launch!" Hitler cried, pounding his fist into his palm and teetering on the brink of a mad rage.

"What I *want*," he snarled, "is annihilation!"

Before the end of that July, Wernher von Braun had received the prestigious academic title of professor—an accomplishment almost unheard of for such a young scientist. Hitler made a point of signing the document himself.

Less than three weeks later, in the early morning hours of August 18, 1943, Bomber Harris's intrepid "warriors of the night" began to drop their payloads on the V-2s at Peenemünde.

Boom!

BUT NOW IT was April 4, 1945, a year and a half after that raid had forced all rocket production underground. The construction of the factory by Work Camp Dora slaves had claimed six thousand lives in the first six months: three thousand men had died in the tunnels, and three thousand more—too exhausted to work—had been sent to Lublin-Maidenek and Bergen-Belsen for gassing and cremation.

Of the sixty thousand slaves who were put to work in the tunnels, twenty thousand never made it out alive.

Throughout that time, Wernher von Braun had come and gone from the Mittelwerk factory. His attendance was vital for quality control. On one of those occasions, the rocketeer had stood with Fritz on the very spot where the Hitler Youth stood now, and he'd gazed up at the clear night sky to proclaim, "One day, men will look back on what we created here and realize that this was the birth of everything to come."

On that same night, he had given the teen a copy of Jules Verne's novel *From the Earth to the Moon*.

Tonight, however, the sky was anything but clear, for while the SS general and his sons had been away meeting Hitler in his bunker in Berlin, Bomber Harris had hit Nordhausen.

The Reich was in ruins, and SS-Sturmbannführer Wernher von Braun knew it. So while Ernst Streicher was absent from the factory, the rocketeer had secretly launched his exit plan.

Pigsticker

THE CARIBOO, BRITISH COLUMBIA
May 25, Now

"Gold!" was the shout that built the Cariboo. In the early 1800s, Indians from British Columbia traded chunks of gold at the forts of the Hudson's Bay Company. In 1858, when the company exchanged that gold for cash at the San Francisco mint, the rumor of untold riches north of the border lured mobs of luckless miners off their California claims. With dollar signs glinting in their El Dorado eyes, they ventured up the Fraser River by sternwheeler and pack mule, hoping to strike it rich in the Cariboo Mountains.

"Eureka!"

Today, the Aryan followed the same route up to the Skunk Mine. It was a nine-hour drive from the Cabaret Berlin to the old gold mine deep in the Cariboo Mountains. The passenger's side had been vacant since the outskirts of Vancouver, when he had stopped in a deserted factory laneway to haul the youth out of the front seat and lug him around to the flatbed of the truck. Stripping the teen naked, the Aryan had dumped him—blindfolded, gagged, and hog-tied—into the large toolbox along the rear of the cab.

For a hundred miles inland from Vancouver, the Fraser Valley stretched east to Hope. That leg of the journey had taken him through fertile farmland. Pre-dawn was smudging the Cascade peaks as he angled north, following

the Fraser River Canyon past the raging fury of the
Hell's Gate gorge, then on up the old miners' road north for
320 miles to Quesnel.

The day was well under way when the Aryan drove out
of the canyon into the vast rolling plateau of Cariboo
country. Groves of aspen and lodgepole pine grew around
sloughs and small, shallow lakes. The sun was toward high
noon when the truck veered east, away from the river and
along Lightning Creek, to snake through the Cariboo
Mountains. From Quesnel to Barkerville, fifty-five miles of
asphalt cut across the maze of streams that drained the
surrounding peaks by gouging gullies and canyons down
the cracked, wrinkled slopes.

Here, the truck abandoned the highway for a rutted road,
bumping off into the mountains along an uninviting rocky
V. Red signs on the gravel shoulders blared: "No
Trespassing! Washout! Open Shooting! You Have Been
Warned!"

Soon, the truck vanished in a haze of dust.

MINERS HAD SAID that Billy Barker was crazy to stake his
claim downstream from everyone else, but in August 1862,
that old fool struck gold and pulled $600,000 out of the
ground. In a blink, those same naysaying miners were
digging near that claim, and by the end of the following
year, the Cariboo Gold Rush had mined $4 million out of
cracks in the granite and the sand and gravel of local
mountains and creeks. In honor of the Cariboo's most
instantly famous man, the miners named the huddle of
saloons, stores, and cabins that grew up around Billy
Barker's shaft after him. Within a year, Barkerville was the
biggest town in the Canadian West, with ten thousand
citizens panning, sluicing, and digging on staked claims. A
day's work was measured in pounds, not ounces, of gold.

So many trees were cut to build houses, shops, and mine shafts that flash floods inundated the town with mud. Everything, wooden plank sidewalks included, had to be raised on posts.

Far and wide, the Cariboo Wagon Road was known as the Eighth Wonder of the World. One hundred thousand drifters were drawn to Barkerville, a boom town in the wilderness where miners threw cash around as if there was no tomorrow. Card sharps took their money in sleazy gambling dens. Whisky flowed like water in smoky saloons. Hurdy-gurdy girls from San Francisco charged lonesome miners a dollar a dance in frilly can-can halls. And in those Wild West days before the Mounties, the law was Sir Matthew Baillie Begbie, the Hanging Judge. In his black legal robes, he would try murder cases off the back of a horse. Sometimes rough justice was carried out on the limb of a hanging tree.

The winter after he struck it rich, Billy Barker met a widow from Victoria. She tossed her curls and got her gold-digging claws into him, then set about spending his cash as fast as it came out of the ground. As soon as the gold was gone, so was she, and Billy's last days were spent penniless in the Old Men's Home. When he was buried in the ground from which his gold had come, it was in a pauper's grave.

And so it was with Barkerville. By the close of the nineteenth century, fortune-seekers had answered the call from the North, and by 1898, the Klondike River was the place to be. As boom towns sprang up to serve the Yukon gold rush, Barkerville turned into a ghost town, and what were once thriving gold claims became Cariboo ranches.

Ranches like the Phantom Valley Ranch, tucked miles away at the end of this rutted road that bounced the truck about as it descended the switchback that zigzagged down to the mountain flats.

The pigs were already squealing as the truck braked to a halt at the mouth of the old gold mine.

WHAT IS IT ABOUT the Cariboo that appeals to the Germanic mind? Are the mountains evocative of the Bavarian Alps? Are the thickets reminiscent of how the Black Forest used to feel? Is it the sense of *Lebensraum* in its wide-open spaces, the yearning for elbow room that drove the Nazis to invade Russia? Whatever it is, German accents are everywhere in the Cariboo today, and that made the Aryan just one among many. For him, the appeal of the Cariboo was basic: accommodation at the Phantom Valley Ranch was free, and any place on earth was a hell of a lot better than the East German pig farm on which he had suffered so much.

Thinking about the pig farm made him tense.

And there was only one way to exorcise that tension.

Unsheathe the pigsticker.

As the Aryan stepped out into the dust, the driver's door squeaked, echoing the squeal of the ravenous pigs in the muddy sty. The pigpen, made from fencing cannibalized from the ranch's disused horse corrals, stood halfway between the maw of the old gold mine and the decrepit ranch house.

The pigs weren't for pork, or for company.

THE MINE WASN'T A RELIC from the Cariboo Gold Rush of the 1860s. The gold came from a vein similar to the one that launched Barkerville, but it had stayed hidden until a single rock tumbling down the slope had bit a chunk out at the bottom to expose ore. The mine was dug in the 1920s and worked until just before the war, when both it and the mine buildings on this range were abandoned. In the aftermath of the war, the mine buildings were dismantled and hauled away. All that remained were the rundown ranch house and some decrepit outbuildings in the overgrown scrub of the valley.

The cross-hatched steel gate that sealed the mouth of the mine resembled the portcullis of a medieval castle. The barricade was now outfitted with a modern electronic lock. The Aryan punched in the release code from memory. The squeaking of the hinges brought more squealing from the pigs.

A few feet inside the steel gate, he flicked a switch to power up a bank of generators. As light began to illuminate the cored-out throat of the mine, he walked to the butcher's station along one rounded granite wall. Specks of gold still glinted in the rock behind a deer-skinning easel frame. The frame was fashioned in the usual X, but the four arms crooked at the tips to form a swastika. Carving instruments hung from hooks affixed to the rock, and an oblong box lay on the seven-foot-long chopping block.

Opening the box, the Aryan gripped a sword by its hilt and scabbard and drew it from its sheath. The portepee around it was caked with blood. Discarding the scabbard, the Aryan swished the rapier about in the air like an Olympic fencer. Light glinted off the SS motto engraved into the steel blade. *"Meine Ehre heisst Treue."*

It felt good to grip the pigsticker in his vengeful fist.

Among the butcher's instruments hung a branding iron with a swastika-shaped head. Pigsticker in one hand, brand in the other, the Aryan moved deeper into the throat of the mine, until it heightened into a glittery cavern.

The cavern resembled a mad scientist's lab from a 1940s B movie. The workbench was spread with German-language blueprints, and a hodgepodge of electromagnetic gizmos had been cobbled together according to the dog-eared plans. Most of the equipment was military surplus or salvage from 1940s warships that had been scrapped in Vancouver's harbor. The vault was crammed with devices worthy of Nikola Tesla, the electrical genius who discovered the rotating magnetic field.

The Aryan wedged the swastika head of the branding iron into the spark-gap of one machine. A flick of a switch induced electric current to jump the gap, and the twist of a dial made the swastika brand glow red hot. Though he was dead tired and desperately in need of sleep, the Nazi knew that first he needed to exorcise his psychological demons, so he set the pigsticker down on the bench in the lab and returned to the truck.

The Aryan used a handcart to remove the toolbox from the flatbed of the truck. Rolling it down a ramp that he'd hooked onto the tail, he wheeled the box and its human contents into the old gold mine, past the butcher's station and through the quantum lab, pressing on into psychopathic shadows. Finally, at the border where light succumbed to darkness, the Nazi stopped pushing and levered the cart upright. As he swung open the lid of the toolbox, the hog-tied youth crumpled out onto the hard rock.

Doubling back to the lab, the Aryan gathered his tools. He had to watch his footing. If he fell while weighed down with so many military props, he might sear himself with the red-hot brand of the iron.

Even tied hand and foot, Yuri was twitching like the electrified leg of a galvanic frog. Ninety percent of crystal meth was artificial solvents. Not only did the drug kill brain cells, but the human body couldn't break it down. So strong was the addiction and so severe the physical damage that detoxing took weeks or months, not days. Just hours into withdrawal, Yuri was a sweaty, jittering mess.

The Internet does a brisk trade in Second World War militaria. All those vets with basement museums. The Soviet colonel's uniform wasn't the real thing, but it was a convincing replica, right down to the last insignia patch.

First, the Aryan locked the steel helmet onto Yuri's head, cinching the chinstrap tightly under his jaw. In the workshop, he had modified the Red Army helmet for the dark pit of the mine by soldering an unbreakable lamp to its crown. When he turned on the lamp to ensure it worked, the street kid's shivering made the beam bounce about like a Second World War searchlight scanning the sky for bombers.

Next, the Aryan clamped a scold's bridle around Yuri's chin. With the blindfold and gag still in place, the teen strained against the chinstrap in protest, and that allowed the Nazi to wedge the bit between his teeth.

At the back of the helmet, the prongs of the bridle joined together to form a handle. A hook like those used by the Gestapo to hang traitors in Berlin was screwed into the granite wall at neck height. The Aryan hung the Soviet colonel's tunic on the hook, then lifted up the street kid and hung him by the helmet handle. That done, the Nazi was able to fit the jacket around Yuri's upper torso, for it had been slit where tied hands would get in the way. Velcro fasteners were sewn on to pinch the openings back together. The belt looped around the waist of the tunic had handcuffs attached.

Snap! Snap! The cuffs locked around Yuri's bound wrists.

From his hips down, he was naked.

It was fantasy time.

WHEN THE BLINDFOLD was torn from the youth's eyes, he came face to face with the Third Reich incarnate. Yuri blinked against the blinding spotlight of the miner's lamp that glared at him from the brow of a Nazi storm trooper's helmet. "Oink, oink," the Aryan grunted in the startled colonel's face as he pulled him off the meat hook. His jelly legs buckling beneath him, Yuri collapsed to the rock floor. Only then did he realize that his feet were free of bonds.

Sssss!

The smell of burnt flesh assailed the Aryan's nostrils as he applied the brand. When he pulled the iron back and tossed it aside, the mark of the swastika smoked black on white. Jerking, staggering, stumbling as he struggled to flee, Yuri scrambled away into the bowels of the mine. Dressed in the full blitzkrieg regalia of Hitler's elite supermen, the Aryan squatted to arm himself with the pigsticker he'd dropped near his jackboot.

The beam from the Nazi helmet zeroed in on the white buttocks of the *Untermensch*.

In a pantomime of *The Triumph of the Will,* the Aryan goose-stepped in pursuit as he extended the blade of the pigsticker along the beam.

Then he charged.

Warrior of the Night

Dane parked his car in front of the house that he had called home for all of his formative years and climbed out into the dusk with a bag of takeout Chinese food and a six-pack of Tsingtao beer. The house was out of whack with the others in the neighborhood. At one time, in the early twentieth century, it could be seen down on Marine Drive, the main drag of the North Shore waterfront. But with the rampant commercialization of that strip in the post-war years, Dane's grandfather had decided to move up—literally. He'd cut the house off just below the subfloor and had it trucked up the hill on a flatbed to this spot. The other homes on the street had been built in the 1950s, so this throwback to Victoria's reign stood out.

The house was steep-roofed from side to side, with dormer peaks at the front. The house was white, the roof two-tone gray, and all the trim and the window shutters forest green. The corners of the yard out front were planted with towering firs and various deciduous trees. The only blemish was the "For Sale" sign.

A half century in one family.

Three generations.

So much happiness and sorrow within these walls.

Dane wondered who would buy it, this old house.

And what their future would hold.

The first thing Dane did upon entering the house was to check on Puss. During the long months of his granddad's cancer slide, a stray cat had taken to entering if a door was left open, almost as if it knew that the old man was in need of its comfort. He was, so Dane had cut a porthole into the backdoor to enable Puss to come and go at will.

"Hello, Puss," Dane said, on seeing the tabby in the kitchen now. "Let me know when it's time, and we'll put the siren on and rush to the vet's."

Puss was pregnant.

That was all he needed.

Dane fed Puss for six kittens or so, then popped the cap off a cold beer and sat down for his takeout feast of Szechuan prawns, with pickles and sweet ginger, and chicken chow mein.

Finished, he cracked the fortune cookie.

"Don't ask, don't say. Everything lies in silence."

TONIGHT, DANE WAS DETERMINED to press on with cleaning out Papa's house to prepare it for sale. Papa, as in the pa of his pa, the father of his father. But in his heart, he knew that he would accomplish nothing more than digging back into his granddad's war record.

Like so many of his generation, Papa had rarely talked about what he'd done in the war. Hidden away with his grandfather's Pilot's Flying Log Book, Dane had found some photos and a square box. Two of the photos now had his attention. One was a black-and-white headshot of a pilot in his early twenties. The pilot wore his peaked cap at a jaunty angle, one side lower to his eyebrow than the other. In the center sat an RCAF officer's badge: the British crown over a pair of bird wings. His uniform was immaculate, and he had a pencil-thin, fly-boy mustache like Clark Gable's.

The patriot with the easy smile who'd come home from war.

The other headshot was much starker. It was a candid shot of a pilot just back from an overnight bombing run, still buckled into the cockpit seat of a Halifax heavy bomber. Gloved and fleeced in a thick bomber jacket against the high-altitude cold, he was turned toward the camera as if spooked by its intrusion into his private hell. His head was encased in a skin-tight leather helmet; on either side, leather earmuffs clamped headphones to his skull. Dangling an obscene corrugated hose as long as an elephant's trunk, the oxygen mask on his lower face dug into the flesh of his cheeks. All you could see of the man within was the intensity in his eyes, and those eyes spoke loudly of what he had just been through.

Dane was eyeball to eyeball with a warrior of the night.

OVER SIXTY YEARS AGO, President Roosevelt called Canada "the aerodrome of democracy." Far from the battle-fields of Europe, this country proved ideal for training wartime aircrews. In all, 131,553 airmen were prepared for combat in Canada. One of those who signed up at the height of the Battle of Britain was Keith Winter, Dane's granddad. From day one of training—January 4, 1941—he was required to keep a pilot's flying log. The log would list every aircraft he took up and every bombing run he made.

This was that book.

The log was bound in black leather with gold type engraved on the cover.

Taped inside the cover were snapshots of two bombing crews, each photo taken in front of the open bomb doors of a Halifax. One crew was bundled up for winter skies over Europe. The other was stripped down to khaki shirts and shorts for the scorching desert sands of North Africa.

Dane settled back with another beer and read through Keith's war against the Swastika.

After he'd completed three and a half months' training in both the Tiger Moth and the Anson—155 hours and 40 minutes in the air—the RCAF had shipped him overseas to Kinloss, Scotland. There, attached to the RAF, Keith was strapped into the Whitley and taught how to fly a heavy bomber. At that point, the monotonous blue ink in the log was joined by red to denote night flights.

September 1941 saw Keith posted to #10 Squadron at Leeming, Yorkshire.

By October, he was outward bound.

"Ops. to Wilhelmshaven. 'Bags of Fun'—Caught in searchlights, but not held."

OUTWARD BOUND was the title of the print on the wall of the TV room in Papa's house. The original painting, all in blue, was as evocative of a night bombing run as war art could be. Every warrior has his weapon, and Keith's was a pair of deadly flying machines. He began bombing with the Whitley and soon traded up. By December, he was in the cockpit of the Halifax.

The painting depicted the estuary of an English river shimmering beneath a Handley Page Halifax en route to enemy territory. A trio of criss-crossed searchlights shot up from the shore below, and silver moonlight shone down through the broken cloud cover to sparkle on the sea. Silver-blue was the painting's only color, except for a hint of yellow around the RAF bull's-eye insignia on the fuselage of the plane. Guns bristled from the see-through turrets in the nose of the bomber and from behind the dual tailfins, where the rear gunner sat. In front of the whirling propellers on the visible wing, Dane could just make out the pilot who was outward bound with the flames of hell in the bomb-bay belly of the beast.

What a beautiful war machine!

Dane recalled himself as a boy asking his granddad where he'd got the picture.

"During the war, it hung in a uniform shop," Papa had explained. "I saw it while on leave. I told the shopkeeper that I flew the Halifax and asked if I could buy it. He said no. It was his window attraction. I left a phone number, in case he changed his mind. On VJ Day—the day the war ended—the shopkeeper called. 'The picture is yours,' he said. 'I'm giving it to you for free. When I see you carry it out of here, I'll know I'm not dreaming that the war is over.'"

THE DESPERATE YEARS.

The years 1941 and 1942.

Hitler was the master of Europe and Britain stood virtually alone when nineteen-year-old Keith volunteered to fly with the RAF. Fifty-seven straight nights of the Blitz had set London ablaze and reduced much of it to rubble. Wolf packs of U-boats under the Atlantic were on the brink of severing the shipping lifeline from America. Rommel and the Afrika Korps, a panzer division trained in desert warfare, had landed at Tripoli. Then Hitler invaded Russia. Kiev fell, and Leningrad and Moscow were besieged. In December 1941, Pearl Harbor was attacked, but even when America entered the war, the bad news kept coming. Japan owned the Pacific. Hong Kong, Singapore, Thailand, Burma, and the Philippines all fell to the Land of the Rising Sun. In May 1942, Rommel went on the offensive and began his push through Libya, which would drive him into Egypt as the British fell back in retreat. By the time the end of May arrived, Keith was in extreme peril. Over ten thousand planes in Bomber Command would be lost in the war. Over fifty-seven thousand airmen would die, and of those, ten thousand would be Canadian volunteers. Proportionately, it would be the highest fatality rate of all who fought in the war. Two tours of duty—which is what Keith flew—and the odds of going home were almost nil.

May 1942.

The record, thought Dane.

He set aside the flying log and picked up the square box that he'd also found in the dresser drawer. Peeking inside earlier, he'd been puzzled by the small disk in the plain brown sleeve. It was the size of a 45. The handwritten center label read, "From Mother to Keith. May 26, 1942. For 21st Birthday." It was obviously a private recording.

Intrigued, Dane went to what had once been his room and fetched the Seabreeze record player, a relic so old that it had probably spun his dad's childhood records. He dropped the disk onto the spindle, set the speed to 45 rpms, and eased down the needle. The voice that spoke to him through time seemed to come from under the sea.

It's warped, he thought.

Wait a sec.

A 45?

They didn't have 45s back then.

Detective that he was, he figured out that the disk was a miniature version of a 78. Sure enough, when he cranked the knob over to that speed, a woman's voice spoke to him from the speaker.

It was Dane's *great*-grandmother.

"Hello, Keith. Mother speaking to you. Happy twenty-first birthday. Hope you received your parcel. If not, it's on its way. No matter what happens, Keith, know Mother is proud of you. Keep the flag flying, son. All long to see you, and hope it won't be long till you and all the other lads come home. It's cold today, but bright. Goodbye, my dear. Keep your chin up. All my love, Mother."

Dane lifted the scratchy needle.

Desperate years.

Desperate days.

Without a victory in sight.

And all those dead fly boys listed in the papers.

So she went off to a recording studio in 1942 and made Keith that birthday greeting—in case it was his last.

May 26?

Dane went back to the log.

Four days after his birthday, Keith entered this:

"May 30. Ops. to Cologne. Over 1,000 A/C on TGT. Beautiful blaze."

THE THOUSAND BOMBER RAID on Cologne on the night of May 30, 1942, was the first turning point in the war. In February, Sir Arthur Harris had risen to the top of Bomber Command, and he was itching for a way to demonstrate to "the Boche" that they had met their match. He planned to overwhelm Nazi defenses with a continuous stream of awesome airpower aimed at one German industrial city. Churchill approved Operation Millennium. When the moon was full, Harris threw every plane he could gather from any source—1,047 aircraft in all—at the third-largest city in the Reich. The raid was a success, and others followed.

"June 1. Ops. to Essen. 1,000 A/C on TGT. Good show. Home on 3 engines."

"June 25. Ops. to Bremen. Another 1,000-plane effort. Excellent trip, but very 'hot.'"

MONTY VERSUS the Desert Fox.

That was Keith's triumphant battle.

A month after the raid on Cologne, Dane's granddad pasted a mimeographed slip of paper into his flying log:

Secrecy

During the course of special operations taking place over the next sixteen days, no communication will be permitted with any person outside the squadron.

Keith's comment beside that, on July 4, 1942: *"Attached to Middle East Command (16 Days?)."*

On June 21, Rommel had captured the British garrison of Tobruk. "Defeat is one thing; disgrace is another," Churchill informed Roosevelt. Hitler was so pleased that he conferred the baton of field marshal on the Third Reich's "hero in the sun." The Desert Fox was on a roll across the sands of North Africa, and by June 30, Rommel had shoved the British Eighth Army back into Egypt. In Cairo, at British headquarters, military documents were being torched to prepare for a full retreat. The burning was dubbed "Ash Wednesday." In front of the Desert Fox lay the Suez Canal and the Persian oilfields. All that stood in his way was the coastal railroad station of El Alamein.

On July 1, he attacked. A sandstorm thwarted that knockout blow. The only way for Britain to hold the line was to maintain air superiority. That's why Keith was on his way down from Britain. Rommel had an Achilles' heel: his long supply line.

"July 12. Ops. to Tobruk ..."

For three weeks, the adversaries engaged in attritional warfare. All through July, they slogged away in the lung-choking, sandy horror that was North Africa. At times, Keith had just one cup of water a day to drink and one more to bathe and shave in.

"July 20. Ops. to Tobruk. Bombed jetties and harbor installations. '16' days up!!!"

Then, on August 3, Churchill arrived in Cairo. Having decided that the Eighth Army required new leadership, he gave the command to General William "Strafer" Gott. Four days later, Gott died in an air crash. So who took his place? Who else? Montgomery. And Monty bombastically declared that he was going "to hit Rommel for six out of Africa."

Some sort of cricket thing.

Throughout August *("Bombed battle lines")* and on into September, #10 Squadron hammered Tobruk again and again and again. All through September and well into October, Keith's plane got shot full of holes and he lost friends *("Ginger missing")*. By then, the focus of the world had settled on the coming battle. If you want to go down in military history, nothing will do it faster than a title match. Wellington versus Napoleon. Grant versus Lee. Sitting Bull versus Custer. Monty versus the Desert Fox.

When the Battle of El Alamein began, on October 23, Keith was in the thick of it. Preening, fussy, and picky though he may have been, Monty had a strategic strength: he knew how to coordinate air power to win a battle on the ground. When the Afrika Korps soldiers turned and ran, instead of surrendering, Keith was on them from the skies, "crumbling" their retreat. Monty preferred to let metal, not flesh, do the blood work of battle.

Keith's sixteen days extended into eight months. He returned to England at the same time that Rommel was called back to the Reich. Not only was El Alamein the turning point in North Africa, but it, along with Stalingrad, was the turning point in the war. "It is not the end," Churchill said. "It may not even be the beginning of the end. But it is undoubtedly the end of the beginning."

Keith was through with operations.

From then on, he trained pilots.

Except for one more raid.

A final entry was made in red, and after that, the Pilot's Flying Log Book in Dane's grip contained nothing but blank, empty pages.

On returning from North Africa in March 1943, Keith was posted to the #6 (RCAF) Group at Topcliffe, Yorkshire. That August saw the only time in the second half of the war when the whole of Bomber Command attempted a precision raid by moonlight on such a small target, so Keith went out for a last hurrah in one of the bomber stream's Halifaxes.

The last entry in red:

"*August 17. Ops. to Peenemünde. Bombed V-2 rocket site.*"

DANE WANDERED into the TV room to stare at *Outward Bound*. From that last entry on, he was left to his imagination, and soon his mind's eye was peering out from the cockpit of Keith's Halifax.

The bomber stream was strung out for miles in front of and behind him. His crew manned their positions within the noisy metal shell. In the cockpit, Keith sat at the heavy controls while the flight engineer monitored the instrument panel and transferred fuel to keep the bomber balanced. In the compartment below and toward the front of the fuselage, the navigator calculated the flight path to and from the target, Peenemünde, and the wireless operator manned the radio. Within the bubble of the nose cone, the bomb aimer hunched over his sight and got ready to drop the payload at the precise moment. He was also the front gunner. Midway back was the dorsal gunner, and way back at the rear sat the tail gunner, in the loneliest and most dangerous place of all. Nazi night-fighters would attack from behind the plane and strafe the tail gunner first.

"Bomb doors open!" the bomb aimer shouted, and they were into their run.

Suddenly, the black void ahead erupted with streaks of fire, as if a giant's sword had been put to a grinding wheel. Chandelier flares flew at the moon, bathing the sky with light to illuminate the bomber stream. Flak flashes ripped apart the dark around their plane as the batteries below riddled the night with anti-aircraft fire. Searchlight beams got a fix on the bombers, then there was a blinding boom, and a Halifax disintegrated into flaming fragments, leaving ugly clouds of ragged smoke behind.

"Bombs away!" the bomb aimer shouted amid the din.

The incendiaries from planes in front of them were already hitting the target. The bombs were bursting like bubbles in a witch's cauldron. It seemed as if every factory, every house, every building was on fire, and still the stream of bombers rained down more ruin. Black smoke billowed up from the raw, red radiance below, and the desperately groping searchlights turned anemic in the glare.

"Night-fighters!" warned the tail gunner.

Keith craned around in time to see a Messerschmitt 109 appear out of nowhere and let loose the stuttering thunder of its underwing cannon pods. The burst blew the bomb aimer in the Halifax next to them against the nose cone, spinning him around so that Keith could see moonlight through the huge hole in his chest. As the Messerschmitt rolled away for another strafing pass, the swastika on its silver tail shone black.

"Corkscrew starboard, Skipper! GO!" barked the tail gunner in his headphoned ears.

Nothing released adrenaline into your bloodstream quite like the sound of fright in a crew member's voice crackling through the intercom. Then blazing tracers zipped past the cockpit on the port side, and Keith knew that another Messerschmitt had come up on their tail. No RAF fighter escort could venture this far from base, so it was the lumbering bomber against the best of the Nazi defenses.

The tail gunner was lashing out with everything he had. Though it was freezing cold back there at this altitude, he'd removed the Perspex panel in front of him before takeoff and braved the bone-numbing wind for better visibility. Evasive action was crucial, so Keith applied violent rudder, aileron, and diving elevators to spiral the Halifax down. That instantly removed the plane from the gunsights of the night-fighter pilot and cascaded them into a deep, deep plunge.

"Pull up … pull up … pull up!" Keith coaxed as fire shot out of the number-two engine. With all that gas in the wings, the plane itself was a flying bomb. If they had to ditch in the sea and take to the dinghy, they could only release their homing pigeons with a message about their general position. Meanwhile, Keith's name would be scratched off the operations blackboard in the squadron briefing room as a skipper missing in action.

The engine fire got doused.

The plane pulled out of its dive.

"Home on 3-engines" would have been entered into Keith's log if the crippled Halifax had made it back to Britain. But the Peenemünde raid was the first time Messerschmitt 110s used their new *Schräge Musik*—"jazz music"—guns. Those upward-spitting cannons ripped into the Halifax's underbelly, where there was no armament or even a window to observe below.

Another engine caught on fire, and the plane rapidly began to lose altitude.

There was no option.

Keith and his crew were forced to bail out over Hitler's Reich.

THE CANADIAN #6 GROUP lost twelve of fifty-seven aircraft in the Peenemünde raid, 20 percent of its fleet. In the box of relics that Dane had found in the drawer with the logbook, there were several mementos from Keith's war against the Swastika. His crest for #10 Squadron had the crown over a winged arrow on the descent, a reminder, no doubt, that the air bomb is a modern rendition of the medieval arrow. The motto was *Rem acu tangere.* "To hit the mark." His six war medals were suspended from multi-colored ribbons. Though time had tarnished their metal, the courage forged into each shone through.

Dane also found several brass buttons embossed with various unit insignias. Among those were two anomalies—a pair of domed metal buttons, each about three-quarters of an inch in diameter. The dome of one was surmounted by a tiny, sharp pin that spiked up when the button was placed flat in the box. Its partner had two dots along one edge and one on the opposite edge. As Dane tried to puzzle out why these buttons were different, he idly placed the dotted one on top of the spiked one. The two dots immediately revolved around on the pin to line up with magnetic north.

Mystery solved, thought Dane.

A pilot shot down behind Nazi lines could cut the buttons off his shirt and use them as a compass.

Unfortunately, that compass hadn't guided Keith to safety. There were no entries in his flying log after the Peenemünde raid because Papa had spent the rest of the conflict in Europe as a prisoner of war—a *Kriegsgefangene,* or "Kriegie"—in a Stalag Luft camp.

DANE WAS SURPRISED, when he glanced at his watch, to see how time had flown. He had his date with the Mountain early the next morning, so it was time to pack it up for the night.

As he closed Keith's Pilot's Flying Log Book on that last entry in red, the Mountie spoke to the cat who'd curled up on the rug.

"Papa had more lives than you, Puss."

He thought it ethical to take the pregnant cat home with him, since the twenty-four-hour vet clinic was near his condo.

Achtung!

✠

NORDHAUSEN, GERMANY
April 4, 1945

Damn Bomber Harris!

SS-Obergruppenführer Ernst Streicher was sorely tempted to draw the Walther from the holster at the waist of his Black Corps uniform and empty it in futile anger at the flaming sky. Last night, while he and both of his sons were off in Berlin, meeting Hitler down in the *Führerbunker,* 247 Lancasters with RAF Bomber Command had relentlessly hammered the Nazi stronghold of Nordhausen, dropping firebombs on what were believed to be the military barracks of Boelcke Kaserne. The barracks, in fact, were a dumping ground for worn-out factory slaves and deportees from the eastern camps that were now being threatened by the Red Army.

"How many killed?" Streicher demanded of an SS bureaucrat with a tally board in hand.

Ordnung muss sein.

Things must be in order.

"Fifteen hundred, General. They hit us on two nights."

Streicher nodded grimly. "At least that's fifteen hundred *Untermenschen* who won't turn on us."

The corpse-counter smirked half-heartedly. There were still almost thirty thousand subhumans alive in the Dora-Mittelbau camp system. That was a lot to get rid of.

"Do we gas the rest of them?" the tallyman asked.

It had taken the general and his sons all night to journey from Berlin back to the V-2 tunnels. The SS car had just pulled up in front of the yawning caverns in the mountainside to disgorge its three passengers. The tallyman had rushed out of Tunnel B to greet Streicher with his death-by-bombing damage report. From the storage area that fed supplies to the factory, the general watched Nordhausen burn a few miles to the south. The sky was fiery and alive with a billion sparks, but Boelcke Kaserne was choked behind a cloud of seething black smoke.

"Fritz!" snapped the general. "Fall into line."

The elder Hitler Youth was standing several feet away, fixed to the exact spot where he and Wernher von Braun had stood, gazing up at the wonders of outer space. Mesmerized by the sparks, Fritz shook his head to clear his mind.

He returned to his father's side like a dutiful son.

Tonight, the general stood resplendent in the black greatcoat of the Black Corps. Double-breasted, with two parallel rows of silver buttons down the front, it had two slanting pockets with flaps on the sides and a half belt at the back. The Death's Head badge leered down from the peak of his high-fronted cap. The silver skull and crossbones matched his silver ring, which had been presented to the general by Reichsführer-SS Heinrich Himmler for his meritorious service to the Swastika.

Here, at Dora-Mittelbau, Streicher stood at the center of his power base. The black holes of the factory tunnels throbbed at his back. A quarter mile to his right, along the Kohnstein's southern slope, Streicher had built a camp to confine the slaves who had worked, lived, and survived in the tunnels during construction.

The camp's entry gate faced the tunnels, and between the two sat the guard compound. The gate was a simple wooden barrier covered with barbed wire. The adjoining buildings housed the Gestapo offices and Camp Dora's administration. Beyond was the *Appellplatz*—the roll-call square—a huge open area carpeted with paving stones. From it, cement walkways led to fifty-eight barracks and down the slope to "the bunker," a prison within the prison that was used for private torture, and uphill to a brothel— the *Puff*—and the crematorium.

The square brick chimney of the crematorium belched oily smoke night and day.

THE SCREAMS!

Fritz was in one of those trances he found it hard to break away from. He had snapped out of it long enough to step back into line beside his father and brother, but the sparks above Nordhausen had hypnotized him again. If he listened hard enough, he could hear plaintive bellows. Shouting from the factory tunnels at his back. Screams from the blazing inferno of Boelcke Kaserne. Shrieks from all the ghosts that haunted Dora's roll-call square.

The square where his *Über*-father had enforced his will. "The Will to Power."

Just as Nietzsche had prophesied—and as Fritz had learned by rote in the Hitler Youth.

Rousted from their barracks before the break of dawn, the factory slaves began each day in the *Appellplatz,* where heads were counted and punishments imposed. Fritz thought back to one cold winter morning that he knew he'd never forget.

"Achtung!"

That day, thousands of wooden prisoners' clogs had smacked the paving stones with the order to stand at attention. The night before, one of the slaves had tried to escape, so all of the prisoners had been awakened early for the punishment known as *Stillstehen*. Freezing sleet had begun to fall as the men came together in the *Appellplatz*. Hemmed in by the dripping, low, flat buildings of Camp Dora, they had waited for hours in a U-shaped formation while the inclement weather got worse.

Standing …

Standing …

Standing still as one by one the weakest dropped.

By the time Fritz had arrived with his father and brother, the sleet was turning to snow. The *Häftlinge*—the prisoners—were clad only in rags, and the biting cold had frozen the stiff tatters to their skin. Some leaned on makeshift crutches because of putrefying wounds. Those with TB spit up the last of their lungs. Those with pleurisy shook from fever. Those with dysentery shitted out their guts, and the yellow discharge hardened to ice on their buttocks. As each weakling dropped, the thinning ranks huddled closer together for warmth. With not an ounce of fat to insulate their bones from the chill, the men shuddered and shook while haggard eyes bulged out of waxy skulls.

"Durch Kamin!"

"Through the chimney."

That's all he had to say, the *Lagerführer* who ran this punishment theater for Fritz's father. The words echoed what every slave had heard in the standard welcoming speech: "You came in through that gate, and you'll leave through that chimney."

To emphasize the point, the *Lagerführer* snapped his swagger stick like a whip at each fallen man, then pointed up to the crematorium on the hill, which even at that early hour belched gray smoke at the tumbling flakes.

Dead or dying, the slaves on the ground would be ash by the next day.

"Auf der Flucht erschossen!"

Another SS expression.

"Killed during an escape attempt."

That was the cue for Horse Face to haul the attempted escapee out into the square, where a trestle had been erected near the central gallows.

Horse Face was the *Lagerältester*, a criminal inmate who wore a black triangle as a sign that he was a hangman and torturer. Strong, swarthy, and dark-haired, he had a face shaped like a horse's, with a low forehead above a prominent chin. Psychologically, he was ideal for this job. The rage that seethed within him could be quelled for a while by the death of a hapless slave.

"Fünfundzwanzig am Arsch!" the guards began to chant.

"Twenty-five on the ass."

Horse Face bent the attempted escapee over the trestle and tore the ragged trousers off his behind. He then lit into the man with his cudgel, thrashing his buttocks and genitals to shreds.

"Fünfundzwanzig am Arsch!"

The screams!

"Pfahlhangen!" ordered the *Lagerführer*, moving the program on to the next act. Fritz felt as if he were Caesar's son in the emperor's box at the Roman Colosseum. Standing in the open end of the U, the Hitler Youth had the best view of the roll-call square. Not only could he watch what went on at center stage, but he could also catch the reaction of the crowd.

Feed him to the lions!

Thumbs-down to any gladiator on the ground!

An icy wind was picking up as the *Pfahlhangen* began. The *Pfahl* was an upright post that had been erected next to the gallows. Horse Face dragged the attempted escapee across to the post, tied the slave's hands together in the small of his back, attached a pulley cord to his wrists, then hoisted him up. So excruciating was the shoulder pain that the slave began screeching again. Before abandoning the man to his fate, Horse Face strung the sign for would-be escapers about his neck.

"Hurra, hurra! Ich bin wieder da!" it read.

"Hurrah, hurrah! I'm back again!"

That done, the time had arrived for the Gestapo to harvest its bounty of flesh. The first fifty rockets, delivered back in January 1944, had proved to be so flawed because of poor welding, shoddy electrical connections, and other factory problems that many disintegrated right after launch. To get to the bottom of the repeated test-fire disasters, Wernher von Braun had sent Dieter Grau, one of his engineers, to the underground factory. After probing its assembly line, Grau had found the cause to be sabotage.

The slaves could undermine the rockets in many ways. They knew just where to loosen or tighten a screw to interfere with a V-2's performance. They would urinate on the wiring to short-circuit electrical contacts. They would accept faulty parts that didn't meet specifications, or fail to install vital components. They would make welds on fins that couldn't withstand launch stresses. No matter the cause, the effect was the same: Nazi rockets blew up or veered off course.

The SS cure for sabotage was to call in the Gestapo, who now ruled the Mittelwerk factory with an iron grip. A network of informers escaped torture and abuse by snitching on others when the rockets failed to work. Von Braun's missiles were so critical to the survival of the Reich that no quarter was given to those who threatened V-2 production. To fool with the Gestapo was to end up like this.

"Stillgestanden!" the *Lagerführer* barked.

Their boots shining like polished black steel, Streicher's Gestapo henchmen marched across to the six-hooked gallows in the center of the quadrangle. The snow was slanting into the square on the wind, piercing the eyes and ears of shivering slaves. Each sub-zero gust made the ropes blow this way and that. Fritz couldn't tell if it was the weather or the Gestapo's list of saboteurs that was wrenching the sobs from frozen lungs.

When the first number was announced, Horse Face grabbed the doomed prisoner from his place in line, cinched his wrists behind his back, then hauled him to the gallows beside the wretch suspended from the *Pfahl* post.

"It was a scrap of leather!" the condemned man shouted. "I didn't do anything wrong. I took it to make a belt. I've lost too much weight! My trousers won't stay up!"

The trembling man faltered and crumpled to his knees. Horse Face kicked him, caving in his ribs. The next kick smashed in the slave's face. The *Lagerältester* yanked him onto a stool beneath one of the ropes and slipped the noose around the groaning man's neck.

Horse Face mumbled as he kicked away the stool.

Slow strangulation was the Gestapo specialty, so they made sure the drop wasn't long enough to snap the cervical vertebra. Instead, the man was left to strangle by his own weight.

Twelve saboteurs were hanged that winter morning. Two gallows' full. Finally, the *Lagerführer* called out, *"Fertig!"* That marked the end of that punishment and time for work, punishment of another kind.

Thousands of slaves from the square were herded out through the concentration camp's gate to march the quarter mile to the mountain tunnels. Those who were snitched on that day by the Gestapo's spies would end up hanging on the gallows at roll call the next morning.

Streicher had consulted his watch. It was almost six a.m. "Fritz, Hans, hungry? Time for a hot breakfast."

As Fritz had turned to walk away that winter morning, he'd glanced back over his shoulder. Snow had turned those who had dropped during *Stillstehen* into heaps of white ice. The same had happened to the first six saboteurs, who'd been cut down from the gallows and discarded on the paving stones. The six who were still hanging from their nooses twirled with the gusts of wind that blew across the quadrangle. The snowdrift at the bottom of the *Pfahl* post was red with blood that had dripped from the would-be escapee's gashes. No longer moving, he'd frozen to death.

If Fritz listened hard enough, he could still hear him scream.

Razorback

At just after dawn on this clear-skied morning, the helicopter lifted up off its pad on Sea Island, in the mouth of the Fraser River, and began a glorious flight up the inland valley. If there were a God, It had ordered up the perfect day, for overnight winds from the west had cleared the valley of air pollution. Sitting in the seat beside the chopper's pilot, Dane faced the dazzling fire mask of the rising sun as it peered over the stockade of jagged eastern peaks.

This flight to the Mountain—for him, it was always the Mountain, with a capital *M*—had actually begun decades ago, when Dane was only three.

They call it "the Graveyard of the Air," that stretch of 120 air miles east from Vancouver to Princeton, in the heart of the Cascade Mountains. Too many pilots have crashed there, and some of their planes have never been found. The dangers are always multitudinous, but winter is the worst. Storms sweeping in from the Pacific are hurled abruptly upward as they batter the precipitous walls of the Cascades. Turbulent air screams over the towering ridges and plummets down the lee side in a whirling maelstrom, just like rapids do over rocks in rivers. Fierce winds race at all angles, for mountains also brew up their own fantastic storms. The result is a standing wave—a waterfall of

wind—that can disappear from under a plane with a
sickening jolt, like a floor collapsing beneath your feet.

And then there's ice.

In an instant, damp mountain air can plaster a plane with
tons of solid rime, weighting it down appreciably and
disrupting the airflow that keeps the wings lifted up.

In 1945, on his liberation from the Stalag Luft POW
camp, Keith had returned to Canada from Bomber
Command and applied to join the RCMP. The Mounties
reorganized Air Division in 1946, staffing it with recruits
who'd flown operations in the war. Keith rose quickly to
pilot staff sergeant on the West Coast, where he flew the
Beaver floatplane on the Fraser River.

Later, Keith's son, Troy, had followed his father into the
red serge and Air Division. Dane's dad was promoted up
the ranks to helicopter sergeant of the RCMP's JetRanger.
He and Papa became known as "the flying Winters." The
winter of the accident, Keith's sister-in-law had suffered a
stroke in Princeton. Because it wasn't known how long she
would live, Troy had rented a private plane to fly both his
mother and his wife inland to be at his aunt's bedside. Papa,
in a cast with a broken leg, had stayed in Vancouver with
three-year-old Dane.

Before that day was out, Keith was a widower and Dane
was an orphan.

In the jargon of pilots who braved the Graveyard of the
Air, Troy and his passengers had run into a "cumulo-
granitus" cloud. The weather in the Cascade Mountains had
changed en route, and the plane, ambushed by the shifting
conditions, had struck a snowy peak. Just to the east of
Mount Slesse—where a North Star had crashed back in
1956, killing all sixty-two people aboard—a search pilot
had spotted a metallic glint in the cirque of the Razorback.
Closer examination revealed it to be the tail section of a

plane bearing the fuselage number of the one that Troy had rented. But before the bodies could be recovered, an avalanche had buried the wreck under tons of snow. To this day, the Razorback remained their grave.

THE FRASER RIVER snaked along the valley like molten gold. Upstream, the bedroom communities of Greater Vancouver gave way to the fertile farmlands of rural enclaves: Langley, Matsqui, Abbotsford, and Chilliwack. Beneath the helicopter, boats and log booms carved wakes along the river while rush-hour traffic began to clog the Trans-Canada Highway. Dead ahead loomed the peaks of the bloodthirsty Cascades, their icy fangs running red with the flush of dawn. Veering southeast off the main artery, the chopper tracked the Chilliwack River past Cultus Lake, whose waters sparkled with silver as if to promote the steelhead angling for which it was famous. The overhead rotor thumped louder as they gained altitude, climbing over Slesse Park, with its monument to those who'd died in the 1956 crash, then soaring up along an evergreen slope and around the shoulder of a wicked rampart of rock.

Dane yawned several times to unplug his ears. The helicopter flew by an ugly scar that had been gouged out of the vertical, gray granite cliff at 7,600 feet. The scar marked the spot where, driven down by a ferocious wave of wind, the North Star had crumpled and broken apart, before plummeting another two thousand feet.

"The Razorback," the pilot said, pointing. And there it was to the east—the Mountain that had crushed the life out of Dane's father, mother, and grandmother.

Like a stegosaurus, the Razorback had staggered triangular plates jutting up along its ridge spine.

"We'll set down there," the pilot told both passengers through the headphones.

Though it was late May, the dead-end valley was still an avalanche cauldron. The chopper closed in on a flattish saddle between two precipitous walls of rock, a spot selected by the pilot because it had no snowcap to drop on the landing site. At 8,200 feet, it was near the summit of the Razorback. So precariously unstable were the snow masses clinging to this horseshoe of icebound pinnacles that the thumping of the rotors as they flew over the cirque sent tons of white thundering down the right-angled cliffs like a waterfall.

As the chopper landed, snow billowed from the ground.

Two men climbed down from the helicopter. The pilot remained in the cockpit … to be ready, just in case. Dane wore the Mounties' famous red serge, an icon almost as internationally recognizable as the Coca-Cola logo. The other man's tunic was also red, but the rest of his uniform differed. Instead of the Stetson, he wore a Glengarry hat with a regimental bison-head badge on the side. Instead of blue breeches with a yellow side-stripe, he wore a kilt with a sporran. Instead of riding boots with spurs, he wore knee-high argyll socks with red garters and white spats over black oxfords. Tucked into the top of his right sock was a boot knife: the *sgian dubh*.

Every thread in the tartan of the kilt had meaning. The background theme color matched Dane's dark blue riding breeches and the saddle blanket of the Musical Ride. The scarlet cross-hatch picked up the red tunic of the frontier riders of the plains. The yellow thread represented Dane's cavalry stripe; the sienna brown thread the bison at the heart of the Mounties' badge; the forest green thread the maple leaves around the edge of their crest; the sky blue thread their new peacekeeping role with the United Nations. The accent color was white, which has spiritual significance for Native peoples and symbolizes strength and endurance. White was also the color of the lanyard that Dane had strung around his neck and attached to the butt of his gun. If he dropped his weapon in the heat of a shoot-out, it would still be at hand.

"Ready?" the pipe major asked.

Sucking in a deep breath, Dane nodded and walked to the edge of a precipice that plunged thousands of feet to the constantly stirring, crevassed snowfield below. Then he crooked his right arm to his hat in the RCMP salute.

The first note of the last post cut cleanly through the thin air of the mountain wilderness. Keith had done his duty both in war and in peace, and the time had come for Dane to do his duty by Papa. Troy had gone to his grave here, so the bugle blew for his duty, too.

Old Celtic legend holds that of all the musical instruments created, the bagpipes speak to the other world. The dead can hear them, and know they are mourned. That's why the lone piper bids farewell to the fallen at Mountie funerals, and it's why the wheeze of filling bagpipes sounded now, followed by drone pipes and the finger-holed chanter mourning Keith and Troy with a Scottish lament, "Flowers of the Forest."

As he listened to the pipes and stood mute in the minute of silence that followed, Dane experienced a strange epiphany. All his life, he had feared this dreaded place, but now that he was up here at the top of the world, where Gabriel could be blowing his trumpet at the gates of heaven, the sergeant was overwhelmed by the awesome energy of the Mountain. We all have to die and rest somewhere, and no place on earth could be more exultant than this.

His soul leaped at the bugle call of "The Rouse"—what the layman incorrectly calls reveille—its stirring notes calling out to the fallen in the next and better realm. Dane found himself awaking to who he was as a man, as if all the threads of his being had woven together into a pattern with as much meaning for him as that tartan had for the Mounted Police.

Reaching into his pocket for his Swiss Army knife, he opened the box of cremated remains and slit the plastic sack with the blade. As the blue windbag of the pipes wheezed again, Dane scattered his grandfather's ashes to the breeze, watching as they drifted out over the valley, then wafted down slowly to rest at long last with the spirits of his beloved wife, his dutiful son, and his daughter-in-law.

With the honors for Keith and Troy complete, the goodbye turned to the mother and the grandmother Dane could not remember. If there was a more inspiring tune in this world than "Amazing Grace" played on the bagpipes, he had yet to hear it. Echoes from the Razorback's steeples joined the notes of the lone piper as the wilderness honored the Winters with its phantom pipe band.

LESS THAN TEN MINUTES after the rotors of the chopper had ceased whirling back at the heliport—and while he was still changing out of the red serge and into plainclothes— Dane got a call on his cell.

"Winter," he answered.

"Dane, this is Rachel. You've got another murder."

The Midas Touch

Leaving the helicopter pad on Sea Island, in the deltoid mouth of the Fraser River, Dane drove straight north across Vancouver with the U.S. border behind his back and crested the harbor on Lions Gate Bridge, parking his car at Lonsdale Quay. As he neared the waterfront high-rise that was the murder scene, he phoned Sergeant Rachel Kidd to come down and meet him.

"Was the scene secured in time?" Dane asked when both sergeants stood face to face.

"Yes. We got lucky. Only two civilians know: the maid who went in to clean this morning and found Midas dead on the bed, and the high-rise manager, a very uptight guy. He's afraid the building will be cursed by the gods of economics if word gets out. He shut the maid up by threatening her job before he called us. The guy's so afraid of a leak that he didn't call 9-1-1."

"Midas?" Dane said. "The exec in the papers?"

The other sergeant nodded. "He really pissed someone off. Wait'll you see what was done to him."

"I hope you're not pissed at me."

"What? For usurping the case?"

Dane nodded in turn.

"It's for the better," Kidd said, shrugging with resignation. A tinge of disappointment lowered her voice. "This murder will be your ticket into Special X. I'm not their favorite poster girl, as you know."

Unlike so many forces around the world, the RCMP remains mostly free of corruption. Its officers take their unofficial motto—"The Mounties always get their man"— very seriously, even when it comes to one of their own. It's a badge of honor in the ranks to take down a dirty cop, but if you go after one of your own, you had better make damn sure that your allegation sticks.

That had been Rachel's downfall.

Until the 1970s, there were no women and no blacks in the RCMP, so Constable Rachel Kidd had been a PR man's dream. Very quickly, she began a meteoric rise up the ranks. Dane had come in to the force at the same time, but he couldn't compete. Everyone understood that Kidd would soon be a dreamboat inspector. But then she overreached by charging Corporal Nick Craven with the murder of his mother, and when that member of Special X walked out of court a free man, his accuser had paid the regimental price. Her booster rocket had sputtered; her career had crashed to earth. And the would-be inspector was now, like Dane, a sergeant with GIS.

"You responded to the first case, so this one is yours. We're cool," Rachel confirmed.

"Good. Beam me up."

"Beam me up" was the ideal way to describe the ascent to the penthouse suite at the top of the most phallic tower in Lonsdale Quay. The suite's private glass elevator waited up at the skyline until the king of the castle summoned it down to one of two levels: the waterfront walk along the harbor, or the access-controlled parking lot below.

The sergeants were on the quayside, and Rachel used a remote control to recall the elevator. It had returned to the top of the tower while they were talking.

"This control belongs to the manager," she explained. "If it's okay for the maid to clean, she gets the control from him. The other control—there are only two—was used by Midas. It's not in the penthouse, but he is, so the killer must have taken it away."

"Security cameras?"

"Uh-huh. But they were turned off. The cameras also work off the remote control."

"The killer turned them off?"

"Midas, probably. That's what he usually did when he escorted his bedmates here."

"That's why the maid had to check?"

"You got it," Rachel said, nodding. "This penthouse isn't where he lived. It's where he came for sex."

"We're looking for a woman?"

"A woman *or* a man. Kurt Midas used sex as a way to flaunt his money and power. Word is that he had a penchant for seducing the wives and lovers of his rivals—and saw it as a coup to bed their yes-men, too."

"That's a lot of enemies."

"The guy was disturbed. You'd have to be to want to ruin as many lives as he did."

"So how do you think it went down?"

"Midas was in the company of someone he wanted to bed. They drove into his private area of the parking lot. He punched off the security cameras, and they rode the elevator up. The attack occurred on the bed in the penthouse. With Midas dead, his killer used the remote to descend to the lot, and then he or she escaped in his car."

"It's missing?"

"Uh-huh. And it's not at his home."

The elevator was tinted so that outsiders couldn't gawk in as it scaled the face of the high-rise. It showed the Mounties a panorama of the inner and outer harbors as it soared.

"Nice view," Dane said understatedly.

"Y'ain't seen nothin' yet."

The doors behind them opened on a single octagonal-shaped room, which, except for the floor, was made entirely of glass. Up here, the view was 360 degrees. Gazing around to take some of it in, Dane felt like the lamp in a lighthouse. For physical setting, globetrotters say six cities are the must-sees: Hong Kong, Sydney, Cape Town, Rio de Janeiro, San Francisco, and the seaport at Dane's feet. Up here, he could see it all, from the ski slopes on the North Shore Mountains to the ships out at sea. An aerie like this was created for an out-of-control ego. From what Dane had heard about Kurt Midas, it fit him to a T.

"Jesus Christ! Is that him on the bed?"

"Like I said," Rachel reiterated, "he *really* pissed someone off."

WHEN DANE WINTER was at the University of British Columbia working toward his law degree, he had to take a science credit. Since he knew he was destined to follow his dad and his granddad into the Mounties, Dane chose zoology as his elective. He figured that all those lab dissections would prepare him for autopsies. The crime scene now before him reminded him of that dissection room more than any of his trips to the morgue ever had.

Smack dab in the middle of the glass-domed penthouse was a king-size bed. At night in that bed, you would be encased by a vault of stars and the moon above, with absolutely nothing to obstruct your view. Because the tower was the highest on the quay, no Peeping Tom could peek in, and the tinted glass would thwart any telescopes aimed down from the North Shore peaks. A square hole in the floor revealed a staircase that stepped down a level to where the bathroom, Jacuzzi, sauna, steam room, and other amenities awaited.

The guy on the bed had been skinned.

When Dane was a boy, Papa had bought him a plastic model kit called the Visible Man. It was a human body with all the internal organs on display through a plastic skin. As he approached the flayed man on the bed, that model came back to him.

"Good morning, Sergeant." Dr. Gill Macbeth, the same sawbones who'd responded to the Mosquito Creek crime and done the post-mortem on the Congo Man, was standing over the body.

"Morning, Doc."

Dane caught the evil eye that Gill flicked at Rachel. The doc had been pregnant with Nick Craven's child throughout his murder trial and had suffered a miscarriage in the aftermath. To make matters worse, Gill was currently in a romantic relationship with Robert DeClercq, Craven's boss at Special X and the man who'd saved him from jail.

Dane felt sorry for Rachel.

She was a good cop.

But a mistake was a mistake, and she'd forever have that albatross around her neck.

"Is there a moral here?" Dane asked.

"Yep," said Rachel. "Fuck with innocent people's life savings, and you could end up like this."

IT WAS LIKE THAT SONG by Johnny Cash, "A Boy Named Sue." If you start a child off in life with the wrong name, there'll be aftershocks. But in this case, it was a family name, so that was a little different. Go through life with the moniker Midas, and you might grow into it.

The Midas touch.

Like in the Greek myth.

When King Midas was granted a single wish by the god Dionysus, he asked that everything he touched be turned to gold. In the world of capitalism and *Forbes* magazine, those with the golden touch—men like Murdoch, Maxwell, Branson, and the Donald—are hailed as gods. Until things went south, Kurt Midas had been soaring to that level. Every deal that passed through his fingers was rumored to turn to gold.

Fool's gold, actually.

Stockholders of Enron and WorldCom know only too well what happens when greedy corporate executives mistake their companies' earnings for their own personal piggy banks. Kurt's company had been listed on the stock exchange, and he had driven it straight into bankruptcy. Its loyal employees had invested their futures in its pension plan. Where all that money was now, no one seemed to know, for just before the gold rush had gone bust, Kurt Midas had mined the company of all that wealth. Perhaps it was squirreled away in some tax haven guarded by a phalanx of lawyers, and by the time prosecutors unraveled his Gordian knot of financial manipulations and extradited him to America to stand trial, Midas would be approaching the age of Methuselah.

In the meantime, Kurt had lived like a king.

Until last night.

"Cause of death?" Dane asked.

"A blow to the head," said Gill. "See where the skull has caved in on one side?"

"Weapon?"

"Ident recovered a bloody champagne bottle from the floor beside the bed," said Rachel.

Identification techs in white coveralls were at work doing forensic tests on areas of the penthouse not yet cleared for the path of contamination. Among the exhibits in evidence bags was a bottle of top-end champagne.

"Prints?"

"Nope. Just the vic's. The killer used gloves or wiped down the scene with a cloth."

"Was Midas skinned alive?"

The pathologist shook her head. "The flaying was post-mortem. If I were to guess, I'd say he most likely stripped off his clothes and climbed onto the bed. Perhaps the killer was supposed to pop the champagne cork. Instead, he or she brained Midas across the head. After he was dead, his skin was peeled away."

The hair remained in place, but the face was gone, as was the skin of the torso and the abdomen, down to, and including, the genitals. The arms and legs were flayed as far as the elbows and knees. But the eeriest thing for Dane was the eyes. They stared up at the glass ceiling from red, raw facial muscles.

"Was the skin taken as a trophy?"

"No," said Rachel. "It's mounted over there."

The sergeant swiveled around to follow the direction of her finger, which pointed toward an octagon window on the right-hand side of the elevator. So shocked had Dane been by the bloody mess on the bed when the elevator doors opened that he had failed to catch sight of it in his periph-eral vision.

"Definitely a case for Special X," Rachel said, ushering him over to the skin display.

"Definitely," Dane agreed. "The international aspect of both crimes—Liberian refugee from Africa and corporate pillager from the States—would transfer it anyway. And then we have the signature left at both scenes."

The skin that had been stripped off Kurt Midas was plastered to the window by its bloody underlay. An aerosol can had been used to spray the human hide with gold paint. The gilded trophy had the torso, genitals, stumpy limbs, and face of a humanoid form. The artwork bore the signature of its creator. Carved into the skin of the forehead was a Nazi swastika.

Wonder Weapons

NORDHAUSEN, GERMANY
April 4, 1945

"Fritz!" Streicher snapped. "Where are you?"

The Hitler Youth returned to the sparks above Nordhausen.

The memory of that winter morning on the *Appellplatz* faded.

"Sorry, Father. I drifted off."

"There'll be no drifting off. I have a task for you."

The Hitler Youth clicked his heels.

"For you *and* Hans."

Jackboots stomping, the SS general led his sons and the corpse-counting bureaucrat into the yawning maw of Tunnel B. As soon as they entered, a deafening din assaulted them. Massive rockets rumbled toward them along the railroad tracks. Each thirteen-ton leviathan received its tail, fins, guts, and open-jawed snout at workshops in the cross-halls as it emerged from the deep. Like an army of ants, thousands of tiny slaves swarmed through the tunnel, one line going in and the other coming out. Lathes, drills, machine presses, jigs, files, and hammers produced a cacophony that ricocheted off the tight confines of the rock walls and down into the bowels of the assembly line. Countless clogs clomped across the concrete floor. Huge slabs of sheet metal clanged and moaned as welders bent and fused them into place. The stench of burnt oil hung heavy in the air.

Up where the tunnel's walls met the rounded roof, ventilation shafts panted like monstrous pneumatic lungs. The tunnel was alight with the brilliant blue rays of the welders and the yellowish cast of the bulbs that shone down from the ceiling. Slaves cried out under the blows of the *Kapos* like the choirboys of some satanic cathedral.

Tunnel A was the supply tunnel. It was used to send parts down to the cross-halls, where they were added to rockets cradled horizontally on railroad bogies that rolled them from north to south along the assembly line in Tunnel B. When a rocket was finished, it was moved to Hall 41, where it would be inspected and approved. Hall 41 had been excavated well below the floor level to give it more than fifty feet of clearance. A giant spanning crane hoisted the rockets off their cradles and stood them up on the tips of their tail fins. Several galleries scaled one whole side of Hall 41. Slaves and Nazi overseers worked on the various levels, inspecting the top-end components of each missile's guidance system and tightening lugs, nuts, seals, and fittings in the open stomach of each upright shark.

Normally.

But not at the moment.

"How many hangings does this make?" Streicher asked.

The corpse-counting bureaucrat consulted his tally board. "Sixteen on March 3. Fifty-seven on March 11. Thirty on March 21. Thirty again on March 22. Plus these."

SS-Sturmbannführer Richard Baer, the commandant of Auschwitz from May 11, 1944, until its evacuation in January of this year, had become the new head of Dora-Mittelbau on February 1. Escaping the onslaught of the Red Army with him had been his SS executioners and thousands of living skeletons—most of them Jews. Days without food in those boxcar pens had taken their toll, and often more dead bodies than live prisoners had come down from the trains. Baer had dumped the hopeless transport cases and Mittelwerk casualties at the Boelcke Kaserne barracks in Nordhausen and left them to die slowly. Ironically, the RAF bombing raid had thwarted that plan. Then, to root out sabotage in the rocket factory, Baer had embarked on a slew of mass hangings in Hall 41.

Hangings like those that the Streichers and the corpse-counter had just walked in on.

The overhead crane spanned the hall like a rolling bridge. Hooked to it was a plank with twelve hangman's nooses attached. The nooses were cinched around the necks of twelve trembling slaves, each with his wrists tied behind his back and his mouth gagged by a chunk of wood that was fastened at the base of his skull like a horse's bridle. The gags were to prevent outbursts that might insult the SS. At the first mass hanging, a Russian had condemned them to eternal damnation, and Baer wasn't the kind of commandant to stomach that.

With a whir, the crane began to rise.

Work had ceased in Hall 41 so that the hangings could be witnessed by all: the twelve slaves who would follow this dozen; their comrades, who would survive to work another shift; and the rocketeers still in the Mittelwerk.

Slowly, slowly, the crane rose to a height of twelve feet, lifting the soles of the hanged men five feet off the floor. At first, it seemed that nothing was happening, that the bodies were inert. But then the wretched marionettes began to stir. They kicked their legs about wildly, as if hunting for a foothold, then lifted their knees to their chests, then dropped them, then lifted them again. As the twitching and twisting continued, the bodies banged about, and legs began trying to climb other legs to loosen the grips of the ropes. Soon, frenzied spasms overwhelmed their muscles. Clogs dropped from feet and loose pants fell to ankles. As if gripped by that winter wind that had blown through Fritz's memory, the hanged men thrashed around and kicked the empty air until—slowly, slowly—the kinetic frenzy waned. One by one, they settled down—a shudder here, a tremble there— with their heads angled sharply from their shoulders, their eyes bulging out of their sockets, and the ropes of the mechanical gallows dug deep into their necks.

With a whir, the crane began to lower.

A loosening of the nooses and the dead fell to the floor, where the undertaker slaves gathered them in their handcarts, heads and feet sticking out, to trundle the "pieces" off to Camp Dora's crematorium.

With a whir, the crane began to rise.

The last twelve men hanged would be left to dangle for days as a deterrent to the other slaves. As each shift came in or went out, the men would have to push through this obscene display, setting the corpses swinging gently from their long noosed ropes in a literal *danse macabre*.

HALL 41 was the climactic fusion of the rocket and the Reich. Here hung the proof that modern industrial technology was morally compatible with slavery, mass murder, and barbarism. The rocketeers, not the SS, had been the ones to suggest solving the war-time manpower shortage by using slave labor to build von Braun's V-2. Arthur Rudolph, the production manager of the assembly line at Peenemünde, had returned from a tour of the slave-driven Heinkel aircraft plant north of Berlin convinced that he held the key to their labor problem. Now that the rocket factory was in these tunnels, so was the office of von Braun's production manager. At least once a day, Rudolph would stroll the assembly line, occasionally stopping to down a glass of schnapps with SS-Sturmbannführer Otto Forschner, the commandant overseeing the horror.

Magnus von Braun—Wernher's brother—was head of gyroscope production. His office, too, was in the Mittelwerk. The guidance system of the V-2—a technical innovation called the *Vertikant*—used three gyroscopes: a pair to orient the missile in outer space and a third to shut off the engine at the correct velocity. The final gyroscopic tests could not be carried out on a horizontal missile, so Magnus von Braun did them in Hall 41.

Because the Baltic had remained the site of rocket testing, Wernher von Braun had stayed behind at Peenemünde. But he'd maintained communication with Hall 41, home of the "cucumber"—as team members had dubbed the olive green rocket. Hall 41 was where every new V-2 had its final tests. Von Braun's plans had suddenly changed in February, however, when the Red Army closed in on Peenemünde. After relocating his staff here to the Harz Mountains, he himself had ended up in one of the small villages near Hall 41.

WHAT MIGHT HAVE BEEN, Streicher wondered, if not for Bomber Harris?

If RAF Bomber Command hadn't stopped Peenemünde in August 1943, V-2 production wouldn't have been postponed until the following year. Because of Bomber Harris, the Reich had missed its best chance to pulverize Eisenhower's D-Day invasion force by plunging a deluge of rockets down on the English ports of embarkation. There was no defense against the V-2. It blasted off to fantastic altitudes, then dropped down faster than the speed of sound to destroy its target before the enemy could hear it coming.

If only …

Instead, the Reich had been forced to rely on the Luftwaffe's V-1. The "buzz bomb" had caused a lot of terror with its ominous noise—it came screaming in, the

ied, and there was an excruciating wait for the
on—but it could be knocked out of the sky by a
ground fire, or by having its wing tipped up by
ing Spitfire. The first pilotless radio-controlled
missile had hit London on June 13, 1944, a week
D-Day. Hundreds more had rained down on Britain
those summer months, but in the end, their military
e was close to nil.

The Allies had landed.

And they were spreading out.

On the other hand, if it hadn't been for Bomber Harris's
run at Peenemünde, where would Streicher be now?
Himmler had used that attack to wrench control of the V-2
away from the regular army and place it in the hands of the
SS. Streicher had built the Mittelwerk in these mountains to
protect it against future Bomber Harris raids, and he'd
engineered this tunnel assembly line to pump out between
six and seven hundred V-2s a month.

That was more than twenty a day.

About a missile an hour.

Streicher was now the most technologically powerful
Nazi in the Reich. After the briefcase bomb narrowly
missed killing Hitler in the attempted coup of July 20,
1944, the führer had appointed Himmler his chief of army
armaments. On August 6, the Reichsführer-SS had
delegated his power to Streicher in order to accelerate
deployment of the V-2.

At 6:43 p.m. on September 8, 1944, a plummeting
thunderbolt had struck London to herald the arrival of the
first V-2. The medium-range ballistic missile had been fired
from Holland. By the end of that month, the SS had ordered
that Work Camp Dora be separated from Buchenwald. That
made it the only SS labor camp set up explicitly for
weapons production. On November 1, the day it went

independent, Concentration Camp Dora-Mittelbau had a population of 32,471 slaves. The sign of autonomy? It got its own crematory ovens.

The tally board in the corpse-counter's hands told it all.

Hall 41 had churned out 5,789 V-2s.

Each rocket had cost the lives of nearly four slaves.

Streicher was proud of the empire of horror that he had created.

But now that empire was about to fall.

"Evacuate the tunnels," he commanded the bureaucrat.

"DO WE GAS THEM?" the bureaucrat asked again.

Himmler's standing order to the SS was that all proof of genocide had to be destroyed. The transport of death-camp survivors from the east had been an interim solution. But a final solution was needed to ensure that the subhumans would not be able to turn on the master race in the event of liberation. And those who had slaved in the V-weapons plant had to be stopped from passing Nazi secrets to the conquering Allies. The best way to accomplish that would be to herd the nearly thirty thousand slaves in Dora-Mittelbau into the factory tunnels along with all the V-2s, then block and seal every possible exit and pump in poison gas—all as a prelude to blowing the wonder weapons to hell and gone.

That, however, didn't fit Streicher's plan.

"No," he said. "Evacuate the slaves, too. Get every freight car you can find and ship them out today."

"Where to, General?"

"Bergen-Belsen. Or any camp with space."

"But that's—"

"Do it!" Streicher snapped. "Or you'll join them!"

Dora-Mittelbau and the Mittelwerk factory were directly in the path of the invading U.S. Army. At first, the deserted valleys of the Harz Mountains had seemed the ideal place to hide the V-2 assembly line. The mountains were a refuge of wild and brooding beauty, of crags, ravines, dark green woods, and snug little towns with half-timbered houses. But now the war had come to the Harz from the air—in the form of the Reich's arch-nemesis, Bomber Harris—and it would be here, on the ground, in a matter of days, when the Americans rumbled in.

Streicher's plan called for them to find the V-2s.

"Where's von Braun?" he asked.

"On his way to Oberammergau," replied the bureaucrat.

"On the Vengeance Express?"

"No, General. The SS major is traveling by car."

"Is he still in a cast?"

"Yes," said the corpse-counter.

It was safe to travel open roads in the Harz only by night. Shortly before his thirty-third birthday, von Braun had been involved in a car accident. His driver fell asleep at the wheel, and the car veered off the road and crashed into an embankment. Von Braun had a broken arm.

"And the other scientists?"

"They're on their way, General."

"Key people?"

"The top five hundred, as you ordered. They're on the Vengeance Express."

Streicher nodded.

The V-2s would be found, but the brains behind them would not.

Bomber Harris, now with the added support of American planes, had set his sights on pulverizing Hitler's Third Reich. The audacity of that bulldog warrior—who was trying now to do to the Reich what the Reich had done to the rest of Europe—had galled the führer past the point of madness. Hitler wanted vengeance at any price. But he knew that his ploy of having Streicher knock the British out of the war in a hail of rockets had failed. So Hitler now obsessed over a new plan.

So did Streicher.

And both exit strategies depended on a new device.

Die Glocke: The Bell.

Golden Fleece

VANCOUVER
May 26, Now

Cort Jantzen got the jolt of his newspaper career when he sat down at his desk at *The Vancouver Times* and checked the overnight e-mails that had been sent to the cyber address at the bottom of his ongoing "Cyclops" column. Someone named Jason had posted a message with the subject heading "The Golden Fleece." Intrigued by what seemed to be a reference to Greek myth, Cort opened both the e-mail and the jpeg file it included, only to drop his jaw at the sight of what popped up onscreen: the skin of a man gilded and plastered by blood to what appeared to be a high-rise window. In the background of the digital photo, Cort could make out the lights of North Vancouver.

The caption beneath the jpeg horror read:

Kurt Midas
A Golden Fleece for a Golden Fleece

A minute later, hard copy in hand, the reporter burst into the office of the managing editor.

"Don't you knock, Jantzen?"

"Stop the presses, Boss!"

THE TWO NEWSPAPERMEN were sitting side by side at Editor Ed's computer when the queen bitch walked in.

"Can't you see we're doing something important, McQueen?"

"Ed, I've got my piece on the stealth killer."

"Throw it in the box. I'll read it later. We got the Scoop of Scoops going on here."

Bess McQueen sulked.

"Scram," growled Editor Ed.

The queen bitch retreated.

The bum's rush, Cort thought gleefully.

Editor Ed had punched the words "golden fleece" into a search engine, and it had come back with 125,000 hits. From among the many condensations of that myth, the précis he'd chosen read:

> To establish that he was fit to be a king of the Greeks, Jason had embarked on a perilous sea quest in a ship called the *Argo*. With the help of his crew, the Argonauts, he was determined to bring back the legendary Golden Fleece. According to myth, the Golden Fleece was the skin of a fabulous flying ram that had been sacrificed to Zeus, overall king of the Olympian gods. It hung from a tree in Colchis, on the Black Sea, where it was guarded by a dragon that never slept. Drugging the dragon with a sleeping potion he'd got from a sorceress, Jason was able to capture the Golden Fleece and sail home, where he was crowned king.

"What an angle!" enthused Ed. "You've got the headline, Jantzen: 'Vigilante Strikes Again and Contacts *Times* Reporter.'"

"Can we put the myth in a sidebar?"

"Whatever you want, sport. You're the golden boy of the moment around here."

"Thanks, Ed."

"Don't get weepy on me. What are you waiting for? It's time to go hunt for *this* golden fleece. You've got a photo of the trophy but no crime scene."

"I'm on it, Boss."

"Set sail, Jason. Get your ass on the street."

Outside the door to Editor Ed's office, the queen bitch was still waiting for her audience with the boss. As Cort came out, he almost bumped into her. The rival crime reporters stared each other down.

"Eat your heart out, baby," Cort finally said with a wink.

Back at his desk, he figured the best place to start was with the North Vancouver detachment of the Mounties. The killer of the Congo Man had struck in their jurisdiction, after all, and the background in the jpeg image clearly showed the North Shore. So the first call Cort made was to North Van GIS.

Bingo!

No need to hunt further.

The general investigation section—the homicide cops—confirmed that Mounties were currently working a murder scene at Lonsdale Quay, in a high-rise penthouse owned by Kurt Midas.

Cort and his spiral notebook were heading for the door.

NORTH VANCOUVER

The crime reporter recognized Sergeant Winter as he strolled out of Kurt Midas's high-rise. Right away, he grasped that Winter had been called in to this case—even if it wasn't his—because it had some connection to the Congo Man's murder.

Had the killer sent a jpeg to the Mounties too?

Or was it something else?

"A moment, Sergeant?" Cort said, homing in on the investigator. The reporter had been lurking about on the quay, probing for bits of information.

"Not now," Winter said, waving Jantzen away.

"Heading for Special X?"

No reply.

This brush-off left Cort no choice, and he went for the sucker punch.

"Did the vigilante carve a Nazi swastika into the forehead of the African cannibal as well?"

Whap!

That stopped the cop in his tracks.

"What makes you ask that?" Winter asked, eyeing the reporter with rubber-hose suspicion.

"Read tomorrow's paper."

"I'd rather read it today."

"This," said Cort, whipping out a copy of the jpeg the killer had sent to him overnight. "See the swastika?" He stabbed his finger at the forehead of the human hide on the window.

The cop was trying to stay cool, but it's hard to shrug off a boot to your knackers. His jaw muscles clenched.

"Where'd you get *that*?"

"From the vigilante. We're pen pals now."

"What else have you got?"

"His reason for skinning Kurt Midas."

"Which is?"

"Read tomorrow's paper."

"Quit screwing around, Jantzen. This is serious stuff."

"No, Sergeant!" the reporter said, flaring. "You quit screwing with me. Two days ago, when you came up from Mosquito Creek, I put to you some questions that

I had a right to ask. You dismissed me like I was shit on your shoe. 'Everyone has the following fundamental freedoms: ... freedom of thought, belief, opinion and expression, including freedom of the press and other media.' Recognize it?"

"Of course. The Charter of Rights."

"You had knowledge I wanted, and I didn't get it. Now the shoe is on the other foot, and you've become the shit. I have knowledge you want, and I have every right to it. Well, Mr. Mountie, here's the deal: either you get down from your high horse and work this out with me, or you wait for the morning paper like everybody else."

"What do you want, Jantzen?"

"The same thing as you."

"What's that?"

"You tell me. Are you on your way to Special X? Would you like this crime to be your ticket into that elite? You know they'll take it from you. Sure, they'll second you to their investigation. They wouldn't want the peons' noses out of joint. You might get to carry their coffee or have some other minor role. But if you were tied to me, and I was tied to the killer, you'd be front and center in the Special X ranks."

"Okay."

"Okay what?"

"Say that's my agenda. What do *you* want?"

"Byline, Sergeant. I'm in a byline battle with a rival reporter. This case is *my* ticket to the top of the front page. If you team up with me to hunt for the vigilante—and I do mean *team up* with me, like Deep Throat did with Woodward and Bernstein—I'll be the go-between who brings you his head on a platter. In return, you will give me an exclusive on how it all goes down from the *inside*."

"In or out? Is that it?"

"Take it or leave it, Sergeant."

"Let me buy you a coffee," said the Mountie.

THE DISCUSSION they were having was supposed to be "off the record."

But these are not the good old days, and nothing is off the record now.

A surreptitious microphone caught every word.

Mr. Clean

SEA ISLAND, BRITISH COLUMBIA

The man who stepped off the flight from the United States had the deepest cover in the black world. The immigration officer at Canadian customs asked him the purpose of his visit to Vancouver, and he replied matter-of-factly, "I'm scouting locations for American coverage of the 2010 Winter Olympics." Satisfied, the Canadian handed him back his U.S. passport, stamped his immigration form, and lettered it in such a way that no one would search his bags. That didn't matter. Check him or not, hell would freeze over before anyone broke his cover. The American president himself would be fooled by the "deep black" smokescreen.

And if something went wrong?

Well, the man would simply walk away. Like a snake shedding its skin, he'd be off to a new beginning. And left behind, with no one to live it, would be an identity as "real" as that of any U.S. citizen.

Nothing stuck to Mr. Clean.

THE OPERATIVES who met him at the arrivals gate were code-named Ajax and Lysol. The black world had many ways to protect its secrets. But this was the cleanup crew Big Bad Bill liked to send in when he was gonna bloodstain the Stars and Stripes.

No fuss, no muss.

Virtually guaranteed.

All three men were dressed in the casual athletic chic that designer labels have perfected—open-throated shirts over buffed torsos, and slacks that brushed sneakers. Ajax and Lysol were a decade younger than Mr. Clean, and he had taught them both how to eradicate troublesome stains. Not a word was spoken in the airport terminal. Mr. Clean stepped into line with his henchmen and followed them out to their rental car in the parking lot. Ajax unlocked the doors, and the trio climbed in. Lysol sat in the back seat with three duffel bags.

"Are we set?"

"It's a go," Ajax informed their leader.

"No problem with the kits?"

"This country has the dinkiest security in the world. They have no idea how to guard a five-thousand-mile border."

"Good," said Mr. Clean. "Here's the plan."

A HUNDRED MILES northwest of Las Vegas, Nevada, Highway 375—or the "Extraterrestrial Highway"—joins the Tikaboo Valley to link the outside world to Area 51, a place that doesn't exist. It doesn't exist because it was the only area in America not revealed by satellite photos released by the U.S. military. So restricted is the no-fly zone over Area 51—which gets its name from that grid on an old Nevada map—that the flats surrounded by the jagged ramparts of the Jumbled Hills and the Groom Range are known to aviators as "Dreamland." Electronic sensors and observation posts high up Bald Mountain offer an unrestricted view of all traffic approaching by land or by air. Try to sneak into the area to get a glimpse of the non-existent runway used to test "deep black" weapons like the U-2, the Mach 3 A-12, the SR-71, the F-117A, and the YF-22, and you could find yourself locked away without a key or sandblasted into kingdom come by Black Hawk gunships.

Where better to ring-fence America's deepest secrets than in the desert? As far back as the Manhattan Project, the deserts of the Southwest had been the black world's black hole. Workers by the thousands were brought in by unmarked planes and buses with blacked-out windows. All were subject to a code of silence enforced as strictly as the Mafia's *omertà*. Each secret learned was kept for life. That's why a squadron of Stealth fighters was able to roam the night skies of the Southwest for a good five years without anyone spilling the beans.

And if you tried?

They'd come for you in the middle of the night. To hard-key the front door, they'd core the lock with a platinum tool driven in by a hammer blow, then snip the chain with bolt cutters and burst into your home like gangbusters. On being wrenched awake, all you'd see would be black silhouettes in body armor and Kevlar helmets. A Colt Commando snub-barreled assault rifle would pin your forehead to the pillow. Dazed and confused, you'd be dragged off into the night to a domestic version of Gitmo or Abu Ghraib. Your trial would be held in secret, for reasons of "national security."

"Pardon our jackboots. They're the price of freedom."

Eradication. Disinformation. Compartmentalization. That was the model the Pentagon had designed to replace the sieve that had leaked the secrets of the atomic bomb. "Plausible deniability." "Need to know." There were now so many layers spread out horizontally in a system meant to be denied that even those who ought to be in the know weren't. Who knew what technologies were being developed in the Pentagon's black world? It was so labyrinthine and unaccountable that even the president was in the dark.

What kept it glued together was phantasmal fear.

Fear of the unknown.

It also helped to have alien fear-mongering in the tabloids. Stories reporting orbs of light hovering in the sky. Stories claiming that the Pentagon was test-flying recovered alien spacecraft. Whistleblowers going public with revelations of secret work being done on otherworldly UFOs near Area 51.

Who knew what to believe?

Occasionally, however, some snoop closed in on the hidden truth. For at the heart of the black world, there sat a secret so dirty and volatile that—no matter what the cost—it could never be allowed to see light. The cover-up had been so successful that the truth had stayed suppressed since 1947. The Weird Shit Division would stop at nothing to keep it that way, so Big Bad Bill's mission for Mr. Clean was simple: Find out what Sergeant Winter knows about the Roswell Incident and the Nazi swastika papers. And if he's within a hundred miles of the truth, take him out.

Mr. Clean had eradicated a lot of stains for Bill.

But this was something special.

Mr. Clean was going to add a Mountie to the many notches on his gun.

Two guns, actually.

One for the hit.

The other as backup.

The gun for the hit was a German-made Heckler & Koch SOCOM (Special Operations Command). When the Pentagon went searching for a new sidearm for special ops groups like the Navy SEALS, the H&K was the weapon of choice. It chambered a .45 ACP-caliber round from a twelve-cartridge magazine and came with both an attachment for a combined laser/infrared spotter and a threaded barrel for a silencer. Resistant to saltwater spray and mud, the pistol had withstood a battery of tests so harsh that it could be said that the Mk.23 was indestructible. It was the ideal down-and-dirty weapon for Mr. Clean.

Ironically, his backup gun was Canadian-made. Who would have thought that a nation bent on gun control would have come on so fast and strong as a manufacturer of quality handguns? Quality counts in a life-and-death firefight, so Mr. Clean—a cautious assassin who valued his own life—packed the Para-Ordnance Warthog as a lifesaver.

A Canadian gun smuggled into Canada from the States to take out the greatest of Canadian icons.

You gotta love it, thought Mr. Clean.

The "kits" that Ajax and Lysol had smuggled across the Canadian border contained more exotic, high-tech spy gizmos than that lovable old coot Q had ever supplied to James Bond. A country that can put a man on the moon and build undetectable bombers can certainly breach any security wall put up by hick cops. The Weird Shit Division had surreptitious access to police communications around the globe. So even before Mr. Clean had driven the rental car off the airport parking lot, he was eavesdropping on both the Mountie dispatchers at Dane Winter's RCMP detachment in North Vancouver and all of Winter's private radio and cell calls.

Ain't technology wonderful?

As Ajax and Lysol were lifting off in a plane they'd chartered to fly them north to the Cariboo, Mr. Clean set off on the same route that the sergeant had driven less than an hour ago, on his return from the Razorback. Intercepted dispatch calls from the detachment told Mr. Clean that a murder had been discovered at Lonsdale Quay. Winter's calls informed him that the sergeant was responding to the new killing, and that it was somehow tied to the murder of the African refugee under the Mosquito Creek overpass.

Mr. Clean knew all about that murder because the photo he'd been given of Sergeant Winter was from yesterday's edition of *The Vancouver Times*. The photo showed Winter and another Horseman, identified as Insp. Zinc Chandler, standing over the corpse of a huge black man who'd been impaled on a riverbank.

Lonsdale Quay.

That was the place to start.

NORTH VANCOUVER

To see him leaning nonchalantly against the waterfront rail, a camera slung around his neck, you would mistake him for a tourist awed by the panoramic spread at the foot of the mountains. Mount Baker, in Washington State, dominated the southeast horizon. The downtown skyline across the harbor reflected back from the sparkling brine of Burrard Inlet. Here the SeaBus chugged toward the North Shore; there a seaplane jumped from wave to wave in its effort to take off for Vancouver Island. The green oasis of Stanley Park and the tented spider webs of the suspension bridge masked the freighters anchored out in English Bay.

In fact, the camera—the eye and ear of the Weird Shit Division—was digitally ogling the two men on the quay outside the high-rise murder scene. One of those men was Sgt. Dane Winter. Mr. Clean recognized the other man as Cort Jantzen, the reporter whose headshot had accompanied his story about the body beside Mosquito Creek.

Built in to the camera lens was a parabolic mike so sensitive that it caught every breath. It sent the words spoken by Winter and Jantzen up to the plug in Mr. Clean's ear. At the same time, audio-visual information was bounced off a military satellite and transmitted in real time to a receiver on the wide desk in Big Bad Bill's office at the Pentagon.

Bill studied the Mountie onscreen.

Bill listened to the reporter describe how he was contacted by the killer who carved swastikas into foreheads.

Bill heard the Mountie ask the reporter for copies of everything to add to his file.

When the conversation was over and the two men onscreen parted ways, Bill called Mr. Clean with pointed instructions: "Get hold of that file no matter what the cost."

Spoils of War

✠

The Nazis had tried to stop them with a barrage of V-2s. Twelve of the supersonic rockets had been launched from Holland toward the Remagen bridgehead, where the U.S. Army was preparing to cross the Rhine. The missiles had landed in a scattered pattern around the Ludendorff Bridge, but just one of Hitler's vengeance weapons had done damage. Striking a house about three hundred yards east of the bridge, it had killed three American GIs.

Still, Major Bill Hawke had been intrigued. The rockets explained why this intelligence officer from something called "Special Mission V-2" was embedded with front-line U.S. troops.

Teamed with the 3rd Armored Division for a rapid advance into central Germany, the 104th Infantry—the so-called Timberwolves—had broken out of the Remagen bridgehead on March 25, 1945, to drive a spearhead deep into the heart of Hitler's Reich. As the Nazi war machine crumbled beneath the treads of their Sherman tanks, the GIs were forced to battle it out with pockets of fanatical SS resisters, desperate, hungry irregulars in the ragtag Volkssturm, and Werewolf commandos in the Hitler Youth.

Timberwolves against Werewolves.

The last howl of Hitler's Reich.

As the American troops rolled inexorably into Germany, Bill Hawke followed the Werewolf phenomenon on his radio. Radio Werewolf—the latest propaganda ploy by Joseph Göbbels—whipped up the clandestine commandos, inciting them to leap out of the woods when the Allies passed by and inflict as many casualties as possible. In the Ruhr, Hawke had witnessed a Werewolf assault. A pack of wild-eyed youths had swarmed a single file of tanks, yowling as they scrambled up to engage the turret crews hand-to-hand. GIs old enough to be their fathers had to shoot them dead in order to survive themselves.

The intel Hawke was receiving reported Werewolf assassination squads creating mayhem all over the Reich. On March 25, the day this drive began, young commandos had taken out Franz Oppenhoff, the new American-appointed mayor of Aachen. A pack of ten-year-olds had ambushed GIs in Koblenz, and Werewolves had killed three of the top brass at Frankfurt am Main. The Yanks were appalled by how young some of their attackers were. Two of those they'd executed as spies for attempting to blow up an Allied supply convoy were sixteen and seventeen, and one young POW was no more than eight.

Hitler as Pied Piper, thought Hawke.

Still, nothing could stop the U.S. juggernaut. The thrust continued through cold, gray drizzle and dark, forbidding nights. Towns with tongue-twisting names—Holzhausen, Niederingelbach, Dalwigsthal, Eibelshausen—were overrun. Easter Sunday and April Fools' Day slipped by in the push. It took only two weeks for the 3rd and the 104th to reach the Harz Mountains, and as they neared the town of Nordhausen, Hawke received an intelligence advisory that he passed on to both commanders.

"Expect something a little unusual in the Nordhausen area."

ON APRIL 11, 1945—the morning the U.S. Army liberated Nordhausen—Maj. Bill Hawke was driven into Boelcke Kaserne in a Jeep. Hawke was a man who physically resembled his name. His hair was so closely cropped to his skull that it could have been the hood of that feathered raptor; his hooked nose mimicked the predator's beak. His shifty eyes were always on the lookout for prey, and the fingers that chain-smoked Lucky Strikes were as long, as thin, and as bony as talons. A comic-strip addict, Hawke was hooked on *Buck Rogers* and *Flash Gordon,* so hunting for rockets was a military mission tailored to him.

Stepping out of the Jeep and dusting off his khakis, Hawke gazed around the charred ruins of Boelcke Kaserne, still smoking from the week-old RAF firebombing. At least fifteen hundred corpses were scattered around ground craters or rotting in the barracks. The four hundred or so survivors were little more than skeletons covered with skin. As the major crossed from the Jeep to a shattered concrete building, he glanced down into a crater that had been converted into an open grave. Some of those at the bottom were still alive. For days, they had been struggling to get out from under the weight of those piled on top, but the task was too much for their starved, emaciated muscles.

"Private," Hawke yelled back to the driver, "they could use some help here!"

He entered the battered barracks.

So this was what the Nazis meant by the term *Vernichtungslager*. This extermination camp for ill prisoners didn't use the poison gas the Nazis saved for Jews, but rather let nature take its course through slow starvation and lack of medical care.

Bedded down on straw in nauseating filth, men too weak to move lay alongside their dead comrades. Some of these wretches were decaying even before they passed on. Others were stacked like cordwood under the staircase to the second floor. Bombs from the British air attacks had ripped large holes through the roof and ground flesh and bones into the cement floor. The stench from the decomposing corpses soured the sooty air, and no matter where the major looked, he saw mouths gaping with horror. It was like stumbling into the midst of the Black Death. Hawke had seen enough.

Lighting a cigarette, the major went back outside.

Now there were zombies lurching around the craters and tripping over the dead lining the ground. These living dead were bug-eyed men in baggy striped rags. Their legs and arms were devoid of flesh, their legs barely able to keep them on feet so swollen that they couldn't take shoes. As they weaved and tottered about Nordhausen camp, Hawke noticed the prison numbers and colored triangles on their ill-fitting coats: green for real criminals, pink for homosexuals, red for political prisoners, and yellow for Jews. Numbers were tattooed on their bony arms as well. The backs of most coats had horizontal stripes crossing the vertical ones, evidence of the lashings that had cut the material and torn into raw flesh.

As Hawke stood out in the bomb-cratered yard, sucking the life out of his Lucky Strike, a shattered man with one foot in the grave shuffled toward him. With tears trickling down his pale, blood-drained face, the shrunken bone-rack stopped in his tracks, struggled to straighten his hunched-over spine, and slowly raised a shaky arm to salute his liberator.

Crushing the Lucky under his boot, Hawke snapped his own hand up to his helmet.

"What's that, buddy?"

The Frenchman was trying to speak English.

"… something fantastic …"

Hawke cocked an ear.

"... inside the mountain ..."

The Frenchman lowered his arm, one knobby finger jittering as it pointed north.

"Major!"

It was the driver.

"The Third Armored liaison is on the radio."

Hawke crossed to the Jeep and took the transmitter. Crooking his thumb back at the liberated prisoner, he told the driver to "Give the frog a drink."

"Hawke," Hawke announced.

"Major," replied the voice on the receiver, "you'd better get up here pronto and see what we've got."

THE JEEP BOUNCED off along the road across this alpine plateau, leaving behind the burghers of Nordhausen to bury the dead of Boelcke Kaserne under the muzzles of outraged GIs' guns. A hundred German civilians had been rounded up on the streets of the deeply Nazified town and were put to work as Hawke and his driver bumped off toward the southern slope of Mount Kohnstein, a broad ridge that hunched up like the hackles of a werewolf about to spring. While the town folks were divided into work crews—some to gather the bodies, others to dig mass graves with spades or their bare hands—the Jeep swung up alongside the railway yard and stopped at a T-intersection in front of the SS camp.

The left arm of the T led to the gates of the Dora compound.

The right arm of the T ran along the face of the Kohnstein to a pair of huge tunnels.

"Turn right," ordered Hawke.

One of the Timberwolves met them in the junkyard at the entrance to Tunnel B. From there, railway tracks ran

into the camouflaged hole in the mountain. While part of
the 3rd Armored Division had battled its way into
Nordhausen, the rest of the tank force and the 104th
Infantry Division had entered this underground works from
the north, through the Junkers Nordwerk. A mile-long slog
through the Kohnstein had brought them out here, and the
GIs had then angled west to liberate the Dora-Mittelbau
concentration camp. What they had seen in the tunnels had
prompted the call to Hawke.

"Show me," the major said.

The Timberwolf ushered the intel officer past rows of
V-2 combustion chambers that looked like hourglasses that
had run out of time. Passing beneath the camouflage netting
that hid the tunnel's yawning mouth from RAF bombsights,
they stepped into the subterranean gloom of a gigantic
limestone shaft with a semicircular roof supported by steel
beams. Electric wires with dim yellow lights dangled down
from the murky ceiling like tentacles. Occasionally, there
were bright bursts from flashbulbs triggered by an army
photographer.

Then Hawke saw them.

"Jesus-fucking-Christ!"

The Mittelwerk tunnels were like a space-age magician's
cave. Freight cars and trucks loaded with long, slender, finned
missiles—there could have been a hundred of them—were
strung along the tracks. Orderly rows of V-2 parts and sub-
assemblies were laid out on work benches and shelves. It
reminded Hawke of the assembly lines in Detroit. Some of
the hardware pieces he recognized from weapons salvaged
after earlier attacks: an Argus pulse jet destined for the
"flying bomb," a gyrocompass destined for the nose of a
rocket, compressed air bottles. His footsteps echoed down
from the ceiling as he walked around, his boots treading
concrete slick with oil.

Drawers, some half-open, were full of tools.

A coffee cup sat on an SS guard's desk beside a tented book.

Signs in German and other languages warned workers not to touch this or to go in that direction.

Work had evidently stopped just the day before. The assembly line still had its power switched on, precision machinery remained in working order, and the ventilation system continued to hum. It was as if the factory force had gone out for lunch and would soon return to work.

Hawke stopped beside one of the railcars to study the guts of the V-2 rocket on its flatbed. The metal outer skin had yet to be welded on, so he could see its internal workings, pipes, and wires. As an intel officer with deep roots in the American Southwest, Hawke had heard rumblings about a top-secret project established to create an astonishing weapon called an atomic bomb. Hitler's Third Reich was in its final countdown, but there would still be war in the Pacific. What the U.S. Army had here was a proven delivery system that could be armed with an atomic weapon—if such a thing was feasible—to blast the Japs back to the Stone Age.

It was true what they said back home.

God *did* bless America.

FROM THE MITTELWERK FACTORY, the Jeep carried Hawke back past the SS camp to the gates of the slave compound. There, flanked by electric fences on both sides, he walked between the administration and Gestapo buildings to the roll-call square, where most of the six hundred remaining slaves could be found.

The major examined the gallows and the *Pfahlhangen* post, then went down to "the bunker" along the southern edge of the camp. This prison within a prison was normally so tightly packed with condemned saboteurs that none of them could lie down and rest. It was all a torturous prelude to slow strangulation on the gallows.

From there, the major strolled up toward the crematorium, a small, shallow-peaked building with a huge phallic chimney jutting up from the roof. As far as he could tell from the ghosts he saw drifting around the barracks, most of those deported to Dora to build the wonder weapons had been Russian, Polish, or French. The Jews came later, after the Nazis had fled Stalin's Commies on the eastern front.

A prisoner, his hands cupped like a beggar's, blocked the door to the crematorium. The skeletal man was among those forced to incinerate their dead friends in the ovens. Twenty thousand slaves had died at Dora-Mittelbau. Quickly, the small crematorium had been overwhelmed. But starvation had shrunken the workers so thin that four at a time could be shoveled into an oven, and soon each oven could process about a hundred bodies a day. Still, the crematorium couldn't keep up with the dead, and bodies lay heaped outside in a gruesome pile. From what Hawke could see, the cadavers had been whipped and brutally abused.

Hawke couldn't tell what the prisoner wanted in his cupped hands. He was hard to understand because of his ghetto accent. Hawke's offer of a chocolate bar was refused. He then knocked a Lucky from his pack and held it out, but the man didn't seem to want a smoke either. As Hawke struck a match with his fingernail to light one for himself, the ghost took hold of his khaki sleeve and gave it a weak tug.

"You want to show me something?"

Out back of the crematorium, the ghostly man showed the major a pit that was about eight feet long by six feet wide by who knows how many feet deep. It was filled to overflowing with ashes from the ovens inside. Small chips of human bone were evidence of that. Bucketfuls, it seemed to Hawke, had been tossed in from a distance, just as you would empty ashes you'd scooped from a hearth.

"Twenty thousand," the prisoner said, "in a year and a half."

As Hawke sucked on the Lucky Strike and let the implications of that sink into his military mind, a puff of wind blew ash from the end of his cigarette onto the mass grave.

Farm Truck

Corporal Jackie Hett was sitting at her desk in the main-floor squad room at Special X when she got a summons from the commissionaire at the front door.

"Corporal, we have two … uh, ladies here at the check-in asking to speak to someone about a missing youth."

"*Ladies!* How archaic, Fred. Call them what they are. Women."

"I wouldn't say that, Corporal."

"Why not?"

"Come out and see."

Jackie pushed away from her desk beside the wall-mounted display of Wild West firepower and strolled out into the entrance hall to solve the gender mystery. A pair of workmen who were taking down the moth-eaten bison head over the lower stairs for transport to the upcoming red serge dinner had paused to gawk at the commissionaire's "ladies."

"I'm Corporal Hett," Jackie said as Fred grinned like the Joker behind the showy cross-dressers.

The taller drag queen introduced herself as Marya Delvard, then shook her wig and clucked her tongue at Jackie in disappointment. "Tsk, tsk, honey. You've let yourself go. What I could do with cheekbones and a set of tits like yours. Lipstick and a little blush? How about a makeover while we talk?"

Jackie smiled. "I play it down in here."

"Shame on you!" Marya exploded, whirling on a high heel to drill Fred with her bitchiest glare. "There's a woman trapped in this uniform, and you force her to look butch!"

"Not me," Fred said. He looked as if he was afraid any further comment would bring charges of sexual harassment his way.

The smaller female impersonator, her splashy wardrobe bright red, stepped forward and introduced herself. "I'm the Queen of Hearts."

"Ladies," Jackie said, sweeping her arm toward the interview room across the hall.

"*Ladies,*" Marya mimicked, chastising Fred. "You should learn to be chivalrous, sir."

"Yeah," scolded Jackie, wagging her finger at the commissionaire. "Archaic is cool."

How strange to be sitting across from two males whose makeup took the art of being female to perfection. Working from the skin out, Marya and the Queen of Hearts had applied beard cover, foundation, and powder for a base. They'd shaped their eyebrows, plucking stragglers and adding on to ends to form arches. Eyeshadow and eyeliner had followed, the bottom lids and outer third of the top lids traced to make their eyes appear bigger, an effect enhanced with mascara and a lash curler. Their lips were lined with sensuous color and shone slick with gloss. Blush topped it all off.

Even more unnerving to Jackie was the way they examined her for faults and blemishes, probing her looks with queer-eye-for-the-straight-gal deconstruction. She felt as if wayward hairs were growing out of her nose and wavy cartoon stink lines were wafting up from her armpits.

"Who's the missing youth?" she asked.

"Yuri," replied Marya.

"Last name?"

"Ushakov. Yuri Ushakov."

"Friend? Relative?"

"A street kid I befriended. I don't want to get him in trouble if you find he's safe."

"What sort of trouble?"

"You know."

"Drugs? Prostitution?"

"He's a good kid. He's had a tough life. His mom's crazy, and she kicked him out when he was thirteen. He lived in foster care for a while, and then tried living with his dad. His dad found out he was gay and beat him up, so Yuri stuck out his thumb and hitchhiked west. He wasn't in school, didn't have a job, wasn't getting welfare, and didn't have a sleeping bag. When I chanced across him, he was living in coffee shops to keep warm. One by one, they all tossed him out."

"You took him in?"

"Uh-huh."

"Why?"

"I've been there."

"Is he still with you?"

"No, I threw him out too."

"Why?"

"Off the record?"

"Ms. Delvard, I'm a homicide cop. I have more than enough to do without hassling street kids. Or you, for that matter. Unless you've done something *very* wrong."

"I'm clean."

"So why'd you throw him out?"

"He got into crystal meth. He promised me he wouldn't. That was the one rule I imposed on him. I used to have a drug problem, and I want to stay clean."

"Where did he go?"

"Boy's town, I believe. That was the only way he could survive on the street and support his habit."

"When'd you see him last?"

"Months ago," said Marya.

"But I saw him yesterday," interjected the Queen of Hearts.

"Where?"

"On the sidewalk out front of Cabaret Berlin."

"I work there," Marya added.

"What time did you see him?" Jackie asked the Queen.

"Early morning. Around two."

"Doing what?"

"Trying to get into the club. He's only fourteen. The bouncer kept him on the street."

"Okay," said Jackie. "Why do you think he's missing?"

"I was crossing the street toward the club when I saw Yuri. I knew him from back when he lived with Marya. He pleaded with me to get a message to her. He said that he had to talk to her, and that he'd be waiting outside the club in an hour. Then he ran across Davie Street and climbed into a farm truck."

"Someone he knew?"

"Doubt it. I think he was turning a trick."

"For drug money?"

"Probably. The kid was in bad shape. He was twitching, fiddling. Know what I mean?"

"Yes," said Jackie.

Marya picked up from the Queen. "I went outside after the show, but there was no Yuri. Then I saw your warning about the boy's town predator in the *Times*, and we've been looking for Yuri ever since. No one has seen him since he climbed into that truck. To play it safe, we thought it best to come here. You *did* ask anyone who's seen anything suspicious in boy's town to report it."

"You did the right thing. But could it be that Yuri got high and is sleeping it off somewhere?"

"Could be," Marya agreed. "But two things trouble us. First, Yuri begged to speak to me."

"Begged," emphasized the Queen of Hearts. "Second, that truck smelled of the stockyard. In jaywalking across Davie Street to Cabaret Berlin, I skirted the back of the truck and got a whiff. No mistaking that stench. I was raised on a farm. My dad slaughtered pigs and sold the pork locally. He took the guts to a rendering plant in our truck. The truck that Yuri got into stank like that."

"Did you see the driver?"

"No."

"Can you describe the truck?"

"No need to," said the Queen of Hearts. Reaching into her red bag, she extracted a camera phone. "That stench made me feel uneasy. So as the truck pulled away, I snapped a photo."

"Get the license plate?"

"See for yourself," said the Queen of Hearts.

IT WAS EASY ENOUGH to uncover the registered owner of the farm truck by punching the license plate into CPIC, a Canada-wide database maintained by the Canadian Police Information Centre. The name that popped up on the computer screen at Jackie's desk belonged to a resident of Prince George, a town hundreds of miles north of Vancouver.

The next step was to run that name through CPIC to check for a criminal record or outstanding charges. When she did that, Jackie got back a perplexing response.

At about the same time that the Queen of Hearts was snapping her camera-phone image of the license plate on Davie Street, a truck with the same plate had been stopped leaving the parking lot of a Prince George pub. And while the drunk sobered up overnight in jail, his vehicle had been impounded by the local Mounties.

Jackie was onto something.

What if … ?

What if the guy who picked Yuri up on Davie Street had *forged* a license plate instead of stealing one? There were only two reasons to go to that sort of effort. First, so the driver couldn't be traced through his real plate number. And second, so the forged plate wouldn't turn up as stolen in a random roadside check.

Jackie's pulse quickened.

The driver had picked up a street kid just a few blocks from boy's town, and the plate forgery meant that he didn't want anyone to know who was actually prowling that area in that truck.

Why? Jackie wondered.

Because he's the stealth killer Special X is hunting?

If so, how do I track him?

An idea sparked in her brain.

As Jackie reached for the business directory and flipped to the Rs, the phone on her desk jangled.

"Hett."

"The chief wants to see you upstairs."

THREE MEN STOOD in front of the Strategy Wall in DeClercq's airy, high-vaulted loft of a corner office.

"Corporal," DeClercq said, "meet Sergeant Winter."

"Jackie Hett," she said, crossing the room with her hand extended.

"Dane Winter," the sergeant replied.

Good-looking guy, thought Jackie. Having him around would be a definite perk of the job.

One day, Jackie Hett hoped to have this office. She coveted the horseshoe-shaped desk and the high-backed chair with the barley-sugar frame. The two window walls looked out on Queen Elizabeth Park, at the summit of Little Mountain. Behind the desk was a portrait titled *Last Great Council of the West*. It showed scarlet-coated Mounties with hands on swords meeting feathered Indians at Blackfoot Crossing in 1881.

The windowless wall was covered from floor to ceiling with corkboard. This was the Strategy Wall, where DeClercq pinned reports and photos to help him and his officers visualize a case. A military strategist, he used his corkboard wall the way generals once deployed toy soldiers on campaign maps.

"Corporal, Sergeant Winter will be seconded to us for the duration of a case," said DeClercq. "Inspector Chandler"—he nodded toward the man standing at the Strategy Wall—"will head the investigation. You know the ropes. Integrate the sergeant."

"Yes, sir," Jackie said, a hint of conflicting emotions buried in her voice.

THE CORPORAL HAD to wait while they finished constructing the Swastika Case on half of the corkboard wall. The other half was occupied by the Stealth Killer Case, *her* case, the case with the hot new lead that might eventually blast her up to DeClercq's corner office. Instead, here she was cooling her heels while the sergeant filled the brass in on *his* murders.

"Where you from?" Dane asked to break the ice as he and Jackie descended the staircase from the chief's office down to the main floor. The bison head above the lower stairs had been carried away.

"From all over," Jackie said. "I have dual citizenship. My parents are American, and my dad was in the U.S. military, high up in NORAD. While my mom was with him on a tour of Arctic defenses, she went into premature labor. Being born here makes me Canadian, but I was raised in the States."

"Why join the Mounted?"

Jackie laughed. "What cop in her right mind would turn down riding horses and wearing red serge?"

"You grow up on a ranch?"

"My granddad had one. In New Mexico. Bought it after he got out of the 509th Bomb Group."

"Did he fly in the war?"

"He was in the crew of the *Enola Gay*."

"Whew! The big hot one. My granddad got shot down over Nazi Germany. Sounds like we have a lot in common."

"Do you have your pilot's license?"

"No," said Dane. "Do you?"

"Uh-huh. Both fixed-wing and chopper."

"How come you're not in Air Services, flying for the Mounted?"

"Because I'd rather be a homicide cop."

"When the chief asked you to integrate me into Special X, I think I caught a hint of disappointment in your voice. Something wrong? If so, spit it out."

"It's just that I got a hot new lead on the Stealth Killer Case, and I was about to pursue it when I got called upstairs."

"Okay, pursue it. Do double duty. No reason why we can't discuss the integration procedure in a moving car instead of a stationary coffee shop."

THE INDUSTRIAL ZONE of this city hugs the commercial docks, along the north edge of a prostitutes' stroll. Even in the middle of the day, hookers hang out on the streets, offering sex to blue-collar workers who crave a quickie instead of lunch.

The neat, tidy buildings of the rendering plant gave no hint of the grisly work going on inside. A dozen storage silos loomed above a low-level complex of reduction stations, pumping equipment, ladders, and catwalks. Raw materials made their way here by train or truck. Big loads or small, the by-products were the same: the waste remains of livestock.

Blood, bones, meat scraps, inedible fats, offal, and guts from meat-packing plants, butcher shops, and supermarkets. Feathers from plucked poultry; innards pulled out of chickens and turkeys. Fish scales and fins from canneries; shrimp shells peeled off seafood. Rancid kitchen grease from thousands of restaurants. All were reduced and rendered here into useful products. From truck and railcar to grinder to cooker to press to centrifuge to drier to mill to storage—waste was recycled into animal feed, cosmetics, soap, shampoo, candles, paint, perfume, plastics, and cleaners. Fats and oils were pumped directly from the storage tanks to boats in the harbor. Solid products were moved in boxcars that shunted between the rendering plant and the railhead, or in sealed containers that were lifted onto ships bound for ports around the globe.

Who says you can't make a silk purse out of a sow's ear?

The foreman's name was Horton Grubb, and he loved fattening beer. A porker with a pig face, he embodied his job. The blood red color of his skin suggested he wasn't long for this world. The Mounties spoke to him out in the chain-link pen of the loading yard while he puffed on a cigarette and watched a line of offal trucks come and go.

"We need to find a truck." Jackie flashed her badge.

"Take your pick. We got lotsa trucks."

"This truck," she said, holding out a blow-up of the image caught by the Queen of Hearts on Davie Street.

"You got the license number."

"It's a forgery."

"You know how many farm trucks pass through this yard? We get product from *every* farm, big and small. Restaurants, too."

"This truck has a dented fender on the left rear and a cracked cover on the tail light."

"That helps," the foreman said sarcastically, dropping the butt and crushing it underfoot.

"It's important. A kidnapping case."

"What makes you think that truck came here?"

"A hunch. Someone smelled guts in the back."

"Kidnapping, eh?"

Jackie nodded.

"Some kinda sex thing?" Grubb said, sneering.

"Can't say."

"If the trucker's a perv, I could run him through the machines and turn him into a bar of soap."

"We don't need talk like that."

"I'm just sayin'."

"We need you to check your records," Dane pressed.

"Got the name of the guy? The name of the farm? The name of the company?"

"No," said Jackie.

"Then you're outta luck. Even the name of the farm mightn't help. Don't keep records of small deliveries."

"Nothing you can do?"

Grubb shrugged. "I'll ask around and show that picture. And keep my eyes peeled."

Death March

"Was ist das hier für eine Judenschule?" the Nazi barked.

"Jewish school" was the usual curse SS officers used when something was not in order, and what was not in order here was this gaunt straggler who'd stepped out of line.

Bwam!

The Death's Head guard shot the Polish slave through the temple, dropping the starving wretch to the side of the bomb-pocked road as the rest of the exhausted Work Camp Dora evacuees struggled on toward the solitary barn.

The medieval walled town of Gardelegen sat eighty miles north of Dora-Mittelbau. The death march now coming to an end in this farmer's field had begun more than a week ago in the V-2 factory, back on the morning that Ernst Streicher and his two sons returned from their meeting with Hitler in Berlin.

On April 4, the SS had begun shipping out Dora-Mittelbau's close to thirty thousand slaves, cramming them into transport trains at Nordhausen station and chugging them off to camps like Bergen-Belsen that weren't as threatened by the American invasion. The same insane logic had earlier brought the Auschwitz deportees to Dora.

"Fritz, Hans," Streicher had said, "use these well."

The SS general had handed each son a 9 mm machine pistol, along with several thirty-two-round magazines. The automatic weapon was capable of firing 180 rounds per minute.

"*Heil* Hitler!" Fritz said, snapping out the flat-palmed salute.

"*Heil* Hitler!" echoed Hans.

With the paratroop guns slung over their shoulders, the two Hitler Youths climbed up into a boxcar.

Clickety-clack, clickety-clack, clickety-clack ...

For days, the train had evaded bombing and strafing by marauding Allied planes. Inside the cars, the overcrowded passengers—exposed to harsh weather and stifling conditions, famished and parched from lack of food and water, and weakened by the rampant spread of various diseases— thinned as the miles slipped by.

Finally, at Letzlingen, the train had been forced to stop because of bombed-away rails. The Dora slaves had been off-loaded to travel the final thirty miles on foot.

The trek to Gardelegen had been grueling. In their striped prison tatters, the doomed slaves had shuffled along the pitted road in an endless line. Stumbling with their bodies hunched over and their heads down, they struggled to put one heavy foot in front of the other. Those who wore *Holzschuhe,* the wooden shoes of the factory, had damaged and bleeding feet. Others flapped along in unlaced boots, or had nothing except rags wrapped around their soles. Their cheeks were hollow, their eyes extinguished.

"*Singen!*" one guard had shouted.

A taunt.

"*Szkop!*" A Pole had insulted him back.

Bwam!

He was gone.

A string of deaths, both natural and not, trailed the walking wounded like the wake of a boat.

The Luftwaffe maintained an air base and a paratrooper's training school at Gardelegen. The ancient town also still kept a relic from bygone wars: the Remount School for cavalry officers. There, in the horse stalls, the SS guards confined the marchers who'd made it to Gardelegen until they decided what to do with them.

The guards were in the same bedraggled shape as the Third Reich. Unshaven and unwashed, in dirty, sweat-stained uniforms that they'd slept in for almost two weeks, all were itching to bring this death march to an end.

The *Kreisleiter* of Gardelegen had raised the alarm. As Nazi Party leader in the town, he was tasked with enforcing Himmler's standing order that all slaves be liquidated in the event of liberation. From the west, the 102nd Infantry Division—the so-called Ozarks—was advancing to take Gardelegen.

So that was it.

The death warrant had been signed.

The only questions remaining were where and how.

"Let's kill them in the stables," suggested the SS commandant.

"No," said the *Kreisleiter*. "That's in the center of town. If you do it there, the blame will fall on me."

"Then where?"

"Isenschnibbe. That's just outside of town. There's an isolated barn on the estate. Shoot them inside."

"No." The commandant vetoed his idea. "That's too many bullets. We have at least a thousand slaves locked in the stables. Gunning them down will take too long. We need every bullet to kill GIs."

The *Kreisleiter* nodded. "Here's what I suggest...."

SO NOW THEY WERE on the final leg of the death march from Dora. It was late in the afternoon of Friday, April 13. In groups of one hundred, just over a thousand slaves were herded from the cavalry stables in central Gardelegen out to the flat farmer's field on an estate called Isenschnibbe. The SS guards were bolstered by twenty parachutists from the Luftwaffe base. Machine pistols at the ready, Fritz and Hans helped bring up the rear.

"It will soon be over," Fritz whispered, antsy to pull the trigger.

"They know it too," replied Hans, nodding ahead.

"They deserve it," Fritz said. "For being subhuman."

"Forward! Forward!" the commandant yelled, lashing his swagger stick across the nearest back. Having been weighed down for days by these outcasts among outcasts, he hankered to dispose of his human freight.

The guards beneath him followed his lead.

Stuck in the middle of nowhere, with flat mud all around, the barn was a shallow-peaked rectangle of brick and stucco. On both longer sides hung two wooden doors suspended from horizontal bars. The doors were about three times as tall as a man and could be rolled back and forth across the opening. Within, the stone-floored storage vault was piled knee-deep with gas-soaked straw.

One whiff of the petrol fumes and several slaves bolted. Machine-gun bursts—

Brrrrrrrrrrrrrt! Brrrrrrrrrrrrrt!

—mowed them down.

Prisoners who balked at entering the barn were shot through the head. It was seven o'clock, and the sky had darkened by the time the thousand-plus were all crowded in. To drive them back, a gunman fired randomly into their midst, then the doors were rumbled shut and wedged fast with stone blocks. All that remained was an opening just wide enough to admit an incendiary bomb, and one of the SS guards tossed in several phosphorous grenades.

Phooom!

The screams of a thousand innocents who'd been plunged into the fires of hell erupted from the torched interior. The blazing fire within could be glimpsed through cracks around the doors. Outside, the SS guards and their Luftwaffe cohorts stood ready to shoot any escapers. Snarling dogs on leashes backed them up.

Shrieks of pain wailed from those being roasted alive in the shed. The heavy doors bulged as the trapped slaves came at them like a battering ram. Spreading flames licked out between the door planks as gray smoke billowed into the black sky. Fritz reveled in the gibbering pleas for mercy and help. He imagined those who had survived the first moments of the conflagration seeking shelter under the charred bodies of those who had perished in the shock wave. How many were being trampled and crushed in the mad panic to find an escape route? How high was the heap of subhuman waste piling up against the doors? He wished he could see them clawing frantically at the stone floor, tearing away the flesh and bones of their fingers in a desperate bid to dig their way out. The sickening stench of burning flesh thrilled Fritz to his core.

There, under the bottom edge of the blackened door. Was that the head of a slave trying to claw his way out? Yes, there was the torso! And there were the legs! And now he was staggering to his feet and weaving this way to escape. Let him come! Let him come! These *Untermenschen* are mine!

The machine gun in his grip erupted with a burst of firepower. The muzzle flashes glinted off the Death's Head badges of the soldiers nearby. As cartridge casings spat out from the ejection port, the slugs ripped through the chest of the fleeing man, throwing him back with arms outstretched like Christ's on the cross. The crucifixion scene was silhouetted against the burning barn.

Clutched by the hand of power, Fritz got an erection.

THE BLAZE WITHIN had raged for seven hours. While Fritz and Hans strolled around the blackened barn, surveying the stinking aftermath of their first taste of combat, civilians from Gardelegen began to arrive to help cover up the massacre. There were bullet-riddled escapees with third-degree burns and peeled skin bleeding in the yard. There were calcified heads and arms poking out beneath the doors, which, remarkably, hadn't been incinerated. Inside, mountains of still-smoldering cadavers blocked the exits.

Those who'd been shanghaied from town—mostly Hitler Youths and Volkssturm irregulars—were in the process of digging long, deep trenches behind the barn when news arrived that the Ozarks were attacking from the north. That was the sign for Fritz and Hans to slip away. Reloading their machine pistols and stocking up on clips—and a pair of Panzerfausts, the Nazis' crude but effective anti-tank rockets—Ernst Streicher's *Über*-Aryan sons morphed from two Hitler Youths into two Werewolf commandos.

Back in November 1944, the SS had established a Werewolf Staff at Hulchrath Castle in the small town of Erkelenz, close to the Rhine. The castle was low profile and out of the way, the perfect spot for a secret demolition school. The first two hundred Hitler Youths to undergo Werewolf training were already proficient in the use of revolvers, machine pistols, and the deadly Panzerfaust. At Hulchrath, they learned how to detonate explosives behind enemy lines, contaminate food and water with arsenic, and disrupt and sabotage the efforts of Allied invaders.

Among those first recruits were Fritz and Hans, and at Hulchrath they had learned how to live a double life. Before embarking from Dora on this SS death march, both youths had been handed passes forged by the Gestapo. These were proof of their "innocent identities" as two ordinary German boys, and had been disguised to help them blend in with other civilians in any town. Safe during the day, they would transform themselves by the light of the moon in outlying woods, retrieving their uniforms and weapons from secret forest caches.

"Bring the radio," Fritz said.

"What about the bodies?"

"They're dead, Hans. Let the Gardelegens bury them and incur the invaders' wrath. We have others to kill."

That night, hidden in the woods, they tuned their portable receiver to Radio Werewolf, the frequency that egged on the Hitler Youth commandos. That's how they heard about the assassinations committed by their brothers in arms.

"Cologne-Deutz!" the radio extolled. "A Werewolf shot dead a Ukrainian as he was taking a piss!"

"Hanover! A mayor who ridiculed Werewolf resistance was shot at point-blank range!"

Day after day, as Streicher's sons prowled south, Radio Werewolf brought more heroic news.

"Rothenburg! Three local cowards were executed in the streets for trying to disarm Werewolves who were on the hunt!"

"Quedlinburg! A Werewolf killed a doctor who betrayed his town and hung his blood-soaked coat in the woods as a trophy!"

"Let's do that," Hans suggested. "With GI uniforms!"

"Yes!" Fritz said. "One for every tree!"

"Hundreds of them!"

"And all dripping blood!"

Exhausted from their trek south, the youths bedded down for some much-needed rest. The woods where they hid were just to the north of Dora-Mittelbau.

"Tomorrow we strike," said Fritz.

Weird Science

THE CARIBOO
May 26, Now

After parting ways with Mr. Clean at Vancouver's airport, Ajax and Lysol had flown north to Quesnel, where they'd rented a car and driven east along the Cariboo Highway toward historic Barkerville. Short of that tourist-infested ghost town, they'd hidden the car in a thicket and hoofed it into the wilderness with their athletic bags.

Thanks to some yellowing 1947 maps, the killers had found the ideal eagle's nest from which to stake out the valley. Except for a V-cleft with the dirt road in from the highway, the Cariboo Mountains encircled the Skunk Mine to cut its secrets off from the rest of the world. From up here on the ridge beside the V-cleft, they had passed the day spying on a pig farmer through a fancy camera that bounced the image off a satellite directly to Big Bad Bill at his Pentagon desk.

"Whatever he's feeding those pigs, they sure do like it," Ajax said mutedly. You couldn't be too careful with your voice on the ridge. The peaks around the Phantom Valley carried sound like a whispering gallery.

The farmer lugged a bucket of feed out of the hillside hole.

Oink, oink.

In and out, in and out, the farmer trucked back and forth from the mine shaft. At one point, he carried out a bulging bag and slung it onto the flatbed of his farm truck, along with a gas-driven grinder. Trailing a pair of ruts in the overgrown grass, he drove across the bumpy range of the Phantom Valley to what appeared to be a bone pile in the distance. There, he revved the grinder to pollute the silence with noise and emptied the bag into a hopper that shot out chipped-up splinters.

"Get me a close-up of his face," Big Bad Bill's voice said through earplugs.

Ajax zoomed the camera in on the farmer's profile. He seemed more like a Eurotrash punk than he did a man of the land, what with his close-cropped *Über*-blond hair and his icy blue eyes. You don't find hicks wearing ear studs like his.

"That's our boy!" rejoiced Bill.

"Yep," Ajax whispered into the little tubular mike that extended to his mouth from the earplug.

The farmer's ear stud bore a swastika.

THE MOON WAS RISING over the Phantom Valley Ranch when the spooks abandoned their perch in the spruce and alpine fir trees. They wended their way down the mountainside to the Skunk Mine. Except for the pigpen between the mouth of the shaft and the decrepit ranch house, the moonlit valley looked natural and untouched. The topographical maps that guided Ajax and Lysol tonight dated back to 1947, yet but for minor alterations caused by passing time, the terrain was the same as it had been half a century ago.

The deep black enforcers kept to the shadows all the way down to the hole in the face of Skunk Mountain.

"Going in," Ajax reported.

In his office at the Pentagon, Big Bad Bill smiled.

The field operatives skulked through the shadows that had gathered at the foot of Skunk Mountain.

Trusting rube.

He'd left the door unlocked.

No need for one of the gizmos they had brought along.

The mouth of the mine could still be sealed by a cross-hatched gate with a new punch-in combo lock, but tonight the barrier stood ajar. As Lysol eased it open, the hinges squealed. Luckily for the pig farmer, no lights came on in the ranch house. Both killers had screwed silencers onto the threaded barrels of their Heckler & Kochs, and they were prepared to shoot, if need be.

Hopefully, not to kill.

Ideally, to maim.

They wouldn't kill the Nazi until they had squeezed every drop of intel out of his balls.

They had a gizmo in their survival kits for that.

Both men had donned night-vision goggles that adapted to any light. With inch-thick lenses that fitted onto the eyes like jewelers' loupes, they made the bug-eyed killers look like jaunty old jalopy men.

The static in their earpieces began as soon as they stepped into the mine, cutting the lines of communication to Big Bad Bill and from mission control to both operatives. The first gizmo they caught sight of through the eerie green lenses was a bank of generators just inside the gate. Were the generators causing this *fzzzzing* in their ears? Before the answer to that question could form in their minds, Ajax and Lysol stopped dead in their tracks.

A butcher's table ran along the concave wall to the left. That was to be expected on a farm that slaughtered pigs. But it wasn't a dressed hog that hung upside down on a stand-up, X-shaped frame. The arms of the X were crooked at the tips to form a Nazi swastika, and the carcass that hung from those arms was that of a gutted youth in his teens.

"Look at his ass," mumbled Ajax, circling the frame.

The buttocks of the carcass had been run through repeatedly with something sharp and pointed. On one of the skewered cheeks was a branding mark in the shape of a swastika.

"He could be a canoe."

Indeed, he could. For the guts from the chest and the abdominal cavity filled a bucket labeled "Rendering Plant."

"There's the brand."

Lysol indicated an iron that was hanging from a hook among various tools for butchery.

"What's in the case?"

On the seven-foot-long chopping block sat a blood-splattered box inset with a silver plaque. When he saw the name engraved into the metal, Ajax turned and retraced his steps to the cave's entrance to get away from the static.

"Bill," he said, covering his mouth to mute his voice. "We found a saber box labeled 'SS-Obergruppenführer Ernst Streicher.' There's static in the mine. I'll report once we're out."

"The moment you find the cache, let me know. Then squeeze that Nazi asshole till he squeals like a pig."

Ajax and Lysol were conversant enough in post-war scientific gadgets to be able to identify components of the equipment they found as they entered a cavern deeper in the mine. The Van de Graaf generator able to blast 250,000 volts DC. The double-headed dumbbell of a Tesla coil on the cave wall around the hole to the inner shaft. Everywhere they glanced, they saw relics from a long-forgotten electromagnetic era. Tuning capacitors, RF coils, magnetrons, high-voltage transmission caps, aerials and dishes aimed at kooky angles, an old rotary spark-plug system to fire off microwaves, big radios and radar screens with dials, valves and analog readouts fit for a scrap heap—

all incestuously connected by coils of wire and cabling joining male and female sockets.

"Holy fuck," said Ajax.

His lenses were locked on a workbench at the center of the subterranean wonderland.

A framed photo of Nikola Tesla, the lab's patron saint, was propped up on one corner. In it, the nineteenth-century master of lightning was alive with sparks, a bolt of generated electricity zapping from his fingertip to illuminate the filament of a lamp. Sparks were active within these machines as well: the banks of receivers and monitors around the workbench chair hummed and pulsed with the electronic rhythms onscreen.

No wonder there was static.

At first, the killers thought the book on the bench was a leather-bound volume of genealogy with a detailed heraldic crest on its cover. The etched crest seemed to represent the architecture of a medieval room. The room's massive fireplace filled one entire wall. Its leaded-glass windows offered no view of the landscape outside, so it was impossible to tell what the building around it was or where it might be located. That the structure was Germanic could be deduced from the Iron Cross—a Maltese cross with splayed arms—engraved over the room-wide mantel.

On closer inspection, the killers realized that the binding wasn't leather.

The binding was human skin.

Nor was the crest heraldic. It was a map-like tattoo stretched over a German-language copy of Hitler's *Mein Kampf*.

Centered on the workbench was a sheaf of Second World War blueprints, calculations, and experiment notes—all printed on paper headed with the Nazi swastika and stamped with the ultra-secret warning of the Streicherstab.

Had they found the Holy Grail?

Like the documents that had been sent to the Pentagon with the extortion demand, these yellowing plans were just the warm-up, not the motherlode.

But where there's smoke, there's fire. Perhaps deeper in the mine. Down where a mysterious 1947 explosion had obliterated sought-after Nazi technology—or so the Weird Shit Division had thought.

"Let's go deeper," said Lysol.

Ajax led.

Flanking the hole in the cavern, where the shaft continued into the black heart of the mountain, were two coat stands. From one hung the uniform of an SS storm trooper, and from the other the outfit of a Red Army colonel. Both were stained with blood, as were the helmets crowning both poles.

"This psycho *needs* a squeezing."

"Coming up," Ajax said.

The blood trail began not far beyond a meat hook that had been screwed into the rock. At this depth, there was no light from any source, but that made no difference to the killers' ability to see. Their night-vision lenses operated on the principles of image intensification and infrared radiation. They amplified small amounts of light from the moon and the stars, and picked up on the energy emitted by all objects regardless of the ambient light conditions. Sensor readings determined which technology was to be used to supply the spooks' night vision at any given moment.

Using infrared, Ajax and Lysol tracked the blood trail down to a barrier blocking the mine.

A blood pool stained the ground.

Here, the shaft appeared to have imploded. Millions of tons of rubble had crushed everything in sight, and the force released by whatever had gone wrong had both fractured and fused the granite into something strange and new.

Weird science.
An untapped force of nature.
The force had a name.
Zero point.

So ACCUSTOMED to the subterranean silence had the spelunking killers become that when the blast of goose-step music roared down into the nether realm, they almost jumped out of their skins. Their cool killer training deserted them with the shock.

The Nazi had returned.

Rammstein was cranked up to ear-splitting decibels.

FZZZZZZZ ...

CRAAACKKKK ...

The master of lightning, reincarnated, was at work.

Their H&K .45s leading the way, the Pentagon hit men retreated from the deep black hole.

Creeper

Mr. Clean had spent the afternoon stalking the meddling Mountie around this one-horse city, gleaning intelligence with his parabolic mike and the other eavesdropping gizmos from his bag of tricks. At Special X and *The Vancouver Times*, Winter had fattened his case file with photocopies of everything pertinent to the swastika killings, then—after dinner alone at a Greek restaurant—he'd taken the file home for bedtime reading.

This spook had a black world answer for every obstacle. Sitting on a seawall bench out front of Winter's home—just another jogger enjoying the balmy late May night with what appeared to be an athletic bag at his feet—Mr. Clean had looked down at what could have been a cellphone but was actually an infrared sensor that was invading the wall of the Mountie's bedroom and tracking his body heat as he sat in bed.

The bedroom light had burned until 10:45, then it went out and the heat signature elongated, a sign that the cop was flat on the mattress.

Sweet dreams, thought Mr. Clean.

Nutcracker sweet.

For over an hour, as the spook's watch crept past midnight, the cop hadn't stirred. Satisfied that it was safe for him to pull a Watergate, Mr. Clean had slinked across the seawall to the shrub garden in front of the Mountie's low-rise condo building. Hidden by the arced tails of a monkey tree, he'd climbed the downspout and pulled himself onto the balcony of Winter's second-story suite.

Having got a floor plan for the suite upstairs off a realtor's website, the skulker knew the general layout of the rooms within. At this end of the balcony, perimeter-alarmed glass doors opened into the living room, with the dining room and kitchen beyond. The hall at the rear ran parallel to the balcony, past a walk-in closet and the bathroom to the Mountie's bedroom in the far corner. There, the cop slept what could be his final sleep.

Time to suit up.

In the moon shadows of the monkey tree, Mr. Clean silently unzipped the athletic bag. He was already sheathed in the armor of his Kevlar jogging suit. A gunslinger holster got clamped around his thigh. Into the holster went the Para-Ordnance Warthog, the hit man's backup iron. Eyepiece, earpiece, mouthpiece. He outfitted his head with the same night-vision goggles and communications paraphernalia that Ajax and Lysol were wearing up in the Skunk Mine. Now he was satellite-tied.

The jogging suit came equipped with Velcro fasteners. The pouch affixed to his left pec held an infrared digital camera with an upload link to the eye in the sky. The pouch affixed to his right pec contained an air-jet tranquilizer gun that would give the sleeping cop a blast that wouldn't leave a mark if that was the knockout Mr. Clean thought it best to use. Attached to the other thigh was a carrying case for the nutcracker. There wasn't a non-eunuch alive who wouldn't betray his own mother if that vicious gizmo had a grip on his balls and was running through its sequence of pressure plates, electric shocks, invasive needles, corrosives, corkscrews, twisters, and shredders.

Mr. Clean was ready for insertion.

He was going in.

A THIN LASER penlight cut cleanly through the glass of one balcony door, and a suction cup pulled the oblong piece out without triggering the alarm in the bottom of the wooden frame. Like Alice in *Through the Looking-Glass,* Mr. Clean put his best foot forward and stepped into the Mountie's living room. He wore skin-tight gloves on both hands to thwart forensic techs. Once inside, he drew his .45 pistol, already muffled with a silencer, from a side pocket of the athletic bag.

Mr. Clean cocked his unplugged ear.

Not a peep.

He crept to the rear of the suite and gazed down the hall toward the Mountie's bedroom.

Not a twitch in the green world of the night-vision goggles.

He surveyed the living room and spotted the swastika file flipped open on the desk.

If the file had been intact, Mr. Clean might have stolen it and slipped away.

By taking the guts of the file into his bedroom to read, the unlucky cop had unwittingly signed his own death warrant.

The creeper entered the hall.

The black world had a secret.

The Nazis had one, too.

The Mountie was sniffing around the former and might have clued into the latter, and he had the file that could unravel both in the bedroom at the end of the hall.

The die was cast.

It was nutcracker time.

Mr. Clean would squeeze whatever the Mountie knew out of him, then cancel his permission slip to live.

So down the hall he crept. The bedroom door was ajar. Just to confirm that the cop was still asleep, the Pentagon hit man reached for the heat detector in the pocket of his pants, and that's when, suddenly, deep black technology slammed into *him*.

Götterdämmerung

Fifty feet above the führer's rat hole, the Russians had overrun the Zitadelle. Operation Clausewitz—a hastily, ill-prepared plan to defend the inner ring of Berlin with a Volkssturm force of old men, young boys, and crippled soldiers—had collapsed before this onslaught by the Red Army.

Berlin was on fire.

Spit-firing Katyushas, known as "Stalin organs," filled the sky with a rain of rockets. As dive-bombers emptied their bellies, Russian artillery hammered the earth where the bunker was buried. Berlin was pounded by the big-bore gun the Soviets had captured at Tempelhof airport and turned back on the capital. Every shell burst shook the sandy soil upon which the city stood, causing it to quake like a shot-put pit. Toppled buildings crumbled into the streets.

Pea-soup green befouled the roiling sky, which was also smeared yellow, red, and orange with flashes and flames. Black smoke smudged the streets around burning ruins, and sulfurous ash alive with sparks and embers swirled through heaps of rubble and choked the air. Searchlights manned by Russians criss-crossed the clouds and the nightscape that cloaked the day. The dark waters of the Spree were stained by war, too. Flares, blasts, and blazing buildings reflected off the river as the current dragged mangled floaters downstream.

Tank traps on Weidendamm Bridge marked the perimeter of the Zitadelle. Streetcars had been tipped over and loaded with boulders to make barricades. Concertina barbed wire coiled like a nest of snakes. Nothing, however, could stop the Red Army tanks from rumbling around the rubble, their turrets swiveling to blast obstacles to smithereens. At ten a.m.—with the Battle for Berlin raging to its climax—the Ivans had launched an all-out assault on the Reichstag, the German parliament, which was defended by several thousand last-ditch SS troops.

The entire city was now a churned-up battlefield. The hellish landscape was littered with crashed planes and abandoned guns, the charred wrecks of overturned vehicles and discarded bazookas. Every street was an open grave-yard. Months of bombardment by the British and the Americans, followed by the Russians' artillery barrage, had left the corpses of soldiers, civilians, and livestock every-where. Sprawled about in ghoulish poses, with their heads blown off, their bellies torn open, and their limbs severed, they polluted the air with an abattoir stench of rotting and roasted flesh.

The bodies of derelict soldiers, most in their mid-teens and still wearing their Volkssturm armbands and Hitler Youth uniforms, hung from the lampposts of cratered streets. "Traitor," "Coward," "Deserter," "Enemy of His People," blared the crude placards that had been strung around stretched necks. Each had been executed by the SS hangmen of the "flying court marshals." Now their bulging blue eyeballs stared blankly at the carnage.

Rape was the Red Army's revenge weapon, payback for what the Einsatzgruppen had done in Russia during the

Barbarossa invasion of 1941. Since January, when Hitler went underground, 675,000 refugees had fled to Berlin, 80 percent of them women. Wearing traditional peasant dress, they trundled in on ox carts and horse-drawn wagons, with cattle, poultry, and swine as company. Some transported their recent dead in homemade coffins, and grandmothers clasped ravished granddaughters.

Today, the hunt was on for the women of Berlin.

Wild Sabine screams pierced the mechanical din of battle—*booms* from the artillery and *rat-tat-tats* from the machine guns at the Reichstag—as terrified naked women ran along rooftops pursued by Russian soldiers. Many leaped five or six stories to escape a dishonor that seemed worse than death.

So phantasmagoric was this Götterdämmerung that it was hard to separate the imagined from the real. In one smoldering tenement, Soviet soldiers blasted through the walls of an old cellar to get at a cluster of Berliners huddled around a candle. The first man to drag one of the women out into the street to be raped was gored through the chest by an elephant tusk and tossed high into the air. Before the woman could escape, a lion was upon her.

Zoo animals—their cages blown open—now roamed the ruins of the Reich.

THE WORD *Klapsmühle*—nuthouse—best described the chaos in the cellar of the New Reich Chancellery. Casualties from the fierce street fighting in the Potsdamer Platz came stumbling into the crude emergency room. The wounded and the dying lay lined up on cots, waiting for the surgeon to clear his bloody operating table. Up to his elbows in entrails and spurting arteries, the doctor struggled to slice and stitch as the battery lamp above the table swung like a jerky pendulum.

Russian planes and artillery were bombarding the area of the chancellery and Hitler's bunker. Concussion after concussion shook the cellar, wobbling the light while torn-apart soldiers babbled about losing battles and chewed-up youths bawled for their mothers.

As casualties died in anguish under the surgeon's scalpel, women fleeing rape burst into the cellar. Some had used lipstick to paint red dots on their faces, in hopes that a simulated scarlet fever would keep them from being ravished.

Soon, more than two thousand Germans were crowded into the cellar. The dying, the mangled, and the raped fused into a distorted chorus. The stress of impending doom disintegrated inhibitions, and before long, orgy became an escape from the waiting. Broken-out liquor released primal instincts. The same women who had just fled their Red Army pursuers now crawled into the bedrolls of the nearest German soldiers. Nazi generals shed their pants to chase half-naked *Blitzmädels*—the women who ran messages back and forth between the bunker and the chancellery—around and over the cots of the dead, the dying, and the wounded. Bodies writhed in group sex off in the corners. The chancellery dentist's chair held an erotic attraction. The wildest of the women enjoyed being strapped in and fucked in a medley of sexual positions.

The madhouse in the cellar had lost all sense of time. The sand in the spectral hourglass continued to flow, but the top bowl never emptied and the bottom bowl never filled. Death was all that would end Berlin's waking nightmare, and until that death was announced to Berliners, the future hung suspended.

Hitler's war had caused twenty million casualties. The past three months saw four million die in Central Europe.

From January to April, half a million were gassed in Nazi concentration camps. But now it all came down to a single murder.

To *Selbstmord* in Hitler's bunker.

FRIDAY, APRIL 13. Seventeen days before *Selbstmord.*

Champagne corks popped deep in the *Führerbunker.* Hitler wasn't a drinker, but he shared in the festive mood. The death of President Franklin Delano Roosevelt was cause to celebrate!

As the party continued into the small hours of the morning, Hitler and Joseph Göbbels, the propaganda minister, retired to the führer's study to thank their lucky stars. While Hitler contemplated the portrait of Old Fritz on the wall, Dr. Göbbels—nattily dressed in a clean shirt, white gloves, and polished boots—read aloud to him from Carlyle's *History of Frederick the Great:*

"Brave king," the Doktor said, addressing Hitler with the words once addressed to Old Fritz. "Wait yet a while, and the days of your suffering will be over. Already the sun of your good fortune stands behind the clouds, and soon it will rise upon you.

"It's written in the stars," Göbbels reminded the führer.

Surely this was the Nazi victory that Hitler's horoscope had prophesied for the end of April. Roosevelt's death would mark the turning point. As Ernst Streicher had predicted on April 3, the U.S. First Army had seized control of the Mittelwerk two days ago, but only the V-1 and V-2 rockets were now in enemy hands.

The most important secret of the Third Reich was still safe in the depths of the Wenceslas Mine, well hidden in the Sudeten Mountains, near the village of Ludwigsdorf, where the German, Polish, and Czech borders converged.

"The *Flugkreisel* works!" Streicher had said.

It would save the Third Reich, just as Hitler's fortune had foretold.

And *die Glocke* ...

"Ah, *die Glocke,*" Hitler sighed, relieved.

That would transport him into the glorious future of his thousand-year reich.

SUNDAY, APRIL 15. Fifteen days before *Selbstmord*.

Hitler called her *Tschapperl,* a Bavarian word meaning "honeybun." Since arriving in Berlin in mid-March, Eva Braun had resided in a private apartment in the chancellery. Now she had her bed and dresser trundled down into the lower bunker. She claimed the small suite just to the left of the führer's quarters, next to the bathroom off his study. Her dresser—which was crammed with enough frilly things to allow her to change five times a day—took up half of Eva's tiny new bedroom.

The manic hope raised by Roosevelt's death was hard to maintain in the face of the relentless Russian advance. Eva's move was a sign that Hitler would not retreat with his "mountain people" to the safety of the Eagle's Nest in the Bavarian Alps, and that had caused the mood in the bunker to slide into depressive fear.

But not for Eva Braun.

To assuage the fear of Hitler's bunker secretaries, Dr. Göbbels had set up a pistol range in the yard of the propaganda ministry, a ruined hulk of a building just next door. There, Eva joined the terrified women for daily target practice.

The secretaries dreaded their fate.

The *Todesengel* was preparing for murder.

WEDNESDAY, APRIL 18. Twelve days before *Selbstmord*.

A loud explosion blasted trees in the already devastated

Tiergarten, beside the chancellery. Russian field artillery. This new threat made the führer shiver. In the closing week of the First World War, when Hitler was a corporal in the trenches on the Somme, he had been temporarily blinded by poison gas. Even then, before the ballistic technologies of today, Germany's "Big Bertha" gun was able to hammer Paris from more than seventy miles away.

The explosion in the Tiergarten rattled Hitler's imagination. Along with deadly gasses like Tabun and Zyklon B, the Nazis had created a knockout gas that wasn't lethal. It merely rendered victims unconscious for twenty-four hours, and could be lobbed in canisters or shells. German intelligence believed that the Russians had a similar gas. Hitler's worst fear—and it would become a morbid obsession—was that their secret weapon, if aimed directly at the chancellery, would enable the Soviets to take him alive, "like a stunned animal in the zoo."

FRIDAY, APRIL 20. Ten days before *Selbstmord*.

With Berlin all but surrounded by the closing iron ring of the Red Army, Hitler celebrated his fifty-sixth birthday in the traditional spot—the Ehrenhof, or Court of Honor of the chancellery. The führer insisted on the attendance of his two most trusted henchmen from the earliest days of his rise to power: fat, preening Hermann Göring, Reichsmarschall of the Luftwaffe, the Nazi air force; and Heinrich Himmler, Reichsführer of the SS.

Hitler's last public act took place in the chancellery garden above the bunker. He awarded twenty twelve-year-old Hitler Youths with the Iron Cross for their heroic efforts in the defense of Berlin. The last photographs of the führer caught by newsreel cameramen were of him patting the cheeks of those Aryan boys.

SUNDAY, APRIL 22. Eight days before *Selbstmord*.

"Verloren!" shrieked Hitler. His color rose to a heated red and his face twisted into an unrecognizable mask. The men gathered in the bunker's main conference room for the afternoon briefing recoiled from the verbal explosion. The führer had taken to carrying a tattered filling-station map of Germany in his tunic pocket, and he began to wave it in the air with his good hand as he bellowed, with spittle flying, "Leonidas at Thermopylae! Horatius at the bridge! Frederick the Great in 1762! Me in Landsberg Prison back in 1923!"

And with that, Hitler slapped the map down on the table in front of his startled generals, then began shouting orders as if in the heat of battle. With his right hand, he started moving phantom Panzer divisions the war had long since destroyed around the map in complicated maneuvers that would surely turn the tide, while his flabby left clutched the table's rim. That whole arm up to his shoulder trembled and shuddered, and he tried to brace his convulsing half by wrapping his left calf and foot around one leg of the table. But that leg was throbbing and shaking too, and he couldn't control it.

Suddenly, Hitler ceased ranting. His face turned chalk white, then went blue as his drugged mind finally grasped what he had just been told by his generals.

The hated Communists were *inside* Berlin.

Hitler was silent for several long minutes before he flopped down into his chair. He nodded.

"Verloren."

Translation: "The war is lost."

HAVING DISMISSED HIS GENERALS, Hitler wobbled into his suite and unlocked the safe. From it, he withdrew most of his private papers, then had them lugged up to the garden and burned in the incinerator. Also in the safe was a large Walther pistol, which Hitler placed on the dresser in his bedroom.

Next, he called Dr. Göbbels.

Later that same day, the propaganda minister moved his wife and their six children into the upper level of the bunker. Each child was permitted to bring a single toy. Before abandoning his home near the Brandenburg Gate, Göbbels announced, over Berlin radio, "The führer is in Berlin and will die fighting with his troops defending the capital city." This was the first time Berliners had heard that Hitler was in their city.

MONDAY, APRIL 23. Seven days before *Selbstmord.*

Blue Monday, as it came to be known by the bunker staff, brought another drug-addled explosion by the führer. The last stand of the Third Reich was under way, and the chancellery was taking sporadic hits from the Red Army's long-range artillery. Suddenly, Martin Bormann stormed into Hitler's study with a telegram in hand.

"Treason, my führer!" he bellowed. "It's a *coup d'état*! Hermann Göring is trying to seize power from you!"

After Hitler's birthday party, the portly Reichsmarschall had fled south to the relative safety of the Bavarian Alps, then he'd sent this telegram suggesting that he—Göring— take over as leader of the Third Reich, "if you, my führer, are now hindered in your freedom of action or decide to remain in Fortress Berlin."

Hitler went berserk.

His blotchy face flushed crimson, his paranoid eyes glaring hate, his mustache, now white, twitching on drooling lips, the führer flew into a wild rage of bitterness and self-pity.

"Göring is a degenerate! A crook! His bad example has led to corruption at all levels. He made a mess of the Luftwaffe and exposed us to massive air raids. He let the barbarians into Berlin. Treason and betrayal are rife in my inner circle! Now Göring has the insolence to try to usurp his führer? The people aren't up to the challenge! Germans are unworthy of me. This war was forced on me by the Anglo-American plutocracy, the Marxist-Bolshevik world conspiracy, Jewish international finance, the Freemasons, the Jesuits—all the enemies who tried to stop me during the great struggle! *Mein Kampf! Mein Kampf!* Is this how my struggle ends? Security leaks everywhere I turn!"

Hitler screamed the words, his fists clenched, his face scrunched, his eyes darting here, there, everywhere, as if he now suspected everyone around him.

The madman dragged his palsied body to the emergency telephone exchange, where he surprised the operator.

"SS-Obergruppenführer Streicher! Have you heard from him?"

"No, my führer."

"Find him!" Hitler bellowed. "And bring him to me!"

TUESDAY, APRIL 24. Six days before *Selbstmord*.

There was still no sign of Streicher by the time the Red Army cut the last overland roads into and out of Berlin.

WEDNESDAY, APRIL 25. Five days before *Selbstmord*.

Having captured Tempelhof airport to thwart any escape from Berlin by plane, the Russians turned the Nazis' big-bore, twin-purpose gun back on the besieged city and began to pound the hell out of Hitler's capital as they breached the Zitadelle.

Still no sign of Streicher.

SATURDAY, APRIL 28. Two days before *Selbstmord*.

Hysteria gripped the *Führerbunker* at nine o'clock that night when a German-language broadcast was picked up

from Radio Stockholm. The story had originated with a San
Francisco–based Reuters man who was covering the organ-
izing of the United Nations. Acting on a tip, he'd reported
that Reichsführer-SS Heinrich Himmler was secretly trying
to negotiate peace with the Allies through a Swedish count.

Pandemonium erupted in the bunker.

Himmler a traitor! There was treason everywhere. No
wonder Streicher had failed to come through for Hitler. Was
it Himmler's plan to use *die Glocke* to save his own skin?

While the führer paced the shrinking confines of his
subterranean hellhole, buttonholing whomever he could to
wave the offending bulletin in their face, a drunken general
raced up and down the central passage, claiming that
Himmler was plotting to deliver Hitler's corpse to
Eisenhower as proof of his intent.

"Body snatchers!" Hitler cried.

That was too much.

A ghoulish SS plot by Himmler to barter the führer's
remains—the sacred ashes of the Third Reich.

"Blood!" Hitler demanded.

"Now!"

Foo Fighters

"What the hell are those lights over there?"

The spook who'd voiced the question was just along for the ride. Seated above and behind the pilot, in what was usually the gunner's position, he was a lieutenant from intelligence.

"Probably stars," the pilot replied.

"I don't think so. They're coming straight for us."

The P-61 Black Widow was on patrol in the pitch-black sky above the Rhineland, where the broad, winding river bordered the wild heights of the Black Forest. Five months after D-Day, the 415th Night Fighter Squadron of the U.S. 9th Army Air Force was hunting for bogies that might attack British bombers on their way to pound the piss out of the Fatherland. If they were lucky, the American aircrew would get a chance to hit a Nazi train or a truck convoy attempting to move men and materiel under the cover of darkness. The intel officer kept mum about why he was really riding shotgun.

What the spook had spied off their starboard wing was a constellation of pulsing lights. The unidentified flying objects jolted the pilot into banking sharply to aim the night fighter's four cannons and machine guns at what had to be Nazi attackers. At the same time, he radioed ground control to get the number of planes caught by radar.

"Negative."

"What?"

"No bogies in your sector."

"There must be."

"No blips. You're on your own."

The Black Widow definitely wasn't alone. True, there was silence except for the P-61's twin engines, but the glowing disks—ten of them—were zooming in fast on this "lone wolf" mission.

"What do you see?" the pilot asked his radarman. The night-sight expert crouched over the scope of his airborne-intercept radar in the well behind the intel lieutenant.

"Negative, Skipper. The sky ahead is clear."

"What the hell … ?"

"Fire!" barked the spook.

Boosting the throttles, the pilot went for the lead UFO, but as the American guns were about to spit tracers into the dark, the exhaust burners of the bogies—or whatever had caused that otherworldly glow—dimmed and snuffed out. The P-61 jinked to check its blind spots. Nothing. Where had those disks gone? They weren't ball lightning, and they weren't St. Elmo's fire, and their darting movement was unlike the flight of any known aircraft in the arsenals of either side.

So what were the UFOs?

No one knew.

But the radarman was able to give them a name. A Chicagoan, he was a fan of the newspaper comic strip *Smokey Stover, the Foolish Foo Fighter*. "Foo" was a bastardization of the French word *feu,* for "fire." Smokey, a fireman whose boss was Chief Cash U. Nutt, drove around in a two-wheeled fire truck known as the Foomobile.

Smokey was fond of saying, "Where there's foo, there's fire." He called himself a foo fighter, instead of a firefighter, and because the mysterious UFOs appeared to be fiery disks of unknown origin, they too were dubbed foo fighters. The name stuck.

PILOTS WHO HAD foo-fighter sightings over Western Europe between September 1944 and April 1945 were consistent in how they described the puzzling UFOs. The phosphorescent balls glowed amber, red, or white and were three to five feet in diameter. Each disk was metallic and seemed to generate light. None made propulsion noise or left a vapor trail. There was something electromagnetic in how they flew. Foo fighters were able to home in on Allied aircraft as if guided to them by remote control. Their rates of climb, maneuverability, and ability to take evasive action were extreme. Steep dives, sharp banks, and defensive tricks couldn't shake them. They tagged along as if magnetized, never fired a shot, and didn't explode in proximity. Then they peeled away and vanished into the blackness of the Third Reich.

THE CARIBOO, BRITISH COLUMBIA
May 27, Now

FZZZZZZZ ...

CRAAACKKKK ...

Even the pounding bass line couldn't suppress the cacophony summoned by this Nazi's infernal machines. At the center of it all, surrounded by the monitors and dials that ringed his subterranean workbench, the Eurotrash freak sat consulting the swastika-stamped plans and tweaking settings and twizzle knobs. As Rammstein rocked out the lyrics of "Amerika," the Aryan's shadow blitzkrieged around the walls of the gold-flecked cave like a ghost from some long-ago battlefield.

The spooks were spooked.

From the standpoint of Newtonian physics, what Ajax and Lysol were witnessing was impossible. This self-trained gizmo addict was able to subvert gravity with just the blueprints from the Streicherstab and an intuitive grasp of electromagnetism. Using a setup cobbled together from supposedly obsolete salvage, he was tapping into the quantum mechanics of Max Planck. Amid the high-voltage effects of a spark-gap, which was snapping ear-splitting shock waves down into the mine, the wizard at the heart of the zone of influence manipulated a forest of humming aerials and dishes. Phantom forces plucked hunks of scrap metal off the rocky floor and levitated them in thin air.

Like foo fighters.

Whatever the Nazi was doing, the fireworks were awesome. In the time they'd spent spying on him from the black hole of the tunnel, Ajax and Lysol had watched the punk maneuver identified flying objects like frying pans and spools of wire as if they were remote-controlled model planes. He could make them slide horizontally or hover in place—and with the flick of a dial that bent aerials toward a target wall, he was able to shoot them in a powerful ballistic arc as if they'd been propelled by a sudden energy boost.

Not only did he levitate objects and move them around, but he also bent them, broke them, and caused them to explode. In military jargon, his was a "lift and disruption" weapon. But how did it work? Did he trigger opposing electromagnetic fields so each canceled the other out? Did he whirl electromagnetic fields in some unfathomed way? Whatever he was doing, he seemed able to channel a flow of zero-point energy toward any object within his zone of influence. By affecting the quarks and gluons of quantum mechanics, did he teeter on the verge of time dilation? Were pockets of space-time being transmuted down here? It certainly looked that way from what the Pentagon spooks saw happen to the anchor.

Rusted and barnacled as if recovered from the bottom of the sea, it was the largest chunk of junk on the ground. It was probably heavier than all three men in the mine combined. To lift it, the Nazi had to crank several dials to their red-line level, and then he cranked several more once the anchor hovered in the air. This appeared to turn the solid anchor transparent, visible in outline yet invisible in mass. It was both there and not there at the same time.

The spooks had seen enough.

It was time for the nutcracker to make the Nazi sing.

Time to give up Hitler's long-lost secret.

The mother lode?

The Nazi was swiveling the antenna farm toward the target wall—in preparation for another cross-cavern hurl?—when suddenly all hell broke loose. The ceiling lights began to glare intensely, as if pushed to the maximum capacity of their filaments, and they soon bathed the floor of the mine with such searing incandescence that illumination burst into the spooks' black hole. Like jailbreakers caught in a searchlight sweep of a prison yard, they froze and hoped not to be seen. The Eurotrash punk aimed a finger of accusation at the intruders, and then he cranked a knob to the max.

FZZZZZZZ ...

CRAAACKKKK ...

"Jesus!"

Both spooks yelped.

The spark-gap exploded with a shock wave of such magnitude that it blew their eardrums. A bolt of lightning zapped from the Nazi's fingertip toward the mine hole. The ceiling lights blew, spewing a shower of red-hot filaments. The cavern plunged into an eerie, sizzling darkness. Tongues of phantom flame licked up the target wall and around the throat of the mine. The lab was sucking energy from who knew where. All at once, the anchor flew across the cavern as if guided to its target by the lightning bolt. One of the arrowhead prongs crunched through Ajax's skull and nailed him to the concave granite.

The shock wave had shattered the lenses of both spooks' high-tech goggles. Lysol missed the plight of his partner because he was plucking at the glass shards in his eyeballs. Then, through pain and blindness, his survival training kicked in.

Where was his gun?

His palm swept the littered floor.

Where was the bag with his backup gun?

He groped around in the dark.

His fingers found the bag where he had dropped it on the ground. As he felt for the zipper, steel punched through the back of his hand like a sword.

A sword!

He recalled the plaque on the blood-splattered box.

SS-Obergruppenführer Ernst Streicher.

A cold voice snarled above and behind his ear.

"Run for your life, pig."

The blade drew back and the bag was kicked away.

"Oink, oink," the Nazi grunted.

Lysol cried out as the pigsticker was jabbed deep into one cheek of his butt.

Hands flailing in front of him, stumbling down into the depths of the mine where Nazi secrets lay, the blind man ran for his life.

Home Invader

Mr. Clean was in peril because of a pregnant cat.

Sure, his parabolic mike had caught what he wanted to hear about the swastika file. And yes, his infrared detector had placed the Mountie in bed. But the Pentagon spook had relied too much on the technological wizardry of Big Brother's eyes in the sky, and not enough on intel from the ground.

For if he had bothered to delve into the emotional landscape of the Horseman, he might have learned that Dane was grieving the death of Papa and had brought his grandfather's feline, Puss, home to see her through birthing her litter. And because Dane knew nothing about pregnant cats, he had put Puss to bed on a blanket in the confines of the hall closet. Birthing might be messy, after all, and he didn't want to foul his entire home.

The Mountie, of course, was in bed when that infrared gizmo had picked up his body signature through the outside wall. But as Mr. Clean was scaling the downspout to the balcony, Puss had let out a mewl of discomfort that woke Dane from sleep. So out of bed he had padded, to check on what was wrong. Figuring time was nigh for the blessed event, he—as he had on many nights of camping on the cold, hard ground with Papa—had lain down on the floor of the walk-in closet alongside Puss, intending to catnap until he knew the expectant mom was stable. That's when Mr. Clean had laser-beamed into his home.

The floorboards of the condo were interconnected.

Dane was lying on the floor when he felt the slight heave come in from the living room next door.

Someone was invading his home.

He didn't know who.

But a homicide cop in the Mounted makes a lot of deadly enemies in the course of his crime-busting career. Dane wasn't about to come out of the closet and introduce himself.

He didn't have his gun.

At night, he kept that close at hand in his bedroom, in case he ran into trouble like this.

So all he had was the element of surprise.

One hand on the floorboards to track approaching vibrations from soft-shoe footfalls, the other clenched around the knob of the closet door, the defender held his breath and waited.

Squeak!

Dane knew that floorboard.

This was *his* home.

He knew every squeak and draft and nook and cranny.

Now! he thought.

And whipped open the door.

The force of the flying door caught the spook completely off guard. The whack from the wood wrenched the H&K from his grasp, triggering a muffled shot as it flew. The door swung wider to slam him full in the face, driving the lenses of the night-vision goggles back into his eyes and smashing the bones in his nose. As the .45 clattered to the floor and Mr. Clean stumbled back in shock, the Mountie grabbed him by the throat of his Kevlar jogging suit and yanked him forward, driving his fist as hard as he could into the shattered pulp of the intruder's nose and the eyeball-bursting goggles. The slug that had torn through the plank of the door left him with little doubt that this was combat to the death, and while Dane didn't have a nutcracker like the one in the pouch on the spook's sneaky uniform, he did have the version that had served Stone Age warriors since war first began.

It was called a kneecap.

The direct hit to the crotch had such outrage behind it that the home invader was lifted right off his feet and propelled out of the bedroom hall to crash down supine at the rear of the living room.

With his blinders on, Mr. Clean couldn't see.

But so incensed was he that some peon had dared to thwart the master plan that he struggled to overcome bunching muscles in his spastic groin and the excruciating pain that tore a battlecry from his throat to go for another weapon.

His hand was closing on the butt of the Warthog at his hip when he heard a sound that was like checkmate to a chessplayer.

Phhhhht!

By reaching for the next generation of black world weapons, Mr. Clean had mistakenly overlooked the firepower still in play.

The H&K .45 scooped up in Dane's fist.

There's only one rule of engagement in the Mounted Police: Don't draw your sidearm except to shoot to kill.

The kill shot wasn't to the heart, which was protected with Kevlar armor. The kill shot wasn't to the brow of the head, which was crowned with metal goggles. The kill shot was to the smashed-in nose, where Dane's skinned knuckles had struck flesh, blood, and bone.

Phhhhht!

Phhhhht!
Phhhhht!

ARLINGTON, VIRGINIA

With the beak of his mouth gaping open and the talons of his fingers clawing the edge of his desk, Big Bad Bill hunched over his satellite speakers.

Ajax had yet to report in from the Skunk Mine. The dead air from that satellite link grew more ominous with each second that ticked by on Bill's watch.

Even more disconcerting was the showdown now going on in the home of the meddling Mountie, every blow of which was being bounced here from the open mike of Mr. Clean's headset.

Phhhhht!
Phhhhht!
Phhhhht!

Thank God, thought Bill.

He recognized the whispering of the silencer-equipped .45 carried by all Pentagon hit men.

"Is he terminated?" Bill asked through the plug in Mr. Clean's ear.

No answer.

Then he heard a voice that was familiar to him from conversations picked up earlier by that parabolic mike, a voice that seemed to be about as far away as someone standing over a body on the floor.

"Who the hell are you?" Winter asked rhetorically.

Selbstmord

BERLIN
April 30, 1945

Only Joseph Göbbels and Martin Bormann had witnessed the wedding the night before last. Snatched from duty to marry Adolf Hitler and Eva Braun, a minor bureaucrat serving with the Volkssturm performed the nuptials. The fiftyish, bewildered man in the brown Nazi Party uniform and swastika armband had asked the two—as required by law—if they were third-generation Aryans. After accepting that their bloodlines were pure, he was able to pronounce them husband and wife.

The bride wore black for their wedding: a short-skirted silk taffeta afternoon dress with gold clasps at the shoulders. It was Hitler's favorite. At long last, Eva had what she'd always desired. The tears that filled her blue eyes were full of joy.

The reception was held in Hitler's study, a room large enough to accommodate a dozen bunker veterans. As the champagne flowed and congratulations were received, Frau Hitler held court with a slight tremor in her lisping voice and tossed back her glass regularly. Not yet drunk, Eva was well on her way.

As a perk for performing the wedding, the Volkssturm official was given a liverwurst sandwich and a glass of champagne, then he was hustled out of the bunker and returned to the streets, where the Battle for Berlin raged on. The man was shot dead on the Wilhelmstrasse, on his way back to his foxhole post.

The night of his honeymoon, the führer dictated his last will and political testament to a secretary. "It is not true that I or anyone else in Germany wanted war back in 1939. It was desired and provoked solely by those international politicians who either come from Jewish stock or are the agents of Jewish interests," he averred. Of those who would succeed him, he demanded continuation of the war, as well as undying hatred of all Jews.

Hitler left his personal possessions to the Nazi Party, or if that no longer existed, to Germany. "If the state, too, is destroyed, there is no need for any further instructions on my part."

Dr. Göbbels witnessed the will.

YESTERDAY, Hitler had awakened to news of what had happened to Il Duce down in Italy. Benito Mussolini—the führer's Axis partner—and his mistress, Clara Petacci, had been killed in Milan by their own countrymen, who then strung their mutilated corpses by their heels from a filling-station marquee so that passersby could jeer and spit on them all day.

Selbstmord would be better.

TODAY HAD BEGUN with the killing of Hitler's dog. Blondi meant more to the führer than even his closest associates. In March, she had whelped a litter of four puppies in the bunker. Though Hitler was afraid of "fresh-air poisoning," he had from time to time ventured out for a few minutes to walk the Alsatian in the chancellery garden. Now it was time to say goodbye.

Besides, this poison had come from Himmler the

Traitor, and so had to be tested.

The vet had to get drunk to do the job. He and Hitler's doctor took Blondi into the toilet. As the first streaks of pre-dawn light fell on Berlin, the dog handler forced the Alsatian's mouth open and the doctor reached in to crush the vial of cyanide with pliers. The poison acted quickly, and Blondi died.

Soon after, Hitler entered the toilet to make sure she was dead. By then, he was so drugged himself that he didn't say a word or exhibit any emotion. Satisfied, he disappeared into his study.

With his pistol, the drunken vet shot Blondi's puppies. Then, prematurely, the man staggered out to the canteen hollering, "The führer is dead, and it's now every man for himself!"

In fact, Hitler had gone to bed.

AN HOUR LATER, at five-thirty Monday morning, April 30, Hitler rose once more. The British–American air bombardment had stopped the week before. The final raid had hammered Berlin on April 21, one day after Hitler's fifty-sixth birthday. That was followed by the 327th all-clear siren of the war. It hadn't taken long to figure out why: the invading Red Army had reached the outskirts of the city. Since then, the Russian artillery had gone to work on the ruins, physically advancing to the edge of Tiergarten park, where the massive outlines of the Reichstag and the New Reich Chancellery loomed. The cannon barrage had reached a crescendo over the past few days, but for some inexplicable reason, it had fallen off during the night. Since the booms of the bursting shells were the only battle sounds to penetrate the bunker, the führer awoke to deathly quiet in his underground tomb.

Der Tag.

The day.

"One must not—like a coward—seek to avoid one's own destiny," Hitler had once told a trusted general. "I shall not join in the battle personally. There would be the dangerous prospect that I might only be wounded, and thus fall into Russian hands while still alive. I do not want to give my enemies any chance to mutilate my corpse. If the end is near, warn me, General."

Today, the general had come to warn him at six a.m.

Hitler was wearing a black satin robe over his white pajamas. On his feet, he wore a pair of patent-leather boot-slippers. The general found him sitting on the edge of his bed. Hitler rose to greet him and moved to the only chair. He motioned to the general to take a seat on the cot.

"How bad is it?" Hitler asked.

"The Reds are in the Wilhelmstrasse, four blocks away. They have penetrated into the subway tubes under both the Friedrichstrasse and the Voss Strasse. Most of the Tiergarten is in enemy hands. Russian troops have encircled our positions on the Potsdamer Platz. They are only three hundred yards from the chancellery. We expect them to storm the Reichstag at any moment."

"Why have the guns stopped?"

The general shrugged. "Tomorrow is May Day, an important day to the Reds. Perhaps Marshal Zhukov plans to hold back for twenty-four hours so that he can present the big prize of Berlin to Joseph Stalin like a shashlik on a spit."

"Too bad," said Hitler, sighing. "I had hoped to make it until May fifth. Napoleon died on St. Helena on that day back in 1821. Another great career that ended in disappointment, disillusion, betrayal, and treason. Fickle Europeans didn't understand the French emperor and his great plans, as they have not understood me and mine. We were both men born before our times. Well, so much the worse for Europe. History will be my only judge."

The bunker staff had shrunk to a skeleton crew. Only the most faithful were sticking around, ready to perish like miserable rats at the hands of the Ivans in this musty cement vault. After the general departed for the Reichstag redoubt, Hitler had wandered listlessly about the lower bunker. His eyes cast to the floor, his hands clasped behind his back, the führer had paced from his cramped quarters to the central corridor, then along the quiet passage, past two staffers asleep in bedrolls on the floor, to the emergency staircase to the garden … before shuffling his drug-ravaged body back to where he had started.

Damn Streicher! he thought.

Never in the history of mankind had a military machine created as astounding an arsenal of wonder weapons as the Nazi scientists of the Third Reich.

The V-1 cruise missile, the "buzz bomb" that plagued Britain …

The V-2 ballistic rocket of Wernher von Braun …

The Me-262, the Messerschmitt jet fighter …

Nuclear energy for bombs and rocket propulsion …

Anti-aircraft rays and laser-guided systems …

The *Flugkreisel* …

And *die Glocke*.

What a colossal mistake he had made when he'd put that entire Pandora's box of weapons under the exclusive control of Himmler's SS, and consequently into the hands of a single keeper—Ernst Streicher. And then he had compounded that blunder on April 3, when the general and his sons had come to the bunker, by leaving it to Streicher to deliver the Reich—or at least its führer—from the forces closing in on all sides.

Damn Streicher!

He had dropped off the face of the earth.

Where were the miracle weapons that would save the Fatherland from annihilation?

Where?

AT EIGHT-THIRTY that morning, while Hitler was still at breakfast, the short-lived respite from artillery pounding had ended. The guns of the 69th Elite Storm Troops, from the Russian Third Assault Army, had opened up on the Reichstag, and ninety minutes later the Red Army's final do-or-die attack had begun.

At noon, suffering from a chronic hangover, Martin Bormann returned from his latest sexual foray into the casualty station in the cellar of the chancellery to caution Hitler that Götterdämmerung had indeed come to the *Führerbunker*.

Hitler's last meal, "for old times' sake," was shared with both of his secretaries and his vegetarian cook at the small table in the map room where he'd been married. Spaghetti and tossed salad. Berlin rape accounts were rife within the bunker, but to avoid distressing the women, the topic was sidestepped. Instead, they conversed about the proper mating of dogs and the fact that French lipstick was made from grease collected in the sewers of Paris.

THE FINAL FAREWELLS were said in the conference passage at just after three in the afternoon. It took less than three minutes.

Eva Hitler had already given away her most valuable possessions. As she presented a silver fox wrap to one of the secretaries, the führer's new wife said, "Traudl, sweetheart, here is a present for next winter—and your life after the war."

The Angel of Death was the only bunker inmate who seemed to be happy. She radiated quiet serenity, and

appeared unaffected by the demoralization depressing
Hitler's staff. Her exultation was born of the fact that
through a morbid pact of death, she would finally get her
way with the only man she had truly loved. It was *Romeo
and Juliet,* with death as the *Erlöser,* the great deliverer.

The führer, too, was calm. Before departing, his
doctor had given him a shot of morphine and a supply of
pills. The man who stood shaking outside the door to his
private suite was in the same condition as his crumbling
bunker and the Reich itself. More shadow than substance,
der Chef seemed hollow and burned out. His face was
puffed, part yellow and part gray. How listless and
subdued his gestures had become. His voice was as flat as
a monotone.

The artillery shells quaking the ground had knocked
mortar off the thick cement walls. A few of the cramped
rooms were painted battleship gray, but now they were as
blotched as the führer's face. A single diesel engine in the
powerhouse ran the utilities that supplied the bunker with
electricity, water, and air. To keep things functioning
throughout the last stand, an electrician had strung light
cables along the floor of the corridor. With all those
comings and goings, the wires had become as tangled as the
spaghetti at lunch, and now—as Hitler spoke his final
public words—the flickering lights dimmed on the dying
moments of his Third Reich.

With Göbbels and Bormann flanking him, der Chef
nodded a cue at his valet.

Heinz Linge opened the door to Hitler's private quarters.

With a chivalrous gesture, the führer directed his
doomed frau to precede him into the anteroom.

"Linge, old friend," Hitler stated, "I want you to join the
breakout group."

"Why, my führer?"

Hitler's final words were "To serve the man who will come after me."

AS FRAU HITLER LED the way into the führer's study, der Chef shut the heavy, vault-like steel door to the corridor and then the door between the small anteroom and the living room, where they would die. Both doors were fireproof, gas-proof, and consequently, soundproof. A narrow blue-and-white sofa ran along the far wall. A small round table and two chairs stood in front of the couch. On the table sat a Dresden vase filled with greenhouse tulips and white narcissi. After rounding the table and chairs, the couple sat down on the sofa.

The foolproof method for *Selbstmord*—according to both Hitler's doctor and his senior generals—was the pistol-and-poison combination. *Selbstmord* was a characteristically German phenomenon. The root word *Mord* meant "murder," rather than *Tod,* "death." Unlike *seppuku,* the Japanese concept of a joyous noble death, "self-murder" was a German's escape from a fate worse than death.

For the past week, Hitler had been carrying two pistols. Concealed in a leather holster sewn inside his trousers by the right front pocket was a Walther 6.35 that he had packed for years. Pulling that pistol from his pants, he set it down on the table beside the vase as a backup should the larger gun jam. The more potent pistol was the Walther 7.65 that he'd removed from the safe on the day of his nervous breakdown. Since then, he had lugged it around in his tunic pocket.

From another pocket, Hitler withdrew two poison vials, each filled with the same cyanide the doctor had used to kill his dog. As a reserve, he placed one on the table between his backup pistol and the vase. The other went into his mouth as he fetched the Walther from his tunic and raised its muzzle to his temple.

"Squeeze the trigger as you bite down on the capsule," his doctor had advised.

Eva Hitler sat in the other corner of the velvet couch, only two feet away from her husband. Dressed in a blue chiffon spring dress, with a raspberry-colored scarf for style, she kicked off her pumps and tucked her feet snugly under her body. She, too, had a pair of cyanide capsules. One she set down on the table, along with the scarf and her own small pistol, also a Walther 6.35. Then she popped the other capsule into her mouth. Unlike her husband, she didn't grip a pistol in her hand.

"Bite quickly into your capsule the second you hear the shot," she had been told by his doctor.

Eva's eyes widened as she watched Hitler intently. She feared that the sight of her dead husband might shatter her resolve. They had to die together, and it fell to Eva to ensure that their deaths were simultaneous. As Hitler put the black muzzle directly to his graying temple and angled the barrel at eyebrow level, she wondered what final thought was passing through his mind.

As his finger tightened on the trigger of the pistol, Hitler imagined Ernst Streicher zooming into the future in the circular shape of *die Glocke,* and he wondered if those in the years to come would look back on him—the führer—as a god.

Bang!

AT 3:40 P.M., the outsiders entered the study. Hitler's instructions had been to wait ten minutes.

So soundproof were the two doors that only Eva Hitler had heard the single shot that millions of people around the globe desired. The first to enter the room was Hitler's valet. Choked by the pistol powder and the poison fumes that made his eyes smart in the airtight confines, he retreated. Martin Bormann led the small group—including Göbbels, the Hitler Youth leader Artur Axmann, the valet, and Hitler's adjutant—that finally entered to survey the carnage.

The führer was slumped over but still seated on the couch. Blood oozed steadily from the gaping hole in his shattered right temple. The drops pooled on the rug at his end of the sofa. It was evident that he had followed the pistol-and-poison protocol as advised, squeezing the trigger and crushing the capsule simultaneously. The pistol had slipped from his right hand and fallen to the carpet at his feet. Since most pistol-only suicides are found still grasping their handguns tenaciously, that meant that the potassium cyanide had accomplished its poisonous job.

Eva Hitler had died painlessly, too. Her body was in the same position she'd assumed when she'd kicked off her pumps, and she looked like a schoolgirl with tucked-up legs on the velvet sofa. She had ingested the poison but chosen not to use her pistol. It was found by the valet on the small table next to the colorful scarf. He checked the chamber and confirmed that it was fully loaded. The Dresden vase, having tipped over and spilled water on Eva's dress near the thigh, had tumbled unbroken to the carpet. Feeling the need to restore order, Linge picked it up, checked for cracks, filled it with the scattered spring flowers, and set it back up on the table.

"Move the table and chairs aside," directed Hitler's adjutant.

That done, he spread two woolen military blankets on the floor and left to summon three young officers from the guardroom to carry the bodies up to the chancellery garden. While he was gone, the surgeon came in to examine the bunker newlyweds.

"Both dead," he pronounced.

Three tall SS soldiers lugged the führer's corpse up the forty-four steps that led to the emergency exit. The cadaver weighed 180 pounds. With no stretcher, it was an awkward task to haul the warm corpse up the spiral staircase. Clutching him beneath the shoulders, two men pulled him from above while the last man shoved from below with a grip on both ankles. The blanket hid Hitler's bloodstained head from view, but not the black trousers of his simple uniform.

Martin Bormann carried Eva Hitler's body out of the study like a sack of potatoes, with one apelike hand clasped over her breast. In life, she had done nothing to mask her loathing for her husband's sycophant, and had complained to Hitler that the lout made constant harassing passes at all the bunker females. Now, in death, Eva was being groped by—in her words—the "oversexed toad," and that so incensed the other males in the funeral procession that they seized her body from Bormann and passed it up man to man.

Her face and shoulders visible, she appeared serene.

On each of the four landings in the stairwell exit, the pallbearers paused to try to catch their breath, but instead they choked on sulfur fumes and smoldering embers mixed with plaster powder and blinding rubble dust. By the time they reached the garden, their eyes smarted and their mouths tasted of ash.

Hell on earth was the only possible description for what they faced above. Berlin was a land of red flames and billowing black smoke. Searchlights slashed the burning sky. The funeral music was supplied by the shrieking Stalin organs as shrapnel zipped through the air. With a brace on his leg, Dr. Göbbels was the last to limp out into the rubble-heaped chancellery garden. This wouldn't be the final macabre requiem for him, however; it would be followed by the *Selbstmord* deaths of his six children, his wife, and himself.

The SS officers lowered the corpses into a shallow ditch less than ten yards from the bunker's exit. Next, they emptied several jerry cans of gasoline over Adolf and Eva Hitler, saturating the blankets that wrapped them like shrouds. The wind made it difficult to light the makeshift pyre, but after several thwarted attempts, Bormann was able to ignite it with a torch of twisted paper.

Whoosh! The bodies in the trench burst into blue flames.

There was no music, no flag, no swastika banner. The sendoff of the führer to his Aryan Valhalla was a brief, spontaneous affair that took place in an interval while the Red Army artillerymen reloaded. Without anyone giving the order, the Nazi survivors, as one man, stood at rigid attention on both sides of the blazing ditch and snapped their right arms out in the stiff, palm-down Hitler salute.

Sieg heil!

Snake Pit

VANCOUVER
May 27, Now

Swastika felt like Perseus on the hunt.

The Nazi motive behind his previous cleansings of *Untermenschen* had been nicely masked by *The Vancouver Times* in its rush to sell newspapers and win the endless media war against its competitors. The parallel to the whitewashing done by the Pentagon when it imported Nazi visionaries and their hardware into the United States in those tumultuous months following the Second World War wasn't lost on Swastika. Satan himself would be transformed into a hero if doing so would advance the agenda of backstage puppeteers plotting to score money or power.

Look what they did for Wernher von Braun and his rocketeers.

Overcast and Paperclip.

And look what they were doing for Swastika now.

Different puppeteers.

Same agenda.

The killing of the Congo Man had been no more difficult for the Nazi superman than the squashing of a bug. That's why he'd spiked the African child-killer to the ground. It wasn't meant to imitate the blinding of the Cyclops in Homer's *Odyssey*. It was to mimic the way an entomologist pins a bug into his collection, so as to attract the attention of Special X.

But Cort Jantzen and *The Vancouver Times* had cloaked his actions in the heroics of classical Greek myth, and the public had concluded that the Congo Man was a monster who'd deserved retribution.

Swastika was a hidden hero in the public eye.

The Vigilante.

The challenge for the Nazi superman was to maintain that crowd-pleasing theme. To do that, he was turning the paper's reportage back on *The Vancouver Times*. Cleansing the crooked business exec whose stock manipulations had ruined so many lives was a no-brainer. With Midas as his name, the "golden fleece" angle had almost suggested itself. Sure, there were those tut-tutting over how he was flayed to death, but that was just another angle from which to sell papers or fill dead air.

Tonight, however, Swastika planned to outdo himself. Hitler's modern-day spawn was enraged that the swastika signature left at his cleansings was being hidden from the world because of an obvious conspiracy between the Mounted Police and *The Vancouver Times*. Why else would the symbol from the jpeg not have appeared in the paper? If Sgt. Dane Winter and Cort Jantzen thought they could suppress and manipulate Swastika's birthright for their own *Untermenschen* ends ... well, each man would suffer for his disrespect.

RATTLESNAKE VENOM has curative side effects. Not only does that serpent's poison dissolve the blood clots that cause heart attacks and strokes, but it also prevents the metastasizing of cancer cells. That's why rattlesnakes—so plentiful throughout the Cariboo region of British Columbia—were being kept in a portable glass vivarium in a medical research laboratory in the department of zoology at UBC. There had been an article on that research in yesterday's edition of *The Vancouver Times*. It was now with the other clippings on the map room table in the replica of Hitler's bunker.

The zoology lab was just a few minutes' drive from the bunker, which was hidden underground on University Hill. In the blackest hours of the night, there wasn't a soul about. Breaking into the herpetology hut was a snap, and Swastika's penlight quickly found the portable vivarium tucked into one corner. The snakes were sleeping soundly in the darkness of the lab. Reptiles become animated in the thermal rays of the sun and turn lethargic when it cools down. Jiggling the case, however, rattled them into a frenzy. Now the serpents were squirming, hissing, and baring their fangs at Swastika. He could hear the death rattle of all those tails thrashing behind a glass darkly.

Medusa

The first thing Corp. Jackie Hett noticed when she walked into the living room of Sgt. Dane Winter's condo was the poster on the wall. The framed bill advertised a 1953 Republic serial film called *Canadian Mounties vs. Atomic Invaders*. In Stetson and red tunic, with his gun drawn, the stalwart hero dominated the upper half of the poster. All warm and fuzzy in her fur-collared white parka, the love interest sought protection behind his broad shoulder. At the foot of the poster, wearing fedora hats, were two dastardly spies intent on setting up a missile base in the wilds of Canada. Somehow, Hett got the feeling that the colorful placard was the film's only claim to fame.

"Taking the myth a little too seriously, I hear," she said.

The redhead nodded toward the poster.

"It's been quite a morning," Dane replied. "First, I had to shoot some government spook playing cat burglar in my home. Then I played midwife to a cat."

"What's her name?" Jackie asked, squatting down beside the mother cat who was kneading her paws as a litter of six sealed-eyed kittens slept close to the warmth of her belly.

"Puss," said Dane.

"Now that's original."

Yesterday after work, they had arranged to meet for breakfast this morning on Granville Island to discuss any questions he might have about integrating himself into the swastika investigation. Since Granville Island was a short walk from Dane's home, it seemed wise to avoid the parking nightmare on that stepping stone in the salt sea of False Creek and have Jackie meet up with him here. Having phoned Special X on the drive over to see if there was breaking news in the case for them to feed in over bacon and eggs, Hett had heard about the assault on Dane. While parking her car out back of his condo, she'd seen the meat wagon from the body-removal service drive off to the morgue.

There were few signs inside Dane's home of what had gone down in the darkness. Bloodstains on the floor where the living room entered the hall to the bedroom. An oblong hole in the balcony door. That was it. The corpse and the clues were gone. To see if the corporal agreed with his suspicion about the origin of the heavily armed intruder, the sergeant now booted up the computer and showed her the images captured by his digital camera.

"Well?" Dane asked.

"You can't buy that stuff at Radio Shack."

"Not a brand name or serial number on any of it. Everything is so high-tech that Ident can't identify what some of it is for. The goggles and the torture device are out of science fiction. That's a laser cutter, and that's a thermal-imaging device. We're going to try to isolate what band the communication equipment links up to, and I wouldn't be surprised if it's a spy satellite."

"Want my gut reaction?" Jackie asked.

"Indeed I do."

"I think you just had a run-in with a hit man from the Pentagon."

"Why send a hit man after me?"

"I don't know," Jackie said. "But I'll hazard a guess. It might have something to do with this file." Her finger moved from the computer screen to the swastika file on his desk.

"Keep going," said Dane.

"Did you watch the Republican National Convention when Kerry ran against Bush?"

"Snippets."

"The speech by the First Lady, Laura Bush?"

"Yeah, she followed Schwarzenegger. I couldn't miss him."

"In rallying the convention to the righteousness of the president's war on terror and the invasion of Iraq, she told the delegates that her father had served in Europe with the 104th Infantry during the Second World War, and that his company had liberated the Nazi concentration camp at Nordhausen. Remember?"

"No," said Dane.

"Well, my dad's uncle helped liberate Nordhausen, too. He spent the rest of his life trying to forget the sickening horrors that he witnessed there. What the First Lady failed to mention was that Nordhausen was the overflow camp for Dora-Mittelbau, the hellhole where twenty thousand slaves died assembling the V-2 rockets of Wernher von Braun. Today, if you were to ask a so-called American patriot about Dora-Mittelbau, chances are he'd say, 'Who's she?' Ask the same patriot to comment on Wernher von Braun, and you'll likely hear, 'He's the American hero who put us on the moon.' My dad won't stomach that."

"Sounds like your dad's an honorable man."

"He's dedicated his life to preserving the values on which America was founded. The way Dad puts it is this: 'If you don't stand for something, you'll fall for anything.' Hundreds of thousands of American heroes died on the battlefields of the Second World War. Every one of them deserved a medal of honor. Instead, in 1975 the president gave one to von Braun, a man who had climbed the ranks of Himmler's dreaded SS. My dad says that action spits on

the grave of all those who died for *something* in the war.
They gave up their lives and got nothing. Von Braun,
however, *did* give us a piece of hardware."

A COP'S MIND works the jigsaw puzzle of a murder case
differently than a lawyer's mind does. The cop in Dane was
trained to follow the clues until they led him to a suspect,
and hopefully proved the offender's involvement beyond a
reasonable doubt. But the lawyer in Dane was trained to
rework the puzzle until the pieces could be used to raise a
reasonable doubt. A defense attorney used his creative
imagination to get his client off. A prosecutor used his to
foresee the defense strategy and undermine it.

At the moment, Dane was tapping into both his cop's
and his lawyer's training to try to puzzle out the pieces on
the computer screen and in the file on his desk.

Two victims killed in Vancouver had swastikas gouged
into their foreheads.

Dane had asked U.S. authorities, through the FBI's
VICAP links, about similar signatures.

A high-tech hit man from what was probably the
Pentagon's black world had invaded Dane's home.

After the Second World War, the Pentagon's black
world had teamed up with Nazi scientists like Wernher
von Braun to beef up space-age ordnance in the arsenal
of democracy.

How the jigsaw pieces locked together remained a
mystery, but Dane suddenly saw another potential link.

The final mission in his grandfather's logbook before he
got shot down and spent a year and a half in a prisoner-of-
war camp said: "*1943. August 17. Ops. to Peenemünde.
Bombed V-2 rocket site.*"

Dane felt as if the octopus arms of the Nazi swastika
were reaching forward in time to wrap their tentacles

around adversaries who were still caught up in the Second World War *today*.

His cellphone jangled.

"Winter," he said.

It was Cort Jantzen.

"There's been another swastika murder."

"How do you know?"

"The killer," replied the reporter. "He sent me a jpeg and an e-mail with directions to the crime scene."

THE CRIME REPORTER was sitting on the porch of a ginger-bread house in the Kitsilano neighborhood of Vancouver when the Mounties pulled to the curb and got out of Jackie's car. With a laptop computer on his knees, he was already at work on tomorrow's story.

Cort was the ideal reporter to play this game of cat and mouse with the Swastika Killer. For as long as he could remember, his taste in reading had centered on heroic fantasy, from childhood superheroes and sword-and-sorcery epics in his teens to the computer-generated spectacles now on the big screen. The Greek myths ran through all of that like Theseus' thread through the labyrinth.

Though it was unclear whether the Swastika Killer had planned the blinding of the one-eyed Congo Man to mimic the myth of the Cyclops, it was certain that he had warmed to his mythological theme on reading Jantzen's coverage of the impaling. The proof was in the MO of his subsequent murders—first the skinning of Kurt Midas, and then what had most likely been done to the woman in this house.

Now, as Sergeant Winter and his sidekick climbed the stairs to the porch, the reporter called up his morning's e-mail and turned his laptop around for the Mounties to see. It read:

Subhumans deserve to die
You'll find Medusa here
My signature is the Swastika
Display it in your story

The address at the bottom of the e-mail matched the address of the gingerbread house.

"Let's see the jpeg," said Dane.

Cort punched a key. The image that appeared was a close-up of a terrified woman's gagged face. Just the flesh, not her hair, with the focus on her eyes. Gouged into the skin of her forehead and still dripping blood was a Nazi swastika.

"Recognize her?" Cort asked.

"No," said Dane.

"*The Times* did a piece on her in yesterday's edition. She strips at a downtown club called the Snake Pit."

"Ah. The extortion."

The reporter displayed the newspaper article on his laptop for the cops:

Snake Pit

A prominent Vancouver dentist, whose name hasn't been released, has filed an allegation of extortion with police, charging that he was enticed by a stripper in a notorious club on the edge of the financial district to join her for a private showing in the back room. A day later, the man was called at his office and ordered to pay $20,000 to a collector who would drop by the next afternoon. If he refused, he was told, pictures of him in a compromising sexual encounter would soon be seen on the Internet.

The dentist refused to give in to the threat, and the photos were posted on the World Wide Web. His wife received an anonymous e-mail directing her to the site, as did other patrons of the club who had fallen prey to similar "honey traps." …

The newspaper photo that ran with the story showed the outside of the Snake Pit. On the billboard beside the door, a naked stripper writhed erotically onstage with a boa constrictor wrapped around her body. The ecdysiast in the photo was the same woman whose terrified face was in the jpeg.

"While I was at the paper collecting this e-mail," said Cort, "news came in that a vivarium full of rattlesnakes was stolen overnight from a lab at UBC."

"A vivarium?" queried Jackie.

Dane introduced them.

"A terrarium. An aquarium. A glass case for animals."

"Who lives here?"

"The stripper," replied Cort. "I checked."

"That's enough for me." Taking care not to smudge any latent prints, Dane tried the door and found it unlocked.

He drew his gun.

Jackie drew hers, too.

"I'll take the point. You back me up," the sergeant said.

WHILE THE MOUNTIES entered the house, Cort stayed outside on the porch and returned to the sidebar he was writing when the cops had pulled up:

A Gorgon is a mythological female monster whose hair is a nest of writhing, venomous snakes. Medusa was turned into a Gorgon for bragging that she was

more beautiful than the goddess Athena. Suitors who
came looking for her turned to stone the moment
their eyes met hers. Medusa lived in a cavern
populated by the statues of men who were petrified
by gazing at her face.

Eventually, the Gorgon was killed by the heroic
Perseus. Using his shiny shield as a mirror so he
could find his way to the monster without looking
directly at her, he hacked off her serpent-haired head
and dropped it into a bag. Later, he withdrew the head
during a battle and defeated his enemies by turning
them all to stone....

THEY FOUND HER in the upstairs bedroom at the front of
the house. Like Perseus in the myth, the cops could see her
plainly without gazing at her face. The ceiling of the
stripper's bedroom was one big mirror, so that action on the
bed was reflected back like a porno movie. What was
playing off the mirror at the moment, however, was a horror
film.

The naked stripper was tied spread-eagled to a four-
poster bed. To stifle her screams, her killer had stuffed a
tennis ball tied with a gag into her mouth. Her hair, as in the
myth, was a nest of snakes, with each serpent cinched
tightly by tresses around its rattle. The rattlesnakes were
trying to break free of their leashes, writhing and slithering
and hissing and baring their venomous fangs. The face and
chest of the woman were punctured by so many bites that
she looked as if she'd died from an outbreak of smallpox.
Some snakes had snapped their bonds and made it to the
floor, and these cold-blooded squirmers—as angry as any
reptiles in *Jurassic Park*—now came charging at the cops.

Dane slammed the door.

"How did the killer do it?" Cort Jantzen asked after Dane had described the crime scene to him.

"Easy," the sergeant said. "If the snakes were stolen from the lab in a vivarium, all he had to do was pump or spray aerosol anesthetic into the glass cage. With the rattlers knocked out cold, he could easily noose their rattles with the stripper's hair. That's probably when he snapped the digital image in the jpeg. That terrified woman is waiting for the snakes to come out of their stupor. When they did, they repeatedly sank their venomous fangs into her."

"And the e-mail?" Cort asked.

"It, like the others, will be untraceable. Stolen computers, Internet cafes, blind servers, et cetera. Where there's a will, there's a way."

"I meant about the swastika. The killer wants it displayed in tomorrow's story. That presents a problem. If I fail to display it, he'll think I'm in cahoots with you and might stop writing. Also, that might enrage him enough to kill again. If I display it, there goes your hold-back evidence. You'll have copycats yearning for his Nazi fame."

"I've thought of that."

"So what do I do?"

"Help us smoke out the killer."

"By doing what?"

"I'll have to get the okay of Special X. But if I do, I want you to go ahead and display a swastika."

Dead Man's Hand

News of Hitler's suicide had reached the SS general a few days ago, on April 30. For more than a month, Streicher had been working out his exit strategy, for it was evident to him—with his knowledge of all the wonder weapons in the SS arsenal—that there would be no last-minute break-through in time to win the war.

Streicher held no illusions about his fate. As the engineer who had conceived the extermination camps, raising the throughput of the gas chambers and ovens to sixty thousand *Untermenschen* a day, he would be high on the list of SS officers to be hunted down by the Allies and hanged for war crimes.

Plus, there was Dora, the slave-labor camp with the sky-high kill rate. It wasn't for nothing that Himmler had rewarded Streicher with the rank of Obergruppenführer. That took the spilling of buckets of subhuman blood.

His only chance at surviving was to bargain. And of all those at the pinnacle of Nazi power—including Hitler and Himmler—Streicher was in the best position to negotiate. Last August, Himmler had named him special commissioner for secret weapons—weapons that had no counter-parts in the arsenals of the three Allied powers. And from the bunker in Berlin, Hitler had just conferred on him his last, highest, and most absurd title: plenipotentiary of the führer for jet aircraft.

Consequently, all wonder weapons in the Nazis' Pandora's box—both those in existence and those in development—were Streicher's to do with as he wanted.

And what he wanted was to save his own skin.

Word that the U.S. First Army was heading for Nordhausen and the V-2 factory in the Mittelwerk tunnels had prompted Streicher to play the first card in his poker hand on Easter Sunday, a month ago. Late in the day on April 1, he had ordered his staff to draw up a list of the top five hundred scientists at work on the V-2 rockets. Then—under the protection of a hundred Death's Head guards—he'd ordered them evacuated four hundred miles south to the Bavarian Alps, where rumor was that the SS had established a redoubt for the last stand of the Third Reich.

Von Braun, still burdened by the heavy cast resulting from his car accident in March, had been driven to Oberammergau. The other chosen rocketeers had traveled in style by train: a sleek, modern engine tugging twelve sleeping cars and a diner that served good food and fine wine. The so-called Vengeance Express.

Despite Hitler's scorched-earth directive—"If the war is lost, let the nation perish!"—Streicher had other plans. His intention was to hold von Braun and the rocket specialists hostage, offering them to the Americans or other Allies in exchange for both his life and his freedom. Killing them all was his backup plan.

But no sooner had Streicher issued his order than he was summoned to Berlin to report directly to the führer in his bunker. With Gestapo meat hooks waiting for those who turned against the Reich to save their own skins, it was probable that the general had doomed himself.

It had been a gamble to take his sons to Berlin, but he'd

hoped that Hitler would believe no traitor would bring his
children along.

The general had been lucky.

His bluff had paid off.

Hitler's sole concern had been *die Glocke*.

Streicher had returned to the V-2 factory early in the
morning on April 4 to find the sky above Nordhausen
aflame from RAF firebombing in the preceding two
nights. The Mittelwerk was safe, but not for long, since the
U.S. First Army was thundering in fast. Himmler's directive—that *Untermenschen* not be allowed to become
witnesses against the Black Corps—dictated that Streicher
herd nearly thirty thousand slaves in the Mittelwerk camps
into the Kohnstein tunnels and blow them and the rockets
up. That, however, would damage his bargaining chip.

Instead, the scheming general had played another card.
Following Himmler's own practise of moving inmates from
threatened camps to safer ones, he had ordered all usable
slaves to be evacuated to Bergen-Belsen by train or death
march. The forty-five hundred rocketeers not chosen for the
Vengeance Express to Oberammergau were to scatter to
villages nestled throughout the Harz Mountains.

The Americans would arrive to find the factory in
working order. The unassembled rockets in the tunnels
would whet their appetite for the men who knew how to
make the missiles blast off. And if they wanted the scientists, Streicher would be ready to deal.

And so the general had seen his sons off on one of the
trains that moved the living skeletons away to other
masters. Then he, too, had left the rocket works for the
Bavarian Alps.

OBERAMMERGAU WAS an Alpine village of peasant
woodcarvers and brightly painted houses. The spiked,

snowy peaks towered high above the SS compound where von Braun and his elite rocketeers were being held. The barbed wire surrounding them was meant to keep the scientists in, not the Americans out. Streicher, meanwhile, was snuggled in at the "Hotel Jesus," nicknamed for its Nazi innkeeper, who played the role of Christ in the village's historic passion play. It was there, on April 11, the day that Nordhausen and Dora fell to the U.S. Army, that SS-Obergruppenführer Ernst Streicher had last met SS-Sturmbannführer Wernher von Braun.

"Schnapps?" the general offered.

"Thank you," accepted the haughty aristocrat.

The SS engineer snapped his fingers at the hovering waiter while his other hand motioned the physicist to a chair by the fire. The chat took place in a cheery room off the lobby, with an SS guard outside the door. Heads of big-antlered trophies hung on the sooty walls, their glassy eyes staring down blankly at the men below. Von Braun's seat faced the machine pistol that Streicher had propped conspicuously against his chair.

"How do you find your accommodations, Major?"

"Secure," von Braun said dryly.

"And your team?"

"They're as comfortable as can be."

"And your broken arm?"

"It's causing me distress. I plan to have it looked at in the hospital in Sonthofen."

"Is your team in a position to recommence research?"

"Yes," said von Braun, mustering as much enthusiasm as he could to reply to Streicher's questions. It was obvious that he was still spooked from his arrest by the Gestapo early last year, after he had tried to retain some measure of control over the rockets he had created. Ostensibly, he'd been charged with treason—for sabotaging the V-2 project by concentrating more on space flight in the future than on crushing the Allies now—with the added allegation that he had a plane ready to fly him to London with blueprints for the Nazi missile that he planned to hand over to the enemy.

Treason was punishable by death, but von Braun was too valuable to be killed. Though spared, the rocketeer was intimidated. That's why Streicher was reinforcing the threat today: to make sure that the uppity baron's son knew that he would be as dead as the trophies on these walls if he stepped out of line.

Streicher played poker for keeps.

"Have you heard of my recent appointment to plenipotentiary for jet aircraft?"

"No," said von Braun. "Congratulations."

Was that a hint of sarcasm?

Streicher rose to his feet, a sign the meeting was over. Von Braun would go without schnapps. No "one for the road" was in the cards that day.

"I will be leaving here shortly for an indefinite period. Production of the Messerschmitt 262 jet fighter requires attention. In my absence, SS-Major Kummer will assume command. If you need anything to boost your work, ask him."

"Thank you, General."

"*Heil* Hitler!" Streicher's arm snapped up and out.

"*Heil* Hitler!" Von Braun returned the salute.

Satisfied, the general watched the major depart, convinced that von Braun had folded his last treasonous hand.

In fact, the rocketeer would soon be calling Streicher's bluff.

IT WASN'T THE MESSERSCHMITT 262 that had lured the general away. It was the top-secret Streicherstab—*Stab,* as

in "special projects staff"—hidden away behind the Skoda
Works, a huge industrial complex in the vassal Nazi state of
Czechoslovakia that manufactured munitions and guns for
Hitler's Reich. This was the black world of the Black
Corps, a research-and-development think-tank so secret
that it might as well not exist.

Had rockets and jets been the only wonder weapons in
Streicher's bargaining chip, the smartest way for him to play
his hand would have been to hole up in his Munich headquarters and wait for the Americans. By April 17, the GIs of the
6th Army Group were days or hours shy of Munich, so why
had one of the most hated butchers in the SS forsaken that
best bet to run east toward the dreaded Russians?

Why indeed!

A good poker player always knows the true value of his
hand. The V-2 and the jet plane were Nazi technologies the
Allies had earmarked for plunder, but Streicher wasn't sure
he had a big enough ante in either to get in the game. The
Me-262, the Arado Ar-234, and the Heinkel He-162 jet
fighters were in widespread use in these closing days of the
war. The Allies could seize their blueprints, along with the
engineers who had designed them, from any number of
factories around the Reich.

But with the V-2, Streicher held a stronger card. The
American army had captured at least a hundred rockets in
various stages of construction at the Mittelwerk, while the
general kept von Braun and his rocketeers at arm's length
in the Alps. The brains behind the missiles were the key to
their future. Yet even if Streicher did hand over the V-2
engineers, what would stop Eisenhower from reneging on
the deal and sending him to the gallows as a war criminal?

Nothing.

Nothing, that is, except a sweetener to the pot, like the
follow-on technology under development at the Streicherstab,

a second generation of wonder weapons that would relegate the V-2 to the slag heap of Hitler's arsenal. Wonder weapons like nuclear power plants for rockets and anti-aircraft laser rays to shoot down planes and—on top of all that fantastic technology—*die Glocke* and the *Flugkreisel*. If Streicher hoped to save his skin, he would need to offer the Pentagon something so spectacular that the U.S. Army would have no choice but to overlook the deaths of those six million Jews and all the slaves killed in the underground V-2 factory.

The first stop on Streicher's Czechoslovakian odyssey had been the twin hubs of Pilsen and Brno.

Death's Head country.

The scientists in the dual and separate think-tanks secreted away at the Skoda Works in Pilsen and Brno were the best brains that Germany had to offer. Selected for their brilliance as engineers and physicists, not for their allegiance to the Nazi Party, the Streicherstab scientists were culled from research institutes throughout the Reich. Geniuses submitted papers to a central office for scientific reports, which promptly passed them on to Streicher for assessment. The general then chose the most promising quantum-leap candidates for his special projects staff at the Skoda Works.

Two think-tanks.

Pilsen *and* Brno.

Rivals competing to create the same quantum-leap weapons.

The central administration building at the Pilsen Skoda Works had been almost completely destroyed a few weeks back in an air raid by American B-17s. The scientists were all away devising tests of *die Glocke* in the Wenceslas Mine, so the general had the secret facility at the central core of the industrial complex all to himself. It had taken him days to bundle up the blueprints generated by the

Pilsen special projects group and load them into his special evacuation *Kommando* plane. Everything else was torched to clean out the lab. Streicher and his six-engine, ultra-long-range Junkers 390 had then flown on to Brno—also abandoned by scientists off at the Wenceslas Mine—to retrieve the secret documents of that group too.

It was at Brno that he'd heard the news of Hitler's suicide.

With no time to lose, an impatient Streicher had mobilized dozing members of his *Kommando* with a burst from his machine gun. This part of the SS domain was neither German nor Czech. The local people spoke German and were terrified of the Slavs to the east, so they didn't know if they should stay or flee to the west. Columns of ragged Wehrmacht troops were in retreat, rolling toward Germany and the relative safety of surrender to American GIs. No one knew whether to fly the white rag of capitulation or the red, blue, and white Czech flag.

The war was all but over. Everybody knew it—except for Waffen-SS fanatics like those at Streicher's next destination. They had announced their intention to defend this stronghold of Hitler's Third Reich to the last bullet.

It was in Prague—while eradicating every reference to his double-barreled Pilsen and Brno special projects think-tanks—that Streicher had received an urgent phone call from a Gestapo spy in Oberammergau, informing him of the treason committed by SS-Sturmbannführer Wernher von Braun.

THE WAY STREICHER HEARD it was this.

On Easter Sunday, April 1—the same day *he* had ordered the evacuation of von Braun and his top five hundred rocketeers to Oberammergau—von Braun had caught a report that American tanks were only a few miles to the south of the Harz. Like Streicher, von Braun had feared that Hitler's scorched-earth policy would destroy his bargaining chip—the tons of irreplaceable V-2 documents and blueprints that were his life's work.

On that same day, it had become obvious to von Braun that he and the other evacuees on the Vengeance Express were to be held hostage in the Alps, so he had decided to create some leverage of his own. With the general on his way to Berlin to meet the führer and he himself on his way to Bavaria by car, he had instructed two of his closest confidants—Dieter Huzel, his chief of staff, and Bernhard Tessmann, the designer of the Peenemünde test site—to hide his treasure trove.

"Did they?" Streicher asked the Gestapo spy.

"So I'm told."

"When was that?"

"April 3."

The same day the general and his sons were in the *Führerbunker*.

"Where did they hide it?"

"No one knows. Our best guess would be deep in one of the abandoned mines in the Harz."

"How many documents are gone?"

"It took three Opel trucks for them to cart them off," replied the spy.

Von Braun had compounded his treason shortly after he met with the general at the Hotel Jesus. With Streicher gone from Oberammergau, the rocketeer had been able to coax SS-Major Kummer to disperse the captive scientists into various surrounding Alpine villages, supposedly to protect them from being wiped out by Allied air raids. Not only had that saved them from annihilation by Streicher's SS, but it had also freed von Braun to wangle his own deal.

"Where did he go?" the general asked.

"Oberjoch," said the spy. "He met his brother Magnus at a resort in the Austrian Tyrol. There, they joined Huzel and Tessmann, the pair who hid the treasure trove for him."

"What did they do?"

"Nothing," said the Gestapo spy. "They lazed about on the terrace of the hotel, sunning themselves, playing cards, and gazing up at the peaks of the Allgäu. Then, yesterday, they made contact with American troops and surrendered."

"How was he received?"

"Von Braun? They didn't kick him in the teeth. I'm told they fried him some eggs."

Good, thought Streicher.

That's what he wanted to hear.

The V-2 might be gone, but he had an ace up his sleeve.

When it came to hardware that took a quantum leap, the Pentagon was obviously willing to fold.

THE FIRST THING General Patton had done when he reached the Rhine was piss in the river to demonstrate his contempt for the Reich. As he landed on the other bank, he had scooped up a fistful of German dirt to emulate William the Conqueror. Then, with his trademark ivory-handled revolvers on both hips, the most pugnacious warrior of the Allied invaders had rumbled his Third Army across the Fatherland. Reports had him gunning down Nazis at a thousand a day.

And now, as Streicher headed for the last stop on his odyssey, he received word that Patton had disregarded agreements made with the exiled Czech government and the Soviet Union and plunged the Third Army deep into the zone designated for Soviet post-war occupation. A forward unit of Patton's army had entered Pilsen, and the people had come out to wave and cheer. As American troops burst into the headquarters of the Nazi commandant,

General Georg von Majewski had pulled a pistol from his desk and shot himself in front of his wife.

Pilsen was famous for its pilsner beer, but that's not what Patton was after. He had occupied the Skoda Works and was searching its interior. Had he somehow heard about the special projects group? And would he next be storming off to find *die Glocke*?

Die Glocke.

The final card in Streicher's dead man's hand.

Eureka

On his way to the Tudor building at 33rd and Heather, Dane made a side trip to the forensic lab. He had already received a report confirming his suspicion that the handwriting on the paper with Zinc Chandler's home address was the Ripper's. The documents section in Edmonton had also matched the order and direction of the cuts in the swastikas in the foreheads of the Cyclops and Golden Fleece victims. Still outstanding were the results of DNA tests on the blood from the splinter on the handle of the stake in the Congo Man's eye.

"You now qualify as a regular," said the petite East Indian woman in the lab's case receipt unit.

"By definition, a serial killer makes a regular out of the cop on his tail."

"What have you brought us this time? Another swastika?"

"No," said Dane. "You'll have to wait for that. First, someone has to wrangle a nest of poisonous snakes."

"You're kidding!"

The sergeant shook his head. "Meanwhile, have your gene jockeys done that blood test yet?"

The woman summoned Dermott Toop from the biology department. Dane knew the light-skinned African-Canadian from after-hours socializing at the detachment. Toop was dating Rachel Kidd, the sergeant from whom Dane had usurped the Golden Fleece Case.

"Hey, Dane."

"Hi, Derm. Whatcha got for me?"

The lab scientist handed the homicide cop his report.

"The blood on the splinter didn't come from the victim."

"So it came from whoever killed him?"

"Most likely," said Toop.

"Good. When we catch him, you can put the final nail in his coffin with his DNA."

"*Their* DNA," the biologist corrected.

"Huh?"

"The test returned a mixed DNA profile."

"*Two* killers jabbed themselves with the same splinter?"

"No, the splinter pierced just a single hand."

"Contamination spoiled the sample?"

"No, the sample's pure."

"I give up, Derm."

"Your killer's genetic makeup is composed of two different and distinct cell lines. I found contributions from *two* people in his DNA."

"What?"

"He's a blood chimera. An example of the genetic phenomenon I know as chimerism."

"What's a chimera?"

"In Greek mythology, it was a fire-breathing monster with a lion's head, a goat's body, and a serpent's tail. In genetics, a blood chimera is a single individual whose cells derive from two distinct embryos, and therefore, two different blood-cell populations circulate in his body. Most of us carry DNA that comes from the union of an egg from our mom and a sperm from our dad, but a blood chimera has a twin within. In other words, the DNA of two individuals is rolled into one."

"How does that happen?"

"A blood chimera begins as non-identical twins who share a blood supply in the womb. Stem cells pass from one embryo and settle in the bone marrow of the other, seeding a lasting source of blood. If one twin dies in gestation and is spontaneously aborted, the other twin—born as an only child—still has the blood of his dead sibling pumping around with his own."

"The kid has dual identities?"

"That's one way of putting it. Genetically, someone with chimeric blood is *two* people."

DANE KNOCKED on the door to the chief's office at Special X HQ and entered to find DeClercq and Chandler moving photos and reports around on the Strategy Wall. The sergeant had spent the early afternoon at Internal Affairs, embroiled in the paperwork and interviews needed to justify his involvement in the second death caused by a Mountie in the past four days.

"How'd it go?" Chandler asked.

"Piece of cake," said Dane. "The guy was in my home and armed to the teeth. I didn't have a weapon, so had to use his silencer-equipped gun against him. Hard to imagine a cleaner kill in self-defense than that, says IA."

"Whoever sent the killer won't see it that way."

"Let 'em try again," said Dane with mock bravado, his arms up in a kung fu stance.

"Be careful what you wish for," cautioned DeClercq. "This guy—whoever he was—was a professional hit man. You got lucky because he thought *you* were a piece of cake."

"No ID?" asked Dane.

"Not a peep. Fingerprints and photos of our mystery man got sent to every agency that might have controlled him. So far, no one has rushed in to claim the body."

"It's gotta be the Pentagon, the way that guy was armed. Corporal Hett suspects spooks in the black world," Dane said.

"Odds are she's right," Chandler replied. "Our military says the gadgets are American-made, and their contacts in the Pentagon deny knowledge of some of the stuff used by the mystery man."

"Hett says the U.S. military is so compartmentalized that no cog has an overview of what all the other cogs are doing."

DeClercq's Strategy Wall represented the opposite approach. It was designed to give the chief an overview of his squad's most convoluted cases. To that end, the collage of the three swastika killings had been joined by a cluster of photos and forensic reports concerning the high-tech hit man. That half of the corkboard wall was labeled "Swastika Killer." The other half, separated by a vertical line, was labeled "Stealth Killer." Pinned to it was the drag queen's camera-phone image of the suspicious farm truck, along with whatever was known about the young men who'd vanished from boy's town.

"Links?" prompted DeClercq.

"Three murders," Chandler offered, "signed with a Nazi swastika. A child killer, a corporate thief, an extortionist. Each murder committed to mimic a classic Greek myth."

"Maybe not," said Dane. "The myths didn't come into it until after *The Vancouver Times* took that angle."

"Why'd he pick up on the myths?"

"The killer sees himself as a hero. He's proud of the swastika. To him, he's killing subhumans. Adding those Greek myths into the mix plays to his Aryan psychology."

"The swastika," said DeClercq. "Let's focus on that. We agree that the hit man can't be the Swastika Killer? He was dead on Dane's floor when the Snake Pit stripper was still onstage."

Chandler and Winter nodded.

"Most likely, he was after the file in Dane's home, and was alerted to it by your VICAP query about U.S. cases with the same signature."

"Had to be," agreed Winter. "Nothing else I'm working on would pull in black world spooks."

"So why did this case?"

"Hett says the Pentagon's black world came into being to take advantage of the weapons expertise of Nazi scientists like Wernher von Braun."

"Those Second World War vets are octogenarians now. I can't see one of them as our Swastika Killer."

"The psycho must *know* something."

"What? A Nazi secret?"

"Could be, Chief."

"Why would the Pentagon suspect that from our Swastika Killer's MO? There was nothing in the query to VICAP except the swastika signature and the fact that the murder took place in B.C."

"A swastika link to B.C. must mean something. If the black world won't tell us, we'll have to ask the killer."

"How?"

"Smoke him out."

Dane approached the Strategy Wall and flicked the latest message Cort Jantzen had received:

Subhumans deserve to die
You'll find Medusa here
My signature is the Swastika
Display it in your story

"I have an idea that might kill two birds with one stone. Swastika wants his signature displayed in the paper. Refuse and he might blow his top. Accept and we might spawn a copycat. So why don't we give him a swastika that will make him wonder. We might buy precious time as he straightens us out."

"Elaborate," said DeClercq.

"The guy's a Nazi. He wants the world to see his mythic symbol. He wants this," said Dane, leap-frogging his finger—one, two, three—from each gouged forehead to the next:

"Instead, let's give him this."

Holding up a blank page in his notebook, the sergeant used a pen to draw a swastika:

"Well?" pressed Dane.

"It's a calculated risk," replied DeClercq.

"The other options are to ignore him or meet his demand. Those pose greater risks. But displaying the *wrong* swastika will make the killer wonder what went wrong. Was the photo mistakenly reversed? Does someone have dyslexia? Is it poor research? The image won't be what he actually carved into these foreheads, and he'll wonder why. Many a slip 'tween cup and lip can occur in the newspaper biz. Instead of going berserk, hopefully he'll contact us again."

The chief nodded.

"Arrange it," he said.

"CORPORAL HETT," said Jackie, cradling the receiver between shoulder and ear as she went on keyboarding at her desk in the main-floor squad room.

"It's Horton Grubb," the caller said. "From Pacific Rim Rendering."

The foreman, Jackie thought. "Yes, Mr. Grubb?"

"That farm truck you were looking for? It dropped off a bucket of product at noon today."

"Get a license plate?"

"It's not the plate in the photo. But it's the truck. Dented fender at the rear. Cracked tail light."

Jackie scribbled down the number on the new plate.

"Describe the driver."

"He's the blondest guy you ever did see. Around thirty. Looks like that space robot in *Blade Runner*."

"Rutger Hauer?"

"That his name? Him, only younger. Guy sure as hell don't look like no rancher to me."

"Get a name?"

"Dirk."

"Dirk what?"

"Straker. Strafer. Something like that. Thick German accent. Hard to tell."

"Know his ranch?"

"That I got. Phantom Valley. In the Cariboo. Up near Barkerville. You think he's running from the law? Seemed to go out of his way to let me know who he was."

"EUREKA!" Jackie announced. "I found it, Chief."

DeClercq, Chandler, and Winter turned from the Strategy Wall and faced Hett, framed in the doorway.

"Found what, Corporal?"

"A Cariboo gold mine, sir. We struck it rich."

"If history serves me correctly, you're about a century and a half too late."

"That farm truck," Jackie said, pointing to the photo on the Strategy Wall, "belongs to the Phantom Valley Ranch, up in the Cariboo. I phoned the commanding officer at the local detachment. It seems that the ranch is an old gold mine. The rancher currently living there is German, a loner and a recluse. Scads of No Trespassing signs on his road. Some kids snuck in a few months back and told their parents they'd seen a pigpen near the mine. The logs around the wallow were branded on the inside with swastikas."

As Jackie finished her report, Dane studied the Strategy Wall. The vertical line separating the Swastika Killer Case from the Stealth Killer Case had vanished in his mind the instant Hett linked the word "swastikas" to the boy's town investigation.

Chimerism?

Doing the switch? wondered Dane.

ON HEARING THAT his grandson planned to follow family tradition and join the Mounted Police, Papa had suggested that Dane arm himself for his chosen career by studying abnormal psychology and criminal law at UBC. "If you aim to rise quickly in the force," said Keith, "you'll need a talent that allows you to shine in the eyes of the brass. For me, it was my flying experience. You say you want to be a homicide crackerjack. Okay, then learn the inner workings of crazy criminal minds, and find out how to build a case that lawyers can't take apart."

To date, the sergeant had had only one case of separate identities. It was a brutal attack in which the suspect had literally torn his victim apart, pulling out organs with his bare hands. A casual laborer, he'd sworn he had no recollection whatsoever of the homicide. He'd thought his hands were sore from doing odd chores.

At trial, his lawyer had tried to get the jury to buy dissociative identity disorder—what used to be called multiple personality disorder, before it was relabeled in the *DSM-IV*, the *Diagnostic and Statistical Manual of Mental Disorders*—as his client's defense. The attorney had used the usual background evidence to establish the split. His client was the only child of a "hard father" who drank to excess and beat up both his wife and his son. The timid boy was terrified of his old man, a towering bully who wielded the threat of death over him. Caught in a mind-trap of never-ending risk, the boy had a fight-or-flight mechanism that never shut off, leaving him only one psychological escape: to *identify* with the aggressive personality of his dad. He would feel safe only if he became a bully himself. According to his lawyer, that set up the split in his personality. The boy both despised and admired his abuser. The good part of him hated his father. The bad part of him yearned to be a thug like him.

The kicker, however, was supplied by his mother.

She, too, was terrified of her husband, but she coped by sexualizing other relationships. Mom's the nurturer, so sexual abuse by Mom breaks the greatest trust bond of all. The confused lad's only psychological escape from *that* Freudian trauma was to hide away the "bad part" of himself as a separate dissociated identity that he no longer knew existed.

And that, his lawyer told the jury, was how the Trog spawned.

Exactly what the Trog was, Dane had little idea. But according to the lawyer, it was the Trog who tore the victim apart with his bare hands. His defense was that the Trog was insane, and since that split-off identity was not recognized by his client, who was legally sane, his client should be acquitted.

The lawyer made it sound as if dissociated identities are separate people, instead of distinct personality states that periodically seize control of the consciousness and behavior of a person with a fractured mind. Arguments like that are largely why the concept of multiple personality disorder is now obsolete.

Dane never did find out whether that jury had bought the "Trog-dunit" defense. Before the verdict could be delivered, the accused had smashed his skull against the wall of his cell and died from a brain hemorrhage.

The classic case of dissociative identity disorder, of course, was Robert Louis Stevenson's *Dr. Jekyll and Mr. Hyde*. The split between good and evil was what dissociated the doctor from the psycho in Stevenson's novel. A similar psychological rift causes most genuine cases of dual personality. A traumatized child copes with overwhelming abuse by not experiencing it. His brain uses the mental mechanism of dissociation to seal off fearful parts of his personality. That evil identity gets locked away from his consciousness like a sleeper cell within his fractured mind. Eliminated and forgotten, the Hyde-like demon lurks unknown for years, or even decades, until some sort of stress forces the dissociated identity to seize control of the imperiled consciousness.

The shift from Jekyll to Hyde and back again was known as "doing the switch." But Dane always thought of it as "*throwing* the switch." In his mind, he pictured the transformation being like a Broadway play performed on a well-lit stage. Soon you know all the characters, and everything appears to be integrated: identity, memory, consciousness, and perception of the environment. Then suddenly the stage goes black and a spotlight glares, and standing there is a terrifying character you've never seen before. The other characters have vanished into the blackness, as if they were never onstage. Then—*flash!*—the lights come on again and the bad guy is gone, and none of the returning characters have any knowledge of having relinquished the stage.

Now, as Dane studied the two case collages on the Strategy Wall, the lawyer in him began to suspect that something psychologically different was going on here.

What if the Nazi monsters they were hunting were like the chimera of Greek myth?

Could it be that the Swastika Killer and the Stealth Killer were not two separate people at all? Could they be a pair of mentally conjoined Siamese twins—two killers rolled into one—mistakenly separated on the Strategy Wall by an illusory dividing line?

Hyde and Hyde?

Die Glocke

Hitler was dead, but still the war raged on.

Having eradicated every trace of his Pilsen and Brno special projects group from records in the Prague offices of the Skoda Works, Ernst Streicher had commanded the pilot of the transport plane to fly northeast to the Sudeten Mountains. There, where Germany, Poland, and Czechoslovakia joined borders, the diehard city of Breslau had held out for over two months against the encircling Red Army. In the dead of winter, with the Oder River frozen over, the city's besieged women and children had tried to escape the vise-like grip of the Soviets, but most were either gunned down as they ran or left to freeze in the sub-zero temperatures. "Every house a fortress!" was now the battlecry. Artillery explosions blew buildings apart, and the fighting in the streets was as ferocious as that at Stalingrad. Five Volkssturm regiments of elderly men and Hitler Youths—the only males left in the city—battled above ground with anti-tank grenades or struggled hand-to-hand with Russians down in the stinking sewers.

The death throes of the Third Reich.

The next-to-last gasp.

Gazing out from the cockpit of the Junkers as they descended into Opeln, Streicher could see the fires of

Breslau in the near distance, then—*bump, bump, bump*—they were on the ground. Opeln was a special evacuation staging area. Heavy-duty cargo planes with the ability to fly thousands of tons of equipment, documents, and personnel to fugitive havens anywhere in the world were being loaded with loot from around the crumbling Reich. The runway was abuzz with activity as the SS general deplaned into drizzling rain. His six-engine Junkers was the largest "truck" in sight—*Kommando* slang for vehicles from the winged motor pool. The four-engine 290s working the escape route up to Norway—which was still under Nazi control—were painted with yellow-and-blue markings to disguise them as aircraft from neutral Sweden. The 290s flying the southern route to Nazi-sympathetic Spain wore green camouflage.

Idling alongside the runway were trucks of the terrestrial kind. No sooner had the cargo bay of the Junkers opened than they drove out onto the landing strip and began to load the belly of the plane with crates of gold and art treasures plundered from the houses of Jews.

Under his coat, Streicher carried a box of blueprints and lab notes from the think-tank at Brno. A truck stood waiting for him in the rain. Ducking out of the drizzle, the SS engineer climbed into the passenger's seat.

"Where to, General?" inquired the driver.

"The castle," Streicher directed.

FROM EAST AND WEST, from north and south, this part of Europe had always been the crossroads for conquerors. Through here had passed the Teutonic knights on their way to challenge the Muslims in the Holy Land. In retaliation, the Ottoman Turks had battled up through the Transylvanian realm of Vlad the Impaler and crossed the Danube at Vienna. To fortify their eastern flank and shield western

Europe from invasion, knights of the Middle Ages had filled these mountains with stone castles on virtually unassailable outcroppings. The central feature of every German citadel is its *Bergfried,* a tall watchtower adapted from Roman forts. The silhouette of each castle is as individual as a fingerprint.

The castle that now towered above the truck as it snaked its way through the teeming rain, its tires clinging precariously to the medieval road, was the headquarters the general had used to oversee various tests in the Wenceslas Mine. The outline of the fortress was the same one that Fritz had tattooed over his heart to look like a family crest.

Just in case …

"Wait here," the general ordered as the driver stopped in front of the dripping gatehouse.

Streicher crossed to the front door and made for the Knight's Hall, where he'd spent many a stormy evening, with schnapps in hand and Wagner on the phonograph, pacing about like Lohengrin, the Aryan knight of the Holy Grail. Now, as twilight grayed the sky beyond the leaded-glass windows, he approached the long mantelpiece that spanned the far wall. With a pocketknife, he opened the hidey-hole to the left of the fireplace, just where the Iron Cross was mounted in the tattoo of the Knight's Hall over the heart of his younger son, Hans.

Just in case …

Removing the blueprints and lab notes from the box beneath his coat, Streicher stashed them in the hole and resealed it. His exit strategy was fraught with danger, so for his own sake, he thought it wise to keep an ace up his sleeve. If the Americans double-crossed him and he got killed, his sons would figure out the puzzle. And though neither of them knew about or had been to Schloss Werwolf, they would be able to fit their tattoos together to identify this hiding place. And once they'd retrieved the blueprints for what would undoubtedly be the most awesome weapon the world had ever seen, they would be able to exchange them with the Pentagon for a post-war life of wealth and freedom.

Mission accomplished, the general turned his back on the Knight's Hall in Castle Werewolf and strode out through the gatehouse to the waiting truck.

"To the mine?" the driver asked.

Streicher nodded.

Down one mountain and up another, the Opel truck labored under a constant shifting of gears. Rain lashed the windshield in such a torrent that they were in endless peril of driving off the road and plunging down into the valley below.

"Stop!" Streicher ordered at the crest of the summit.

The truck braked.

"Hurl this over the edge," Streicher commanded, passing the empty document box to the driver. "Make sure you toss it out far enough that it will never be found."

Rain slanted into the truck as the driver swung open the door and jumped down into the mud. The wail of the wind drowned out all sounds as he approached the ledge. As he threw the box into the air above the cliff face, his body absorbed the dual sucker punches of a bullet to the back of his head and a flat-footed stomp against his spine to propel him over the precipice.

A secret is guaranteed only if one person alone knows it.

That person climbed back into the truck and drove it the rest of the way to the mine.

LIGHTNING FORKED and thunder grumbled as the general splashed the truck through pockmark puddles along the road southeast of Waldenburg, a coal-mining town close to the Czech frontier. The single-lane route followed the tracks of an old prewar railway, built to link the region's resources to the outside world. As he wound his way up into a valley flanked by tall trees, Streicher passed through three checkpoints of strict SS security. Cleared of suspicion, he curved around a bend, and there the valley opened into a camouflaged marshaling yard. Turf-topped wooden planks called sleepers roofed six lines of track where the railhead met the shaft of the Sudeten coal mine. A derelict building with high arched windows loomed next to the pit, while across the valley stood a red brick house that dated back to the nineteenth century, just like the workings below ground. Spotted from the air, this operation would look like it always had, but down here you could see the concrete bunkers and blockhouses that Streicher's slaves had built into the thick hillside.

The tunnels in the Sudeten Mountains—this one especially—were the core of Streicher's high-tech kingdom, the places where the best brains in Germany had been testing the next generation of weaponry, including *die Glocke*.

But now those brains were packing up.

A convoy of Opel trucks occupied the railhead yard. Positioning his vehicle so that it could be loaded too, the SS general stepped out into the rain and marched directly into the yawning mouth of the Wenceslas Mine.

Having developed the cruise missile—the V-1—and the ballistic missile—the V-2—the Nazis had pressed on with other futuristic gizmos in Streicher's eastern realm. Unbelievable gadgets like an atomic bomb and a supergun called the "Busy Lizzie," which could hit most cities in Britain from gun placements in France, as well as sound waves, air vortices, jets of compressed air, and a death ray (a focused beam of light called a laser) to bring down Allied aircraft. Another plan involved turning the upper atmosphere into a high-voltage conductor that would fry the enemies' Lancaster, Halifax, Flying Fortress, and Liberator bombers before they reached their targets. Preposterous weapons that no rational mind would accept, but the scientists of the Streicherstab had conceived them anyway.

Along with *die Glocke*.

The Bell.

Blueprints for those wonder weapons had been sent from the think-tanks in Pilsen and Brno to an underground weapons plant—code-named "Giant"—clawed into the core of a Sudeten mountain by Gross-Rosen slaves. The Bell, under development in the Wenceslas Mine, was to have been connected to Giant by a six-mile tunnel, but time had run out on the Third Reich before Streicher's complex could be completed.

Now, as the last of the crates containing the dismantled Bell were carted up to the convoy of trucks from the experimental chamber deep in the mine, the general descended against the scientific exodus for one last look at his handiwork. If his exit strategy was to succeed, no trace could be left behind.

The chamber was hundreds of yards below ground, and the deeper the general sank, the colder it became. Thick cabling had once fed power into the mine, but now, with that rolled up and hauled away, Streicher had to rely on the flashlight in his hand. Entering the chamber, he swept the beam around. All the light illuminated was naked rock.

"Good," he told himself.

Streicher's imagination recalled what had been. The dome of the vault was covered with ceramic tiles overlaid with thick rubber matting. At the center of the chamber had sat *die Glocke,* a bell-shaped, metal gadget fashioned around a pair of concentric cylinders that spun in opposite directions. A tall, yard-high, Thermos-like flask encased in lead had jutted up like a phonograph spindle at the core of the bull's-eye.

A violet-colored metallic liquid something like mercury was stored in the flask. Each R&D test lasted a minute and involved covering the Bell with a ceramic shield and whirling those cylinders until the device emitted an eerie pale blue glow. During the tests, any electrical equipment within a radius of five hundred feet short-circuited, and five scientists exposed to electromagnetic side effects from the original test had died excruciating deaths.

So unhealthy was exposure to the Bell that after each test, Gross-Rosen slaves spent an hour hosing down the chamber with brine. The rubber matting on the ceiling had to be replaced after only two or three tests, and the entire setup—except for *die Glocke* itself—was dismantled and reinsulated after ten whirls.

In November 1944, the tests had expanded to include experiments on plants, animals, and human tissue. Initially, everything placed within the electromagnetic field of the Bell had been destroyed. The plants turned white as their chlorophyll decomposed, eventually disintegrating into a puddle as thick as axle grease. Animal blood gelled and distilled into separate components, while a crystalline substance hardened within the human tissue samples to decay them from the inside with no abhorrent smell. By January 1945, Streicher was ready to test the Bell on human guinea pigs, and luckily for him, the Red Army was about to liberate Auschwitz, necessitating a Nazi retreat to Gross-Rosen.

OF ALL THE MONSTERS spawned by Hitler's Third Reich, none surpassed Dr. Josef Mengele. Calling Eva Braun the Angel of Death was an SS joke. The infamous doctor at the most horrific of the Nazi extermination camps was the *real* Todesengel.

As the trains pulled into Auschwitz from mid-1943 on, they began disgorging bewildered wretches who had endured a day's-long ride with no food, no water, no toilets, and no fresh air, in cattle cars that packed them in a hundred to a crate. The doomed were met by cudgel blows from shouting guards and the snapping fangs of snarling German shepherds that herded them up a ramp to the SS officer waiting serenely above.

"Raus! Raus!"

Out! Out!

As the tide of human misery stumbled up from the trains, special guards searched the prisoners to cull the matching pairs.

"Zwillinge! Zwillinge!" they bellowed.

Twins! Twins!

Seemingly oblivious to the stench of burning flesh that belched from the smokestacks of the crematoria, the officer at the top of the ramp whistled an operatic tune. How surreal he looked in the midst of this devastating scene, with his polished black boots planted slightly apart, his Death's Head cap worn to one side of his perfectly styled dark hair, and his handsome face that made women swoon. His signature was the white cotton gloves on his hands. The thumb of one glove rested on his pistol belt. The fingers of the other held a riding crop that flicked left or right as each new arrival passed.

Links oder rechts.

Left or right.

Death to the left. Life to the right.

With each snap of the riding crop, the Angel of Death chose who went directly to the gas chambers and who went to the barracks.

That was Streicher's first view of Mengele on his visit to Auschwitz to engineer a greater throughput for the camp's killing machine.

The general liked what he saw.

For what he saw in Mengele was a duplicate of himself.

There was so much about Mengele for the general to admire. The doctor had studied eugenics at the University of Munich so that he could unlock the source of human imperfections and develop his "theory of unworthy life." He had earned his Ph.D. for his enlightening thesis, titled "Racial Morphology Research on the Lower Jaw Section of Four Racial Groups." After receiving his medical degree at the University of Leipzig, he was awarded the position of research assistant in the Third Reich Institute for Hereditary, Biological, and Racial Purity at the University of Frankfurt. In 1938, at age twenty-seven, the doctor had joined the SS as a genetic purifier, and he had welcomed the establishment of concentration camps during the war because they provided the opportunity to experiment *in vivo* on subhuman beings. In May 1943, Mengele arrived at Auschwitz with a mandate "to unlock the secrets of genetic engineering and devise methods for eradicating inferior gene strands from the human population as a means for creating a Germanic super-race."

Links oder rechts.

Left or right.

The 70 to 90 percent directed left were killed.

The 10 to 30 percent directed right were spared.

So fast had Mengele overwhelmed the Auschwitz ovens that it soon became necessary for the doctor to have trenches dug and filled with gasoline. As trucks backed up and dumped their loads of dead and living into these monstrous pits, they were set alight. Mengele oversaw the makeshift incineration, while guards roamed the rims of hell with long poles, ready to shove back the screaming *Untermenschen* who tried to claw their way out.

And then there were "Mengele's children."

Test subjects for *die Glocke*.

The twins, along with other "exotic specimens" like dwarfs and cripples, were kept in a special barracks known as "the Zoo." One of each pair would serve as a control subject while the other, with the identical genetic fingerprint, was used for Mengele's experiments. In this way, twins were the ideal double subjects for the doctor's research into the secrets of human genetics.

Streicher had marveled at the intellectual breadth of the Auschwitz experimenter's scientific methods. To see if eye color could be altered to more Aryan shades, he injected dye into the eyeballs of the guinea-pig twin. Once it died or went blind, he harvested the eyes and pinned them to his office wall, like a collector of bugs. To study the dangers inherent in transfusions, he injected the blood from one twin into an unrelated twin with a different blood type, and then reversed the procedure with the remaining odd two. He injected twins with infectious agents to see how they would compare with their healthy siblings. By castrating boys without anesthetic and sterilizing girls with X-ray machines, by shocking both sexes with high voltages to test their endurance, and by cutting off limbs and removing organs to see what troubles ensued, the doctor advanced Nazi science to its depraved outer limits.

Youngsters were locked away in isolation cages, then bombarded with harsh stimuli and their reactions observed. After those tests were finished, Mengele himself escorted the youngest to the gas chambers in a game that was called On the Way to the Chimney. With the older twins, he would snuff the healthy control subject with a shot of phenol, then perform double autopsies—unless science was better served by vivisection. In one stroke of brilliance that impressed the general no end, the doctor had created an artificial Siamese twin by sewing the veins of the pair together.

At Auschwitz, Mengele had whittled three thousand individual twins down to just over two hundred survivors. After he fled to Gross-Rosen, where the Angel of Death's medical expertise was put to work by Streicher in the Wenceslas Mine, the doctor went through a lot more twins. Now, Mengele's tests, combined with the modifications of the Bell, had reduced the electromagnetic damage done to the twins to around 3 percent, and then mainly muscle spasms, loss of memory and balance, troubled sleep, and a weird, permanent metallic taste in the mouth.

Die Glocke was ready.

STREICHER EXITED the mouth of the mine to find the truck convoy in final preparations. All sixty-two scientists from the think-tanks in Pilsen and Brno were climbing into three Opel trucks, pleased to be escaping the horrors in the oppressive chamber below, and to be getting out before the Russians could get their vengeful hands on them. In other vehicles, the crates containing the Bell were being cinched down for the bumpy exodus through the mountain passes. The evacuation involved two kinds of troops: logistics personnel to accomplish it, and armed Sonderkommandos for protection.

Still, the rain poured down.

Rat-a-tat-tat, like a machine-gun spray.

At the far end of the valley stood a power station capable of burning a thousand tons of coal a day. The experiments with the Bell had required massive amounts of electricity, which is why Streicher had chosen this place to be the crown jewel in his high-tech kingdom.

Now, as the troops began to flood the mineshaft with pumps and hoses, the general sloshed along a prefab roadway that took him past the station and through a thicket of woods to a clearing beyond. There, like Stonehenge, rose a concrete structure about a hundred feet wide and thirty-two feet high. It, too, had thick columns and horizontal beams, and it appeared to be waiting for Druid priests and their human sacrifices.

A closer look, however, revealed a more modern purpose. A rut in the ground fed cabling to the camouflaged pagan henge. The floor within the circle had been excavated down several feet and covered with ceramic tiles like those in the mine chamber. And super-strong steel hooks, designed to restrain something with extraordinary thrust, were fused to the tops of the upright columns.

A test rig for Hitler's ultimate wonder weapon.

A rig that Streicher would leave as it was in case the Pentagon needed convincing.

NOT ALL THE TRUCKS would make it out of the mountains with their cargoes intact. Along the way, as the Opels ground their gears up and down the stormy, dark grades, the three vehicles with the sixty-two scientists in back—the only ones other than Streicher who understood the quantum mechanics behind the Bell—peeled away from the convoy and bounced off into a forest where a line of executioners were awaiting them.

The Einsatzgruppen—four mobile killing squads that had preyed upon Russia—had refined these exterminations to an art. The trench had already been dug to the proper size—thirty-odd feet long, six and a half feet wide, three and a half feet deep—so no time was wasted. The first thirty-one scientists were marched to the edge of the ditch and dispatched in quick succession, four seconds apart, by bullets to the back of their skulls. The second thirty-one tumbled in on top of the corpses, then the mass grave was filled to a mound a foot and a half high.

By this time next year, the decaying bodies would level the grave into flat ground.

And buried with the scientists was the secret behind the mechanics of the Bell and its follow-on weapon.

HITLER'S GOLD and Hitler's loot and Hitler's time machine were safely stored on board as the six-engine Junkers 390 roared along the runway and lifted off into the rainy night. The long-range transport could fly with a heavy payload for thirty-two hours. Two men sat in the austere living quarters in the rear of the plane, and they spoke through microphones in the muzzles of their oxygen masks. One passenger was Streicher. The other wore the uniform of a Waffen-SS soldier and, from the bandage covering most of his face, might have been wounded on the crumbling eastern front while heroically defending the Fatherland.

"Where are we going?" the masked fugitive asked as he eased the bogus bandage off his uninjured skin.

"Paraguay."

"A long flight."

"That it is," said Streicher.

"A long way away from here is good," said Dr. Josef Mengele.

Human Soap

Stealing the Mounties' bison head had been easy enough. Earlier this week, *The Vancouver Times* had done a feature article on the RCMP's Wild West traditions as a prelude to Special X's upcoming regimental dinner. Traditionally, the function was held at Minnekhada Lodge, a retreat nestled between the heights of Burke Mountain and the marsh flats of the Pitt River, a few miles up the Fraser River Valley. As always, the red brick fireplace of the lodge was to be ornamented with the huge stuffed bison head from the stairwell at Special X. Watched over by this shaggy mascot, the hearth would burnish the rustic hall with its copper glow. Filling the vaulted loft, the wail of bagpipes would herald a procession of commanding officers through the ranks of red serge to the head table.

While scanning the *Times* to select his next subhuman victim, Swastika had chanced across the photo of the bison head. A few casual phone calls purportedly on behalf of the organizers of the dinner and he knew when the movers planned to drive the mascot to the lodge. As luck would have it, those movers had stopped for coffee along the way, and that's when Swastika heisted the moth-eaten trophy off the bed of their truck.

Now, with the bison head firmly in his lap and a box of tools open at his feet, the psycho sat on a chair in the map room of the mocked-up *Führerbunker* and used a chisel to pry off the mounting plate behind the neck. Swapping that implement for a trowel and a knife, he then scooped out the sawdust that stuffed the bison head until he had a hollow large enough to accommodate the skull and shoulders of a man.

The black walnut case holding the SS dagger still sat in the center of the map table. The silver plaque set into the lid could no longer be seen, for the box had been draped with a circular doily of tanned human skin tattooed with what seemed to be the battlements of a medieval castle. Neatly arranged along one side of the case were the clippings from *The Vancouver Times* about the three Swastika killings: the Cyclops, the Golden Fleece, and Medusa. Scrabbled together across the front surface of the table was the word *"Untermenschen."* On the other side of the dagger case was the layout of a garden maze at UBC and a volume from the department of classical studies. This was open at the Greek myth about Theseus' hunt for the Minotaur in the labyrinth on Crete.

The bison head was prepared.

The psycho set the hollowed-out Special X mascot face up on the floor.

The head required a victim to fill the hole.

Swastika left the bunker to venture out into the night.

"Jantzen."

"Cort, it's Dane Winter."

"You get a copy of the story? Is the swastika okay?"

"It's fine."

"We'll go to press shortly. The paper will hit the streets in the wee hours."

"Good, but we might not need it."

"Why?" asked the reporter, his grip tightening on his cellphone as he sensed another story.

"I'm making good on my promise. We might be taking the psycho down tonight. Meet me in the parking lot beside Special X within half an hour. Clear your schedule until noon tomorrow. I might give you the scoop of the year."

FROM THE MOMENT he walked into the lot at Special X, the reporter knew something major was in the works. The Mounties were ramping up for an emergency response team assault, and there were enough gunmen in gear to launch a guerrilla war. The strike-team members were outfitted in black. Each wore a rolled-up cap that could be tugged down into a balaclava for camouflage. The uniform was a combat jacket over a turtleneck and combat pants with cargo pockets tucked into heavy-duty army boots. The tactical vest over top was known as "the beast." The words "POLICE RCMP" in bold white letters were hidden behind a pull-down flap, waiting for exposure. Velcro pouches could be filled with as much firepower as tactics required, and these cops were slapping on tear gas, pepper spray, extra ammo clips, and stun grenades. Holstered on each hip was a SIG/Sauer P226 pistol; that was backup for the Heckler & Koch MP5 submachine gun with the pressure-activated bulb that would help them aim in the dark.

As he weaved through the "mount-up" in the tree-lined parking lot, Cort deduced, from the pair he saw calling the shots, that this was no urban takedown. Only a country that still has an untamed frontier could spawn these hunters.

A full-blooded Plains Cree from Duck Lake, Saskatchewan, Inspector Bob "Ghost Keeper" George had as a boy ventured out alone on a spirit quest to survive by his wits in the threatening northern woods, and there he had found the supernatural soul that would guide him through life and beyond.

The son of a Yukon trapper who had grown up in the North, Sergeant Ed "Mad Dog" Rabidowski could take the eye out of a squirrel with a .22 at a hundred yards before he was six.

Those who followed the exploits of Special X understood from the standoff at Totem Lake and the storming of Ebbtide Island that these two enemies turned unlikely friends were locked in a modern contest of frontier one-upmanship. That both had been called in to mount up for whatever was going down tonight boded well for another Jantzen scoop in *The Vancouver Times*.

"What's up?" Cort asked as soon as he located Dane and Jackie by their car.

"I'll tell you on the way."

"OFF THE RECORD," Dane said, "until we have proof."

"Off the record," Cort confirmed.

With Jackie at the wheel, they were speeding south along Cambie Street en route to the airport.

"I suspect that we're going after a killer who was sexually abused as a boy, in circumstances somehow linked to Nazism. Because of that abuse, the boy split off an evil Nazi identity from his consciousness to form a secret repository for all the shame, guilt, anger, and homicidal impulses generated by the sexual trauma. That Nazi Mr. Hyde is the Stealth Killer who's preying on runaway teens in boy's town. He kills them in a revenge fantasy that parallels the abuse. The murders take place at a ranch in the Cariboo that has a pigpen with swastika brands along the inside of its fencing."

"That's where we're going?" Cort asked, excitement in his voice.

"Yes," said Jackie.

"The Stealth Killer," Dane continued, "has been at work since the early 1990s. Judging by his choice of victims and the fact that the bodies are never found, we can assume he doesn't want notoriety or attention from the police. Instead, he gets a thrill from something he believes we don't know about."

"But we do?"

"I can hazard a guess. I think he's a Cariboo rancher who feeds his victims to hogs. Except for the guts, which he trucks down to Vancouver and drops off at a local rendering plant to have reduced into human soap."

"Holy shit! Why?"

"Because it's a very Nazi thing to do. In multiple personality—or dissociative identity—disorder, the psycho creates a *new* identity for his Mr. Hyde, and he can give it whatever background seems to fit. In the case of our Stealth Killer, I'll bet he cooked up a family history linked to the Third Reich."

"The truck," said Jackie, "is how we located the ranch. A witness saw it snare a runaway youth near boy's town. Earlier today, it dropped off a load of guts at the rendering plant."

"Human guts?"

"No way to tell. To control obnoxious smells, the drop-off zone is hermetically sealed. Whatever got dumped went into a hopper system that hides it from sight."

"You got the license?"

"Uh-huh."

"And traced the registration to the ranch?"

"Where we hope the killer is heading now," said Dane. "We have an alert out for the farm truck, but he might be using other wheels."

"It's possible he *wants* to be caught," Jackie said. "He went out of his way at the rendering plant to reveal who he is. Perhaps his dissociation is reintegrating."

"You mean Hyde is becoming Jekyll?"

"Not exactly," said Dane. "I think the evil Nazi is psychologically bleeding into the good Nazi."

"The *good* Nazi?" Cort queried. "Isn't that an oxymoron? What sort of fucked-up mind spawned that?"

"You did," Dane replied.

JUST AS HENRY JEKYLL'S HOUSE had front and back entrances—a front door so the respectable doctor could come and go as a productive member of polite society and a back door so his alter ego, the depraved Edward Hyde, could sneak in and out for debauchery and brutal murder—Fritz Streicher's Point Grey home was a genteel mansion with Hitler's bunker recreated in its cellar.

On his release from a Nazi prisoner-of-war camp run by the U.S. Army after the fall of the Third Reich, Fritz Streicher—who'd had no ID on him when he was captured in the woods north of Dora-Mittelbau—had made his way back to where he and Hans had stashed their civilian clothes and false papers. At the time of his capture, Fritz was dressed in the winter uniform of the Hitler Youth.

Ironically, the skills that teenager had acquired in the Hitler Youth had helped him survive the austerity of Allied occupation, when the Fatherland had sunk into a dismal and impoverished state. Then one day, out of the blue, Ernst Streicher's elder son had been accosted on the street of a Bavarian town by a man from Zurich who said he'd been sent to find Fritz by the phoenix of the Fourth Reich.

"How do you know who I am?"

"I know the name on the papers your father gave you the last time you saw him."

"Is my father alive?"

"Yes," replied the stranger.

"Where is he?"

"Far away in a foreign country. One day, he'll send for you. In the meantime, come with me."

Years of schooling had followed in neutral Switzerland, where the young man had majored in modern German history. Once he'd graduated and was securely established in his new Swiss identity, Fritz—not the name he used— had flown to Vancouver, then a little-known city lost in the forests of nowhere, to get a Ph.D. from the department of history at UBC.

"I have some bad news," said the next stranger, who had met him at the airport.

"My father?"

The man nodded. "I regret to inform you that he died several years ago in the cause of the Fourth Reich. It was the general's hope that one day you would carry on the struggle."

"*Mein Kampf,*" Fritz said absently, still absorbing the shock.

The Nazi gripped his shoulder. "The torch passes to you."

From the airport, Fritz was chauffeured to what was then a brand-new house. Here, he resumed his Swiss identity in a style suitable for the son of a rich Zurich lawyer. As far as authorities knew—and the curtain still held today—this estate on the slope of University Hill, looking over the whitecaps of English Bay and across to the snowy peaks of the North Shore Mountains, was part of the real-estate portfolio of a Swiss corporate law firm. Bought back when land was as plentiful as the trees on the West Coast, the Fourth Reich's underground railroad station was now worth ten million bucks.

And so it was that young Fritz Streicher had gained in reputation, accepting an academic position at UBC and working his way up through the department of history until he was a full professor and *the* authority on modern

Germany. In and out of the front door of this mansion on the bluff, Fritz had maintained his Jekyll face, and all the while he'd lived a secret life down in Hitler's bunker, where post-war Nazi fugitives had gathered periodically to plot a return to the glory days and pick up some gold.

The location was ideal.

This was about as distant as Hitler's henchmen could get from the post-war Nazi hunters.

And Fritz was the perfect stationmaster.

Too young to have taken part in the Nazi atrocities, he was below suspicion.

The back entrance into the mansion was through this coach house halfway up the drive. Just as Hyde had come and gone unseen by those who used the front entrance to Jekyll's house, so had the fugitives of the Third Reich come and gone from Fritz's mansion. The coach house hid a tunnel that had been burrowed into the slope. Wheel a limo with darkened windows up the drive and into the coach house's garage, and you would end up in the Fourth Reich's bunker.

Tonight, it wasn't a limo that wheeled up the drive. It was a dusty farm truck with a broken tail light, the rear bed laden with branches cut from pruned trees. The sky had clouded over and it was beginning to rain, a light drizzle that splattered the windshield that masked the Aryan's face. As the truck approached the garage under the upper-floor living quarters of the coach house, the psycho punched the button of the remote control to open the mouth that swallowed him like Jonah into the whale.

Seconds later, the door closed behind the truck.

THE SAME SWISS corporate law firm that owned this mansion also owned the Phantom Valley Ranch in the Cariboo. That purchase, however, had predated this one. Title to the ranch went back to 1945, and since then, it had been held by a string of dummy companies scattered around Europe. There was no way to link the two properties together, and in all the years that Fritz Streicher had lived here on University Hill, he had rarely journeyed up to the Cariboo.

Better safe than sorry.

But of Fritz Streicher's two Swiss-held estates—this city mansion and that Cariboo ranch—the latter better suited the Aryan's psychology, because he'd grown up on an East German pig farm. So for more than a decade, ever since he'd come to B.C. after the fall of the Berlin Wall and the reunification of the Fatherland, the psycho had spent most of his time at the old Phantom Valley ranch house, guarding the entrance to the mine.

To amuse himself, and because German was his mother tongue, he had begun experimenting with the Streicherstab blueprints that he had recovered from Castle Werewolf in the Sudeten Mountains. What the Aryan had discovered about himself as he tinkered around in the Phantom Valley mine was that, like Nikola Tesla, he was blessed with an intuitive grasp of electromagnetic quantum mechanics. Only when he had learned to tap into the zero-point energy in the Skunk Mountain lab did he comprehend the full space-age potential of the Streicherstab treasure trove.

By luck and family background, fate had given him the means to fulfill his Nazi fantasies.

Revenge against the Russians was the be-all and end-all of the Aryan's existence. With growing anticipation, he had watched America shift toward the political right. To his mind, the war in Iraq was simply a war of revenge. America had far deadlier enemies in the nuclear states of North Korea and Iran than it did in the tinpot dictatorship of Iraq. With all its satellites and state-of-the-art spy technology, America must certainly have known that there were no weapons of mass destruction moving around that landscape of flat, visible sand. No, that war was perpetrated to fix the mistake of not having crushed Saddam Hussein in the first Gulf War, and to wipe the smirk off that nose-thumbing *Untermensch*'s face.

Give America the means to disarm the Russians, and to exact revenge for Soviet anti-Americanism throughout the Cold War, and the hawks in the Pentagon today would pull the payback trigger in an instant.

It was to further his *own* desire for Götterdämmerung for Russia that the Aryan had sent the Pentagon a peek at the Streicherstab blueprints, with an offer to forward the mother lode in exchange for a billion dollars.

A billion dollars was a drop in the bucket to Uncle Sam, while no amount of money, no matter how big the pile, could ever compensate the Aryan for the post-war hell that he and his family had endured at the hands of a Soviet colonel.

All because of the line between.

But instead of welcoming him with open arms, what had been the Pentagon's response?

They had tried to kill him!

He figured the hit men had traced him through Switzerland. He had used a dummy address to forward his extortion demand to U.S. authorities—a subterfuge that had worked so well for Fritz Streicher, the post-war paymaster, when he needed to contact Third Reich refugees—but the Pentagon must have leaned on the Swiss postmaster to find out the source of the package. When that was exposed as a post office in central British Columbia, someone must have linked the location to the 1947 Skunk Mine explosion.

Or had he been betrayed?

Only one person knew his Nazi secret.

THE ARYAN'S TRIPS to Vancouver to find stand-ins for the psychodramas he acted out in the mine always involved the same ritual. First, he dropped off the soap-makings at the rendering plant. It thrilled him to think of all those pampered human pigs rubbing their porcine bodies with luxury soap made from *Untermenschen* fat. Then he passed a day or two at Fritz's mansion, sleeping in the living quarters of the coach house and sneaking into Hitler's bunker to fantasize about what it must have been like to be the spoiled *Über*-child of Fritz Streicher and his bleach-blonde wife. And finally, he would set out on another hunt for a boy's town youth to pigstick back at the Skunk Mine, for that gave him his only temporary release from the horrors of his past in East Germany.

But no more.

Pentagon hit men would return to the mine to finish the job, so he knew he could never go back to the Phantom Valley Ranch. That's why he had left the spooks a surprise up there, and why he had dropped off soap-makings harvested from one of the gunmen at the rendering plant earlier today. If the Americans were tailing him, he wanted them to know that one of their own had been converted into bars of human soap. That's why he had talked up his link to the ranch at the reduction works.

This time, instead of coming to town to hunt for another victim, he had brought a victim down with him. The pigstuck hit man was stored in the tool box behind the cab. Might as well let the Pentagon think that he had a hostage squealing all their secrets—and use the body to confront his betrayer, if this was a turncoat's game.

To make sure no one tracked the truck to the coach house—the last thing he needed was to have the ranch connected to the mansion—he had switched the license plate, then parked the vehicle at a beach where gardeners were pruning the trees. Having watched the lot for hours from woods bordering the shore, he felt it was safe to drive the truck up to the top of the bluff and—shrouded by this misty drizzle—along the shadowed driveway to the coach house garage, where he now alighted from the cab.

With a box and a book under one arm, the psycho crossed directly to the entrance to the subterranean tunnel. Swinging wide on oiled hinges, the door opened into a dank passage. He followed a flashlight beam into the heart of University Hill, his footsteps echoing as he walked, until he reached a steel door with a punch-coded lock. In went the code, and in went the Aryan.

A flick of the wall switch and Hitler's bunker was flooded with murky light. Ahead of him ran what would have been the conference passage. The entrance to this bunker was by the door that had led up to the chancellery garden where the remains of Hitler and Eva Braun were burned and buried. The first door to the right ushered the Aryan into the map room where the two had married.

He almost tripped over the bison head on the floor.

Another switch flicked and the map room jumped to life. Standing over the table, he took in its arrangement, then he sat down on the chair and shuffled items around. Along the far edge of the cluttered surface, he placed the oblong box that he had brought down from the mine; sheathed within was the bloody sword of SS-Obergruppenführer Ernst Streicher. On top of that he piled the box that was already on the table, the case storing the general's companion dagger, which had remained here at the UBC mansion.

In front of that, he displayed the two tattoos: the one he himself had skinned from Fritz Streicher's heart and tanned into a circle, and the one from the skin of Hans Streicher that had bound his copy of *Mein Kampf*. The outline of the castle in Fritz's tattoo had, after a little pictorial research about German medieval strongholds, lured him to Castle Werewolf, where the cross above the mantle in Hans's tattoo had taken him to the hiding place.

Having read the newspaper clippings and the story of the Minotaur in the UBC book, the Aryan studied the layout of the labyrinth, just a mile or so from here.

Then he went out to the truck to drag in the corpse.

"THE GOOD NAZI," Dane said, "is the general consciousness of our killer's split identities. He's no different from the millions of German civilians who embraced the Nazi Party before and during the war, but didn't know about Nazi atrocities and weren't involved in the killings. The evil Nazi is the half who embodies all of that, and he's involved in his own 'final solution' vendetta using 'subhuman' stand-ins for the one responsible for his early sexual abuse. And that was all kept secret while the Stealth Killer preyed in boy's town for far too many years."

"So where do I come in?" Cort asked.

"It wasn't just you. It was Special X too. But the threat began with the series of *Times* articles that you and Bess McQueen did on 'disposable people.' Bess's piece on the boy's town disappearances, especially, threatened to bring to light the Stealth Killer's crimes."

"Blame Bess," said the reporter.

"Not so fast," Dane countered. "Threatening the Stealth Killer also threatens the good Nazi, for even though they see themselves as separate people, they share the same haunt—the home where they live—when they do their switch. So if the Stealth Killer, the evil Nazi, screwed things up and led the cops to their door, he would also expose the secrets of the good Nazi."

"Like Siamese twins," said Cort.

"Right. They're subconsciously joined. So it was self-preservation that turned the good Nazi into a killer as well. To distract attention from the missing boys, he killed someone who deserved to die in a spectacular fashion."

"The Congo Man."

"Which gave *you* a story."

"So why did he carve the swastika?"

"To repatriate the Nazi symbol. He's the good Nazi. The other guy is the evil Nazi. And if he needed reinforcement in that twisted thinking, he got it in spades when you wrote up his crime as a vigilante killing on a par with a Greek myth."

"You're saying that's why he killed again?"

"No," replied Dane. "By then, we had told the *Times* that Special X was after the Stealth Killer too. The good Nazi had ample motive to keep us looking his way. Through murder, his fate was in his own hands, and not the other Nazi's. And when you and the *Times* kept writing him up as a Greek hero, ridding the earth of monsters who prey on innocent people, that meshed with his view of himself as an Aryan superman."

"Why would both identities reintegrate now?"

"Because that's what dissociated multiples do when they have no further need for the split-off identity. In psychological therapy, that's the goal. Here, the good Nazi has become a killer too, so if the Swastika Killer can take over victimizing the stand-ins for whoever sexually abused him as a boy, what further need is there for the split-off evil Nazi?"

"It fits," said Jackie, by way of punctuation.

Cort held out his wrists for handcuffs. "Does that mean I'm off to jail as a journalistic abettor?"

"No," said Dane. "You're embedded with us. Just like reporters on a modern battlefront."

"Why?"

"Because that was our deal, and I like to keep my word. And when I ran it past the brass, they agreed. Find the Stealth Killer and—if my theory proves true—we'll find the Swastika Killer as well. Still, there might be hostages from the boy's town abductions. And if the evil Nazi is integrating into the good Nazi, you're the one he'll trust for hostage negotiations."

"Another myth," Jackie said as she parked the car in the lot of the RCMP runway.

"How so?" the reporter asked.

"You're our Trojan Horse."

AIR SERVICES had several aircraft warmed up on the Tarmac. The PC12 Pilatus, which would hold eight assault cops with their duffle bags of gear. A Twin Otter. A Eurocopter. And a LongRanger. Air Services had mount-ups like this one down to a science. Each ERT cop had been weighed with his weapons to "weight and balance" the aircraft. Before he let a passenger board his bird, each pilot asked, "Have you got your minimum specs?" to make sure that his part of the air cavalry "stayed within its envelope."

Cort buckled in with a grin plastered on his face. If the gods were smiling, he would have the byline of the year. Not only would the cops take down his killer—the Swastika Killer—at the Cariboo ranch tonight, but in doing that, they would also take down Bess McQueen's killer— the Stealth Killer—and he would royally scoop the queen bitch.

The plane took off.

AS THE ARYAN DRAGGED the dead weight of the Pentagon killer into Hitler's bunker, the RCMP planes and helicopters droned northeast toward the Cariboo ranch, their engine noise muffled by the buffer of earth. Dropping the body onto the floor in front of the trio of waxworks that represented the ideal Aryan family, the East German returned to the map room for the hollowed-out bison head and the sail-sewing kit in the tool box beside it. Then he came back and knelt down by the corpse.

While the vacant eyes of the wax figures watched him work—the man in Hitler's uniform, the woman in Eva's black dress, the boy in his Hitlerjugend clothes—the Aryan fitted the Mounties' bison head over the dead spook. With a big sail needle and threads of black cord, he began to sew the mutant monster together to mimic the myth of the Minotaur, half bull and half man.

Zero Point

THE CARIBOO
May 28, Now

With the gunning down of Mr. Clean in Sergeant Winter's condo, the shit had hit the fan for the white world of the Pentagon. Fingerprints and photographs taken from and of the corpse—along with images of the high-tech gadgets seized by the cops—were being circulated among U.S. authorities by RCMP investigators hoping to identify the gunman on the floor. Uncle Sam's black world rested upon plausible deniability, and now not only was Big Bad Bill's Weird Shit Division being exposed to prying minds outside and inside the Pentagon, but there was a possibility—a *probability,* maybe—that Bill had fumbled the ball on the two blackest secrets of the Second World War.

Bill's main concern, however, wasn't Mr. Clean. It was the silence from Ajax and Lysol up at the Skunk Mine. "Bill, we found a saber box labeled 'SS-Obergruppenführer Ernst Streicher,'" Ajax had phoned in. "There's static in the mine. I'll report once we're out." And since then, nothing.

Slowly, Bill had started to put the pieces together. The Pentagon had received a demand from Switzerland for one billion dollars in exchange for the secret of zero-point energy. The note was clipped to a sheaf of random photocopies that the extortionist claimed were notes and blueprints from a Nazi think-tank that General Patton's

Third Army had failed to find in Czechoslovakia. The true mailing address behind the Swiss front was in the Cariboo region of British Columbia, where the Weird Shit Division had covered up the Phantom Valley mine explosion of 1947. In that same valley, a Nazi punk was now raising pigs out front of the abandoned mine where Ajax had found Streicher's sword.

Conclusion: That Nazi had the mother lode of Streicherstab papers, and the only way to seize them if Ajax and Lysol were dead was to send in a strike force.

Like Bill had done when the Stealth fighter crashed in 1986.

And like Hardware had done in 1947, when alien monsters had crashed at Roswell, New Mexico.

IF YOU WANT a job done right, do it yourself.

That's why Bill had scrambled a jet from Arlington up to Alaska, where he was met by a surgical strike team and a chopper with the authorization to pass through B.C. airspace in the black of night. Just your friendly hawkish neighbor flying a little hardware from state forty-nine to the lower forty-eight.

A report of mechanical problems was radioed to the Canucks as the chopper flew over the Phantom Valley Ranch, and permission to set down and check things out was granted. Bill would have preferred to have backup surveillance from his eyes in the sky, but storm clouds over the Cariboo had blinded the satellites. Still, he had stale-dated intel from Ajax and Lysol's reconnoitering the night before, so he figured he knew the lay of the land.

"Let's go!" Bill ordered.

The helicopter came swooping down out of the clouds like a bird of prey. It landed beside the ranch house, spraying needles of rain out as a starburst. The red team jumped down into the mud and hit the building hard, bursting in doors, front and back, to storm the Nazi's home. Moments later, they rushed out and signed the all-clear, then sloshed past the pigpen to the mouth of the mine. With a sharp bang and a soggy flash of light, the portcullis was blown open by an explosive device. Gung ho, the Pentagon red team got swallowed into Skunk Mountain.

The pilot remained in the chopper as Bill splashed off toward the mine. The ranch was hauntingly dark. With night-vision lenses over his eyes so he could see, a communication plug in his ear so he could hear, and a pistol in his fist so he could kill, Bill lurked outside the yawning hole until he was summoned.

"Colonel, you gotta see this!"

Stepping into the tunnel, Bill recoiled from the stench. An X-shaped frame with swastika arms was the source, and upside down on it were the rotting remains of a gutted teen. Pressing on, Bill entered the ruins of what looked like a mad scientist's lab. It had been torn asunder, as if Frankenstein's monster had gone berserk. At a constricted hole in the facing wall, the soldier who had summoned Bill crooked his arm in a "come here" motion.

At first, Big Bad Bill didn't recognize Ajax. All he saw was a body impaled to the concave rock by a rusted, barnacled anchor that would need three men just to lift it. One prong of the anchor was spiked through the skull, so the body hung from it like a limp rag doll. The stripped-off clothes lay jumbled on the ground amid shattered teeth and shards of bone. Like the youth on the X-shaped frame, the dangling man had been gutted, scooped out like a human canoe, the offal carried away. He'd been repeatedly branded with swastika marks, and among them Bill spotted Ajax's military tattoo. The clothes on the floor were black world camouflage.

"Weird, huh?" the soldier said.

"Yeah," Bill grunted.

"It would take Superman to hurl an anchor like that."

This anchor *had* been hurled by a superman. A Nazi superman tapped into quantum mechanics. The force behind the hurling—of this, Bill had no doubt—was the Holy Grail of aerospace engineers: zero-point energy.

ZPE, thought Bill.

Germany was the place where quantum mechanics was born. Nazi physicists looked at gravity from a perspective unlike everyone else's. They saw space as a plenum filled with energy, where particles flashed in and out of existence around their zero-point baselines. Even at the zero point of existence—a vacuum chilled to absolute zero, or −273.15° C—ZPE was present. In the atoms of our bodies, in the air that filled our lungs, in the outer limits of the cosmos, the quantum vacuum was a quantum sea full of quantum foam. Billions of fluctuations occurred every second from particles popping in and out of existence.

ZPE was invisible.

Zero-point energy could not be seen.

But it could be heard in the background hiss on a transistor radio.

Zero-point energy—the Nazis had grasped—was the pulse of the universe.

So what if gravity was a zero-point fluctuation force? That's what the best brains of Nazi Germany had pondered in the two Streicherstab think-tanks in the climactic months of the Second World War. Since gravity, electromagnetism, and space-time are interrelated, could there not be an electromagnetic device that would mesh with those fluctuations in the zero-point energy field to cancel out the properties of gravity and inertia around a vehicle? In perturbing ZPE and distorting space-time, wouldn't this device yield an anti-gravity effect, freeing the vehicle to levitate and—*zoom!*—take off?

The answer was yes.

As those Nazi scientists and the Weird Shit Division of the Pentagon knew only too well.

As did this enigmatic Nazi punk, judging from the weighty anchor that had been propelled across the lab to pin Ajax to the Skunk Mine's rock.

So where was Lysol?

Big Bad Bill ventured deeper into the mine. He followed several trails of blood of different vintages down to a barrier blocking the shaft. Here, the rock floor was caked with pools of blood, but there were no bodies. Ahead of him, the mine had imploded, and millions of tons of rubble had crushed any secrets that were buried beyond. Bill knew the secrets behind nature's cover-up, though, for they were the same ones that his predecessor had suppressed in the surface world.

Still, it was astounding to see the havoc wreaked by *die Glocke* as it had spun out of control, decades ago.

Zero-point energy had fractured and fused the rock into something from another dimension.

From hyperspace.

Bill retraced his steps to the subterranean lab, where he paused for a moment to assess two bloody uniforms hanging on a pair of coat stands at the entrance to this dead-end tunnel. One was the uniform of an SS storm trooper; affixed to the helmet was a miner's headlamp. The other was the uniform of a colonel in the post-war Red Army, but there were no trousers to go with the jacket. The Russian's helmet also included a lantern.

Role-playing? wondered Bill.

Only then did he notice the workbench in the middle of the ruined lab. It was as if a vortex of destruction had whirled around its four edges and not disturbed its surface. As he approached the bench, Bill saw why. Damn if the Nazi punk hadn't left *him* a message.

Ringed around two sheets of paper like the circles on a bull's-eye were the high-tech gadgets from Ajax's kit and a jumble of unidentifiable metal objects. Somehow this weird scientist had transmuted the molecular composition of one material into that of another. An incredibly strong molybdenum rod, like those used in nuclear reactors, had been bent into an S-curve as if it was made of soft lead or tin. Bits of one metal were embedded in another. A length of steel had turned to lead at one end, as if an alchemist had been at work.

Bill's gaze, however, was drawn to the center.

Stamped with a Nazi swastika and the ultra-secret warning of the Streicherstab were two blueprints. One depicted the circular exterior of *die Glocke*. Scrawled across that in blood were the English words "You fucked up!" The other blueprint was more alarming. On it was drawn a design for the *Flugkreisel,* its silhouette remarkably unlike that of the prototype that had crashed in New Mexico in 1947.

A single bloody word was smeared across the image.

The word was "Roswell."

"COLONEL! Something's up!"

Bill caught the adrenaline surge in the voice of the guard stationed outside the blown-open gate to the mine. Pressing in his earplug to hear the sentry better, Bill barked into his helmet mike, "What's going on out there?"

"Motion in the dark."

Gotcha, punk, Bill thought as he snapped the general order. "Red team, out of the mine! Go! Go! *Go!* Our guy must have slipped away as the chopper came down."

Single file and weapons at the ready, the strike force members dashed through the bowels of the mountain and out into the night, prepared to fan out in whatever direction the guard indicated. But no sooner had the last man exited than Bill found himself in a predicament that was going from bad to worse.

"Halt! Police! Drop your weapons!" a disembodied voice ordered from the dark.

One of the red team members spun around and opened up with an automatic in what he hoped was the right direction. In a flash, he was dropped by dual sniper shots. The rear of his helmet blew out as shrapnel.

"Halt! Police! You're surrounded!"

Again, they got the yell.

And suddenly Bill and his team were caught in a pool of blinding light, about as naked as Gypsy Rose Lee in her burlesque routine. Every weapon in the blackness surrounding them had its sights lined up on one of Bill's men.

Another soldier reacted.

Another soldier went down.

Bill's mind kicked into overdrive to work out the permutations. It was a choice between fight, flight, or give up.

By elimination, flight was the viable option.

The pilot already had the rotors of the chopper turning. But before Bill could bark the "Get outta here!" order, something streaked across the darkness and leaped up through the open door into the cockpit. Cries of pain and the sounds of a struggle filled the wilderness quiet as the fly boy was dragged out through the far fuselage door. If Bill had bothered to study the myth of the Mounted Police, he'd have known full well that—like Sergeant Preston of the Yukon and his trusty mutt, King—they usually send in the dogs.

Flight was no longer an option.

Bill had more than enough guts to call for a last stand. He and his team would gladly go down swinging like the Texans at the Alamo. The only problem with going for that gold in this fucked-up situation—given the blueprints on the workbench back in the mine—was that Bill could take close to three hundred million Americans down with him.

"Don't be a knob!" warned the voice from the darkness.

Not the most historic of battlecries, but that about summed up the *realpolitik* of Bill's situation. So although it went against every fiber of his being, he reluctantly commanded his team to drop their weapons.

Bill was stunned by the number of shadows that emerged from the nightscape. He had way too few troops on the ground to cope with such an insurgency.

What a mess!

Within minutes, the Mounties reduced Bill's chaos to order. From their hiding places, marksmen "covered off" the invaders with bright red laser spots. The red team members dropped to their knees, their hands high in the air. One by one, they were cuffed and searched by cops.

"Who's in charge?" asked a mean-looking Mountie with the voice of prior commands.

"I am," responded Bill.

Wrists secured behind his back, Bill was grabbed by Mr. Mean and his Native sidekick and hauled off to their commander.

"I'm Chief Superintendent DeClercq," announced the cop who confronted Bill. "You're under arrest for the attempted murder of one of my officers, terrorist offenses under the Criminal Code, and whatever we uncover in the Skunk Mine."

Russkies

NORDHAUSEN, GERMANY
July 5, 1945

The first thing Maj. Bill Hawke had done when he saw the V-2 factory buried in Kohnstein Mountain was report the news back to the Pentagon's chief of Ordnance Technical Intelligence in Paris. That was on April 11, the day the 3rd Armored and the 104th Infantry had liberated Nordhausen and Dora-Mittelbau.

"Hot damn!" the colonel had said. "Good work, Major."

"Thank you, sir."

"You've got a future in the Pentagon, son."

"I hope so, sir."

"How many rockets are there?"

"Hard to tell, Colonel. Most are in pieces. A few are half-built. It's an assembly line."

"Are there a hundred?"

"Probably."

"That's the magic number we've been given by Army Ordnance at the Pentagon. We're to grab a hundred of the Krauts' V-2s and ship them off to the White Sands Proving Ground in New Mexico for detailed study."

"Can do, Colonel. If I get support."

"You'll get support, Major. But we gotta move fast. Germany was divided up at the Yalta yak in February. Nordhausen is in the Reds' zone of occupation."

"The Russkies get the rockets?"

"Fuck those Commie bastards. What you do is steal the V-2s in a way that doesn't look like we looted the place."

SPECIAL MISSION V-2 had swung into action. As Army Ordnance assessed the inventory in the subterranean tunnels and tried to figure out how best to disassemble a huge quantity of parts and sub-assemblies and transport them to the port of Antwerp, a call went out for GIs with basic mechanical skills. The 144th Motor Vehicle Assembly Company was soon brought in. By rounding up captured German rolling stock and clearing the tracks to the factory, the Americans were able to trundle off the first forty-car trainload of Nazi rocket hardware.

Meanwhile, Hawke was in command of the "gypsy team," a band of roving experts who could be deployed on a moment's notice to check out interesting discoveries. Their primary task was to find and interrogate the missing rocketeers.

On May 2, Hawke struck gold.

Two days after Hitler's suicide in Berlin, an anti-tank company of the 44th Infantry was on patrol just over the Bavarian border with Austria when a cyclist came down the road. The man on the bicycle was Magnus von Braun, Wernher von Braun's English-speaking brother. He informed the surprised Americans that just up ahead at an Alpine hotel, the brains behind the V-2 was waiting to surrender to them.

Hawke met von Braun the following day, in the Austrian town of Reutte, where the rocketeer had been taken for interrogation by Army Intelligence.

"You're top on my list," Hawke said, tapping the roster of names of Nazi scientists given to him by the Pentagon.

"And so I should be," said von Braun.

"What do you expect from us?" the major asked, getting straight to the point.

"To give me the opportunity to conquer outer space." Von Braun pointed his index finger toward the ceiling.

"Why us?" Hawke asked.

"We discussed that."

"When?"

"Early this year."

"Where?"

"Peenemünde."

"Who?"

"My chief assistants and I."

"Huzel? Tessmann?"

"And others."

"Why?"

"I had received conflicting orders from the SS. Ernst Streicher, special commissioner for the V-2, had sent a teletype directing me to move my rocketeers to central Germany."

"To the Mittelwerk?" said Hawke.

"To the Harz," replied von Braun, side-stepping that trap.

"And the other order?"

"From the Reichsführer-SS himself. Himmler told me to command all of my engineers to join the Volkssturm and help defend that area against the Red Army."

"What did you decide?"

"I told my staff that Germany had lost the war, but that we should not forget that we were the first to succeed in reaching outer space. We had suffered many hardships because of our faith in the peacetime future of our V-2s. Now we had a duty. Each of the conquering powers would want our science. The question we had to answer was, To which country should we entrust our heritage?"

"That's why you followed Streicher's order, not Himmler's?"

"Certainly. To move west. We despise the French. We are mortally afraid of the Soviets. We do not believe the British can afford us. So that, by elimination, left America."

The Pentagon, of course, welcomed Wernher von Braun with open arms.

SPECIAL MISSION V-2 had raced against the clock.

On April 25, a patrol from the U.S. 69th Infantry had met a lone Russian horseman in the village of Leckwitz, not far from the Elbe River. The next day at Torgau, as part of the official link-up ceremony, Major General Emil F. Reinhardt had swapped salutes with Major General Vladimir Rusakov of the Soviet 58th Guards Infantry Division.

The Russians were coming!

To Nordhausen!

Sometime around June 1!

"Fuck those Commie bastards," the colonel had told Hawke. So the GIs looting the factory tunnels had toiled night and day until they had enough components for a hundred V-2s loaded into railcars bound for Antwerp, where sixteen Liberty ships were waiting to sail for New Orleans. From there, American trains would trundle these spoils of war to the White Sands Proving Ground.

The last train left the future Soviet zone on May 31.

The cupboard was all but bare.

VON BRAUN WAS PLAYING COY. A big negotiator, he was refusing to tell Hawke the whereabouts of his V-2 blueprints and other important papers. He was trying to make sure that without him and his rocketeers, the U.S. would be unable to make its captured hardware blast off.

Arrogant prick, thought Hawke.

The five hundred rocket scientists who were Streicher's hostages on the Vengeance Express had been corralled at the Alpine resort of Garmisch-Partenkirchen for interrogation by Hawke and his intel experts. But there were still the thousands left behind around the Mittelwerk, and one of them, as it turned out, knew where Huzel and Tessmann had hid von Braun's treasure trove. Through a little trickery—Hawke convinced him that the SS major wanted him to reveal where the archives were—that man directed the Americans to an old mine in the isolated mountain village of Dornten, several miles northwest of Nordhausen.

There they encountered a new problem.

The mine was in the future British zone of occupation.

And the Brits were to arrive on May 27.

Back on April 3, it had taken Huzel and Tessmann, with their little convoy of three trucks, thirty-six hours to transfer the fourteen tons of V-2 documents into a small locomotive and haul that cache down into the heart of the mine. There, von Braun's assistants had carried his rocket records by hand into the shaft, which was then dynamited shut to conceal their treasonous secret.

Hawke had only a week to go before the Dornten mine would fall into British hands, so there was a frantic scramble to evacuate the demolished tunnel and transport the recovered document crates back to Nordhausen. That was accomplished on May 27, as the British were setting up roadblocks to mark their occupation zone. All that Nazi paper—like all that Nazi hardware—was soon en route to America.

Fuck those limey has-beens too, thought Hawke.

Pax Britannica, your time has passed.

Pax Americana, your day has come.

TIME WAS RUNNING OUT.

They called the Pentagon's plan to export the Nazi rocketeers to *Amerika* Operation Overcast.

On June 8, senior engineers from von Braun's inner circle had returned to Nordhausen to help Major Hawke identify which of the thousands of Nazi technicians in the Harz should be evacuated to the American zone. Less than twenty-four hours before the Soviets were to arrive, some one thousand German V-2 personnel, and their immediate relatives, were boarded onto a fifty-car Nazi train, which chugged them forty miles southwest to the town of Witzenhausen.

The town was just inside the American zone.

With the rockets safe, the archives safe, and the brains in custody, it was time for Hawke to deal with von Braun.

Army Ordnance had sold the Pentagon's Joint Chiefs of Staff on Operation Overcast. The official plan was to exploit the Nazi specialists to defeat Japan. As a reward, Hawke got a permanent post-war job at the Pentagon and a code name befitting all that he had accomplished in Special Mission V-2. Thenceforth, he was known as "Hardware."

"What is this?" von Braun asked, glancing down at the papers that Hardware had dropped on the table.

"A contract for you and your rocketeers to work in America."

"For how long?"

"Six months, it reads. But let's agree on five years, between you and me."

"How many rocketeers?"

"Your quota is one hundred."

"I'll need at least ... a hundred and fifteen," said von Braun.

This Nazi jerk is pulling my chain, Hardware thought.

"We won't let orders get in the way."

"Good," said von Braun.

Hardware held out his hand.

The SS major shook it.

"So who do you want from this list of POWs?"

As Hardware watched the Nazi physicist put together his dream team from the brain trust of Hitler's Reich, his mind filled in the war crimes certain names had committed.

Yep, thought Hardware. This cover-up will take more whitewash than young Tom Sawyer and his dupes slapped on that fence.

A lot more.

IN THE END, the clock was not running as fast as Army Ordnance had feared. It wasn't until today—July 5—that the Red Army reached Nordhausen to assume its occupation from U.S. forces. As he waited for the Russkies to arrive for a tour of the tunnels, Hardware brushed his palms together and thought to himself, with righteous pride, Spic and span. Fuck these Commie bastards.

Tasked with handing the stripped-down Mittelwerk over to the Russians, Hardware had tapped some of the local prisoners to "sanitize" the tunnels of rocket secrets.

The warm summer sun was shining down on what had not so long ago been the industrial storage area outside the mouths of the Mittelwerk tunnels. The slaves were gone and the bodies were buried, but this former SS enclave still had a haunted atmosphere. Even in the sunshine, it seemed oppressively gray.

The Russian colonel drove up in a dust-caked jeep. His name was Boris Vlasov, and Hardware thought he was a nasty piece of work. He wore the shit-colored uniform of the Red Army, with the same flared jodhpurs and knee-high jackboots as an SS goon. On the brow of his peaked cap sat a big red star. The high Slavic cheekbones of his bloated face were red and raw from shrapnel wounds. The undamaged flesh around his intense squint seemed to bear the permanent mark of a tank commander's goggles.

No salutes were exchanged.

Vlasov's cohorts didn't fool the major one bit. Sure, they drove up in a jeep and packed pistols, but their new, oversized uniforms and lack of battlefield decorations betrayed them as closet civilians. U.S. Army Intelligence knew all about the Soviet "trophy battalions." The job of these Russkie counterparts to Uncle Sam's V-2 detectives was to ferret out Nazi rocket technology for Joe Stalin's Chief Artillery Directorate. No doubt these thick-set peasants all carried Commie wish lists of Fatherland hardware and rocketeers.

Tough luck, Colonel.

Hardware sensed the growing tension as he ushered the colonel and his trophy hunters through the Mittelwerk. It was a lot colder in the tunnels than the temperature dictated. The Russkies got an eyeful of the factory assembly line, but just a few indications of what had been there when the Yanks arrived. When they emerged from the dark, shielding their eyes against the blazing sun, the Commies were no more enlightened than they'd been before they went in.

"How many men did you lose in the war?" Vlasov asked through his interpreter.

"Three hundred thousand," Hardware said proudly.

"We lost eight and a half million!"

Hardware flicked out a Lucky Strike and offered it to Vlasov. The Russkie ignored the smoke.

"When we took Berlin, where were you?" Vlasov asked in a voice shaking with clenched rage.

Hardware ignited a match with the nail of his thumb.

"Holding back on the Elbe," Vlasov scoffed.

"Ike gave you the glory. Be thankful," the major said. No way was he going to take shit from this borscht-eating peon. "If it was up to me, the Stars and Stripes would have flapped on top of the Reichstag, not the hammer and sickle."

"This"—Vlasov jerked his thumb toward the tunnels—"is all we get!"

The major stared the Russkie dead in the eye.

"Be thankful you're getting anything," he said, winking.

Official Secrets

THE CARIBOO
May 28, Now

Time was ticking down on the deadliest secret in the
Pentagon's closet, and Bill was pissed that that time was
being wasted by this straight-arrow Mountie. By the time
Uncle Sam got through with him, Chief Superintendent
DeClercq wouldn't be able to get a job scooping poop at the
Calgary Stampede.

Bill paced the interview room.

From the Phantom Valley Ranch, the Lone Ranger and
Tonto had driven him in an unmarked police car along the
Cariboo Highway toward the former ghost town of
Barkerville. At Wells, the cops had locked him up in the
hoosegow of the local redcoat detachment, and he was now
heating his heels as he watched precious minutes tick away
on the wall clock. With each jerk of the minute hand, Big
Bad Bill imagined the secret cache of Streicherstab
documents slipping further away.

In frustration, he slammed his fist down hard on the table.

Bill would tear the balls off this yokel.

So where the hell was he?

DECLERCQ WAS DECKED OUT in the red serge tunic of
Review Order No. 1. With a weaponless Sam Browne,
riding breeches, high boots, brown leather gloves, the felt

Stetson, and several medals on his chest, he came down the hall toward Dane, Jackie, and Cort. It was rare for commissioned officers to don the historic color—their everyday working uniform was blue—but the chief had carried his red serge north just in case he was called upon to address the media following the arrest of the Stealth Killer. *The Vancouver Times* had accused the Mounties of ignoring "the less dead," "the disposable people," so the chief had planned to give that case the full Monty.

Instead, Special X had trapped a different quarry.

And now DeClercq had a different use for the iconic uniform.

"Chief," said Jackie, standing up, "I just got a call. Another Greek-myth corpse was dumped overnight in Vancouver. A bunch of high-tech gadgets were found on the body."

"Dumped where?" DeClercq inquired.

"In a maze at UBC. If you don't need us here, we want to fly back down."

The chief turned to the reporter. "Do you have a camera on you?" he asked.

"Yes," replied Jantzen.

"Good. Here's what I want from you...."

OH, SWEET MOTHER of Jesus, thought Big Bad Bill. What does this redcoat prick hope to do? Relive the War of Independence? Refight the Battle of Saratoga? Get real, pal.

The Mountie crossed to the recorder and punched it on.

"Chief Superintendent DeClercq has entered the room." He turned to his suspect. "You know my name. What's yours?" he asked.

"That's classified information," Bill replied.

"Classified by whom?"

"That's classified, too," parried Bill.

"Name, rank, and serial number. Let's start with that."

Bill was sitting. The redcoat was standing. So Bill pushed back his chair and stood up to face the Mountie eye to eye.

"I demand to speak to your commander-in-chief."

"So speak," said DeClercq.

"Not you. A *military* man. I demand to speak to someone with real authority."

"I'm listening."

"Get off it. You're just a cop. I want the man in command of your armed forces."

"It doesn't work like that up here."

"It does where I come from."

"But you're not down where you come from, are you? This is *my* jurisdiction. You will obey Canada's laws. So I'm asking you one more time, what's your name?"

"I refuse to answer. Turn that thing off." Bill crooked his thumb at the recording device.

"This interview is terminated," said DeClercq, and he punched off the recorder as requested.

"Okay, Mountie-man, listen up," said Bill. "You have no idea who you're fooling with. You've got five seconds to read me my rights, then I want the American ambassador on the phone. If you know what's good for you, you'll quit jacking around. The last thing you want is a fight with Uncle Sam."

"What's your name?"

"Fuck off."

"Is that your final answer?"

"Give me my *rights*."

"What rights might those be? Only people have rights. So until I get a name out of you, those rights are in abeyance. And I *will* get your name—and get to the truth— one way or another. Just so you know what you're fooling with, I'll lay my cards on the table."

DeClercq opened his briefcase and withdrew several photos.

"Yesterday, this unidentified hit man broke into the home of one of my officers and tried to kill him. No one does that unless they want to deal with me."

The redcoat dropped a crime scene photo of the dead Mr. Clean onto the table.

"This high-tech spy gear was found with that body."

The redcoat dropped a photo of the contents of the black world's cleaning kit onto the morgue shot.

"The unidentified hit man was after a file containing photos of murder victims with swastikas gouged into their flesh. The question is, Did you order these killings?"

The redcoat dropped photos of the Cyclops, the Golden Fleece, and Medusa onto the pile.

"The swastikas in those photos led us to the Skunk Mine, and what did we find there but this gutted corpse branded with swastikas and stripped of clothes identical to those worn by the burglar killed in the condo."

The redcoat dropped a photo of Ajax onto the rapidly rising pile of images.

"The high-tech spy gear seized in the mine matched the gear we found at the attempted hit."

The redcoat pulled a number of see-through evidence bags out of his briefcase.

"These gadgets were ringed around this."

He dropped a photo of the blueprint scrawled with the words "You fucked up!" onto the table.

"And around this."

He topped the pile with a photo of the blueprint with "Roswell" smeared across it.

"I'd say that looks like a flying saucer, wouldn't you? And what I see stamped on both blueprints are Nazi swastikas. The same sort of swastikas as those carved into the bodies that brought you and your hit men here. Why, I wonder? But you're not talking. So I have someone for you to meet."

The redcoat gathered up the photos and stuffed them into a brown manila envelope. Backtracking to the door, he swung it open to reveal a man with a digital camera. Bill couldn't move fast enough to cover his face, so—*flash!*— the spook's mug shot was captured by the lens.

"Tell our suspect who you are," the Mountie said.

"Cort Jantzen," replied the reporter, flashing a press card. "I work for *The Vancouver Times.*"

"Thank you, Mr. Jantzen," the redcoat said. "If you wait a minute, I'll have a scoop for you."

DeClercq shut the door and held up the envelope. "That reporter is on his way down to Vancouver, where we've just discovered the body of the next swastika victim. I suspect that victim is another of your hit men, since we have recovered the same spy gear as that found with the other two."

Lysol, thought Bill. "Let me go!" he ordered. "This case is a matter of national security."

"So you did screw up?"

"Get out of my way, Redcoat!"

"One way or another, I *will* get to the truth. While you're sitting in a cell thinking you pulled one over on me, the contents of this envelope will be published around the globe—along with the headshot just taken of you. Then we'll see who'll come forward with information that will rip the mask off your face."

"You're bluffing."

"Watch me," said DeClercq.

Big Bad Bill looked on as the Mountie moved toward the door. If what was in that envelope escaped from this room, he would never be able to get the genie back in the bottle.

"Whoa!" said Bill as the Horseman opened the door.

DeClercq turned.

"Whoa *who*?" he asked.

"Whoa, Chief Superintendent."

As Bill uttered those pacifying words, which came so hard to his lips, he prayed to America's God that they had some sort of Official Secrets Act in this godforsaken wasteland.

Minotaur

The labyrinth at UBC reminded Dane of the yew-treed maze at Hampton Court, King Henry VIII's royal palace on the Thames, to the west of London. Dane had tried to maneuver his way through that twisting puzzle with a sexy Swede he'd met at a London club the night before. Dilly-dallying along the way, they had finally figured out that the trick to threading the maze was to keep your touch brushing the hedgerow to the right. Leaving Hampton Court, they had navigated the turns of London's transportation system, until they'd finally ended up entwined with each other in bed in Dane's hotel room.

He wondered where Kadriin was now.

Probably married, with three blond kiddies and a husband smiling in perpetual satisfaction.

He sighed.

Today, Dane entered another maze with another attractive woman. But this was strictly business, and Cort Jantzen was along as a third-wheel chaperone. The three of them had just flown down from the Cariboo, having been released to return south to this new murder scene. Landing out of an overcast sky sodden with rain, the trio had driven across the Fraser River to Point Grey and around the peninsula to the maze in the gardens out at the tip of the tongue.

"You three look bagged," said Gill Macbeth as Dane, Jackie, and Cort splashed into the labyrinth. There was no danger that they would get lost as Dane had in England, for the body was sprawled in the mud just around the first turn. Ident had erected a makeshift tent over the victim to keep any forensic evidence from being washed away by the deluge.

"Didn't sleep," Dane responded over the downpour's patter on the dripping tarp.

"None of you?"

"Uh-uh."

"We were up north," Jackie explained. "With the chief. Looks like the guy we were after was busy down here."

The corpse in the labyrinth was garbed in the same midnight black camouflage as the two prior Pentagon spooks. But stitched over the head and shoulders of this cadaver was the bison head mascot of Special X.

"Another Greek myth," suggested Gill.

"The Minotaur," Cort expanded. "Half bull, half man, the creature was a monster that haunted the labyrinth under the palace of King Minos of Crete. This killer is *really* into myths. I grew up on this stuff. Odysseus, Jason, Perseus, Theseus—Greek heroes one and all. It was Theseus who slew the Minotaur."

"How?" asked Jackie.

"The labyrinth was supposed to be impossible to escape, but Theseus unwound a ball of string that would later guide him back out. When he found the monster, he ran it through with his sword."

"This victim was impaled too," the pathologist said. "From the look of the wounds in the buttocks, he was spiked from back to front with a similar weapon."

"Time of death?" Jackie asked.

"Judging from rigor and body temp, I'd say more than twenty-four hours ago. Sometime in the early morning of

the night before last would be my rough guess. The body
was found when a gardener walked into the maze earlier
today to continue trimming the hedge. It wasn't around
when he quit work yesterday afternoon and cordoned off
the entrance."

"So the victim was killed elsewhere and dumped here
overnight," said Dane.

"Had to be," Gill agreed.

Before flying down from the Cariboo, Dane had
assumed the role of exhibit man. He'd carried with him the
high-tech gadgets they'd recovered from the mine so that he
could convey them to this crime scene and see if they
matched the hardware still on this latest victim. Crouching
beside the Minotaur, he compared them now, confirming
that every device from the Cariboo had its twin here, and
also that both twins had a triplet in what was seized off the
spook who had burgled his condo.

"Is there a swastika gouged into the forehead of the
bison?" Dane asked Gill.

The pathologist examined the matted fur.

"No," she reported.

"Ident will want to examine the stitching and other
forensic clues before the head is removed from the corpse,
so after you do the autopsy, would you call me and confirm
whether the Nazi signature is carved into the brow
beneath?"

DANE, JACKIE, AND CORT returned to Special X for their
respective cars. Before they parted company, the three laid
out a game plan.

"The first thing we need to know," Dane suggested, "is
whether or not the Swastika Killer sent you another jpeg.
When he saw that reversed swastika in this morning's
Times, did he slip up in a quick shoot-from-the-hip reply?"

"I'll phone if he did—or if he does," said Cort.

"Next, we need to anticipate where he will strike next time. It seems his MO is to choose his victims from the *Times*. So far, each victim was killed soon after a story about him or her appeared in the paper. This psycho picked up the myth angle in your Cyclops story, Cort, and that's why he homed in on you as his confidant. So I think the name of his next victim is buried somewhere in the *Times*."

"The body in the maze doesn't fit your theory, though. There was no story about a Pentagon hit man in the paper until this morning. And even then, it was about the killer who came after *you*."

"That proves my other suspicion. Remember what I said about the good and bad Nazi killers being one?"

"You told me it was off the record until we had proof," said the reporter.

"Well, it's on the record now. The proof is the guy dumped in the maze. The Stealth Killer Nazi has been playing out his revenge fantasies up at the Skunk Mine for years. The Swastika Killer Nazi came into play only recently, to throw us off the trail of the other identity. He's the killer who communicates with you. For some reason, the Pentagon spooks want our Siamese twins, so they sent a hit man after me for the Swastika Killer's file and two hit men after the Stealth Killer up at his home next to the Skunk Mine."

"But he killed them both," said Jackie.

"Right. In the mine. He left one for us to find and brought the other down with him in the back of that farm truck. While the three of us were flying up to the Cariboo last night, hoping to grab the Stealth Killer on his return to the Skunk Mine, he stayed down here in whatever hiding place he has in Vancouver and switched into his Swastika Killer identity to dump the second hit man."

"He's reintegrating," said Cort. "The killers are fusing together."

"And it's probably a struggle between both identities, with neither actor willing to be upstaged."

"So where do we find him?" asked Jackie.

"The only place left," said Dane. "He won't return to the Stealth Killer's lair in the Skunk Mine, so we must locate the Swastika Killer's hideout down here."

EDITOR ED was waiting to pounce when Cort rushed into the newsroom of *The Vancouver Times*.

"What have you got?" he demanded. He almost drooled when his star reporter told him.

With his boss staring over his shoulder, Cort checked his e-mail for another jpeg from the Swastika Killer.

Nothing.

What did that mean?

As Cort reached for that morning's *Times* to search for articles that might point to the next victim, Bess McQueen sidled up to his desk.

"What's up?" she asked.

"The Stealth Killer and the Swastika Killer are the same guy, Ed," Cort said, addressing their boss. "Since both have fused into one and I was at both scenes—the mine up north and the maze down here—I think the scoop and the byline should both be mine."

"You got 'em," said Ed.

"Hey, that's not fair!" fumed the queen bitch.

"All's fair in love and war," said the old newshound gruffly. "And it's a market-share war out there, Bess."

"I'LL TAKE THE FIRST WATCH," said Jackie. "You go home and sleep. Both of us were up last night, but thanks to that hit man at your home, you lost the night before too."

"You'll phone if anything breaks?"

"Sure. Now go home to Puss and the kittens."

As Dane was driving down Cambie Street, Gill Macbeth called his cell. "There was no swastika carved into the forehead underneath the bison mask. Does that make sense in light of the previous signatures?"

"Yes," replied the sergeant. "This psycho is losing his shaky grip on the switch that controls his dissociated identities."

"He no longer knows who he is?"

"And we don't know either," said Dane.

By the time he reached his condo, his imagination had come up with a way to kill two birds with one stone. Dr. Kim Rossmo was at work on a geographic profile that would reveal the most likely anchor points for the Swastika Killer. Dane was no profiler, but he had noticed something. The rattlesnake research lab, Medusa's home, and the maze at the tip of Point Grey were all geographically linked to UBC. The university, he believed, also held a key to the next victim of the Swastika Killer. So before he climbed into bed to catch up on his lost sleep, the sergeant phoned the university. That done, he set the alarm on his clock-radio.

The moment his head hit the pillow, Dane was out.

SWASTIKA STARED in disbelief at the swastika on the front page of *The Vancouver Times*. The symbol sat front and center for readers to see, just as he'd demanded in his last e-mail communication with Cort Jantzen, but it was the *wrong* symbol, and that error had spun his message around 180 degrees.

The swastika in the Western world dates back to the Crux Gammata, a pre-Christian cross composed of four Greek capitals of the letter gamma. The arm of that third letter in the Greek alphabet bends to the right, so the swastika turns clockwise. When Hitler appropriated it for the Nazi Party, he twisted that swastika forty-five degrees. But instead of signifying the racial purity advanced by Hitler's Third Reich, the swastika on the front page of the *Times*—with its counterclockwise arms—evoked the contentment sought by subhuman religions.

Hindus!

Buddhists!

Native Indians!

Untermenschen all!

Because it wasn't composed of the Greek letter gamma, the *Times'* subhuman swastika—from the Sanskrit word *Svasti,* which means "happiness" or "well-being"—could turn either way. The most common Asian/Native version— the one used in the *Times*—turned in a counterclockwise direction, with the tip of one arm pointing straight up.

You stupid fools!

But as his rage began to cool down into cold, clear logic, Swastika grasped that he was being played for a fool. This mistake wasn't caused by dyslexia or some printing screw-up. It was a deliberate betrayal by Cort Jantzen. Swastika had courted arrest by linking up with the reporter because he thought the newspaperman was a vigilante like himself, an Aryan crusader who understood that only the master race created supermen.

Okay, thought Swastika. We'll play it your way. If betrayal is the game, so be it.

His previous victims had all been chosen from stories published in *The Vancouver Times.*

His next victim would come from the *Times* too.

From a byline.

The byline of Cort Jantzen.

The Line Between

NORDHAUSEN, GERMANY
July 5, 1945

The formal handover of the Allied occupation took place in the roll-call square of Dora-Mittelbau. Beside the gallows and the *Pfahlhangen* post, liberated Poles had erected a huge crucifix to symbolize their suffering.

The Nazi POWs were lined up single file and flanked by a detail of GIs with automatic weapons. Hardware was about to command the column to march when Vlasov growled something in Russian to his interpreter.

"We demand our share," the mouthpiece translated.

"Of what?" Hardware asked. The V-2s, he predicted.

"These prisoners of war."

Hardware shrugged his shoulders and said, "Take your half."

The two Allies stood face to face at the approximate center of the line of ragtag POWs. As the Russkie stepped back a few paces to count off from both ends of the line, Hardware studied the two youths directly in front of him. Both were sweating in the winter uniform of the Hitler Youth, and neither was more than fifteen. They were probably Werewolves, for they had been caught napping in the woods with their Panzerfaust bazookas. They might have carried out an attack if exhaustion hadn't knocked them out and a U.S. patrol hadn't pounced on them in their sleep. Blond-haired, blue-eyed, and with similar features, they could have been brothers.

The Pied Piper, thought Hardware.

The way the American saw it, Hitler was the Pied Piper of Kraut youth. He had put these punks under his spell by playing his seductive flute. They had only to listen, and they would follow him anywhere. Never before in history had a generation of young people lived and breathed the propaganda of war for so long that they couldn't recall the innocence of childhood. As the Nazi war effort grew more desperate, and adult men were killed off, the SS had been forced to seek its recruits from the ranks of the Hitlerjugend. These two had been captured with no ID papers in their pockets. As Hardware wondered what hid behind their hateful glowers, Colonel Vlasov rejoined him in front of the prisoners and sliced his arm down like a guillotine to divide the line into equal shares.

The line between separated the two *Über*-Aryan youths.

Vlasov shoved his to the left.

Hardware moved his to the right.

Minutes later, the transfer complete, the Americans and their POWs left the roll-call square.

His job done, Hardware was going home.

BARBAROSSA—which sounds like "barbarism"—had been a fitting code-name for the Nazi invasion of Russia in 1941. Droning bombers, diving Stukas, blitzkrieging panzers had torn into the flesh of the Motherland, launching the biggest battle in the history of the world. And in the wake of Hitler's conquering army had come the Einsatzgruppen, Reinhard Heydrich's mobile killing squads. The four "special action groups" had two orders: first, to "cleanse" Russia of its Jews; and second, to secure political order by liquidating every perceived enemy of the Reich.

Most of Vlasov's family had gone to the pits. The Einsatzgruppen killers had herded them, along with thousands of other men, women, and children, to the edge of huge graves to be shot one by one in the presence of the others. Large *Aktions* that cleansed thousands in Lvov, in Rovno, in Kharkov. The one that took all of Vlasov's family, except his sister, was the massacre at Babi Yar, near Kiev, where thirty-five thousand people were shot in just two days. The killing squads had to work in shifts to complete the job.

Vlasov had been a butcher before Barbarossa. It was hard enough to slaughter livestock day after day. But to slaughter *people,* to order them to strip naked and march them down to a mass grave … Well, Vlasov had learned to wreak revenge.

More than a million Russians had died to defeat the Nazis at the Battle of Stalingrad. Like Napoleon's army, Hitler's had misjudged the onslaught of winter, giving Vlasov and his troops the strength to push forward, slowly and remorselessly, in the teeth of retreating rifle fire, spitting machine guns, shrapnel bursts from hand grenades, and the shocking booms of percussion artillery shells. But on they had pressed, through rain, snow, freezing temperatures, and soft, muddy ground, while the beleaguered Nazis ran short of manpower, oil, and ammunition. And now, the Red Army at last had the Third Reich in its grasp and was ready to strip it of every armament. But when Vlasov had taken control of the rocket works, the spoils of war had all been stripped away by "American rules."

The scheme was obvious.

The Americans were doing backroom deals with any Nazis who could help the United States create the most powerful arsenal the world had ever seen.

An arsenal they planned to use against Russia.

It all made sense.

So enraged was Vlasov by this capitalist deception that as soon as Hardware, his troops, and their half of the Nazi POWs had vanished from view, he whipped out the Nagant revolver holstered at his left hip—the gun he carried specifically for times like these, when the Tokarev semi-automatic pistol at his other hip wouldn't do—and flipped open the cylinder to empty six of its seven chambers of bullets. After spinning the cylinder clockwise, he snapped it shut.

The first to feel the cold muzzle pressed up against the flesh at the bridge of his nose was the *Über*-Aryan youth. The eyes of the fourteen-year-old widened, but he didn't flinch.

Click!

Vlasov moved left to the next POW and aimed at his brain.

The shaking man pissed his pants.

Click!

Five chambers left. The next POW was defiant.

Click!

The next.

Click!

The next.

Before Vlasov could pull the trigger on one of the last three chambers, the POW in front of him cried out in Russian—he must have learned it from Slavic slaves in the Mittelwerk—"Don't kill me! I'll buy my life from you!"

Vlasov paused. "With what?"

"Information."

"Speak," he demanded.

"Him!" the terrified man barked, pointing back to the *Über*-Aryan youth. "He's Ernst Streicher's son."

The words so jolted Vlasov that he actually winced. His head jerked to the beginning of the rank, just this side of where his hand had marked the line between.

"Streicher's son?"

"Hans Streicher. Can't you see it in him?"

"Yes," agreed the Russian, and he pulled the trigger. The revolver bucked in his hand as a blood red spray exploded out the back of the whistleblower's skull.

On the Soviet colonel's order, Hans Streicher was grabbed by two soldiers and hauled away from the line of POWs.

"Kill them," Vlasov commanded, and the machine guns opened up on the prisoners with successive bursts of fire until Streicher's son was the only one left alive.

TRINITY TEST SITE, NEW MEXICO
July 16, 1945

At 5:29:45 a.m. on this Monday morning, God spoke to Hardware for the first time. The lieutenant colonel—Hawke had been promoted for his new Pentagon job at Army Ordnance—was in New Mexico to prepare for the arrival of SS-Sturmbannführer Wernher von Braun and his team of rocketeers so that work could begin on beefing up the "arsenal of democracy." Thanks to his top-secret clearance level, Hardware had earned a special invite to the Trinity test site to witness the birth of a weapon that promised to shock the world.

So here Hardware stood in the early dawn light, as tense as he had ever been in his entire life, counting down the longest ten seconds in history.

Three …

Two …

One …

BWAM!!!

First, there were just a few streaks of gold to the east, and it was so dim that you could barely see your neighbor. Then suddenly there was an enormous flash of searing light, the brightest light that any living creature had ever witnessed. That first atomic explosion created a blinding fireball that fused the desert sand into a green glass-like solid. The sacred blast bored its way through Hardware and produced a vision that was seen by more than the eye. What was a measly burning bush compared with a crater nearly twenty-four hundred feet across and ten feet deep? Hardware heard the word of God in that two-second revelation.

Glory hallelujah!

LOS ALAMOS PRODUCED two atomic weapons.

The first—nicknamed "Little Boy"—was a gun-style weapon that used uranium 235. A slug of U-235 was projected down a gun barrel into the center of another chunk of U-235. That collision produced a nuclear explosion.

At eight-fifteen in the morning on August 6, 1945, a B-29 bomber, the *Enola Gay,* dropped the Little Boy uranium bomb on the Japanese city of Hiroshima. Half of the city was leveled, and somewhere between seventy thousand and a hundred and thirty thousand men, women, and children died instantly.

The Japanese had no idea that such a weapon existed.

On the night of the day that the world got news of this bomb, Hardware had a dream. In it, he saw an internment camp at Ground Zero. Prisoners scurried around like ants, and a huge chimney loomed up from the center. All at once, the bomb went off—its thirteen thousand tons of TNT like the world's largest blast furnace. And when the face of God retreated back to heaven, all that remained of the camp conjured up by his mind was a swirl of ash and bits of bone.

Hardware awoke with a start, and the biggest erection he could ever remember.

Waking up the wife to get a little relief, he spread her legs and climbed on top and launched his own V-2—for that's the sexual fantasy that sprang to his mind, a rocket like the one the Nazis of Dora-Mittelbau were going to build for the land of the free—and he came in a nuclear blast of his own.

THE SECOND WEAPON—nicknamed "Fat Man"—used implosion to detonate plutonium. Explosives surrounded a plutonium ball, and when they were detonated, they compressed the ball to cause a nuclear explosion.

With its large harbor and many hills, Nagasaki was called the San Francisco of Japan. On August 9, 1945, three days after Hiroshima, Fat Man dropped out of the belly of another B-29 to devastate more than two square miles of the city. Exploding with a force equal to twenty kilotons of TNT, the plutonium weapon was more powerful than Little Boy. Forty-five thousand citizens died instantly.

Five days later, Japan surrendered and the war was over.

NINE MONTHS AFTER Hardware's nuclear explosion inside his wife, his son was born.

They named the baby after his dad: Bill Hawke, Jr.

A chip off the old block, the kid required a nickname.

Hardware considered calling him Little Boy.

But instead, the boy ended up with another handle.

Big Bad Bill.

Deep Black

"But can I trust you?" Bill Hawke, Jr., asked.

"You don't have a choice," said DeClercq. "I swore a declaration under the Security of Information Act. It's in your pocket. And you have my word. I'll keep my word if you don't try to lie to me. But be warned. When I came out of retirement to head up Special X, I was hard at work writing a history of the Second World War. And if there's one thing a Mountie knows, it's the smell of horseshit. So what's your Nazi secret?"

"Overcast," said Bill. "What does that mean to you?"

"It's the operation in which the Pentagon spirited Nazi scientists like Wernher von Braun from the ruins of the Third Reich to America at the close of the war."

"Basically, we fucked the Russians."

"That you did," said DeClercq.

"But we had to do it under restrictive rules. Bleeding hearts in the White House and Congress tried to tie our hands."

"That didn't stop you."

"We did what we had to do. The American eagle rules the world's skies thanks to its beak and talons."

To DeClercq's way of thinking, warlords like Bill Hawke were to blame for the dirtiest cover-up in U.S. history.

Hundreds of thousands of American patriots had died making a heroic stand against the tyranny of the Swastika. Before they were even cold in their graves, however, the Pentagon had hatched a plan to absorb Nazi scientists into military think-tanks in the United States. Von Braun flew to America in September 1945. Shortly thereafter, he was joined by the rocketeers on the list that he himself had drawn up at the time of his surrender.

Prisoners of peace.

That's what they'd called themselves.

But it wasn't the idea of using Nazi scientists to advance the development of U.S. missiles that disgusted DeClercq. It was the deception used to con the post-war world, paid for in the blood of honest men who had fought for truth and democracy. Many a time, he had made his own pacts with the devil—plea bargaining with criminals, for example, to catch more vicious predators—but in every case, the deal he'd made was scrutinized by those he served.

DeClercq abhorred liars.

Lying spread like cancer.

The cancer had begun in 1946. The Pentagon had yearned to recruit more former Nazis for the Cold War arms race that was just beginning. But U.S. immigration laws barred entry by former Nazi Party officials, so President Truman expanded Operation Overcast into Project Paperclip, a top-secret mission to bring in Nazis who were supposedly untainted by war crimes.

In April 1946, von Braun's group test-fired their first reconstructed V-2 at the White Sands Proving Ground in New Mexico. Once they had their Nazi wonder weapon, the Arlington warlords had no intention of laying it down, so they authorized Bill Hawke, Sr., and his cleaning crew to rid the immigration files of Hitler's rocketeers of anything that might rile the sensibilities of Americans who truly believed in truth.

Red-lining, the Pentagon called it.

There was so much to red-line out of the Nazi rocketeers' files. It was von Braun's team—not Himmler's SS—that had thought to use concentration camp labor to produce the V-2 at Peenemünde. Arthur Rudolph, the production manager, was the master of those slave workers. That's how the V-2 group linked up with Ernst Streicher, the engineer behind Hitler's final solution and the architect of twenty thousand slave deaths at Dora-Mittelbau.

With the switch to the underground factory in the tunnels north of Nordhausen, Rudolph became production director. Though based at Peenemünde, still the site for rocket testing, von Braun was a force at the Mittelwerk. There, at a crucial meeting in May 1944, he and Rudolph decided to enslave eighteen hundred more skilled French POWs to bolster the workforce. To accomplish that, von Braun went to Buchenwald and spoke to the commandant. All the while, Rudolph was passing on sabotage reports to Streicher's SS. That was the problem confronting Hawke and his red-line spooks. Instead of taking orders, many of their not-so-nominal Nazi golden boys had been issuing them.

In the rewritten version of history, lies trumped the truth. The use of slave labor had been forced on "our Nazis" by Himmler's SS. Von Braun's arrest in March 1944 was a blessing. Hawke spun the real reason—Himmler's desire to take control of von Braun's V-2—into an anti-Nazi mythology about apolitical space enthusiasts who were forced to develop weaponry at the expense of their dreams of interstellar flight.

But a threat to that myth presented itself in 1947. The war crimes trial of those who'd headed up the rocket works at Dora-Mittelbau took place at Dachau. To protect the lies that ring-fenced his sanitized Nazis, Hawke rebuffed the prosecutors' request to have von Braun appear as a witness. And when those prosecutors went hunting for Georg Rickhey, the general director at the Mittelwerk, they found he was doing research on underground factories for the U.S. Air Force at Wright Field in Dayton, Ohio. Most of the men on trial went free.

Expediency over principle.

The unexpected explosion of the Soviet Union's first atomic bomb in 1949 sent shock waves rattling through the Pentagon. The following year, von Braun and his rocketeers were transferred to Huntsville, Alabama, to develop nuclear-tipped missiles to counter the Red threat. Anti-Communist sentiment slapped the last coat of whitewash onto the post-war conspiracy, and the truth about the Mittelwerk vanished into the black hole of the black world.

So impenetrable was the cover-up that by 1955, DeClercq—then a boy in a coonskin cap like Davy Crockett wore on the new medium of TV—could watch Wernher von Braun, his handsome face above the slide rule in his pocket, on a trio of popular Walt Disney shows: "Man in Space," "Man and the Moon," and later, "Mars and Beyond." That same year saw the opening of Disneyland. There, DeClercq had tilted his head back in Tomorrowland to take in the sleek metal skin of the Moonliner, a needle-nosed rocket that soared higher than Sleeping Beauty's castle. Designed for Disney by von Braun, that rocket was touted as the future of America's space program.

That's about as squeaky clean as you can get.

"Pearl Harbor of the Stars!" and "Red Conquest!" blared headlines across America on the morning of October 5, 1957. The Russian satellite Sputnik, developed from the V-2s left behind in East Germany, was orbiting the globe. When the Pentagon freaked and tried to launch its own Vanguard rocket, it exploded on takeoff and was christened

"Stay-putnik" by the press. So von Braun got the go-ahead to give it a try, and on January 31, 1958, his Jupiter-C rocket—really a modified V-2—blasted off from Florida to put Explorer 1 in space.

By 1960, von Braun was the head of NASA's George C. Marshall Space Flight Center, a civilian agency that usurped the Pentagon's role in the space race. With Arthur Rudolph as the project director, the whitewashed Nazi rocketeers helped create the mighty Saturn 5 booster, which put Americans on the moon in 1969. "That's one small step for man, one giant leap for mankind."

In the realm of science, von Braun was a genius. Every rocket that first shot into space off American and Russian launching pads had its origin in his brain. America loves its heroes—no matter what the truth behind the myth—and von Braun had become an American citizen in 1955. *Life* magazine crowned him one of the one hundred most important Americans of the twentieth century, and the Daughters of the American Revolution bestowed on him their Americanism Medal. Lionized, glorified, and showered with honors, SS-Sturmbannführer Wernher von Braun died of stomach cancer in Alexandria, Virginia, on June 16, 1977.

Rudolph wasn't as lucky.

His past caught up with him.

Between 1946 and the 1960s, the story of the underground rocket factory was written out of history. The Cold War and the arms race made sure of that. In the 1960s, the East Germans tried to blow the whistle on von Braun's membership in the SS and his links to Dora-Mittelbau, but the American media wouldn't touch that exposé with a ten-foot pole. By then, von Braun was an American god. That's why they say you can fool all of the people some of the time, and some of the people all of the time. The Pentagon wanted to fool all of the people all of the time.

The first memoir by a Dora survivor was published in English in 1979, two years after the death of von Braun. Congress had just created a new Nazi-hunting agency, the Office of Special Investigations, or OSI. Rudolph was persuaded to renounce his U.S. citizenship and flee to Germany, in lieu of standing trial for war crimes at the Mittelwerk.

It was that background that had brought DeClercq and Bill Hawke, Jr., to this interview room, where they sat staring each other down with the tape recorder turned off, since official secrets don't exist. If von Braun represented the depths to which Pentagon patriots would sink to hide un-Americanisms in the white world, how far, DeClercq wondered, would the spooks of the black world go to bury their own dirtiest secrets?

On the table between them lay the pair of blueprints from the bench in the Skunk Mine.

"Roswell," said the Mountie. "Tell me the truth."

"Do you know what a torsion field is?"

"No," replied DeClercq.

Bill explained the quantum mechanics of zero-point energy. Space isn't a vacuum; it's a quantum foam, with nanoparticles popping in and out of existence billions of times a second on every conceivable frequency and in every possible direction. Those fluctuations generate a field of zero-point energy. "At the end of the Second World War," Bill informed the Mountie, "the Nazis were hard at work on an electromagnetic device designed to tap into ZPE."

He rapped the blueprint of *die Glocke*.

"The Nazis called it the Bell."

"Where did they build it?" asked DeClercq.

"In the Wenceslas Mine. In the Sudeten Mountains of what is now Poland but then was Nazi Germany."

"How did the Bell work?"

"As you can see in the blueprint, it's in the shape of a disk. That's because anything that spins can create a torsion field. Vortexes—energy spirals—are what nature uses to funnel energy. Inside the Bell were two cylinders that spun in opposite directions. By whirling them at twenty-five thousand to fifty thousand rpms, the Nazis created an electromagnetic device that tapped into, drew energy from, and altered ZPE."

"How did a spinning superconductor do that?"

"Spin polarization."

"Draw me a simpler picture," said DeClercq.

"Imagine a mixing bowl full of zero-point energy. Now imagine a whirling blender dipping into the contents of the bowl. The Bell was a Mixmaster that spun to generate a whirlpool of electromagnetism—a torsion field, in other words. And when Nazi scientists dipped the energy spiral of their man-made vortex into the mixing bowl of quantum foam, the ZPE reacted, meshed, or aligned with the Bell in such a way that it produced magical effects."

"What sort of magic?"

"Basically, they were experimenting with the hidden properties of space-time. If you generate a torsion field of sufficient force, it's possible to bend the three dimensions of space and the fourth dimension of time around the generator."

"The Bell was a time machine?"

"That became Hitler's obsession during his last days in the Berlin bunker. He sank into madness before he put a bullet in his brain. Time, like gravity, is a variable of hyper-space. Hyperspace is best visualized as a fifth dimension where the binding mechanisms of the universe do their work. The Nazis knew that quantum particle fluctuations slow down when they are affected by a torsion field. If the Bell was able to slow time *within* its vortex to a thousandth of the speed at which time was advancing *outside* its influence, Hitler thought he would be able to save himself by switching bunkers to the Wenceslas Mine and living down there for a year. When he stepped out of his time machine twelve months later, he would see the apex of his thousand-year Reich."

"How?" asked DeClercq. "A time machine can transport you to the future, but it can't actually *change* the future. Why wouldn't Hitler find himself in the Germany of 2945—a Germany that still would have lost the Second World War?"

Hawke shrugged. "Because that's not what his horoscope foretold. He expected a miracle, like what happened with Frederick the Great."

"Megalomania."

"The guy was nuts," said Hawke. "But with reason. The science is sound."

"Gravity," probed DeClercq. "Where does that fit in?"

"You caught that, huh?"

"It wasn't hard," said the Horseman, tapping the *Flugkreisel* blueprint on the table in front of him. "It's staring us in the face."

"Gravity, like time," said Hawke, "is a variable of hyperspace. The Holy Grail of aeronautics is, and always has been, an *anti*-gravity device. Every aircraft in the skies today, from supersonic jets to the space shuttle, is the same as the Wright brothers' biplane. All are powered gliders.

"But imagine if we could develop a craft that sucked—instead of pushed—its way through what's up there. A device that not only negated the force of gravity, but also canceled out the sluggishness of inertia, an object's innate resistance to acceleration. Such an aircraft would in effect have *negative* weight. And without inertia providing resistance, it would continue to gather speed all the way up to the speed of light. No more jet engines, rocket blasts, or nuclear power. No more propellant fuel of any kind. We'd be flying a machine that drew its power from the pulse of the universe, the ultimate quantum leap in aircraft design. It would be the biggest transportation breakthrough since invention of the wheel!"

Having made up his mind to come clean with DeClercq—national security depended on this, and so did the black legacy of Hardware and son—Hawke was manic in his enthusiasm. He had the look of a zealot in his eyes. DeClercq had a question he was itching to pose, but now wasn't the time to risk turning off the verbal tap.

"Sounds fantastic," he said.

"Not really," Hawke replied. "Think about it. What happens when you bring the same poles of two magnets together? North meets north? Or south meets south?"

"They repel each other and bounce apart."

"Opposites attract. Likes diverge. So electromagnetism both pulls and pushes things. Gravity, inertia, and electro-magnetism are component forces of zero-point energy. By spinning the Bell at high speeds, the Nazis created a coupling device that *directed* the flow of ZPE, exploiting those fluctuations in the quantum sea as they blinked in and out of existence in hyperspace. The most efficient shape to whirl up electro-gravitational lift is a disk. Charge a saucer-like disk positively on the top side and negatively on the lower, and it will exert thrust from the negative to the positive and rise skyward. In other words, it will manipu-late gravity for an anti-gravity effect. Divide the disk into segments and dispatch part of the charge around the outer rim, and the saucer can be made to move in any direction."

"Sounds simple."

"It's not. No more simple than splitting an atom. The device must be tuned like a radio to interact with the gravity and inertia components of the ZPE field. Tune it right and you can cancel them out. Tune it wrong and what you've got is useless."

"Is that what the SS was working on in the Wenceslas Mine? The nuts-and-bolts hardware of a time machine for Hitler and an anti-gravity war machine for use against the Allies?"

"Down in the mine and above," said Hawke. "They also fashioned a Stonehenge-shaped test rig on the surface. A rig sturdy enough to hold down the lift of a flying saucer."

Now's the time, thought the Horseman.

"So tell me about Ernst Streicher."

The Pentagon spook blinked.

DeClercq cinched the hangman's noose. "And don't try to play me for a fool."

Mein Kampf

For as long as the Aryan could remember, pigs had been his best friends. Even back when he was just a young boy living on a pig farm in East Germany, with his broken father and his simpleton of a mother. That his father was crippled both physically and mentally was evident as they went about their chores, mucking out the wallow in their scrub patch of a yard, birthing litters of tiny piglets in the barn, and hanging the pigs up from hooks in the slaughter-house to slit their throats and butcher the carcasses down to pork.

Hunched and dragging one leg behind him like a ball and chain, the Aryan's father had struggled through every workday aided by his only son. His wife stuffed the sausages they sold on market day. The tears that ran down his father's face as each strung-up pig squealed for its life exposed how fragile he really was. Only later, when the boy was older, did his mother tell him that his father had spent twenty years enduring torture and humiliation in Moscow's notorious Lubyanka prison after the war.

Seared into the Aryan's memory was the one time he'd met his father's tormentor.

Colonel Boris Vlasov.

It was December 1979, and winter held East Germany in its hoary glove. The landscape behind the Iron Curtain stood frozen in time, locked forever in May 1945, on the ignoble day that the Third Reich had crumbled into ruins. Time had moved forward in the zones occupied by the United States, Britain, and France. But in the grim, gray zone occupied by the Soviet Union, where Red Army jackboots continued to stomp Germans in their homes, you could still dig war-time bullets out of most of the shell-shocked walls. Only on days like this, with fresh snow blanketing the earth and icicles glittering everywhere else, could a boy fantasize that he was in wonderland.

It was slaughter day, and all three were in the barn. Each wore the leather apron of that messy work, with traditional German rural clothing underneath. Forsaking lederhosen because of the cold, both he and his father wore brown trousers with suspenders over wool vests. The barn doors were open to the snowy countryside, but inside it was misty from the plumes of their breath and the condensation rising from the pools of warm red blood on the floor. The pigs were making such a racket that the family didn't catch the sound of footsteps entering the barn.

Bang!

A shot was fired through the roof to grab their attention.

A line of icicles crashed to the ground and shattered into a thousand ruby red diamonds.

"Drop your knives," the gunman yelled.

Russian soldiers quickly moved forward and cuffed the hands of the boy and his parents in front of their waists. Then one by one, starting with his father, they were hoisted up by their wrists like the hog-tied pigs still squealing fearfully on the slaughterhouse hooks. The Germans, however, weren't hog-tied. Their legs hung free, so that they could just touch the blood-soaked floor. Hanging so their backs were to the open door, the terrified boy and his mother faced his father, six feet away.

The change in his father's expression clearly signaled that worse was to come. The eyes widened in disbelief, as if he had just glimpsed a ghost, and the lips began to tremble. Soon his father broke into gibbers while trickles of urine ran down his toes to mix with blood on the floor.

"No, Vlasov!" he wailed.

His legs jerked this way and that like a marionette trying to break free of the strings that held it prisoner. The boy saw the shadow of the puppet master creep across the floor before he saw the man behind it. When he finally got a look at his father's demon in the flesh, he was surprised to see that the man was little more than a walking, cancer-ridden skeleton.

"Yes, Streicher," Vlasov snarled as he sucked in a final puff from his cigarette and dropped it in the gore at his feet. "Why do you think I released you from prison, if not for this? For you to experience what your father made me suffer in the war, I had to let you start a family."

Vlasov unbuttoned his greatcoat to expose the outdated Stalinist uniform underneath. Through a hacking fit violent enough to cough up both lungs, he motioned his thugs to attack the boy and his mother.

"Rape them," he rasped.

The boy was still wondering why the Russian had called his father Streicher—that wasn't the name they went by— when the soldiers grabbed hold of his mother and ripped off her clothes. As she hung naked from the hook, they moved across to her son and stripped him, too.

"The boy first," Vlasov ordered. "Remember, Streicher? How you screamed at Dora-Mittelbau?"

The last sound the boy heard before he passed out from shock was the high-pitched squeal from his own throat.

THE BOY HAD EMERGED from unconsciousness to find his father gone. The hook in front of him no longer held the

.

crippled wreck of a man. Beside him, his mother hung bleeding, and that's how they'd stayed until someone arrived to buy a meal of bratwurst.

That Christmas, a package addressed to the boy came in the mail. He opened the paper to find what at first seemed to be a leather-bound book. But the crest engraved into the cover was one he knew well, since it was the tattoo from the skin over his father's heart.

What Vlasov had sent as a keepsake was a blood-splattered copy of Hitler's *Mein Kampf.*

NOW IT WAS HIS CHORE to slaughter the pigs for pork. But instead of stringing them up by their hind legs, as his father used to do, he hoisted them up by their front legs so he could pigstick them in the butt first. As he did, he fantasized about doing that to the Russian colonel.

Only pigsticking released the rage inside him.

With Russian spies everywhere in East Germany, it was too dangerous to dig too deeply into the name Streicher. Libraries were monitored and history books rewritten. He didn't dare try until he reached high school, and even then he didn't reap much of a payoff. Just one Nazi of consequence had borne that name: SS-Obergruppenführer Ernst Streicher. According to the book the Aryan read, that general had "died in the same cowardly way as Adolf Hitler. Two days after the Nazi surrender, he committed suicide in a forest somewhere between Prague and Pilsen."

The Aryan hadn't learned the truth until 1989.

Shortly after the fall of the Berlin Wall on November 9, he and his mother were eating lunch in their farmhouse kitchen when a fancy BMW drove up and stopped by the pig wallow. The sexiest woman he had ever seen climbed out from the passenger's side and swept her eyes around the yard with distaste.

The Aryan thought they were lost.

Seconds later, however, the driver stepped out, and the instant the pig farmer saw him, he knew this man was his dead father's brother. No mistaking the Nordic blond hair, icy blue eyes, and Aryan bone structure of the stranger's face.

"Hans!" his mother gasped, stumbling to her feet and dropping the bread knife to the grimy floor. She saw the resemblance, too, and thought her husband had returned to her. His ailing mother had never recovered from that horrific visit by the cancerous colonel and his gang-raping thugs.

"Say nothing," the Aryan silenced her. "Leave all the speaking to me."

The visitors from the West rapped on the kitchen door. That they had come from the other side of the Iron Curtain was evident from their car and their fashionable clothes. The woman cast her gaze at both pig farmers and around their kitchen as if she feared catching a sewer disease. Her luscious figure complemented her sable coat. The man wore an elegant gray leather jacket over matching slacks; a charcoal turtleneck was visible in the V at his throat. In East Germany, survival taught you to spot a hidden gun, and the Aryan caught the telltale bulge in one pocket.

"Bratwurst or blutwurst?" he asked on opening the door.

"Neither," replied the man. "I'm here because I believe you're the son of my brother, Hans."

"Hans Streicher?" the Aryan said.

"We don't use that name, do we?" cautioned the stranger. "That's why I had a devil of a time tracking you down. But with the fall of the wall, certain Communist archives have cracked open. It took a chunk of cash to uncover the name your father assumed after the Russians released him from prison."

"What's your name?"

"Fritz. But I don't use that either. May we come in? It's chilly out here in the yard."

The Aryan stood aside so they could enter. He noticed that the woman was careful not to brush against him. She wrinkled her nose as if she could smell pig shit in the kitchen.

"Hans!" his mother cried again, tears welling up in her eyes. "I knew you'd come back to me. We still have your tattoo. Let me sew it back on for you."

"My mother isn't—"

But that's all he got out. Fritz Streicher elbowed the Aryan aside in his haste to engage the feeble woman.

"Show me," the intruder from the West demanded.

"Stay put, Mother!" ordered the Aryan. "Why have you gone to the trouble of finding us after all this time? And how do I know you're who you say you are?"

The man purporting to be his uncle turned his attention back to the son. "I've come to make you rich. Did your father never tell you how we got separated?"

The Aryan shook his blond head.

So Fritz Streicher told a story about two Werewolves captured by the Americans in the woods near Work Camp Dora. His story ended when the POWs were divided by the line that Colonel Vlasov cut between the Streicher brothers. With one gesture, he sent Fritz off with the GIs to a post-war life of luxury on Canada's West Coast and condemned the Aryan's father to Lubyanka prison and then a scrub existence on this pig farm.

Vlasov!

The mere mention of the name caused the Aryan to tense up tighter than the mainspring of a watch.

"You know that name?" Fritz Streicher asked, picking up on his nephew's discomfort.

"Vlasov flayed my father and used the tattoo over his heart to bind a copy of Hitler's *Mein Kampf*."

"You have the book?"

"It was sent to me as a Christmas taunt."

"Let me see it."

"How will that make me rich?"

"*Us* rich," corrected Fritz. "We'll split the treasure."

"What treasure?"

"Do you know who your grandfather was?"

A flash of insight. "SS-Obergruppenführer Ernst Streicher," the pig farmer said.

"Near the close of the war, Hans and I were tattooed with different crests. The last time we saw our father, he told us that if anything should happen to him, we were to look to our legacy. And then he tapped us both on the heart."

"The tattoos hide a map?"

"Half a map," said Fritz. "Mine shows the outline of a castle. But I can't recall what was hidden in Hans's tattoo. We were too embroiled in events of the time, and then we got caught and separated by the line between. Only later did I work out the mystery behind the tattoos. Each by itself kept our father's treasure hidden, but together they are the pieces of a jigsaw puzzle. Solve the puzzle and we will share the legacy left by him."

"You've done well for yourself."

Fritz Streicher shrugged. "Your grandfather smuggled out Hitler's gold to finance the Fourth Reich. After your father and I got separated, I was asked by those who remained of the Third Reich to become paymaster for those on the run."

"Why didn't you save my father?"

"You're far too young to know how impenetrable the Iron Curtain was in the decades after the war. The Russians, not the Germans, kept all the secrets. And even when the grip loosened in the late sixties, it would have been suicide for me to go to the East. Besides, your father dropped our name long ago. How would I have found him?"

"Show me your tattoo."

The four of them were still standing in the kitchen. The woman in the fur coat seemed disgusted and antsy. She kept shifting her weight from foot to foot as if she was ready to go. The Aryan's mother was nibbling her lower lip and wringing her hands in the apron of her grubby dirndl. Then she noticed the bread knife on the floor and crouched to pick it up from the dirt.

Fritz Streicher opened his jacket and tugged his turtle-neck up from his belt. For a man verging on sixty, he was exceptionally lean and taut. Just as he'd said, the tattoo over his heart was a crest showing the battlement towers of a castle.

"What castle is that?"

"Not so fast," said the Aryan's uncle. "Get *Mein Kampf* and we'll fit the jigsaw together."

The pig farmer left the kitchen for his ground-floor bedroom, returning a minute later with the skin-covered Nazi bible. As his uncle began to slip his hand into the pocket with the telltale bulge, the Aryan held the book out on that side. So as not to arouse suspicion in the wary German, Fritz detoured his gun hand to receive the offering.

"Which castle?" his nephew pressed, refusing to release his grip on *Mein Kampf*.

"Castle Werewolf," Fritz said. "In the Sudeten Mountains."

He yanked the book free from the young man's fingers and passed it across to his other hand.

"During the war, the general had his headquarters there."

As Fritz's hand went back to the pocket with the bulge, a blur of motion passed in front of his eyes. Before he even realized that his throat had just been cut, the book was wrenched away from him. Slitting throats came naturally to the pig farmer, who had armed himself in the bedroom for a counterattack.

There were several reasons why Fritz had to die. First, he should have used Hitler's gold to bribe Soviet officials into turning Hans over to the West. Second, he was certainly not intending to let his nephew and his sister-in-law live once he got what he wanted. Third, the Aryan was so wound up by the unfairness of having been abandoned to the atrocities of Colonel Vlasov that he could no longer restrain himself. And finally, he couldn't imagine why he should split the treasure in the castle with somebody who already had too much.

So Fritz Streicher had to die.

And so did his wife.

The rage that powered the whirling sweep of the razor-sharp blade was so intense that it almost severed the sexy woman's head right off her furry shoulders. *Lustmord,* the Germans called it, this feeling of absolute power that turned the Aryan into a superman, unleashing the killer within.

"Hans!" his mother wailed, dropping to her knees beside the dead man on the floor.

How pathetic.

How unworthy of the master race.

Ashamed of this feeble woman, the Aryan crouched down and slit her throat too.

TO BE A SAUSAGE-STUFFER in post-war East Germany was to be ribbed about Georg Grossmann. Many a time had the Aryan heard about how Georg had ground up and sold more than fifty people as frankfurters on the platform of the Berlin train station. Inspired by that story, the pig farmer had skinned Fritz's tattoo from over his heart, then processed his victims as he had so many pigs before them, grinding the meat into sausages and the bones into meal. Both products sold out at the farm's stall the following market day.

Getting rid of the car was easier. He drove the BMW to a destitute city and left it unlocked, with the key in the ignition. In the blink of an eye, it vanished forever.

The reunification of Germany saw East Germans flooding to the West for a better life. The Aryan let it be known that his mother had joined the economic exodus. West German relatives had taken her away to Cologne. Soon, he'd follow.

When he arrived at Castle Werewolf in what was now Poland, the former pig farmer matched the dark outline against the tattoo from his uncle's chest. The castle was being renovated to capitalize on a burgeoning tourist trade in unshackled Poland, so the Aryan managed to get work on the site. He was guided by the inky cross in his father's tattoo to the mantle in the Knight's Hall and what he thought would be a cache of gold. Instead, he found nothing but scientific papers.

Cheated again!

Well, not quite.

There was still a chance that Hitler's gold could be mined on the West Coast of British Columbia. His uncle's pocket had given up a sizable wad of ready cash, some traveler's checks, and several credit cards, as well as a Canadian passport with an address in Vancouver. Packing up the scientific papers, which had to have *some* value, the Aryan had abandoned the Fatherland for this *Lebensraum* half a world away.

His dreams of Hitler's gold, however, were not to be.

By 1990, the bullion vaults hidden behind the walls of the replica bunker were empty of Nazi loot. It didn't really matter. Psychologically, the Aryan was more suited to the isolation of the Phantom Valley Ranch, so over the intervening years, the Cariboo mine had been his home base.

But now the phoenix of the Fourth Reich was dying.

Hitler's bunker was where the Aryan would make *his* last stand.

First, he would kill the traitor who betrayed him.

Then he would kill every cop and Pentagon hit man who came to take him down.

The Roswell Incident

Before he entered the interview room to offer the Pentagon spook a choice between public exposure or private confession, DeClercq had delved into the Roswell Incident and reduced it from all its gobbledygook down to a set of solid, confirmed facts.

Those facts were these: Sometime in the first week of July 1947, the morning after a fierce overnight thunderstorm, a New Mexico rancher named Mack Brazel saddled up a horse and rode out to check on his sheep. He found some unusual debris strewn around one pasture. Whatever crash-landed there had gouged a shallow trench for hundreds of feet across the hard ground. After taking a few pieces to show his neighbors, Brazel drove into Roswell to report the incident to Sheriff George Wilcox. Wilcox passed the information on to officials at Roswell Army Air Field, home base of the 509th Bomb Group, the air unit that had dropped the atomic bombs on Hiroshima and Nagasaki.

The U.S. military locked down the crash site and retrieved the wreckage, which was first moved to Roswell Army Air Field, then later was flown to Wright Field in Dayton, Ohio. On July 8, 1947, the commander of the 509th, Colonel William Blanchard, issued a press release stating that the wreckage of a "crashed disk" had been recovered. The news made headlines in thirty afternoon papers across the nation.

Within hours of Colonel Blanchard's press release, the commander of the Eighth Air Force, General Roger Ramey, issued a chaser release explaining that the 509th Bomb Group had misidentified a weather balloon and its radar reflector as a crashed disk. To prove the point, Ramey displayed the balloon's remnants in his office and allowed some photos to be snapped. The press reported the correction on July 9.

To this day, that remains the Pentagon's official position.

Case closed.

Those facts, of course, gave rise to wild speculation about a top-level cover-up.

According to the legend of the Roswell Incident, Glenn Dennis, a young mortician working for the Ballard Funeral Home, received several telephone calls from the mortuary officer at Roswell Army Air Field. He wanted to know about the availability of hermetically sealed caskets and the best way to preserve bodies that had been exposed to the elements for a few days without altering the chemical composition of the tissues. That evening, Dennis drove to the army hospital, where he saw two military ambulances stocked with pieces of wreckage marked with weird symbols. Inside the building, he began speaking with a nurse he knew, but MPs threatened him physically and forced him to leave. The next day, he met the nurse in a coffee shop, and she told him that she had assisted two doctors doing autopsies on several non-human bodies. One body was still in good shape, but the others were mangled. She drew a diagram of these non-human creatures. Within days, she was sent to England, and never returned.

Similar strong-arm techniques were used on other Roswell witnesses. Mack Brazel was sequestered for a week by the military, for example, and sworn to secrecy on his release. Sheriff Wilcox was told that he and his family would be killed if he ever talked about what he had seen while investigating the crash. Any bits of wreckage that surfaced were immediately seized. But none of that could squelch the rumor that there were *three* crash sites. The debris field that Brazel had found was in the middle. Thirty miles to the southeast, investigators had come upon what remained of the flying disk and its crew. And a few miles northwest, there was a touchdown point of fused sand and baked soil.

DeClercq, however, was most intrigued by Major Jesse Marcel. As the intelligence officer at the 509th Bomb Group, he was involved in the recovery of the Brazel wreckage. On July 8, the day of the Blanchard press release, Marcel took some of the debris to Texas to show to General Ramey. In his office, that debris was switched for the weather balloon that later appeared in the press photos. When he was interviewed about the wreckage in 1979, Marcel stated, "It was not a weather balloon. Nor was it an airplane or a missile." The debris "would not burn. That stuff weighs nothing. It wouldn't bend. We even tried making a dent in it with a sledgehammer. And there was still no dent."

In 1994, a U.S. congressman asked for "information on the alleged crash and recovery of an extraterrestrial vehicle and its alien occupants near Roswell, N.M., in July 1947." That spawned "The Roswell Report: Case Closed," a paper released by the military later that year. "There is no dispute that something happened near Roswell in July, 1947," it concluded. "The Roswell Incident was not an airplane crash ... a missile crash ... a nuclear accident ... [or an accident involving] an extraterrestrial craft." Instead, it was an accident that resulted from a "Top Secret balloon project designed to attempt to monitor Soviet nuclear tests, known as Project Mogul." The so-called Roswell Incident, the report concluded, grew out of "overreaction by Colonel Blanchard and Major Marcel, in originally reporting that a 'flying disk' had been recovered." The report dismissed rumors of the recovery of "alien bodies" at Roswell, insisting the wreckage was from a Project Mogul balloon. "There were no 'alien' passengers therein," it stated.

Case closed. Again.

The following year, a British film producer allegedly discovered footage of the alien autopsy. Widely considered a fake because the surgeons disregard conventional autopsy techniques, the film nonetheless contributed to a strange epilogue.

In 1997, the Pentagon revisited "The Roswell Report: Case Closed." It concluded that "'aliens' observed in the New Mexico desert were actually anthropomorphic test dummies carried aloft by U.S. Air Force high-altitude balloons for scientific research." In other words, the Roswell Incident was really just an accident involving *two* balloons: one from Project Mogul, the other full of test dummies.

Case closed.

This time, we *mean* it.

ROBERT DECLERCQ did not believe in little green aliens in flying saucers. He did, however, believe in conspiracies and cover-ups.

During and after the Second World War, the U.S. government had used its own personnel for radiation experiments. The CIA had secretly tortured drugged-out mental patients to test mind-control techniques.

Disinformation, the chief knew, works best when mixed with the truth. Something had crashed at Roswell in 1947, *and the rumors surrounding the Roswell Incident were generated by rival press releases issued by the Pentagon.*

No balloon could gouge a trench hundreds of feet long into desert shale, scattering debris over a large area. A flying disk, on the other hand, would skid across hard shale like a skipping stone. But the official position of the Pentagon is that the "crashed disk" story was an "overreaction" on the part of Colonel Blanchard. So prone to overreacting was William "Butch" Blanchard that he was chosen to supervise the dropping of the first atomic bomb on Hiroshima. In the post-war years, this hysterical man was given command of *all* atomic bombers. And then—*having overreacted at Roswell*—he went on to conduct atomic tests on the Bikini atoll, to train the crews of intercontinental nuclear strike forces, to set up Strategic Air Command, and to rise to the level of vice chief of staff of the United States Air Force.

Overreaction?

DeClercq didn't believe it.

Assuming a "flying disk" did crash, and Blanchard's press release was true, how would the Mountie—were he a Pentagon spook—cover up what had occurred? How better than to hide the truth in plain sight?

A few weeks earlier, on June 24, 1947, pilot Kenneth Arnold had reported experiencing a mid-flight flashing in his eyes, "as if a mirror was reflecting sunlight at me." Then he saw what he thought were nine luminous aircraft flying near Mount Rainier, in Washington State. Each craft seemed to be shaped like "a pie plate" and flew "like a saucer would if you skipped it across the water." A press report of his remarks gave birth to the term "flying saucer," and by the end of July, Arnold's one sighting had exploded into more than 850 reports of unidentified flying objects.

By suppressing the truth behind a cover story about a weather balloon, the Pentagon had tapped into the rising hysteria over aliens from space. If the cover-up succeeded, mission accomplished. And if it was exposed by conspiracy theorists as an attempt to cover up something *unbelievable,* rational minds would conclude that the outlandish incident was fabricated by kooks.

A win-win situation.

But what really piqued DeClercq's interest was the fact that fifty years later—in 1997—the Pentagon was *still* playing that spin-doctor game. Why would "The Roswell Report" undercut the "weather balloon" story by introducing Project Mogul and *then* engage the "alien" issue with some drivel about test dummies and the unlikely simultaneous crashing of two balloons, unless there *actually* was something being covered up?

The Pentagon doth protest too much, thought DeClercq.

Okay, a "flying disk" crashed at Roswell. If there were *three* crash sites leading from northwest to southeast, that would line up with Mount Rainier in the Pacific Northwest. If you continued to follow that line farther north, you'd eventually arrive at the Skunk Mine in British Columbia. In that mine, the Mounties had found this Pentagon spook, whose motive for being there was hidden somewhere in Nazi blueprints for a flying saucer. Those blueprints were stamped with swastikas and had been drawn at the Streicherstab, the brain trust of the man in charge of all super-weapons at the close of the Second World War— SS-Obergruppenführer Ernst Streicher.

"YOU KNOW ABOUT STREICHER?" said Big Bad Bill.

"To my mind," DeClercq replied, choosing his words carefully so as not to expose his bluff, "what became of Ernst Streicher is perhaps the most puzzling mystery to come out of the fall of the Reich. As Nazis fled west to be captured by you Americans instead of the Russians, Streicher went east, to the most dangerous place there was for him. Czech partisans were summarily executing every Nazi they seized. But Streicher's body was never found, and we don't know how he died. One version has him bursting out of a cellar in Prague, charging the Czechs like a Norse hero bound for Valhalla, then being shot in the back by his aide-de-camp to give him as glorious a death as Hitler's. In other versions, Streicher killed himself in various Czech woods."

"What's wrong with that?" said Bill.

"There are too many clues that suggest he survived. First, for no discernible reason, General Patton's Third Army crossed the Czech frontier on May 6, just two days before Nazi Germany surrendered, to penetrate deep into the future Soviet zone and search the Skoda Works."

DeClercq tapped the word "Streicherstab" on the blueprints on the table.

"Patton was after Streicher because of all the sightings of 'foo fighters' over the Reich by American pilots. And you did make contact with him. That's obvious because you failed to try him *in absentia* at the Nuremberg war trials. Martin Bormann's body was never found, despite reports that he'd died while trying to break out from the *Führerbunker*. Streicher's corpse also never turned up. So why try Bormann at Nuremberg, but not the monster who engineered the concentration camps and the gas chambers? There's only one reason. Streicher offered the Pentagon—"

Again, DeClercq tapped the Streicherstab blueprints.

"—something so spectacular that your predecessors had no choice but to deal with him."

It was Hawke's turn to tap the blueprints.

"Do you not grasp the implications of a war machine like this? A *real* flying saucer propelled by fuelless power? There would be no limit *at all* to what you could do. It would take off like a rock out of a slingshot and turn on a dime. The rate of acceleration would defy your imagination. In flight, it wouldn't make a sound. No one would hear you coming. It would stop abruptly, but there'd be no need for seatbelts. Your cockpit crew would feel nothing more than what we feel now from the tremendous speed of our orbiting, revolving earth. Arm it however you want—guns, bombs, lasers. Or nuclear weapons. A fighter like that would rule the world."

The glittering eyes were back.

"So Streicher made you an offer you couldn't refuse?"

"Could you?" said Hawke. "Remember the Cold War? The Cuban Missile Crisis? Nuclear terror?"

DeClercq nodded. "When was contact made?"

"The summer of '45."

"Where?"

"South America. In the dying days of the war, Streicher had flown the Bell to Paraguay. The Pentagon had no one else to deal with. Before escaping from Nazi Germany, he had killed every scientist who'd worked on the project."

"Except himself," said DeClercq.

"He *was* an engineer."

"What deal was struck?"

"What you'd expect. If he could produce a functioning anti-gravity war machine, we'd give him the same break we gave scientists like von Braun—a clean slate. History would record his death in Prague in the final days of the war, and he could live out his life under a new identity, free of Nazi hunters."

"So you let him into the States?"

"Fuck no!" said Hawke, genuinely affronted.

"He stayed in South America?"

The spook shook his head.

That's when it dawned on the Mountie.

"Christ, *we* took him in?"

THERE GOES THE MORAL high ground, thought DeClercq.

As he listened to Hawke describe the ins and outs of the Streicher conspiracy, he began to grasp the unwitting complicity of his own country, and even of the Mounted Police, in the cover-up. So secret was the project that only those directly involved knew it existed. The spook who ran it out of a maverick division of the Pentagon, and was the only American who knew that the engineer of the Holocaust was involved, was someone called Hardware. In the 1940s, there was no better place for the Chronos Project than the Phantom Valley Ranch. Buried in the hinterland of British Columbia, the Skunk Mine was the perfect replacement for the Wenceslas Mine. So throughout the summer and fall of 1945, the last Nazi U-boat in operation went up and down the West Coast of North America, transporting Bell components under the green sea with the blessing of the Pentagon.

"Who owned the ranch?"

"Streicher bought it."

"How?"

"Through an impenetrable false front in Switzerland. It went 'deep black.' A 'denial program.' Streicher picked the scientists and forged the papers. No one knew who was there, or what they were really doing. The only thing we— *and* you—provided was security for a nebulous post-war defense project."

"Who owns the ranch now?"

"Wheels within wheels, it seems. After 1947, we forgot about it."

"What happened?"

"Streicher reassembled the Bell in the Skunk Mine. He picked up where the dead scientists had left off in the Sudeten Mountains. He was able to sneak in a new team of quantum physicists. The coast of B.C. is a smuggler's dream."

Hawke rapped the blueprint of the Bell.

"In their desperation to win the war, Hitler's SS had fooled around with a branch of physics that we still don't comprehend. Out of that cauldron of weird ideas had emerged a method for cracking the code of electrogravitics. Based on that, the Skunk Mine scientists were able to build two flying prototypes."

"Anti-gravity platforms?"

"Right," said Hawke. "The first was the Fireball. Unpiloted, it was remotely controlled. The Nazis had flown it at the end of the war. It had a metallic surface that reflected light like a mirror. In daylight, it looked like a shiny disk spinning on its axis. But at night, it turned into a burning globe."

"The foo fighter?"

Hawke threw DeClercq a thumbs-up.

"The Streicherstab had designed it to be a flying bomb. It had a guidance system called *Windhund*—or wind-hound—that locked onto the change in polarity around our planes like a dog's nose locks onto a strong scent. An oscil-lator canceled out our radar blips. Black Widows over the Reich got tailed by these strange orbs of light."

"Is that what the Skunk Mine scientists flew past Mount Rainier?"

"A Fireball. As proof of concept."

"The witness, Kenneth Arnold, saw nine saucers."

"The rest were coruscations. Mirror images."

"What became of that disk?"

"Anti-gravity worked, so they ditched it out in the Pacific."

"And the other 850 sightings of UFOs that July?"

"It only took one visionary to spot Elvis alive at the mall," replied Hawke.

"There are no little green men?"

"None that I know of. And believe me, I'd know," said the spook.

DeClercq believed him.

"So what crashed at Roswell?"

"The *Flugkreisel*. The Flightwheel. Streicher's ticket to freedom."

"Was that its first flight?"

"Uh-huh. It was being blooded. Tested."

"Why New Mexico?"

"In 1947, that was *the* state. Von Braun and his rocketeers were at White Sands, launching V-2s. And the world's only nuclear strike force was at Roswell. The *Flugkreisel* looked like a flying top. It left a vapor trail of bluish-white ionization in its wake. The plan was to zoom the Flightwheel—with two flight engineers and a doctor in the cockpit—over both New Mexico locations, blow the minds of those below, then fly it north, back to the Phantom Valley."

"What went wrong?"

"Who knows? Some monkey wrench in hyperspace. The team that finished the Flightwheel wasn't the same team that had dreamed it up, so it might have been human error. More likely, the design was flawed. When the craft was found, some metals had transmuted into others. Disrupted hardware had torn apart. And if that wasn't 'extraterrestrial' enough, the flesh of the crew had morphed into otherworldly shapes. If you didn't know what had really happened, it wouldn't be unreasonable to assume that an alien spacecraft had landed."

"Was Streicher on board?"

"No, he was back at the ranch. The crash of the *Flugkreisel* put his immunity deal with us in jeopardy. So that same day, he gathered every member of his new team in the experimental chamber of the Skunk Mine to work on adjusting the torsion field in the hope that would solve the problem. But they must have pushed the gadget too far. There was a huge implosion that turned the whole chamber into a tomb of fused rock."

"That's what blocks the mine today?"

"It's like it never happened."

"And anti-gravity?"

"It's still the Holy Grail. The Flightwheel that was recovered from Roswell was too far gone to reverse-engineer. And all the blueprints from the Streicherstab were with Streicher and his team when they ceased to exist in the depths of the mine.

"Breakthroughs, by their nature, are quantum leaps that short-circuit the evolution of science. The trouble with Nazi technology was that it took *Nazis* to make it function. We couldn't replicate the successes of the Streicherstab, so we returned the Skunk Mine and the Phantom Valley Ranch to the way they were. Then we boxed up the remnants of the Flightwheel and buried everything away until our physicists were able to make a breakthrough of their own. By flatly denying that anything had happened at Roswell, we goaded the conspiracy theorists into making wild claims that have allowed us to keep the truth secret since 1947."

"You're still keeping it from me."

Hawke frowned. "What makes you say that?"

"Come on. No one knew about Streicher, and he never set foot in your country. You say that all you hid were some pieces of scattered debris and three anonymous corpses. You could have claimed you had a broken arrow—a wayward atomic bomb. Or an American saucer that didn't work. Lots of hardware failures have made the news. With Roswell, something *forced* you to bend over backwards to hide the truth. I'll bet your secret involves the Flightwheel's crew."

Hawke snorted.

"Come clean," warned DeClercq. "In for a penny, in for a pound."

"The doctor in the cockpit?"

"Yes?"

"Was Josef Mengele."

THAT'S WHAT HAPPENS, DeClercq thought, when you climb into bed with Nazis.

Mengele epitomized the depravity of Hitler's Reich. Somehow, he was able to elude Nazi hunters for close to thirty-five years. And even when he allegedly died from a stroke while swimming in Brazil in 1979, it took six years before a combined force of American, German, and South American authorities was able to locate his grave. In 1992, DNA tests on the recovered remains confirmed his identity. But now, Hawke was telling DeClercq that all of that was a lie to cover up the fact that the most hunted Nazi in post-war times had actually been killed during a Pentagon super-weapon test in 1947.

No wonder the Roswell Incident was still being spun today!

"How'd you pull that off?"

"With a lot of help," replied Hawke. "Mengele was obsessed with doubles and twins. The Mengele that history tracks across Europe and South America was actually a doppelgänger chosen by the doctor himself to mask his escape. For various reasons, the thirty-odd folks who knowingly or unknowingly aided that deception never said a word. Meanwhile, the Roswell remains were kept in a freezer, and their DNA was preserved."

"So you seeded the grave in Brazil with Mengele's DNA?"

"Brilliant, huh? His skeleton hadn't changed, so his DNA could be compared with that of his known son."

"Why was Mengele aboard the Flightwheel?"

"That was Streicher's doing. We were shocked. The doctor was smuggled in on one of the U-boat runs to assess the impact of the *Flugkreisel*'s test flight on the crew. Not content to stay on the ground, he wanted in on history in the making."

"What do you make of these?" DeClercq asked, indicating the two bloody blueprints.

"The Streicherstab must have done with the Flightwheel what we did with the bomb. Manhattan Project scientists pursued more than one approach to splitting the atom. One method produced Little Boy and the second created Fat Man. Streicher must have done the same with anti-gravity, pursuing one approach at Pilsen and the other at Brno. I guess he didn't trust us not to welsh on the immunity deal, and so held back notes and blueprints generated at Brno. That's the site name stamped on these papers."

"Someone found them."

"Yeah, and tried to blackmail us. We received a sample, along with a demand for a billion dollars, earlier this week. That's a lot of dough for what could be junk, so when we got your swastika query, we took the less costly route of trying to get hold of your file and searching the Skunk Mine. The anchor in the rock must have been moved by anti-gravity, so it's possible that the Brno papers do correct the flaw that caused the Flightwheel to crash."

"You should have paid the billion."

"In hindsight, yes. But now we've really pissed off the extortionist and the papers are still out there. The only operatives killed so far have all been Americans, and they knew the risks. No Canadians have been killed in this operation, so I ask you to honor your deal with me and help the Pentagon recover the Brno blueprints. Imagine what will happen if they're the real McCoy, and they fall into the wrong hands."

Argonauts

No sooner had Dane crashed into sleep than the alarm seemed to go off by mistake. No such luck. It was time to get up if he was going to catch Robson MacKissock.

But first, a quick call to Special X.

"Corporal Hett."

"It's Dane. I'm awake," he reported.

"You don't sound rested."

"I'll catch up later. There's someone I have to see. Nothing new on your front?"

"Nada," said Jackie. "No Swastika Killer e-mail to Cort. No Stealth Killer truck sighted."

"Bedtime for you, then. I'll take over the watch."

"Call if things get exciting?"

"Will do."

Do TEACHERS COME any more old school than Professor Emeritus Robson MacKissock? Though in his eighties, the man was still larger than life, his leonine head crowned with a mane of wavy white hair, his body still robust from youthful development by rugby, soccer, and punting the backs while he was earning top place in classics at prewar Oxford.

The most enthralling lecturer at UBC in his heyday, MacKissock drew hundreds of auditors to his small classes.

Sporting the full regalia of an Oxford don, he would stride the pit of a lecture theater way out here on the colonial edge of the civilized world and boom out his oratory as if he were Marc Antony begging friends and countrymen to lend him their ears. Greek gods like the old prof were hard to find these days, so even though the university had long since put him out to pension pasture, the students had him back for a roundtable in the classics reading room once a month. That's where Dane found him after the meeting tonight.

"Harpies!" announced MacKissock, fluttering his fingers above an article in *The Vancouver Times*. He and Dane were encircled by shelves of dead-language texts, study carrels, and portraits of past department heads, the most imposing of which was the one of MacKissock himself. Outside, rain splattered the windows.

"Gang Girls Bully Blind Boy to Death" blared the headline that had caught MacKissock's eye. "Lunch Money Stolen," added the subhead. According to the report by Bess McQueen, a gang of girls from junior high had waylaid a special-needs student at a bus stop near his school and demanded all his money under threat of "de-panting" him. In a sightless effort to flee from them, he had darted out into rush-hour traffic and was run over by a car.

"Harpies?" echoed Dane.

"Fierce, filthy, flighty females," expanded MacKissock. "Hideous haggish heads on the torsos of vicious vultures, with talons intent on tearing a man's flesh from his bones."

The professor flapped his robes like wings, billowing out what seemed to be decades of chalk dust and baring see-through patches in threadbare fabric.

"And the myth?" said Dane.

"Homer refers to Harpies in the *Odyssey,* but the best-known story involves Jason and the Argonauts. Harpies haunt an island in the Aegean Sea. There, they peck out the eyes of a king named Phineus and repeatedly snatch his food. When Jason rids him of the hateful demons, the blind man helps him find the Golden Fleece."

By seeking out this expert in the field of Greek myths, Dane hoped to be able to predict who the Swastika Killer would choose as his next victim. If that psycho was preying on people selected from the pages of *The Vancouver Times,* who better to connect those articles to ancient mythology than Robson MacKissock? Harpies did fit the gang-girl angle nicely.

"Anything else?" the Mountie asked.

"Not that I can discern."

The sergeant, however, had a second reason for this visit. The Swastika Killer appeared to have links to UBC: the vivarium was stolen from a university lab, and the Minotaur corpse was dumped within the labyrinth. If his knowledge of Greek mythology had an academic plinth, he had probably studied classics at UBC and had MacKissock as his prof.

"Did you ever teach a student who was pathologically obsessed with Greek myths?"

The classical scholar peered quizzically over the spectacles perched on the tip of his Roman nose.

"Do you suspect that *I* spawned this killer?"

"No," said Dane. "But serial killers get psychologically tangled up in fantasy, and what fantasy world is more inspirational than the one you taught?"

"A moth to the flame?"

The Mountie nodded. "Greek heroes lend themselves admirably to role-playing."

"Are you alluding to the alleged rape at the Argonauts party?"

Dane had no idea what MacKissock had in mind. But it sounded promising, so the sergeant played along.

"Tell me about it, Professor."

"The Siren—that's what we called her—was a remarkable student. Not only was she super-smart, but like Helen of Troy, she had a face and a figure that would launch a thousand ships. In fact, one of our colleagues became so besotted with her that soon after she graduated and joined the faculty, they tied the Gordian knot."

"He married his student?"

"More precisely, I'd say she married him. Pulchritude that alluring has its pick of men. She was half his age, so I'd venture to say there was role-playing in the marital boudoir."

"When was that?"

"The early seventies. The decade of free love."

"And the rape?"

"*Alleged* rape. There was no charge or trial. The Siren was teaching a seminar on Greek and Roman myths. There were twenty registrants, and each assumed a character to dramatize in class. The seventies, you'll recall, were awash with psychotropic drugs. The role-playing of the Argonauts—that's what the students called themselves— spun out of hand and transformed into a quasi-cult. The Siren threw an end-of-term party at her home, and that's where a female student playing Circe alleged she was raped by a classmate playing Odysseus."

"Why no trial?" asked Dane.

"Circe was the enchantress of Homer's *Odyssey*. Circe turned men into swine and tried to seduce Odysseus. The role, it seems, fit the claimant too well. Both her prior sexual history and her drunken behavior at the party scotched the likelihood of a conviction. The Argonauts disbanded, and the Siren, under a cloud of scandal, abandoned the faculty for married life."

"What became of her?"

"She vanished in Europe. After the fall of the Berlin Wall in 1989, she and her husband took a trip to East Germany. When the next term started, he wasn't back to lecture. As far as I know, they never returned to Canada."

"He taught classics?"

"No, modern history. The Siren did a double major in both fields. She took a course in modern Germany under her soon-to-be husband. Swiss fellow. Brilliant. Independently wealthy. She married well. Owned a huge house near campus. Fit for a king. His seminal work is still a leader in its field. *Hitler and Eva Braun.*"

Wolf's Lair

Come tomorrow morning, Cort Jantzen would *own* the front page of *The Vancouver Times*. Editor Ed was so pleased with the stories his golden boy was hammering out that once the edition had been put to bed, he actually unlocked the right-hand drawer of his cluttered desk and offered Cort one of the Havana cigars that he hoarded in a wooden box.

"Go home. Smoke this. And get some rest. You'll wake up to your byline on the scoop of scoops."

Before he left the newspaper building, Cort checked his inbox one more time to see if there was another e-mail from the Swastika Killer.

There wasn't.

What did that mean?

THE WALTHER PPK lay hidden from sight under the driver's seat of the empty car. The myth among the post-war Nazi fugitives who had slipped in and out of the bunker beneath Fritz Streicher's mansion was that the gun had once belonged to the führer himself, and had been presented to Ernst Streicher for his unflinching devotion to the Fatherland. Somehow the gun had survived the fall of the Third Reich and made its way to Vancouver in the 1950s, where it was presented to the new paymaster of the Swastika.

From father to son to grandson, the Walther PPK had passed through three generations, and now it lay in the car outside *The Vancouver Times* building, waiting for the moment when it would blow out Cort Jantzen's brains.

THE RAIN WAS COMING down so hard when Cort exited the building that he could see nothing but blurry outlines in front of him. Popping open his umbrella as a shield from the biblical deluge, he sloshed in the general direction of his car. Climbing in without getting soaked took some maneuvering—a dance of unlocking the door and swinging it wide, protecting himself with the umbrella as he swiveled into the driver's seat, and then furling the umbrella and giving it a good shake to fling off the raindrops before depositing it in the foot well of the passenger's seat.

As Cort reached back to close the driver's door and shut out the raging storm, he felt a circle of cold steel press against his temple.

"Straighten up slowly," Swastika's voice commanded. "If you try anything, I'll empty your skull."

Carefully, Cort sat up in the driver's seat. As he caught a quick glimpse of himself in the rear-view mirror, he spied the Walther PPK aimed at his brain.

"You drive," Swastika ordered.

EVEN ON HIGH SPEED, the windshield wipers of Dane's car couldn't sweep the glass fast enough for him to be able to absorb any more than a vague outline of the mansion on University Hill. In driving around the property on odd-angled hillside streets, the sergeant deduced what he couldn't take in because of the curtain of rain: that this estate on grounds that swept down the slope of Point Grey would offer breathtaking views of the ocean, the mountains, the park, and the harbor on a good-weather day. He parked his car a block away and walked back through the blustery storm to the foot of the rear driveway.

Time to flex the law.

No way would he get a warrant on the basis that a couple who specialized in Nazi Germany and Greek myths had resided on this property prior to 1989. Nor could he do a perimeter search to see if he was able to spot something suspicious in plain sight. He'd have to get really lucky to find that farm truck with its broken tail light, and already he could see that there were no vehicles parked outside.

So, hidden by the deluge and trees alongside the driveway, Dane crept up the gurgling black ribbon to what seemed to be a coach house tucked in an evergreen thicket. The windows were dark. Circling around to the side of the building most shrouded with greenery, Dane shone his penlight in through the glass and …

"Yep, that's a farm truck," he whispered.

Still, all Dane could see was a side silhouette. He couldn't swear that this was *the* truck.

Not without breaking in.

Burglarizing the coach house was a snap, thanks to the laser beam device he'd seized from the Pentagon spooks. Cutting out the window, the Mountie climbed in.

The flatbed of the truck reeked with the stench of death. From the tool box just behind the cab all the way back to the tailgate was a smear of blood. From there, the smear continued across the floor and around the side of the truck, seeming to disappear under the wall in front of the windshield. Before following the trail any farther, Dane checked to make sure that one of the truck's tail lights was cracked exactly as it was in the snapshot taken outside Cabaret Berlin.

It was.

Raindrops on the hood meant that the truck had been out in the storm. The engine was still warm.

A quick call to a justice of the peace and a little creative editing to avoid telling *how* the farm truck was spotted secured Dane the legal right to search the wolf's lair under a telewarrant.

"MMM?" Jackie mumbled into the phone.

"Wake up, sleepyhead. I found the farm truck."

"Uh. Bad connection."

"No, it's the rain. My head's sticking out a window, and I'm whispering to muffle this call."

"Where are you?"

"Got a pen?"

Dane gave her the address.

"We have a telewarrant to toss this estate. Secure the perimeter as quickly as you can so no one can escape. But don't send the gangbusters storming in until I give the word. And you'd better call Cort so he can be in on the action."

"What are you gonna do?"

"Scout around."

As soon as Jackie disconnected from Dane, she punched in the number for Cort's cellphone.

No answer.

CORT JANTZEN turned his car off the street and drove halfway around the U in front of the sprawling Point Grey mansion. The porte-cochère welcomed visitors to the university side of the residence while the coach house lurked out back, where the bluff fell away.

"Get out," Swastika ordered, waving the pistol.

THE MOMENT HE UNLOCKED the door and stepped into the front vestibule of his hideout, Swastika knew that the Aryan was lurking downstairs.

The alarm system wasn't engaged.

Only one other person on the face of the earth knew the code to shut it off. Ever since that dark day when Hans Streicher's East German son had rapped on the door to the post-war domain inherited by Fritz Streicher's Canadian son, Swastika had lived under the constant threat of exposure. By using the tattoos from both their fathers, the Aryan—for that's what he called himself—had found a cache of mysterious documents in their grandfather's Sudeten headquarters. The Europunk had squirreled away the documents, along with a handwritten letter detailing Streicher family Nazi secrets revealed to him by Fritz moments before he died, in a safe new hidey-hole, and there they would remain so long as no one tried to betray him.

"Do we understand each other, Cousin?"

"Yes," Swastika had replied.

"If I go down, you go down. And it's goodbye to all of this."

In the end, they had divided their legacy in half. The country cousin got the Phantom Valley Ranch in the Cariboo; the city cousin got this mansion near UBC. The Fourth Reich bunker they had to share, with Swastika gaining access by way of the hidden staircase from the mansion upstairs and the Aryan by way of the underground passage from the coach house in which he stayed whenever he came to town. The Aryan also relieved his cousin of Ernst Streicher's sword, while Swastika retained the dagger and this gun.

If the Aryan had been content to putter around like a low-profile hick, the Mounties of Special X would not now be cinching this double noose around their necks. But instead, he had been compelled by whatever demons tormented his psyche to drive down to the city periodically to pick up prey in the tenderloin district of boy's town.

As soon as it became evident that they had picked up the Aryan's trail, Swastika had done his best to keep the bloodhounds at bay. The vigilante killings had given him a sense of Nietzschean purpose, and they had also diverted the Horsemen from the exploits of his reckless cousin. But now the Aryan had stolen that from him too, by using the bison head that Swastika had left in the map room to usurp *his* Minotaur myth.

Cort Jantzen had betrayed him.

So had the Aryan.

The time was nigh to execute *both* traitors.

The Fourth Reich wasn't big enough for two supermen.

THE BLOOD ON THE FLOOR of the garage could mean only one thing: another victim had been dragged into this lair. If the victim was dead, Dane could afford to wait until Jackie had the perimeter cordoned off. But if the victim was alive, and he or she died because of some hesitation on Dane's part, the Mountie would never be able to wash that guilt from his mind.

He followed the smear to where it seemed to vanish under the wall, then felt around the panel until it gave way under his fingers. Unaware that by dislodging the door he would cause warning lights to flash in the bunker, he swung the camouflaged entrance wide to reveal a subterranean passage that swallowed the beam of his penlight.

Racked and ready to point and shoot, Dane drew his gun.

The Mountie was inward bound.

THE ARYAN was ready for whoever came to get him. Pentagon pigs or Mounted pigs, he'd pigstick them all the same.

Hours ago, he had run a whetstone along the blade of his grandfather's sword until the cutting edge was as sharp as a

razor. For well over a decade, his cousin had lived in fear
that the Aryan would expose the secrets that bound them
together like Siamese twins. Although it was possible that
his ploy to extort a billion dollars from the Pentagon had
lured the pair of hit men to the Skunk Mine, he suspected
that his cousin had betrayed him to the Yanks. Pay me
handsomely for the treasure trove the Aryan will hand over
if you squeeze his balls hard enough, he imagined him
saying, and you can have whatever he retrieved from the
Sudeten castle.

Well, no more.

The documents were gone.

Before returning to the bunker to die like a hero, just as
the führer did, the Aryan had removed the Streicherstab
blueprints from their current hidey-hole and done with
them what would do the most damage to the Pentagon.

Then, having set a trap in this version of Hitler's
bedroom, he sat waiting to kill.

THE PENLIGHT in one hand and his Smith & Wesson in the
other, Dane followed the blood smear along the dank
tunnel, closing on the flashing light ahead. As his footsteps
echoed within the claustrophobic confines of the underground passage, he reached an open steel door with a
punch-coded lock and stepped across the threshold of time
into Hitler's bunker underneath the chancellery garden.

Sweeping the gun before him, he almost opened fire on
three people who appeared in the flashing pulse of the
1940s-vintage overhead bulbs. But he realized in time that
one was just a boy, and then it sank in that all three were
wax figures.

Hitler.

Eva Braun.

And their illegitimate son?

The corridor straight ahead presented no immediate peril. If an attack were launched, it would come from one of two doors in the wall to his right. As Dane side-stepped to clear the first chamber, like a dancer slinking through a strobe light in a disco, the steel door swung shut behind him and he heard the beep, beep, beep, of the punch code imprisoning him within the bunker.

THE ALARM INFORMED Swastika that the tunnel door was ajar, so the Nazi hit the button that closed it by remote control and then entered the security code.

Beep ... beep ... beep ... beep.

If the Aryan was down in the bunker and wanted out, undoing the alarm would give him away. If the Aryan was out on one of his prowls, disarming the alarm would announce his return.

Walther in hand, Swastika crossed to the secret panel in the side of the vestibule and popped it open to expose the staircase to the bunker below.

He waved the gun.

"You first," he ordered.

With the muzzle of the firearm pressed against his skull, Cort Jantzen stepped into the hollow wall and, step by step, began the cold descent into the pit of University Hill.

THE FIRST DOOR to the right ushered Dane into a mock-up of the map room where the führer had married Eva Braun. A table and chair to the left, a settee to the right. Nowhere to hide except under the table, and a quick crouch convinced the cop that no one hid down there. The tabletop was bare but for a wooden box with the words "SS-Obergruppenführer Ernst Streicher" engraved on the lid. Dane flipped it open to reveal perhaps the finest dagger he had ever seen.

Stepping out of the map room, he hugged its outer wall with his gun hand extended, ready to fire at anything that emerged from the next door.

The closer he got to the wax figures, the sharper the features became. Dane could see now that the Hitler mannequin bore the face of the UBC professor, whose photograph Professor MacKissock had retrieved from faculty files. The wax sculpture of Eva Braun, he assumed, resembled the wife of the history professor, the Siren. The third figure was a boy in a Hitler Youth uniform, and the blood trail ended directly at his feet. The large sail needle and threads of black cord in the blood suggested that that's where the Swastika Killer had sat to stitch the bison head onto the Pentagon hit man.

The Swastika Killer?

Or the Stealth Killer?

It no longer mattered which, for this was clearly where the man who'd grown out of the waxworks lad split into a pair of Nazi killers. This bunker, thought Dane, is where the psycho does his identity switch.

Under the throbbing overhead lights, Dane switched the gun to his left hand and swung it around the jamb of the adjacent door.

Nothing.

Darting into the antechamber, the Mountie shielded himself behind the wall that separated it from Hitler's study, waiting for a counterattack that didn't come.

Another peek convinced him to rush the mock room in which Hitler and Eva Braun had killed themselves. It, too, was vacant of life. The door to the left, which should have led to Eva Braun's boudoir, was bolted shut. Faint music could be heard from the room to his right, where the beam from a film projector seemed to animate the ceiling.

Hitler's bedroom.

Dane peered in.

The chamber was empty.

Or so he thought.

For what the Mountie didn't see was the eyeball at the peephole in the false wall that hid the staircase to the mansion on University Hill.

Crouched in the well at the bottom of the secret staircase, the Aryan was ready to spring his trap. His eye followed the Mountie as he entered the bedroom and checked beneath the cot to make certain that no one lurked there. That done, the cop stood up and turned to face the bed, where the Aryan had arrayed a collage of artifacts on the blanket to distract the intruder so his back would be to the peephole.

Having searched the bunker for danger, Dane felt safe enough to let down his guard. His gun hand lowered to his side until the muzzle was aimed at the floor. Obviously, the Nazi killer was in the mansion above, where he had just reset the perimeter alarm, unaware of Dane's presence down in the bunker. Since the blood smeared across the floor belonged to the Minotaur victim, there was no hostage for Special X to worry about. Dane could call Jackie and have the ERT team storm the mansion so the Mounties would once more get their man. And if it came to a prosecution, there was evidence spread all over this bed.

With footage from Leni Riefenstahl's *Triumph of the Will* flickering over his head, Dane perused the newspaper clippings from *The Vancouver Times*. Individual letters had been cut out and arranged to form the German word *Untermenschen.* They encircled a leather-bound book engraved with some sort of family crest. Only when he picked it up and flipped to the title page did Dane realize that the hide was human skin.

Another patch of flayed skin, with a different crest, stuck out from where the lid met the bottom of an oblong case like the one that held the dagger back in the map room. The plaque on the lid also bore the name of SS-Obergruppenführer Ernst Streicher. As he raised the lid to see the full tattoo, and noticed that the scabbard inside was empty, Dane thought, I wonder if the weapon is in the killer's fist?

The answer to that question came swift and sharp. The split-second warning of a squeaky hinge galvanized Dane to action. But before he could whirl around to face whatever had caused that squeak, he felt the cold steel of a sword blade run him through from back to front.

Überman

The sharp pain caused Dane to drop his pistol to the floor. A moment later, as the sword was wrenched back from his midriff for a second lunge, he inadvertently kicked his only weapon and sent it spiraling under the bed. If only he hadn't left those Pentagon gizmos back in the coach house! Before the swordsman could finish him off with a more severe stab, Dane dodged to his right through the door he had entered, grabbing the frame with his fingers to stop himself from crumpling to the floor, and swinging about at ninety degrees to propel himself toward the corridor.

Again, he caught the jamb to break a sprawling tumble. The resulting quarter turn flung him along the corridor wall. Just behind, the tip of the sword scraped across his back as the lunging fencer overreached his mark.

His pursuer stumbled trying to recover from his forward motion, and that gave the bleeding cop a chance to claw along the wall toward the sealed tunnel door. In jerking sideways at the squeak of the hinge, Dane had caused the sword to miss his spine. The blade had passed through one kidney, and maybe his bowel, in the space between his ribcage and his pelvis. A potentially fatal wound if he didn't get help soon, but it didn't cripple him in this desperate run for his life, powered by the biggest surge of adrenaline he had ever felt.

Gasping, Dane pivoted around yet another doorframe. Crying out in pain, he stepped up onto the seat of the chair in the map room and scooped the SS dagger out of the open wooden case with his free hand.

With Ernst Streicher's razor-sharp sword gripped in both hands to cut off the Mountie's head, the Nazi rushed into the map room for the kill. But before he could take a swipe, he was struck from above by the plunging dagger. With all his might, Dane drove the dagger's SS motto, *"Mein Ehre heisst Treue,"* down into the Aryan's brain.

The dead man and the bleeding man crashed into the corridor, one on top of the other. Struggling to push himself away, Dane puzzled over this guy's identity.

He had never seen him before tonight.

Right now, however, Dane had a greater concern, for he knew that his wound was potentially fatal, and that if he didn't get medical attention soon, his blood pressure would plummet as his system bled out.

Luckily, he had phoned no one since his call to Jackie, so he fished his cellphone out of his pocket …

God, don't let it have broken in the fall.

… punched the Send button, and was connected to her.

"Corporal Hett."

The weak signal was barely audible in the bunker.

"It's Dane. I've been stabbed, Jackie. I'm in a bunker beneath the address I gave you. The passageway in from the coach house out back is sealed. Break into the house and see if a dog can find another way down to me."

"What about the killer?"

"I killed him," said Dane.

"Keep the line open. We're coming in."

DANE THOUGHT he was hallucinating from loss of blood when he saw Cort Jantzen step into the corridor with a gun pointed at his head. Stark fear caused the reporter's face to twitch, and his voice cracked with strain as he begged the wounded cop, "Don't try anything stupid, Dane."

It took a moment for the Mountie to grasp what was going on. The lawyer in him had outsmarted the cop in him by dreaming up a more exotic psychological profile for the Swastika Killer than was necessary. He should have remembered the principle of Occam's razor: "Assumptions introduced to explain a thing must not be multiplied beyond necessity. When multiple explanations are available, the simplest version is preferred."

The blood on the splinter from the stake in the Congo Man's head had led Dane astray. The lab tech's description of the DNA "twin within" had induced Dane to theorize that their quarry was two dissociated Hyde identities in one fractured mind. In fact, the Swastika Killer and the Stealth Killer were actually two separate and distinct psychos, both working out of this Nazi bunker.

Dane concluded that the blond lying dead on the bunker floor was the Stealth Killer. Not only did he match the descriptions of the Phantom Valley Ranch suspect provided by the upcountry Mounties and those at the rendering plant, but the sword he'd used to attack Dane would cause the kind of pigsticker wounds they'd seen in the Skunk Mine.

That left the Swastika Killer.

It took little imagination to conjure up the psychological traumas that the parents in the waxworks exhibit had inflicted on their son in the Hitler Youth uniform. His hard Nazi father and his oversexed mother had fractured the boy's mind not into good and bad Nazi killers, as Dane had originally theorized, but into a good crime reporter and an evil Nazi killer.

Now that he saw them side by side in the flickering corridor, Dane caught the features of the waxwork boy in the flesh and blood of the man he knew as Cort Jantzen.

Who was aiming the pistol at his own temple.

THE GERMANS have words for concepts that have no direct translations in English. Words like *angst, schadenfreude, zeitgeist,* and what was going on here.

Selbstmord.

The noise of glass smashing from an all-out ERT blitzkrieg on the mansion above echoed down into the bunker. As he watched the face before him "do the switch" between the Jekyll of Cort and the Hyde of the Swastika Killer, alternating almost as quickly as the light and dark throbbing of the bunker bulbs, the sergeant grasped the connection between the psychological Siamese twins.

To cope with whatever his parents had done to create an *Über*boy worthy of the master race, the kid had dissociated all that fascist trauma into a Swastika identity. The peril that came from being tied to the Stealth Killer had probably forced Cort to protect himself by working as a crime reporter for *The Vancouver Times.* The news media would be the first to know if Special X picked up the trail of the Stealth Killer. When that finally occurred, Cort's stress level reached a crisis point, and the split-off identity of the Swastika Killer had to seize the spotlight and launch a spree of killings that would draw the attention of the psycho-hunters away from the Stealth Killer until both halves of the fractured mind figured out what to do.

What had Cort said as they were standing over the Minotaur in the UBC labyrinth?

"This killer is *really* into myths. I grew up on this stuff."

So strongly dissociated were their separate identities that the Swastika Killer had ended up playing a cat-and-mouse game with Jantzen over the myth angle of the vigilante killings. Each identity remained so tightly locked in his mental bunker at this precise moment of the hostage-taking crisis that neither realized that they occupied the same brain.

A brain at which the muzzle of the pistol pointed.

"It's over," said Dane.

The sound of army boots descending the staircase from above filled the bunker.

"Then we'll all die together," snarled the Swastika Killer.

The lights pulsed brighter.

"No!" beseeched Cort, doing the switch. His face twisted with fright.

The lights dimmed to herald the fall of the Fourth Reich.

"Yes!" the *Über*man shouted triumphantly, switching back. "They didn't take Hitler alive, and they won't take me! A bullet for you, then a bullet for the cop, then a bullet in my brain!"

The lights pulsed brighter.

"No!" Cort screamed, caught in the spotlight of consciousness. "I don't want to—"

Bwam!

War Machine

May 29, Now

Editor Ed was in a foul mood as he ripped open the pile of morning mail on his desk. The identity of the Swastika Killer had not become clear until after last night's deadline for today's press run of *The Vancouver Times*. Tomorrow morning would see everything revealed on the front page of the paper for which Cort had worked. Hard to think of a worse case of investigative reporting than that.

How embarrassing.

While he was still in that funk, Ed tore open an envelope with no return address and read the Aryan's letter detailing the history of the Streicher Nazis.

Who says you can't make a silk purse out of a sow's ear?

Ed got up, opened his office door, and yelled across the newsroom to his golden girl, "Bess, get in here!"

BEIJING, PEOPLE'S REPUBLIC OF CHINA
June 5, Now

In the world-view of the Red Guards, space belonged to China.

A crater on the moon is named for Wan Hu, a legendary Chinese explorer who was killed in an ill-fated attempt to reach the heavens by strapping forty-seven rockets to a chair. The Maoist anthem "The East Is Red" still broadcasts to the heavens from a satellite that was launched back when China began space exploration, in 1970. China's program to reach the moon is called Chang'e, for the fairy that soared heavenward after mistakenly eating medicine that made her fly. "I will not disappoint the motherland," said Yang Liwei, the first Chinese *taikonaut* to orbit the world, in 2003. "And I will gain honor for the People's Liberation Army and for the Chinese nation." His spacecraft, carried aloft by a Long March rocket, was named *Shenzhou,* meaning "divine vessel." Plans were now afoot to send a rocket to the moon, to ring the globe with satellites aimed at improving the accuracy of Chinese ballistic missiles, and to build a space station within ten years.

Chairman Mao would have been honored.

In the world-view of the Red Guards, China should also dominate the earth.

For most of the four thousand to five thousand years of recorded time, China was history's preeminent culture. The Chinese saw themselves as a middle kingdom between heaven and the rest of barbaric humanity. Their long humiliation began in the 1840s, when British invaders seized Hong Kong after the first Opium War and imported that addictive drug from India to foist on the Chinese. A pack of European and American plunderers had followed. Were it not for the revolution led by Chairman Mao, those jackals would still be feasting off the middle kingdom.

But no more.

Today, only one adversary persisted: the United States. America had assumed the threat where the Europeans left off. In addition to its military bases in Japan and South Korea, the U.S. was now aligning with the Philippines, Singapore, Thailand, Pakistan, Afghanistan, and the warlords of Central Asia. These alliances were supposedly meant to help the Americans hunt the terrorists of the post-9/11 world, but in reality they were designed to contain China within its present borders. Why else set up listening posts in Mongolia, just across the border from China's Lop Nor missile- and nuclear-testing sites? Why else bury silos in Alaska for the Pentagon's Missile Defense Shield?

One reason.

To dominate China.

In the world-view of the Red Guards, a giant was rising in the East to overtake the globe.

China's economy was expanding so fast that it would soon dwarf America's. The People's Liberation Army had several million boots on the ground, and it was firmly in control of China's space program. In the 1960s, when Chairman Mao had loosed the Red Guards of the Cultural Revolution on the land, the men in this room, then in their teens, had stomped out counter-revolutionary tendencies with bloodthirsty brutality. The Red Guards today, a faction of the People's Liberation Army, were charged with arming China to the teeth. As a superpower, China would succeed in its fanatical quest for respect, and world dominance could be wrenched from the hands of the lesser race that had caused its humiliation.

In China, it was most important to have face.

And the Chinese take the long view when it comes to revenge.

It was to that end that these men met in the Beijing headquarters of China's "black world" to assess the documents that had been delivered anonymously to the country's consulate on Granville Street in Vancouver. Written in German and stamped with the Nazi swastika, the papers seemed to be Second World War blueprints and notes for an otherworldly war machine.

"What powers it?" one Red Guard asked the German translator.

"Anti-gravity."

Beneath the red stars on their caps, these twenty-first-century warmongers passed curious glances around the circle of the new master race.

"What's it called?" another asked.

"The Flightwheel," replied the translator.

AUTHOR'S NOTE

This is a work of fiction. The plot and the characters are products of the author's imagination. Where real persons, places, incidents, institutions, and such have been incorporated to create the illusion of authenticity, they are used fictitiously. Inspiration was drawn from the following nonfiction sources:

Agoston, Tom. *Blunder!: How the U.S. Gave Away Nazi Supersecrets to Russia*. New York: Dodd Mead, 1985.

Béon, Yves. *Planet Dora: A Memoir of the Holocaust and the Birth of the Space Age*. Translated by Yves Béon and Richard L. Fague. Boulder, CO: Westview Press, 1997.

Berlitz, Charles, and William Moore. *The Philadelphia Experiment*. London: Souvenir Press, 1979.

———. *The Roswell Incident*. New York: Grosset and Dunlap, 1980.

"Bomber Command, 1939–1945." www.raf.mod.uk/bomber command

Bower, Tom. *The Paperclip Conspiracy: The Battle for the Spoils and Secrets of Nazi Germany*. London: Michael Joseph, 1987.

Cook, Nick. *The Hunt for Zero Point: Inside the Classified World of Antigravity Technology*. New York: Broadway Books, 2001.

Cook, Stan, and R. James Bender. *Leibstandarte SS Adolph Hitler: Uniforms, Organization and History*. San Jose, CA: Bender Publishing, 1994.

"Death by Moonlight." *The Valor and the Horror*. Directed by Brian McKenna. Toronto: National Film Board of Canada, 1992.

Dornberger, Walter. *V-2*. Translated by James Cleugh and Geoffrey Halliday. New York: Viking, 1958.

Dungan, Tracy. "A-4/V-2 Resource Site." www.v2rocket.com.

Egger, Steve A. *The Killers Among Us: An Examination of Serial Murder and Its Investigation*. Upper Saddle River, NJ: Prentice Hall, 2002.

Holmes, Richard. *World War II in Photographs*. London: Carlton, 2000.

Hunt, Linda. *Secret Agenda: The United States Government, Nazi Scientists and Project Paperclip, 1945 to 1990*. New York: St. Martin's Press, 1991.

Jaroff, Leon. "The Rocket Man's Dark Side." *Time* magazine online edition. Posted March 26, 2002. www.time.com/columnist/jaroff/article/0,9565,220202,00.html.

"The Language of the Camps." www.jewishgen.org.

Lasby, Clarence G. *Project Paperclip: German Scientists and the Cold War*. New York: Atheneum, 1971.

Lewis, Brenda Ralph. *Hitler Youth: The Hitlerjugend in War and Peace 1933–1945*. Osceola, WI: MBI Publishing, 2000.

Lomas, Robert. *The Man Who Invented the Twentieth Century: Nikola Tesla, Forgotten Genius of Electricity*. London: Headline, 1979.

Longmate, Norman. *Hitler's Rockets: The Story of the V-2s*. London: Hutchinson, 1985.

Lusar, Rudolf. *German Secret Weapons of the Second World War*. London: Spearman, 1959.

Mann, Chris. *SS-Totenkopf: The History of the "Death's Head" Division 1940–45*. Osceola, WI: MBI Publishing, 2001.

Maule, Henry. *The Great Battles of World War II*. Chicago: Regnery, 1973.

McGovern, James. *Crossbow and Overcast*. New York: William Morrow, 1964.

Michel, Jean, with Louis Nucera. *Dora*. Translated by Jennifer Kidd. New York: Holt, Rinehart & Winston, 1979.

Middlebrook, Martin. *The Peenemünde Raid: The Night of 17–18 August 1943*. London: Penguin, 1988.

National Timberwolf Association. "Mittelbau Dora Concentration Camp." www.104infdiv.org/CONCAMP.HTM.

Neufeld, Michael J. *The Rocket and the Reich: Peenemünde and the Coming of the Ballistic Missile Era*. New York: The Free Press, 1994.

O'Donnell, James P. *The Bunker*. Boston: Houghton Mifflin, 1978.

Peden, Murray. *A Thousand Shall Fall*. Toronto: Stoddart, 1988.

Petrova, Ada, and Peter Watson. *The Death of Hitler: The Full Story with New Evidence from Secret Russian Archives*. New York: Norton, 1995.

Piszkiewicz, Dennis. *The Nazi Rocketeers: Dreams of Space and Crimes of War*. New York: Praeger, 1995.

———. *Wernher von Braun: The Man Who Sold the Moon*. Westport, CN.: Praeger, 1998.

Randle, Kevin D. *The Roswell Encyclopedia*. New York: HarperCollins, 2000.

Report of Air Force Research Regarding the "Roswell Incident" (1994). www.af.mil/lib/roswell

Rhodes, Richard. *The Making of the Atomic Bomb*. New York: Simon & Schuster, 1995.

Rossmo, D. Kim, and Anne Davies. "Stealth Predator Patterns." *Crime Mapping News*. Volume 3, Issue 4 (2001). Pages 6–7.

The Roswell Report: Case Closed (1997). www.af.mil/lib/roswell

Saler, Benson, with Charles A. Ziegler and Charles B. Moore. *UFO Crash at Roswell: The Genesis of a Modern Myth*. Washington, DC: Smithsonian, 1997.

Sellier, André. *A History of the Dora Camp: The Story of the Nazi Slave Labor Camp That Secretly Manufactured V-2*

Rockets. Translated by Stephen Wright and Susan Taponier. Chicago: Ivan R. Dee, 2003.

Simpson, Christopher. *Blowback: America's Recruitment of Nazis and Its Effects on the Cold War.* New York: Weidenfeld & Nicholson, 1988.

Speer, Albert. *Infiltration: How Heinrich Himmler Schemed to Build an SS Industrial Empire.* New York: Macmillan, 1981.

———. *Inside the Third Reich.* Translated by Richard Winston and Clara Winston. New York: Avon, 1970.

Stolley, Richard B. *LIFE: World War II.* Boston: Little, Brown, 1990.

Time Life/BBC. *Secrets of WWII: Adolf Hitler's Last Days.* London: Nugus/Martin Productions, 1998.

Time Life/BBC. *Secrets of WWII: How Germany Was Bombed to Defeat.* London: Nugus/Martin Productions, 1998.

Trevor-Roper, Hugh. *The Last Days of Hitler.* London: Pan, 2002.

Warriors of the Night. Directed by James Hyslop. Toronto: Nightfighters Productions, 1999.

Williamson, Gordon. *The SS: Hitler's Instrument of Terror.* Osceola, WI: MBI Publishing, 1994.

World at War: An Illustrated History of the Second World War. New York: Dorset, 1991.

The V-2 was called the A-4 until it was renamed the Vengeance Weapon 2 and began to be used against Britain in retaliation for nighttime raids against the Reich by RAF Bomber Command. To avoid confusion, only the term V-2 is used in the novel.

For those of you interested in delving into the truth that inspired this fiction, I recommend several books. O'Donnell's *The Bunker* captures the madhouse atmosphere of Hitler's last days underground in Berlin. The author was there in 1945, and he also interviewed those who endured that experience. A stiff drink is advisable before you sink into Michel's *Dora* and Béon's *Planet Dora*, two hellish memoirs about what went on in the V-2 production tunnels at Work Camp Dora, both written by prisoners of war. Although SS-Obergruppenführer Ernst Streicher and his sons are fictional, that non-existent Nazi engineer is based on a real-life monster in Hitler's Reich: SS-Obergruppenführer Hans Kammler. In *The Rocket and the Reich,* Neufeld, a curator of Second World War history at the National Air and Space Museum, Smithsonian Institution, details the involvement of Kammler and Wernher von Braun in building the V-2 and explains what happened when the Pentagon moved in at the close of the war. Finally, to answer the question that tormented Jean Michel for decades—what became of Hans Kammler after the fall of the Third Reich?—you definitely want to read Cook's *The Hunt for Zero Point*. Written by the aviation editor of *Jane's Defence Weekly,* the world's top journal of military affairs, it's a work that would impress Sherlock Holmes.

Hans Kammler? Work Camp Dora? The Mittelwerk?
Never heard of them?
I wonder why.

Slade
Vancouver, B.C.

If you enjoyed this book, read Michael Slade's

KAMIKAZE

Turn the page for an excerpt

Zero Hour

Like a swarm of hornets buzzing in from the north, the Japanese planes dove out of a Sunday morning sky to bomb and then strafe the hangars and aircraft that lined the bottom edge of the A-shaped runways at Hickam Field. *"Tora! Tora! Tora!"* While Commander Mitsuo Fuchida repeatedly signaled the code word "tiger," meaning "total surprise," back to Admiral Chuichi Nagumo on the *Akagi,* flagship for the strike force, Corporal Joe "Red" Hett was shaving in his digs on the Hawaiian air force base. Having spent Saturday night at liberty in the bars, brothels, dance halls, and clubs of Pearl City, the airman was nursing a hangover from consuming too much booze at a late-night poker party in the new enlisted men's beer hall, dubbed the Snake Ranch.

"Damn Marines!" Hett muttered on hearing the first boom. "Some trigger-happy jarhead must've let one go."

Boom! Boom! Boom!

As the coral foundation beneath the barracks shuddered, Hett cut his cheek.

The flyboy glanced at his watch beside the sink.

7:56.

Then the concussion from a closer blast crashed the ceiling fixture to the floor.

The "Red" in Red Hett was a reference to the fiery hue
of his hair, which was almost as crimson as the blood that
now streaked his shaving cream. At this moment, Joe wore
khaki trousers and loafers, and had U.S. Army Air Force
dog tags strung around his neck. Bare-chested, he sported
the deep tan he'd earned from goofing away his days off on
the sands of Waikiki. That's where he was destined now—
to doze in the sun and wake up to an eyeful of wicked
wahines in skimpy beachwear. What better peacetime
posting was there than this?

BOOM!

The Hale Makai Barracks, Hickam Field's newest structure, was a huge, octopus-like complex with wings jutting
in all directions. It served as quarters for more than three
thousand enlisted men. So violent was the explosion
caused by the direct hit on the mess hall at its center that it
blew soldiers out the windows of the upper floors. On the
ground floor, the bomb scattered diners, tables, chairs, and
trays of grub, and shrapnel killed thirty-five men as they
gulped down their bacon and eggs. Machine-gun bullets
rat-a-tat-tatting through shattered windows ricocheted off
metal footlockers to perforate bunks. By the time Red
Hett, razor still in hand, got down the stairs and out the
door, blood-spattered survivors in tattered clothes were
already crawling amid the rubble or staggering around in
a daze.

Chaos!

As his eyes adjusted to the glare, Joe caught sight of a
young GI, a Colt .45 flapping in a holster on his hip,
dashing hell bent for leather along the road between the
barracks and the hangars that bordered the airfield. He was
obviously on guard duty.

"The Japs are here! It's war!" he shouted as he ran past,
a modern-day Paul Revere raising the alarm.

As Joe turned to watch the guard sprint down the street, the roar of an airborne engine zoomed in from his other side. With tracer streaks leading the way, bullets stitched across the ground, throwing up puffs of asphalt dust in their wake. They drilled through the guard as red mist and continued on ahead. A Zero fighter shot by Joe and soared over its kill before the GI crumpled down dead. So close to the road was the plane that it almost seemed to be landing, and through the open cockpit, Hett got a glimpse of the pilot. With his helmeted head and square goggles, he resembled a creature from outer space. Wrapped around his brow and rippling in the breeze was a white scarf, the *hachimaki,* a traditional symbol of courage. Hell, Joe could even see the gold in his teeth!

"Meatballs," Hett cursed as the plane began to climb. The word was slang for the Rising Sun painted on the underside of both wings.

Clang! Clang! Clang!

Shiny shell casings ejected by the Zero's guns showered the street and bounced around until motionless.

Casting aside the razor, Joe ran to the cut-down guard. The corpse lay sprawled beside a patch of green grass littered with petunia blossoms and red hibiscus. Crouching, the flyboy relieved the holster of its .45 and craned his neck around.

Sandwiched between Diamond Head to the east and Pearl Harbor to the west, Honolulu's Hickam Field was home base for the U.S. Army Air Force's bombers on Oahu. From the plumes of thick, oily smoke mushrooming ominously into the sky above the anchorage, Joe knew the ships of the Pacific Fleet were sunk or damaged. Ahead of him, at the end of the barracks, the Stars and Stripes hung limply at the top of its flagpole. Nearby, a sergeant was struggling to mount a machine gun in a bomb crater. The

attack had blown open the guardhouse, releasing its
prisoners, and the escapees rushed to help the sarge set up
the .50-caliber weapon.

Save the planes, thought Hett.

A row of double hangars lined the curb to his right.
Between the tent-roofed buildings fronting the flight line, Joe
saw the Zeros flash by with their wing cannons blazing and
heard the shriek of dive bombers jazzing the base. Hickam
had no anti-aircraft guns, no air-raid shelters, no slit trenches.
The guard force was armed solely with pistols. As a defense
against sabotage—the only threat contemplated by those
in command—Hickam's twenty B-17 Flying Fortresses,
thirty-two almost obsolete B-18s, and twelve A-20s were
dovetailed wingtip to wingtip out on the concrete mat.
Sparkling in the sunlight and easy prey, they'd be smashed to
smithereens by this sneak attack if something wasn't done.

The boom-booming and bang-banging was loud enough
to rupture eardrums in the iron alleyway between the
hangars. With one fist gripping the .45, Joe covered his ears
as he darted for the runways. He burst out onto Mat A to
find it hell in the Pacific.

Bombs fell like black rain from a cloud of high-altitude
Japanese planes. Looking up, Hett had the sensation that
every bomb was heading straight for him. Dive bombers off
the *Shokaku* had launched the initial assault on Hickam Field
while twenty-four men labored in Hangar 11 to roll out
B-18s for an eight o'clock training flight. A bang-on strike
through the roof had killed twenty-two outright and cut the
legs off the other two. Now, as the hangar's twisted frame-
work licked the sun with tongues of flame and ongoing
explosions blew out skylights, windows, and doors, officers
and enlisted men in a hodgepodge of Sunday attire—
uniforms, skivvies, aloha shirts, and pajamas—fought the
fire, salvaged equipment, or tended to the wounded.

His bathrobe gaping to expose his nudity, a captain came reeling out of the smoke with blood streaming down his face, shaking his fist at the planes and bellowing, "I *knew* the little sons of bitches would do it on a Sunday! I *knew* it!"

Bwam! He got mangled by a fragmentation bomb.

From Joe's standpoint, the base was a sea of fire. Every swoop by a Val dive bomber took out something else: a supply building exploded in a hail of nuts and bolts and wheels; the chapel succumbed, even with the supposed protection of God; the Snake Ranch beer hall had served its last drink; the firehouse and its engines were made permanently unavailable to fight this inferno, while broken water mains uselessly spurted geysers into the air. Down, up, and away screamed the bombers, dipping so low that some struck telephone lines, then tore off with wires tangled around their wheels.

Until now, the Yanks had scoffed at the skill of Jap pilots, and blood was the price of that arrogance. After each Val dropped its load on a target, it veered into a figure eight to strafe the field repeatedly, winging back and forth, its guns chattering, along one cross-leg and then the other. The gunners, riding backward in the rear seats, glowered at Joe with each pass and tried to pick him off with bullets that zinged from the concrete just as they do in the movies. Meanwhile, the Zeros flashed around like silver mirrors, their aerial ballet tightly choreographed as they fanned over the bomb-cratered moonscape to rip the flight line to pieces.

Zoom, circle, *fire* …

For a moment, Joe thought one Zero was sprinkling toothpicks on the roof of Hangar 9, but then he grasped that it was sending the structure up in splinters.

One tin hangar still under construction rattled hollowly, as if stones were hitting metal, then suddenly bullets were ricocheting around inside like the balls in a pinball machine.

A blinding explosion of gasoline *foomed* up from the flight line as ground crews dodging bullets tried to haul machine guns and ammunition out of the disabled Flying Fortresses. *Foom! Foom! Foom!* Off went a chain reaction as bomber after bomber was consumed by the ravenous fire. Flaming, gibbering men were hurled away from the wrecks, flailing their arms like phoenixes desperate to rise from red hot ashes.

Acrid smoke choked Joe's lungs.

Blasts were coming at him from both above and below ground, quaking the concrete under his shoes as the terrible concussion and the deafening pressure wave of each massive explosion blew his breath away. Through gaps in the white pall that roiled across the mat, Joe watched an improvised crew scramble into an undamaged B-17. As guns poked out of the turrets, the pilot got three engines going and taxied off across the pitted battlefield, but he was unable to coax the recalcitrant engine to kick in. Splats of lead from vulturous Zeros soon tattooed the plane's wings.

Into the thick of this flew a dozen more planes.

The Japs are really coming now, thought Hett.

Then he wondered, Where did they get four-engine bombers?

When he recognized the new arrivals as B-17s, Joe grasped that they were twelve Flying Fortresses the base had expected from the mainland.

The crew members probably thought the approaching planes were a meet-and-greet from the U.S. Army Air Force, until the Japanese Zeros opened up with their wing cannons.

Low on fuel and with their turret guns packed away, the B-17s had no choice but to go for emergency landings.

Zeros strafed one as it ran the gauntlet down to the field, setting off magnesium flares in the radio compartment. A fire broke out in the midsection of the lumbering bomber, and as the burning plane thumped down heavily onto the runway, the tail section snapped off. As it skidded to a halt, what was left of the forward fuselage stood up like a penguin, forcing the battered airmen out to run for their lives. As they scampered across the Tarmac, a fighter pounced down and took out the flight surgeon in a withering hail of bullets.

Another Flying Fortress was also in deep trouble. Three Zeros were clinging to it like vampire bats, slamming slugs from their nose guns into its engines. Flames erupted from one cowling, then a second. Joe saw the white star on the blue circle as the crippled U.S. bomber passed directly overhead, and that galvanized him into action.

By chance, a freelance photographer was at Hickam Field to shoot a pictorial spread on Pearl Harbor for *Life* magazine. Cowering in one of the hangars, the cameraman spied the shot of a lifetime passing right before his eyes, so he bolted from his bomb shelter to follow the bare-chested airman out onto Mat A.

As he snapped his first picture, a discus of spinning shrapnel came whirling toward him from the fiery flight line. Dropping his camera, the photographer stretched out on the concrete as if sunning himself on a quiet Sunday morning. Though his severed head and hands plopped down next to his body, no blood appeared. So hot was the shrapnel that when it decapitated him and sliced off his hands, it cauterized his neck and wrists. The blood coagulated before it could spurt.

The sole image captured in the now broken camera was of Joe "Red" Hett standing defiantly in the open, the blasted bombers of Hickam Field ablaze beyond him. Legs astride and back arched, he was emptying the Colt .45 as fast as he could pull the trigger into the belly of a Japanese Zero above his head. Ejected shell casings spat from the pistol. His dog tags bounced off the muscles of his chest as he swiveled to give the muzzle enough lead on the plane. His half-shaven face was a symbol of the sneak attack. Outrage flashed in his eyes, and his lips snarled back from his teeth. Whatever Joe was yelling at the pilot whose head stuck out of the cockpit, those words would never see print.

The photo, however, made the next issue of *Life*.

By capturing America's reaction to the Day of Infamy, that image became an icon of the war.